UNDER *your* SCARS

ARIEL N. ANDERSON

UNDER YOUR SCARS: A DARK ROMANCE NOVEL

Self-Published in 2023 by Ariel N. Anderson

Cover design and graphic design by @artscandare

Paperback ISBN: 979-8-9882962-0-1
eBook ISBN: 979-8-9882962-2-5

First Edition: September 2023

10 9 8 7 6 5 4 3 2 1

PROCEED WITH CAUTION

This is a dark and smutty **romantic tragedy.**

The Silencer is a morally black psychopath who displays signs of a severe, untreated mental illness that manifests in a violent manner. Some of you may find his actions disturbing, and this book is not suitable for readers who are sensitive to such topics.

CONTENT WARNINGS INCLUDE :

rape/sexual assault, graphic violence, drug use, graphic murder, toxic/abusive relationships, stalking, terminal illness, Stockholm syndrome, suicide, and self-harm; with themes of grief and depression.

This book contains explicit sexual content, including gun play, slapping kink, and dubious consent.

This is a book with adult themes and is intended for mature readers only.

If you have any questions about sensitive content, please reach out to me on Instagram: @ariel.n.anderson

PLAYLIST

Gangsta's Paradise – 2WEI

Whispers in the Dark - Skillet

Not Strong Enough – Apocalyptica

My Demons – STARSET

Popular Monster – Falling in Reverse

Painkiller – Three Days Grace

THE DEATH OF PEACE OF MIND – Bad Omens

Punch Drunk Love – Magic Whatever

Numb – Linkin Park

Call Me – Shinedown

City – Hollywood Undead

Anthem of the Angels – Breaking Benjamin

Save Yourself – My Darkest Days

Hymn for the Missing – Red*

* Listen during the epilogue if you want to cry harder ☺

"I am equal parts impressed and concerned that you wrote this."
-My Husband

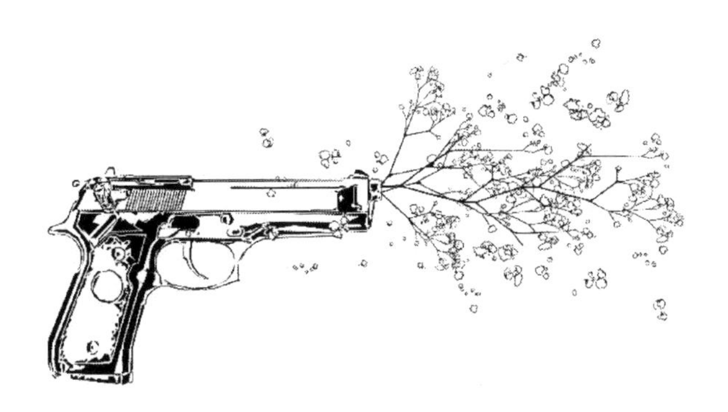

PROLOGUE

THE FATHER

I've learned after eighty-seven years on this earth to trust my gut in all things.

Where my son is concerned, I've become clairvoyant.

At my age, I've got nothing better to do all day than make peace with death. I can smell it. Always polluting the corridors of my home like a miasma of despair.

I can feel his pain lingering in the air long before I see him.

Tonight though, I do not feel his pain. Not a physical pain, anyways. More akin to…frigid anguish.

It feels like guilt. It feels like horror.

It feels like resignation.

My bones are aching something fierce. I can feel something wrong deep in the pit of my stomach, causing me to clutch my rosary to my chest. I take a deep breath as I sit up from my bed, my knees cracking loudly as I use my walker to steady myself. I can't walk very well on my own anymore, but something gives me the strength to stand and step into the corridor.

My son isn't here. He's never here at night. His absence in the dark doesn't bother me. Never has. What bothers me is his bedroom door. It's fully ajar. He never leaves it open.

My walker clacks against the tile floors as I slowly make my way to the open bedroom door, tapping on the wooden frame with my knuckle as I peek in. Empty. Like it always is.

There's a piece of paper neatly laid on the edge of his bed, the creamy custom embossed parchment a stark contrast to the burgundy comforter. My heart sinks, and I rush over to it as fast as my old legs will carry me. I know what this is before I even read the first line.

Wherever my son has gone, I'm already too late.

Friday, September 6, 2019.

I, Christian Thomas Reeves, being of unsound mind and a broken spirit, declare this my last will and testament, as well as a goodbye.

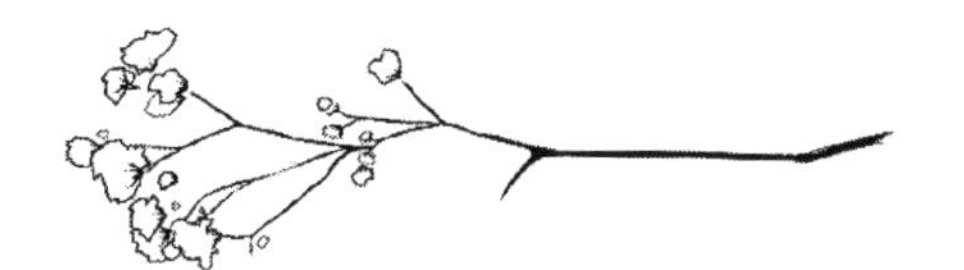

PART I

CHAPTER 1

THE ANGEL

I glance at the clock in the bottom corner of my computer. It's 8:37 PM on a Friday night. I groan quietly to myself. I've been at this desk in this uncomfortable office chair since nine this morning. You'd think with all the money flowing in and out of this place, they'd be able to provide their staff with chairs that don't cause early-onset arthritis. I take an exhausted breath and finish up an email to my boss, Neil, before shutting down my computer and grabbing my things.

Five months ago, I landed this job out of pure dumb luck. I applied for an open position at Reeves Enterprises to be a secretary for one of the senior attorneys. During my third round of interviews, I bombed it. Hard. My nerves got the best of me, and I formed one coherent sentence through the entire thing.

That sentence was my name.

Good morning. My name is Elena Young. I want to work at Reeves Enterprises because....because I...um....

After that, I fell apart. I only got this job because the other two candidates got stuck in awful lunchtime traffic downtown and missed their interviews. I can't afford a car, or even the three dollar per hour parking meter outside the building, so I walked.

During the interview process, the entire legal department seemed so welcoming. Unfortunately, the supervising attorney I was assigned to wasn't in any of my three interviews, so I never got the chance to meet him. If I had, I might have dropped out of the candidate pool entirely. I didn't realize how difficult my new boss would be. Neil Hayden's ego is bigger than the Atlantic Ocean, and he absolutely hates me. I can do no right in his eyes, and he berates me in front of my other coworkers on a regular basis. It's embarrassing and demeaning, but I need this job. For my career and my survival.

So, I'm forced to overlook Neil Hayden's clear distaste for me and pretend I don't notice his extra-long pinky fingernail or the way he's always sniffling when he comes back from the bathroom.

At fifteen dollars an hour, I'm making double what I was as a receptionist at my last job. It's not a glamorous lifestyle by any means, but I can afford my rent and I can feed myself.

Instant noodles and tap water mostly, but it could be worse.

I can also earn unlimited overtime, which is why I work so late most nights. It's not like I have anything better to do. I like to have fresh flowers in my kitchen, to bring life to my dull, gray, 300-square-foot studio apartment. It's got a single window, a shitty water heater, and the bathroom is so small that I can barely squeeze in, but it's home.

Most of my excess income, I spend on baby's breath, ice cream and Twizzlers. It makes the long hours bearable.

Sometimes it's the simple things, you know?

I live in Meridian City, New Jersey, the crime capital of the United States. It's an island off the mainland of New Jersey, as Staten Island is to New York. Meridian City is about twice the size of Staten Island with a population of almost three million.

Meridian City is divided into four 'sides', North, South, East, and West. The North Side is home to a billionaire's philanthropy project. The South Side is where the wealthy live, and the East and West Sides are where plebians like me live. Druggies litter the streets. Robberies happen nightly. We have the highest murder rate in the country. The police force is stretched so thin that calling for help is a crapshoot on if they'll actually show up.

I'm convinced I have the best luck in the world, because the most uncomfortable interaction I've ever had in this cesspool of a city is a few homeless men offering me a hit of whatever they were smoking.

I always carry a taser with me though, just in case someone decides to try and make me a statistic.

My father insisted when I moved halfway across the country for school that I always carry some sort of protection with me. He lost his first family—a wife and two daughters—to a lunatic with a gun, and he's very protective of my brother and me.

I'm sure every time his phone rings from an unknown number, he thinks he's getting the call that I'm dead.

My father is a world-famous plastic surgeon in Houston, Texas. My mother is a therapist. I grew up in a big house on a large plot of land, and my parents never denied me anything growing up.

When I told them I wanted to move to the most dangerous, crime-ridden city in the United States, they looked at me like I had grown a second head and murdered a kitten in front of them.

Meridian City is objectively a terrible place to live, but for some god-forsaken reason, it's home to the best law school in the country.

Guess what I want to be someday?

I moved here five years ago after I graduated with my bachelor's degree from UT Austin in public relations to chase my career in law, and I graduated with my JD two years ago.

Sometimes I wonder why I decided I wanted to be a lawyer when I'd rather stick pins in my eyes than stand in front of a group of people and argue on behalf of someone else. I also get horrible testing anxiety, which is probably why I keep bombing the bar exam. I've failed it twice and I'm too insecure to retake it again without a prep course. I've been saving up for one, but it's nearly four thousand dollars, and I have about seven in my bank account.

The most valuable thing I own is my coffee maker; a custom-painted purple Keurig my parents gave me my freshman year of undergrad.

Everyone in my family has a successful, thriving career, and I'm tolerating verbal abuse during business hours so I can afford my rent.

Fortunately, my job at Reeves Enterprises is a foot in the door—even if Neil is insufferable. I'm trying to work as hard as I can to make a good impression so that once I'm finally licensed to practice law, they'll take me on as their newest associate attorney. Maybe I'll even take Neil's place one day—who knows?

Unfortunately, I have to actually *pass* the bar exam before that dream comes even close to being a reality.

It's just past 9 PM when I make it to the downstairs lobby of my office building, and it's pouring down rain. I stupidly forgot my umbrella at home this morning, as if it's not raining every other day in this decrepit city. Taser in hand, I step outside into the dark of the night, soaking wet by the time I make it to the crosswalk.

Snap.

I hear the strap of my old, battered purse break and it sends my phone and the rest of my things into a puddle at the curb. I look up and whine in frustration, before bending down to scoop up my belongings into the purse. I reach into the puddle and grab my phone. When I try to unlock it, the screen flickers a bit before distorting, and then goes black.

Shit. I really do not need this in my life right now. I can barely afford ramen noodles for dinner. How am I supposed to afford a new phone? If the old rice trick doesn't work, I'll be screwed.

I'm about halfway home when I get a *feeling*. The kind where the hairs on the back of my neck stand up. The kind where I just *know* someone is watching me. I try my best to resist the urge to look around, but I fail. My eyes snap to my right, and three figures are walking towards me from the cross street. I clutch my broken bag a bit tighter to my chest and walk with a new sense of urgency.

I try to tell myself that they're just passing by, that I'm being paranoid, but the pounding of blood in my ears is so loud that I begin to panic. I can hear them cackling and whooping behind me, and my heart sinks into my stomach. My conscience tells me to run.

So I run.

Receipts, tampons, and lip-gloss fall out of my bag as I do, leaving a convenient trail for the three men to follow. I can see my apartment building in the distance. I'm less than a block away, but a lump forms in my throat at the thought of leading them right to where I live.

What if they wait for me? What if they come back? What if they break in and come get me in the night?

I make a split-second decision to dart into an alley, but I nearly collapse with fear when I'm met with a dead-end brick wall. There's a dumpster to my left. I crouch behind it and cover my mouth, staying perfectly still and trying not to make a sound as the rain ruthlessly pelts down on my trembling body.

My attackers catch up and surround me. I dropped my taser while running, and I'm defenseless. One of the men grabs my arm roughly and yanks me to my feet. His grubby fingers dig into my flesh so hard I'll have bruises in the morning.

I scream louder than I ever have before. Louder than I thought I was capable of. I yell for help as two of them each grab one of my arms and hold me in place. The third twists his hand into my braid as if it's a rope and forces me to look at him. He looks me over and licks his lips. He caresses my cheek and I scream again before he presses the cold blade of a pocketknife to my neck.

"Shut the fuck up! Nobody's coming to help you, sugar."

I shake, but I don't make another sound. I wait in horror, in silence, as he traces the tip of the knife over my neck, down my chest, and in between the valley of my breasts, ripping the fabric of my blouse enough for it to fall open and expose my bra.

I close my eyes tightly and accept the inevitable, tears streaming down my face. I pray that whatever they're about to do to me, they will make it fast.

"Oh shit!" I hear one of them yell.

The knife that was at my chest gets yanked away, followed by the hands holding my arms in place. My eyes are still closed and I'm shaking violently from fear and the cold rain.

I hear three rapid gunshots, three sickening squelches, and three thuds on the pavement.

It goes eerily quiet, save for the sound of rain on the concrete.

I open my eyes, and I gasp.

My lips quiver and tears sting in my eyes as I look up at my savior, standing just a foot away from me. I'm in a state of shock, I'm sure, because I look up and see his throat bob like he's speaking, but I don't hear words.

Meridian City, and all its crime-ridden glory, has something else that makes it absolutely unbelievable.

The Meridian City Silencer.

A serial killer in a red mask that patrols the streets at night, beating up criminals and dishing out bullet-shaped justice to anyone he feels deserves it.

The red mask covers the bottom half of his face like a muzzle. His tactical pants are pitch black and covered with dozens of knives and guns, bulky from whatever equipment he keeps stuffed in the pockets. His combat boots are caked in mud. He's got on a jacket with the sleeves cut off, exposing his vascular arms, and the hood thrown over his head. With every breath he takes, I can see the gentle separation of scales that make up his shirt, hugging his muscles like snakeskin. His dark hair falls over his forehead and sticks to his skin from the rain.

The wanted posters don't do him justice. Not his beauty, nor the malice in his eyes.

My heart is beating so fast I can hardly think. I might have thanked him for saving me if I wasn't utterly traumatized from nearly being gang raped.

A burning, itching sensation cuts through my chest and I look down to see a bright red welt in my skin where the knife was dragged down my sternum. I cover the welt with the shredded parts of my top.

"Superficial."

My eyes snap up to him and I shake my head in confusion. "What?" I ask, my voice unsteady.

"It's a superficial wound. It will heal fast. You won't even feel it by morning."

All I can do is stare up at him. His eyes are an artificially bright green. Dark paint in his eye sockets has streaked down his face from the rain like blackened tears. "Are you okay?"

My eyes flicker down to the three bodies that are scattered around us, lying face down in the dirty alleyway. My breathing heightens into panic again when I notice the subtle red pools mixing with the thin layer of rainwater.

"Don't worry. They won't touch you again."

I stand there unmoving for so long I think I've forgotten that I even have legs. Every sense in my body is telling me to run, but I'm frozen in place, shaking like this is the first time I've stood on my own in my life. My bottom lip quivers and I recoil into myself when he brushes away a strand of my loose hair with his knuckle.

"You're scared."

I can hear in his voice the rest of the sentence he didn't say. '*Of me*'.

Fuck yes, I'm scared of him. He murders people that look at him funny, and right now, *I'm* one of those people. I've got my gaze locked on him like I'm a deer in headlights. Rain drips off the edge of the mask covering his mouth and jaw.

"Do you live close?"

I don't answer his question. He nods as if he already knows the answer.

"Go home. I'll make sure no one else follows you."

Before he can even finish his sentence, I dart away from him and around the corner. All I want is to be alone, safe, in my tiny apartment. Mercifully, my keys are on a stretchy wristband around my arm, and I run the next street over to my apartment building. I'm shaking so violently that I type in the wrong code to open the outer door three times before I get it open.

With a slight sense of safety behind the door, I sink onto the small staircase in the lobby and cry as the reality of what just happened—and what could have happened—washes over me.

I sit on those stairs for a long time, and when I manage to get enough of a grip to stand again, I run upstairs to my apartment, lock the door, collapse against the thin wood, and cry some more.

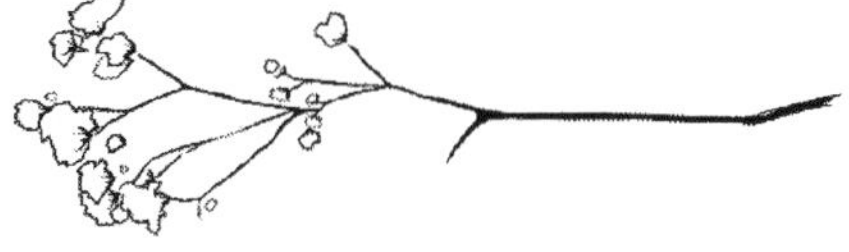

The next morning, my eyes are painfully puffy. Thank God it's the weekend, so I have some time to properly cope before pulling myself together for work. I turn on the news and my heart plummets at the coverage.

It's Saturday, September 7th here in Meridian City. MCPD detectives are investigating a triple homicide that occurred last night on the 1700 block of Season Circle. Three men were found shot to death in an alleyway with red duct tape over their mouths, the distinctive calling card of the Meridian City Silencer. The police are asking anyone with information to call the MCPD tip hotline and ask for Lieutenant Martinez, the investigator on the case.

My body shakes as I watch the morning news on my 20-inch TV I found in the dumpster my first week living here. I blink and swallow the bile in my throat.

I think I was in such a state of shock last night that I was desensitized to the fact that I was standing a foot away from a serial killer that shot three men in front of me.

I pull out my phone on instinct to call the hotline. I'm stopped when it's nowhere to be found, and I realize I dropped my phone, my purse, my wallet, my *everything* in that stupid alleyway and was so preoccupied with staring at my savior that I forgot to gather it all before I ran away from him.

I consider knocking on my neighbor's door and asking to borrow their phone, but what the hell am I supposed to say?

Oh, hi. I witnessed a triple murder last night and my first instinct was to wrap myself in blankets and cry instead of going to the police.

There's a one-million-dollar reward sponsored by the MCPD and the local government for any information leading to the arrest of the Silencer. I'm pretty sure he's on the FBI's most wanted list. I could use a million dollars, but I don't think telling them I was almost gang raped but was saved by the resident serial killer is going to do anything except get me locked in a mental institution.

No. I need to keep this to myself. Pretend it didn't happen. If the police saw me on any cameras or any witnesses saw me running, they would have already come to question me about it. I'm fine. I just need to stay calm and forget this whole thing ever happened.

I go downstairs at midday to my building's lobby to check my mailbox. There's a business card and a pink slip indicating I have a package waiting with the receptionist.

I don't remember ordering anything, but maybe it's something from my parents or my brother. I bring the slip to the helpful, scrawny blond man at the desk, and he hands me back a medium sized box. He holds onto it for an awkwardly long amount of time, staring at me and flashing me a crooked, unnerving smile. I uncomfortably laugh and tug the box free from his hand and then look down at it.

Plain brown box, addressed to me with no return label or any other indication of where it came from. I don't think much of it and gather it in my arms before heading back up to my apartment. When I get back, I load my coffee maker with fresh water and let my beloved Keurig work its magic.

I take a look at the business card. It's not uncommon to get them in the mail, especially from the surrounding businesses. Hell, I have a stack an inch high of business cards from the pizza shop across the street in my junk drawer.

The business card is a shiny, metallic gold, embossed with black lettering.

Hellfire Lounge: Bartenders Wanted! Ask For Frank!

I put the card to the side and keep it in the back of my mind. Bartenders make great money; I would know from experience. Maybe it's something I could do on the weekends for extra cash, to help me move out of this terrible neighborhood sooner. I've never heard of the Hellfire Lounge, but if it's as luxurious as the business card, maybe it wouldn't be the worst place for a second job.

My spine tingles as I look at the mystery package on my kitchen counter. I take a sip of my coffee and open the box, praying it's not a bomb.

Though in this city, I honestly wouldn't be surprised.

I close my eyes when I open the top, only peeking when I'm sure nothing's going to explode. My jaw drops to the floor when I examine the contents.

My wallet, my phone, and my taser all lay inside. I check my wallet, and my ID is still there, along with all my cards and the same three dollars cash I always keep for the vending machines at work. Everything seems to be accounted for.

My heart squeezes. It had to have been the Silencer, right? No person in Meridian City would have returned my things without at least taking the cash from my wallet.

A *serial killer* went out of his way to return my most important belongings.

The thought alone is unsettling.

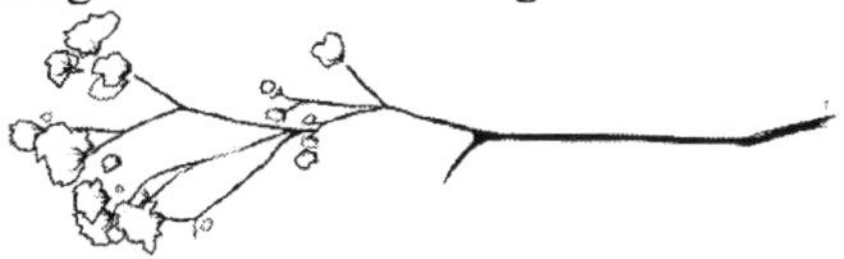

When the sun goes down, the rain finally stops. I need to take my garbage out, and I would rather get it done before it inevitably starts raining again. I'm on edge after last night, but I think I can muster up the courage to go outside by myself in the dark.

When I dump my garbage into the vile smelling dumpster, I hear a groan down the alleyway from me. I don't look at first, tensing every muscle in my body. Nothing is worth the trouble. Meridian City is the type of place where you ought to mind your business.

I hear another groan, followed by a thud and a small splash.

I can't help it. I squeeze my eyes tight and then open them and whip around, taser out in front of me for protection. Just a few feet away, there's a vaguely human shaped lump in the alley.

"Hello?" I call out, getting no response. I tip-toe two steps closer. "Hello?"

Still no response. I adjust my grip on the taser and step even closer. I gasp when I finally make out the figure.

The Silencer.

No. *Absolutely not.* I didn't intend on meeting him last night and I'm not going to get myself tangled in whatever the fuck he's been up to. I hold my breath and tiptoe backwards. I let out a shrill of fear when the Silencer's hand catches me by the ankle and tugs me so hard that I lose my footing and fall onto the concrete next to him. I barely manage to catch myself before I completely eat it.

I try to crawl away quietly, but his grip on my ankle isn't letting up. I kick him roughly in the head and he looks up at me, half-annoyed with his brows knitted together. That's when I notice the blood on his hands—blood that is now coating my ankle. I stare at him for a while, my chest heaving as I try and consider alternate methods of escape.

Without thinking about the fact that it's raining or that the Silencer has an iron grip on my ankle, I press the prongs of the taser into the meat of his arm and shock him. The electricity travels through his arm and up my leg, causing me to drop it. He loosens his hold just enough for me to wiggle out of his grasp, scramble to my feet, and start running.

I'm functioning on pure adrenaline as I sprint towards the back door of my apartment building. As my fingers wrap around the handle, I feel the Silencer grab my waist and clasp his hand over my mouth. I let out a useless cry for help and he presses me against the door. The sharp metallic smell of blood taints my senses as the warm liquid on his fingers smears across my cheek. I'm letting out panicked breaths, and I cower away from him best I can when he leans forward and whispers into my ear.

"Shut up and take me to your apartment."

On instinct, I shake my head vehemently. He engulfs me in the scent of faded cologne, gunpowder, and cigarette smoke.

"Open the door. *Now*. Don't make me ask again."

My life comes down to two options in this moment.

I can continue to be defiant and die in this disgusting alleyway, or I can let him follow me into my apartment, in which case he'll kill me in the comfort of my own home.

It's not like it matters. My phone is broken, so I have no way to call for help, and everyone in this damn city fears this psychopath. No one with any sense of self-preservation is going to help me.

With a shaky hand, I type in the code to open the back door and walk inside with my mouth tightly shut. My apartment might as well be a portal to hell because as soon as we're both inside, I hear him shut the door behind him and lock it.

I close my eyes and take a deep breath, trembling on the inhale and exhale. I can feel him circling me like a predator.

"Please don't hurt me," I beg with a whisper. "I promise, I didn't see anything. Just—just leave. I won't tell anyone you were here."

I tense up when I hear him turn on my kitchen sink, and a moment later, he rubs a warm rag over my cheeks and lips. The action is so tender that my eyes fly open in confusion. He's standing in front of me with one of my dish towels in his hand.

He's wiping the blood off my face.

It catches me so off guard that I stumble backwards, suddenly feeling lightheaded but refusing to let myself pass out. I might never wake up again if I do. I use the door to prop myself up as the room spins.

"Don't be scared," he says, closing the distance between us and continuing to gently wipe my face. "Take a deep breath. I'm not going to hurt you."

My lip trembles and more tears fall. "Why?"

He laughs, and it feels so out of place considering I'm shit scared and fighting the undeniable urge to scream.

"Did I hurt you last night?" he asks, and then he kneels, carefully removing my shoe and sock and cleaning the blood from my ankle, too.

"No," I squeak.

"Do you have a first aid kit?"

The entirety of my vocabulary escapes me, and I can't think straight. The room starts to spin again and unease twists in my gut.

"Look at me," he commands, snapping his fingers to get my attention and then standing to his full height. "*First aid kit.*"

"Under the bathroom sink," I manage to choke out, and the corners of his eyes crinkle as if he's smiling under that mask. His gloved thumb traces over my lips.

And that's when I finally black out.

CHAPTER 2

THE ANGEL

I sit up abruptly, gasping for air.

I'm covered in my comforter and tucked into bed. It takes a while for everything to come rushing back to me, but when it does, my eyes finally adjust to the darkness, and I see the Silencer sitting on the floor, slumped against the wall like he's asleep. A plethora of first aid supplies lay scattered around him; bloody rags, alcohol wipes, and a sewing needle with fishing wire attached.

He's got a large, nasty gash on his right bicep that he's haphazardly stitched up himself in a jagged line that will leave him with a scar that only serves to make him appear more dangerous.

I untangle myself from the sheets and throw my legs over the edge of the bed. I brace myself as I experimentally poke his arm with my sock-covered foot. He doesn't move. I rest my feet firmly on the floor and before I attempt to stand up, I poke him again, this time in the cheek with my index finger. His head sways slightly, but he doesn't wake up. I sigh a breath of relief and sink to the floor on my hands and knees.

Wait.

What the fuck is happening right now? Am I dead, and this is just some fucked up purgatory?

The serial killer in my apartment tucked me into bed after I passed out *and* he made sure to put my socks back on my feet so they wouldn't get cold.

The hardwood floor digs into my knees and palms. I poke him again with my finger, making my touch a little firmer against his tactical pants. He's still not moving. He's either unconscious or he's one hell of a deep sleeper. Though why he chose to take a nap in my apartment is a question I'll have to ask myself later.

Before I crawl away from him, I make a decision to grab one of the many pistols he has strapped to his thighs. I'll be damned if this psycho catches me off guard without a weapon. I quietly check the chamber. It's already loaded.

Something is stopping me from moving, and I think I know exactly what it is: greed. One of the most notorious serial killers in the United States is unconscious in my apartment, and if I can press that tiny button on the side of his muzzle and give the police an accurate description of him, I could be a million dollars richer. It would be so easy for me to peek. He'd never know.

I bite my lip and my hand is unsteady as I reach a finger towards him to press the lock.

As soon as my finger touches his mask, his eyes fly open and he lunges for me with a growl, grabs my wrists, and flips me onto my back. He's straddling me, his thick thighs caging my arms down by my sides. He has one hand cupped over my mouth to stop me from screaming, and another hand white knuckling a serrated knife that's now pressed firmly against my jugular. He uses his boot to kick away the gun that I stole from him.

Tears prick in my eyes as he stares at me, wild and terrifying.

He takes three deep breaths and I see his green eyes soften. He lowers the knife from my throat, placing it back into his thigh sheath, followed by the discarded gun I stole. He's got so many weapons strapped to his legs I don't even know how he can move properly. He's still holding me down with nothing but his body weight and his hand firmly over my mouth.

I watch his Adam's apple bob when he swallows. "I'm going to let you go. Scream and I'll tape your mouth shut. Nod if you understand."

I do.

He hesitates, but he lets me go and lifts himself off me, and I roll over and take in a huge breath of air. He's standing now, while I'm cowering on the floor, and if he looked big before, he looks massive now. He's got to be at least six-three, maybe even taller. He's built like a truck, and I think he could pop a balloon between his pecs.

He looks down at me with an amused glint in his eyes. "Your curiosity almost got you killed."

I eye him with confusion. *Almost* got me killed? That's actually a terrifying fucking point. Why the hell hasn't he slit my throat yet?

My cheeks heat up from the intensity of his stare.

"Did you tell anyone I was here?"

I shake my head and finally work up the nerve to stand, scurrying to the kitchen. My apartment is so small that even though he's by the bed and I'm by the kitchen counter, I could still touch him if I reached out a hand. "No. I can't even if I wanted to. My phone is broken from Friday night."

He takes a half-step towards me to close the gap. "If you're lying to me, I'll find out, so I'm going to ask you again. *Did you tell anyone I was here*?" He enunciates each word as if I didn't hear him the first time, his voice low and gravelly behind that mask.

"No!"

He's looking at me like he's plotting my murder. *God, why didn't I just fucking run when I had the chance?*

I notice his fingers poised over the guns strapped to his legs.

One wrong move, and I'm dead.

"Is this the part where you murder me?" I ask, letting out a trembling exhale. "Because I'll fight back." I grab the taser resting on my kitchen counter. He must have grabbed it from the alley. I turn it on and let it crackle with a charge. He takes a step closer to me until my hips are pressed tightly against the kitchen counter and my only way out is through him.

"You wouldn't make it a single step."

I hold out the taser to warn him.

His hands stay at his side, and he steps even closer to me, pressing his chest directly into the teeth of the charged taser. I look up at him, and he doesn't even blink. Once the charge is finished, and he hasn't moved, I drop the taser at my feet and gulp.

"I swear on my life, I didn't tell anyone you were here."

"Where's all that bravery now, huh?"

He leans over me as if he's considering breaking my neck. Quick, easy, painless. That's how I would want to go anyways. His eyes flicker to the counter behind me and I shiver as his arm brushes past mine to reach around me. He rubs over my access card to the Reeves Enterprises building with a gloved hand.

"You work at Reeves Enterprises?"

"Yes," I say breathlessly.

His head snaps to me. "Don't tell strangers so much about yourself."

"You asked!" *As if the card wasn't already a dead giveaway.*

"Do you tell every person you've ever met where you work?"

I don't have an answer for that. Considering he murders people on a regular basis, he's the last person I should be telling about my life. He slinks back to my bed and sits on it with a heavy sigh and so much force it scratches across the floor. He manspreads on the mattress like he owns it, and I cross my arms over my chest.

He looks up at me and has *the nerve* to *wink* at me from behind his stupid little mask. I run my fingers through my hair and look down at myself and cringe. I had forgotten I had his blood all over my clothes and I'm suddenly itching to take a shower. I'm not stupid enough to put myself in that kind of position though. Naked with a serial killer on the other side of the door? No thanks.

"Why do you do it?" I ask, the words spilling out of me faster than I can put a filter on them. His predatory gaze flickers to me and there's something vulnerable in his expression that I can't quite describe.

"I like it."

I don't know why I expected his answer to be something profound, but even murderers have a story. I want to know his. "Why?"

He scoffs. "If you're expecting me to tell you some sob story to justify what I do, don't."

I tilt my head to the side slightly, trying to read him—to understand his intentions behind what he does. "Someone you love was killed." I don't expect him to confirm or deny my observation, but something in the way he stiffens tells me I'm right.

He cracks his neck. "Doesn't matter why I do it."

"If you hadn't been there the other night those men would have gang raped me and left me to die in that alley. Is it bad to admit that I don't feel guilt over their deaths?"

"No. You did what anyone in your situation would have done. You called for help. I made the choice to kill them, and I'm the one who has to live with it. You have nothing to feel guilty for."

"Do *you* feel guilty?"

"No," he answers, almost scoffing when he does as if he can't believe I'd ask such a stupid question. I stiffen up as I remind myself that he's not my friend and even though he saved me last night, he's not a hero.

I can't meet his gaze, so I keep my attention on my hands wrapped in my sweater. It's quiet for a long time, so long that my feet begin to ache from standing. His muffled voice cuts through the silence.

"Do you like working at Reeves Enterprises?"

I perk up at his question and narrow my eyes, resisting the urge to tell him *I shouldn't talk to strangers*. After a moment of trying to hold his gaze, I lose our staring contest.

"It's a foot in the door. It's better than a lot of jobs here." I glance at my JD hanging on my wall. "My boss Neil is awful, but I want to be a lawyer, and working for him will look good on my résumé."

"*Neil Hayden*?" The Silencer asks, and my blood instantly runs cold when he says that name, because he knows exactly who I'm talking about. "What does he do that's so awful?"

"Nothing. It doesn't matter."

"Yes, it does."

"Why?" I ask, and he stands up slowly. Pushing off his thighs with his fists, he takes a large step towards me. My stomach flips, and I cower further into the wall, quickly letting an answer escape my chest before he comes any closer. "He just does everything in his power to make me feel small and useless. That's it. It's really not a big deal."

He leans closer to me, lifting a gloved finger to lightly touch my chin. "Everything that happens to you is a big deal. Say the word, and I'll take care of him."

"No! God, what is wrong with you? Neil Hayden being a dickhead isn't grounds for murder."

He lets out an amused huff and I think if he didn't have that mask covering his face, I'd see a sinister smile painted across his lips. "Well, you're no fun at all, angel."

My throat goes dry, and I lean away from him again. Panic rises in my chest. He reaches for my hand, and I snatch it away. Our eyes meet and the tension between us cracks. He pounces on me and when he pins me down to the bed, my chest heaves and I whimper in fear, trying to wiggle out of his grasp. He's too big. Too strong. I struggle and struggle to no avail and finally, I give up, going slack under the fiery intensity of his stare.

Tears slide down the sides of my face, disappearing into my hairline.

"Are you scared?"

I start nodding before he finishes his question. I see the corners of his eyes crinkle as he lets out a low chuckle. "I promise, I'm the one thing in this city you never have to be afraid of." He cocks his head to the side. "Why'd you try to take off my mask?"

All I do in response is bite my lip in an attempt to get it to stop quivering. I search through my brain for every possible lie I can come up with. Telling a serial killer that I was planning on turning him in for money seems like a quick way to end up with a bullet in my skull.

"I wanted to see the face of the man who saved me," I say cautiously.

He gives me a dangerous glare and goes completely still. I gulp, because I can just see it in the tension of his shoulders that I've crossed a line I shouldn't have touched with a thirty-nine-and-a-half-foot pole.

"You've got it backwards, angel."

Before I have a chance to ask him what he means, he lets go of me and leaves my apartment so fast I'm not sure he's even human.

CHAPTER 3

THE ANGEL

Sunday passes in a blur. I spent the entire day trying to get the blood off my floors, to no avail. My apartment looks like a crime scene, and I'm honestly pretty upset about it.

When I get to work on Monday morning, I head straight for the coffee pot. Reeves Enterprises spares no expense when it comes to coffee. In our department break room, there are so many options for creamer and sugar and syrups that for my first two months working here, I tried a different combination every morning. I'm a sucker for the hazelnut creamer though, and I can't afford my own at home, so I always savor it here.

I wonder if anyone would notice if I took off with the container.

There's also a Starbucks in the downstairs lobby, and each employee at the R.E. headquarters gets credit for one free drink per month, but Neil always steals it.

Yes, he *steals* it. Will swipe it right off my desk. Doesn't matter what's in the cup, he steals my coffee because he lives off my misery.

I'm not a violent person, but I'd pay good money to have someone knock out his front teeth or hit him in his bald head.

Neil Hayden is Reeves Enterprises' best attorney. He's so good that at Meridian Law School, there's literally an entire module in our 2L curriculum dedicated to him and his legendary representation. His previous employer got busted for using illegal child labor, and Neil managed to get them out of it without so much as a fine. Charges dropped; civil case dismissed. *With prejudice*. The man is legendary, and he knows it, which is probably why he's so damn awful. He could slit my throat and watch me bleed out all over the marble floors and nobody would bat an eye.

I'm not even sure *why* he hates me. I'm not totally incompetent when it comes to my duties here. My best guess is it's because I'm not fun to look at. I've got as much curve as a two by four, and the sex appeal of a plastic bag.

With my hot mug of hazelnut creamer with a splash of coffee in hand, I walk to my desk, and I nearly drop the mug when I get there.

A large bouquet of flowers is sitting on my desk. Scratch that—a fucking *massive* bouquet of flowers is sitting on my desk. Bright, beautiful peonies, roses, gardenias, and baby's breath in varying shades of purple and white are neatly arranged in a heavy marble vase.

I blink in shock and I'm not sure what to think. There's a light purple notecard sitting upright against the vase. I hesitantly open the envelope and inside is a card with messy, yet perfectly legible handwriting scribbled across it, almost like it was written with a non-dominant hand.

For my angel.

I throw the card haphazardly in my bag and push the heavy bouquet to the corner of my desk to try and get it out of the way as I power on my computer.

Okay, Elena. Breathe. Don't panic.

I tap my fingers against the desk and stare at those flowers while I wait for my computer to boot up. I'm not sure if I should be flattered or terrified that the Silencer sent these to me. There's no business card indicating he hired a service to deliver them. Besides, he'd have to put in contact information and his whole thing is remaining anonymous.

He must have brought these himself, which is an even more unsettling thought because I know there are at least a dozen cameras in the lobby.

How the hell did he get in here?

I don't have much time to consider it, because before my computer even fully boots up, I hear Neil shouting my name.

Judging by his tone, he's clearly on the warpath. I take a deep breath and brace myself as he stomps towards me from his office. I turn slowly in my chair and force a smile. "Yes, Mr. Hayden?"

"Where the hell have you been?" he shouts, his tone already drawing the attention of curious eyes across the office. His nostrils are flaring, and he points a crooked finger at me. "I've been trying to call you all weekend! I had court this morning and needed you to file an order before I got there. Where the fuck have you been, Eliza?"

"Elena," I correct. He hardly ever gets my name right. It's not even a complicated name, he just likes to get under my skin. "I'm sorry…I broke my phone on Friday night and I haven't—"

"I'm getting real sick of your excuses, *Elena.* You know what? It's not working out for you here. Pack your things and leave. See HR on your way out."

My heart sinks to the floor. "What?" I ask with a quiver in my voice. "Please," I start begging. "I really need this job. I'm sorry about this weekend. I'll get a new phone and–"

"This is not a negotiation."

I look at his stern face for another moment before I sigh a breath of defeat. I don't keep many personal belongings at my desk—just a few of my favorite gel pens and a framed photo of my dad and I at my college graduation. I shove it all into my purse and stand up, blinking away a stray tear to try and maintain some dignity while I leave.

When I turn to make a break for the elevator, I run face first into an Armani suit and a cloud of *absolutely divine* cologne. Large, warm hands hold me steady by my upper arms when I lose my footing and nearly fall over.

I gasp. "I'm sorry!" I crane my neck to look up at the man holding me. My lungs seize up. I feel as though I've just been punched in the stomach.

Christian Reeves is standing before me in a well-tailored gray suit and a black turtleneck.

The Christian Reeves, as in, the man who owns Meridian City and whose name is plastered on the side of the building I'm standing in.

The Christian Reeves as in, the CEO.

The Christian Reeves as in, the richest man on the goddamn planet.

I swallow the lump in my throat and all I want to do is sink seamlessly into the floor and perish. He gives me a dazzling, perfectly straight, bright white smile, and says, "It was my fault."

His voice slices through my resolve like butter. I can't help the blush that rises to my face. He's not just handsome. He's stunning. Godlike. His jawline could cut diamonds. Waves of dark brown hair frame his face in a '*I styled my hair but don't want to look like it*' sort of way. He's clean shaven and his eyes are such a pretty shade of blue the ocean would be jealous. His whole demeanor screams wealth. The grin on his face oozes confidence.

He's tall. A full foot taller than me and then some, and he's so broad I'm not sure how he can fit through a door frame.

He smiles at me warmly and patiently waits for me to stop ogling him. All the while, Neil Hayden is witnessing this extremely awkward interaction. My eyes go down to Christian's chest and blow wide when I see that I ran into him so hard I left smudges of my makeup on the lapel of his expensive suit. His eyes go down to his chest too, and he stifles a chuckle and wipes the makeup away with his thumb. I realize one of his hands is still firmly on my arm and I subtly wiggle out of his grip.

Christian glances at the bouquet on my desk and nods towards it. "Pretty flowers..." He rubs a finger over the acrylic nameplate next to the vase. "*Elena*."

Holy shit. Holy fuck.

The way this man just said my name was pure sex. I take one small step backwards to try and relieve some of the tension that's pooling between my legs.

What I wouldn't give to have him say my name like that again. Like it's the prettiest sound in the world. Like it's coated in sugar and dripping with honey, and he's got a massive sweet tooth.

I blink and look at the flowers, cotton mouth stealing my ability to speak. "Thank you."

Christian looks at my purse hanging off my shoulder. His brow arches. "Surely you're not already leaving the office? It's nine AM on a Monday."

"I'm…I'm…no longer employed." My face heats up at the admission. Christian Reeves has more important things to worry about than an entry-level employee, but it's still embarrassing to admit that I just got fired to the CEO.

"She was just on her way out," Neil interjects, pulling Christian's intense eyes away from me and I almost thank him for it, because I can finally breathe again. "Weren't you?"

I nod. "Yes, sir."

I move to leave, but Christian steps in my path. I look up at him and my brow knots, because I really can't tell what he's thinking based on his expression. "I think the three of us should take this discussion to your office, Mr. Hayden," he says to Neil, though his eyes are fixated on me.

"The three of us?" Neil asks with an eyebrow raised.

"I don't believe I stuttered," Christian says, giving him a threatening glare that has Neil shrinking in his shoes. Neil leads the three of us to his office, and in a gentlemanly fashion, Christian holds the door open for me.

I really wish the building would catch on fire or Godzilla would attack. Anything to get me out of this. I pray silently for an act of God to save me. Neil takes a seat at his desk, and Christian sits down in a low back leather chair across from him. I stand awkwardly in the corner of the room, and Christian turns in his seat to flash me that billion-dollar smile.

"Come sit," he commands, pointing to the chair next to him, still smiling. My legs feel like jelly, but I take a shaky breath and slowly sit down in the matching chair next to him. I'm so out of place right now. An entry level nobody, with the boss that just fired me and the CEO who has more dollars to his net worth than there are stars in the galaxy.

Neil frowns at me and we all sit in uncomfortable silence. He finally softens his face when he looks at Christian. "Mr. Reeves, I wasn't expecting you here today. Is there something I can help you with?"

"Let me stop you there, Mr. Hayden." I can tell from Christian's tone that I really shouldn't be in this room right now. The door is *right there*. I could make a break for it. "I'm going to do the talking, and you're going to do the listening."

Neil nods at Christian for him to continue, looking like he's seen a ghost. He's sweating profusely. Neil has a giant ego, but at the end of the day, Christian is the CEO, and he wouldn't risk pissing off the one person at this company that has the power to put him in his place.

Christian pulls a silver cigarette case out of his pocket and proceeds to light one of the sticks, taking a long drag and puffing out the smoke hard enough for it to waft into Neil's face across the table. "You will rehire Ms. Young, immediately, with double pay and full employer-paid benefits."

Settling back comfortably into his chair, he waits patiently for Neil to answer.

My mouth falls wide open in shock as Neil's judgmental gaze flickers to me and then back to Christian. "I see what this is," he says, lacing his fingers together and resting his elbows on the arms of his chair. "What did she tell you about me?"

Christian raises an eyebrow. "She's told me nothing."

Neil chuckles to himself, scratching the top of his shiny bald head. "You're telling me Christian Reeves is giving Eliza Young her job back out of the kindness of his heart? I wasn't born yesterday."

"What are you implying, Mr. Hayden?" Christian asks in a low growl, his tone as toxic as the stick between his teeth.

"I'm just saying she's got one hell of a mouth to have a man like you pulling strings for her, that's all." Neil shrugs and pumps his fist near his mouth in a vulgar gesture so that it's incredibly clear what he's implying.

Christian laughs, but there's no humor in it. He stands up, sauntering around Neil's desk. When he's at Neil's side, Christian grabs him by the back of his blazer and shoves his head onto the thick glass of the table, cheek first. He whimpers, and I gasp with my hand over my mouth. I can't say I'm not happy to watch Neil get what he deserves, but I'm not sure what to do except keep my mouth shut and try really hard to pretend I don't see the CEO of the company assaulting his top attorney.

Christian leans over him to speak in his ear, to ensure he hears every word. The ash from the cigarette hanging out of his mouth lands on the side of Neil's face.

"Mr. Hayden, her name is *Elena.* I have never slept with her. If that implication ever leaves your mouth, or this room, or you so much as *think* it again, I will shove a lawsuit so far up your ass you'll be able to taste paper. You will rehire her, and if you retaliate in any way, I will know, and you will regret it. Is this in any way unclear?"

"You're crazy!" Neil whimpers against his desk.

"Call the police if you want. But I can make or break your career. You piss me off, and all it takes is a few phone calls to have you blacklisted from the legal field in under an hour. If you want to keep your seven-figure salary, I suggest you do what I say, keep your mouth shut, and start treating Ms. Young with a little respect. Clear?"

Neil nods his head against the glass of his desk and Christian lets him go. I shake in my seat as Christian sits back down in his chair, and then he turns to face me, smiling as if I hallucinated what just happened. "Elena, would you be so kind as to make Mr. Hayden and I some coffee? I'll take mine black, thank you."

I give him a shaky nod and stand up, my ankles wobbly like a newborn deer in my heels as I walk to the coffee maker that's in the corner of Neil's office.

I'm so nervous that I drop a mug, shattering the ceramic all over Neil's black laminate flooring. If beating your employees was legal, I'd have two black eyes by the end of the day with the way he's glaring at me. Once the remains of the mug are in the small bin next to the coffee machine, I go back to preparing the drinks.

Neither of the men speak, and it's so awkward I would rather be thrown off the side of a bridge than bear witness to this cock fight that Christian Reeves is clearly winning.

When I get to Neil's coffee, I freeze. It's either three creamers and two sugars, or three sugars and two creamers. It changes depending on his mood, and I'm always somehow wrong. I choose two sugars, three creamers, and pray he will save the reprimand until later.

With shaky hands, I give Christian his coffee first in a black mug with the Reeves Enterprises logo on the side. He thanks me, and I hand Neil his mug much less politely, practically throwing it in his hands. I was hoping it would slosh over the rim and stain his pants, but no dice.

Neil takes a small sip before dramatically groaning.

Of fucking course. It's like I said, it's always wrong.

"I'll sprout wings and learn to fly before you get my goddamn coffee right, Eliza." He glares at Christian as I stand awkwardly to the side of his desk. "Of all the bitches in this building for you to bang, did you have to choose this one?"

"My name is Elena!" I shout, my voice breaking on the last syllable.

Neil glares at me. "Don't you raise your voice at me."

"My name is *Elena*," I repeat, my face surely as red as a strawberry as anger flares across my chest. "I *did* get your coffee right; you just change your preference every day because you get off on making me miserable!"

It's so silent in the room you can hear the fucking earth spinning on its axis. I have never lost my cool like that, on anyone, but to hear Neil call me a bitch and accuse me, *twice*, of whoring myself around for my position was the last straw for me. I don't even care that the CEO is witnessing my breakdown.

Fuck this job.

Neil's nostrils flare and he points at me, but I cut him off. "Yeah, yeah, I know. I'm fired." I move to stomp my way out of the room, but gentle, calloused fingers wrap around my tiny wrist, and I freeze. Christian is examining my hand like it's the prettiest thing he's ever seen.

"No," he purrs, as if he's seducing the inside of my wrist. He looks up at me like a puppy and it makes me want to fall to my knees. He moves his eyes slowly to Neil, still fuming at his desk as Christian's gaze darkens, and the entire room crackles with tension. "She's not fired. *You* are."

Neil's mouth falls open, and for the second time, so does mine. My wrist is still in Christian's firm grip, like he's afraid I'll make a run for it if he lets me go, and honestly, I might. I want to be anywhere other than in this room right now.

Neil scoffs in shock. "You're really going to fire me over this airhead? How good is her pussy?"

Protest is on the tip of my tongue. I've never even met Christian Reeves, let alone been in the same room as him before today. Where is Neil getting the idea that I would have found the time to sleep with him?

Christian flicks the butt end of his cigarette at Neil, and the ashes spread across his suit, burning a small circle in the expensive fabric. "If you don't stop talking about her like that, I'll break your nose," Christian threatens, and his voice is filled with so much venom that I believe it. "And for every minute it takes you to get the hell out of my building, I'm going to break one of your fingers. I'll give you a thirty second head start."

Neil begins to laugh humorlessly. Christian releases my wrist and I breathe a sigh of relief. He reaches into his blazer and pulls out a golden pocket watch with a monogrammed 'R' engraved into the metal.

"Sit," he commands, and the last thing I want to do is get on Christian's bad side, so I take a seat in the chair next to him again. He leans over and hands me the pocket watch, opening it for me and wrapping my fingers securely around it. It's heavy. It must be solid gold. "Elena, every time the small hand passes the twelve, tell me."

I tremble as I look down at the watch, my eyes following the small hand as it clicks around the clock. "It passed," I say quietly, looking up to Christian, who's stuck in a staring match with Neil.

"That's one finger," Christian says, taking a sip of his coffee.

I look back down at the watch just as it passes the twelve again. "It passed."

"Two. Better hurry, Mr. Hayden, or I'll have to move on to toes."

"You've got to be shitting me!" Neil says. "You can't do this!"

"I own this company, I assure you, I can do whatever the hell I want, and what I want is you off of my payroll."

"It passed."

Neil must begin to worry that Christian's threats towards his fingers aren't hollow. He stands, muttering expletives about Christian being a 'rich prick' and loudly announcing that he's calling the police. His office door quietly shuts itself, and

Christian and I are left alone in the room. Christian takes another long sip of his coffee and sighs contently.

"I was worried I was going to have to get security to drag him out," he says with a sexy smirk, brushing off a piece of lint from his pants. He's so collected, like the last ten minutes didn't happen. The corners of his mouth quirk into a smile as he turns his head to look at me. "I was never going to break his fingers."

I don't believe him for a second. I sit, frozen in place in the chair. Christian leans over, clasping his hands around mine and freeing his pocket watch from my stiff fingers. He rubs over the monogram on the front and smiles softly down at it. "I'm not a fan of gold. I think it's a harsh, ugly color, but this was my father's."

"Yeah, I'm more of a silver girl myself," I reply nervously, thankful I managed to form a coherent sentence as I look anywhere but him. My foot bounces with nervous energy, and Christian's large hand comes to rest on my knee, halting my movement.

"He won't bother you again."

I look up at him through my lashes, slowly, like he's a snake and I'm trying to avoid sudden movements.

I chew on my bottom lip. "You just fired your best attorney."

He chuckles. "He's not going to make accusations like that to my face and get away with it." His tone comes out nonchalant and suave, all the while I'm strung tighter than a drum. "The way he spoke about you made me want to throw him off the roof."

"I don't understand why you'd do something like that for a nobody like me."

His answer is immediate, like it's been rehearsed. "You're so much more than a nobody, Elena."

"I should get back to work."

I quickly leave with my hands crossed over my chest so he can't catch my wrists again.

Today was an absolute shitshow.

Mondays, am I right?

I'm out the door of the building at exactly five and get home as quickly as possible. Flopping on my bed, I take a long breath and stare up at my ceiling.

I instinctively go to pull out my phone, to text my brother, but then I remember that my phone is, in fact, broken and sitting in a bag of rice on my countertop. I stand up and make my way over to it, and I stand there, in shock, unable to breathe when right next to the rice bag is a brand-new phone, sitting neatly in a factory-sealed box. I blankly read the sticky note resting on top of the box.

Stay safe, angel.

I scoff at the note in a slight panic and crumple it before shoving it into my trash can. Then, I pull my old phone out of the rice bag and pray with everything in me that it still works. I press the power button and hold, and hold, and hold, waiting for the screen to turn on, but it doesn't.

I take a deep breath and lean over to hit my forehead against my countertop several times in frustration. Maybe I don't have the best street smarts in the world, but the Silencer clearly broke into my apartment, and I'll be damned if I turn on this replacement phone and start using it. What if he's got some sort of spy software installed on it? He's already given me enough red flags as it is. I really don't want to give him another outlet to stalk me. I'm going to end up as one of his victims if I'm not careful.

I throw the box in my nightstand and try to forget about it. I get paid on Friday. If I can just make it to Friday, I'll go to the store and buy a new phone on my lunch break. I make a mental note to email my mom and dad to let them know my phone is broken so that they don't worry if they call or text and I don't answer.

If I buy a new phone, I'm going to be way behind on my rent and my landlord is not exactly an understanding guy.

I need a second job, badly, if I want to avoid getting evicted, and I am way too stubborn to ask my parents for help. Unfortunately, there's not a lot of jobs floating around this city. An idea pops into my head and I search around my kitchen until I find that business card that I got in the mail. I take note of the address on the back. It's on the other side of the city, in a secluded corner near the shoreline.

I throw on a coat, shoes, and a bit of eyeshadow to look a little sultry, grab my purse, and make the long trek there.

I have to walk the entire way, so it's nearly eight PM when I make it. I can hear loud bass behind a large steel door. I take one deep breath and knock.

It takes a minute, but a man opens the door and gives me a once-over. He meets my eyes and smirks. "How can I help you, pretty girl?"

I gulp and get a feeling at the base of my spine that this is a terrible idea. That I should just walk away right now. But then I remember my rent, and I push the feeling to the back of my mind. I hold up the business card. "I'm here about the bartending position."

The bouncer wordlessly beckons me inside before leading me further into the club.

I *definitely* should have backed out when I had the chance.

I'm not one to judge people for the way they live their lives, but this is not the place for girls like me. It's a Monday night and the patrons are so drunk they're falling over themselves. Exotic dancers in lingerie line the walls on light-up platforms in neon colors. The music is so loud it makes my ears hurt. Some of the patrons follow me with their eyes like they're a predator and I'm the prey.

The bouncer leads me to a glass room overlooking the dance floor, where I can see men on the floor below grinding against drunk women with cigarettes hanging out of their mouths and their skirts hiked up revealing their underwear.

"Mr. Valenti, I've got one for you," the bouncer says to a thin man sitting on a plush couch with two passed out women next to him. He looks up from the stack of money in his hands that he was counting, does a double-take, and gives me the most awful smile I've ever seen.

"Hey beautiful," the man greets in a thick Jersey accent as he licks his lips, his eyes trailing over my body. "You're a pretty little thing, ain't ya?"

I don't acknowledge that. "I'm here for the bartending job." I look anywhere but his eyes when I speak. "I have experience. I did it in college."

"How soon can you start, gorgeous?" His gaze leaves me as he takes a drink of his whiskey. I can smell the high proof alcohol from across the small room.

"As soon as possible. But don't you need–"

"Be here tomorrow night when the sun goes down, ask for Kate. She'll show you around."

I realize this establishment is probably not legal, considering there's no paperwork and he hired me without even knowing my name. The man who brought me up here puts his hand on my lower back to push me out of the room.

"Congrats on the new job, baby," he says, notably staring at the curve of my ass in my tight slacks. "Make sure you wear something…a little juicier. Better tips."

CHAPTER 4

THE ANGEL

My next shift at Reeves Enterprises is thankfully, uneventful. I'm not sure I can handle any more drama in my life. Between the Silencer stalking me and whatever the hell that was yesterday between Christian Reeves and Neil Hayden, it's all way too much for me right now.

I leave promptly at five again, having already packed something 'juicier' to wear for my shift at the Hellfire Lounge, and I make the long trek across the city to the club.

When I get there, the same bouncer from last night lets me in and leads me to the locker room, where women scantily dressed sit at vanity mirrors while they do their makeup and hair. They must not all be bartenders like me, because a few of them are in matching showgirl costumes. Topless.

"Hey Kate!"

A curvy strawberry blonde woman whips her head around to us. She frowns when she looks at me, and the bouncer roughly pushes me further into the room.

"Show the new girl around, will ya?"

Kate walks up to me and crosses her arms, sizing me up. "I hope you brought something else to wear, pipsqueak. You'll never make any tips with all those clothes on."

I shake my bag on my shoulder. "Right here."

She nods and points. "Our bathroom is there. Pick an empty locker. Mr. Valenti likes to keep the girls rotated constantly to keep the patrons entertained, so your shifts are only five hours. You get one five-minute break. One. Five minutes. That's it. If you need to take a piss or something and you've already taken your break, tough luck. Patrons are allowed to touch you, dance with you, buy you drinks, but all clothes stay on. Don't come crying to me if someone smacks your ass or cops a feel of your boobs. You want to make good tips? I suggest you pretend to be into it. Cash tips are yours, house gets a hundred percent of your card tips, no exceptions."

She takes a deep breath to think through if she's covered everything, and my legs are shaking so bad I'm not sure how I'm standing up straight. She groans and rolls her eyes. "God, you new girls are such babies. Get dressed. You're working the bar, right?" I nod. "You got experience?" I nod again. "Good. I'll show you how the sections work, then you'll be on your own."

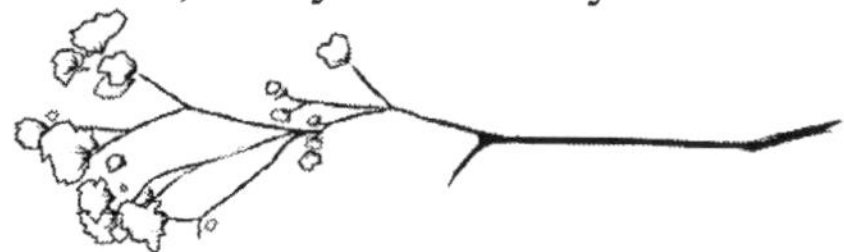

By the time Friday night rolls around, I'm exhausted. I work my normal 9-5 at Reeves Enterprises, and then go straight to the club after. My shift starts at eight, and ends at one in the morning, and then I'm up by seven the next morning to do it all over again.

We don't get normal days off at the club. The 'boss', Frank, decides when you can take the night off. Other than when he hired me, I haven't seen him again, which is A-okay with me. He gives me the creeps. All the girls here seem terrified of him, only talking about him in hushed tones as if he can hear them whispering over the bass of the music.

Kate is the only one that doesn't seem bothered by him. She's kind of like the mom friend around here. She cares about us, but she doesn't take any of our shit, and she definitely doesn't tolerate laziness. Everyone has to pull their own weight. I wonder if she's the way she is because Frank made her that way, or if she's just trying to look out for us.

I used to be a bartender when I was at UT Austin, and on a *good* night, I'd come home with over two hundred dollars in tips.

But I make two hundred dollars here within my first hour most nights. I haven't had a day yet where I didn't leave with at least twice that. I'm not even sure how most of the men here can afford to throw money at all the girls. They don't seem like the rich types. In fact, most of them are pretty rough looking.

It's not my business though. I came here to make money, and that's what I got. I can't complain.

While I'm cleaning off a table in my section, in the corner of my eye, I see five men sitting in loungers in a circle across the room with their hungry gazes on me. Every time I bend over a table to clean or take an order, their eyes follow me, drink me in, all trussed up in a mini skirt and a magical skin-tight crop top that transforms my A-cups into C's.

I try to ignore those gazes while I work, and halfway through my shift, I notice two other men have joined the group. One is Frank. He's tall and skinny, with a thin, almost bird-like face. He's much older than the rest, his hair white and gray and the skin of his cheeks slightly sagging.

The other man makes my heart skip a beat.

Christian Reeves.

Frank has his arms around Christian's shoulders and is smiling, though Christian's mouth is in an unimpressed line. His eyes shoot up like he can feel me staring at him, and our gazes collide. His jaw goes so tense that even from across the room, I'm wondering if he's cracked his teeth.

He says something to Frank and then all of them look at me again, and I quickly turn my back. My heart skips a beat and I suddenly realize I'm in deep shit. Not only is this club bad news, but now the CEO of my other job has seen me here with my boobs popping out of my shirt. He is one-hundred percent regretting giving me my job back. Panic begins to set in, and while I still have my back turned, mixing another cocktail, I subtly tap my hip against Kate's. She hums at me while she leans far over the bar to hand someone a drink.

"Psst. Hey. Does Christian Reeves come here often?"

Kate's eyes glance up at the mention of the name of the richest man in the world. "No. Not often. I've seen him around a handful of times but he's never here long."

Her voice is so quiet I can barely make it out over the loud bass bumping through the speakers. I peek over my shoulder to see Christian with his eyes glued to me as he takes a sip of his drink. He's lounging on a leather sofa, one arm thrown over the back of the seat, and an ankle propped on his knee.

He very subtly tips his glass to me—so subtly I might have imagined it, but his eyes are still hot against my skin as the corner of his mouth quirks, giving him the smallest hint of a devilishly sexy smirk.

"He and his friends won't stop…looking at me."

Kate looks in their direction and then 'accidentally' yet very intentionally drops a glass and tugs me down with her to help her clean it.

"Listen to me, Elena. If Valenti ever tries to take you downstairs, you run. You run away from him and hope that while you're running, he shoots you in the back. It's better than what's waiting for you down there. I don't know if Reeves is a part of it or what, but just…stay away from them."

I gulp. "What happens downstairs?" She doesn't answer me, so I pinch her arm lightly. "Tell me."

She sighs. "Valenti always has a '*favorite*'. She becomes his personal bartender for a while, and then if he takes her downstairs, I never see her again, and he comes back out of that elevator with duffle bags full of cash. You can let your imagination fill in the rest." She pinches me back. "Tell anyone I told you that, and I'll shank you."

My stomach flips. If what Kate says is true, I'm praying I'm not Frank's next bartender.

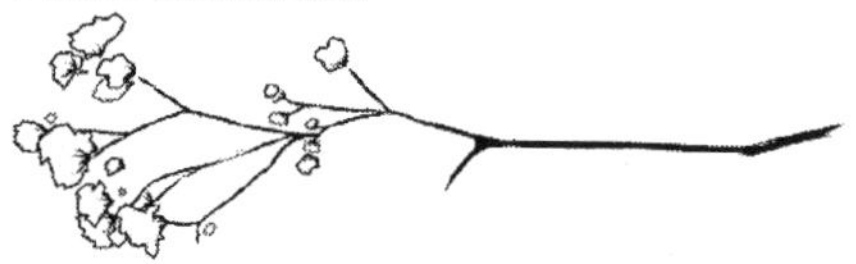

I spend the next hour trying to bribe Kate with my tips to get her to tend to Christian Reeves and the men with him. I offered her five hundred dollars, but she says it's my turn for that section and won't budge. I can't put it off anymore, so I try to hide my fear as I walk towards the group of men that have been eyeing me all night.

"Hey, fellas," I say, trying to raise my voice an octave to mask the nerves. "Anybody need anything?"

Christian won't stop staring at me, and I'm certain he recognizes me now. I can't read his face, but I think it's safe to assume I'm no longer employed at Reeves Enterprises. None of the men say anything to me, they simply stare with wicked little grins.

"Well, just flag me down if you do, okay?"

With a small wave over my shoulder, I turn to leave, and a familiar calloused hand wraps around my wrist, just like it did at the office. I take a breath, trying to find some courage in the air and turn to him. He's got a new intensity in his stare when he looks at me this time.

"What's your name, beautiful?" he asks, and my brow furrows. Does he really not remember? *Ouch.*

When I hesitate to answer, he very subtly rubs my wrist with his thumb and tilts his head towards me, and I understand that he doesn't want our audience to know that we've met before.

"My name is Elena."

"Elena," all of the men say in unison, and I nearly shit my pants. My stomach hurts, I can't breathe. I have a terrible feeling about all of this.

Christian, without taking his eyes off me, speaks again. "Let's dance, Elena," he says as he stands, towering over me. He tugs me to a secluded, empty corner of the club. Though we've got some privacy, the other men can clearly see each brush of his fingertips as he grips my waist and pulls me close to him. "What are you doing here?"

I try to think of any plausible excuse, but I come up empty as we sway to the song. All I manage to choke out is my job. "I'm bartending."

Christian's hands pull me closer to his chest, his hot fingers feeling like molten lava against the exposed skin between my skirt and my top. "How long have you been working here?"

I gulp. "Since Tuesday."

"Since Tuesday," he hums back. His hands graze over my hip and down my bare legs. He wraps his arms under my thighs and lifts me up, pinning me against the wall and his body with laughable ease. The action causes me to gasp. He clicks his tongue. "Tell me why."

I dig my nails into his biceps. Even from under his shirt, I feel the ripples of muscles on his arms while he holds me up. His body radiates so much heat I don't know how he hasn't broken into a sweat.

"On Friday I broke my phone, and I couldn't afford to buy a new one and still pay my rent, so I got a second job here to make some extra money."

He hums again. "Is thirty dollars an hour not enough for you, Elena?"

"Of course, it is," I say, hoping to maybe sweet talk him into letting me keep my job. "I really appreciate you giving me a raise. Please don't fire me. I'm…I'm saving up to move back home anyways. Just please let me keep my job until—"

In the middle of my sentence, he shoves two fingers into my mouth and presses down on my tongue to keep me quiet. I whine at the intrusion. "Where is home?" He pulls his fingers out of my mouth and grips my thigh again, my saliva smearing across my bare leg.

"Houston," I breathe.

"Put your fingers in my hair, Elena. Make it convincing."

Hesitantly, I do as he says, tangling my thin fingers in the hair at the nape of his neck, letting my nails scrape across his scalp. My eyes skate over the five men and Frank Valenti, still carefully watching the interaction, and I understand why Christian's being so…bold. We're putting on an act. He lowers his head so that his mouth is right at the shell of my ear, his hot breath fanning over my exposed neck. "What's it going to take?"

Goosebumps prick over my exposed skin. The bottom of my spine tingles. "What?"

"For you to stay in Meridian City. What's it going to take?"

I don't know what to say. I don't know how to answer that. The only reason I'm in Meridian City in the first place was because of law school, but now? I don't have a reason other than my dream position at Reeves Enterprises.

Though the fact that the CEO of Reeves Enterprises currently has his groin pressed against mine, that dream is just a sexual harassment lawsuit waiting to happen.

He's so close. So close that I can feel a bulge in his pants where he's holding my legs up, my center slotting against his. My mouth falls open and a heavy breath of desire escapes from my lungs.

Christian Reeves is a fucking masterpiece, all hard muscles and charming smiles, effortless swagger and a panty-melting voice. I'm inclined to believe that he was sculpted by the gods for the sole purpose of putting every other man on the planet to shame.

His lips ghosting over my neck sends my senses into overdrive and it's taking everything in me to stay still and not grind against the considerable tent in his pants. I tug on his hair slightly to pull him away from my neck, and it only brings a wicked, hungry grin to his face. He uses one of his hands to grab a fistful of my own hair and tug my head to the side, exposing my neck further. I feel his teeth lightly graze against my skin and his tongue follows the same trail. My eyes close, and I let out a breathy moan.

"Are you friends with Frank Valenti?" I ask quietly. He stops his gentle assault on my neck with his teeth and wraps a large hand around my throat, squeezing enough to make the pressure in my skull skyrocket, but not enough to cut off my air supply.

"I don't want to hear another man's name out of your mouth again, Elena."

"I'm sorry," I shudder, and he lets my throat go, his fingers digging into the curve of my ass. I'm going to have bruises in the exact size and shape of his fingers all over my legs. The thought alone has my mouth watering. A heady feeling settles low in my stomach when his mouth goes back to my neck and he kisses me right below my ear.

"I'm here because he invited me, not because we're friends. He's been trying to be my business partner for years."

"What kind of business could you have with a place like this?"

Illicit nightclubs aren't exactly the type of establishments Reeves Enterprises invests in.

I hear him laugh against my neck. "I wonder," he mumbles, and then he looks back up at me. His eyes have been invaded by his own pupils, gone so dark and large with lust that the blue of his eyes is nothing more than a thin line. "Does that bother you? That I'm here with him?"

I keep my mouth shut. I remember what Kate told me earlier, but if I say anything and it gets around to him, there's no telling what Frank will do to me. Christian ruts against me to catch my attention again.

"Are you scared of him?"

I shake my head. "I don't want to start rumors."

His mouth hovers millimeters from my lips. I can taste the whiskey on his breath, but he doesn't kiss me—only lets me bathe in the ghost of his lips against mine. "It'll stay between us. I promise."

My breath shudders again. "All night, his friends haven't taken their eyes off me. He won't either. I…I pointed it out to one of the girls here and she said that sometimes if he really likes a girl, he eventually takes her downstairs, and she's never seen again."

Tension fills every line of his body, and his eyes darken again, not with lust, but with anger. "What happens downstairs?"

"Kate told me to use my imagination."

Christian finally sets me down, and I'd be lying if I said I didn't miss the heat of his chest against mine—the heavy weight of him straining behind his zipper against my core. He lifts a thumb to trace over my bottom lip, and then with the same hand, he laces his fingers with mine and tugs me over to Frank and his friends, who have watched the entire interaction with curious eyes. Christian stops at his chair, fumbling through his suit jacket until he pulls out a small bank roll secured with a rubber band.

He slowly stuffs the roll down the valley of my breasts, and then uses his thumb and forefinger to lift my chin. He gives me that billion-dollar smile that makes me weak at the knees.

"Until next time, *Elena*."

Oh yeah, I'm definitely going to imagine him saying my name like that with my vibrator against my clit tonight.

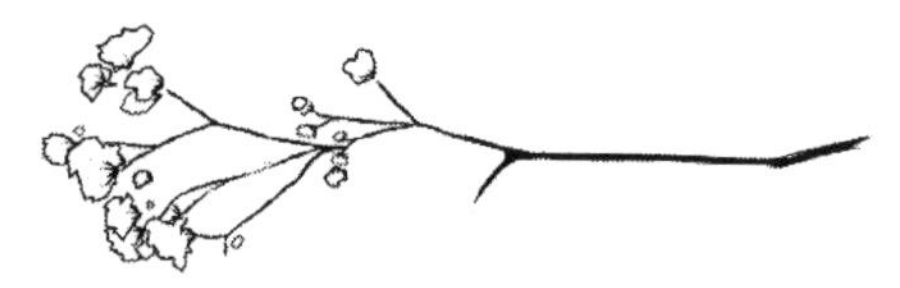

After my shift is over and I'm back home, I sit on the floor of my apartment and count the roll of bills Christian stuffed into my bra. I'm pretty sure I blacked out for a second.

One thousand dollars. He tipped me *one thousand dollars* for…whatever the hell we did tonight.

Rich people are nuts.

I wonder if the richest man in the world even knows other denominations of bills exist, or if he's only ever seen Benjamins. The latter wouldn't surprise me.

While I appreciate his generosity, I'm actually fucking mortified at the thought of ever running into him in the office again. I really don't know how we're going to come back from our 'dance' tonight. For a dance, there sure wasn't a lot of dancing but a whole lot of him making out with my neck and grinding his dick against me.

Not that I minded it.

I shove all my money into my nightstand, and I take a long shower. I'm so exhausted I barely have the strength to wash my hair. I want a night off from the club so bad, but I know if I asked, I'd probably be skinned alive or something equally as terrible. I should have never gone to that club. I should have just swallowed my pride and asked my parents to front me the money for a new phone.

But I unfortunately inherited my father's stubbornness.

When I get out of the shower, I wrap one of my fluffy purple towels around my body and step out of the bathroom to grab some clothes from my dresser. When I open the door, two large hands grab me, one going over my mouth to cover my scream, and the other holding me flat against the wall next to my nightstand.

I'm forced to choose between holding up my towel or fighting against the Silencer's grip, and I choose my towel easily. I use my foot to kick him in the shin and he chuckles before letting me go.

"Get out," I snarl. "How the hell did you get in here? Don't you have someone to murder or something?" I narrow my eyes at him and cross my arms over my chest. I glare at him while he looks me up and down, and I feel unnervingly exposed in nothing but my towel. "Why don't you go bug someone else and leave me alone!"

"Now where would be the fun in that?" He quirks up an eyebrow at my frustrated stance. "You look adorable when you're trying to be intimidating."

"Yeah, and I bet you'd look real adorable bleeding out in the alley again with a knife in your gut, which is exactly where you're about to end up if you don't get the fuck out!"

He plops down on my bed across from me, and I stay with my back against the wall with my arms and ankles crossed.

"Aw, not happy to see me?" I roll my eyes at his teasing tone. I want to smack the smile off his face that I'm sure is under that mask. "You looked real cozy with Christian Reeves at that club tonight. No wonder you haven't been home all week."

My face drops. "How...how do you know about that?"

"I can't say I was expecting to see such a clean-cut girl like you in that place. Tell me why you started working there."

I bite my cheek. "I needed a new phone."

"I *bought* you a new phone."

I scoff. "You're deranged if you think I'm putting any of my personal information into that thing."

He laughs. "That's not the reason I'm deranged, angel. And you don't have to worry, I didn't do anything to it. Didn't you see it was still factory sealed?"

"I'm not using it." I go to my nightstand and pull out the box from under my money and throw it roughly into his lap. "Here. Go get your money back or something and get out!"

He lets the box fall off his lap and onto the floor. "How much did Reeves pay you for your little tryst in the club? I'll pay double for a lap dance."

"I'm calling the police."

"With what phone, Elena?"

God fucking damn it. I groan in frustration, and then take a deep breath. "Please, just go, okay? I'm tired and I don't want to deal with you right now. I'm asking you nicely to please leave me alone. I have a life to get back to, and you're not a part of it."

In an instant, the Silencer is on his feet, across the room, and has me lifted up and pressed against the wall in the same fashion that Christian Reeves did in the club, only this time the only thing preserving my modesty is a towel. My bare center is pressed tightly against his tactical pants.

"You have no idea how wrong you are about that," he says into my ear, his voice low and dangerous. Then, in an unceremonious fashion, he drops me on my butt. I land with a thud on the hardwood floor and rub the sore spot. I freeze when he grabs me by the jaw in his thick hand and jerks my head up so I'm looking at him towering over me.

"You know, Elena, I don't think I ever heard you thank me for saving you and returning your things."

My blood runs cold and my breath quickens. My heart begins to thud and my cheeks turn red. I shake my head best I can in his iron grip. "Please," I beg. I can tell what he wants by his shift in energy alone, though the growing bulge in his pants makes it clear, too.

He growls. "You're begging, angel, but you're begging for the wrong thing." He runs a finger over my bottom lip and it makes me shiver. "Such a pretty mouth."

"Please," I beg again. "Thank you for saving me. I appreciate what you did. Truly. Please don't make me do this."

"I'm not going to *make you* do anything," he sneers. "You're going to do it because it's the *polite* thing to do." He looks up as if considering another option, and then his bright green eyes meet mine again. "You can thank me with your mouth or with your blood." He pulls a knife from his thigh and flips it in his hand for emphasis.

"You said you wouldn't hurt me."

"That's true, but you misunderstood, angel. I won't hurt you, if not for the purpose of our shared pleasure."

I scoff. "It's not shared if you take it. Put your dick near my mouth and I'll bite it off."

"Fine," he concedes. I sigh a breath of relief when he moves away from me to sit on the edge of my bed. "You can thank me with your mouth, or you can show me what's hiding under that towel."

This psychopath is clearly not leaving until I choose one of those two options. Or the third option which he's notably left out. He could also just kill me.

He's not even doing anything except sitting there, and I've never felt so helpless—not even when those men had me cornered in the alley.

At least the Silencer is giving me a choice.

I make the obvious one, which is to drop my towel and look away, pretending I don't feel his gaze glued to every inch of me.

"Beautiful," he whispers, and I think I might be going crazy, because the way he said it didn't feel sexual in the slightest. It felt tender. I peek from under my lashes at him. The look in his eyes isn't feral and hungry like it was a few minutes ago.

Now it feels almost…raw. Like he's experiencing seeing color for the first time. Like he's looking straight through me and admiring my soul instead of my body.

"Spread your legs," he commands.

Why did he have to ruin it? I scowl at him and wrap my towel back around my body.

"No. I delivered on my part of the deal. I thanked you. Now get out and leave me alone."

He chuckles. "You really think you're capable of getting rid of me so easily?"

He sinks to the floor and crawls on top of me before I have a chance to move, using his entire body weight to hold me down. I can feel every part of him pressed against every part of me. Every hard, rigid muscle. He cradles my head in his hands as I take a trembling breath in.

"Here's the thing, angel. I'm not going anywhere," he whispers, running his thumbs against my scalp. "I'm going to stay right here where I belong." His green eyes drink me in, committing every inch of my face to memory. "You're beautiful. How did I get so lucky?"

I try to push him off me. "You're not. I don't owe you anything."

"You're right. You don't, but I do. You're not the only one that needs to show your appreciation."

"What the hell does that mean?"

"It means that I'm going to make you want me as bad as I want you. I'm going to make you fantasize about how it feels to have my fingers in your greedy little cunt. I'm going to make you beg for my tongue against your clit. I'm going to make you so wet and needy for me that you'll do anything to get me to relieve that hot, achy feeling inside you. Once you admit you want me, that's when I'll show my appreciation. With every part of me. On every part of you."

My breath shudders. My heart is beating so hard that I think the downstairs neighbors can hear the thud in their ceiling. The filth of his words gathers a primal reaction from me against my will. He leans down to whisper in my ear.

"Is that what you want? You want me to taste and feel every inch of you until you're begging for my cock?" I stay quiet, willing myself not to react. He lets out a malicious laugh. "I promise angel, the next time you touch yourself, all you're going to be thinking about is me."

And then he lifts himself off me, throws me a wink, and crawls through my window and disappears into the shadows like nothing happened.

The first thing I do on Saturday is buy myself a new cell phone and call the police.

I'm put on hold for two hours before the line goes dead.

CHAPTER 5

THE ANGEL

I finally, *finally* get Monday night off from the club. I plan to take full advantage of my freedom by going to bed as soon as I get home.

Neil Hayden's position still hasn't been filled, and since I was *his* secretary, I have absolutely nothing to do except play solitaire on my computer. While that sounds great, it got old after about three days.

I FaceTime my father on my lunch break as I do every Monday, but I don't dare say anything about the past week. My dad would *flip* if he found out about those guys that cornered me in the alley, the Silencer, Christian Reeves, or my new job at the Hellfire Lounge. My father is extremely overprotective of me, and while I love him, he can be overbearing. He wasn't even happy for me when I told him I got a job at the biggest, most successful company in the world. He's been wanting me to move back to Texas for five years, literally since the day I moved to Meridian City. He can't have a single conversation without trying to convince me to come home.

After I hang up with my father, I toss the remains of my frozen microwavable lasagna in the break room trash can, and just like last Monday, when I turn, I run face first into an expensive suit.

"I'm sorry!"

I can't say I'm surprised to see Christian standing there looking down at me with a curious gaze. He leans against the doorframe and crosses his ankles, and because he's so broad, he effectively blocks my way out. "Mr. Reeves," I greet, clearing my throat. I try my best to not let my eyes trail down his body and drink him in, but what can I say? He's hot, and I have eyes. And a vagina. The whole '*master of the universe*' vibe that he gives off spreads heat through my whole body. He's wearing a proper suit today, charcoal gray in color with a red silk tie.

He greets me back with a curt nod. "Elena. Just the person I was looking for. Though I think you're running into me on purpose now." He winks at me to indicate he's only joking. He probably didn't think twice about it, but the action sends my heart racing.

I swallow nervously. "Can I help you with something?"

"Yes, actually."

He motions with his head for me to follow him. He leads me to the elevator and presses the button for his private office. I've never actually seen the CEO suite. It's the entire top floor of the building, and you need special permission on your access card to get up there. My office and the rest of the legal department is the floor directly below his, so the elevator ride is, thankfully, short. The doors open and I can't help the gasp that leaves my lips as I take it in.

His office is glass on three sides, overlooking the city. There's a large, mahogany conference table directly in front of me, the rich wood a nice contrast to the perfectly shined marble floors. He takes a seat in his plush leather office chair and props his feet up on the glass top of his desk. His red bottom shoes stick out amongst all the neutral colors of the office.

I sit in the chair across from him at his desk and fold my hands politely in my lap. "What can I do for you, Mr. Reeves?"

"First of all, Elena, stop calling me that. I have a first name for a reason."

I nod apprehensively. "Okay."

He narrows his eyes for a second, but then softens them again. "Second, I could use some help arranging a…field trip of sorts, for some of the people in your department. The Thomas and Elizabeth Reeves Memorial Orphanage—you know of it?"

I breathe easier knowing he invited me in here to talk about something *work* related. "Of course, I do."

The orphanage he's talking about is one of the most philanthropic things I've ever seen a rich person do. It opened five years ago, right around the time I moved here. Christian bought out the northern half of Meridian City that was mostly abandoned from crime and vandalism, stripped it, and turned it into a sanctuary for orphans, juvenile delinquents, and otherwise underprivileged kids.

The orphanage has its own accredited academy, a grocery store, fast food restaurants, and a bowling alley to give them work experience. It's a haven for kids with nowhere else to go, and though I'm intimidated by the man sitting across from me, he's giving them a chance, and that's really admirable of him.

He's got a soft spot for the kids there because he *was* them. He's lived it— experienced some of the worst pain a child can go through.

When Christian was six years old, his parents were both murdered in front of him. According to the police reports, they found him sitting in a puddle of his parent's blood, and when the police asked him what happened, all he said was that a man with a gun ambushed his father and shot both of his parents in cold blood.

I can't even begin to imagine what that was like. My parents mean everything to me. If I lost either of them so tragically, I'm not sure I could come out of it. He *watched* them die. It probably still cuts him like a serrated knife if he thinks about it too long.

He takes a silver case out of his jacket pocket, pulls a cigarette from it and lights it. Finishing half the stick in two drags, he glances back up at me before taking it between two fingers and blowing the smoke to the side. "I'd like to take the attorneys to tour the campus, connect with some of the kids there, and then have a meeting with them to make sure we're still perfectly in compliance with the law. Have them spot any potential lawsuits, that kind of thing. Think you can arrange it for me?"

"Yeah, absolutely. I think that's a great idea." My words get caught in my throat, but he politely grins and waits patiently for me to finish my thought. "Do you think I could come too? I've always wanted to see it in person."

"You don't even have to ask. I'd be lost without you by my side. In fact, I'd like to promote you. Since you no longer have a supervising attorney, I'd like you to be my personal secretary instead," Christian suggests casually, as if his words didn't just sucker punch me square in the mouth.

I'd be lost without you by my side.

He couldn't have meant that the way I took it. He just means that he needs someone to keep his schedule straight for him. He's a busy man, lots of appointments. I think his calendar would give me anxiety just by looking at it.

He gives me that damn smile again, and I almost accept. The agreement is on the tip of my tongue, but I get to thinking about my future and why I came to this company in the first place, and I shake my head. I give him an apologetic sigh. "Mr. Reeves,

I really appreciate the offer but…I'm actually committed to the legal department, and I'd like to stay there."

"*Christian*," he corrects as his face falls, seemingly disappointed in my response. "Is it because you want to be a lawyer here? You already have your JD."

My brow furrows in confusion. "How do you know that?"

Something unknown flickers across his eyes and then he chuckles. "I've read your résumé, Elena."

Right. Of course, he did. Probably read it the day he fired his top attorney for insulting me, to make sure I really wasn't an airhead like Neil claimed.

"Well, I haven't passed the bar exam yet, but yes, I'd really love to be an associate here one day. I came to Meridian City for my career, and I'd like to stay where I am, if that's okay with you."

His eyes darken a bit. "On one condition."

Oh fuck, please don't ask for something sexual. Please don't ask for something sexual. Please don't—

"I want you to quit your job at the Hellfire Lounge, and I want you to promise me you'll never go back there."

I gulp. That's not an unreasonable request. That place is shady as hell. "Um…okay. Yeah, I can do that."

His eyes go back to that stunning shade of light blue, and he smiles. "Great. Perfect. I'd like to visit the orphanage within the next week or two, do you think that's enough time to plan everything?"

"Yes." I stand to leave, and he takes his feet off the table.

"Come here," he commands, his tone leaving no room to argue, and I follow him to the wall of windows directly behind his desk. It's a beautiful view of this city of nightmares. From way up here, you can see almost the whole island—you might even be able to see the mainland of New Jersey if it's a clear and sunny day.

There's not many of those in Meridian City, though.

"It's so pretty up here you might forget how terrible this city is."

I don't particularly expect an answer. Just an observation.

"It's not so bad, I think."

I turn my head to look at him. "Maybe not up here from this ivory tower, but people like you and people like me see this city differently for a reason." I rub my fingers together to emphasize that I'm talking about money, and how he's jaded from it.

"I see a lot more than you think I do," he says, and then we both look out over the city for a long time. He brushes a strand of my hair back from my shoulder. "Come to dinner with me, Elena."

I shudder from the unexpected touch. My eyes blow wide, and I take a step away from him. "What?" I ask, my chest heaving. "Why?"

He chuckles and takes me lightly by the waist, pulling me closer again, his thumbs rubbing small circles onto my hip bones. "Because *I want to* take you to dinner."

"I…I work for you," I remind him. "I'm pretty sure there's a clause in my employment contract that says if I so much as breathe in your direction outside this building, I'll be sued so aggressively my grandchildren won't be able to afford to eat much more than dirt. And not to mention what happened at the club."

"With a napkin and a flick of my wrist I can make you the exception to all of those rules."

I tremble, my body suddenly feeling like it's entered fight-or-flight mode because of a dinner invitation. Why the hell would the richest man on the planet want to go to dinner with *me*?

He takes a deep breath, softening his voice to something velvety and warm. "I haven't been able to get you out of my head since we met." He twists a finger in one of the loose curls in my hair. "Let me take you to dinner. Please?" After a second, he adds, "I'm not a man who says please often."

I shake my head. "I can't go on a date with you. I'm sorry."

"Not a date. *Dinner*."

I try to wiggle out of the hold he has on my waist, but he lets me go only for his hands to cup my cheeks. My breath catches in my throat as he looks down at my lips and then licks his own. "Are you sure you don't want to come?" he asks, and I nod as he presses a light kiss to my mouth. Featherlight and cautious, like he's afraid he'll hurt me. It's over in an instant, and he looks back down at me. "Are you still sure?" he asks again, and I nod, to which he presses his lips against mine again, soft, like the first time. "How about now?"

I nod, and he kisses me again, longer this time, and I suck in a sharp breath as he takes a step and presses my back to the glass of the floor-to-ceiling window. He capitalizes on the gasp that escapes my throat by shoving his tongue in my mouth, exploring the new territory. I can't help the way my hands tangle in his lapels, pulling him closer. I feel him smirk and his kisses become hungry, ferocious, and needy. A small moan escapes my mouth, and my cheeks heat up in both embarrassment and desire.

He lifts me up like he did at the club and deposits me on top of his glass desk, slotting himself between my legs, all without taking his mouth off mine. I gasp again when I feel the hard length of him straining against his pants as he brushes up against me.

"Stop. Stop!" I gasp between our kiss, and he pulls himself away just enough to look at me. His eyes are lust-blown, his lips swollen, and I'm sure I look the same. I take a deep breath. "I can't go on a date with you. I'm sorry," I repeat, jumping off the table and making a break for the elevator, sighing in relief when he doesn't follow me.

When I get back downstairs to my desk, I find an instant message request from Christian's work email to my own.

Christian Reeves: **If you change your mind**, **I'll be waiting in the lobby at 5 PM**.

I do not change my mind.

In fact, I'm so committed to *not* changing my mind that I stay glued to my desk chair until 7 PM to avoid him in the lobby.

Regret twists in my gut.

You'd think as a billionaire, he'd be dripping in women wherever he goes. Women that are beautiful and successful, with long legs and big boobs that never have a hair out of place.

But Christian has never been seen with a woman at his side. The paparazzi haven't even snapped a photo of someone leaving his mansion doing the walk of shame at nine in the morning.

That alone makes it a huge deal that he even asked me in the first place. How many women get to say Christian Reeves invited them to dinner?

He's the CEO, and I'm an entry-level nobody that's been here since April. People like him don't waste their time with people like me. It will only end badly, and I don't want to put myself through that.

With all the craziness that's been going on in my life, I decide to reward myself with my favorite pizza for dinner: ham and pineapple. I'm a savage, I know, but I can't get enough.

After dinner, I shower and start to think about my brother, Travis, and his wedding in December. He's marrying his longtime boyfriend, Justin, at a beautiful vineyard in California. I run through all the shoes in my closet and think about which ones will look best with my dress. Nude pointed-toe heels are always a good bet, and mine are well broken in from all the love I've given them over the years. I wore them to prom, and my high school, college, *and* law school graduations. Nothing better than a good pair of heels.

My dress is sunflower yellow, despite the wedding being in December. Travis proposed to Justin in a field of sunflowers, so they've decided to make that their wedding theme. I don't think I've ever even glanced at a yellow dress before, but when I found it hanging on a rack in a thrift store six months ago, I snagged it. It's pretty damn ugly. Lacking in shape with unflattering fabric. Looks like something my grandmother would wear, but I didn't have a lot of money to spend at the time. I'm stuck with it now.

Speaking of my ugly dress, I need to hem the bottom so that I'm not scrambling to do it right before the wedding. I take the dress out of my closet and set it on my bed along with my sewing kit. I mark the new hemline and start to sew it by hand, the cool breeze fluttering into my apartment through the cracked window. Every few minutes, I pause to look outside and up at the sky like I'm a princess waiting for Prince Charming.

I used to do this all the time back in Texas. I could see all the stars in the sky from my bedroom window. We lived just far enough from the big city to avoid the light pollution. Here in Meridian City, I don't think I've ever seen a star in the sky. Just police helicopters and reflections of red, white, and blue emergency lights.

I sigh as I stare out the window, and my mind wanders back to Christian. I'm not stupid enough to believe he's Prince Charming in my story. Whatever his attraction is to me, I have a feeling it will pass soon, and I'll be back to daydreaming.

My Prince Charming is *not*, however, the herculean asshole in a red mask that refuses to leave me alone. His sudden appearance outside my window has me gasping, and I frown at him from behind the windowpane. I shut it before he manages to slide in, making eye contact with him as I lock it. He points at the lock. I shake my head and cross my arms. He has the fucking nerve to wink at me, and then holds up three fingers, and then two. I roll my eyes and unlock the window before he gets to one, because he's broken into my apartment before, so I wouldn't put it past him to do it again.

He slides through the narrow frame and closes it behind him. He reaches out to tap my nose with a gloved finger as he settles onto the other end of my bed. "Hey, angel. Miss me?"

"*Pft.*" I stick my tongue out at him in disgust. "You fucking wish. What the hell do you want?"

He pushes my dress and my sewing supplies to the floor to make room for his massive body. "Hey!" I protest. I use my foot to kick him in the chest to get him off. My bed is not made for two people and I'm certainly not going to extend neighborly hospitality to my stalker. He barely moves as the heel of my foot meets his broad chest wrapped in Kevlar. A vibration murmurs through my bones like I just kicked a hunk of steel.

"Such a sour puss tonight. What's got you all worked up, angel?"

I roll my eyes at the nickname. "Why would I tell you?"

"Because that's what good girls do."

My cheeks flush and I kick him again when he shuffles closer and closer to me. He catches my ankle and spreads my legs, getting into my personal space until I'm nearly folded in half between him and the wall.

"How about a deal?"

I quirk up my eyebrow.

"You tell me about your day, and I'll stop breaking into your apartment. There's not much to look at anymore, anyways. Not surprised your vibrator is purple."

I try to shove him away from me, but he doesn't budge. "God! Get out! I can't stand you," I huff, still all scrunched up into a pretzel against the wall. "I have a phone now. I'm calling the police."

"I dare you," he challenges, and something low and dangerous can be heard in the back of his voice. "You really think I'm scared of a few pigs?"

"I don't understand what your deal is with me. Please just leave me alone."

"Tell me about your day and I'll *consider* it."

I take my bottom lip in my mouth. At this point, I'd eat rat poison to get him out of my life. "Promise?" He holds out his gloved pinky to me, and I frown, but I take it in mine. I huff. "I don't even know where to begin." He waits patiently for me to get my thoughts together. "You know how Christian Reeves was with me at the club the other night?"

"Yeah."

Nervousness brews in my stomach. If I admit to the Silencer what happened today, is Christian going to be found murdered in the morning? I *cannot* have that on my conscience.

I sigh. "He asked me to dinner."

The Silencer stares down at me with an eyebrow raised. "*That's it*? That's what you've got your panties in a twist for?"

"Why on earth would someone like him want to be seen in public with me? I'm not his type."

"How would you know what his type is? Maybe he's into short brunettes with…" He makes a pinching motion to insinuate that I have small boobs, and well, he's not wrong, but I scowl and swat at him anyways, still trying to push him off me. He sits back and it gives me the opportunity to sit up a little, though my legs are still spread wide open like an invitation.

"He kissed me," I blurt out without so much as a second thought. I hold my breath as the Silencer looks down at me, his body tense, and if he didn't have a mask on, I know he'd look absolutely devilish.

"Did he, now?" He hums in amusement. He grips the flesh of my thighs harshly, tugging me a little closer to him. "He could give you everything, you know. Treat you like a goddess. You deserve nothing less."

"You're just saying that because I saved your life." I tap his bicep where his admittedly minor injury is healing. He lost a lot of blood, but he wasn't close to death by any stretch of the imagination. I was just teasing. I didn't do anything to help except direct him to the first aid kit, but his body goes rigid, and his green eyes meet mine. Whatever is about to come out of his mouth, I'm equally intrigued and terrified to hear it.

"That's why I call you angel," he admits, so quietly it feels like he's confessing to a horrific crime.

My heart skips a beat, and my body relaxes slightly. I'm not sure why, but I suddenly feel safe with him. I have no idea what the hell I'm supposed to make of that. Not even five minutes ago, I feared him. Now, I'm not sure how I feel, and that's even more terrifying. My mind brings back the hazy memory of him wiping off my face with a warm rag before I passed out. How I woke up tucked in bed like I had fallen asleep on the couch during movie night.

"I thought you'd be mad," I admit, changing the subject. "About me kissing someone else."

He chuckles. "You're nothing but trouble, Elena Young. Want to know why?" He leans over, folding me in half again so he can whisper into my ear. "Because I know there's a part of you, deep down, that's upset I don't have you bent over my lap right now, punishing you for letting another man touch what's mine."

I frown, my earlier sympathy gone. "You want to know a secret, asshole?" I mumble, pushing him away from me, and this time, he sits back. "Remember how you said the next time I'd touch myself, I'd think of you?"

He nods enthusiastically, and I sit up completely, pushing him again until he's flopped onto the bed, his head and shoulders hanging off the edge, and I straddle him. I lean far, far over until my chest is pressed against his, and the vein on his neck is thick and protruding against his throat.

And then I slowly reach to his thigh, pull a knife from the sheath, and press it against his neck with the sharp blade digging right into that vein. I do it slowly because I know if he was truly worried about me slicing open his throat, he would never have let me wrap my fingers around his knife.

He's giving me an illusion of control, and I can feel a bulge pressing against my center, telling me that he's just a little too into it.

I lean down to whisper in his ear. "You were wrong. I didn't think about you. I thought about *him*," I purr, making my voice as sultry as I can with that knife pressed dangerously against his jugular. "Now leave."

I don't know how this man manages to move so damn fast, but in less than a second, we're on the floor, flipped over, with my cheek against the hardwood, my ass in the air, and that knife now against the side of *my* neck instead of his. I yelp as he pins my arms to the base of my spine with one hand.

"Sounds like I need to teach you a goddamn lesson," he growls, sheathing the knife. I feel his large hand land with a hard smack against my ass, so hard that it pushes me forward on the floor a few inches. I choke out a whine and tears prick in my eyes.

He lets me go, and I turn over, the cold wood of the floor soothing my tender flesh. He only slapped me once, but I swear to God, any harder and he would have broken a bone. He's lounging triumphantly on my bed, his massive body nowhere close to fitting on the twin sized mattress. His arms are propped behind his head, and he's got a tent in his pants as tall as a skyscraper.

"I've got something for you."

"No," I growl. I'm horrified. I can't believe that just happened. He spanked me so hard I felt it in my teeth and he's acting like we're roleplaying or some other twisted shit.

"Get your head out of the gutter, Elena, and get up here." He pats the bed next to him. "Now. Or I'll drag you up here myself."

"Don't fucking touch me," I snap back on instinct. In an instant, he's sitting up on the bed, and his arm snaps towards me lightning fast, tangling his large hand into my hair.

Without saying a word, he uses his firm grip in my hair to drag me up to the bed with him, careful not to break eye contact. His stare burns right through me as he lays me down flat against the mattress. Only after he cages me in with his thick thighs does he release his grip on my hair, and my chest blooms with redness. There's a stirring deep in my stomach.

He reaches out a finger to run along my jawline, and then in his other hand, he holds up a thin silver bracelet between us. It has a small circular charm no bigger than a dime dangling from it.

He drops it on my chest unceremoniously.

"It's in case you ever need help," he explains. I lift the chain to examine it. "The charm attached is a silent panic alarm. You turn it on by clicking it five times. You'll feel it vibrate, and it will send me an alert with your exact location. If you press it, I'll come. No matter what."

Unease flips my stomach as I stare at the device. "How do I know you're not just using it to track me all the time?"

"I guess you'll just have to trust me." He takes a deep breath, his body unnaturally rigid. He nods towards it. "Put it on."

"Give me one good reason why I should."

My attitude never seems to faze him, and he grips my jaw roughly. "Because if you were really scared of me, you would fight harder. You would run when you see me. You'd scream and beg for your life, but you don't, Elena." His voice is gravel behind that mask, but it doesn't lack finesse, and it envelops me like a snake strangling its meal. Its rough edges trail up my spine like phantom fingers, coming to rest on my blushed cheeks. "You're all alone in this city. If I killed you, it'd be days before anyone found you." His fingers sensually trace my neck and the collar of my shirt, coming to rest along my throat like a necklace. He squeezes so gently, just enough to quicken my heartbeat but not enough to steal my breath. "I don't want to kill you, angel. I want to keep you all to myself. You'd better take off those rose-colored glasses and accept that the only place you belong is in my black heart."

Gone is the wit and the teasing glint in his eyes. He sighs, and his tone softens. "I'm not strong enough to stay away from you. I couldn't live with myself if someone came after you because of me."

"Why would anyone come after me?"

"Because I care."

Though he doesn't say it out loud, I know he wants to finish the sentence with '*about you*'.

I don't know what comes over me, but I carefully reach up to run my fingers along his mask. When my fingers touch him, he closes his eyes and practically purrs.

"Are you trying to say I'm important to you?"

He opens his eyes and I swear he's burrowing into my soul. "Yeah."

"Important enough to know your name?"

Though a mask is covering his face, I can see it in the way his eyes sparkle that he's smiling behind it. He laughs and shakes his head. "We're not there yet, angel."

I wiggle away from his legs, and he lets me sit up. We're both crossed legged on the mattress now, and I hold the device between us. I glance up at him from under my lashes and my tongue wets my bottom lip. I fasten the chain around my ankle, and then rest my foot against his chest to examine it. "Ugly," I hum, unimpressed. "I would have preferred diamonds."

My comment pulls a chuckle from deep in his chest and he pushes my ankle to the side. He focuses on the dress discarded on my floor. "You going somewhere?"

I shrug. "A wedding."

He hums and picks up the ugly garment from the floor, raising an eyebrow when he looks it over. "Elena, you're way too beautiful to wear this abomination."

"You offering to buy me a dress?" I snap back. He stays quiet. "Then shut up."

He tosses the dress into my face. I roll my eyes when it falls and lands in my lap. He clears his throat. "I have to go. But remember what I said—if you press that button, I'll come. I promise." He makes a move for the window and without thinking, I catch him by his large bicep, at least what I can grab in my small hand. He looks at me and raises an eyebrow.

"I'm going to figure out who you are under there." I tap his mask. "I don't just mean your name."

"What will you do once you know who I am?"

"Easy. I'm going to collect that one-million-dollar reward for turning you in to the police."

I can tell that he's got a smirk painting his lips from the crinkles at the corners of his eyes.

Before he steps onto the fire escape outside my window, he blows me a kiss from behind his mask.

"Until next time, angel."

CHAPTER 6

THE ANGEL

I haven't seen the Silencer since our last emotionally charged meeting when he gave me the tracking device that now sits around my ankle.

Ever since he gave it to me, I've found myself becoming more aware of my surroundings. I think I'm trying to catch him following my every move, to find a reason to be upset at him, but the stupid anklet actually gives me some semblance of security—like I've got my own personal bodyguard on speed-dial.

I take a break halfway through my shift at the Hellfire Lounge like I normally do, and when I put my phone back into my purse, I hear Frank's voice behind me. "Hey, pretty Ellie." He gives me that disgusting smile and wraps an arm around my shoulders as he drags me to an elevator. The panic in my chest rises even more, but I manage to suck in a breath of relief when the elevator goes *up* instead of down.

We ride in silence, and the elevator door opens at the top. He leads me into a penthouse-like private lounge. It's gaudy, with way too much gold covering the walls and floors. "Here's the deal, Ellie. I like you a lot, and I'd like to give you a promotion. Two grand a night to be my personal bartender, plus tips."

My blood runs cold. "Actually, Frank…" I fumble over my words, "I was hoping I could, you know, move on? I don't think this job is for me."

The words were hard to get out, but once they're in the air, he pauses, turning to face me directly. The look on his face tells me that leaving is not something people do here. Especially not girls like me.

The girls he wants.

I try to bring an innocent grin to my face, like I don't know what tonight will eventually lead to.

Frank's friends, the five that never stop looking at me, are here already. They greet me in unison, calling me *'pretty Ellie'* and it almost makes me hate the nickname I've had since I was a child.

All five order a whiskey on the rocks. Easy. Simple. The private bar in the space is huge, and the smooth jazz is a welcome break from the obnoxious techno that plays downstairs. Balancing the glasses on a tray, I try to appear sexy as I saunter over to them.

I give a shy smile as I hand them their drinks. One of them stuffs a hundred-dollar bill so far down my bra that he grazes my nipple with it. I gulp and try to hide the uncomfortable shiver. As I hand the last man his glass, I hear Frank's footsteps come to a stop directly behind me, and his cold hand smacks my ass so hard I drop the empty tray and fall across the lap of one of his friends. They all laugh at me, and I blush, embarrassed as I stand back up and turn around.

Frank rubs a thin finger from my waist to my chest, and then lifts my chin with a too-long fingernail so that I have to look him in the eyes.

"Bet those pretty brown eyes would look even prettier if you were on your knees," he hisses. I suck in a shaky breath and Frank laughs, very lightly slapping my cheek. "Whiskey."

I walk to the bar to silently pour his drink. It doesn't take me but a second, preparing it like I would any other. I smile politely when I hand it to him, and he takes a sip. He glances up at me from behind the glass.

"Ellie," he says, and the hairs on the back of my neck rise in high alert at his poisonous tone. He sounds *furious*. "Ellie, baby, there's a small box on the bar top. Bring it to me." I do as he says as quickly as I can without tripping over my own two feet. When I bring it to him, he sits up slightly in his chair and motions for me to stand in front of him. My legs feel heavy as I do. When I'm in front of him, he gives me further instructions. "Get on your knees and face away from me."

I hesitate, and he takes his whiskey glass and throws the amber liquid in my face. I gasp in shock as the cold ice falls over my body.

"Did I fucking stutter?"

I kneel so fast my bones groan against the cold floor, and I turn to face his friends like he said. They're all reveling in my humiliation. I try not to cry, but I've accepted that I've gotten myself into deep shit.

Frank gathers my hair in a tight fist and wraps something around my neck. The men watching all smile at me and Frank tugs on the back of my head so that I'm forced to look up at the ceiling. I start to hyperventilate when I hear a jingling at my throat.

He's fastened a fucking *leash* around my neck.

"Vic?"

A man, Vic, hands him a knife that he promptly waves in my face. "Now, Ellie, I'm going to let you off easy because it's your first night up here, and you're just so, *so* pretty. I don't like ice in my whiskey."

"Please, Mr. Valenti, I'm so sorry," I beg with tears streaming down my face, my neck aching from his hold on me. "I'll remake it. I'll—"

He takes the knife and slices my top off, pulling the leash tighter as he cuts off my bra and then my skirt, followed by my underwear until I'm completely naked in front of all of them.

He stares down at me for a while, and then releases me. I instantly fold in over myself to try and cover my naked body.

"Go make my drink, Ellie. *Correctly* this time."

I realize that he intends to make me finish my shift completely naked, with nothing but my hair to provide me with modesty, and a leash around my neck. I scurry back to the bar, and I make his drink again as fast as I possibly can. No ice. I bring it over to him with shaky hands and he takes a long sip.

"Perfect."

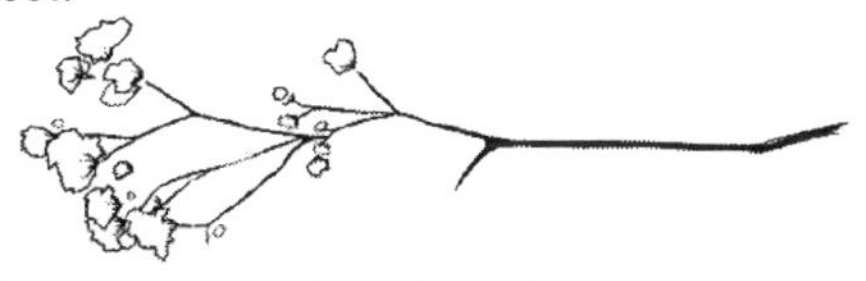

I've been groped a few times in my twenty-nine years of life. Every woman has. But tonight, I've been humiliated and violated more times than I can count.

Every time I brought one of Frank's friends a drink, they'd grab a handful of ass or tits. A few of them licked my nipples. One tried to stuff a twenty in my fucking vagina, but mercifully, he was drunk and missed.

Frank was the worst. Not because he was touching me all night. He didn't touch me at all after he cut off my clothes. No, he was the worst because all he did all night was stare at me, and I know exactly why. I could see dollar signs behind his dead eyes.

The horror of my shift tonight is burned into my brain forever.

When I'm finally allowed to go home, I rush downstairs to the locker room completely nude, and cry into my knees until I have a headache from hell.

"Hey girl," Kate says, kneeling next to me in a corner of the locker room. "You okay?"

I bite my lip and shake my head. Not that being naked in front of another woman really bothers me, but I find myself cowering away from her trying to cover myself, cold and humiliated and violated. She reaches into her locker to give me a spare shirt. I cry on her shoulder and give her all my tips in gratitude.

Kate is curvier than I am, and quite a bit taller, so her shirt acts as a dress. Kate bids me goodnight and heads home, and it takes me another fifteen minutes before I work up the courage to leave the locker room.

I walk home as fast as I can, dead tired but desperate to get home before one of the lunatics in this city realizes I'm a woman without any underwear on in the middle of the damn night.

Once in the safety of my apartment, I curl up into a tight ball on my bed, gripping my soft purple blanket tightly to try and give myself a bit of comfort as I cry into my pillow. I'm sticky and smell like whiskey from where Frank threw his drink in my face. I don't even have the willpower to change clothes or shower.

I'm staring at a chip in the paint on the wall across from me when I hear a sharp tap on my window, causing me to jolt out of my memories of the night. I know it's the Silencer, but I don't make a move to let him in or even acknowledge that he's there. Maybe he'll just assume I'm asleep and leave me alone. I don't have the strength to tell him to go away.

I hear him mess with the window and after a few seconds, I hear the lock click open behind me and then feel the cool breeze at my back. The bed dips when the Silencer kneels onto it, propping himself up over me.

I feel his fingers brush a strand of hair away from my face. "Are you drunk?" I hear him sniff loudly. "Didn't take you for a whiskey kind of girl."

I tug my blanket over my head to try and hide my tears as a quiet sob wrecks through me. He pushes my shoulders until I'm flat on my back, and then he easily tugs the blanket away from my face. I bite my lip and turn my head, knowing that if I look at him, he's just going to make me cry some more.

"What happened?"

My lip quivers and my voice cracks. "How was I supposed to know he doesn't like ice?"

"What?" He leans closer to me and tilts my chin with his hand to make me look at him. I think he's looking in my eyes to see if I really am drunk. As I predicted, the moment our eyes meet, I cry harder. He takes off his gloves and wipes away my tears with both hands, rubbing his thumbs soothingly across my cheeks. "Angel, tell me what's wrong."

I let out a deep breath and finally sit up, letting the blanket drop around my waist. I move my sticky hair out of my face and without thinking, my hand rubs over the raw spots on my neck from where Frank and his friends kept roughly tugging on the leash. I feel the Silencer stiffen, and he moves my hand and softly brushes his fingers over the red marks littering my skin. I whimper softly.

I muster the courage to look at him, his eyes fixated on the marks around my neck. His gaze goes dark with fury, and that's when I notice something odd about his eyes. A soft film of green overlaps his dark pupils.

He's wearing colored contacts.

The unfiltered rage in his eyes scares me to death. "Who did this to you?" he asks quietly, though his tone couldn't be any more venomous.

When I don't answer, he sends his fist flying into the wall next to us so hard that I'm confident I heard his knuckles break. I get the faintest glimpse of blood smeared over his fingers when his hand goes back to my cheek.

"If you don't tell me the truth right now, I will find out myself by burning this fucking city to the ground."

"It was a leash. I got in trouble for messing up a drink and it was my punishment. I had to wear a leash and work completely naked. They threw whiskey in my face and cut off my clothes with a knife." I motion down at the large shirt I'm wearing. "I had to borrow this from my friend Kate so I wouldn't have to walk home naked."

He looks like he's gone completely feral, and I begin to shake under his intense gaze. He grinds his teeth, his words dripping in pure venom. "I want names, Elena."

"Frank Valenti. He owns the place. And then his friends…Vic, Mike, Oliver, Simon, and Mario."

"I'm going to kill them," he growls, ready to set the world on fire with his rage.

He reaches for the window, but the last thing I want him to do is leave. If he leaves this apartment, there isn't a single soul in the Hellfire Lounge that will survive the rest of the night, guilty or not.

He killed three men for chasing me into an alley for Christ's sake. I wouldn't put it past him to kill everyone in that club simply for the crime of being in the same building as me without his permission.

I can see it in his eyes that he's gone blind with rage. It's terrifying and exhilarating all at the same time, to see him so unhinged over something that happened to me. "Wait," I beg, wrapping my arms tightly around his neck, trying to hug him close to my chest. My voice seems to snap him out of whatever chaos is in his mind. I feel his shoulders relax, *slightly*, and then he looks at me.

"They need to know what happens when they touch what's mine, Elena. They're going to convert religions, because they won't be praying to God, they'll be praying to me. Begging for my fucking mercy after I hunt them all down and show them the true meaning of fear."

"Okay," I breathe, and with trembling hands, I cup his masked jaw and force him to rest his forehead against mine. I don't know what else to do to calm him down.

He grips my wrists tightly, squeezing and then relaxing and squeezing again, as if he's trying to ground himself. "I can feel them, you know."

"Feel what?"

He takes a shuddering breath. "I designed the mask myself. There are sensors on the outside that project whatever is touching the mask onto my skin. It tingles. I can feel your fingers. I can feel your little breaths across my face." He presses closer into me. "I can feel it all."

I run my fingers along his cheek and then I gulp before pressing my lips to the front of his mask where his own would be. I look up at him from under my lashes. "You can feel that?"

By the way his shoulders slump, it had the exact reaction I wanted—it calmed him down. He chuckles sadly and nods. "Yeah. I can feel that." He runs his hand over my hair, smoothing out the tangled, sticky strands. "Why didn't you press your panic alarm?"

"Because you would have come in there and gone on a murder spree to get to me, and I didn't think it was enough of an emergency for that. I'm okay. It could have been worse."

"If your safety is even slightly in jeopardy, it's an emergency to me. Next time, press the goddamn button."

"I don't want to be the reason you lose your humanity."

He rubs my bottom lip with his gloved hand. "If you're so concerned about my humanity, Elena, then reach into my soul and find it, because I'm not sure I have any left."

CHAPTER 7

THE SILENCER

Victor Moreno. Mike Jones. Oliver Priest. Simon Wayne. Mario De La Cruz.

Frank Valenti's friends are all quite the characters. Criminal records the size of phone books and about thirty active warrants between the five of them. They're all rich like their boss, but what his friends don't have is his influence.

Valenti's got the MCPD by the nuts and all the judges in New Jersey in his pocket. Nobody's going to go after him. His friends are fair game though, so they cozy up to their boss in hopes to stay on his good side. They're almost always on the top floor of the Hellfire Lounge. They have no need to leave. They have goons to do everything for them. The second any of them steps outside, they run the risk of going to prison.

Prison is the least of their fucking problems right now.

Can't go to prison if you're dead.

Valenti keeps the club heavily guarded on the ground, but fortunately for me, he skimps on the security for the rooftop. Once inside, all I have to do is use the rafters of the industrial style building to navigate my way to Valenti's private suite.

These men live off whiskey and cigars. I'm not sure how they don't give themselves alcohol poisoning when all they do is sit on their asses and drink.

I've watched them grope the poor bartender at least fifty times. It doesn't require much critical thinking to conclude that Elena was subject to the same abuse when she was here a few short hours ago. Their inability to keep their hands to themselves is precisely the reason they're going to have bullets in their brains soon.

When I saw those fucking marks around her neck, my body was no longer running on blood and oxygen, but fury and vengeance. If she hadn't begged me to stay with her until she fell asleep, I would have torn apart every person in this club, limb from limb, until I got to Valenti and his friends and strangled them with their own intestines.

That rage never subsided, and now that I'm here, I'm certain that after I'm done with Valenti's friends, I'm going to need a long shower to wash off all the blood.

I watched Valenti leave thirty minutes ago, and it doesn't seem like he's coming back anytime soon. I wish I had dished out my revenge while he was here, but I was stuck trying to come up with a plan that involved incapacitating him and his friends so I could torture them.

Unfortunately, I am not superhuman. I'm one man and taking out six armed men without killing them isn't easy. Not killing them is a very important part of the equation for me. I like to play with my food.

At this point, I'll just have to go after Valenti later. I move silently through the rafters above their heads, and I land with a heavy thud directly behind the unsuspecting bartender. Before she has a chance to turn and scream, I grab her from behind in a chokehold and keep her steady until she falls unconscious.

Valenti's friends are all so drunk they're falling over themselves trying to get away from me. One of them pulls out a cell phone and I throw a knife at his hand with such precision that the blade goes straight through the screen. The way they scramble away from me fills me with extreme satisfaction.

I like taking my time with my victims. I enjoy the hunt just as much as I enjoy watching the life leave their eyes after I listen to them beg me for mercy.

I love making them feel helpless, like I felt all those years ago.

Two of Valenti's men make a break for the elevator. I let them get close enough to press the button, allowing them to bask in the illusion of relief, thinking they'll escape me, and then I send a bullet right through the meat of their thighs. They fall to the ground with cries of pain, and I growl in satisfaction at the sound.

One of them tries to sneak behind me with a tiny pocketknife. I block his swing with my forearm and then crack my fist against the center of his face. His nose breaks and blood gushes over his lips and chin. I languidly pull the pocketknife from his grasp and shove it into his gut and twist it, and then, just because I feel like it, I slice off his ear, too. He drops, moaning in pain and writhing on the ground like a grub worm.

The two remaining men both have their guns up pointed at me. If I didn't have a mask over my face, they'd see a wicked smirk painting my teeth. I take one heavy step forward.

"Stay the fuck back!" They back up against the wall behind them as I stalk towards my prey. "I'm warning you!"

I let out a dark laugh and make my steps even slower. The man keeps spewing miniscule threats as I get closer, and he finally shoots me. The bullet lands dead over my heart, crumples against my chest, and falls with a clink to the floor.

Can't remember the last time someone had the balls to shoot me. Respect.

The clothes I wear when I don this mask look completely normal. A black moisture-absorbent shirt, black tactical pants, and my zip-up hoodie with the sleeves cut off. The material that makes up my outfit is a special triple-weave Kevlar that I designed myself. I've made thousands of individual scales from the Kevlar, with thin plates of titanium woven into the fabric. The scales are doubled up on the most vulnerable parts of me. My heart. My spine. My dick. All the important things. The titanium/Kevlar weave protects me without weighing me down as much as steel would, and the scales allow the material to hug my body, keeping me agile and comfortable.

There's no such thing as bulletproof. Bullet resistant is a much more accurate term, but bulletproof sounds a lot fucking cooler, and I'm as close to bulletproof as anyone can get.

Combine that with my six-five stature, a body built like a tank, and a little bit of adrenaline ordered on the dark web, and I'm practically unstoppable.

The goon continues to empty his clip into my torso instead of using his fucking brain and aiming for my face or my exposed arms—somewhere that I'm vulnerable. He stares at me in shock when the bullets do nothing but make me suck in a sharp breath.

This is my favorite part. The part where they realize their fate is sealed with red duct tape, and I'll be the last fucking thing they see on this earth.

I raise my own pistol and send a bullet through both of his kneecaps, and he lands with a thud on the floor. His friend, the last man standing, drops his gun and holds his hands up in surrender. Smart man. I'll kill him last for having a few working brain cells.

Valenti's men squirm around in bloody heaps around the floor, groaning. I move some chairs from a table to my left and put them all in a line facing the elevator, so that when Valenti comes back, the first thing he'll see is his dead friends.

One by one, I secure them to their chairs by their wrists and ankles with zip ties. The one who surrendered pissed himself, the dark gray of his slacks gone black from the warm liquid seeping through the fabric.

I take another empty chair and place it in front of them before sitting on it backwards. I stay quiet as I reload my gun and then start flipping it in my hand. I can see it in their eyes that they're wondering what they did to land on my shitlist.

I've never bothered Valenti or the Hellfire Lounge. Valenti is the East Coast's drug trade. It all goes through him, and in the grand scheme of things, the drug trade isn't high on my list of concerns, which is why I haven't done anything about it.

I knew this place was shady, but it wasn't until I met Elena that I realized something sinister went on here, hidden by the stench of alcohol and the thrum of the bass. I can't just kill Valenti. I've got to destroy this place from the inside out, brick by brick, until there's nothing left to salvage.

Taking down what I suspect is a bidding house for the skin trade is going to take a lot of meticulous planning and even more patience. I don't have any hard evidence yet, and what I'm about to do to Valenti's friends is going to make it that much harder to gather information.

I can't risk waiting too long to strike, though. If there's even the smallest fraction of a chance that Valenti plans on trafficking Elena, this planet will know the true meaning of fury and malice as I tear it apart in retaliation. What he's done to her tonight is bad enough, and I need to come up with a plan before he puts a price on her head.

Quitting isn't an option for her. I know that. Valenti would just send his goons to kidnap her and drag her back to this wretched place. It's better that he thinks she doesn't suspect anything. If he thinks she'll run, he will chase her.

And that's my fucking job.

Sweat drips from my brow after hauling up Valenti's friends into chairs and strapping them down. I look up at the ceiling and take a long, deep breath.

"This is for Elena," I whisper to myself. Even with my voice dripping in venom, her name tastes so sweet on my tongue.

I open my eyes, my glare so frightening that some of them are shaking in their seats as I look over them, one by one, deciding what form of torture they each deserve.

"Welcome to the slaughterhouse, gentlemen."

It's moments like this that I wish I didn't wear a mask, because I want them to see my wicked smile. "I'm going to kill each of you. Want to know why?"

One of them whimpers and it pulls a satisfied chuckle from me. Keeping my voice calm and collected, I crack my neck.

"My angel told me that Valenti made her work naked, and you assholes touched her all night. That was a big fucking mistake on your part. Elena is *mine*. *Mine* to scare. *Mine* to chase. *Mine* to touch." I choose one of the men at random, the one second from the right with the stab wound in his stomach and the missing ear, and I point my gun at him. "Tell me which one of you touched what's mine first."

The five of them all tense up together and they begin looking down the line frantically, begging each other to keep quiet because none of them want to admit the truth to me.

"Start talking," I threaten, my gun still aimed for the fucker's massive forehead. He says nothing, trying to force his face to go blank. If he's trying to convince me he's not scared, he's doing a terrible job. I can see it in those green eyes of his that he's on the verge of pissing himself too. After about a minute of silence, my patience wears dangerously thin. I shoot him right between the eyes, the force of the gunshot sending him and his chair toppling backwards. His friends cringe as his skull cracks against the ground and his blood pools under him.

I point my gun at the man whose kneecaps I shot out. "I said *start talking*."

"Mike!" he shouts. "It—it—it was Mike! He slapped her ass!"

Mike whimpers and starts writhing in his chair. "You dirty fucking liar!" he growls at his friend. Mike then looks me dead in the eye. "Look man, I promise I didn't touch her."

Another bullet leaves my gun and lands in Mike's brain for the crime of lying to me. I look back to the one who sold out his friend. "Who touched her next?" His breathing hitches and becomes erratic. I narrow my eyes. "Was it you?" I ask quietly. The man bites his lip and trembles as he nods. I slowly stand up from my chair and take two big steps towards him, circling him like a hawk. "Tell me what you did to her."

He stays quiet, so I come to a stop behind him and pull his head backwards with his hair, forcing him to look up at me. "Don't make me ask again."

A pungent odor fills my nostrils through my mask. He's pissed himself too.

He gulps as well as he can with his neck bent backwards unnaturally. He admits to me that he licked Elena's nipples. I proceed to cut his own off and feed them to him, before slicing his throat and watching him gurgle and choke on his own blood.

Dickhead number four made Elena sit in his lap with her ass against his dick and grinded into her until he was rock solid before rubbing one out in the bathroom thinking about her.

He told me that Valenti said she was off limits from raping. I asked him if he wanted to.

His small intestine is wrapped around his throat, so I trust you can imagine what his answer was.

The man I promised to save for last, who surrendered when I came here, told me he tipped Elena by shoving bills in between the lips of her pussy and her asscheeks.

I cut a hole in his chest and shoved a Benjamin into the bleeding wound before slitting his throat, groaning with satisfaction when his arterial blood spurts across my chest and neck.

Bloody. Just the way I like my kills.

I stand in front of the carnage I just inflicted on five men for touching my angel, and I wish I was a good man. I wish I could say I felt any semblance of guilt, or remorse, or hell, even nothing. I'd take feeling numb over loving the taste of death.

But what I feel when I kill can only be described as relief. Relief that the monster inside me has been fed and will recede back into his decrepit cave until he's hungry again, and that's when I'll kill next.

Eight. I've given him eight souls since September sixth.

It should have only been one.

It should have only been me.

Taking a deep breath after a moment of reflection, I plaster red duct tape over the mouths of the five men I just turned into the past tense. It's the icing on the cake of my kills.

Valenti will eventually come back, and the first thing he'll notice isn't his dead friends, but my sadistic calling card and his name spelled out on the walls in their blood.

Over. And over. And over. And over again.

CHAPTER 8

THE ANGEL

I don't remember falling asleep last night, but I do remember the Silencer holding me to his chest and stroking my hair. By the time my alarm went off for me to get ready for my *actual* job, he was gone.

Exhaustion hits me hard while I'm at my desk. I can feel my eyelids grow heavy as I stare at the Reeves Enterprises logo on the wall across from me.

After I chug my third cup of coffee, I'm certain my ability to be a functioning human being does not exist anymore.

I'm so tired I can hardly keep my eyes open. I'm pretty sure I've dozed off on five separate occasions, and it's not even noon. I don't even answer my dad's FaceTime, texting him back that I'm too busy. I'm looking forward to taking a nice long nap on my lunch break.

That is, until three minutes *before* said lunch break, I get an instant message.

Christian Reeves: Come to my office.

I groan quietly to myself and blink away some of the exhaustion. Letting out a sigh, I stand up and make sure to bring my access card with me. When I step into the elevator, I click the button for the top floor, the shiny golden plaque next to it reading *CEO - Christian Reeves.*

The button turns yellow, and I swipe my card against the scanner. After a second, the button turns green, the elevator closes, and it goes up one floor to let me into Christian's office. Clearly, he gave me access between the last time I was up here and now.

I wonder what kinds of eyebrows that raised in the building security department.

He's at his desk, and when we make eye contact, he flashes me those perfect teeth. He's got his feet propped up on the tabletop again, and I have half a mind to ask him if he does anything up here all day except sit there and look pretty. He's got a cigarette between two of his fingers and the composure of a man who knows exactly what he wants and how to get it.

I walk around the conference table separating us and stand in front of his desk with my arms crossed over my chest. "Yes, Mr. Reeves?"

"*Christian*," he corrects.

Normally, I'd at least attempt to be nice, but I was looking forward to that nap that he's stolen from me, and bitter irritation is surely painted all over my face. "Can I help you with something?"

"Drop the attitude and sit, Elena."

I do what he says, my stomach turning at his commanding tone encased in honey. When I sit, he stands, walking around his desk and snuffing out his cigarette in an ashtray. He comes to a stop directly behind me, and I hold my breath when his large, warm hands rest on my shoulders.

"What are you doing?" I ask, trying to shrug him off, but then his thumbs dig into the sore, stiff spot at the base of my neck, and I melt into the touch, my eyes closing and my head falling forward in sweet, sweet relief.

I'm so tired and lost in the way his fingers dance across my skin, that the last thing I remember is warm hands catching me when I slump over.

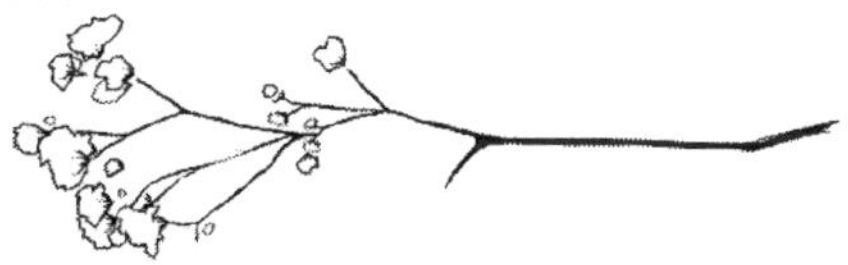

I wake to the sound of thunder rumbling loud and menacing in the sky. I sit up with a gasp and rub my cheek. I look around the room and panic a little bit, relaxing slightly when I realize I'm just in Christian's office.

But instead of sitting in the chair where I fell asleep, I'm now lying across a long couch on the right side of the room. My heels and purse are neatly placed next to the foot of the sofa. There's a buttery-soft navy-blue blanket draped over me.

"Welcome back to the land of the living."

I jump at the voice. Christian is leaning against the conference table with his hands in his pockets. He's no longer wearing his suit jacket, and he looks just as delicious as he did in the club—those thick, muscular arms straining against the custom dress shirt embroidered with his initials on the cuffs, now pushed up to his elbows. His red tie is a stark contrast against the pristine white of his shirt.

I blink, trying not to stare at the very obvious self-harm scars across his forearms. "What time is it?"

He pulls out his left hand from his pocket to check his watch. "Seven."

"Seven!" I scramble to my feet. "Oh my God. I can't believe I fell asleep. I'm so sorry." I grab my shoes and hop on one foot and then the other to put them back on. I fumble over my own feet as I stumble around still half-asleep in a panicked circle. "Why didn't you wake me up?"

He laughs and catches me by the elbow as I walk past him towards the elevator. "Because you were tired, and I wanted you to get some sleep."

I suck in a shameful breath. "I'm so sorry. This was unprofessional. It won't happen again, I swear."

He laughs again. "It's fine. I promise. Stop apologizing. You woke up just in time, anyways. Dinner just got here."

"Dinner?" I repeat quietly, still in a haze, and he turns his shoulder to reveal two to-go containers, hot and steamy with fresh lasagna. My stomach growls.

"No more of that microwaved crap you eat at lunch every day." He pokes my grumbling belly.

"Hey! I really like those things. Plus, they're only a dollar."

He scoffs at me. "You'll never want another microwaved lasagna after you taste this one. There's an Italian restaurant on the South Side that was my mother's favorite. The owner's a good friend—I asked him to make this one special."

He got me lasagna from his late mother's favorite restaurant after letting me sleep in his office all day? Can this guy get any more perfect?

"Not a date. Dinner," I say, and he smiles down at me, remembering what he said to me the day I rejected his dinner invitation. Seems he found a way to make it happen regardless of my prior objection. Standing up to his full height after pushing off against the table, he pulls out a chair for me.

"Not a date," he confirms, and I slowly sit down as he pushes in my chair so I'm comfortably snug against the table. Along with the lasagna, there is a box of garlic knots, two fruit tarts for dessert, and a bottle of red wine with two delicate glasses. As he pours the wine, I look out the window and listen to the rain pelting onto the side of the building.

"Don't worry. I'll take you home."

I can't help it, I scoff. He raises an eyebrow in confusion. "A guy like you will get robbed in my neighborhood."

He smiles and sets down the wine bottle, handing me a plastic fork. "I can take care of myself, Elena."

I take a small bite of the pasta, and I groan obnoxiously. "Oh my God!"

"Amazing, right?"

I nod. "Mhm."

I haven't eaten since yesterday afternoon, so the conversation is minimal as I stuff my face with the decadent, cheesy lasagna, the garlic bread, and my fruit tart. I lean back into my chair with a satisfied huff. "That was so good," I say, taking the last sip of my wine. "Thank you, Mr. Reeves."

"Elena, my name is *Christian*."

I playfully roll my eyes. "I know what your name is."

"Then use it."

"I did, actually." He raises an eyebrow in confusion as I bite my lip. "Name dropping you has its perks. I finished all those plans for the orphanage. We're going tomorrow, *Mr. Reeves*."

I watch him grin and bite the inside of his cheek. I refuse to call him Christian to his face, because I'm still his employee, no matter how nice he is to me. If I started using his first name, it would open the door wider and wider until we can't close it again, and one of us is going to get hurt.

Me. *I'm* going to be the one to get hurt, because he's the untouchable Christian Reeves and I'm nobody.

It's still raining when we leave, but he doesn't lead me out the front door of the building. Instead, we go to the private parking garage reserved for the most important people in the company. He has an entire floor of the garage dedicated to him, which is overkill since he's only one man and can only drive one car at a time. Perks of being rich, I guess.

He opens the passenger door to his Aston Martin for me, and my old heels and thrift store outfit feel horribly out of place against the pristine leather seats and shiny black exterior of the luxury car.

I shrink into my seat as reality comes crashing back to me.

What does he really want from me? My body, most likely. What else do I have to offer him?

I feel his finger poke my temple and I blink at him. "Where'd you go? I lost you in here." He taps my temple again.

"Sorry," I mumble. A horrible, sickening feeling makes its way into my gut, and I check my phone. It's almost nine. I'm an hour late for my shift at the Hellfire Lounge. "Oh God, oh shit!" I grip Christian's arm as tight as I can and shake him. "Please, you have to take me to the Hellfire Lounge right now! Frank's going to kill me!" Christian doesn't start driving and I lean over the center console and shake him again by the front of his shirt, disturbed by his lack of distress at this extremely dire situation. "Please! You have to take me there now—*mmph*!"

He shuts me up by pulling my head close to him and capturing my lips in a kiss.

"I already took care of it, Elena." He wraps his hands around my waist and hoists me from the passenger seat and into his lap like I weigh nothing. In the process, my head bumps against the roof and he tenderly rubs the spot for me, though it didn't hurt. "Your friend Kate is covering for you."

I scoff in disbelief. "Kate doesn't cover for anyone."

"Well, I asked nicely," he says, tucking a loose strand of hair behind my ears and cupping my cheeks. I assume *'asking nicely'* is rich people speak for *'bribed'*. I turn my head and even though it's dark outside, I shudder. *What if someone comes out here and sees me with him?*

"Don't worry, no one can see in," Christian says, as if he can read my thoughts. "It's five percent tint. I single-handedly fund the MCPD from all the tickets they give me for it, but it's worth it. We could get up to all kinds of nefarious things in here and nobody would ever know."

I gulp, nodding, trying not to think about the fact that I'm straddling the CEO's lap right now in his expensive car after he just bought me dinner and let me sleep in his office all day. I'm really asking for things to go wrong at this point.

I try to climb back into the passenger seat, but his grip on my waist is firm. His lips go to my neck, lightly nipping at my pulse point. "Where do you think you're going?"

I part my lips slightly and let out a small puff of breath. "Home."

Christian removes the elastic band holding my braid together and loosens the twists, letting my hair fall free over my shoulders and down my back. "Are you sure you want to go home?" he asks, his voice low and husky. His cologne wraps around me like a mist of hot lust and any common sense I have left gets lost in his blue eyes looking up at me. He glances at his watch. "It's 8:54. How about I take you home at nine?"

My voice falters. "What are we going to do for the next six minutes?"

"I'm sure we can get creative," he laughs, flashing his perfect smile at me. "Do I make you nervous?" I nod. "Because I'm the CEO?" I nod again. I feel his fingers untuck my shirt from my pants and he lifts it over my head, tossing it into the passenger seat. He pulls his bottom lip in between his teeth when he spies my lacy shelf bra I had hiding under my top, and my core turns molten and achy with desire. "This is very inappropriate for the workplace, Elena. What am I going to do with you?"

I gulp. "It's easier to change at the club when—"

He presses his finger to my lips and shushes me before kissing me softly, letting his hands trace up my back, unhooking the lingerie top. He takes his lips off mine to watch my chest fall free. "I hate knowing other men get to see you like this every night," he growls, kissing my chest. "You were supposed to quit."

"I know," I whine, with an apology on the tip of my tongue. "I will. I promise I've tried. It's not as simple as handing in a two-week notice."

His mouth goes back to my chest, sucking one of my nipples into his mouth. I can't help it; I grind on his lap. He groans against my chest, his fingers digging into my waist. He drags his teeth lightly across the perky rosebud he's holding hostage in his mouth.

Fear, insecurity, and common sense all surge back into me and I reel back from him, gripping my bra close to my chest to cover myself. Without letting him protest, I clip it in the back and then pull my shirt on.

"Please take me home."

His face falls, but he doesn't push me to go any further. He cups my cheeks, places a featherlight kiss to the tip of my nose, and then he helps me climb into the passenger seat.

I glance at the clock.

It's nine on the dot.

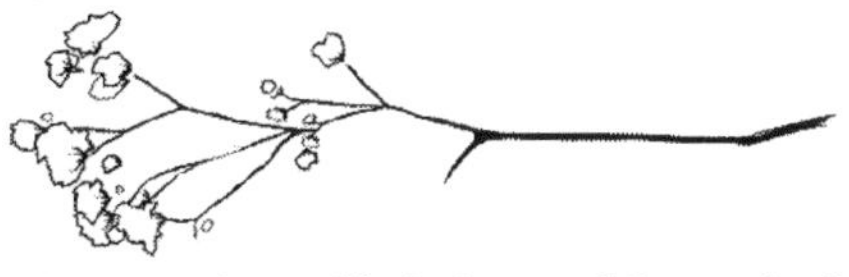

I don't know where Christian and I stand after our 'not-a-date' in his office followed by our 'six minutes in heaven' in the parking garage yesterday. The only way I can describe how I feel is confused. I've caught the attention of the most eligible bachelor in the world, and I can't figure out why.

I will never belong in his world. That's a fact. His life is all champagne and diamonds and unprecedented wealth. Parties and high-profile dinners. Interviews and business trips all over the world.

My life is so utterly normal in comparison that it's almost laughable.

Regardless of whatever is going on between us, I'm excited for our planned visit to the orphanage.

Christian had to add us to an approved list of visitors to even get through the gates. I had to gather everyone's driver's license numbers and their full names, and they had to run a criminal background check on all of us before we were allowed to even be considered as an approved visitor.

The only person that came back with a criminal record is Christian himself, but when have the rules ever applied to him?

He has fifteen separate instances of assault in the past decade. In interviews, Christian is open about being suspended from school on multiple occasions for fighting, and even recreational drug use when he was a minor. Once he became an adult, he gave up marijuana in favor of cigarettes.

His most recent arrest is from the day I met him, when he assaulted Neil Hayden. I went through the public jail records and found out that Christian spent a total of two hours in a holding cell before getting bailed out, and the charges were dropped the next day.

It didn't even make news because everyone was still focused on the Silencer killing those three men from the alley.

Yeah, those men that he killed for *me*.

God, I must have hit my head that night I met the Silencer, and I just can't remember, because I can't imagine there's any other plausible excuse for why I haven't reported that I'm being stalked by a serial killer. I make a promise to myself that the next time I see him, I'm giving him an ultimatum to stay away from me.

Shaking my head, I try to forget about him for the day, attempting to stay focused on the opportunity of a lifetime—getting to visit the Thomas and Elizabeth Reeves Memorial Orphanage with the man that willed it into reality.

I've fleshed out the itinerary for our trip today, down to every last minute. It wasn't easy coordinating Christian's schedule with seven attorneys, but I managed to make it work.

We're going to tour the entire campus, and then our first activity will be at the academy where we'll shadow a preschool class. Then we'll have a meeting with the Board of Directors, and then I arranged a bowling tournament for the high schoolers, where the winner will get a letter of recommendation from Christian himself for their college applications. With the weight the Reeves name carries, that's nothing less than a guaranteed acceptance to any college of their choosing.

Christian finds me lingering in the lobby waiting for all the attorneys to arrive, and insists I ride with him to the orphanage. When I agreed, I thought he meant that he just wanted to be in whatever SUV I chose. Instead, what he *actually* meant was he wanted me all to himself, because while the other attorneys load in to two vehicles, Christian takes my arm and leads me to a third, blacked-out Escalade.

I'm wearing a knee-length pastel purple dress, my favorite nude heels, and a camel-colored peacoat. My hair is up in a French twist with loose strands framing my face, my makeup light and fresh.

This orphanage is Christian Reeves' legacy, and I want to make sure I represent him well. The usual business attire I wear to the office won't do.

Oddly enough, Christian is wearing a purple tie that matches the color of my dress almost exactly. It's quite a jarring contrast to his black suit, but he couldn't have known what I chose to pull out of my closet today, so I convince myself that it's simply serendipity.

"You look lovely, Elena." He helps me into the passenger seat, his warm hand lightly holding me steady by my waist. "Sophisticated and beautiful."

"Are you trying to say I don't always look sophisticated?"

"I've seen what you wear under your shirt," he quips, winking at me when the blush across my face turns three shades darker. He's laughing at my embarrassment as he shuts the door before hopping into the driver's seat.

As he drives us to the North Side of Meridian City towards the orphanage, Christian asks, "If you could go back and time and change one thing, what would it be?"

My heart aches at the question, and my response is immediate. "That's easy. I'd save my father from so much pain by stopping his first family from being murdered. I mean, if they weren't he wouldn't have met my mom and I wouldn't exist, but that's beside the point."

"Murdered?"

I know he wants more details because my answer is almost exactly the same as his, I'd imagine. I'd want to prevent my dad's first family from dying, and he'd want his parents back.

I nod and take a deep breath. "Sorry, I didn't mean to make the mood so heavy. My dad had a family before he met my mother. A wife and twin girls. They were found shot to death in their home in 1989. My dad never talks about it, and I've never asked him because he's got severe PTSD and I don't want to upset him. He didn't even tell me about it until I was eighteen, and of course, I wanted more details, so I requested the police records, but they didn't say much. It was weird. The entire investigative file redacted all suspect names, and when I begged the MCPD for more information, they told me there wasn't any. I didn't want my father to know I dug into his past like that, so I dropped it, but I've always wondered if he knows who did it."

Christian is quiet for a long time.

"I'm no fan of the MCPD. They're useless in my opinion, but I'm...*acquainted* with the Chief. If you want, I can ask for a favor, maybe get some more information for you?"

I shake my head. "No, that's okay. It's redacted for a reason, and it's a sensitive subject for my dad. It's not my story."

"I understand. My answer would be the same, but I'm sure you already knew that. September 6, 1989. I'd change everything about that day."

I let out a sympathetic sigh and lightly rest my hand over his on the center console. "I'm sorry. For what it's worth, I think you're amazing for what you've built out of all that pain. This orphanage isn't just some publicity stunt you're half-committed to. I'd bet my life that you know every single one of the kids there like the back of your hand. You're...you're a hero."

"*Hero*," he hums back, almost like he can't believe I just called him that. I couldn't think of another word. Maybe it wasn't the right one, but I think he understands what I mean. His fingers loosely tangle with mine, the touch sending white-hot jolts of electricity through my veins. He begins to chuckle to himself as his hand tightens around mine.

"What's so funny?"

"You're calling me a hero when the only person worthy of that title is you."

"Me?" I ask, so off guard that I scoff. "Are you sick? Do you even hear yourself? What have I ever done?"

"More than you could ever possibly know."

My heart thumps so hard in my chest that I'm sure he can feel it where our hands are connected.

You'd think we were entering a military base with how much security we have to go through at the orphanage. At the gates, our IDs are checked, our vehicles searched, and my purse is sent through a scanner TSA-style. Then, once we get to the main campus, we have to go through a metal detector.

There is a good reason for the security measures. It's called an orphanage, but there are more stories than just absent parents here. A lot of these kids have been abused, neglected, and forgotten for most of their lives. Some of these kids have already been to the juvenile justice center. There are even children here that have been rescued from sex trafficking. That fact alone makes my heart ache for them. The trauma living in these walls is so heavy you can almost feel it in the air.

While the attorneys are all getting the grand tour from a staff member, Christian tugs me away from the group and the unexpected action makes me gasp loudly.

I bite my lip nervously. "What are you doing?"

"I want to show you something."

"But—" I protest, knowing the tour is going to move on with or without us because we have a tight schedule to keep to.

"It'll be fine, Elena. I'll show you everything, I promise."

With his fingers laced in mine, he leads me back outside and along a narrow concrete path leading from the main campus to a garden filled with what seems like miles of flowers. A low white-brick wall surrounds the garden, separating different types of flowers in every shade imaginable. How they've managed to get them to grow when Meridian City is cloudy and rainy most of the year, I don't know.

The path through the garden is all pristine white, until we reach a section of incongruous gray concrete like the rest of Meridian City. There's a bronze plaque in the ground that reads *In Loving Memory of Thomas and Elizabeth Reeves*.

I suppose Christian finds whatever he was looking for, because I hear him mutter an 'ah-ha' under his breath.

My eyes go wide, and I gasp in awe.

It's a section of the garden dedicated solely to crisp white baby's breath. Fluffy bushes of it grow up to my waist, and I feel over the soft flowers with a joyful giggle. I've never seen baby's breath if it wasn't in a bouquet. It's beautiful. This entire section of the garden is like stepping into a fairytale.

"I want to jump in it so bad," I exclaim with glee, though I'm really only joking.

"Your wish is my command," he purrs, and before I have a chance to comprehend it, I feel him wrap his arm around my waist, spin me to face him, and then with a devilishly handsome smile, he sends us tumbling down to the ground into the whimsical blooms. He catches the weight of us both with ease and I land with a tiny thud on my back. He's leaning over me, resting his weight on one forearm as he uses his free hand to stroke his thumb across my cheek with gentle tenderness. We exchange that cliché moment where our gazes flicker to each other's lips, and he presses his mouth to mine with something I can only describe as adoration. It's light and chaste—nothing like the way he kissed me in his car last night.

That kiss had been lustful and harsh, full of intoxicating desire. The way he's kissing me now feels like a promise of something more. It feels like the future.

"How did you know I love baby's breath?"

"You have a picture on your desk at your college graduation holding a bouquet of it. It's also your desktop background on your work computer."

I have to say that I'm shocked that he actually paid attention to something like that.

I see more than you think I do.

He said that to me the first time I was in his office, and I foolishly thought he was talking about the city. I didn't realize he was committing tiny details about *me* to memory.

Christian checks his watch and sighs. "We should go back," he murmurs against my lips, and then pushes up onto his knees before helping me to my feet.

Before we leave the garden, we do our best to fix the crooked and squished flowers we were lying in. He plucks a stem from the plant and gently sticks the buds into my French twist.

As much as I'd love to spend more time with him, he's right—we need to go back. The rest of the tour is probably getting ready to shadow that class right about now, and it will look bad if we're missing. He takes my hand again and leads us back to the campus, cutting through a few quiet corridors that let us out right next to the classroom, arriving there seconds before the rest of the tour meets us.

As we're all gathered in the hallway, I can see a few of the children in the classroom excitedly pointing at Christian. He must be a regular visitor if seeing him lights them all up like this.

We're there for a few long minutes, the attorneys now talking amongst themselves while Christian's attention is wholly occupied by staring at me. I pretend not to notice by taking my time to observe the artwork on the walls of the hallway. Finger paintings and coloring book pages, macaroni art and construction paper flowers, watercolors and charcoal sketches.

I flip open an old Valentine's Day card stapled to the wall and smile at the cute poem scribbled inside. I feel a soft tug on the bottom of my skirt. I look down to find a girl, no older than four, with the cutest button nose I've ever seen and a purple bow in her hair looking up at me with curious eyes. A bunny stuffed animal is tucked into the crook of her elbow. I squat down.

"Hi. What's your name?"

She blinks, her blue eyes sparkling. "Caroline."

"Hi Caroline. I like your bow. Purple is my favorite color."

"Mine too!" she excitedly squeals. She looks at Christian and then back at me and gives me an adorable, toothy grin. "You're pretty. Are you Mrs. Reeves?"

I clear my throat uncomfortably with a nervous flush pooling in my cheeks. "Thank you, sweetie, but no, I'm not Mrs. Reeves. My name's Elena."

She tugs me closer and cups her hand around my ear as if to tell me a secret, and she *very loudly* whispers, "Mr. Reeves thinks you're pretty too, 'cause he won't stop looking at you."

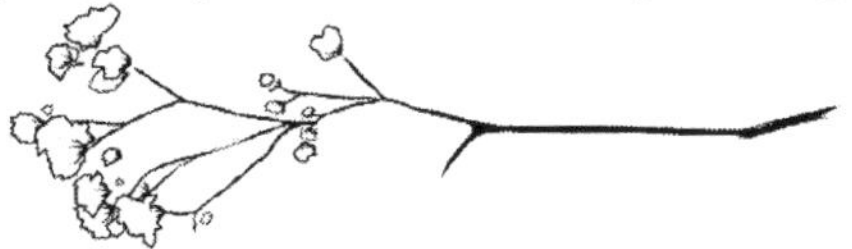

While I knew that there was a bowling alley within the campus, I expected five lanes, a small concession stand, and maybe a little arcade.

What I did *not* expect was the most insane looking bowling alley to exist in the universe. There are at least twenty lanes, two different fast-food restaurants, an arcade the size of Alaska, and an indoor go-kart track. Christian certainly spared no expense when it came to this place.

The attorneys all left after the meeting with the Board of Directors, of which he is Chairman, leaving Christian and I alone. The bowling tournament is down to the quarterfinals. I'm halfway into a strawberry milkshake when Christian slides into the booth next to me, his arm resting on the backrest and his hand thrown over my shoulder.

"So? What do you think of everything? Did I do good?"

I blink at him and swallow a mouthful of my shake. "You mean with the orphanage?" He nods, and I sigh. "God, Mr. Reeves, this is amazing. I've heard about everything you've done for these kids but to see it for myself…I have no words. Also, this milkshake?" I hold it up for emphasis and sing in a one-woman chorus like angels are descending. "Ten out of ten."

I lick the whipped cream off my straw. He's got a mischievous glint in his eyes and a smile on his face that screams trouble.

"What?" I ask around a mouthful of sugar. He lifts up his thumb and gathers some stray whipped cream from the corner of my mouth. Then, he innocently licks his thumb, though my damn vagina couldn't have found the action any more obscene judging by the way it just fluttered.

He nods towards one of the empty lanes. "Do you bowl?"

I scoff. "Do *you* bowl? Kinda seems like an activity that's beneath royalty such as yourself."

"How about a wager? Let's play one full game. If I win, I get to take you on a date."

I hum. "And if I win?"

"Whatever you want," he answers, far too easily.

"*Whatever* I want?" I repeat with a mocking gasp, and his eyes gleam with curiosity. I think about it for a minute. "Alright, Mr. Reeves. If you win, we go on a date—but if *I* win, I want an office with a view just like yours."

"You're on, Elena."

He grabs my hand and I giggle as he brings us to one of the free lanes.

Christian rolls first, lining up his shot and hitting nine pins on his first, and the last pin on his second for a spare. He winks at me, and I wink back, taking the ball in my hand and lining up my own shot.

I hit a perfect, clean strike.

I turn around to see Christian's mouth hanging wide open, and I give him a triumphant smile. "How did you do that?"

I tug my bottom lip between my teeth. "I was on my high school's bowling team. National champions three years in a row."

He smirks. "How convenient of you to not bring that up until now," he mumbles as I roll another strike. He gives me a playfully pained expression. "Best two out of three?"

"No take-backsies. I'll expect to move into my new office on Monday morning, Mr. Reeves."

And then I play a perfect game.

CHAPTER 9

THE ANGEL

As I approach the Hellfire Lounge for my shift, I scold myself for daydreaming about Christian. I cannot get feelings for the CEO. I just can't. It would be detrimental to my career when things inevitably go bad. I haven't put myself through hell for the past five years to have everything I've worked for come crumbling down because I got horny for a billionaire.

But he's so damn dreamy I can't help all those butterflies going nuts in my stomach every time I think about him.

All the warm fluttery feelings disappear the moment I see our resident masked asshole that *still* won't leave me alone. He grabs me roughly by the arms and shoves me into an alley when I'm a block away from the club.

He presses me against the wall so hard my head knocks against the brick, but his hand cups the back of my head to soften the blow. "Ow!" I mumble, rubbing the spot. "What do you want, asshole?"

"I need your help with something. And don't be dramatic, I made sure to protect your pretty little head."

I roll my eyes. "You need *my* help? With what?"

"Frank Valenti is up to something, and I want to know any information you can get me about this place. If you see or hear anything weird, I need to know."

A knot twists in my stomach and I rip my arm out of his grasp. "How exactly do you expect me to get this information? Why don't you just break in, since you seem to be such an expert at that?" I mock, bitterly pointing out all the times he's broken into my apartment.

"I'm not exactly welcome here. It's not as simple as walking in the front door."

I chew on my bottom lip. "What did you do?"

"Exactly what I told you I would. I killed all Valenti's friends. Spelled his name in their blood so he knows I'm coming for him next."

I shudder. "You can't just keep killing people for—"

"I *can* and I *will*, Elena. Until there's no one left that can hurt you. That's a promise."

I push him roughly away from me. "So, what, next time my father and I get in an argument are you going to run to Texas to kill him too?"

He huffs, pressing himself into me and caging me between his body and the brick wall. He softens his voice. "No, angel. I would never hurt your family."

He looks at me for a long while, his green eyes bright behind the dark paint that surrounds them. I take a deep breath. "Look, I'll try to help you, but only if you make me a promise." He says nothing, but he nods for me to continue. "You have to promise me that you won't hurt Christian Reeves. Ever. I *like* him. I don't want to wake up one morning to see that you murdered him because you're jealous I'd rather fuck him than you."

He raises an eyebrow. "Is that right, Elena? You'd rather fuck him than me?"

"Yeah, I would. He's actually nice to me, unlike you. And he's not a fucking psychopath."

He raises both eyebrows this time, and then slots his knee between my legs to spread them slightly, the action causing my mini skirt to get dangerously short.

"I can be nice, Elena. Want me to show you?" I instinctively shake my head. His hand snakes up my leg, stopping right at the bottom of my skirt. "You want me to make you cum so you can compare notes? Are you scared I can fuck you better than your boyfriend can?"

"He's not my boyfriend."

He chuckles against my neck. "I love how that's the only thing you decided to respond to." His hand brushes up my skirt, causing it to pool around my waist, my white cotton thong now exposed. He looks down and growls to himself, and I swear, even behind his mask, I can practically see him hungrily lick his lips. His fingers ghost over the front of my panties.

I grab his wrist with both of my hands to get him to stop, and to my surprise, he does, glaring at me with those artificial eyes like he's waiting for an invitation.

"When will you admit to yourself that you want me?"

I scoff. "I don't."

He raises his voice enough to cause me to nearly jump out of my shoes. "Don't fucking lie to me." His hands come to rest on the brick wall on either side of my head and he presses his chest into mine. His proximity sends my senses into overdrive, and that part of the brain where arousal and fear get muddled together makes my legs clench and my pulse skyrocket. "I have a confession," he says, his tone hard with need as he whispers his dirty confession directly into my soul. "Did you really think it was a coincidence that you found me in that alley the night after I saved you? No, angel. I had been watching you from your open window all night. Were you thinking about me saving you when you used that cute purple vibrator on your pretty cunt? Were you wet thinking about using your body to thank me?" My breath quivers as his hand travels up my thigh again, and this time, I don't stop him. "I stabbed myself in the arm and waited for you to find me, and I forced you to help me."

"You're fucking insane," I mumble, trying to find any rational thought in my brain. His left hand lightly squeezes my neck as my pulse thrums under his fingers.

In my neck and my underwear.

"Yes, I am," he whispers breathlessly, grinding himself into me so I can feel his erection digging into my stomach. "And you are the object of my insanity."

With an abrupt change in mood, he takes a purposeful step back from me. "Get me that information, Elena."

I start to make several undiscernible noises as I attempt to form a sentence to even begin to *try* and comprehend what just happened. *Did I really almost just let a serial killer feel me up in a dank alleyway? What the fuck is wrong with me?*

The Silencer turns and walks away without another word, and I make a mental note to research psychiatric hospitals when I get home, because I need serious mental help.

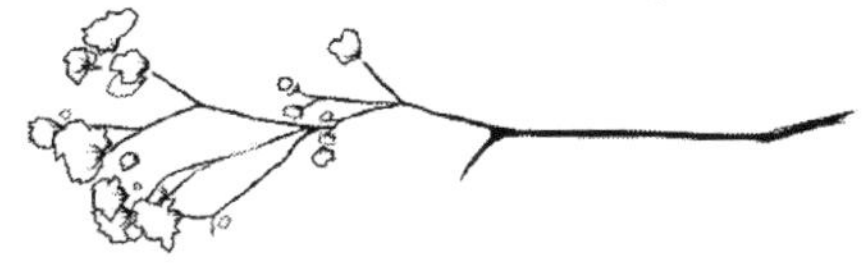

Two hours into my shift, Kate taps me on the butt and shoves a piece of paper into my hands. My eye twitches when I look at her, and all she does is shrug. I open the folded-up paper to find the Reeves monogram at the top, and underneath, the number six.

My brow furrows for a brief second, and then I look across the room and up, to where private suites look out over the dance floor. Those things are hardly ever used because they're fifty thousand dollars to rent, but the rules in those suites aren't the same rules that apply down here.

There's a very strict 'clothes on' policy on this level. Anyone who gets too adventurous gets immediately thrown out, because there's a strip club one floor up where men can get their rocks off to naked women. This floor is mostly just a bar and dance floor.

Those suites though? Rule free zones. That's why they're so expensive.

Six. He's in suite six.

I take a deep breath of courage and leave the bar, walking up the steps until I reach the corridor that leads to the suites. It's completely soundproof, and slightly unnerving how quiet it is. The only indication of any life is the very faint thump of the bass from the club. I reach suite six, and before I have a chance to knock, Christian opens the door and wordlessly lets me inside. He's wearing the same thing he was earlier, sans his jacket. His shirt looks rumpled, his hair is a mess, and I swear it looks like he has a dark shadow under his eyes. I've never seen him so unkempt.

"Hi," I croak.

"*Relax*," he laughs. "I won't bite." He points towards one of the couches. "Sit."

I do, and he hands me a glass of champagne, taking a sip of his own before slumping into the seat next to me with a smile. I eye him suspiciously. "I'm confused. What are you doing here?"

"Sharing a bottle of champagne with you."

I raise my eyebrow, making an obvious show of looking around the room, taking in the various bondage supplies and the stripper pole in the center on a raised platform. "You rented a fifty-thousand-dollar suite in a shady nightclub to have champagne with me? Sorry, I'm not buying it."

Christian holds up his hands in surrender and then playfully clutches his chest. "On my honor, I have no ulterior motives other than seeing you again."

"You saw me this morning. We spent the entire day together. Was it really so forgettable?"

He gives me a crooked smile. "Not in the slightest. I like spending time with you. Is that such a crime?" He sets his champagne glass down on the table in front of him, wraps his hand around my thigh, and pulls me into his lap. I'm straddling him, his mouth mere inches from mine. He caresses my cheeks with a featherlight touch and presses his lips to mine—soft and sensual. I don't fight it. I let him explore my mouth as our tongues tangle together. I can taste the champagne still lingering on his breath and my hands fist into the front of his shirt.

He pulls back with an abrupt hiss, like he's in pain.

I let him go immediately. "I'm sorry."

He shakes his head and grabs my cheeks again. "It was nothing. I'm just sore from a workout," he quickly says, not missing another beat before crushing his lips to mine again in a hungry and ferocious kiss before finally confessing. "I rented the suite because I wanted to kiss you again, and I couldn't wait until tomorrow."

"You paid fifty grand to kiss me," I repeat breathlessly, less of a question and more in a statement of disbelief.

Silence fills the air between us for a heartbeat, and then the next whispered sentence out of his mouth is so sinful it makes my core ache with desire.

"I'd pay even more to touch you."

His warm hand cups my pussy and any reservations about him being my boss crumble to dust. "I want to touch you here." I whimper when his fingers leave my achy cunt to squeeze my ass. "And here." He pulls my shirt over my head and then pulls down my bra, so my breasts are spilling out over the top. "And here. And everywhere in between."

A shaky moan escapes my lips when his hot mouth licks up my chest, from my sternum to my pulse point, where he nips and sucks until I'm sure there will be a bruise in the morning. I feel the heaviness of him between my legs, begging to be free of his slacks.

Playing along with him, I ask, "How much would you pay?"

"Name your price."

There's a lust in his eyes that won't be easily extinguished, and a sharp jolt of power zaps up my spine. I take a quick second to think of the most outlandish thing I can conjure up, and I smile wickedly.

"Yacht."

A feral growl emanates from deep in his throat and his hot hands feel up my bare back and unhook my bra, tossing the fabric to the side.

"*Done*."

In half a second, my panties are ripped to shreds, the elastic snapping against my thigh as he tears them off me and his fingers expertly stroke the skin near my center, yet not close enough. I don't care that he's the CEO and I don't care that this is only going to complicate things further, and I don't care that I'm going to be alone in dealing with the aftermath when it all goes wrong.

All I care about are his fingers and his mouth and the hard length of him straining against his pants. I throw my head back and let out a breathy moan that only urges him on. He sticks his sinful middle finger in my mouth, silently telling me to get it wet for him, and I do as we make eye contact that has him burning a hole in my resolve and my self-control. I grind down onto his lap, just knowing I'm leaving wet spots of my arousal all over the front of his pants. He uses his free hand to hold my hips still.

"Beg for it, Elena."

My eyes snap open and I look at him with defiance. "That costs extra."

He chuckles darkly, and I know I'm utterly fucked. He ghosts over my clit with his middle finger, slick with my saliva, and I moan again. His free hand goes to my jaw and grips me tight, pushing my cheeks together with his thick fingers that I'm dying to feel inside me. "I've got all the money in the world. Now *beg*."

He can't make this easy, can he? But God, if it doesn't light me right up and set my center on fire as I think about the thousand different dirty things he might say to me when he plunges his fingers inside me and sees how absolutely drenched I am when he hasn't even *touched me* yet.

Swallowing the remains of my stubborn pride, I soften my face and flutter my thick lashes. I make sure I look pleading, simpering, and whiny, and I raise my voice an octave higher. "Please make me cum. I want to feel your fingers inside me. I want you to ruin me, Mr. Reeves."

He chuckles like a goddamn maniac. "Fuck, Elena, don't worry. I'm going to do that and so much more."

He plunges two of his thick fingers inside me, and the sound that escapes my throat is so obscene that I don't think the soundproof barriers of these suites are hiding it. I twist my fingers in his hair and pull as he pumps his fingers in and out of me at a brutal pace. I can feel myself dripping down my thighs and all over his hands and pants. When those sinful things curl inside me and press down on that sweet spot, I come undone. I cum so hard I can practically see stars. I convulse with his fingers still deep inside me, still pumping, pulling sweet aftershocks from my needy hole. I lightly graze my teeth over the side of his neck and whimper softly when he removes his fingers from me.

The space between my thighs is hot and sticky in the most delicious way. With a content sigh, I lean back, only for my mouth to fall open in horror when I see the mess I made all over his lap and abdomen.

"Did I—"

"*Yes*," he breathes, his cheeks flushed a dark shade of red and his light blue eyes gone sharklike with lust. "*Fuck yes* you did. I want you to do it again when I fuck you with my tongue."

He flips me onto my back, pulling off my skirt so that I'm completely bare to him while he's still fully dressed, his clothes soaked with my release. My cheeks heat with embarrassment. I've never done that before, and he pulled it out of me so easily you'd think I was trained to squirt on command.

Judging by the tent in his pants, he loved it.

My center tingles with anticipation as he begins to slowly kiss down my body. My skin erupts into goosebumps and I lick my lips when I look down to see him staring at the space between my legs.

"Fuck, you're beautiful."

He admires me like my pussy is the finest work of art he's ever seen. He licks his middle finger, still damp with my release, and slowly pushes it into me again.

"Oh, *God*," I cry out, my back arching off the leather sofa. "Please, Mr. Reeves. Please."

"I don't think you even know what you're begging for."

He looks up at me from between my legs and keeps eye contact with me as his sinful tongue lightly circles my throbbing clit. My eyes roll back in my head and my hands shoot to his hair, pulling him closer. I feel him chuckle against my pussy and the vibrations cause me to buck against his chin. "Do you know what I want, Elena?"

"What?" I ask—no I *plead* for him to tell me. "Please, whatever you want, God, please just taste me."

"Don't worry, baby, I'm going to stay down here for as long as it takes. I want to spell out my name with my tongue against your clit, Elena, over and fucking over, until you're screaming it."

He uses his free arm to pin down my hips and he finally licks a thick stripe up my wet slit. I moan loudly as he begins to trace letters on my clit. I'm so clouded by pleasure that I've forgotten the alphabet. I've forgotten his name. I've forgotten *my* name. All I can do is gasp and grip at his hair and grind against his face as he sucks on my clit and pumps his middle finger in and out of me so fast and so hard I'm convinced he has the strongest forearms on the goddamn planet.

"What's my name?" he asks, and I only moan in response as his finger curls inside me.

"*Oh my God*," I gasp. The sounds I'm making are downright pornographic and dirty. He's eating me out like I'm his favorite meal, licking and sucking my clit and plunging his expertly skillful tongue into my dripping cunt along with his finger.

My legs clamp shut against the side of his head. He uses his free hand to push them open again. "Not quite. Let me start over."

He begins to trace his name over my clit again.

C. H. R. I. S. T.

Christ is right.

That's as far as I make it before I cum again, all over his mouth and chin and hands. I really should be embarrassed by how messy and filthy it is, but when he crawls back up my body and I see that his face is soaked with my essence, all it does is make me want him more.

"Say my name," he whispers.

"Mr. Reeves."

He growls and flips me onto my stomach, delivering a sharp slap to my ass. I hear him begin to unbuckle his belt, and it makes my pussy quiver with anticipation.

"*Say my name*," he commands.

"Mr. Reeves."

"Goddamn it," he growls, landing another harsh slap against the tender flesh of my ass, hard enough to make me whimper.

That's when I feel the silky length of him rut against my weeping core. The tip of his cock catches against my entrance and we both moan at the same time.

He reaches under my body and up my chest to wrap his hand around my throat, gently squeezing until he has complete control of me. He tilts my head to the side to kiss me, all tongue and teeth as he slams into me in one harsh thrust. It causes me to rock forward with so much force I nearly fall over the arm of the sofa.

Holy fuck, he's huge. I don't have to see it, I can feel it in the deepest, most primal part of my body. He's stretching me deliciously, hardly meeting any resistance from how drenched I am. My body opens up to him like I was made exactly to fit his throbbing length. He pounds into me at a brutal pace, so hard that my loud moans get cut off each time he slams into me. So hard that the couch scuffs along the floor with each thrust.

He hits that perfect spot inside me over and over again until I'm writhing around him, and my release launches me into space.

"*Fuck*," he spits out through gritted teeth. "You're on the pill, right? Fuck, fuck, fuck."

"Yes," I breathe, skipping over how he knows that. "Yes. I promise I am."

"Can I—"

"God, yes. *Please*."

"Only if you say my name. Fuck, Elena, please, I'm so fucking close. Say my name, baby."

When I don't, another sharp slap lands across my ass, the hardest of them all. It hurts so good that another small orgasm rolls through me, and this time, when I fall over the edge, he falls with me, spilling inside me without warning and with such vigor I think he caught himself off guard.

"*Fuck*," he groans, falling over me and resting his head on my back. "Jesus Christ. You are fucking perfect."

Still inside me, he kisses up my spine until he reaches my cheek. My body begins to tremble with not only the brutal crash from an incredible high, but also fear.

Fear. Because what did I just let happen? This is wrong for so many reasons.

Panic overtakes me and I hiss when he pulls out of me. I scramble to try and find my clothes scattered across the room.

"Elena."

I ignore him as I look for my bra. *God, where the fuck did it go?*

"Elena."

I ignore him again, finally opting to just say fuck the bra and wear my hair down for the rest of my shift to cover my boobs. "I have to go," I choke out.

"*Elena*," he repeats, gently catching me by my face and stroking his thumbs across my cheeks. "Take a deep breath. Everything's fine."

"No, everything is not fine!" I exclaim, my voice a clear indication of my distress. "Holy shit, what have we done?" I grab my forehead like my brain has fallen out of my skull.

"Tell me I didn't completely read the situation wrong."

He stuffs his hands in his pockets, his belt still unbuckled around his waist. Guilt traces his features, and it hits me that he thinks he took advantage of me. Not in the sexy way, but in the '*I'm going to the police*' kind of way.

"*No*. No…I promise it's not that. Everything we just did was consensual but so, so stupid. You have no idea what kind of danger I just put you in."

"Elena, breathe," Christian coos, cupping my cheeks again. "Relax. Tell me what's going on."

"I have a stalker." I take a deep breath. "It's…it's the Meridian City Silencer." As hard as that was to admit, my chest immediately feels lighter. I've been keeping it to myself for weeks. Christian's face softens. "He's killed eight people for touching me. He killed three people for chasing me into an alley and then he killed all five of Frank Valenti's friends for groping me during one of my shifts. He's dangerous and I…I just don't want him to find out about this and come after you, too. This can't happen again."

Christian wraps his arms around me in a comforting gesture, coaxing me to rest my head on his broad chest and listen to the thump of his heart. "I am not scared of the Silencer, Elena. Nothing is going to happen to me."

Big tears find their way to my eyes and drip down my cheeks. "I made a deal with him to keep you safe," I admit shamefully, like I've done something wrong. "He wants some information about Frank and this club. I told him I'd help if he promised not to hurt you."

Christian looks down at me and tilts my chin up to look into my wet eyes. "You made a deal with a serial killer to protect *me*?"

I get it. He's a rich man and he thinks he's untouchable, but no amount of money will save him if the Silencer chooses him as his next victim.

Christian uses a hand on my lower back to lead me to the sofa, instructing me to sit and hands me the glass of champagne I've barely touched. He downs his own glass in one gulp, then pours himself another.

He hands me his cell phone and unlocks it for me. "Text yourself." He walks over to the in-suite sink to clean himself up. He glances at me through the mirror and watches me bite my lip.

"You want my phone number? We must be getting serious, Mr. Reeves."

"I've been serious about you from the moment we met."

He takes a seat next to me, champagne in hand, and glances at his watch. "I'll take you home after your shift. You get off at one, right?"

I raise an eyebrow. "How do you know that?"

Something unknown flashes across his gaze. "Kate told me."

That doesn't surprise me. I told Kate that I had a thing with a rich man from work, and I'm sure once Christian came here to bribe her to cover for me yesterday, she put the pieces together.

He smiles at me, warm and genuine, and I can't deny it anymore. I have a big crush on the CEO of my company. It's probably way too late for that realization considering we just fucked in a shady nightclub.

"What are you thinking about?" he asks. I take a sip of champagne to try and hide the shy smile creeping up my face.

"This. Us," I admit. "What does this really mean to you? I won't hold it against you if you feel differently, but I'm not really into the idea of being the CEO's mistress. I know it's such a turnoff to ask what we are after sex, but I just…I have to know. I don't want either of us to get hurt."

"I'd never hurt you." He scoots closer to me and caresses my cheek with the back of his hand and tucks a strand of hair behind my ear. "If you want to know what we are, I'll answer your question with another question. Would you like to go steady with me?"

I violently choke on my champagne. "Go steady? What is this, 1945?"

He smirks. "I'm serious, Elena. You wanted me to be straightforward about my intentions, and that's what I'm doing. If you want to be together, then let's be together."

Insecurity creeps up my spine. "Why me?"

He takes a deep breath. "My parents died when I was six. For the past three decades, all I've done is focus on the past. You are the only thing in my life that's ever made me consider the future. At first, the future was just the next day. I started sleeping better because I knew falling asleep would make tomorrow come faster and I would get to see you again. I wanted to get a glimpse of you, to see you smile, to hear you laugh. I made a game out of trying to guess how you'd wear your hair to the office. I was always looking forward to the next day because I wanted to discover one more piece of the puzzle that made up Elena Young."

He reaches across the space between us to tenderly hold my face in his hands. "And now I've got a whole section of my brain dedicated solely to you, and I think about more than just the next day. I see next week. I see next month. I see next year. I see you in every possible version of my future." He presses a chaste kiss to my lips. "I've never been in a relationship. I can't promise it will always be easy, but I can promise that I'll always try to be the best version of myself for you." Another chaste kiss, this time he keeps his lips ghosting over mine when he breaks it. "That's why."

I wipe my face, trying not to look like a complete mess after this man just said the sweetest thing I've ever heard. "Yes, Mr. Reeves. I'll go steady with you." He flashes me that brilliant smile, and with a gentle tug on his tie, I pull him closer to me. "Now about that yacht…"

Our laughter fades into the steady bass of the club. When he takes me home and he kisses me, I'm taken back to that kiss we shared in the garden, and how that moment felt like he was promising me a future—because he *was*.

CHAPTER 10

THE SILENCER

This is wrong. This is so fucking wrong, but I can't help myself.

Frank Valenti is a pervert. He exploits all kinds of people in Meridian City by sticking cameras in the private suites at the Hellfire Lounge. Probably to catch powerful people participating in all manner of perversions so he can blackmail them.

Christian Reeves doesn't know how fucking lucky he is to have Elena and all of her affections. Yes, he's charming and hot and rich and blah, blah, blah. But he doesn't deserve her and it's not fucking fair that he gets to have her, and I don't.

I don't deserve her either, but that's beside the point. She's *mine*. I don't have to deserve her for her to belong to me.

It's because she belongs to me that I have a sick obsession with seeing her beautiful face whenever and wherever I can.

Even if that means I have to be a pervert myself and hack into the Hellfire Lounge cameras to find and download the recording of Christian Reeves fucking her in one of those plush private suites. I knew the second Kate handed her that piece of paper that she wouldn't need much convincing to go find that rich asshole waiting for her. I knew the second she stepped into that suite that he'd touch her, and she'd let him, because all those nights alone with her vibrator aren't enough anymore.

The video footage is crystal clear and ultra-high resolution. There's no sound, though, and that's a damn shame, because fuck, what I wouldn't give to hear her pretty little moans as she came undone.

I need to taste her. I need to feel her around me. I need to worship her the way only I can.

I need to love her so violently that it breaks her, and then fill in all those cracks with gold until the only thing holding her together is me.

I sit on my bed with my laptop to the side where the video plays, my cock out of my sweatpants and in my tight fist. I stroke my shaft, using my thumb to spread the precum around the tip, zooming in on Elena's face twisting in pleasure.

Fuck Christian Reeves. Fuck him for bulldozing his way into her life at the exact moment I started to.

Most of all, fuck him for getting to taste her first. I don't share. I've never had to share, and I'm not about to start.

Her dark brown hair frames her round face in a beautiful fucked-out way that makes her even sexier. Her plump bottom lip is between her teeth. Her thick lashes graze her cheeks as her lids flutter closed, hiding those honey brown irises from me.

My fist begins to make wet slapping sounds as I touch myself to a video she doesn't even know exists. I deleted it from the Hellfire Lounge server, so nobody will ever see it but me.

With a loud grunt, I explode, cumming in hot, erratic spurts all over my hands and abdomen and chest, the milky white strands standing out against the purple bruises littering my torso.

The release is unsatisfying to a point where it's almost frustrating, but my angel is a stubborn little thing, and she needs more…*convincing* before she lets me take what's mine.

She's going to fight me every step of the way, but it's fine. I love it when she fights. I love it when she thinks she's being intimidating and when she foolishly thinks her threats have any weight to them.

She's the only person who commands my self-control just as much as she makes me lose it.

I clean myself up with a towel, and then I close the video, keeping it in a password-protected file that happens to be Elena's birthday. 0211. Not very secure, I know, but she has consumed every single facet of my life and it's hard not to tie everything to her. My passwords. My computer screen. The fucking wallpaper on my cell phone.

She's everywhere, and it's still not enough. It will never be enough. Not until she loves me.

With a sigh, I navigate through the computer to the files I downloaded earlier. My pulse thrums with anticipation as I pull up a police report.

Hacking isn't as easy as the movies make it seem, but the MCPD firewall is made of popsicle sticks and hot glue. Not surprising, considering everyone in Meridian City hates the local police department and they haven't had decent funding since Christian Reeves pulled his yearly billion-dollar donations to the department over a decade ago.

I click through the poorly scanned records and begin to dig through pages and pages of seemingly useless evidence logs before finding the actual narrative.

As expected, all the names are redacted, but it doesn't stop me from reading through the entries and taking meticulous notes as I do.

On August 15, 1989, I, Officer Harold Fischer, reported to the lobby of the Meridian City Police Department to take a harassment report.

Diana Louise Young, date of birth 12/17/1960 explained that soon after starting a new job, the owner, [REDACTED], began making unwanted advances towards her. She described the first few conversations they had as typical of an employer-employee relationship. They would exchange small talk and he would often bring her coffee before going to his office. As the receptionist in the lobby, they crossed paths often.

[REDACTED] extended a dinner invitation to her. She politely declined, stating to him that she is happily married with two young children, and reminded [REDACTED] that he has a wife and six-year-old son.

Mrs. Young claims that he handled this initial rejection well, and she blew it off. Several weeks passed, and [REDACTED] began to extend dinner invitations again, sometimes multiple a day. She declined all of them, once again reminding him that she is happily married and committed to her family and advised him that he should focus on his wife and son.

Mrs. Young claims the invitations turned into lavish gifts, including flowers, jewelry, and presented me with statements that show her bills had been paid in several yearly sums, totaling several hundred thousand dollars. Mrs. Young made a report to the company's HR department. She was told that an investigation would be conducted. Three days after making the report, she was informed that the investigation was closed, and that no inappropriate behavior was found. She was given a written reprimand for making a false report.

I assured Mrs. Young we would investigate the matter and advised her to report any more harassment to us. I provided her with my business card.

On August 20, 1989, I, Officer Harold Fischer, responded to a 911 call at the Young residence. Mrs. Young states that [REDACTED] showed up unannounced and uninvited to her doorstep demanding to be let in. She refused, and she claims he grabbed her by the wrist so hard it caused her immense pain. I observed several bruises consistent with fingerprints around her right wrist.

I interviewed [REDACTED] and asked him for his side of the story. He admits that he was at the residence, but denies grabbing Mrs. Young. He claims she was shocked to see him at her doorstep and was so 'frazzled' that she tripped on the doorframe and fell, so he caught her by the wrist. I informed him that his story was not consistent with her injuries and placed him under arrest for Misdemeanor Assault. While booking him into the Meridian City Jail for overnight processing, I filled out a request for the arraignment judge to issue a temporary no-contact order on behalf of Mrs. Young.

I informed Mrs. Young about the arrest. She advised that she told her husband, Elliot Young, about the situation, and he had some questions about the investigation. I told her he is free to call me when he is able. Mr. Young is in the United States Army and currently deployed in Korea, so I will not be interviewing him at this time.

17 hours after [REDACTED] was taken into custody, Judge Willis, who handles arraignments, dropped the misdemeanor charge and denied the no-contact order on the grounds of insufficient evidence. I informed Mrs. Young of the outcome. I later received a call from Mr. Young, who was infuriated at the outcome of the arraignment hearing. I informed him that the charges were dropped at the judge's discretion and there was nothing I could do except wait for further evidence.

I received a records request from [REDACTED], who states in her request that she would like the entire investigative file for this matter as her husband intends to open a defamation lawsuit against Mrs. Young. I informed her that we do not release records of ongoing investigations, and that she would need a subpoena to obtain them.

Subpoena received in the matter of [REDACTED] v. Diana Louise Young. Investigative file produced to Plaintiff's attorneys.

On August 26, 1989, I, Officer Harold Fischer, responded to a 911 call at the Young residence. Dispatchers informed me that Mrs. Young called the emergency line screaming for help, and they heard several gunshots in the background. Five units responded to the residence, where Mrs. Young was found face-down in the kitchen. She had three gunshot wounds in her chest and no pulse. Officers checked the rest of the house and found Lisa and Mary Young, both age 6, with gunshot wounds in their chests and unresponsive. All three were pronounced dead at the scene.

I made an emergency call to the American Red Cross who assisted in informing Elliot Young about the deaths of his wife and children.

[REDACTED], when interviewed, admitted to the murder of Diana, Lisa, and Mary Young. He was taken into custody on three counts of first-degree murder.

Under advice of the county attorney, Judge Willis, and my superiors, this investigation has been changed from confidential to highly classified. Due to the sensitive nature of this crime and the high-profile suspect, an emergency meeting of the Grand Jury was called, and the jury found insufficient evidence to indict [REDACTED]. The charges were dropped, and this case is now closed.

I set the laptop to the side and scan over my notes, tapping my pen to my temple. It's not going to be easy to unravel this mystery that's haunted the Young family for Elena's entire life.

What I do have is a year, and Diana's full name and date of birth. The police report mentions that this all went down in August of 1989, and that whoever her stalker was, he had a six-year-old child. Perhaps I can cash in some favors and gain access to confidential police and court records from that time, and then if all the stars align, maybe find out the name of her murderer.

The police report mentions he was a high-profile business owner, and there weren't many of those in Meridian City in 1989. There are a few old money families that inhabited the island before Thomas Reeves made it the center of his empire, so maybe those names are a better place to start.

Of course, the easiest way to get the name of the man who murdered Diana Young is to simply ask Elliot himself, but he sure as hell isn't going to divulge the name of the man who haunts his nightmares to the man that haunts Elena's.

I'd bet my life that he knows the person who did this.

I'd also bet my life he took his own revenge.

I understand now why Elena is so afraid of me. She's worried about history repeating itself. She's worried that I'm one of those stalkers that will eventually grow to resent her for not loving me back and then ultimately kill her, but it's not like that. It's not like that at all.

I'm different.

I'm in control.

Maybe not when it comes to my murderous impulses, but I'm in control when it comes to loving her. I'm in control when it comes to keeping her safe.

Though the Youngs have a history of stalkers, I'm not in this because I have some indescribable obsession with Elena.

I know exactly why I desire her in my soul, and I'll tell her about it one day, because she deserves to know why I call her angel.

CHAPTER 11

THE ANGEL

Friday morning, when I arrive at work, Christian is lounging in my office chair with a wide grin on his face that has me blushing the second I step out of the elevator.

"Good morning," he greets casually, dropping a small paper bag on the center of my desk. "Got you breakfast."

I peek inside the bag to find a blueberry muffin. The corner of my mouth quirks up. "Thank you."

He stands up and buttons his suit jacket before placing a tender kiss to the crown of my head. "I just wanted to say hi before I got trapped in meetings all morning. I'll see you later."

"Okay," I whisper, my cheeks going pink as I notice several other people on my floor turning their gazes to us. "See you later, Mr. Reeves."

He tightens his jaw and sighs heavily at the teasing way I say his name. He lightly pinches my chin between his thumb and knuckle of his index finger before leaving, and I sit down in my office chair wondering how the hell I got so lucky to capture his attention.

I boot up my computer and then head to the breakroom to make my coffee, where I'm met with curious eyes and low whispers as I pass by. I try to ignore them best I can. I keep my gaze to the floor like I've got something to be ashamed of.

I had assumed Christian wanted to keep our new relationship private for as long as possible, but bringing me breakfast and kissing me in front of everyone isn't exactly inconspicuous. I suppose I'll have to get used to the judgment and the whispers—it comes with the territory of dating arguably one of the most recognizable people on the planet.

When I get back to my desk, I spend the morning transcribing all the notes the attorneys took on our trip yesterday. It feels good to have some work to do again. It takes me a few hours, but I get it typed out and dispersed amongst the department. Around the same time, I receive an email from Christian asking me to proofread his recommendation letter for the winner of the bowling tournament. The junior who won wants to go to MIT, which is coincidentally where Christian went to school, too. His recommendation letter is closer to a thesis. I don't know how the hell he managed to get it written so fast. It's flawless too. He had to have stayed up all night writing it, because I didn't get off from the club until one in the morning and his estate is on the other side of the island from my apartment. It had to have been close to 2 AM before he even got home.

At lunchtime, Christian texts me to come up to his office. I don't have any hesitation when I step into the elevator and swipe my access card. I'm practically bouncing on my toes.

Christian is leaning against the conference table in his perfectly tailored suit with a cigarette between his smile. I've never really liked smokers. My father is one, and I've always detested the smell, but Christian makes it look sexy.

He makes everything look sexy. He's just fucking standing there and my panties are wet. I'm truly, utterly down bad for this man.

When the elevator closes behind me, I cross my arms over my chest and raise an eyebrow. "Yes, Mr. Reeves?"

He uses one finger to motion for me to come to him while he places the nub of the cigarette in an ashtray, and I take a few steps until our legs are lightly brushing together. "I have something for you." From behind him, he pulls out a box from Tiffany's and holds it in the space between us.

I suck in a sharp breath. "I—"

"It's to say thank you. For organizing everything yesterday. You're great with the kids there. They all love you. I never would have thought to have a bowling tournament."

I meet his eyes. "You paid me thirty dollars an hour yesterday to kick your ass in that bowling tournament. You didn't have to get me anything." I gulp and look down at the iconic blue box. "Especially not something expensive."

"Something tells me you could use a few diamonds in your life."

Ignoring my protest, he nudges my hand with the box, his bottom lip between his teeth like he's nervous. As if *he's* the one that needs to be nervous in this situation. I open it slowly, like I'm afraid something will bite me. I lift the lid to find a diamond tennis bracelet inside.

"I *cannot* accept this."

He once again ignores my protests and takes my left wrist in his hands, fastening the silver and diamond bracelet around it. It's so sparkly that it glimmers with the smallest movement.

I sigh. "It's beautiful."

"Like you," he whispers, lifting my hand to his mouth and placing a small kiss on the inside of my wrist. "Now…how about lunch? What are you in the mood for?" I open my mouth and he presses his finger to my lips. "If you say you brought a frozen lasagna again, I'll rip my hair out."

I gulp. "It's actually a pot pie this time."

He shakes his head in feigned disappointment and chuckles. "There's an old woman that sells homemade tamales outside the lobby on Fridays. They're amazing. What do you say?"

I lick my bottom lip. "I'm fine with my pot pie, Mr. Reeves." I glance down at the bracelet on my wrist. "Or maybe I'll pawn this and buy myself a five-course steak dinner."

"*Or*," he draws out the word playfully, "you can keep the bracelet and let me buy you a five-course steak dinner on that date you owe me."

I *tsk*. "I don't owe you nothin'! You owe *me* an office though. *And* a yacht."

"Working on it, baby. You owe me a date as a consolation prize for hustling me at the bowling alley." His hands drift down to my waist, and he rubs gentle circles with his thumbs against the fabric of my white dress.

I get a small surge of confidence and reach out to straighten his tie. "If you let me drive one of your fancy sports cars, I'll go on a date with you."

"Done."

He laces his fingers with mine and drags me into the elevator, stopping one floor below so I can grab my things, and then we giggle like kids as we stumble together to the parking garage.

I spy his black McLaren, and my heart skips a beat.

This is his favorite car. His signature car. His baby, according to the interview he did when he was named Sexiest Man Alive a few years back.

There is no way in hell he's actually going to let me drive this thing, right?

As always though, Christian has a way of totally throwing a curveball at me, and he tosses his keys high into the air. I catch them with shaky hands, and he opens the driver door for me.

"Wait. I…I can't drive this. What if I wreck it?"

He blinks as if that's a ridiculous question. "What do you think insurance is for? Come on, Elena. Don't tell me you're scared!"

"I'm scared," I squeak, and Christian lightly kisses me. All my nerves fade away and turn into butterflies in my stomach. He doesn't take his mouth off mine as he leads me to the passenger side and only releases my lips once I'm safely buckled into the seat.

"I'll give you a driving lesson some other time." He pecks me on the cheek and closes the door. He gets in on the driver's side and revs up the engine. "Where to?"

"The orphanage."

"The orphanage? Why?"

I smile at him with a mischievous glint in my eyes. "Because I want everyone there to know you're just as bad at skee-ball as you are at bowling."

He licks his teeth. "We'll see."

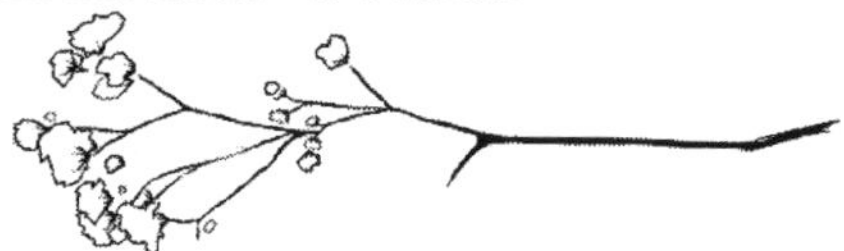

We did see.

I got my ass beat. Thoroughly. Repeatedly. At skee-ball, basketball, Space Invaders, *and* ring toss. We shared a basket of cheese fries and a club sandwich for lunch, and I got myself another strawberry milkshake.

Christian and I are playing footsie while I obscenely lick the whipped cream off the straw. Christian's jaw is tight as he glares at me from across the table.

"Mr. Reeves! Mr. Reeves!"

I turn my head to find Caroline standing next to our table with her stuffed animal in her arms. She waves at him.

"Hi Caroline," he greets. "What are you doing here? Shouldn't you be in school?"

She shakes her head unconvincingly. Christian and I share a look and smile. "Miss Kelly said no math class today."

Christian raises an eyebrow. "If I go find Miss Kelly, she's going to say the same thing?"

"Okay!" she whines. "I sneaked out 'cause I don't like math." Christian snorts, and Caroline turns her attention to me, climbing into the booth next to me. "Hi Elena. Are you Mrs. Reeves yet?"

I laugh at her. "No, Caroline. Mr. Reeves and I are just friends." I watch as Christian raises an eyebrow at me and bites his cheek. Caroline gasps dramatically with her hands over her mouth.

"Stay here. I'll be right back!"

She runs off before either of us can protest, and Christian glares at me. "Just friends?" he repeats with a half-smile he's trying to hide. "I'm wounded, Elena." He grabs his chest over his heart. "It hurts right here."

I lightly kick his shin under the table as Caroline comes running back, placing two plastic spider rings from the prize counter on the table between us, and forcefully tells Christian he needs to take a seat next to me. He does, and Caroline crawls into the booth opposite us, placing her hands on her hips.

"Mr. Reeves, you have to marry Elena right now!" She pushes the two plastic rings closer to us. "Hurry! Before she marries someone else!"

"Caroline!" I hear a woman shout from across the room sternly. She's clearly pregnant. She's got that waddle from a belly that's keeping her off center. She approaches us and her eyes blow wide when she spies Christian. "Oh! Mr. Reeves, I'm so sorry. Caro likes to slip away when no one's looking and steal Tootsie Rolls from the prize counter."

"It's alright, Kelly," Christian assures her. Kelly takes Caroline's hand, and Caroline's lip quivers slightly as she gets led away by her teacher and she waves us goodbye. Christian laughs quietly while poking one of the spider rings on the table for a second, and then holds it up to me. "Elena, will you be Mrs. Reeves?"

The giggle that escapes my throat is one of genuine amusement, and I playfully hold up my left hand to let him slip the plastic around my ring finger. I look at my hand and hum. "It's beautiful."

"Thanks, it's a Harry Winston," he deadpans. "By the power vested in me by that four-year-old, I now pronounce you, Mrs. Reeves. May I kiss the bride?"

I bite my bottom lip and nod, and he cups my cheek before kissing me deeply. I grab him by his tie and pull him a little bit closer. "I'm not signing a prenup."

He laughs against my lips. He lets me finish my milkshake and then we leave, driving through the city towards the office. About halfway there, Christian stops in a random parking garage and rolls his seat back as far as it will go.

"What are you doing?" I ask, but then I notice the bulge in his pants.

"We need to consummate the marriage, Mrs. Reeves."

I hesitate at first, but then his cock twitches in his pants and the space between my legs begins to ache with need. I lick my lips and crawl on top of him, straddling his lap and taking the initiative to kiss him. It's heavy and needy and I scrape my nails down his chest, earning a hiss from him before my fingers begin to work the buckle of his belt so I can pull his throbbing length free.

He throws his hands behind his head like he's lounging and watches as I stroke his thick cock in my hands a few times, spreading his precum over the tip before grinding my pussy along his length.

He moans my name. "Fuck, Elena. You haven't had panties on this whole time? I could have pulled up your skirt and fucked your wet little pussy hours ago?"

I throw my head back when I seat myself on his shaft, relishing in the fullness only he can give me. He touches every delicious inch of me, and the mere thought that he's so deep combined with the stretch makes my cunt clench around him.

I begin to bounce shamelessly on top of him, biting my lip as he kisses along my neck and licks my pulse point. His arms are still behind his head and I preen at the feeling of control over one of the most powerful men in the world.

"That's it, baby, ride me like a good girl. Make yourself cum. Yeah, just like that. Just like that. Fuck, don't stop, Elena."

His praise only serves to make me bounce faster, grind harder, moan louder. When I'm right on the edge, I press our lips together, pulling his face close to mine as I grind my clit against his pelvis and let go, crashing into a thick wall of pleasure and letting him swallow every sweet sound I make for him. He follows just seconds later, spilling into me with a grunt that resonates through the car like a gunshot.

We share heavy breaths as we gather air into our lungs, and when a group of people walk past the car, paying no notice to us in the front seat, I thank God for that five percent tint.

CHAPTER 12

THE ANGEL

When Monday morning comes around, all I can think about is seeing Christian again. It still baffles me that he's asked me, of all people, to be his girlfriend. Everything that's happened in my life over the past few weeks has felt like a fever dream. I'm not sure which parts are real and which parts I've hallucinated.

I'm still waiting for the ball to drop. I've been in this city for five years, and suddenly, I have a stalker who happens to be a serial killer and a boyfriend who happens to be the richest man on the planet. Oh, also can't forget that I started working at a shady nightclub where the owner sees me as nothing but a price tag.

All of that would give anyone whiplash.

I'm worried about what the Silencer will do once he finds out my relationship with Christian has become serious. I have a feeling that if I try to break it off, he's going to take out that anger on Christian.

Christian says he can handle himself, but I know first-hand that the Silencer isn't afraid to get his hands dirty, especially where I'm concerned. If he thinks he might lose me, there's no doubt in my mind that Christian's going to be his next victim, and that terrifies me.

When I walk into the office building, I spy Christian waiting near the elevators, smiling brightly when he meets my gaze. He says nothing to me as we enter the elevator together, and he scans his access card and presses the button for his office. I furrow my brow.

"Excuse me, Mr. Reeves, but you owe me an office," I tease, elbowing him lightly.

He elbows me back. "Shut up and take a closer look, Elena."

A closer look at what? At him? I blink twice, and he must sense my confusion, because he nods his head towards the elevator directory. I cup my hand over my mouth and gasp. "Tell me you didn't."

The gold plaque that used to read *CEO - Christian Reeves* now reads *Christian Reeves & Elena Young.*

"A deal is a deal, Elena." He wraps his hand around my waist. "Even if you made that deal in bad faith, you won fair and square, and you said you wanted an office with a view just like mine."

"It wasn't in bad faith!"

He laughs, and when we finally ascend to the top floor, the elevator opens, and I swoon. The entire office has been rearranged. The conference table is now on the left side of the room, and the right side has been made into a small break area. There's a coffee machine, a microwave, and a mini fridge.

Curiosity tingles in my spine and I open the mini fridge to find a large container of hazelnut creamer amongst a pitcher of water and an unopened bottle of expensive champagne. In the small freezer, a selection of my favorite dollar-store frozen meals. I bite my lip to stifle a giggle.

I see more than you think I do.

He really does pay attention, because how else could he have known that I have a monopoly on the hazelnut creamer downstairs? I don't think I've ever even had coffee in front of him.

Closing the fridge, I turn back to face the office. On the other side of the room, closest to the back wall of windows, the office is divided down the center, the left side for him, the right side for me. We now have matching desks that are facing each other, and my new office chair is custom monogrammed with my initials, E.L.Y, in a purple embroidery thread.

"You don't do anything halfway, do you?" I ask, my hands on my cheeks to hide the blush as I walk to my new desk and set down my purse.

"No, I don't do anything halfway. Especially when it comes to you." He stands directly behind me and brushes my hair off one shoulder. I shiver when his fingers graze the skin there. I feel him lean down, and in our reflection in the windowpanes, I watch him press a kiss to the side of my neck. His fingers ghost down my arms before resting on my hips.

I take a deep breath when he sucks on my neck slightly, sending electricity down my spine straight to my core. His hands on my waist grip tighter and spin me around so that we're chest to chest. I look up at him from under my lashes as he lifts me up and takes us across the room to set me on the conference table. "I'm so glad you're all mine now, because I get to do this." He crashes his lips to mine, all tongue and teeth, and trails his hands under my dress until he finds my panties, ripping them off without a second thought and throwing the ribbons of lace haphazardly across the room. "Whenever I want. As much as I want."

My stomach plummets as his knees hit the marble floors and he takes me in, all bare and already weeping for him. I feel his hot breath fan across my core, and it makes me clench my legs together slightly, and he wraps them around his broad shoulders to keep them open.

His tongue licks a thick stripe up my aching core. I fall back against the table and moan loudly. Christian ravishes me like he's been starving for months. He licks and sucks on my clit and plunges his tongue into my needy hole as deep as he can manage. My hands find their way into his hair, desperate to hang on to something, pulling him closer. "You taste so fucking good, Elena. I could stay down here forever."

He plunges a finger into me and curls it as he sucks on my clit, and I cum with a wail loud enough to wake the dead.

I hear Christian moan in delight as he laps up every drop of my release and stays there until I'm begging him to stop. He gets up, standing like a god over me while I'm splayed out on the conference table like a harlot. My cheeks and chest are no doubt flushed bright red from desire and my breaths are heavy with anticipation and need.

He quickly gets to work on his belt. "I need to be inside you. *Right fucking now.*"

When he frees his cock from his pants, he's eight inches of solid titanium, thick and leaking precum. My chest begins to heave faster, and his hands snake up my back until they reach the zipper of my dress, tugging it down and then exposing my chest to him.

Instead of doing what I expect him to do, which is pull me closer to the edge of the table to reach me, he crawls onto the table with me, covering my body with his. His cock twitches against my core and I let out a whine of anticipation.

He pulls back and slaps the tip against my swollen clit. He smirks and gathers some of my wetness on his fingertips, smearing my arousal over his cock. He throws his head back and sighs. "God, you're so fucking wet, angel."

I open my mouth to ask him what he just called me, but all that escapes is a cry of agonizing pleasure when he presses into me without warning, seating himself fully inside me in one fluid motion. He captures my shallow breaths with one kiss after another as he rails me so hard I nearly go blind. I hold onto him for dear life, clutching at his suit and dragging my nails down the expensive fabric.

Christian fists a hand in my loose hair and exposes my throat to him, licking and sucking until he marks me as his. He sucks in a sharp breath. "*Fuck*, you were made for me. Your pretty pussy was made to be mine."

I know I'm dripping obscenely onto the conference table, and I pray nobody sitting here will be able to see the imprint of our passion on the rich mahogany. With his hand still in a tight fist tangled in my hair, he lifts my mouth up to his and swallows my desperate moans. We share breaths. My inhale is his exhale. He's drinking in the noises I'm making like they're a symphony made just for him.

In a way, I guess they are.

He uses his free hand to trace my bottom lip as I stare up at him, half delirious from pleasure.

He begins rolling his hips again, slowly grinding into me, catching that sweet spot inside me. My brow furrows and I let out another breathy moan, wrapping my arms around his neck and tugging on the locks at the base of his head.

He finishes inside me with a loud groan at the same time I throw my head back in pure euphoria. My bones almost crack under his unyielding grip as he twitches inside me. A mixture of our release drips onto the table when he pulls out. He licks his lips as he looks between my legs, gathers some of it up on his fingers and shoves it back inside me. I hiss from the sensation.

He tucks himself back into his pants, his hair a dead giveaway of our rendezvous, and I'm sure I look like a chaotic fucked-out mess.

"I think I'm beginning to like Mondays," Christian teases with a wink, taking a seat in one of the chairs at the conference table. He takes a cigarette from a silver case in his pocket and lights it.

I playfully roll my eyes. "You owe me a new pair of underwear."

He blows smoke to the side. "You don't need them. If you thought that was the only time I was going to fuck you today, you're dead wrong."

I can feel our combined release leaking slowly out of me and onto the table. I cross my legs to try and keep it contained, and Christian growls, rolling his chair directly between my legs after uncrossing them. He flips up the bottom of my skirt and places my feet on the arms of his chair, exposing my center to him again. His eyes catch on the ugly anklet the Silencer gave me, but he doesn't comment on it. He shrugs off his suit jacket and tosses it carelessly behind him as he looks me over.

Blush creeps to my cheeks in the most delicious way. This feels absolutely filthy, his gaze nothing short of feral. It's like he's committing this moment to memory, the way my pink folds look after being abused by him. He lightly brushes his thumb across my clit, and I nearly jump off the table from the hypersensitivity.

He takes another drag of his cigarette and leans back in his chair, one hand still firmly on my thigh, while I'm still presenting to him.

"Touch yourself," he commands. Slowly, I drag my fingers through my sensitive folds and gather some of the wetness on my fingers, smearing it over my clit and sucking in a sharp breath at the sensation. Christian's mouth is partially open, his cigarette between his teeth as he uses his large hands to keep my legs widely parted so he can get a perfect view of me. When he blows out smoke, some of it wafts up to my face.

I hate cigarettes, but he makes it look so goddamn sexy that I really don't care. With the way he fucks me, he can do whatever the hell he wants.

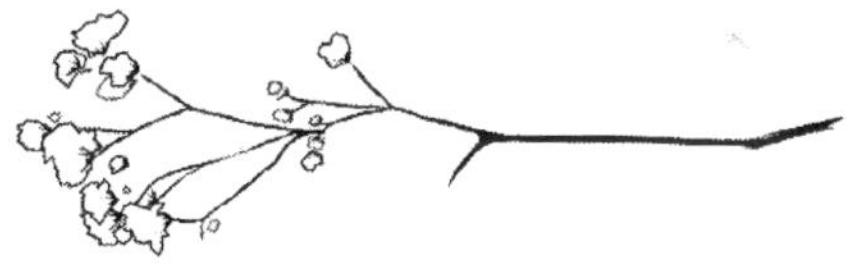

Christian absolutely ruins me two more times before lunch. Once on his desk, leaving an imprint of my asscheeks on the glass, and the second time on the couch.

I catch a glimpse of myself in the mirror of his private bathroom, and I *definitely* look like I've been railed multiple times before noon.

Christian is insisting that we go out for lunch. It's easy for him to suggest when he looks deliciously sexy with that ruffled hair and I look like I just came off a porn set. Despite my protests, Christian laces his fingers with mine and tugs me along with him to the garage. Today, he's driving a blacked-out G-Wagon.

I wonder how he decides to pick a car every morning. I don't think I've seen him drive the same car twice since I met him. Maybe he uses a spinning wheel of car keys or pulls them out of a hat.

I had forgotten how nice it is to not have to walk everywhere. It's super mundane, but my feet thank Christian every day for the fact that he drives me most places, and when he can't, he sends a cab for me. He even sends them for my shifts at the Hellfire Lounge, but I am not going to put myself in the vulnerable position of being trapped in a car with a stranger while wearing a mini skirt. I'd rather take my chances on the street.

I'm sure the Silencer is lurking somewhere anyways, watching me go to and from the Lounge and probably jerking off to the sight of my toes in my heels or some weird shit like that. He seems like the kind of man to have very weird fetishes. That's probably one of the reasons why he murders so many people. It probably gets him rock solid, and then once he's worked up, he comes to me hoping I'll put out for him. He hasn't left me alone since we met, so that's got to be the only plausible explanation.

Christian and I are in a secluded corner of a small cafe. He brought us here after I offhandedly mentioned tomato soup and grilled cheese sounded good. He drove around the city for an hour before we found this place, to which the owner, upon seeing Christian Reeves walk into his restaurant, claimed he had the best tomato soup in the world.

Then he proceeded to serve us the most pathetic looking soup I've ever seen. It was bland and unremarkable, but we silently giggled to ourselves over it. The owner even asked Christian to take a picture with him, to hang up on his wall. Christian politely agreed even though I could see in his face that he thinks being associated with this man's tomato soup is going to plummet his stock prices or something.

After we finish lunch we talk for a while, and before I even have a chance to think about what I'm saying, I ask, "What was your mother like?"

I want to know more about Christian, of course, but the second those words fall out of my mouth, the way he looks at me has me wishing I kept my mouth shut. It's like he'd rather drink acid than answer me. "I'm sorry!" I apologize frantically. "You don't have to answer that."

After a moment of painfully avoiding each other's eyes, Christian's face softens, and he reaches across the table to take my hand in his. His thumb brushes over mine, but I don't interpret it as a gesture of comfort for me. It's for him. I rest my other hand on top of his. I try to give him an apologetic look, but he grins down at our hands.

"You don't have to be sorry. It's just...nobody's ever asked me that before. My mother was...extraordinary. At least to me. I know that my parents' friends thought she was high-strung and pretentious, but I don't have any memories of that. To me, she was a loving, doting mother. But I was only six when she died, so my recollection probably isn't perfect." He sucks in a breath. "I still remember the way her hair bounced when she walked. She loved that old Hollywood glamor, and I don't think I ever saw her without red lipstick on. Now that I think about it, that's probably why it's my favorite color."

I feel something crack inside him from across the table, and it occurs to me that if nobody's ever asked him what his mother was like, he's also never talked about what it was like to lose her or his father. Christian doesn't strike me as the kind of person to cry often, but if there was a moment where he would, this would be it. I move from my side of the booth to sit next to him, trying to bring him some comfort with my presence.

Christian wraps his arm around my shoulders and tugs me close. His right hand is clenched into a tight fist on the table, and that's when I notice the knuckles on his left hand are bruised and freshly scabbed over.

He takes a deep breath before speaking again. "I remember the last thing my mother ever did before she died was kiss me on the forehead. My parents had been fighting for a few days. I don't know why, but they always seemed so upset. Of course, my six-year-old brain came to the conclusion that they needed a burger, because burgers always made me feel better. I *begged* them to take me to this shitty place on the North Side I used to love. We never went out to eat because we always had private chefs to make us whatever we wanted, but I was convinced that it would stop their arguing, even if it was just for one night. We ate, and they even let me get a meal to-go so I could have it the next day too. My mother kissed me on the forehead before we got up from the table, and the moment we stepped outside, a man with a gun confronted my parents and told my dad he *deserved it* before shooting him." He takes a shaky breath. "They died because I wanted a fucking burger."

I take his cheeks in mine and press my forehead to his. "It's not your fault. You couldn't have known. You were just a kid."

"You want to know the first thing I did when I turned eighteen and inherited my dad's fortune?" I wait in silence, because I know whatever he's about to say will break my heart for him. "I paid the owner of that restaurant a million dollars to hand me the deed, and then the next day I took a sledgehammer, some gasoline, and a lighter, and I burnt the building down."

Realization pours into me.

"When we went to the orphanage…there was an out of place slab of concrete in the rose garden. That's where they died, isn't it? That's why you chose to build it there." Christian looks down, and nods. I sigh apologetically and stroke his cheek with my thumb. "I'm so sorry."

It's all I can say to try and comfort him, but I know it will never be enough. I knew the bare-bones version of the story. Everyone in this city does. I had no idea the kind of deep-seated guilt he felt about unknowingly choosing his parents' deathbed. I can't imagine the kind of pain he's kept locked away in his chest all these years. I can tell by the way he talks about it, that I'm probably one of the few people that even know that detail.

His eyes are stuck on the booth opposite of us, with a haunted look on his face. It's like the ghosts of his parents are sitting there, and he's begging them to hate him so that he can justify the guilt he's felt all these years.

So he can justify the scars on his wrists.

"What about your mom?" he asks, looking up. The wetness in his eyes is gone, like it was never there in the first place. "You have a picture of your dad on your office desk, but not your mom. Are you close?"

I give him a weak smile. "Yeah, we're close. I'm just a daddy's girl, even though he's impossible to get along with. Sometimes I think he believes he's used all his luck in this world by getting my mom to marry him."

Christian goes back to stroking his thumb across my hand. "What do you mean?"

"My mother met him when he was deep in his depression, and from what she tells me, he was nothing like the man he is now. She says she knows he's her soulmate because she fell in love with him anyways. Demons and all."

"Do you believe in soulmates, Elena?"

I think about it for a long time. *Do I?* Everyone wants to believe they exist. Everyone wants to believe that there's someone out there that was always meant to love them.

"I think if two people are meant to be together, then they will be. I don't know if that makes them soulmates though. I feel like a soulmate implies some sort of…divine intervention. I think the best love stories come from the people who say that love came out of nowhere for them, not from the people who were looking for love in the first place." I squeeze his hand in mine. "Do *you* believe in soulmates?"

The corner of his mouth tilts into a smile. "Not until I found you."

CHAPTER 13

THE ANGEL

The past few days have been a fairytale and I don't think I've ever been happier.

The sun is shining bright over the island, and I consider it a good omen. It's never sunny in Meridian City, New Jersey.

The elevator opens to my shared office, and I raise my eyebrow when Christian is lounging in his chair, feet propped up on his desk with a cigarette in between his lips at 8:45 in the morning. He gives me that brilliant smile that makes me weak at the knees and I quietly set down my purse.

"What, no good morning kiss?" he purrs.

I narrow my eyes at him and take a seat in my office chair, propping my feet up on the desk just like him and lightly nip at my nail on my index finger. "Seems like your mouth is already preoccupied, Mr. Reeves."

He blows out a long puff of smoke. "I'm a wonderful multitasker. Come here and I'll show you."

I roll my eyes. "I have work."

"Your job is to sit there and look pretty, Elena." He looks me up and down from his desk, his gaze predatory and dark. "You're very good at it. Now come here."

He puts the butt of his cigarette in an ashtray and takes his feet off the desk, sitting now like a king on a throne. I suppose he is, in a way. The King of Meridian City. The King of the East Coast. The King of the World.

I decide that I'm in a particularly mischievous mood. I push back from my desk and then slowly slide to the floor on my hands and knees. I watch his eyes turn hungry. He leans back into his chair with his arms behind his head and watches intently as I crawl to him, his only indication of approval the tent now in the front of his slacks.

"*Seems like crawling is an activity beneath royalty such as yourself.*"

I pause just inches away from his legs, sitting back on my heels. "Do you want me to stop?"

"Fuck no," he growls back, his voice husky. "Crawl to me, Ellie."

I cock my head slightly, and I hear him breathe out an '*oh fuck*' as I bite my bottom lip. "Say please, Mr. Reeves."

Christian reaches forward and shoves two fingers into my mouth, like he did that first time at the club, and pushes down on my tongue. His cheeks are flushed red with desire, and it's something that makes me drenched every time—the way his face always gives away how needy he is. I wonder if he even knows he does it.

I let out a whine as he tugs me forward, until I'm directly in between his legs. "Elena, if you don't stop fucking calling me that–"

I shake my mouth free from his grip and lick my lips. "What will you do?"

"Do you want to be punished? Is that why you're being so goddamn mouthy today?" His hand grips my chin. His hold is firm and commanding, but far from painful. I tilt my chin down and suck his thumb into my mouth, and he groans. "Since you're down there already, might as well make yourself useful, yeah?"

With blush-stained cheeks, I reach for his belt first and then his pants, popping open the button, tugging the zipper down, and freeing the full length of him from the fabric. It bobs invitingly in front of me, and the mere sight of it has my face flushed as red as Christian's is. My eyes go to the thick vein prominent up the underside of his cock, and my mouth waters.

I glance up at Christian from under my lashes and his hand goes to my hair, grabbing a gentle fistful and tugging my mouth exactly where he wants me. I lick my lips and brace my hands on his thighs, and I keep eye contact with him as I lick up that throbbing vein, from base to tip, and then suck his angry, leaking head into my mouth. Christian throws his head back and lets out a satisfied grunt.

"This is a much better use of that pretty mouth of yours, Elena."

The praise has me even more determined to take more of him. We've barely begun, and my jaw already aches. His eyes screw shut when I take in another two inches. I quietly moan as I pull back and then try to take more of him.

He can't help himself. His hips buck forward and cause me to gag, but he holds my head firmly in place. My eyes begin to blur as tears prick in my eyes and I dig my fingernails into his thighs to try and brace myself as he begins to thrust into my mouth. He goes slow at first, telling me how pretty I am, telling me how perfect I am, and once my jaw relaxes, he gathers my hair and stands up to chase his pleasure, and I do my best to keep up with the relentless pace.

The room fills with filthy grunts and my desperate gasps for air. Saliva breaks free from the corner of my mouth, dripping down my chin and onto my chest, webbing sloppily between my mouth and the base of his cock.

I force myself to look up at the man before me, and I try to keep myself from going stupid at just how fucking godlike he appears above me. Here I am, on my knees for the richest man in the world, and I'm lucky enough to call him mine. His face is twisted into a beautiful piece of artwork, jaw slack, cheeks red, sweat gathering on his furrowed brow.

He pumps into my mouth twice, and then with a loud grunt that I swear has the glass of his desk vibrating, he spills down my throat without a warning. His cock twitches and pulses with satisfaction against my tongue, and he hums when he pulls back, gathering a few errant strands of his milky semen and shoving it back into my mouth with his thumb.

He lets go of my hair and tucks himself back into his pants, and then with the utmost care and concern, he trades places with me, making me sit in his office chair while he cleans my face and chest with a tissue.

"You're nothing but trouble, Elena Young." I blink at him, zoning out for a second, feeling like I've got the most uncertain hit of déjà vu in my life. I don't hear the rest of his words. I don't even realize I'm staring at nothing until he taps my nose. I bite my lip, embarrassed that I missed everything he said.

He saves me from having to ask and repeats himself. "We're going out tonight. I'm giving you the rest of the day off to get ready."

"Get ready? Where are we going?"

He pulls out his wallet and proceeds to shove a black American Express credit card between my lips, and then completely ignores my questions. "Go shopping. There's a car waiting downstairs to drive you wherever you need. Find something pretty to wear tonight. Be ready to go at six."

My jaw falls open and the card slides from between my lips and lands in my lap. "You're joking," I scoff, wide eyed and confused while he stares with what I can only describe as pure adoration in his eyes as he kneels in front of me. "You're giving me your credit card?"

He raises a brow in confusion. "You want cash instead?"

I giggle. "No!" I lean forward and kiss him, my mouth aching. "Is this a test? Am I supposed to say '*no, don't spend your money on me*'?"

"Elena, let me be very clear." He stands up and leans against the desk, and then rubs his thumb over my cheek while I look up at him. "I will never, ever deny you anything. I don't give a fuck how much it costs. You can buy the entire Chanel catalog and I wouldn't bat an eye. Actually, please do that. My cock is already getting hard again thinking about you spending all my money."

I pick up the card and twist it, the heavy plastic gleaning against the light from the window. His name is printed neatly at the bottom of the card.

Christian Thomas Reeves.

I peek at him from under my lashes and give him the most mischievous look I can manage. I wave the card in the space between us. "I think my first purchase will be a penthouse." He tucks his wallet back into his pocket and laughs. "Can I at least know what kind of attire I should be wearing? Are we talking Miss Universe or cocktail party?"

Christian hums to himself. "Wear something sexy and easy for me to get you out of."

He winks at me, presses a quick kiss to my lips, and lightly smacks my ass, warding me towards the elevator door.

There's one mall on the rich side of Meridian City, the kind of mall filled with designers and overpriced food courts.

The driver Christian sent for me followed me into the mall, which I thought was weird. It was only after I clocked the outline of a gun in his pants that I realized he must be private security.

He's big and burly and never takes his eyes off me while I shop. Not in a creepy way though, more like a '*Christian Reeves will kill me if anything happens to you under my watch*' kind of way.

After some prying, I learn that the massive man's name is Gavin. He's a retired Marine. Has a wife and a newborn. He's been working for the Reeves Estate for six years. Started out as perimeter security for the mansion and is now one of Christian's most trusted bodyguards.

Gavin tells me that Christian doesn't use his security to protect himself, but rather the people he cares about. Well, *person.* Christian has a godfather named Edwin, who has been with the Reeves family since his father, Thomas, moved to Meridian City. Edwin was Thomas' private secretary and raised Christian after his parents died. Gavin used to tag along when Edwin wanted to get out of the mansion to make sure he didn't fall or get bombarded by reporters or mugged outside a coffee shop. Edwin has become frail in his old age and has trouble walking, so he never leaves the mansion anymore.

If Gavin is following me around a mall, it's not lost on me how that must mean *I'm* included among the people Christian cares about. The thought alone makes me blush and smile like an idiot.

I'll be the first to admit that I love shopping just as much as the next girl, but when your ultra-rich boyfriend hands you his credit card and tells you money is no object, it's a whole different world. I'm not typically one to spend so frivolously, but Christian was very encouraging. I jokingly texted him that I couldn't decide between the black Louboutin's or the nude ones, and he simply texted back '*get both*'.

I shop for five hours. Three of those, I spend on trying to find the perfect dress. I still don't know where we're going tonight, so I hope my choice of attire doesn't have me making a fool of myself.

"He talks about you all the time," Gavin says in his thick Jersey accent, causing my head to snap up to him in curiosity as we walk back to the car, a dozen shopping bags in his hands. "Don't think I've heard him get through a sentence without mentioning your name."

"Really?" I ask, insecurity prominent in my voice. Gavin laughs quietly to himself as he opens the car door for me. I slide in and he walks around the hood to get in on the driver's side. "What's so funny?"

"He's down bad." He takes off towards my apartment. "He was…different before he met you."

"Different how?"

Gavin takes a deep breath as if he's considering how much he should say. "Sad. Violent. Angry. I don't think he's smiled *once* in the past thirty years, but then he met you. I don't mean that fake shit he does for the press. I mean a real smile."

Sad? Violent? Angry?

I would have *never* used those words to describe Christian. But I suppose now that I think about it, I don't actually know anything about him. At least not anything that the general public doesn't already know. I guess he must be a little violent to have accosted Neil Hayden the day we met, but otherwise, he's been nothing but charming. He's a sweetheart.

"I think it's that southern charm," Gavin chuckles. "My wife's from Texas too. You southern belles have a knack for taming us feral brutes from MC."

I laugh. "We're three for three. My dad is from Meridian City and married the *queen* of the southern belles."

Gavin chuckles. "See? You Texan ladies are like sirens. It's the accent."

"I do not have an accent!" I protest, and he does nothing but laugh.

Gavin drops me off at my apartment and I thank him politely for entertaining me all day. He reminds me that Christian will pick me up at six and waits patiently until I'm safely inside the building before driving off. I haul my shopping bags up the stairs and jitter with excitement as I do my makeup and hair, styling it into big, loose curls.

I'm pinning the last one up to set the curl when my phone starts ringing. It's my father. I smile lightly and press the answer button, and then put the phone on speaker as I rub moisturizer over my freshly washed face.

"Hi, dad," I giggle into the phone speaker.

"Hi, sweetheart. You sound happy today."

I bite my lip. "I'm just having a good day. What's up? Anything fun happening there?"

"Tomorrow is our wedding anniversary," he quips. "I'm taking your mother to upgrade her wedding ring. I'm thinking five carats is sufficient, don't you?"

My father absolutely adores my mother. Would do anything for her. He's sixty years old, but doesn't look a day over forty-five, despite his nasty habit of smoking and a lifetime of hurt.

Because of his past, he's incredibly overprotective of his family, and it's one of the main reasons he and I argue. He hates that I live in the most dangerous city in the country. He's just itching for an opportunity to force me to move back. I think sometimes he wishes something bad would happen to me, to scare me into coming home.

My dad's a good man, but he lets his own paranoia rule his life.

I hold up my hand to try and imagine a five-carat diamond on my mother's dainty fingers. Even my humble, 'southern belle' of a mother can't resist the appeal of diamonds. "I think that'll do just fine."

"How have you been? I haven't heard from you in almost a week. You don't got time for your old man anymore?"

"Dad, I told you I was busy. Things are finally starting to look up for me out here."

"You certainly sound happier. What's going on? You got a promotion or something?"

I suck in my cheeks to try and avoid blushing. "Sort of. I got a raise. And I'm uh…I'm actually…seeing someone now."

I can practically hear my dad's brain short circuit, and I brace myself for the incoming interrogation. "Name?"

"Christian."

"Age?"

"Thirty-six."

"Too old."

"Dad—I'm twenty-nine!"

I hear my dad mutter incoherently into the phone. "Yearly salary?"

"He's…*comfortable*. I met him at work."

"No good will come out of dating your coworker, Ellie."

I uncomfortably frown at myself in the mirror because he's probably right—and Christian isn't just my coworker, but the CEO.

"Everything's going to be fine, dad. I promise. Maybe you can meet him soon. At Thanksgiving or the wedding."

I hear my dad sigh. "I miss you. I hate that I only get to see you on holidays. I hate that city you're living in. Scares me to death. Anytime I don't hear from you for a while, I think you're rotting in a dumpster somewhere. There are plenty of law firms here in Texas. You could come live with your mother and I while you study for that test. You could get a good job that pays you better than Reeves Enterprises."

I sigh quietly and roll my eyes in the mirror. My father really can't resist trying to guilt me into coming home. "*Dad*."

He never seems to get it through his thick skull that the bar exam is state-specific, so, one, I'd have to start my studying from scratch, and two, if I passed the bar exam in Texas, I wouldn't be able to practice in New Jersey. I moved here because I wanted to be an attorney for *Reeves Enterprises.* The best attorneys in the country work for Christian. I'm in the best place I could possibly be for my career.

My dad concedes, and he suddenly sounds sad. "I know, I know. Just don't be a stranger. I'm not getting any younger, El. I won't be around forever."

"You're going to live to a hundred, mark my words," I tell him. I tap my phone to check the time. It's 5:15 and I've barely started my makeup. "I have to go, but I promise I'll call more. I love you, dad."

"Hey, Ellie?"

"Yeah?"

There's a long pause on the other end. "Never mind. I love you too. I'll hug your mother for you. Be safe, sweetheart. Talk to you soon."

The phone call ends, and I take a breath before getting to work on the rest of my face. I want to look perfect tonight for whatever Christian has planned. As if he can feel me thinking about him, my phone buzzes with a text and his name flashes on the screen.

Christian: Hi beautiful.

Christian: I can't wait to see you tonight.

I smile to myself and send a winking emoji back to him. It's been ages since I've been on a date, and I don't think I've ever been so excited for one. I'm going out with the richest man in the world. He's unimaginably wealthy. One quick google search will tell you that he's worth almost half a trillion dollars. Not million. Not billion. *Trillion.* With a capital T.

Reeves Enterprises makes other Fortune 500 companies look like they're working with Monopoly money. There isn't a single industry in the world that R.E. isn't involved in. He even has a 250-billion-dollar contract with the Pentagon.

The most powerful man in the free world?

It's Christian Reeves.

Obviously, he doesn't have half a trillion dollars sitting in his personal bank account, but I can't even imagine the number of zeroes he's got in there. Would it be inappropriate to ask? Now I'm curious.

Pushing Christian's crazy wealth to the back of my mind, I continue to blend my eyeshadow. I keep my makeup simple, a light brown smokey eye to pair with my bright cherry red lipstick. When I let my hair down to examine my work, I'm damn proud of the way it turned out. I look fantastic.

I really need to get dressed. It's 5:50 and Christian will be here any minute. I frantically try to zip up my dress while simultaneously hopping around the room to put my brand-new nude Louboutin's on.

My dress is a beautiful shade of red silk. It fits every small curve of my body perfectly. It's knee-length, off the shoulder, and has a small slit on the side. At precisely six, while I'm fastening the diamond bracelet he gave me to my wrist, Christian texts me that he's coming up the stairs, and I do one last look in the mirror to make sure I look picture perfect.

I open the door slowly, gazing up at Christian from under my thick lashes and give him a shy smile. He says nothing to me at first, but I swear to God, his jaw hit the floor once he finally took me in.

I've never felt so beautiful in my life, to have someone like Christian Reeves looking at me like he's never seen the sky before—and I'm a bright, vibrant, sunny day.

"Holy *fuck*, you're beautiful."

I giggle and use one of my well-manicured nails to close his mouth. "You like?" I ask, twirling in a circle to show off all sides of my dress and flash him my new red bottom shoes. Christian bites his fist as if he's trying to keep some semblance of a filter on his mouth.

"Baby, we've got somewhere to be in a few minutes and my dick thinks that somewhere is buried inside you." My face heats up at his words and he runs a hot hand over my hip. He grinds into me once for emphasis, and I gasp quietly at his rock-hard length. Christian ghosts his mouth over my lips. "If I'm not careful we're going to miss our reservation and that pretty dress is going to be in shreds on this floor."

I let out a small giggle and he lightly kisses my cheek to not mess up my makeup, and then moves his lips down to my neck to leave a wet, open-mouthed kiss on my pulse point. I know he can feel it fluttering wildly when his lips curl into a smirk against my skin. I scrape my nails against his belt, catching on the buckle, and Christian tugs me out of the apartment before we get too handsy.

He leads us downstairs with our fingers laced together. Tonight, he's driving his Lamborghini. The paint matches the finish of the bottom of my shoes almost exactly.

"Where are we going?" I ask as he helps me into the passenger seat. The corner of his mouth quirks into a smile.

"Dinner with some friends," he vaguely tells me. If I know one thing about Christian Reeves, it's that his dinner guests are almost always high-profile celebrities, government officials, and business partners. When Christian slides into his driver's seat, he leans over me to reach into the glove compartment, pulling out a box from Tiffany's and softly dropping it in my lap. "Thought I should complete the set."

I stare at him with wide eyes. He's already covered me in diamonds, and I've only known him for a few weeks. I bite my bottom lip lightly and open the box to find a diamond necklace and stud earrings from the same collection as my bracelet. My gasp can be heard over the purr of the engine. "Thank you but…you didn't have to do that."

Christian chuckles quietly next to me, pulling the necklace from the black velvet and fastening it around my neck for me while I put on the earrings. "Ellie, if you don't think I'm going to spoil you rotten you are sorely mistaken."

A teasing scoff escapes my lips. "I think you already have."

"Diamonds are just the tip of the iceberg. What color do you want your McLaren?"

I lightly swat at his arm, pulling a laugh from him. The sound warms my heart as I remember what Gavin said at the mall, about how he didn't think Christian ever smiled before he met me. I find it hard to believe that someone so suave and charming never found a reason to smile in the past thirty years.

"White," I tease. "The pearlescent kind that sparkles in the sunlight." The corner of his mouth quirks up into a smile, and the butterflies in my stomach go wild.

Christian drives us through the busy streets of Meridian City, his hand not once letting mine go.

As we get closer to the restaurant, I grow more and more rigid in my seat. Christian glances over at me and quietly says my name to catch my attention. "What's wrong?" he asks, squeezing my hand even tighter.

I let out a defeated sigh and embarrassment pools in my cheeks. "I'm just worried about not measuring up. You can have anyone you want and…I feel like I don't belong in your world."

"Our world," he corrects quickly after I finish. "*Our world*, Elena. There isn't a you and me anymore. It's us. You're worried about not measuring up, but there's no competition. Don't compare yourself to women that don't exist. We're together now, nothing else matters. I know it's easier said than done but try to let go a little bit and have some fun. This is a different life than you're used to, and I get that, but it's your life now too. You don't have to feel bad about enjoying it."

The embarrassment in my cheeks turns into a blush. "I find it so hard to believe you've never been in a relationship when you always know the right things to say."

"I think I was saving all the charm for you."

I take a deep breath, trying to keep myself from vibrating in my seat. "I'm nervous." Christian smirks and bites his tongue. I narrow my eyes at him. "What?"

He lets go of my hand and squeezes the flesh of my thigh. His pinky and ring finger run along the hem of my dress, and I know exactly where his hand is going.

"I know the perfect distraction," he says, his voice low and husky.

When his fingers trail under my dress, his jaw tightens when he discovers I'm not wearing any panties.

CHAPTER 14

THE ANGEL

When we step inside the restaurant doors, the entire place falls dead silent and all eyes land on Christian and I. They're all sizing me up, wondering where I came from and how someone like me wound up at his side.

"Don't worry about them," Christian quietly whispers in my ear as the hostess leads us to our table. The walk is short, but with each step I attempt to make myself as mousy and unnoticeable as possible under the intense glares of all the patrons.

Our table is in the dead center of the dining room. Circular, with ten chairs evenly spaced out. Eight of them are already occupied. As we approach, a man I recognize as the Mayor of Meridian City, Ronald Goldstone, stands from his seat and smiles at us.

"Mr. Reeves!" he exclaims excitedly. "Great to see you, sir. Glad you could join us tonight." He shakes Christian's hand and then his eyes go to me. "And who is this lovely young woman?"

"Elena Young," I say politely. The mayor kisses my knuckles.

"Otherwise known as my better half," Christian quips, and my eyes snap up to him, wide with shock. We're together, so it shouldn't be such a surprise that he talks about me like that, but I don't think it will ever fully sink in.

Christian told me on the way here that he doesn't like the term 'girlfriend' because he thinks it sounds juvenile. He also hates 'partner' because it sounds too emotionally detached and 'significant other' sounds too corporate. He made a joke that he couldn't wait to refer to me as his *wife*, and I swear I stopped breathing for so long that I turned purple.

The mayor leads me to my seat and Christian pulls out the chair for me. I'm sitting next to Ronald's wife, Jeannine, and Christian sits to my right. He rests his arm on the back of my chair and grazes his fingers over the exposed skin of my shoulder.

The rest of the table exchanges pleasantries with me. We're sitting with both New Jersey senators and their wives, and the Reeves Enterprises PR representative and her fiancé.

I'm trembling in my seat. I'm completely out of my element. My father is a world-famous plastic surgeon, but I never meet any of his clients, so I really don't know what to expect coming into this. My stomach flips and I'm forever thankful that Ronald is leading the conversation and the table seems to be ignoring me. I don't know how to talk to people like this, way out of my social class. I also don't want to embarrass Christian with my awkwardness, so I simply do my best to make it seem like I'm invisible.

Ronald addresses Christian and asks him about the vacancy on the Board of Directors at the orphanage. It's for the secretary position, someone to handle all the ins and outs and legal paperwork.

Christian scoffs to himself. "I was going to offer the position to Neil Hayden, but I've had a falling out with him." Christian says that so buttery smooth, like their '*falling out*' didn't end in him getting arrested for assault. "They're hard shoes to fill. That position comes with a lot of responsibility." Christian's arms roam across my back, rubbing a gentle circle on the base of my neck. "I think I'm going to offer it to Elena when she passes the bar exam."

I'm in the middle of a sip of water that I nearly choke on. I look at him, my eyes screaming '*what the fuck*?'.

Ronald looks at me and gives me a warm smile. "Elena, I didn't realize you were such an accomplished young woman. You want to be a lawyer?"

I nod shyly. "Yes. I graduated from Meridian Law School. I'm taking the bar exam in February."

"Are you a native to Meridian City?" Jeannine asks.

"Oh, no. I only moved here for school. I'm from Houston, Texas. My dad is from here, though."

"Ah!" Ronald exclaims loudly. "I knew you looked familiar! You're Elliot's daughter!" Ronald roughly pats his wife on the back. "Dr. Young does Jean's liposuction."

A small round of laughter popcorns around the table as Jeannine lightly scolds her husband. She smiles brightly at me. "Oh, your father is so proud of you. Last time I saw him for a touch up he wouldn't stop talking about how he couldn't wait to see you for Thanksgiving. You'll tell him hello for me next time you talk to him?"

I nod. "Sure."

Jeannine goes back to scolding her husband and I take one more bite of my dessert before resting my hand on Christian's thigh and whispering in his ear. "I need to use the restroom. I'll be right back."

Christian stops me from standing by tenderly holding my jaw, stealing a deep kiss before letting me go. A bright red blush forms across my cheeks and I try to pretend I don't notice the entire table fall quiet at the gesture.

After I take care of my business, I wash my hands and the restroom attendant hands me a warm towel to dry them with. I don't understand why rich people are okay with having someone listen to them pee. It's wildly uncomfortable.

After I dry my hands, I give myself a once-over in the mirror to make sure I still look nice. I twirl one big curl with a finger to shape it and touch up my lipstick, slightly smudged after my meal, and then check my teeth for any food or rogue makeup.

Once I'm satisfied that I can still blend in as one of Meridian City's elite, I awkwardly thank the bathroom attendant. *Am I supposed to tip?* I honestly don't know. I leave the restroom before I can think twice about it.

The restrooms are tucked away in a long hallway far away from the dining area. My heels click against the shiny floors as I make my way down the corridor. As I pass the men's room, the door swings open abruptly, and my eyes nearly burst out of my head when Neil Hayden comes stumbling out, sniffing and rubbing his pinky along his nose. He doesn't notice me at first. He's clearly drunk, and maybe even high, too. Once he manages to stand up straight, we make eye contact, and he frowns at me like he always does.

"Look what we have here," Neil boasts. "It's the little whore that got me fired." The way he says '*whore*' sends white hot rage through me. He's such a dickhead. I don't know how I tolerated his verbal harassment for five months before Christian fired him.

I don't know what to say to him. He's drunk, so I doubt he'd comprehend anything that comes out of my mouth. He's always hated me, and that clearly only got worse after he was fired. I tilt my head down and stare at the floor and try to step around him, but he steps into my path. I try to go the other way, and he blocks my path again.

"Where do you think you're going?"

"Back to my table," I snarl, and I'm proud of myself for sounding firm even though my anxiety is at twelve on a scale from one to ten. I try to step around him again, and he blocks my path again. "Move, Neil."

"Just tell me one thing, Eliza." He lifts his hand to drag his finger along the diamond necklace around my throat. The touch sends a cold chill down my spine. "How much does Reeves pay you for a night?"

"*Pig*," I mumble as I push past him as hard as I can, and in his drunken state, he stumbles backwards, giving me enough time to quickly scurry down the hall before he can straighten up. The moment I take a step back into the dining room, I feel Neil's grubby hand grab my elbow and tug me back. It startles me enough to make me let out a yelp, drawing the attention of the two tables closest to us.

"Let me go," I demand, trying to rip out of his grip.

Warm, large hands circle my waist and pull me back a few steps. I sigh in relief that Christian's come to my rescue, but it quickly turns to heightened panic as he puts himself between Neil and I, grabbing Neil by the back of his neck and slamming his face down into the table closest to us. Neil's ear lands in a poor lady's hot soup, and he lets out a wail. Christian lift's Neil's face again, only to slam it back down into the soup bowl hard enough to break the ceramic.

Christian growls, leaning down until he's inches away from Neil's other ear. He twists one of Neil's arms unnaturally over the edge of the table, pressing it until it's on the cusp of breaking. "You listen to me, you fuckhead. If you *ever* touch her again, *I will kill you*. Do you fucking hear me? I will make you regret your entire miserable existence and then I will kill you. Slowly. Don't even fucking breathe in her goddamn direction or I will rip your heart out of your chest with my bare hands."

Before I even have a chance to step in to try and calm Christian down, he takes Neil's arm and breaks it over the edge of the table. The snap is loud and sickening, and the witnessing tables gasp in horror as Neil lets out a loud groan of pain. Christian lets him go, pushing him down to the floor and then without even sparing me a second glance, he grabs my hand and wordlessly leads me outside.

I struggle to keep up. My legs are so much shorter than his and my heels feel like they're going to fly off with how fast he's walking. Once we're in the cool air of the night, I let out a shiver and cross my arms over my chest to hide my quickly hardening nipples from the temperature.

Christian paces around in a small circle while the valet disappears to go get his car. His eyes meet mine and notices my shivering, tension so hot on his body that steam is radiating off him. He shrugs off the jacket of his suit and drapes it over my shoulders, rubbing my arms twice with his large hands to try and warm me up with friction.

He growls and his eyes shoot back to the front doors of the restaurant. He presses his forehead against mine and squeezes his eyes shut as he holds his jacket around me in a white-knuckled grip. I might have found the embrace beautifully intimate if he weren't seething with rage.

"Elena, talk about something. Distract me so I don't go back in there and break his neck," he says softly to me, almost pleading for help. My chest heaves with so much panic and confusion. What the fuck am I supposed to say?

My voice trembles when I start talking, not even trying to make my thoughts coherent. "Okay, um…sometimes I think about stealing the hazelnut creamer from the office because I can't afford my own, but I'm always afraid that if I do, you'll go bankrupt and it will be my fault, and I'd go to jail over coffee creamer."

Christian lifts his head off mine and stares at me like I'm a fucking idiot. Of course, stealing creamer wouldn't put Reeves Enterprises out of business, and nobody in their right mind would waste time with sending me to jail over creamer when there is an *actual* serial killer running around this horrible city.

If my stupidity prevents Christian from going in there and giving Neil Hayden a broken neck to match his broken arm, it's worth the momentary humiliation.

Christian grabs me by the cheeks, closes the mere inches of space between us, and kisses me so hard our teeth clack together. He holds me impossibly tight to his chest as he steals the air from my lungs.

He only lets me go once the purr of his car's engine comes around the corner, but before he pulls away completely, he shakes his head roughly, and I hear him murmur through gritted teeth, *"You're the mistake."*

His voice was so quiet, I don't think he meant for me to hear it, and with that, any hope I had of him being my future shatters.

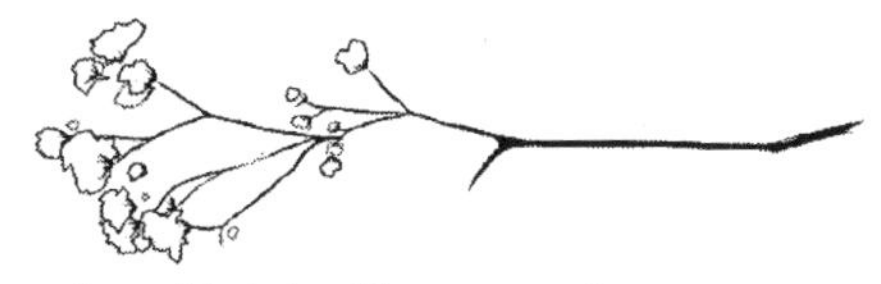

It's nearly midnight. I'm a wreck.

Christian dropped me off at my apartment without a word, and I barely had my footing on the ground before he started driving off, and I haven't heard from him since. It's only been a few hours, but I suspect I won't see him again for a long time. Maybe ever.

He got what he wanted from me, after all.

I'm sitting on the floor of my apartment, my back against the cabinets of my small kitchen. I've gone through three pints of chocolate chip cookie dough ice cream, an entire pack of Oreos, a cold, leftover pizza, and I'm two thirds of the way through a bottle of bitter tequila. I'm calling out of work sick tomorrow anyways, so I really don't care if I'm hungover with a stomachache from hell.

I'm mourning, okay?

Mourning the loss of my dignity. Christian took it with him when he ruined my vagina and then called me a mistake.

My dress and heels are thrown carelessly across the room. All I'm wearing is the jewelry Christian gave me, and his suit jacket. My hair that I spent so much time curling is now messily covering my tits. I scoop another spoonful of ice cream into my mouth and hear a tap at my window. I don't even glance up. My fuzzy brain is concentrated on one thing and one thing only: shoveling as much junk food as I can into my mouth and seeing if I can make it through this entire bottle of tequila before passing out.

Another tap comes from my window that I ignore.

Finally, after it's obvious I'm not moving, I hear the Silencer wedge something under my windowsill, unlock it from the inside, and let himself in. I don't look at him, but I can see him from the corner of my eye as he takes me in from the other side of the room. I'm sure I look like I'm in the middle of a mental breakdown. Not only am I naked, surrounded by junk food and alcohol, but dozens of discarded tissues circle me like I'm performing a seance with my tears and snot.

His heavy boots stomp against the floor and he kneels next to me. I feel the back of his gloved fingers brush along my cheek to move a strand of hair that's been stuck to my face from tears.

"*Who do I need to kill?*"

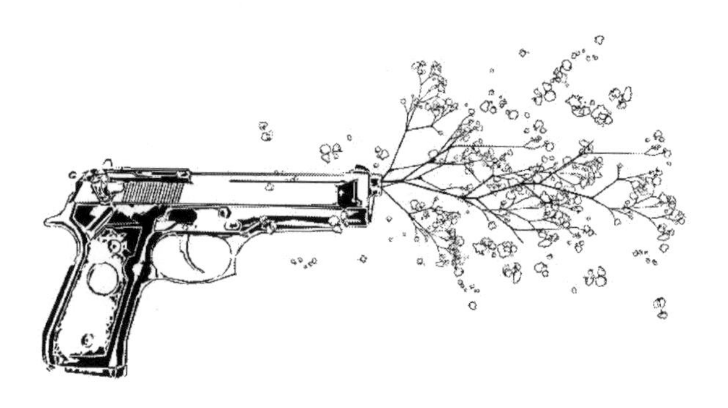

CHAPTER 15

THE SILENCER

One thing I cannot stand is the sight of Elena crying. It does unnatural things to me. Turns me into a feral beast. Makes me want to set the world on fire.

She's naked, her long, bouncing curls resting over her tiny, perky tits and a large suit jacket covering her arms. She's got big tears in her eyes and all I want to do is tear this mask off my face so I can kiss them away.

"Who do I need to kill?" I repeat, my voice laced with pure venom.

She makes a very unattractive snorting sound as she shovels another spoonful of ice cream into her mouth. "Christian Reeves," she mutters, in that softspoken voice that makes my dick hard every time I hear it. She repeats his name quietly into the tequila bottle like it's an ancient curse as she takes a swig. "Him and his shiny shoes and his perfect teeth and his pretty blue eyes."

She's almost all the way through that tequila and I'm impressed that her tiny body is still functioning. I take a seat next to her, my legs straight out in front of me, spread wide. I grab Elena by her waist and drag her into the space between my legs so she's lounging with her back against my chest. I nudge the top of her head with my masked chin.

"What did he do?" I ask softly.

She scoffs. "I had sex with him." Tears betray her and start falling down her cheeks as she hiccups through her words. "Really good sex. *A lot* of really good sex. We had a lot of really good sex and then he took me out to dinner with his friends, and when we left, he said I was a mistake." She laughs like she's gone crazy and wipes her face with my forearm, and then her voice breaks. "I'm a mistake."

My heart twists at the pain in her voice, but at the same time I resist the urge to laugh. She's leaving out a lot of details, like the fact that Neil Hayden confronted her at the restaurant or that her boyfriend got arrested for aggravated assault for breaking his arm.

"He didn't mean it," I mumble into her hair.

"Why are you defending him? You're supposed to be on my side!"

"He wasn't talking about you. I'd bet my life on it."

"Newsflash, asshole—you weren't there."

She takes another sip of the alcohol and her face twists in disgust, like she's only just remembered that she hates tequila. She slumps against me and spreads her legs in a very unladylike fashion. "God, I'm such an idiot for thinking someone like him could actually have feelings for me." Her lip quivers and she tilts her head back to look up at me. "Do you think I'm a mistake too?"

I rub a gloved finger along her jaw. "Of course not. You're the best thing that ever happened to me."

She scoffs. "You're crazy. You don't even know me," she protests with a sniffle. "I really thought I was special, you know?"

"You are."

"Not to *you*, to *him*."

"You *are*."

"You know what? I don't even care anymore." She sits up abruptly, swaying gently from the alcohol in her veins. She straddles my lap and then flips her hair over her shoulders to fully expose her chest to me. "I want *you*," she whispers, trying to sound sexy and enticing even with the slur in her words.

"You're drunk, Elena," I tell her, and it fucking hurts because if this were any other circumstance and she put her naked body in my lap and gave me a green light, I'd already be inside her. But I can't do that. Not when she's drunk and upset.

"So?" she challenges.

I chuckle and wrap my fingers in the lapels of the suit jacket she's wearing. "So the only thing I'm doing to you tonight is tucking you into bed."

She frowns at me. "Oh, so now you want to take the moral high ground instead of punishing me for having hot, steamy sex with a billionaire?" She grinds down on top of me again and it takes considerable effort for me to not react, but she can feel the bulge in my pants. I'm a man, after all, and she's the object of all my affections.

My eyes close and my head tips back into her cabinets, and my dick nearly drills a hole in my tactical pants when she lets out a tiny, breathy moan.

"*Fuck*," I groan, drawling out the word. "Elena. Stop."

My hands curl into tight fists as I attempt to keep myself from doing something stupid but fuck, she looks so goddamn beautiful on top of me. I can't help it—I grab her perfect little waist and dig my fingers into her soft flesh. If it's to stop her or urge her on, I'm not sure.

I wish I was a good man.

I push her lightly until she's on her back against the floor, taking care to protect the back of her head. "You have no idea what you do to me, angel."

Lying next to us in a wrinkled pile of silk is Elena's pretty red dress. I take it in my hands and then rip it into ribbons.

"Hey!" she protests, trying to slap my hands away from her dress in an uncoordinated fashion.

"Shut up," I command, and she crosses her hands over her chest in a drunken tantrum. I take one of the strips of her dress and tie it around her eyes like a blindfold. My cock is begging to be let free from the prison of my pants, and I'm so fucking close to taking it out and just sinking into her. Her pussy is all bare and begging for my attention, her legs spread wide in invitation. Once I'm sure the tie around her eyes is fully blocking her vision, I press the locking mechanism for my mask and let it fall to the floor with a clatter. "Open your mouth, Elena," I command. She doesn't listen. I use my fingers to roughly press her cheeks together and then I take a long swig of the leftover tequila. I lean over her and then let the alcohol fall from my mouth into hers in one continuous stream and then force her lips shut. "Swallow." She has no choice, and she does, earning sweet praises from me. "*Good girl.*"

I lean down to run the tip of my nose along the underside of her jaw. She smells so fucking sweet, like cotton candy.

I pour a tiny puddle of tequila in the hollow of her throat, and then lick it from her skin. She sucks in a sharp breath when my tongue traces up her neck, along her jaw, over her chin until my mouth meets hers and I steal the air from her lungs with a searing kiss that has my head spinning.

She whines for more tequila, but I put my mask back on and then rip her blindfold off and hold the bottle out of her reach. "You've had enough. Now get in bed."

"Only if you come with me."

I grab her threateningly by the jaw again and pull her to her feet with me. "Fine. Bed. Now."

I let her go, and she stumbles to the tiny twin-sized mattress on the other side of the room. She climbs into the bed and then makes grabby hands at me. I chuckle, crawling into the bed next to her.

I wrap her tightly in a blanket burrito until she can't move. For good measure, I hook a heavy leg over her waist and wrap my arms around her shoulders and tug her close to my chest, rendering her immobile and effectively trapping her.

She wiggles against the cocoon to try and break out, but my grip is solid, and she soon realizes her attempts are worthless. She gives up with a huff. "Go to sleep, Elena."

She huffs again. "You're no fun at all. I hate you."

When those three words leave her lips, my entire body tenses. It feels like she plunged a dagger straight into my heart. She has every fucking reason to hate me, but it still hurts.

"I'm sorry. That was really mean. I don't hate you. I promise."

I exhale deeply and pull her impossibly closer. Her head sinks into my chest. "It's okay, angel. I could never be mad at you."

I feel her snuggle into me and it sends warmth from my chest all the way down to my toes. Her breath begins to steady out as my heartbeat lulls her to sleep.

"Hey," she says quietly. "You'd do anything for me, right?"

"Anything, baby," I repeat with certainty.

"Will you punch Christian Reeves? I'd do it myself, but I don't think I can reach. You're at perfect punching height."

My chest vibrates with laughter. "Sure thing, angel."

Elena falls asleep in record time, curled into a ball next to me. I nudge the top of her head with my masked chin, like an animal marking its territory.

The only sounds in the tiny apartment come from the street below and the leaky kitchen sink.

Plop. Plop. Plop.

It reminds me of all the blood I've had dripping from my fingertips. All the lives I've taken in an endless attempt to control this city through fear.

I've never cared about making a difference in Meridian City. I've only ever cared about becoming a ruthless god amongst men. I wanted control. I wanted the scum of this city to feel helpless as I wring their fight from their necks.

But then I met Elena, my perfect little guardian angel. I don't just want to be a god anymore; I want to worship my goddess. I want to protect her. I want to take care of her. I want her to be mine. I want her soul to belong to me as mine belongs to her, even if she doesn't realize she holds that power over me yet.

I still crave control, though. Not only over this city.

I want control over *her*.

I only move from the bed when I hear Elena begin to softly snore. I carefully remove my arm from under her head and take off the suit jacket she's wearing.

Before I tuck her in, I take my time tracing the lines of her body. Even in her drunken sleep, her body craves me. I can see it in the way her skin breaks out into goosebumps when I run my fingers along the delicate flesh of her breasts, the softness of her stomach, and her lightly toned thighs.

I bite my lip. I have to taste her skin again. In all the places that are close, but not close enough, to the parts that want me most. When she wakes, she'll have that ache between her legs that she'll remedy with that cute purple vibrator she loves so much, and I'll fucking love the satisfaction of knowing I'm the reason she's so desperate for release.

Quietly, I remove my mask again.

I'm not worried about her waking up. She's consumed way too much alcohol for that to be an issue. Even if she did, she'd be so out of it that I wouldn't have to worry about her remembering my face.

I lightly push her until she's flat on her back, and then I kiss up her body, licking and nipping at her thighs, her stomach, the space between her breasts, until I get to her neck.

And then I bite her. Hard.

Hard enough to leave bruises.

A soft moan escapes her lips. If it's one of pain or pleasure, I really don't give a fuck. She'll have *my* bruises on her body, one thing I get to claim before Christian *fucking* Reeves does.

I lean back from her sleeping, angelic body. Her rich brown hair frames her face, still holding the curls she so carefully crafted for her date. Mascara tears streak down her face, but the rest of her makeup is still perfectly intact, especially that *fucking* lipstick.

I swipe my thumb across her plump lips, gathering some of the cherry red pigment and swiping it across my neck. She gets to mark me too. It's only fair.

I didn't just come here tonight to see my angel. I came here on a mission. I expected her to be asleep when I got here, but I like this reality better.

I make my way into her bathroom and flick on the single dim lightbulb above her sink. I flip open her medicine cabinet to find the packet of pills I need and place them foil side up on the counter. I flip open the sharpest of my pocketknives and then pull out a tiny plastic bag of blue and white pills from my tactical pants.

Carefully, I wedge the knife between the foil and the plastic of the packet and peel it back from the glue. I dump the old pills into the toilet and then replace the unused pills in the packet with the corresponding blue and white placebos. Then, I take a lighter to heat up glue stuck to the foil before sealing it down.

It's not perfect, but I imagine for someone who has probably been on the pill since she was a teenager, some crinkled foil isn't going to rouse any suspicions.

I place the packet back in the medicine cabinet where I found it, flush the old pills down the toilet, and place a kiss to her lips before grabbing my mask, and crawling out the window.

It's a shame I'm already destined for Hell, because it's not where angels belong.

But I'm not going anywhere without her.

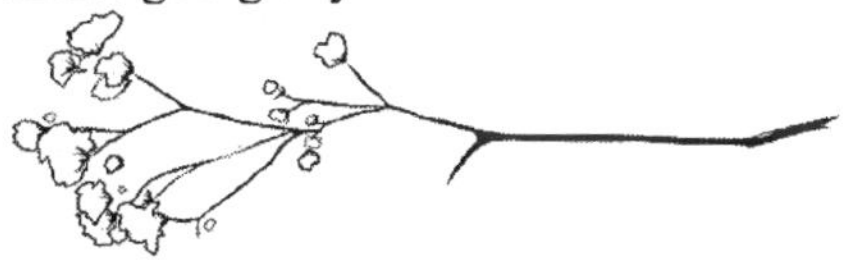

The Silencer was born out of an unnatural thirst for violence. I had the urge to feel bones crack under my skin, and for a while, that's exactly what I sought out. I made my targets the scum of this island and broke bones in my free time. I was angry at this city and thought I could make it better by wiping criminals off the map.

I tried for a few months to do what the MCPD couldn't; capture wanted felons and deliver them to the police headquarters with zip ties around their wrists and ankles, and broken noses. When that didn't sate the urges, I moved on to less peaceful methods.

I needed to watch the life leave my victim's eyes. I needed to feel them take their last breaths, but strangling wasn't bloody enough for me.

Slitting their throats—now *that's* satisfying. It's a lot messier and takes a lot longer than a bullet to the brain, but it is without a doubt the most *satisfying*.

It's like playing a fucked-up game of tag, only if you get caught by the psychopath in Kevlar, your blood will paint the pavement.

The duct tape didn't always have significance. I used red duct tape to shut my victims up simply because it was what I had at the time. When I was still new to this, still scared of getting caught, I'd use the tape to keep my victims quiet. I like taking my time and there's no greater buzzkill than police sirens. The media took off with it though, claiming I was a serial killer that used the tape to 'silence' my victims, and voila—overnight I became public enemy number one to the MCPD.

After my tenth kill, the mayor banned the sale of red duct tape on the island.

That was nearly two years ago. My current kill count is at sixty. *Eight* of those have been since I met Elena last month.

Now I have to fulfill the promise I made to her before she fell asleep.

I crack my neck, walking in a tight circle. The marble floors beneath my boots shudder when I take a step.

I pause in front of him. His stare is as unwavering as mine. Christian Reeves is not a man that's afraid of many things, but he should be afraid of me.

I send my fist into his face, my knuckles leaving streaks of blood across his skin.

"You had everything." I punch him again. My hands flair off my head in a 'mind blown' gesture. "She was wrapped around your fucking finger and all you had to do was keep her happy! You can't even do that right. This is why I fucking hate you."

I pace around the humid, steamy room, sweat dripping down my brow and temples. Dripping off my chin and onto my chest.

I have problems. Really big fucking problems.

Christian Reeves is one of those problems. He's perfect. He's everything Elena could ever want. Handsome. Rich. Doting. He'd do anything to see her smile—to see the way those subtle golden flecks in the brown of her eyes sparkle when she's happy.

I'm not perfect. Far from it—I am unstable. I am broken and my soul is empty. I have nothing to offer her except pain and suffering and lies.

Yet I can't stay away from her.

The only reason I haven't killed Christian Reeves is because of her, so he should consider himself fucking lucky.

The man across from me has said nothing. He doesn't react. He doesn't fight. He just…takes it.

I land three more punches in rapid succession, each one leaving more of my blood smeared across his face. I headbutt him, splitting my lip open in the process and watching in satisfaction as blood drips from his nose, over his chin and down to the floor.

I lean over to pick up a reflective shard from the ground. I grip it tightly in my fist until it breaks skin, and then watch my hot blood pool into a small puddle at my feet, mixing with his.

I look back up at him, and he's staring back at me with a frown. I wave the shard in his face, running my forearm over my nose to wipe away the blood dripping into my mouth. Blood smears across my scarred wrists.

I tear off my shirt and adjust the grip on the shard. I grit my teeth and growl at the sharp pain as I carve my angel's name into my chest, right over my heart to cement her into my life.

"I'd bleed for her," I spit at Christian, raising my eyebrows in a challenge. "Would you?"

"Gladly," he snaps back, spitting out a mouthful of blood that's stained his perfectly white teeth. I growl, pushing him over and holding him down by his throat as my blood drips onto his bare chest.

"You don't deserve her!" I shout, my voice echoing off the walls as blood from my mouth lands on his face. "I had her first!"

I begin to relentlessly beat my fists into his face, and I don't stop until my fists are annihilated and the reflective shards are nothing but dust covering the floor.

The hardest part about falling in love with an angel isn't making her accept the fact that I kill people. It isn't even keeping the identity under my mask a secret from her.

It's accepting the fact that Christian Reeves makes her happier than I ever could. It's accepting the fact that I am not Christian Reeves.

I am not Christian Reeves.

I am not Christian Reeves.

I. Am. Not. Christian. Reeves.

CHAPTER 16

THE ANGEL

When I wake up, my head is *throbbing*.

My apartment is a mess. Snacks, a tequila bottle, and dirty tissues litter my kitchen. My red dress is in shreds on the floor.

What the fuck happened last night?

I remember taking off my dress, and eating until I felt sick to my stomach, and I briefly remember waking up in the middle of the night shivering because I was naked, but otherwise, nothing seems out of place or abnormal despite the gaps in my memory. I stumble to the bathroom, where I cringe when I see myself in the mirror.

I look, and smell, and *feel* like shit.

I take a shower and brush my teeth, *twice*, because I feel *that* gross.

It's only when I emerge from the shower that my eyes finally focus on the world around me, and I let out a shriek when I notice a giant bruise on the curve of my neck. I slap at it with my hands as if that will make it go away, but any hopes I had of it being some rogue makeup disintegrate when I notice fucking *teeth marks*.

My stomach curdles then, and I lean over the toilet just in time to empty my guts out. When I look back up in the mirror and get ready to brush my teeth for the third time, my lip begins to quiver and a few tears escape my eyes.

I bang my fists on the counter. "Why me?"

I know it was the Silencer. I have the sneaking suspicion that it's not the only thing he did to me. My fingers graze between my legs, poking to try and find any physical evidence that I was touched by him, but I'm not sore and there's no burning. I even take a hand mirror and double check, but I don't see anything that would lead me to believe he took advantage of me last night. I find it hard to believe he fucking *bit me* like a savage and did nothing else to me.

I'm going to give that bastard hell the next time I see him.

My stomach hurts and I can't drink enough water to quench my thirst. Clean and fresh, I make my way to my freezer and pull out two frozen sausage croissants and stick them in the microwave. While I'm waiting for them to heat up, there's a knock on my door. I flip my hair over my neck to cover the bruise.

I open it, and a sweet older man greets me. "Elena Young?"

"That's me." My eye twitches when he hands me a beautiful arrangement of purple and white roses wrapped in ivory parchment paper. I close the door and notice a tiny purple envelope is taped to the bouquet. I rip it open to find expensive parchment paper embossed with the Reeves monogram inside, with Christian's neat handwriting scribbled across the page.

I'm sorry.

I throw the note in the trash. I scoff when I find twenty missed calls from him and a dozen texts that get increasingly more desperate between last night and this morning.

Christian makes my insides twist in all the wrong ways, and if he thinks some flowers will heal the ache in my chest, he's dead wrong.

I had to cut up my favorite turtleneck sweater to turn it into a makeshift crop-top to hide the bite mark on my neck, because makeup did nothing to cover the deep purple bruise.

Just another thing to my list of grievances against our resident homicidal maniac.

Every night when I arrive at the club, there's always a moment of tension right as I walk through the doors. I always expect Frank has somehow tied the Silencer's retaliation back to me and will punish me for it.

Thankfully, Frank has been keeping to himself atop the Hellfire Lounge. He hasn't had me come up there since his friends were killed, which doesn't make me feel any better. It only makes me feel like he's plotting his revenge.

Kate and I have bonded a lot since I started. At first, I didn't think she liked me because I kept stealing all her tips. She was short with me like the other girls here, but after I was forced to work naked, I think she realized that I wasn't her enemy. She's become my sister in a really fucked up '*we're prisoners here but pretend we're not*' sort of way. I asked her about covering for me the other night when I missed my shift, and she said Christian waved too much money in her face for her to resist. Everyone has their price, I guess.

Kate elbows me. "Hey, your sugar daddy is here."

Speak of the fucking devil.

I frown when I make eye contact with Christian on the other side of the circular bar. My heart skips a beat when I spy a split lip and a bruise on his cheekbone. *Did he get in a fight?*

"*Pft.*" I roll my eyes and release myself from the tight grip his eyes had on me. "He is not my sugar daddy. He's not my anything."

"Really?" Kate asks, handing a drink over to a patron. Her voice hitches as she teases me. "That's not what it looked like the other night when you came out of those private suites with that post-sex glow."

"Fine. Yes, we had a thing, but it's over now," I mumble. "Can you–"

"I'll get him off your back for a hundred bucks," Kate proposes, and I happily pull a Benjamin from my bra and hand it over. She smiles and plucks it from my fingers, stuffing it in her own bra. "Pleasure doing business with you." She saunters over to where Christian is sitting, has a short conversation with him, and like magic, he stands from his seat and leaves. Kate turns around and playfully bows. "You're welcome."

I make a noise somewhere between a scoff and a laugh. "What did you say to him?"

"Told him you'd meet him outside in five minutes."

I give her a teasing scowl. "You know if I don't meet him, he's just going to wait outside all night for me, right?"

"So let him," she mumbles, going back to work as if it never happened. She smacks my ass lightly. "Make him work for it." We share a laugh and then go back to making drinks, exchanging small talk with the patrons and each other. I glance at the panic alarm around my wrist and clear my throat.

"Hey Kate?" I ask, trying to sound nonchalant, but I know she can see right through me. I should really tell the Silencer to go fuck himself, especially after whatever the hell he did to me last night, but something in my gut tells me this might be my only chance to get some information about the club. Maybe I can use it as leverage to get him to leave me alone. "What can you tell me about the club downstairs?"

Her eyes glance up and around to make sure there are no wandering eyes or ears. "Not much. Our locker room is right by the elevator, and I've been here a long time so…sometimes I hear things. If you want to get in, you have to be invited by Valenti, and there are only two keys. That's all I know." Kate gives me a sympathetic look. "I'm so sorry."

"For what?"

"I knew the second Valenti got a look at you that you would be next and, well, I'm just sorry. I wish I could tell you I knew how to get you out of his grasp. You'll eventually get a price on your head, Elena, and that's when he'll take you downstairs."

"Kate, I'm…" I hesitate. I want to tell her so badly that I'm going to help put a stop to it, but I don't want her to judge me for teaming up with a serial killer. She's never mentioned the Silencer before, but for all I know, he could have killed someone she knew. That's the thing about this city—everyone has an opinion on our resident psychopath. I think I only have a soft spot for him because he saved me the night we met. I don't think that's enough to erase his sins. "Never mind. Just…whatever happens to me, it's not your fault."

I begin to wonder why Kate has never been taken downstairs. She's a beautiful girl, and the patrons here love her. She's the perfect, curvy physique with thick thighs and the sexiest bit of tummy jiggle a woman could possibly have. She's also nine inches taller than me and has the prettiest strawberry blonde hair that always looks amazing. She has big blue eyes she adorns with massive fake eyelashes and eyeliner sharp enough to slice through skin.

Not that I would wish that fate on anyone, but to put it bluntly, she seems like the kind of girl that would fetch a high price. Certainly higher than me.

Oh my God. What the hell is wrong with me? Am I so screwed up from working here that I'm comparing our imaginary price tags based on our looks?

I'm disgusted with myself. I need to get away from this club before I start getting delusional. I bet this is exactly what Frank wants, so that we don't start forming alliances or friendships that could compromise his money.

I tell Kate I'm going on my break, and hastily make my way to the locker room. I sit on the bench and pull my phone out of my bag. I have two text messages from Christian begging me to come outside, and then another message from an unknown number.

Unknown: I've got your boyfriend's head in my scope. Want me to take him out?

I know he's entirely serious. I don't even think twice about the fact that he has my phone number. I'm honestly more shocked that he hasn't used it until now.

Me: No, asshole. Leave him alone. Meet me after my shift, we need to talk.

Me: Maybe starting with the bite mark on my neck you psycho.

Unknown: Don't act like you weren't begging for that and more last night. You're lucky that's all I did.

Me: What are you talking about?

Unknown: Don't remember throwing yourself at me? Shame.

What the fuck? He's lying. He must be. I was drunk, but I wasn't that *drunk.*

Me: You're lying.

I immediately get a reply. A photo. I'm curled up next to him, using his chest as a pillow while his arm is wrapped around me.

Me: That doesn't prove anything.

That fear I felt when I first met him is back, and I delete the text thread and shove my phone back into my locker as if that will also rid me of him.

Back at the bar, I get to work helping Kate with the endless stream of orders. As we're mixing and pouring and serving, I ask her about her life away from this Lounge. We never talk about normal things.

"Have you always lived in Meridian City?"

"Nope," she says, popping the 'p'. "After I got out of high school, I wanted to see the world. My sister moved out here for law school just like you. I came with her, to keep her company and help her out with the bills, you know? We were poor as fuck and with all the studying she was doing, she didn't have much time to work. I learned through the grapevine that girls make lots of money here, so I convinced her to start working here with me. She…" Kate clears her throat. "She didn't last long, but the money was good enough for me, so I worked, she studied."

"And where is she now?"

Kate humorlessly laughs. "Got pregnant her last year of law school. The guy left her, she miscarried and got really depressed. Started doing drugs. Can hardly hold a job. We still live together, but I almost never see her. When I do, she's high out of her mind." Kate shrugs. "We're just not that close anymore."

"I'm sorry," I say, handing a drink to a patron with a polite smile that earns me a five-dollar tip.

She makes a face like I'm being ridiculous. "Don't be. It's life. I'm happy where I am. I don't need anyone's pity. Especially not my friends."

I smile. "Friends, huh?"

She bites her lip and giggles. "Okay, truthfully pipsqueak, the only reason I like you is because I'm hoping your sugar daddy has a long-lost twin that needs a sugar baby. Because I call dibs."

I laugh too. "I'll keep that in mind."

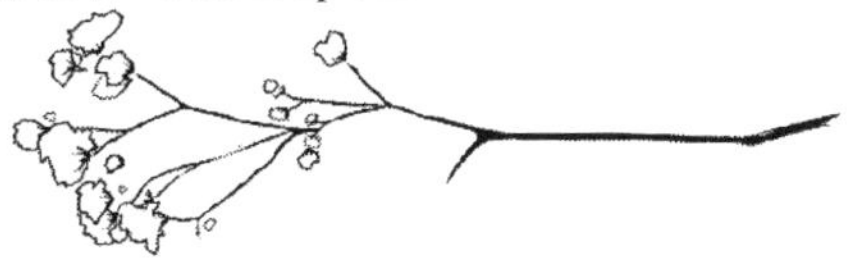

As expected, after my shift, Christian is waiting for me outside the club with a cigarette hanging out of his mouth and his hands in his pockets as he leans against his cherry red Ferrari. We stare at each other for a moment, and then I continue walking as if he's not even there.

"Elena," he calls after me, and judging by his footsteps, he's right on my heels. "Elena, stop." He grabs my arm and I tug it out of his grasp. "Elena, listen to me."

I turn abruptly and shove him away from me. "Just go!"

"No. Not until we talk about this," he says, throwing the butt of his cigarette into the street, joining the hundreds of others stuck on the curb.

"Talk about what? You made yourself *very* clear the other night. Leave me alone."

"What I said at the restaurant, Elena…I didn't mean it. I didn't mean that *you* were a mistake."

With the look on his face, the plead in his voice, I almost believe him.

Almost.

"Yeah, screwing your employee was the mistake. I got it. Well, I'm quitting. Consider this," I give him my middle finger, "my resignation."

I can't help the tears that prick in my eyes.

Christian really did a number on me, didn't he? He's got me crying over a fling that went bad because I was stupid enough to believe a billionaire's honeyed words. He got what he wanted out of me, and left me with nothing but an ache in my chest and bitter longing for a man who doesn't want me.

It begins to rain, and I throw a small tantrum and stomp my foot. "Now I have to walk home in the rain because of you!"

I would have walked home in the rain regardless—it's not like he can control the weather—but it feels nice to blame him for it anyways.

I huff and try to shove him off me again, but Christian catches my wrist and tugs me along with him towards his car. "Let me go!" He opens the passenger door and practically shoves me inside, buckling my seatbelt for me. I cross my arms when he slams the door behind him before sliding into the driver's seat as it begins to rain harder.

He takes a deep, frustrated breath and rests his wrists on the steering wheel. "I'm not letting you out of this car until you talk to me."

"That's called kidnapping," I snap back. "I'm not your hostage."

He scoffs. "*Hostage.*" He turns in his seat to face me, and I make an obvious effort not to look at him. He gently grabs my chin with his fingers and forces me to meet his intense gaze. "Elena, I'm trying to communicate with you and you're throwing it in my face. You won't answer my calls or texts. You blow me off when I try to see you in person. You're refusing to look at me. What do you want from me?"

Tears sting in the back of my eyes and I blink them away, pushing his hands away from my face and sinking into the leather seat. "I want you to take me home. *Please*," I beg quietly.

The way he aggressively puts the car in drive tells me he's pissed, but I can't find it in me to care. I wipe away a stray tear that's fallen out of the corner of my eye and quietly sniff. There's a moment where the air goes stale and then Christian sighs.

"I'm sorry if I hurt your feelings. What I said…it had nothing to do with you."

I laugh sarcastically to myself. "*It's not you, it's me.* Right? That's really the best you can come up with?" I turn my head to finally look at him and he tightens his jaw. My eyes catch on the cut across his lip and the bruise under his eye. "What happened to you?"

"The Silencer."

"What do you mean?"

He lets out a deep sigh. "I got arrested last night for breaking Neil Hayden's arm. After I bailed out of jail the Silencer found me and punched me in the face. At your request, according to him."

"What do you mean, *at my request*?"

"He said you asked him to hurt me for hurting you."

"No...no I didn't. I didn't! I...I...I can't remember anything."

All the terror and panic and unease that comes with being stalked crashes down on me all at once, and my body starts trembling. My hands begin to tug at my hair, and I tuck my knees up to my chest in the seat.

"Oh God," I croak. "*Christian*."

The car lets out a loud screech as it skids to a stop from how hard Christian hits the breaks.

Because that's the first time I've used his name.

He puts the car in park and faces me, his eyes dark with worry.

I stare at him for a moment, taking in the bruise on his face that's apparently my fault. The cut on his lip is my fault. Everything is my fault. All eight of those people, dead, because of me.

"I'm scared," I admit, my voice cracking.

Christian sighs and then reaches across the car to tuck a strand of hair behind my ear and then cradle my face in his warm, gentle touch. Salty, cold tears trail down my face as weeks of emotion overtake me.

"I'll protect you," he declares, and I wish I could believe him. I want to believe him so bad that it almost hurts. "I swear it on my life."

"You can't."

"Yes, I can."

I take a deep breath and wipe my face with the back of my hand while he watches me with a careful gaze. He settles back into his seat and begins to drive again. I don't say anything else to him, keeping my face tucked into my knees.

"Elena?"

I turn my head to face him. He reaches across the console to take my hand in his. "I can't be a good partner if you don't let me fix my mistakes. Next time, talk to me."

He's right. It wasn't his fault everything went badly at the restaurant, yet I've been blaming him for a comment he probably said because he was high on adrenaline. "I'm sorry."

He kisses my hand as he drives past the intersection to get to my street. I wait two more blocks before I realize he's not attempting to turn around.

I uncomfortably clear my throat. "You...you missed my street."

"I know. I'm not taking you home."

My stomach flips. "Where are you taking me?"

"My place."

Apprehensively, I squeak out an 'okay', and then the rest of the ride is spent in awkward silence.

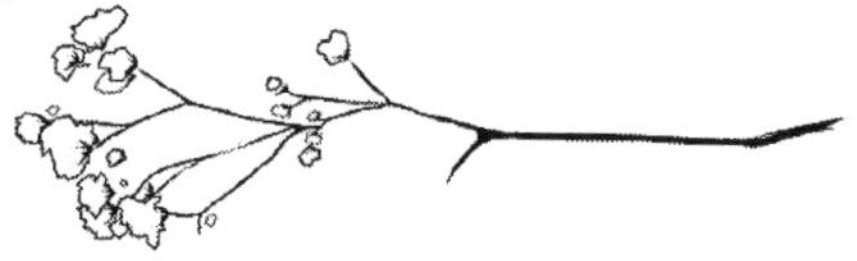

The Reeves Estate is the southernmost peninsula of Meridian City. The property is currently valued at $300 million. When we approach the gates, it's even more beautiful than the pictures online. A large, wrought-iron gate opens to let us into the grounds, lush and green and beautiful. Well-trimmed trees line the long driveway. It feels like an eternity before the mansion comes into view, and it simply takes my breath away.

Bright white stone covers the exterior of the massive two-story mansion. It's bigger than any home I've ever seen by at least five times. Wings are jutting off in every direction, and the square footage is probably a number that would make my head spin. There's a large fountain out front in the middle of the circular driveway, with a gargantuan marble statue of an angel in the center, pouring water out of a gold decanter. I have half a mind to ask if it's real gold.

I wouldn't be surprised.

The double front doors of the mansion are black wrought iron with ornate sconces on either side, a matching chandelier hanging above the porch to provide a warm glow. Christian exits the car and opens the door for me, holding out a hand to help me out of my seat.

I nervously take his hand and a valet manifests out of thin air, giving me a once-over as Christian hands him the keys. I know how it must look. I'm in a mini-skirt and a crop top. He thinks I'm a hooker. He doesn't let any emotion show on his face as he takes off in the car, leaving Christian and I alone. He opens the front door and leads me inside with a gentle hand on the small of my back.

I look up and I can't help the sound of awe that escapes my lips. The foyer of the mansion is something directly out of a movie. A double staircase leads up to the second floor. Pristine hardwood floors under our feet reflect the sound of my heels with each step. Directly across from us, beyond the staircase on the other side of the mansion, I can see a wall of windows, displaying the massive backyard with the biggest pool I've ever seen and a hot tub the size of my apartment.

"*Wow*." Red blooms across Christian's cheeks, as if he's embarrassed by the grandeur of it all. "I think I'm going to need a map," I joke, trying to ease the tension between us, and it pulls a soft laugh from him.

"You get used to it," he says, lacing his fingers with mine and pulling me towards one of the long corridors. It feels like I've walked a mile before we come across a set of double doors. It must be his bedroom.

There's a fireplace crackling on the far wall, framed by two floor-to-ceiling windows, with blackout drapes tied away to let the moonlight shine through the room. The furniture is rich brown wood and black leather. The only slice of color in the room is the burgundy comforter neatly made on the California-king sized bed. There's a table and two chairs in front of one of the windows, and a loveseat tucked into the corner near the other. On either side of the bed sit two nightstands.

There's a bookshelf directly next to us. It's covered in photos. So many photos of his family. His parents. His accomplishments. His life. His mother and father on their wedding day. Him as a baby in his mother's arms. A family photo of him, no older than five, in an adorable little suit with a bowtie, matching his father. His mom is wearing her signature red lips in all of them, and her short black hair is styled in big, glamorous curls.

"Your mother is beautiful."

He has his mother's eyes. That unique, vibrant light blue with a dark rim around the iris that had me swooning from the moment I collided with him at Reeves Enterprises.

There's a photo of his MIT graduation, standing next to an older man that I guess is his godfather, Edwin. He's got a proud smile on his face, though Christian's mouth is in a hard line. I'm glad Christian had at least one person to love him while he grew up. I can tell just from this one photo how much Edwin adores his godson.

"Why did you bring me here?" I ask, my fingers tracing over the framed photos on the bookshelf. He wraps me in his arms from behind and the embrace feels like home.

"There's someone I want you to meet," he whispers against my neck. "At breakfast."

"Oh," I whisper nervously. "You want me to stay over?"

I feel him smirk against my neck. "Yes."

I turn to face him, and his hands instantly go to my waist. He lightly pushes me backwards until the backs of my legs hit the bed and I sit down. I gulp, swallowing the massive lump in my throat as he kneels in front of me and tenderly unbuckles the strap of my heel to take it off my foot before moving to the other. "I don't have anything to sleep in. Or makeup wipes. Or a toothbrush. Or anything."

He shushes me, kissing my ankle when it's free from my shoe. "I'll take care of it. Wait here. I'll grab you something to change into."

He stands up and pads over to his closet, flipping on the light. Even from across the room, I can tell it's as over the top as the rest of the house. He disappears and I run my hands through my hair as my phone vibrates. I absentmindedly pick it up and my heart stops when I read the message.

Unknown: You're going to regret blowing me off for him. You think I'm scared of those armed guards?

Unknown: Sleep with one eye open, angel.

My heart starts pounding so hard in my chest it makes me dizzy. The phone slips from my hand onto the comforter and I push it away from me like it's a bug. I completely forgot that I told the Silencer that I was going to meet him after my shift, so distressed about the fact that he was in my apartment last night and I don't remember it.

He's not actually stupid enough to try and break into the mansion, right? It's suicide. He'd get shot dead two steps past the fence. I start to fidget nervously, and that's when Christian emerges from the closet with a t-shirt far too big for me.

Christian is being awfully quiet, and I hate it. I hate that things are weird between us, and I hate it more that it's almost entirely on me. I take a deep breath and crack him a small smile.

"So what's for breakfast?"

"Anything you want. Paolo makes the best eggs on the East Coast."

"Can Paolo make French toast?"

Christian's dazzling smile is all the answer I need. He caresses my jaw and captures my lips in a searing kiss.

"I missed you, Elena. I don't care that it's been less than a day. I fucking missed you," he whispers against my mouth, and I mewl when he lowers me backwards onto the bed. He holds himself up and I tangle my fists in his dress shirt. The kiss turns hungry, and he wastes no time pulling off my shirt and bra, followed by my skirt and thong until I'm completely bare to him.

His eyes glue themselves to the bite mark on my neck, and I suddenly feel defensive. "It's not what it looks like."

Christian gently leans down, cradling my head to the side as he tenderly kisses the bite mark and then licks along the bruise, as if to reclaim my skin as his. He nips lightly, and the ache causes me to hiss, but he shushes me by connecting our lips and grinding against my center.

I fumble with his belt and unbutton his slacks. He helps me pull them off his legs to free his hard cock and my pussy instantly clenches at the anticipation of feeling him inside me again. The space between my thighs is already growing hot and wet. I reach for his shirt buttons, and he grabs my wrists with one hand, pinning them above my head so fast I yelp.

His blue eyes bore into me, and his gaze is practically seducing my soul as he licks two of his fingers and rubs a circle against my clit. It throbs with need, and I moan into his mouth.

"That's it, baby. Let me hear how good it feels."

His fingers curl inside me, expertly finding that sweet spot that has me arching off the bed. He removes his fingers just as I'm about to cum and I let out a dissatisfied grumble. He licks my arousal off his fingers, and it only makes my pussy slicker.

He grabs my hips and flips me over onto my stomach, hiking my ass up. When he rubs my clit and plunges his tongue inside me, I moan so loud into the sheets that I think I've broken the sound barrier. He sucks on my clit so hard the pain and pleasure mix together into something delicious.

"Cum for me, Elena."

And I do. I cum so hard that I see stars and I have to bite the comforter to keep myself from sounding ridiculous. Christian pulls away and smacks my ass.

I've decided that I love this rough side of him. He leans over and uses his large hand to turn my head so he can shove his tongue down my throat. The arms of his dress shirt are messily pushed up to his elbows and the scars along his wrists and forearms are on full display. I can taste myself on his lips, and I'm so desperate for him to be inside me that I can feel my juices dripping down my legs.

He releases my mouth and looks at the mess between my thighs. "Your pretty pussy is *crying* for me."

I gasp when he enters me in one easy swoop, effectively stealing the breath from my lungs and any coherent thoughts from my head. Once he's buried to the hilt, he pauses, our pants the only sound in the room. I wiggle my ass against him to get him to move, and he stops me by roughly pressing his thumb against my tight untouched hole. I let out a sound of protest and pleasure. His cock twitches inside me as he rubs my rosebud like he's considering fucking me there.

"Beg," he demands.

"Please," I immediately respond, my voice raising an octave when he presses his thumb harder into me. I'm on the verge of tears from how bad I want him. "Please fuck me, Christian. I need you. *Please*."

The satisfied groan that escapes his throat has me clenching tight around his rock-solid length, and I think I could cum from that sound alone. He leans down and nips at my ear. His smooth voice cuts through the air thick with sexual tension. "Don't worry, angel. I'm going to send you straight back to heaven."

"Oh God!" I scream through gritted teeth when he begins to pound into me, his cock hitting my g-spot with each relentless thrust of his hips. He's fucking me so hard I'm concerned he's going to cause the bed to go straight through the wall and into the next room over. He seats himself inside me one, two, three more times as hard as he can, and then the world stops spinning, time freezes, and he launches me into the fucking stratosphere. His hips snap against mine so fast that my pussy is making obscene noises as I gush around him and arousal drips down my legs enough to form a pool on the comforter below. My thoughts have been reduced to nothing but his name—*Christian. Christian. Christian.*

"Oh fuck," I whine. "Please. Fuck, I need to cum."

"Not yet," he growls. He pulls my head back to kiss me again, and his mouth is a complete oxymoron to the abuse he's inflicting on my pussy. His mouth explores mine slowly, savoring every inch of it. I can still taste the remnants of myself on his tongue and it has me mewling and my pussy clenching around him again. He moans a breathy '*fuck*' into my mouth, and it's the sexiest sound I've ever heard.

It sends me over the edge before I even realize what's happening, and I cum around his thick cock so hard I can't breathe. He slows down, grinding himself into me as I ride out the aftershocks of my orgasm. He roughly flips me over and my entire body freezes.

He's got a dangerous, fiery look in his eyes.

"Did I fucking give you permission to cum?"

The pure venom dripping from his voice has me trying to skitter away from him on the bed. Pure, icy-cold fear replaces the blood in my veins. "I–I'm sorry," I blubber out. His hand tightly wraps around my neck, squeezing until my body tenses up. "I'm sorry," I repeat with my last breath, and then he lets me go. I inhale a mouthful of air so big I'm gagging on the oxygen.

He holds my legs open wide, exposing my still-weeping pussy to him, and his fingers roughly circle my sensitive clit, still pulsating from my orgasm, and he shoves himself inside me again. I scream from the girth of him splitting me open, so deep it's painful, and he fucks me even harder than he was before, holding my hips still to meet each of his thrusts.

It feels so good and I'm quickly cascading towards another orgasm. I bite the insides of my cheeks so hard my mouth fills with a coppery tang. If I cum again without his permission, he might snap my neck.

So naturally, I almost *want* to defy him, to test his patience with me. As my eyes roll back into my head, I feel my pussy start to flutter around him again.

"Don't you fucking dare," he warns coldly.

My reaction is completely lacking in self-preservation, and I know I'm going to regret it, but I do it anyways. I sensually bite my bottom lip, make direct eye contact with him above me, and I cum again with an obnoxious moan just to piss him off. He pauses, fully seated inside me, and I feel his cock twitching with the need to cum too, but I know he's far from done with me.

He laughs with so much malice that I don't even recognize him. "Fuck, Elena," he growls. "I hope you weren't planning on using your legs tomorrow."

I whimper in equal parts fear and ecstasy, and by the time he's done with me, he's fucked me so hard I can feel him in my soul.

CHAPTER 17

THE ANGEL

"Good morning, beautiful."

Christian's voice floats into my dream, smooth like honey as his breath fans across my neck. Blush paints my cheeks and I smile to myself, rolling over to rest my head on his chest.

"Good morning," I whisper back, burying my face into his shirt that still smells like fresh laundry.

"How'd you sleep?"

I moan with delight. "So good. This bed is amazing."

"It's a Hypnos. Worth every goddamn penny."

"Do I even want to know how much it cost?" I tease, pulling a small laugh from him.

"No, probably not," he mumbles into my hair, checking the time on his phone. He kisses my forehead with so much tenderness that my heart does cartwheels. "Let's get up. Breakfast is served at eight."

With a grumble, I sit up in the bed and rub the leftover sleep from my eyes. There's a satisfying ache between my legs and when I attempt to stand, I nearly fall over. Christian laughs at me and I narrow my eyes at him.

It's easy for him to stand up when he didn't get railed all night by eight inches of steel. Ever the gentleman, he rescues me from my predicament by lifting me into his arms bridal style to carry me into the bathroom. Like the rest of his house, the bathroom is grand. The bathtub is the size of the bed, and the shower could fit at least ten people inside. There's a double sink with bright white lights surrounding it, making it perfect for getting ready.

And the window? God, I've never seen the Atlantic Ocean look so stunning. I am making myself a promise that I'm going to run myself a bath one day and look out over the water for hours.

Christian flicks a switch on the wall, and a minute later, the cold marble tiles under my feet radiate a pleasant warmth that has my eyes rolling in sweet delight.

"I could live in this bathroom."

Christian laughs again and nods towards the countertop. "I had someone take your keys and grab some things from your apartment. It should be everything you need to get ready." He nods in the opposite direction, towards the shower. "Be careful with the water. It gets hot."

I take my bottom lip between my teeth. "You could shower with me," I suggest.

"No," he snaps with a tone change so abrupt I need a chiropractor from the whiplash he gave me.

"Oh. Okay."

"I'll wait for you," he says dryly, and then leaves, shutting the door behind him. My brow furrows with utter confusion. I don't know what I did or said to make him change his attitude so quickly. It can't be the fact that I asked him to shower with me. He had his dick inside me and his tongue on every sinful place he could manage last night. Showering together seems pretty PG in comparison.

Maybe I'm overthinking it. Maybe he's weird about his shower time. For some people, it's a way to unwind, and having me there might mess with the peace it brings him. I sigh to myself and turn to the countertop.

Whoever he sent to my apartment, I can tell it was a woman, because my pack of birth control pills is sitting neatly on top of a stack of clean clothes. My toothbrush, hairbrush, and my makeup bag are all there.

I pull Christian's shirt off and toss it into the hamper near the door, and my gaze lands on something peculiar.

There's a freestanding frame leaning against the wall. I run my hands along the sleek black frame. There's a nail high above my head. That must be where it came from. It doesn't have any artwork in it. Weird.

My eyes catch on something reflective in the frame. I lean in to look closer. It's a tiny piece of a mirror. I raise an inquisitive eyebrow and look up at that nail again.

How did a mirror hanging that high up on a wall shatter?

On the floor, near the frame, there's another tiny shard. I bend down to pick it up, not wanting Christian or anyone else to step on it, and when I turn it over in my hand, I notice that there's a red smudge across the reflective surface.

Fifteen minutes later, I emerge from the bathroom with damp hair, fresh breath, and clean clothes. I'm not exaggerating when I say that it was the best shower I've ever had. I feel like an entirely new woman, and most importantly, I smell like Christian. I used his body wash and shampoo, and it feels so…domestic. It feels like I belong here, and when my eyes meet Christian's, sitting on the bench at the edge of the bed, I can't help but smile.

His hair is damp, so he must have showered in some other room in the mansion.

He smiles back. "Hungry?"

He's returned to that charismatic side of him that's always made me weak at the knees. I nod, and he holds out his hand for me to take. He pulls me into his lap and I giggle when his fingers dig into my ticklish sides. "I have it on good authority that there's the world's best French toast waiting for us in the dining room."

Yeah, I was definitely overthinking it—he just values his private shower time.

"*The world's best*?" He captures my lips in a searing kiss, and I can feel him grow hard against my center. "Jesus, how is your dick still working? My vagina has never been so sore."

He sensually licks up the column of my neck. He grabs a fistful of my hair to tug me closer to him, and as I begin to grind into his lap, there's a sharp knock on the door. It swings open a second later, and a middle-aged woman in scrubs walks in.

"Oh! Mr. Reeves, I'm so sorry." She quickly turns around. "I thought you were alone. Pardon me, I only came to tell you that Mr. O'Donnell is being difficult about his medicine again."

I'm mortified, and Christian buries his face in my chest and quietly growls before letting out a soft chuckle. "I'll be there in a minute," he tells the woman, and she's out the door a second later. "Sorry. The nurses always come get me when Edwin's being testy."

"Edwin? Your godfather?"

He nods. "He's probably having breakfast. Come meet him."

I crawl off his lap, and Christian laces his fingers with mine as he leads me leisurely through the mansion. It's so bright and open in the daytime. We pass by so many bedrooms that I begin to wonder if his parents intended on having more children. I can't imagine that a family of three needs so much space, but then again, the Reeves legacy is dripping with so much wealth that they might as well spend it. We pass game rooms, libraries, studies, home theaters. Yes, all plural. There's even a ballroom. I repeat, he has a *ballroom* in his house.

My stomach grumbles as we approach the dining room. I can smell the cinnamon and the bacon from the foyer. When we round the corner, the same nurse that barged in on Christian and I is sitting in a chair next to an absolutely ancient man. His gummy smile and the way his eyes are slightly squinted reminds me of a garden gnome, complete with rosy, plump cheeks. He's the epitome of a cute old man.

He points to Christian with a bony finger. In a grumbly Irish accent he says, "You've got some explaining to do, son."

"Uh oh," Christian says, pulling me closer. "I must be in trouble."

"The nurse said you had a pretty lass over! Why didn't you introduce us?"

"Edwin." Christian motions towards me. "This is Elena."

Edwin stares at me for a long, long time, saying nothing as his eyes stay fixated on my face. After what feels like an eternity, he flashes me an elated grin.

"Helen! Oh, Helen, look! Our boy's home," he says to me, pointing at Christian.

"No, Edwin, this is *Elena*," Christian says lightly. "Remember me telling you about her? About how she beat me at bowling?"

I raise my hand and wave nervous fingers at him. "Hi Edwin." I cautiously approach him and take a seat at his side. He reaches for my left hand and feels over my ring finger. His face falls into a frown.

"Where's your wedding ring, Helen?"

Christian opens his mouth to speak, and I suspect he intends to correct his godfather, but I shush him. "I just took it off to do laundry. You know I don't like getting it wet."

Edwin's face lights up. "Isn't our son handsome? We have to find him a wife. He's getting old like me."

I giggle softly to myself and throw Christian a look over my shoulder. "Yes, he's very handsome, but his wife won't be half as beautiful as yours. Isn't that right?"

Edwin smiles again, his eyes crinkling in the corners. "No one will ever be as beautiful as you, my darling."

I feel something shift in Christian's mood, like my acceptance and understanding of Edwin's spotty memory is infuriating. My grandmother had memory problems too, and I learned during her last few years of life that sometimes it's better to go along with whatever reality they believe in, than risk aggravating them with contradiction. Edwin doesn't seem like the combative type, but you never know. "Let's have breakfast," I suggest as Christian's gaze on me softens.

Platters of warm French toast, crispy bacon, fresh berries, and a pitcher of hand-squeezed orange juice next to a coffee pot sit on the table ready for us. It seems like way too much food for three people, but maybe they make an excess for all the staff on the property.

Christian takes the liberty of making my plate for me, his mouth quirked up into a wistful smile. "He's known me since I was born. Raised me after my parents died. Stuck by me while I was a delinquent in school and always came to bail me out of jail." He chuckles to himself at the memory, and then he lowers his voice enough that someone as old as Edwin can't possibly hear. "Helen died before I was born. He rarely talked about her when I was growing up. When he started calling every brunette by her name, I knew his memory was slipping."

My heart swells when he talks about Edwin. It relieves me to see that they have such a good relationship. I can tell by the way he talks, that Edwin considers Christian his son, but I don't think Christian considers him a father figure.

I suppose it's hard to call another man 'dad' after watching yours get shot.

After he sets my plate in front of me, he makes his way around to the other side of Edwin and hands him a small plastic container with all his pills—at least a dozen of them in a million different colors.

"Take your pills, Edwin," Christian commands. He grumbles in protest, but swallows each pill with a sip of water in between until they're all gone. Christian gives him an encouraging pat on the back.

So he's got a soft spot for old people *and* kids. Talk about dreamy. He's the perfect man and I swear I can feel my ovaries release a bunch of eggs at the thought of a house full of miniature versions of him.

I shake off the thought. I can't think about babies when we've only just made up. I'm not even sure I want them. I love kids, but I always imagined I'd be the rich aunt that travels the world and only shows up on Christmas with a million gifts for my brother's adopted kids.

Hell, if Christian really is my future, maybe we'll just adopt, too. There's no shortage of kids in need of homes, and this house is plenty big. I hum to myself and try to hide the blush in my cheeks at the thought of a future with him.

Christian has always been open about how he feels about me. It's almost surreal to know that he's so wrapped around my finger when I haven't got much to offer him. I care about him, deeply, and of course I want this to work out. He's everything I could ask for in a man and he's already given so much of his heart to me.

I've noticed that Christian is intense about everything. It's like all his emotions are immediately dialed up to eleven. Anger, sadness, frustration, happiness. He feels everything so wholly.

"Christian?" Edwin asks into the comfortable silence. Christian hums and turns his attention to Edwin. "Will you do a puzzle with me?"

"Of course," Christian answers between a bite of French toast. "It will have to be later though; I have some stuff to do today. I promise we will when we get back. Why don't you pick one out and get it ready for us? Elena can help too."

"Who's Elena?" Edwin asks. It doesn't faze me in the slightest. This is the first time we've met, and he's clearly got severe memory problems. I can't blame him for not remembering. Christian purses his lips like he's frustrated.

"She's right next to you, Edwin," Christian mutters. I reach behind Edwin's chair to run my hand along Christian's arm.

"It's okay," I whisper. "It's not a big deal."

Abruptly, Christian stands up from his seat and stomps out of the room. I don't understand why he's been so weird all morning. I excuse myself from Edwin's side and the nurse comes to take over talking to him. I wander through the house until I find Christian. He's in the backyard smoking a cigarette while standing near the edge of the pool. I hesitantly approach him. He looks over his shoulder at me, but he says nothing.

"Hey. Are you okay?" I cross my arms over my chest to keep my hands warm in the cool air and wait for him to answer. The wind carries the smoke from his cigarette directly into my face.

"It's nothing, Elena. Drop it."

"And here I thought we were working on our communication skills." He turns to face me, and his eyes trail up and down my body before settling on my face. He pulls the cigarette out of his mouth with two fingers and scratches over his eyebrow.

He takes a deep breath. "It's just…I don't appreciate when people go along with whatever bullshit Edwin's brain is making him believe. I don't think it's good for him. The point of hiring 24/7 care for him is that it gives him a routine to stick to, and routines are easier for him to remember. I've fired a dozen nurses for pretending to be Helen. I don't allow people to lie to him."

"Oh," I say, my heart squeezing painfully. "I'm sorry. I didn't know."

He looks up at the sky and sighs. "Just don't do it again."

"Okay," I concede. I understand Christian's position, even if I don't agree with it myself. But that's the reason he's the one making all the decisions. He knows Edwin best, and he's clearly well taken care of. I need to respect this boundary Christian's put in place. I apologize again softly, to let him know I mean it, and his face instantly softens. He takes my chin between his thumb and knuckle and tilts my face up to kiss me.

"I'm sorry too. Edwin's all I've got. I'm sensitive about him, is all. I didn't mean to storm out."

"It's okay. I understand."

Satisfied with our apologies to each other, we fall into comfortable silence while he finishes his cigarette. When he's done, he discards the end and takes my hand to lead me back into the mansion.

"I'm going to grab my suit jacket from my room before we leave," he says, letting go of my hand and walking up the stairs.

"Leave? If wherever we're going requires you to wear a suit, shouldn't I wear something a little more professional?" I ask, motioning down at my long sleeve t-shirt, leggings, and sneakers.

He smirks. "You look *perfect*. Always."

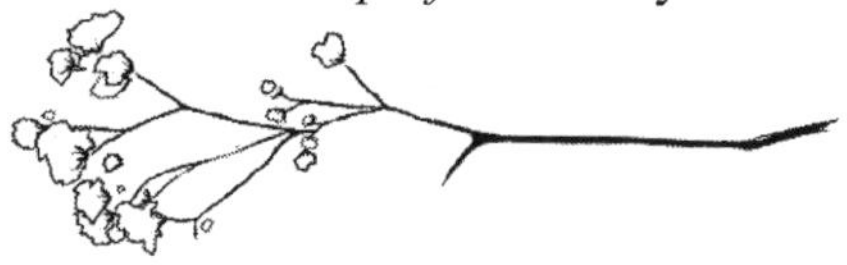

Four hours later, we're seven interviews deep into candidates for the new Secretary of the Board for the orphanage. Christian told the mayor he was going to offer the position to me, but February is still a few months away and he needs someone now.

When he asked if I was disappointed, I smiled and truthfully told him I didn't mind. I'm not sure if I really would have been a good fit for the position when I have zero experience. He promised me that if I ever changed my mind, he'd make a co-chair spot for me.

I rub my fingers against my scalp and groan when the last candidate leaves the room. "If I hear the phrase *'I'm a team player'* one more time, I'm going to stab myself with this pen."

Christian chuckles and rolls his seat over to me, where I've been taking notes for him while he conducts the interviews. "That was the last one. Promise." He kisses my cheek and tells the assistant in the office building to scan my notes and email them to him as we're walking out the door. As we approach the car, I tug backwards on his hand to stop him.

"Before we go…can I please get a milkshake from the arcade? I think they put crack in them here, because they're so good."

Christian laughs. "Whatever you want. Come on."

One milkshake in hand later, I check the high scores for bowling, giving Christian a satisfied grin when I'm still number one.

"Still miffed about that," he mumbles into my ear.

"Hey, you got off easy. You said I could have anything I wanted if I won, and all I asked for was an office. I should have asked for a zebra or something." I gasp. "No wait! I should have asked for all your stock in your company." I fall into the small couch in front of one of the bowling lanes dramatically and sigh. "Wow, I really blew it, didn't I? I could be rich!"

Christian sits down next to me and lets me rest my head in his lap while I lick whipped cream off my straw. "It would have been a waste, baby. My stock will be your stock once we're married."

I playfully roll my eyes and wave my bare ring finger at him for emphasis. "I don't see you asking."

Suddenly, I feel a small finger poke my cheek and turn my head. I smile when I see Caroline standing next to us with a big smile on her face.

"Hi Caroline," Christian and I say in unison. I sit up on the couch and she takes a seat between us. I tap her on the nose, pulling a giggle from her. "What are you up to?"

She sighs and kicks her feet back and forth over the edge of the couch. "Miss Kelly said she would take us to the park, but she broke her ankle, so we came here for free time instead."

I look around the room to see the arcade filled with children around Caroline's age, and then Kelly at the back with a casted foot.

"We can take you to the park," Christian says, lifting Caroline up to carry her and then lacing his fingers with mine. On our way out, he lets Kelly know we'll take good care of her, and then we make the short walk to the park. Caroline wiggles out of Christian's arms and makes a break for the empty playground set. She puts her hands up like she's on a rollercoaster when she goes down the spiral slide.

She's so cute it hurts. Her joy is infectious.

Caroline goes down the slide several more times, and on her fifth time down, I notice she has some dirt on her arm. "Come here, sweetie."

I try to wipe it away before I realize it's not dirt at all.

It's a tattoo of a serial number.

I gasp quietly and let her go, mumbling about how a bug landed on her and then turn around quickly to hide the brewing tears in my eyes. I feel like all the breath has been stolen from my lungs and my milkshake threatens to make a comeback. I try my best to blink away the stubborn tears. Christian immediately notices and subtly pulls a handkerchief out of his pocket and hands it to me. "Take a deep breath," he whispers quietly. I can still hear Caroline giggling behind me and I'm so glad she hasn't noticed my breakdown, because that's exactly what this is. I feel dizzy as a hot flash spreads through my body. "*Breathe*," Christian whispers again. "No one can hurt her here, Elena."

"How can people be so fucking evil?" I whisper back, a new wave of tears slipping down my cheeks. I dab them away and finally catch a steady breath. I sniffle once and then turn around as Caroline comes down the slide again. I give her a small smile and try to let her radiating happiness fill my heart again. Caroline asks me to take the next trip down with her, so I crawl onto the steps and take a seat behind her. As I push off to go down, I feel my phone vibrate a few times in my pocket, but don't think anything of it. Once we're back on the ground, Caroline jumps into me and gives me a big hug. A folded-up piece of paper falls out of her jacket pocket, and I pick it up for her.

"Oh yeah! I forgot! I drew this for you, Elena. It's safe!"

Safe? I wonder to myself what she could mean by that when she unfolds the paper to show me the drawing.

There's a big yellow sun in the corner, grass on the ground, and three stick figures sitting on a bench. On the bench is a woman that has long brown hair and comical eyelashes, a man with a red tie, and a smaller person with a blonde ponytail tied with a big purple bow.

Caroline points at the stick figure in the middle. "That's me." She points at the man. "That's Mr. Reeves." She points at the woman. "And that's you, Elena!"

Caroline holds up her drawing proudly. I nearly burst into tears again when I spot that serial number on her arm, and I understand what she means now.

She drew what makes her feel safe.

"Oh, Caro, it's beautiful. Thank you so much," I coo, giving her another big hug. Christian squats down next to us, kissing my cheek. Caroline says my name to get my attention, to which Christian and I both give to her.

"Will you be my mommy?"

My lungs seize up again, and I frantically look at Christian, hoping he can telepathically tell me what to say to her. "Um..." I mumble, trying to buy more time. "Well, I don't think I can, honey. My...my house is too small. Don't you want a big room all to yourself?"

"No!" she loudly whines, hugging me tight around my neck. "I want you to be my mommy. Please? I'll be good, I promise."

My shoulders slump in defeat and I pull her onto my lap to hold her close, trying to disappoint her in the most delicate way I can think of. "Maybe someday?" I gently suggest, but I can tell she doesn't like that answer, because she pushes away from me to retreat into Christian's arms instead. He hugs her close as she cries into his neck and I feel horrible, but I know that I couldn't tell her yes. I can't give her hope. I barely have my own life together. Adopting or fostering her just isn't a possibility. All I can promise her is to visit often, but not much more than that.

"I'm going to take her back inside," Christian says. I nod and he gives me a sympathetic smile, because he feels the same way I do. While Christian is gone, I move to the swings and sit down in one, kicking my legs back and forth to create a gentle momentum.

Pulling out my phone to check it, I see several missed texts. Two from my brother about wedding nonsense, and two from the Silencer.

Unknown: I'm running out of patience, angel.

Unknown: Don't keep me waiting much longer.

I delete the texts and wait on the swings for Christian to come back. As I stand up to leave, I freeze.

No. No, no, no.

I tell Christian I need to use the restroom, and when I get into a stall, I pull down my pants to find the red wave has come almost three weeks early.

I've been on the pill since I was fifteen, and I've never gotten my period in the middle of a pack—not even spotting.

Luckily, I have a tampon and a change of underwear in my purse. Even though my period is like clockwork, I always seem to forget and have found myself in one too many situations like this to not be prepared.

After I wash my hands, I pull out my phone and dial the number for my gynecologist's office. I explain the situation, and the receptionist tells me they have an opening in a month.

That's the downside of living in a huge city. I can never get an appointment for anything in a timely manner. I tell her to get me on the books and let me know if anything sooner comes up.

I hang up with them as I walk out of the bathroom and Christian furrows his brow.

"What was that?"

I shrug. "Oh, you know. Girl stuff."

"You look worried." I shrug again. "Elena, tell me."

"It's really nothing." I sigh. "I just…started my period early, which has never happened. I just called my doctor for an appointment to make sure everything's fine. Especially since, you know, I'm…sexually active now."

"You started your period early," Christian repeats.

"Sorry, I know men don't like to hear about the horrors of being a woman."

Christian chuckles and throws his arm around my shoulder as he leads me back to the car. "It doesn't bother me, I promise. It was just…*unexpected*."

A few minutes later, as we're driving back to his estate, he says, "I wanted your input on something."

"Okay," I reply, tilting my head in curiosity.

"This is going to sound weird since we haven't been together that long, but since we are, your opinion matters to me." He takes a deep breath. "The orphanage has a foster program sponsored by the State. It's always been in the back of my mind, but I've never committed to it because of work. Caroline just…she got me thinking about it again and I want to go for it."

"To foster? I think that's wonderful."

He chuckles. "Of course you do, because you're perfect. I'm asking because you're the most important part of my life and I want to make sure you're okay with it. Don't feel like you have to say yes. It's a big commitment."

"So what you're really asking is if I'll foster *with* you?"

"We're together, so it's a decision we should make together," he clarifies. "Caroline loves you."

I laugh wistfully, my heart squeezing at the thought of everything Christian could give her. I take a deep breath. "Let me think about it?"

He nods and laces our fingers together, and once again, it feels like he's promising me a future.

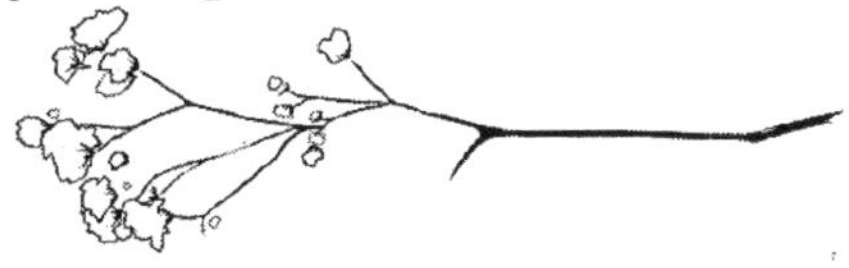

"Do you have a passport?" Christian asks while I'm typing away on my keyboard. It's raining outside, the storm pelting against the windows of our office hard enough that it makes the glass of my desk vibrate.

"Yeah. Why?" I reply, not looking up from the rejection emails I'm writing to the candidates that weren't selected for the Secretary of the Board position. It's been a week since we conducted the interviews.

"I'm going to Greece to meet with some investors," he says, walking across the office and moving my keyboard away from me so my attention is solely on him. I lean back in my chair and cross my arms, looking up at him with a defiant raised brow.

"What does that have to do with me?"

He growls and takes my jaw in his large, warm hand. "It is way too early in the morning for you to be so mouthy. Remember what happened last time?"

The corner of my mouth quirks up into a smile and I tug my chin out of his grasp with a laugh. "So you're going to Greece? When?"

"Tomorrow. I'll be gone three days, five if you count travel, and I want you to come with me. It's not going to be stuffy board meetings like we have here. Mostly business dinners and yacht parties."

With disappointment, I shake my head. "I can't miss three days of work at the Lounge."

Christian tightens his jaw in frustration, and his entire mood shifts. "That fucking club," he growls. "You know what? No. You're done working there. I'm going to go talk to Valenti and work out a deal."

I scoff. "I assume by '*deal*' you mean you're going to ask him to name his price for letting me go?" Hurt twists in my chest. "I'm not an object, Christian, you can't just buy me."

He narrows his eyes at me. "You don't seem to have a problem with other men throwing their money at you while you're there, but when it's me you suddenly have an issue with it? I'm trying to get you out of that place. If paying him is what does it, I'm not losing any sleep over it, and neither should you." The backs of my eyes sting at his accusatory words. He doesn't get it. I've been stuck there from the moment I walked through those doors. Leaving has never been an option for me. Christian softens and then rubs a knuckle across my cheek. "I didn't mean it like that, Elena."

"I know what you meant," I snap back. "I get it. I just…I hate feeling like a burden to you and a price tag to him."

"You're not a burden to me." He takes my cheeks in his hands and makes me look up at him. "You're my everything, and I just want you all to myself."

"What if he wants something stupid like ten million dollars for me?"

"Then I'll have ten million less dollars but something that's worth a hell of a lot more than that."

He always knows the right things to say to make my entire body tingle. He always talks about me like I'm the most precious part of his life. He leans down to kiss me softly. "If I'm not back by the time you get off, Gavin will take you home to pack your things. You're going to love Greece, and I have a surprise for you when we get there."

"A surprise? What kind of surprise?"

"A big one."

Dissatisfied with his answer, I playfully huff. He kisses me again and then leaves. I finish out my day by sending the last of the rejection emails, scrolling through Instagram, and taking an extra-long lunch. Dating the CEO has many perks, but it feels sleezy to waste my days away doing the bare minimum when I'm trying so hard to build my career. I probably shouldn't make a habit of it and try to find some real work to do.

I call Gavin to pick me up early, and he takes me home. I check what the weather is like in Greece in October and pack accordingly. Looks like the temperature will be pretty mild, so I pack some jeans, a few nice dresses, a jumpsuit, and a couple sweaters in case it gets chilly. I find my passport buried deep in a box in my closet and make sure to put it in my purse for easy access.

My phone dings with a text message.

Christian: It's done. I'll pick you up tomorrow at 6.

Me: Too early. You better bring coffee.

Christian: You got it, gorgeous.

Me: Which part of Greece?

Christian: Mykonos.

Me: Mykonos! I've always wanted to go there!

Christian: Then you're going to love the surprise.

There isn't a single part of him that isn't insanely perfect. It's so unfair. I don't even think he realizes just what an amazing partner he is. I don't know how I got so lucky. I've only known him for a few weeks, but at this point, it feels like the life I had before him was a prologue and I'm dying to turn to the next page to start the rest of our fairytale.

"What's got you so smiley, angel?"

I let out a startled scream and turn on the floor. I clutch my hand to my chest and suck in several deep breaths, trying to catch my heart before it leaps out onto the floor. I blink up at the Silencer, looking down at me with an amused glint in his eyes.

"Jesus Christ, you asshole! You scared the shit out of me! What the fuck is the matter with you?"

"Oh angel, you don't know how much I miss hearing you pretend you aren't happy to see me," he teases, and my eyes roll so far back in my head it hurts. "I'm here because we have unfinished business and you've been avoiding me. You wanted to talk, so here I am."

"I changed my mind," I tell him, cocking my head to the side and giving him a seething scowl. "Now get out."

"Not how this works, angel," he says, kneeling down to cage me between his legs. I lean so far back to get away from him that I'm flat on the floor and he's holding himself over me by his elbows, barely supporting his weight. I struggle to breathe as his massive frame crushes me. "Tell me."

"I want something in return first." His eyes widen in playful excitement. I push on his chest but he doesn't move an inch.

"You're negotiating with me?" he asks. "Okay, I'll bite. What do you want, baby?"

"I want you to leave me alone!"

He laughs menacingly. "No. Try again."

"Fine," I sneer. "Tell me your real eye color, then. Give me a part of you that no one else has."

He stares at me for a long while, as if to question himself how I know he's wearing colored contacts. "You don't get it, do you? You have every part of me already."

"Not your eye color, though."

He growls and grabs my face with his left hand and squishes my cheeks together, and I get a weird flashback of him doing this before, leaning over me with a tequila bottle in his hand.

"Blue."

"Blue," I repeat. "Can I see?"

"No," he snaps. "Now tell me what I want to hear. I don't have all night."

"Got a date with a murder victim?" I sneer. His patience is wearing thin, and his grip leaves my mouth to my neck, where he squeezes, and I begin to worry that he's not going to stop. He doesn't let me breathe until I'm in a full panic, writhing under him and weakly punching his chest. I suck in a deep breath when he lets me go. "The club!" I gasp. "To get downstairs, you have to be invited in by Valenti, and there are two keys."

"Who has the keys?"

"I don't know!"

He's quiet for a moment. "That wasn't so hard, was it, angel?" He lets me go and gets off me. He leaves my apartment without another word, and I scramble to grab my phone with my hands trembling. I finish packing as fast as I can while the phone rings.

"Hello, Ms. Young. How can I help you?"

"Gavin! Can you please come pick me up? I know you just left and it's a long drive but—"

"Of course, I can. Are you okay?"

"Yes. Well, no, but…just, come as soon as you can."

"I'll be there in forty-five minutes," he promises, and then hangs up. Two minutes later, my phone rings again and I answer it.

"Hey," Christian greets, his voice sounding robotic and muffled. "Are you okay? Gavin just called and said you wanted to be picked up."

I wipe away the wetness on my cheeks with the sleeve of my sweater. "Can I stay at your house tonight? The Silencer…he's…I'm scared, and I just don't feel comfortable here right now."

He shushes me. "It's okay. It's okay. Yes, you can stay at my house. You don't even have to ask. You can come over just to raid my fridge and do cartwheels by the pool if that's what you want."

I let out a sad laugh. "But I don't know how to do cartwheels."

I hear him laugh too. "I'm finishing up some stuff before we leave for our trip so I might not beat you back to the mansion. Gavin's on his way, baby. Just sit tight. I—" He takes a deep breath. "I'll see you soon."

The line goes dead. Exactly forty-five minutes after I called Gavin, he knocks on my door and helps me with my luggage, loading it into the trunk and then driving me back to Christian's mansion.

When we get there, waiting in the foyer is Paolo, with a diner-style glass in his hand.

"Miss Elena, Signore Reeves asked me to give this to you."

It's a strawberry milkshake, complete with whipped cream and a cherry, and a thick red and white striped straw.

My mood instantly improves.

CHAPTER 18

THE ANGEL

Soft kisses peppered along my jaw rouse me from sleep. A pleased smile makes its way to my face, Christian's gentle stubble tickling the tender flesh of my neck.

"I know it's early, but we need to get up."

I groan in protest. "Sleepy."

"I know, baby. You can sleep on the plane. Come on."

A poke to my side has me fully awake in a millisecond, and Christian laughs as I playfully whack him with a pillow. He's already dressed in black slacks and a black dress shirt. I glance at the clock. It's 6:15. He must have let me sleep until the last possible second and I appreciate the consideration.

I rub the sleep from my eyes. "I was promised coffee," I grumble, and a second later, a cup of it appears in front of me. Christian looks at me as if he wants me to praise him for remembering, and so I kiss him on the cheek before taking a sip. It's perfect. Just the right amount of hazelnut creamer. I sigh contently and smile. "Should I wear something nice too? Are we going somewhere after we land?"

"Wear whatever you want. The plane ride is long and we're just going to relax tonight. We don't have any obligations until tomorrow."

Long plane ride and relaxation sounds like leggings and a sweater to me. Christian always dresses with finesse. It doesn't really surprise me that he's boarding a plane at six in the morning looking like he's about to visit a country club.

I get ready as quickly as I can, and we get into an unassuming Escalade. "What's so important about this business trip?" I ask, finishing my coffee as I watch the mansion grow smaller in the side view mirror.

"Nothing special. We're trying to open a satellite office in Greece and the investors there just want to have a few more casual meetings before they sign contracts. That's really just an excuse to spend three days drinking on the company's dime."

"They couldn't have picked a better location. Mykonos is my number one dream destination."

Christian smiles. "Any other dream destinations?"

"Pretty much anywhere in Europe. Oh! New Zealand. The only place I've ever traveled to outside of the US was the Bahamas. It was a college graduation present from my parents, and it was such a nice escape before I started law school. I haven't had the chance to travel since I moved to Meridian City."

Christian hums. "Well, that'll change. I travel all the time. Pretty much my entire life as CEO is meetings, meetings, and more meetings. We will see so much of the world together."

Together. I love that word. I love how casually it rolls off his tongue—like it's set in stone that we're spending the rest of our lives with each other.

The drive to the Atlantic City airport is shorter than I thought, and before I know it, we're driving straight onto the tarmac towards a large black private jet with the Reeves Enterprises logo on it.

"I can only imagine the headlines that will emerge once it gets out that you're getting on your private jet with some woman."

"*Some woman*?" Christian emphasizes, hitting the brakes so hard I jerk forward violently in my seat. "Elena, you listen to me. Don't you *ever* refer to yourself as 'some woman' again. You are the only woman I have eyes for. You are the only woman I've ever considered sharing my life with. I knew from the second I met you that I wanted to make you mine forever. You are *everything* to me."

I sit in my seat and stare at him, wide-eyed with my mouth hanging open in shock. Everything he just said feels like it came straight from his heart without a filter, and I really don't know what to say or do except look at him.

My car door opening breaks me out of my hypnotic gaze and I step out onto the tarmac without a word, Christian following close behind. He leads me to the stairs of the jet with a hand on the small of my back. Once inside the warmth and privacy of the jet, he spins me around to face him.

"Elena, look at me." I bite my lip nervously as my eyes meet his. "I meant every word."

I nod. "I know. I'm sorry—I just…I don't know what to say."

He leads me to one of the many plush seats and I take one by the window, and he sits across from me. A flight attendant brings a small tray with two glasses of sparkling champagne for us. I take mine with an unsteady hand and take a long sip.

Bleh. Champagne and coffee do not mix. The flight attendant notices this and offers me an array of different beverages. Orange juice, coffee, water, soda. I shake my head and put the champagne in a cup holder. I stare out the window as we ascend, and Christian lightly taps my ankle with his foot.

"Are you okay?" he asks quietly. I give him a nod, albeit unconvincing. "Talk to me."

"I guess I'm just a little…shocked that you feel that way about me. We haven't known each other very long." I shrug my shoulders to convey that I'm not sure if what I'm saying even makes sense.

"You shouldn't be shocked. You're extraordinary, Elena. I know you don't see it, but I adore everything about you, even the parts of yourself that you're insecure about. I know precisely how much creamer you put in your coffee because your nose does this crinkling thing as you pour it until it's enough. I know you tend to forget your lip balm because you've got a dozen tubes of it all over our office. You lightly chew at your bottom lip when you're concentrating and when you bowl you always double tap your foot before you roll."

I can feel my eyes sparkling from just how wonderful it is to know he commits all those seemingly unimportant details to memory.

"I see more than you think I do," he adds, and a stray tear falls from my cheek. I nod and wipe my face.

"Do I at least look cute when I crinkle my nose?"

"Fucking adorable," he confirms. Once we've reached our cruising altitude, he leans over.

"Want to join the mile-high club?"

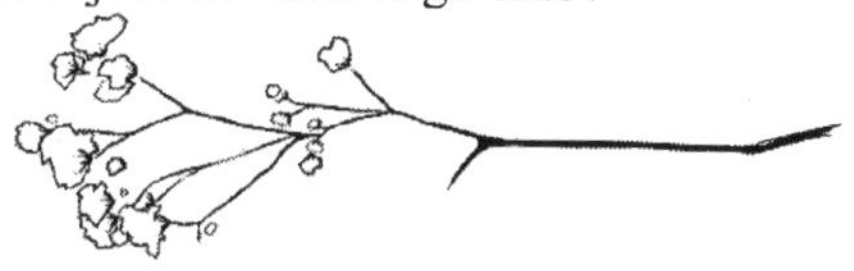

Fifteen hours later, we land in Mykonos. Our jet pulls in next to a dozen other private flights and we emerge onto the tarmac, where a black Rolls Royce is waiting for us. It's late and dark outside, but I wish it was daytime because all I want to do is stare at the ocean.

"Is the car ride to the hotel long?"

"Who said we're staying at a hotel?"

"Oh sorry, is that not what rich people call the Ritz?"

Christian playfully rolls his eyes. "There isn't a Ritz-Carlton in Mykonos. Get in the car."

I narrow my eyes at him, suddenly realizing that he's up to something. "Make me."

He picks me up and throws me over his shoulder and I let out a fit of giggles as he shoves me into the back seat, silencing me with a kiss before buckling my seatbelt for me. He drapes his arm around my shoulders and the driver takes off.

A short while later, the driver mutters something in Greek, and Christian answers back casually before turning his attention to me.

"Close your eyes," he commands.

"Why?"

"Because you'll ruin your surprise if you don't."

I smile and then close my eyes. He warns me not to peek and it feels like an eternity before the car stops.

He helps me out of the car and holds me to his side as he steers me towards wherever we're going. When we finally stop walking, Christian angles me towards something and then wraps his arms around me from the back, using his hands to cover my eyes. I smile with anticipation.

He places a kiss to the shell of my ear. "When we met, I knew you were going to be the most important thing in my life, but I didn't realize just how much I'd be wrapped around your finger. I'd do anything for you." He kisses the curve of my neck. "You've always wanted to visit Mykonos, right?" I nod and jump excitedly in his arms. "Well now we have somewhere to stay every time we visit."

He lowers his hands, and my eyes fly open. I suck in a sharp breath and my hands both immediately go to my chest in awe. My eyes turn glassy. Blush creeps to my cheeks and my knees feel weak.

I'm staring at a massive, and I mean *gargantuan* white yacht gently swaying in the tide.

"Christian…" I gasp, unable to form words or sentences. All I can do is stare in utter shock and amazement. "Oh my God. It's beautiful."

"Just like its namesake," he says into my neck. I turn to him, and he simply turns my head back to focus on the words painted on the side of the boat.

The Elena.

I laugh through my tears at just how surreal it feels. I turn again to face him and rise up on my toes to kiss him fiercely, because it's the only thing I can do to convey every emotion running through my veins that I can't put into words. "You're so perfect it makes me angry," I mumble against his lips. "You could have bought me a tub of ice cream and I'd be happy, but this? Christian, I have no words."

He kisses me again, smirking. "You have a billionaire worshiping the ground you walk on, flying you all over the world on his private jet and buying you a hundred-million-dollar yacht, and you're thinking about ice cream." He takes my hand and leads me onto the boat, keeping me steady as I adjust to the gentle sway.

Despite how late it is and the jet lag, I'm wide awake. On the main deck, a bottle of champagne is sitting in a bucket of ice, and a soft melody of violins dances through the speakers. Between the moonlight and the beautiful ambience, I've never felt happier than I do right now. There's nothing but joy in my heart. Christian twirls me in tight circle before pouring us each a glass of the light, sparkling drink. He wraps his arms around me, and we sway to the music, his chest to my back and his head resting on my shoulder.

"I could stay here forever, just like this," he whispers into my ear. I turn my head to look at him, cup his cheek, and press a long kiss to his lips. He whisks me into his arms, pulling a giggle from me as I wrap my legs around his waist. I pepper kisses to his neck as he carries me through the yacht, stumbling into a large bedroom and depositing me near a tub. "Take off your clothes."

I do as he says, stripping down sensually, slowly, relishing in the way he watches me as I undress for him. When I'm naked, I lick my lips, growing wet at the sight of his bulge behind his pants, aching for me as I am for him.

"Your turn," I breathe.

He gives me a wicked smile and takes a step towards me, pressing a soft kiss to my lips before slowly sinking down to his knees, trailing kisses down my body as he does. His fingers dig into the backs of my thighs and his tongue just barely grazes over my clit. I throw my head back and sigh in delight, and then he turns on the water and lets it fill the tub as he licks me—not so much to bring me to release, but still enough to bring me pleasure. My knees go weak, and I sit on the edge, perching my legs wide open on the rim to give him better access, trying to urge him to give me more.

It almost brings tears to my eyes from how bad I want it. How bad I want him to take me right here on the floor of this grand yacht, to christen it as ours.

"Get in," he commands. I step into the perfectly hot bath, sighing as I lower myself into it. He stays kneeling next to the tub, dipping his fingers into the water and playing with one of my nipples until it's an aching peak.

"Why won't you get in with me?" I ask. Another wicked smirk comes to his face, and he toes off his shoes, removes his belt and his watch, and then gets into the tub fully clothed. I laugh as the water sloshes over the side, and he settles his weight on top of me.

"Is this what you wanted, Elena?"

I giggle. "You know what I meant. You don't…you don't ever take your shirt off around me."

He takes a deep breath and his lips pucker in a way that makes me regret bringing it up. I seem to have a tendency to do that with him.

"I have scars," he offers vaguely. I pull one of his arms out from under the water and run my fingers along his forearm, mangled with years of self-harm and hatred. I kiss his wrist.

"If it's because you're afraid it will run me off, you're wrong. I won't judge you if that's how you chose to cope with what happened to you."

"It's not that," he answers, moving to rest against the other side of the bath, making no effort to take off any of his clothes. He runs a finger across his lips in thought. "I have to tell you something."

My heart sinks as my shoulders fold forward. Those words never mean anything good. "Oh."

"It's two things, actually," he adds, "but…I don't know which one to tell you first."

"Bad thing first," I suggest, assuming there is one.

"If I tell you the bad thing first, it will ruin the good thing."

"Good thing first?"

"If I tell you the good thing first, you won't believe me after I tell you the bad thing."

I think about it for a long time, and then I cross the space between us to sit in his lap. I lean in closer until our lips tingle with the anticipation of a kiss. "How about a compromise?" He nods, running his hands along the length of my bare back. "Tell me the good thing first, and then tell me the bad thing when we're not in a foreign country. That way, I can run away if it's *really really* bad."

He laughs with a smirk against my lips. "If you run, I'll catch you."

I hum and then close the gap between our lips, moving my hips in time with our mouths until he's rock solid beneath me. I pull away just enough to whisper, "Tag, you're it."

I poke him in the chest, hop out of the tub and grab a towel on the way out, squealing as I wrap it around myself and run through the yacht. I'm sure I'm leaving a trail of water wherever I go, but it doesn't matter. I see Christian for a brief second through a window, traveling in the opposite direction as me, so I make a big loop around the deck back to the bedroom.

"*Boo*."

I scream so loud I think I ruptured my own ear drum when Christian pops out from behind the door and grabs me by the waist, still soaking wet from the bath. He tosses me onto the bed and rips my towel away from me before spreading my legs. He eye-fucks my bare pussy and I think I could orgasm just from the sight of him so hungry for me.

"Can this be my reward for catching you?" he asks, running a finger along my slit and laughing when he finds I'm already soaked. "You like being hunted, baby?"

"By *you*."

My mouth falls open in silent pleasure when he lightly kisses my clit and then licks a broad stripe up my cunt. My fingers tug on his hair and I can't help myself—I laugh.

"What's so funny?" he asks in between licks.

I sigh as his tongue continues to explore me. "I can't believe a billionaire flew me all the way to Mykonos on his private jet and is currently—*fuck*!"

"Finish your sentence, Elena. What am I currently doing?" He shoves two thick fingers inside me and curls them to seek out my g-spot. When he finds it, I arch off the bed.

"Making me feel good. *Fuck*, it feels so good."

He kisses up my body, latching his teeth onto my neck and clumsily unbuttoning his pants before pulling them down. The wet fabric makes it difficult for him, but he finally removes the offending material and rubs the tip of his cock along my folds. He slowly pushes into me, making sure I feel every single inch of him buried in my center. I grind against him, urging him to move, but he doesn't. "Fuck me. Please."

"Elena."

He cradles my head between his forearms and rests his forehead against mine. The way he said my name, so tender and soft, makes my eyes glassy.

My hands reach up between us to caress his cheeks with the same tenderness with which he cradles my face. "Tell me the good thing."

Time freezes as we stare at each other, and my heart flutters when the corners of his mouth quirk into a smile, before his face hardens with nerves.

"I am painfully, catastrophically in love with you."

My throat aches with raw emotion and tears escape my eyes, falling to the comforter below us. I open my mouth to say something back, but no words come out.

"I love you," he whispers against my lips. It doesn't feel like a declaration this time, but rather, a desperate attempt to get me to say it back. Because that's what you do when someone says they love you. You say it back. *But I can't.* I can't, and I think he and I both realize it in horror at the same time, because something in his face changes.

There's something brutally betrayed in the unique icy blue of his eyes.

I want to love Christian. I want to have a life with him, and I want him to show me every side of him, even the parts he thinks are unlovable. Because that's what he feels for me, and I want him to know that I cherish his love by reciprocating.

But I don't love him. Not yet. Not when everything between us is so new and raw.

While I'm lost in thought, Christian begins slowly grinding into me. This isn't anything like all the other times we've been together. This isn't boundless euphoria. This isn't getting lost in each other's bodies to sate the carnal desires we feel for each other.

This is him making love to me. This is how he's choosing to show me that he means it. It's beautiful and passionate and tender and gentle. I mewl as he grinds into me, seated as deep as he can manage—so deep until I'm not sure where he ends, and I begin. I wrap my arms around his shoulders. I moan quietly each time he drags his pelvis across my clit.

"Christian." He shudders at the way his name falls off my lips. "Tell me again," I beg him, my voice breaking.

He rests his forehead against mine and my pussy flutters at the pure intimacy of this moment that has nothing to do with sex and everything to do with our hearts morphing together.

"I love you, Elena."

He waits. He waits and waits and waits for me to say it back. More tears spill from my eyes, pouring down my face now. My lip quivers and I sniffle. "I'm sorry."

He shushes me with a soft kiss and begins to thrust into me again, leaving kisses over every inch of my skin he can reach.

His moan when he finishes inside me doesn't hide the shattering of his heart.

CHAPTER 19

THE ANGEL

When I wake up with the bright sun reflecting off a beautiful blue ocean, I feel peace. I feel serenity. The sliding glass doors that make up a full wall of the bedroom of the yacht are open, letting a cool breeze flutter around the room. I sit up in the bed, finding it empty.

"Christian?" I call out towards the bathroom, but the door is closed, and the light is off. His side of the bed is cold. He must be somewhere else on the boat. I stand up with the sheet wrapped around my naked body and walk out onto the balcony of our room, inhaling the refreshing, clean ocean air.

After I take a moment to breathe and compose myself, I go back into the room to take a proper shower and get ready for the day. I dress myself in a cornflower blue jumpsuit, classy enough for a luncheon but still cute and casual. It's got a mock neck, short sleeves, and an open back. I pair it with nude strappy heels, light makeup, and throw my hair into one long braid down my back.

I carry my heels as I walk around the deck, feeling over the glossy, pearlescent paint of the yacht. I still can't believe Christian bought this boat, much less believe that he named it after me. What did I ever do to deserve that man?

I think about what he said to me last night. Now that I know the 'good thing' was a confession of love, anxiety spikes in my veins, wondering what he could possibly tell me that would be so bad I'd no longer believe it.

I think I knew that he loved me before those words fell from his lips, but to hear him say it felt surreal. I will love him back, in time. I just don't feel as intensely as he does about everything.

One day, when I'm sure of it, I'll tell him '*I love you too*'.

I find Christian on the main deck, looking out over the ocean. When I notice we're no longer near the island, it occurs to me that we must have gone out to sea while I was sleeping. Christian has a white-knuckled grip on the railing of the boat, and a cigarette between two of his fingers. I watch him for a while. The steady rise and fall of his torso as he takes deep, even breaths. He's not even smoking the cigarette; the ashes are simply landing on the deck as the flame slowly eats away at the paper and toxins until it's nothing but a short nub.

I make myself known by wrapping my arms around him from behind and pressing my cheek into his back. "Good morning."

"Good morning."

My body tenses. He sounds so cold, and my heart begins to ache at the thought of how hurt he looked last night when he realized I wasn't going to tell him I love him.

"Christian…"

"You don't have to explain yourself," he says with a sigh. "I get it."

A knot ties itself inside my throat, making it hard to swallow.

"Edwin always used to say that I was intense in all aspects of my life. I always thought he was full of shit. He was an old man, trying to be a father figure to a punk ass kid who didn't want to listen. It wasn't until I got older that I started to notice it. Anger. Guilt. Jealousy. Pride. Then I met you, and falling in love was like some nuclear catalyst inside me. I've been consumed by it—*by you*. I can't think about anything else except how much I want you to be mine to love, forever." He takes a deep breath. "I mean that in the kind of way that's going to suffocate you one day but I can't stop. I can't fucking stop. I won't be satisfied until I am every part of your existence as you are mine."

Hiding my own tears, I pull away from him and force him to turn around and face me. He's got his head turned away like he's ashamed of feeling so strongly for me. I run my fingers along his jawline in a way that has him purring under my touch.

"Look at me," I demand, my tone soft but firm. "I am so, so sorry that you trusted me with your heart and that I didn't give you mine back, but I promise I will. I *promise* we'll have that all-consuming love that gives us cavities and I promise we'll build a life and a home and a family together if that's what you want. I just need a little time to learn how to love you back."

Christian rests both of his hands on my hips as he leans against the railing. "How much time?"

My shoulders slump in defeat. "I can't answer that. I don't know. I can't put a timeline on it."

"You really want all those things? A family?"

The corners of my mouth quirk up at the way he hangs onto that declaration. "If that's what you want."

He doesn't hesitate when he answers. "*Yes*. Yes, I want a family with you. I want you to have ten thousand of my babies."

I laugh quietly. "Ten thousand seems like a lot."

"Meet me at fifty?"

I raise my eyebrow. "How many guest rooms do you have in that mansion of yours?"

"Fifteen."

"Let's compromise at ten, then," I suggest, even though that's still a shit ton of kids and my poor vagina is cringing in horror at the thought. "We could always adopt, too."

Christian laughs and kisses my knuckles like a knight greeting a princess. "I see Caroline's gotten into your head."

I huff playfully. "I know, I can't help it. She's adorable." When Christian looks at me, I know he can see in my eyes exactly the thought that crossed my mind.

"Have you been thinking about what I said about fostering?"

I nod. "Yeah. I have."

"And?"

I smile softly and cup his cheek. "I think you'll make a wonderful father."

His face lights up like fireworks in the night sky on Independence Day. He takes my face in his hands and kisses me passionately. "Caroline is going to be so happy."

I raise an eyebrow. "How do you know you're going to foster Caroline?"

He runs a finger along my bottom lip. "Because I'm Christian Reeves."

I giggle softly. "Touché," I whisper, then my face turns down with nerves. "You told me you believe in soulmates."

"Because of you."

"Then that means I'm destined to love you no matter what, even if it's not right now."

Christian's shoulders slump, but he accepts it. If anyone deserves love, it's him, and I'm so lucky that he trusts me enough to let his heart be vulnerable around me. I will never take that for granted.

For both of our sakes, Christian changes the subject. "Chef's making breakfast. We'll have a few hours to ourselves before the investors get here, and then we'll have lunch and meetings with them for the rest of the day. Tonight, we'll go to the island for dinner and then to a nightclub. Tomorrow we'll have a grand tour of the island and brunch, and then the next day will be the most boring one. We'll flesh out all the details of the deal and then go out to celebrate when we're done."

I wrap my arms around his neck and stretch like a cat before standing up straight again. "How much is this deal worth?" I ask in curiosity.

"Three hundred million."

"*Dollars*?"

"No, chickens. Yes, dollars. Don't give me that look. I don't even consider deals unless there's at least seven zeros at the end of it."

"I do hope I get a bonus for being your most loyal assistant on this business trip, Mr. Reeves."

Christian grabs my braid and tugs my head back, exposing my throat to him. He licks along the column of my neck and then whispers deliciously into my ear, "After I close this deal, I'm going to fuck you so hard they'll be able to hear you screaming in Meridian City."

On our third day in Mykonos, my father calls me. We're eight hours ahead, so while the sun just came up for me, it's nearly midnight in Texas.

"Hi dad," I answer delightfully. Christian grumbles and rolls over to cover his face with a pillow. He's got a hangover and I poke him in the side just to hear him grumble again. I get out of bed and walk to the balcony, closing the door behind me so that Christian can sleep.

I apologize for the awkward pause, and, sounding distressed, my dad gives me his 'stern father' tone. "Elena, I've been texting you for days. Where have you been?"

I sigh. He's probably right, I've barely checked my phone since we got to Greece. "I'm sorry, dad. It's kind of a funny story but I'm actually not in the States right now. Christian and I are in Mykonos. It's beautiful here. You should see—"

"You flew all the way to a foreign country halfway across the world without telling me?"

My eyebrows knit together and I grow irritated with his tone. "I'm a grown woman, dad. If I want to travel, I can. And I told Travis."

"You didn't think to tell *me*?"

"It's not a big deal," I snap. "Relax. It was a last-minute thing. It's just a short work trip. We'll be back tomorrow."

"Didn't realize you had that kind of money." I try not to audibly huff at his tone. "You can never afford to hop on a flight to come see your mother and I, but you're traveling across the world with your boyfriend? Is your family not good enough for you anymore?"

"Dad!" I snap loudly, turning to make sure Christian didn't hear through the glass. "That's unfair and you know it. Not that it's any of your business, but Christian paid for my flight."

"You're my daughter, so it is my business."

"Yes, your *adult* daughter." Before this turns into a screaming match, as these types of conversations normally go, I huff. "Look, I have to go. I'll text you when we get back to the States."

I hang up and stomp back into the bedroom, tossing my phone on the nightstand and then holding a pillow to my face to scream in frustration into it. Christian grumbles again and turns over, wrapping an arm around my waist and hoisting his head up to rest on my lap.

"What's going on?"

I groan. "My father is so…impossible sometimes! He treats me like a child."

"He'll get over it, whatever it is," Christian mumbles into the soft flesh of my thighs, placing a kiss to the skin there.

"You haven't met my father," I say back. "Elliot Young does not get over things." I look out the window and let the pretty view of the bright blue ocean calm me down. I run my fingers through Christian's hair, and he purrs like a cat at the touch. "Can we come back here in the summer?"

Mykonos is beautiful, but the weather in October isn't exactly suitable for swimming and tanning.

"Absolutely. I'll block off a week for us, maybe even a month. We can go all over Europe."

I laugh. "I don't think your company would appreciate you taking a month-long vacation to tote your leech across Europe."

"It's my company, Elena. They'll get over it. You'll be my wife by then anyways, so consider it our honeymoon."

My jaw drops open. "Is that a proposal? Because I still don't see a ring on my finger."

Christian grumbles and grabs his phone from the nightstand. After a few seconds of scrolling, he tosses it onto my lap. I'm staring at an email thread with a photo of an absurdly massive purple diamond. When I see the eight-figure price tag for said diamond, I dramatically roll over the edge of the bed and land on the floor.

"I think I'm gonna hurl," I say into the rug.

I feel Christian land on top of me, supporting most of his weight on his arms and legs so that he doesn't fully crush me. "Because you're pregnant?"

I make a noise of disgust. "No, because you're insane." I tease. "I'm on birth control, remember? This uterus is not open for business."

"*For now*," Christian says, kissing my cheek. He inhales the scent of my hair, still smelling of my lavender shampoo from my shower last night. "We don't have any meetings until one. Want to go to the island, just you and me?"

I nod. "Yeah, sure."

He flips me onto my back and kisses me, slow and deep.

"I love you."

The tenderness in those three words makes my heart flutter, and it would be so natural and feel so right to say it back.

I don't know why I can't, and that frightens me—because what if he's right about the bad thing he wants to tell me?

What if I stop believing him?

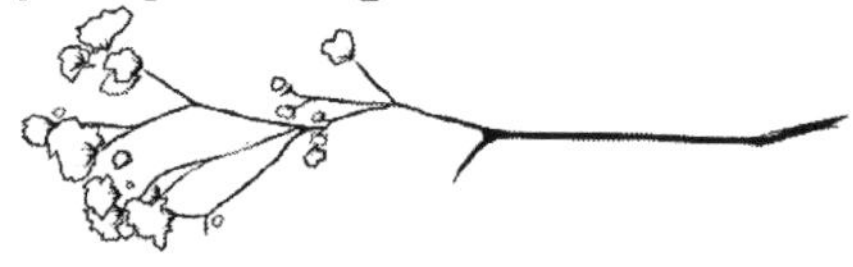

Mykonos truly is as stunning as the photos.

I never really thought I'd have a chance to visit. At least not for a long time. My dream destination was simply that. A dream.

But Christian and all his irritating perfection, makes all my dreams come true.

We have brunch at an oceanside cafe with the breeze flowing around us. I have the most delicious Croque Madame on the planet, and a mimosa. After our meal, we walk along the beach, hand in hand. By the time we circle back to the dock, we need to prepare for the meeting this afternoon.

Christian dresses behind the closed—and locked—bathroom door, only emerging when he's fully dressed in a suit, sans his signature red tie. It's loosely slung around his neck. I approach him slowly, already primped and ready to go. I tie a neat Windsor knot around his neck, straightening it for him and then fastening his initial-monogrammed cufflinks around his wrists.

"Did you know you have the same middle name as my dad? I think if we have a son one day, we should keep the tradition going."

"There you go, talking about kids again." He pokes me in the stomach. "Is there something you're hiding from me in there?"

My face turns bright red. "No! No, I'm not…I didn't mean…"

"I'm *kidding*," he says, kissing my forehead, and leading me to the office where the meeting will be held as the investors start arriving.

Much to my dissatisfaction, the investors were very adamant that they wanted a private audience with Christian, so I was shuffled out of the room along with the two other women that tagged along. I linger in the hallway outside of the office.

After about ten minutes, I'm bored out of my mind. I understand that it's an important meeting, but I'm going to remind him about what he promised to me the day we got here. If he closes this deal, he's going to fuck me so hard they'll hear me across the world. I pull out my phone and send Christian a text that he may just ignore, but I don't care.

Me: My fingers don't feel the same as yours.

I pair the text with a quick photo I snapped of my fingers just under the waistline of my underwear, easily accessible from my short dress. I press send before I can think twice about it.

I decide to stop lingering in the hallway like a maniac. As I walk past the door to the office, it flies open, and Christian grabs me by the scruff of my neck and forces me to my knees right there in the hallway, where anyone can see us.

"Take off my belt," he growls down at me, his eyes dark and his jaw tight. "Now."

I do as he says, keeping eye contact with him as I unbuckle it and then slide it out of the loops. He takes it from me, wraps it around my arms, and buckles it again so that my arms are fully restrained at my sides. He begins to pull his cock out of his pants, and when it's free, it's already hard and red and angry.

"You wanted my attention, baby, and now you've got it. Now be a good girl and suck." He grabs a fistful of my loose hair and tugs me to his length, and I welcome him into my mouth. I smear the salty drop of precum along my lips and then lick up the bottom of his shaft before taking him fully in my mouth. "*Fuck*," he groans, throwing his head back as his eyebrows knit together.

My arms are pinned to my side, so I have no choice but to stay still and take it as he fucks my mouth like he's furious with me for interrupting his meeting. He pulls out of my mouth and jerks me up to my feet, before roughly pulling my panties down my legs and making me step out of them.

I expect him to pocket them, but he shoves them in my mouth and then presses my chest into the wall of the hallway. "Don't make a sound, Elena, or I won't let you cum."

I'm completely at his mercy like this, gagged and bound and pushed against a wall of the office where his investors can very possibly hear everything that's happening on this side.

Christian doesn't draw this out. He fucks me deep and hard in the hallway. My arousal is dripping down my legs and he's growling into my ear, trying to keep quiet himself. Finally, he snakes his hand around to rub my clit. "Cum," he demands, and the feeling of him spilling inside me sends me over the edge, my pussy fluttering and squeezing until he has nothing left to give me.

I'm still pressed against the wall, trying to catch my breath as he loosens his belt and puts it back on, adjusting his slacks and shirt to hide that post-sex state of unkempt that I'm still fully in.

He spins me around and gently tugs my panties out of my mouth, pressing his lips to mine with a satisfied breath. "Behave," he warns, and then with a smirk, he goes back into his office like nothing happened.

A half hour later, I'm sipping on a glass of wine and scrolling through Instagram, when a notification pops up.

I click the notification and see that Christian has tagged me in a photo—one of me in this exact moment. My eyes shoot to the other side of the deck, where Christian is leaning against a bar top, ankles crossed, holding up a wine glass as if to toast me, with a smug grin on his face. I look down at my phone. The caption of the post simply reads, *Mine*.

In an unexpected turn of events, that tiny glimpse into his personal life sent his stock prices skyrocketing. The growth is so explosive, that by the time we board the plane to go home, Christian is worth *500. Billion. Dollars*.

He chooses to celebrate his historic success with a bottle of red wine and his tongue on my clit because, in his words, I'm '*the single best pairing with a good Cabernet*'.

CHAPTER 20

THE ANGEL

When we land in the states, Christian says he needs to go to the office and sends me home with Gavin. He just closed a massive deal for the Mediterranean region, and he wants to make sure he's tied up all those loose ends. The business stuff bores me to tears, so I didn't mind his sudden need to run off. I'm out of clean clothes anyways, so heading home for a few days doesn't sound like a terrible idea.

Gavin drops me off at my apartment, and I walk up the stairs with my suitcase trailing behind me, thumping against each step. When I reach my floor, from across the hall, I see a bright pink sheet of paper on my door. I hurry over to it, frustration and confusion racing through my veins.

EVICTION NOTICE.

Eviction? There's no way. My lease is in good standing. I've always paid my rent on time. I've been living here for five years, and I've never had any problems with the landlord or the other tenants. I've gotten a couple of noise complaints, sure, but it's not my fault the walls are paper thin.

I immediately rush downstairs and bang my fist on the property manager's office. A greasy looking man that smells like stale beer begrudgingly opens the door and I shove the paper in his face.

"You've made a mistake. This is a mistake!" I seethe, anger pooling in my bloodstream. "I've been here five years and suddenly you're evicting me? For *what*?"

The man scratches his belly and slow blinks at me like he just woke up from a nap. "Apartment number?"

"Thirty-two."

The man goes digging through his office for a file and then comes back to the door. "Says here you've been behind on your rent for three months. Sorry, sugar, looks like it's not my problem."

"That's not true! None of that is." I pull out my phone and open my bank account to show that I've paid my rent, on time, for the past three months and the money left my account. "See?"

The manager shrugs and holds in a burp. "Not. My. Problem," he repeats, and then slams the door in my face.

"Asshole," I mutter under my breath and kick the worn-out wooden door. I grit my teeth and let out a guttural groan of anger and stomp away from the office.

I go back upstairs to my apartment, my eyes burning from unshed tears as I slump against my wall and pinch the bridge of my nose.

"What's wrong, angel?"

I growl at the Silencer without opening my eyes. "Go. Away."

"But I missed you while you were gone."

I open my eyes and hope that the glare I'm giving him will cause his brain to melt inside his skull. "Do I look like I care?"

"I see you didn't appreciate my surprise."

I freeze. My body goes numb, and I think my fury could demolish nations. "You got me *evicted*?" I snarl, standing up. I grab one of my purple kitchen knives from the block on my counter and swing at him. He dodges me easily, but I don't give up. I swing and chase him around my tiny apartment until I'm drenched in sweat and panting. "Come here, you motherfucker."

He laughs at me as if he's bored with my attempts to chop him into tiny pieces and flush him down the toilet. "Are you done, angel?"

As a matter of fact, I'm *not* done, and his calm demeanor is pissing me off. I swing again, this time narrowly missing his face. He catches my wrist and twists it until the pain causes me to drop the knife. Then, he wrestles me to the ground as I furiously fight back, clawing at him with my nails hoping to catch some of his DNA.

When he pins me to the ground, I start hollering for help. He clasps his hand over my mouth and growls viciously in my face.

"You just have to make this difficult, don't you?" he asks, and then takes his red duct tape, plasters it to my cheek and rolls it tightly over my mouth and rips it off the roll in one fluid motion.

He tosses the tape and it lands with a thud on the floor, then he sits on my hips to hold me down with his weight.

I scream again, but the tape muffles me. It's no use, and I can't fight him anymore either. My body is tired and he's too strong.

Then, he flips me onto my stomach, and I begin to panic. *Holy shit. Holy fuck. He's going to kill me.*

He binds my wrists together with zip ties at the base of my spine, and then binds my ankles together before connecting them to my wrists with a third tie.

The position is painful and awkward and dehumanizing. Humiliating and frustrating. I'm thoroughly immobile. I stop trying to fight and give myself a chance to catch my breath. If I want out of this, if I want to *live*, I have to give him what he wants.

He flops down onto his back next to me, takes one of his knives, and starts flipping it into the air above him, seeing how high he can toss it without it impaling himself in the chest. I can practically see my name invisibly etched into the handle of that knife as if it's been meant for me all along, and this was just one long game of cat and mouse to him.

If I'm ever going to see the sun come up again, I have to beat him at his own game. I do my best to soften my face despite the ice-cold fear in my chest and knit my brows together. I raise my voice and octave and begin to whine against the tape covering my mouth.

That catches his attention, and he leans over to get closer to my face. "What's wrong, angel?" he taunts, and it takes considerable effort not to snarl back.

From under the tape, I whine, wiggling my hands behind my back for emphasis.

"It hurts?" he asks, and I nod. I quietly sigh in relief when he leans over with the knife, and I expect him to cut off the ties that have my hands and feet connected. It's not like I can run away with my ankles still tied together.

I cry out in pain when he tightens the ties instead.

"Nice try. Playing with my soft spot for you. I'm touched, truly." He clutches his chest in feigned awe. "You're going to stay like that all night. Sweet dreams."

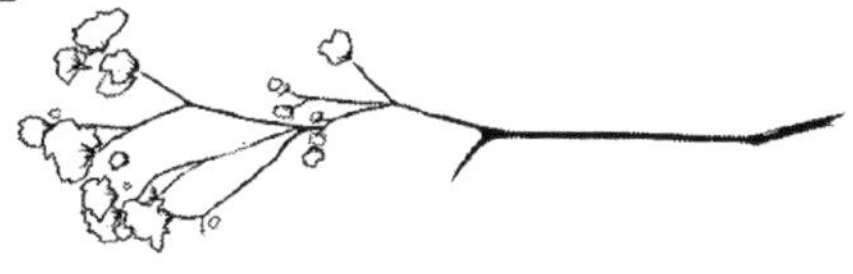

I don't know at what point I simply gave up and fell asleep awkwardly tied up on the floor, but it must have been after hours and hours of fighting because my body fucking hurts.

We make eye contact, and I snarl at him. He rolls his eyes and cuts all the ties to let my limbs free, and I gasp at the sudden mobility. I scramble away from him. The burning ache in my limbs makes it impossible to walk, so I crawl until I reach the other side of the room. There's no way I can make it to the door without him catching me.

I rip the tape off my mouth, and like I've just drilled a hole through a dam, I shatter. I start sobbing so hard I can barely breathe. My hands grasp at my chest and hair and my entire body is trembling.

Something changes in the room. The tension breaks and suddenly, he's rushing to my side and cradling my cheeks in his hands. I shove him away as hard as I can.

"Don't fucking touch me!" I growl, cowering against the wall, still sobbing.

"Elena, I—"

"Shut up! I hate you! Get away from me you sick fuck! You're a twisted fucking psychopath, and I hope you die. I hope you never experience love or happiness, and you die young and alone."

I shakily stand and waddle towards the door, my knees buckling after being in an uncomfortable position all night. Two large hands wrap around my waist, and I start thrashing again. "Let me go!" I cry through gritted teeth, emotionally exhausted.

"Elena, look at me," he demands into my neck. His grip against me is firm, but not rough or angry.

I turn around and shove against him, but he only tightens his grip on me. More frustrated tears fall down my face and I avoid his intense glare.

"Look. At. Me."

I bare my teeth and meet his eyes, ready to rip him apart for what he did to me, but something stops me dead in my tracks. I freeze, the whole world seeming to disappear until it's just me and him.

Looking down at me isn't a set of artificial green eyes, but a set of dazzling blue. Bright and vibrant and dynamic like the ocean. A vivid shade of aquamarine stands brilliantly against the dark paint in his eye sockets. They're devastatingly beautiful.

My face turns down into a scowl as I look away. "Let me go."

"I went too far, and I am sorry."

"You're *sorry*?" I repeat, disgusted.

I make a split-second decision that I'm absolutely going to regret, but I want him out of my life. I wrap my fingers around the handle of one of his guns and shove him away from me with one hand and then point the gun at him with the other. He steps towards me, and I take one step back.

"Don't fucking move," I warn. "I grew up in a gun-loving state with a father who spent thirteen years in the Army. He taught me how to shoot pistols when I was a teenager. I'm a good shot. I could hit you between the eyes with mine closed."

The Silencer puts up his hands in surrender, but I know if I give him even a second of opportunity, he's going to take advantage of it and take back his gun before I can blink.

"What the fuck do you want with me? What is your endgame? You…you expect me to fall in love with you or something?"

His distractingly pretty blue eyes darken. His hands are still up by his head, but he relaxes his stance like I don't have a gun pointed at his fucking forehead right now.

"Yes, I want you to love me. I want…no, I *need* to be your *everything*."

I laugh sarcastically, because how could I love someone like him? "Why am I so important to you?"

"Because you saved my life."

I scoff. "You know, you always say that, but you've never actually told me what that fucking means!"

There's a pause between us. In the split second of distraction, he lunges for the gun and twists my arm around my back, spinning me in a half circle with it. We stumble to the wall, and he presses my chest up to a large mirror hanging there, staring at me through the reflection. He wrestles the gun out of my grip and puts it back into its holster. In one smooth movement, he wraps his left hand around my body and holds me against his chest by my throat. His other hand laces our fingers together and trails our hands up my body agonizingly slowly.

"You're not just some obsession I picked up out of boredom. You're my life essence. The air in my lungs. The beating heart in my chest." Goosebumps erupt over my skin as our hands trace over my stomach. "You are my everything. Mind. Body. Soul. I fucking love you, Elena, and you *will* love me back. I don't care if I have to destroy you in the process." He moves our hands even slower across my breasts, and I hate the way my nipples harden into tight peaks under the sensual touch. "You'll be mine one day. Fully. I love it when you fight me, but if you would just shut up and stop, even for one second, you might see what's right in front of you."

Then he releases me. I stay pressed against the wall long after he leaves, shaking, exhausted, and scared.

Fear is such a strange emotion.

I think the Silencer knows that, and I think he's very good at manipulating my fear. I don't think I will ever be able to trust my own emotions for the rest of my life.

Taking a deep breath, I pull out my phone and call the police. I don't get put on hold this time.

Instead, when I tell the dispatcher I'm being stalked by the Silencer, she laughs at me, and hangs up.

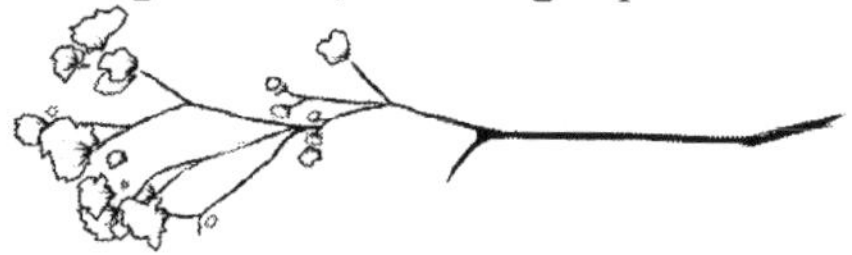

I spend four hours crying, lying down on my back against the hardwood floors of my apartment, staring up at the ceiling. I think for a long time about how I ended up in this situation and how I can get out of it.

I do the only logical thing I can think of. I call Christian.

As expected, he answers almost instantly, his voice sounding tired. "Hey, beautiful." I don't say anything back to him, and I can feel tension through the phone. "What's wrong?"

I rub over my face with exasperation and sigh. A pathetic, humorless chuckle leaves my throat. "I don't even know where to begin." I sniffle, trying not to cry and doing a terrible job at it. "I got evicted. Or should I say, the fucking *Silencer* got me evicted."

God, no wonder the dispatcher laughed at me. I sound like a lunatic.

"I don't know how, but he got me evicted and I don't know what to do."

"Stay with me," Christian suggests immediately. "Move to the Reeves Estate."

"I can't ask you to do that for me."

"You're not asking, I'm offering."

I take a deep breath and attempt to make a joke to cheer myself up. "You'd better clear out half of your closet. I have a lot of shoes."

He laughs. "I'll pick you up in thirty minutes. Pack an overnight bag, and I'll have people come move your stuff in the morning."

"Okay," I say, hanging up the phone.

I should be excited, right? I'm moving into a billionaire's mansion. That's like, every normal person's dream. Something feels…sinister about the whole situation though. It sits in my stomach like curdled milk. The Silencer probably did this to me with the expectation that I'd end up on the street so he can whisk me away to his secret lair like some kind of fucked up white knight.

Or red knight, if we're staying true to his modus operandi.

At least once I'm living at the Reeves Estate, I'm safe. He knows he can't get in or out without getting seen by the security cameras or getting his head blown off with a shotgun by one of the guards.

I pack my overnight bag and mess with the chipping paint on the wall next to me while I wait for Christian to pick me up. When he does, the first thing I notice about him is the way he looks at me. It's…strange. Almost like I've said something to hurt him.

He's still upset that I didn't say I loved him in Mykonos.

He looks restless, and the skin under his eyes looks gray. He doesn't make any effort to compliment me or flirt like he normally would.

As we drive towards his house, I start to fidget with my braid, and its only once Christian gently tugs my hands away from my hair that I realize I've got a handful of strands that I've absentmindedly pulled out.

"He came to my apartment," I admit into the stale air of the car. "He told me that it was him that got me evicted and I tried to fight him off. He held me down and tied me up. When he finally let me go, I called the police and they just…laughed at me."

Christian is stiff and completely silent for a long time. "You called the police?" he asks, almost sounding offended. "The MCPD is useless. You shouldn't have got them involved."

"Well what else was I supposed to do?" I ask, frustration rising up through my throat.

"*Not* call the police."

His tone has turned dark, and I feel anger brewing in my chest. "Let me get this straight. You broke Neil Hayden's arm for grabbing me in a restaurant and threatened to kill him if he touched me again, but you draw the line at reporting a *serial killer* to the police?"

Now that I'm riled up, I think about how nonchalant Christian has been about the whole stalker situation. To be honest with myself, he's never once shown concern for it. Like it's an afterthought to him when it's been tormenting me for months. "Do you not care that the Silencer is stalking me? Do you even understand how hard it is to not feel safe in your own home?"

"Fuck, Elena! Of course I care!" Christian shouts, and it's the first time he's ever raised his voice at me. He didn't even sound this terrifying when he was threatening Neil. Cold shivers trail up my spine and I cross my arms over my chest, shrinking into the door of the car. After a moment, he reaches across the expanse between us that feels about a mile long, and lightly squeezes my thigh.

For the first time, his touch doesn't bring me comfort. It only makes me colder.

I stare out the window, and once we reach the Reeves Estate, I don't say a single word to Christian as I pick a guestroom, slam the door behind me, and lock it.

I collapse against the cool wood of the door and tuck my knees into my chest. The door moves a few times as Christian tries to open it, but the lock keeps him out. I hear a small thud when he takes a seat against the door on the opposite side.

"Christian?"

"Yeah, baby?"

"Will you tell me the bad thing now?"

It's quiet for a moment. "Only if you let me in."

I don't even have to think about it. I stand up from my place on the floor, walk to the bed, and bury myself under the covers.

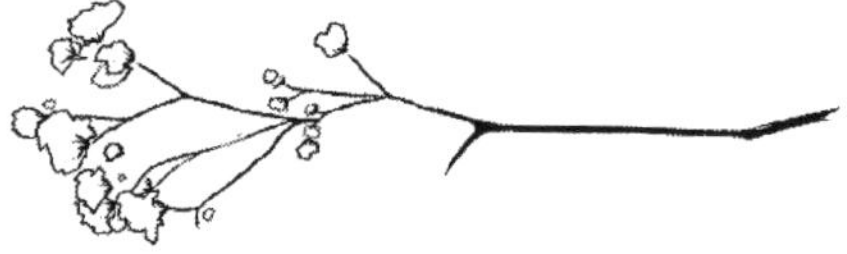

After a few hours of feeling sorry for myself I decide I need to talk to Christian. I need to understand why he got so upset about me calling the police. It can't just be that he doesn't like them. *Nobody* likes the MCPD.

I take a deep breath, trying to build up some courage before I go find Christian. I don't know what I'm going to say to him, but I know for sure that if there was ever a moment where he should tell me the '*bad thing*', it should be now. This strange limbo we're in seems like a good time to share all our demons.

Well, for Christian to share his.

I pull myself together and walk to Christian's room with my heart pounding in my chest. I knock on his bedroom door and poke my head in. It's empty, but the light is on in his bathroom. I can hear his voice on the other side.

It almost sounds like he's weeping, and if my life were a movie, this is when the suspenseful music would start. I reach for the door, slowly, like a horrible monster is waiting on the other side for me. I suck in a sharp gasp and jump back when I hear something shatter.

I gulp and carefully twist the handle. It's unlocked. I push the door slowly until it's fully open.

Christian is standing in the middle of the bathroom. His hair is wet from a shower that's still running. He's wearing nothing but a pair of black sweatpants. I've never seen his naked torso. His back muscles are beautiful like the rest of him.

Blood drips to the floor from his knuckles. The bathroom mirror is in shards across the countertop. He's facing away from me, tugging on his hair, hitting the side of his head, and mumbling quietly to himself.

"Christian?" I ask, reaching out to lightly grab his bicep.

He whips around abruptly, and nothing could have prepared me for what I saw when he turned around.

The look on his face—*God*, I've never seen anyone look so broken and uneasy. Tears stream down his cheeks, dripping off his chin and landing on his chest.

It's not just his knuckles that are bleeding. He's got a shard of the mirror in his hand and three cuts along his left forearm.

My eyes trace over his body, lingering on his broad, strong chest.

His *entire* body is covered in scars. Not just his wrists, but his *everything*. His chest is littered with bruises in various stages of healing. I swallow when my eyes land on the marred skin where his heart is.

Five scars.

Five jagged letters of the alphabet, pink and healing.

Five letters that spell my name.

I think I'm in shock, but something compels me to trace my fingers over the letters and Christian trembles under my touch, sucking in a sharp breath.

"Is this the bad thing?" I whisper.

He shakes his head and inhales a harsh breath. "You said you hated me."

I shake my head in confusion. "What? No, Christian—" I take his face in my hands. "I don't hate you."

He cradles my cheeks with the same tenderness I'm holding his. With his lips ghosting over mine, he whispers, "The day we met…I was going to kill myself."

My throat tightens and tears prick in my eyes. "What?"

He holds me close to him, his trembling breaths telling me he's terrified. Wet droplets of water drip from his hair and mix with his tears.

"I had the gun to my head. I had my finger on the trigger, and I was about to pull it. The bad thing, Elena...is that the only reason I stopped was because I heard you screaming for help." His voice cracks as a violent sob wrecks through him. "That's why I call you angel. Because you saved my life."

The horror stings up my spine like I've just been cracked with a fiery whip. My heart is beating so hard I think it might jump straight out of my ribcage.

"*You're the Silencer.*"

My voice is so soft, like the floor might cave in from the weight of the truth. He doesn't answer me, but his silence is answer enough. My vision goes black around the edges and I'm on the verge of passing out, but I *refuse* to let this man do any more damage to me or this city.

So I shove him away from me, smack him hard across his wet cheek and I run.

I run as fast as I can out of his room and through the mansion to the garage, ignoring the stares of the staff as I loudly sob. I reach the garage and pull a set of keys off the wall.

I don't even know what car I chose or remember leaving the estate.

The only thing I'm certain of is that I'm driving straight towards the police station and never looking back.

CHAPTER 21

THE ANGEL

I make it about halfway to the city before I have a complete mental breakdown and have to pull over. I cry into the steering wheel so hard that I get sick and have to open the door of the car to vomit on the side of the street.

I'm hyperventilating and I don't think I've ever felt so betrayed and used and horrified in my life.

Christian was the man I could see myself spending the rest of my life with. He was the man I wanted to marry and have babies and adopt Caroline with.

This whole time, he's been a fucking psychopath, and I was so blinded by the jewels and the charm and the love that I didn't see what was right in front of me.

My head is throbbing. I'm dizzy, exhausted, and all I want to do is hug my dad and tell him how right he was about this city.

Police first. I'll tell them everything I know regardless of if they believe me or not. Then I'll go home to Texas so I can be far, far away from this city and from Christian.

I'm a few blocks away from the police station sitting at a stoplight when the phone calls start. Christian's name pops up on my screen over and over and over again. I ignore it every time. I don't know why he thinks I would listen to anything he says right now.

The light turns green, and I cruise into the intersection. From the corner of my eye, I see two bright lights approaching me lightning fast, and I think I watch my life flash before my eyes before those lights slam into the side of my car so hard that I go skidding across the road, rolling over three times before coming to a stop upside down on the other side of the intersection.

For a while, all I can see is white, and there's a loud ringing in my ears. Soft plumes of smoke and dust from the airbags flutter around me. My hands tremble as I brace myself against the roof of the car and unbuckle my seatbelt, landing with a thud on broken glass.

One time, when I was in high school, my brother and I went four-wheeling on our parents' land. Travis was driving and he lost control of the ATV and we both went flying off. I fractured one of my ribs. It was the first time I had ever broken a bone, and it was one of the worst physical pains I've ever experienced, second only to appendicitis. The inability to breathe without pain was awful, and I had only fractured it—didn't even break it all the way. I was able to stand up and walk back to my parents' house, and we calmly drove to the urgent care.

I'm feeling that pain again, in my ribs, but it's at least five times worse. I crawl out of the mangled car on my stomach. I try to keep air in my lungs, but it feels impossible. My body is shaking. I've never been in a car accident before. Not a bad one. A tiny fender bender when I first got my license, but that's it. I've never had to drag myself out of an upside-down vehicle.

The car that hit me is still upright, the bright headlights shining down on me. Two people emerge from the SUV.

I hold up my hand to try and shield my eyes from the light. It's covered in blood from the glass digging into my skin.

This is really just my luck, isn't it? To get in a car accident on my way to the police station to tell them their resident billionaire is also the serial killer that's been terrorizing the city for the past two years.

I take a deep breath and lie on my back to try and relieve some of the ache in my body. If I can just relax until the police and ambulance get here, I can kill two birds with one stone.

They can patch up my injuries and then lock me in the psych ward for dating a serial killer.

I hear footsteps running towards me. I turn my head towards them to show that I'm not unconscious. Yet.

I wince in pain when one of them steps on my stomach to hold me down, and then another one kneels next to me and whispers in my ear.

"Hey, Eliza."

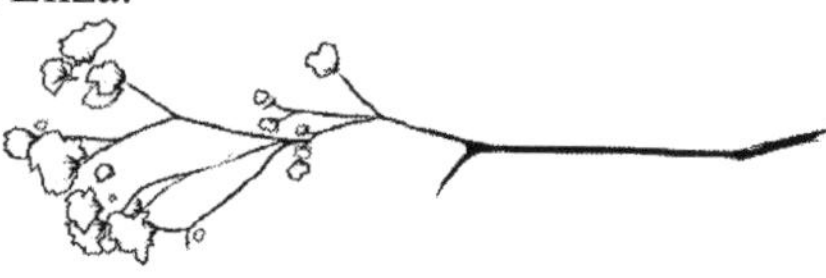

I wake up with a headache and my body is freezing. My eyes take a few seconds to adjust to the ambient yellow lighting of the room. I'm on a leather couch, my cheek stuck to the seat. I sit up slowly, my ribs throbbing as my blood begins to circulate fully through my body. I must have been asleep for hours.

No. Not asleep. *Unconscious.*

I gasp and I feel over my body for injuries, whining when I touch my torso. My arms itch from all the glass that sliced me up. I'm still shoeless and braless like I was when I left the Reeves Estate.

I look around for my phone and all the color drains from my face when I realize where I am.

I'm in Frank Valenti's private suite on the top floor of the Hellfire Lounge.

Fuck. This is bad. This is so fucking bad.

Frank's friends were probably murdered in this very room, judging by the burning scent of rubbing alcohol and bleach in the air.

Cold, thin, bony fingers wrap around my shoulders, and I stiffen.

"Don't panic," Frank whispers into my ear. "Don't you worry about a thing." I shiver against his touch, and his breath fans over my neck in a cruel, malicious way. Without looking at him, I take a deep breath to try to keep myself calm.

How the hell did I get here?

I was downtown when I got in that accident, miles away from the Hellfire Lounge. The police would have found me before Frank did.

Then I remember the voice right before I passed out.

Hey Eliza.

Neil. Neil was there. He crashed his car into me. But for what? So he could bring me to Frank Valenti? What do either of them want with me?

While Frank has his back turned, I do the only thing I can think to do—press the panic alarm on my wrist and hope Christian will come. I don't know why I didn't rip it off when I was running away from him, but I'm so glad I didn't.

Frank takes a seat next to me on the couch and pulls me closer to him by my shoulders. "Did you know that the poverty divide in Meridian City is bigger than anywhere else in the country?" he asks rhetorically. "In this city, you're either filthy rich, or dirt poor. And when pretty young women are dirt poor in this city, they come to me. Just like you did." He brushes some of my hair away from my neck. "My personal record for the selling price of one of my girls was two hundred thousand. She was a beautiful redhead with bright green eyes and plump lips." I tremble and tears fall out of my eyes, soaking the collar of my sweater. "Do you want to know what my new record is? *One million.* One million dollars. Cash. That's what Christian Reeves paid for you."

"If he bought me, why am I here?"

He chuckles to himself and runs his hands along my chest, gripping and squeezing my boobs. "Because you're a very valuable girl, Ellie. You see, you're worth so much more than money to me. Tell me, how good is that cunt of yours? Do you drip gold when you're wet? Not only is a billionaire dropping a million dollars to have you all to himself, but the Silencer is willing to cross me for you, too. What's so special about you?"

My stomach drops and I begin to tremble. "I'm not…I don't know what you're talking about."

Footsteps slowly tapping along the polished floors cut me off, and I turn my head slightly. My entire body goes numb when the man approaching us has a sinister grin to match his broken arm.

"Hey Eliza," Neil sniffs. His pupils are dilated. He's got a tiny dry drop of blood in his nose. He sits on the cushion next to me, both of them surrounding me like lions cornering a gazelle. Neil clicks his tongue against the roof of his mouth. He smiles at me, and I hate it, because it's disgusting. His smile is nothing short of creepy, and he only solidifies that thought by running his hand across my collar bone like he did at the restaurant. He runs his hands all over my body as he speaks, like he's restless and can't keep himself still. "Did you know that after I was fired from Reeves Enterprises, I bought a security company?" he asks, though he doesn't wait for me to acknowledge him before he continues speaking. "There's an ATM right next to the club. You know what that ATM camera is pointed at? An empty, unassuming alleyway."

Neil pulls out his phone, and my eyes go wide when he presses play on the screen. It's a video of the night the Silencer cornered me in the alley and asked me to help him with taking down Frank. The video cuts off while he's pressed against me.

Even though nothing happened that night, it certainly doesn't do me any favors of proving my innocence. Frank and Neil make me watch every second of that footage, staring down at me with satisfied smiles on their faces.

I swear I see Frank adjust himself in his pants.

He squeezes my neck lightly, causing my horrified gaze to meet his eyes. "Neil here came to me with a proposition to get a thorn out of my side. I give him drugs, he gives me you. That psychopath killed my friends because of you, Elena."

"And I got fired because of you," Neil interjects.

"So here's how this is going to work, beautiful," Frank says, grazing his cold, thin finger across my cheek. "Neil here is going to blackmail your rich boyfriend into giving him his life back, and I'm going to use you as a bargaining chip. That messy business with my friends can be left in the past. All I want is the Silencer's loyalty, and he can have you. I'd be invincible with him on my side. But I need something from you too, pretty girl, to ensure he knows who holds the leash. Since you're my favorite…I've decided I'm going to give you a chance to make this easy. I'm only going to ask you one time, Ellie. What's his name?"

I gulp again. Frank stares at me while I very clearly consider my answer. Tears prick in my eyes. I shake as I answer him, trying to keep my face blank. "I don't know who he is."

He laughs. "You know what, Ellie? I'm not even mad." He runs his hands up my bare thighs. "If you don't want to tell me yourself, we're going to enjoy fucking it out of you."

"Wait! Please!" I shout as his fingers graze my shorts, and he stills. "Please don't."

"Reconsidering?" Neil asks, rubbing my shoulders as if trying to get me to relax.

Frank's hands trail slowly up my shorts, giving me more than enough time to tell them what they want, but I know him, and I know that if he intends to rape me, he's going to do it. It doesn't matter if I tell him the name or not.

I screech loudly when Frank grabs me by the neck and forces me to the floor onto my stomach, my chest aching and sore from the accident. Neil holds me down by pressing a gun to my temple. Tears stream down my face as I writhe and scream as Frank pulls down my shorts and underwear and forces my hips up.

"I should have done this a long time ago, Ellie," he mutters, before pressing himself into me.

My body shuts down. I don't think I can force my limbs to move even if I had any fight left in me. I cry softly against the cold tile floor and stare out the large window, trying to distract myself by counting the windows on the building across the street.

I get to thirty-seven when Frank grunts loudly and empties himself inside of me.

And then Neil gets a turn. He sighs in pleasure and chuckles to himself. “I see why Reeves kept you around,” he whispers into my ear as he thrusts into me.

I go back to counting windows.

When I run out of windows, I count my tears instead.

CHAPTER 22

THE SILENCER

It's been over an hour since Elena left.

I can't blame her. I'd leave me too. I've never been worthy of love, and this proves it.

I didn't even have the strength to follow her, because I knew that no matter where she was going, there would be nothing I could do or say to get her to come back. Not anymore.

When we were in Mykonos, away from this cursed city, I'd never seen her so free of burdens, and for the first time in my life, I didn't let Meridian City and the filth of my past pollute our happiness.

I think she could have loved me if I could control *him*.

But I can't. He's the stronger one. The inmate runs the asylum and all I can do is sit and watch him destroy my life.

I've smoked two packs of cigarettes in the hour she's been gone. I tried calling her, but she wouldn't answer. What does it matter anyways? I don't even know what I would do if she answered.

Beg for forgiveness that I don't deserve?

I take a swig of whiskey, and another drag of the stick between my teeth. There's a knock on my bedroom door. I don't answer it. It goes quiet again, and then another knock comes. And then another, and then another, until they're practically pounding on my door. I stomp to it, unlock it, and swing it open, throwing my whiskey glass at the floor to shatter it in the space between us.

It's Gavin.

I seethe. "What the fuck do you want?"

The look on Gavin's face is unamused. Like how someone would look at a pathetic wet rat of a man drowning his sorrows at a bar. "One of your cars went missing. The black McLaren."

I shrug my shoulders. "So?"

"Ms. Young was seen leaving in it an hour ago."

"Yeah, Gavin, I know. She left me and took off with my car. What the fuck does it matter?"

He huffs. "The GPS tracker went offline downtown. Thought you'd want to know the MCPD were called out to work a major accident in the area involving a black McLaren."

That makes me pause and blow my smoke into his face before pushing past him. "Why the fuck are you just now telling me this?"

"I've been trying to call you about it for fifteen minutes." Gavin sighs as he trails me. "Police scanner's pretty vague but they haven't called any ambulances yet."

"Yeah? That's because they're saving them for you after I rip your spine out of your back for not telling me sooner. If there is so much as a hair missing from her head, you're dead."

I pull my phone out of my pocket to call Elena, but there's no answer.

Fuck.

Fuck, fuck, fuck.

Snuffing out my cigarette in one of the ashtrays in the foyer, I jog to the garage and grab the keys for an Escalade and pull up the location information Gavin texted to me. It's only a fifteen-minute drive.

I make it there in eight.

My hair falls onto my forehead in messy strands. My hands are tight around the steering wheel, the smooth leather warping and groaning under my grip.

No ambulances my ass. My McLaren is fucking *upside down.*

"Jesus Christ," I mutter to myself.

I lunge out of my car, barely remembering to put it in park before I'm running towards the car. An officer catches me by the arm and yanks me back.

"No civilians," he shouts into my face like I'm not two fucking feet from him. I shrug his grip off my and give him a snarl. I take another step towards the car, and he grabs me again. "You deaf or something? Back off."

"You must be new here," I tell him, glancing down at the fabric of his uniform. No decorations. No awards. No medals. Rookie. I pull my ID out of my wallet and flash it at him. His eyes go wide with realization. "That is my car, so get your hands off me."

He lets me go, and I hear him mutter a quiet '*prick*' under his breath. I get closer to my McLaren, three officers huddled around it talking amongst themselves. Thankfully, one of them recognizes me.

"Mr. Reeves," he greets.

"Where did you take them?"

"What?"

Is he fucking serious right now?

I enunciate each word carefully. "The *occupants*. Which hospital did you take them to? Elena Young was driving, where is she?"

He furrows his brow and pulls out a notepad from his pocket. "Elena…Young, you say? Do you know her middle name or date of birth?"

"Elena Louise Young, February 11, 1990. *Where. Is. She*?" I ask again, my patience thinner than a razor.

"Sir, there were no occupants when we got here."

"What?"

"The accident was called in by someone going through the intersection, and when we got here, there were no occupants in either car."

"What the fuck do you mean, *there were no occupants*? She didn't just vanish into thin air!" I growl and let out a roar of frustration. "Fucking useless pigs."

"I'm going to need you to step away now, Mr. Reeves," the cop says, glaring at me angrily.

That's when I hear it. Elena's panic alarm.

The horrible, blood-curdling, high-pitched ringing that emanates from my cell phone. My body goes rigid, and my blood runs completely cold. I pull out my phone and with trembling hands, I watch a red dot blink rapidly on the screen at the precise location of the Hellfire Lounge.

"Fuck!"

I take off in a sprint towards my car and hop in, my wheels screeching harshly against the asphalt as I drive. *This is bad. This is fucking bad.*

After I told her the truth, Elena left my house with the intention of never seeing me again. I know that in my bones. The way she looked at me felt like my heart had been ripped out of my chest.

If she pressed her panic alarm after that, she is in danger. Not just *scared*, but actual, mortal *danger*. '*I'm calling the one person on this earth that I hate for help*' kind of danger.

She's calling me for help because she thinks I'm the only one who can save her.

I will not let her down.

The first thing I do when I get home is rush into my basement. The official property records indicate that my mansion doesn't have a basement. It wasn't easy—or cheap—to forge the documentation that I had it sealed up. The entrance is now hidden behind a fake bookcase, spy movie style, in the second-floor library. The staircase is thin and steep, and my knees ache painfully when I jump down one story at a time until I reach the bottom.

My basement is where I keep all my gear. Guns, ammo, grenades, adrenaline, knives. Anything and everything I could possibly need to do what I do. I change and strap everything I can to my body and inject myself with a shot of electrolytes and chug a bottle of water to fight the alcohol in my veins. I need a clear head for this.

I check Elena's tracker again. She's still in the Hellfire Lounge, which is a small relief. It means at the very least, she's still on the island.

In an abundance of caution, I call 911 and make a fake report from a burner phone that I've placed bombs along the bridges leading to and from the island, so that they're forced to shut them down to investigate. I'm not above actually blowing one up later if I have to.

I'm coming for her, and nothing will fucking stop me.

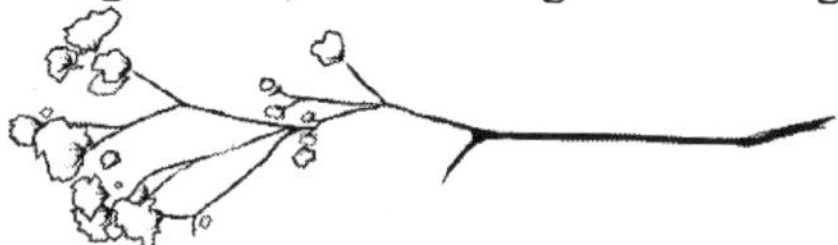

I bring so much fury with me to that fucking club that I can hardly think straight. The only thing bouncing around in my mind is her name, and what I'm going to do to the motherfuckers that dared to try and take her from me.

Elena. Elena. Elena.

My brain chants her name like she'll appear in front of me if I say it enough times.

I slice open the throat of the bouncer at the door and stomp through the club until I reach the main dance floor, hot air leaving my nose with each exhale like a dragon. Once I'm in the direct center of the club, I rest my M4 in the crook of my arm, point it towards the rafters, and spray a dozen bullets into the ceiling.

Sparks erupt from the lights above me and screams fill the club before the music cuts off and the room goes silent.

"Somebody take me to Frank Valenti. *Right. Now*," I yell into the air. "*Now*! Or I'm going to kill every single person in this fucking room!"

Three armed bouncers come running down the walkway on the other side of the room. They have pistols, and I have a rifle. The three of them go down in nine easy shots.

Two to the chest, one to the head.

Two to the chest, one to the head.

Two to the chest, one to the head.

"Hey!"

A woman's voice behind me has me spinning and pointing my gun at her head. It's Kate. I take three deep breaths, my eyes wild as I stare her down. She has her hands up in surrender.

"Where is he?" I growl, my voice dripping in venom—laced with adrenaline and fear and anger. "*God fucking damn it*, tell me now or I'll blow your head off!"

"He's downstairs!" Kate tells me, her voice timid under the threat of the barrel shoved in her face. She points to a corridor diagonal to me. "The elevator is over there. Here." She hands me a key card. "I stole it off the bouncer that guards the door. It should unlock the VIP room. That's where Valenti is." I step around her and she grabs my arm, and I come dangerously close to pulling that trigger. "Hey! They took my friend down there. Her name's Elena. She's got long brown hair and she looked hurt. Please, please, *please* get her out of there."

They. She said *they* took her down there. "Was there someone else with Valenti?"

She nods. "Yes. Yes—a bald man. With a broken arm."

Neil. My chest ripples with unfiltered rage. "I'll get her out. I'll fucking get her out," I growl, though I think I'm telling that to myself more than Kate.

Valenti's goons have shit aim and most of them have never been in a shoot-out before. I cut down all of them, leaving a trail of bloody carnage in my path as I fight my way to that elevator.

As it descends, I reload my rifle. My blood is thrumming in my ears, and my head is still chanting Elena's name.

I'm coming, angel. Just hold on a little longer.

When the door opens, I'm almost knocked back by the change in atmosphere. This place reeks of sex, cigars, and liquor. The music is a smooth jazz, and the lights are dimmed. There's a stage on the far end of the room, bright panels of light making up the floor behind a thick glass pane.

Bidding will begin soon.

That's what a bright red neon sign says on the other side of the room.

In the center of the stage, curled up in the fetal position, is my perfect little angel. She's completely naked.

I do the same thing I did upstairs, shoot into the ceiling to get the attention of all the men sitting in plush leather chairs scattered around the room. Most of them dive for cover, while others try to run. There's not many. Six or so.

All of them get a bullet in their brains, and I fucking relish in watching them bleed. When they're all dead, I throw my gun over my shoulder by the sling and run to the front of the room, up onto the stage, and I fall to my knees in front of Elena, that glass the only thing separating us.

She's so dissociated that she doesn't even realize I'm here.

"Elena," I say as I knock on the glass. It earns me no reaction. I lie with my masked cheek flat against the floor to try and get level with her eyes and line myself up with her blank stare. I put my hand against the glass. "Angel, come on, look up." I pound my fist against the glass. "Elena look at me!" I shout, and her eyes finally snap to me. Her face twists into a look so full of hopelessness that it makes my own chest feel like it's being ripped open. Big tears fall out of her eyes as she reaches for the glass, the very edges of her fingertips grazing the barrier between us. I shake my head in response. "Don't cry, baby. I'm going to get you out. I'll fucking get you out of there." I use my hands to make a gesture for her to cover her face, so that when I break this glass separating us, none will get into her eyes. I don't humor myself trying to ask her to move when she's so clearly hanging on to her mental stability by a goddamn thread.

I step back a few feet and point my gun at the glass, sending several bullets in rapid succession into the thick panes. The glass webs slightly where the bullets collided with it, but otherwise, it's still holding up. I shoot again. And again. And again, until my mag runs out of bullets on my M4. I pull out my pistol next, emptying it into the glass too.

It's fucking bulletproof.

My chest heaves with worry when I kneel back down to meet Elena's eyes. "Baby, how did you get in there? Show me." I put my hand flat against the glass again to attempt a comforting gesture.

That's when I hear Valenti laugh through the speakers, and he emerges from a velvet curtain behind Elena. He's got his hands in his pockets as he takes slow steps towards her, and I know if looks could kill, Valenti would be six feet under. "Well if it isn't the man of honor." He nudges Elena with his dirty shoe until she's lying flat on her stomach. She's so limp and lifeless. If I couldn't see the rise and fall of her bare chest, I might think she was dead. "Glad you could join us."

"You'll let her go, and you will do it now."

Valenti cocks his head to the side as if he's considering it, and then he flashes me a poisonous smile. "No, I don't think I will. I got a question for you though, Silencer. Is her mouth as good as her cunt? She's got a few holes I haven't tested yet."

My heart skips, and if I was angry before, the fury now coursing through my veins will burn down the world. "Don't you fucking touch her again." I bang my fist on the glass. "Let her go now, asshole, or I'm burning this place to the ground with you in it!"

Valenti laughs. "How does it feel to know you can't get to me, while I can touch her all I want?"

Valenti bends down and begins to unbutton his pants. I bang on the glass with my fist, over and over again. I reload my pistol and shoot it. Throw a chair at it. Pull an emergency axe off the wall and began beating at the stupid glass that *won't fucking break*. It won't break and Elena's in there with him, her hips lifted into the air as he fucking rapes her in front of me.

"Stop!" I scream, ready to resort to begging if that's what it takes. "What the fuck do you want? I'll give you fucking anything! Please!"

Valenti grabs Elena by her hair and lifts her up, still inside her with her back pressed to his chest. The look on her face is devastating. Fractured. Hopeless. "Here's what I want," he says, loud enough for both of us to hear, then leans down and whispers something into her ear that I can't make out. She shakes her head as he pushes her face down onto the floor again as he continues to thrust himself inside her.

"Whatever he wants, just give it to him, angel. I'll fix it. I promise." I press my hand flat against the glass again. lining myself up with her defeated face—the glass now cracked but still a barrier between us.

Fuck. What do I do? What do I do? What the hell does he want, and how do I give it to him?

I pound my fist on the floor in frustration to desperately try and get her to listen to me. "Fuck! Elena, please!" Tears drip onto the bright white floors from both of our eyes. I can't take mine off her terrified face as she shakes her head again. My hands shoot up to grip at the hair on the side of my scalp.

I grab that axe again and start wailing on that fucking glass over and over and over again, until it's so broken that I can barely see through it. "Fuck! What the hell do you want, asshole? Tell me and it's yours. Do you hear me? I will do *anything*."

Valenti pauses his assault on Elena just long enough to meet my eyes and give me a wretched smile, and then presses himself into her three more times before he finishes inside her. He pulls himself out and tucks himself back into his pants and rolls Elena onto her back. Her eyes are open, but her body is limp. I think she's gone into total shock at this point.

Valenti slaps her, and I pull out another gun to empty it into the glass, as if it will do any good. He punches her then, so hard she coughs out blood, and then he stands up and kicks her in the stomach. She's in the fetal position again, crying out in pain, blood dripping out of her mouth forming a puddle on the floor.

It's then that Neil emerges from behind the curtain, though instead of the suave, careless look Valenti has on his face, he looks enamored by me.

"Never thought I'd see the Meridian City Silencer up close." Neil snorts. "Huh. The police sketches never quite capture the exact green of your eyes. What do you think Christian Reeves will pay to get his bitch back?" he asks, and it takes every ounce of self-control I have in my body not to respond. Neil laughs. "Or do you think he'll even want her back?" He presses down on her stomach with his foot, causing her to wince and fold over herself. "I never understood why he was into her. I always thought it was because of her pussy, but I wasn't sure until I tested it myself." He kneels down next to her and then backhands her with his cast, and then he looks at me again. "Do you and Reeves have joint custody of her? You get her on weekends, he gets her during business hours?"

I shoot another round into the glass at his head, knowing full and well it won't do anything. He jumps back and smiles with relief when the bullet gets stopped by the glass, perfectly lined up with his forehead. Neil unzips his pants and pulls them down, uncoordinated with his broken arm.

"*Don't you fucking dare*. Don't. Fucking. Touch. Her."

"What are you going to do about it?" Neil snarls, pulling his puny dick out of his pants and pumping it a few times. I can't let this happen to her again. I won't be able to live with myself. I frantically look around the room, trying to find anything to help me break the glass. I can't find anything. Nothing but a dozen dead men scattered around the room and an axe held tightly in my fist. My breath turns panicked as Neil lines himself up with Elena's entrance.

I reach into my utility belt and pull out a small vial of strange clear liquid. I bought it on the dark web, and it's said to push your body to its limits. I don't know what it's made of. It could be straight meth for all I know, but I don't care. I'm fucking desperate. I plunge the needle roughly into the meat of my bicep and press down to release the contents into my veins.

It burns, and then I feel my heart begin to race. My vision tunnels and my body begins to tremble. The axe suddenly feels featherlight in my hands and I start swinging it against the glass again. At first, it does nothing, merely bounces off the surface with a loud thud—but as my body grows accustomed to the mystery substance each strike of the axe makes the cracks grow wider and deeper. I start grunting and roaring like a wild beast to try and push out every last drop of strength in my body.

I swing again, and nearly faceplant onto the stage when the glass shatters, covering Elena in dozens of cuts. A thick shard implants itself into the meat of her thigh and she barely flinches. Valenti breaks out into a sprint, disappearing behind the velvet drapes. Neil cowers backwards, his hand over his dick as he scoots back and back as I stalk towards him like a predator that's finally cornered its prey. I shoot him in both his kneecaps, and he writhes against the floor, screaming out in pain and crying for help.

"Please!" Neil begs as I take his arm and handcuff him to the decorative brass pipe along the edges of the stage. "I—I—I have a wife and kids, man. I'm sorry!"

"I don't give a fuck! Now shut your goddamn mouth or I'll kill them too."

He bites his lips to keep silent as I quickly kneel in front of Elena, my hands hovering above her in caution. She's trembling, rocking herself back and forth in the fetal position. She's pressing her head into the fluorescent white tiles beneath her. Her eyes are shut tight, tears leaking from them and dripping off her nose and cheek to the floor. With my own trembling fingers, I slowly push a strand of hair out of her face.

"*Angel*," I coo softly. Her bottom lip trembles and then a guttural sob escapes her throat, so extreme that it wrecks through her body, and she chokes on her own broken spirit. "Baby, it's over."

"Hey."

A feminine voice from behind me has me spinning on my heels and aiming a pistol at her head. "God damn it," I grunt at Kate. "I almost blew your brains out."

I notice she's holding some clothes in her arms, and she very cautiously peeks over my shoulder to look at Elena. Her eyes flicker back to me, like she's waiting for my permission, and I give her a subtle nod. She tip-toes around me like she's still afraid I'll shoot her. She crawls onto the stage and kneels next to Elena's naked body.

"Hey, pipsqueak," she murmurs, carefully squeezing Elena's scratched up and lightly bleeding hand. "Don't go all looney on me, you'll get through this."

Elena slowly opens her eyes, bloodshot and glassy with tears still profusely leaking from them. She makes eye contact with me, but there's no emotion in her honey brown irises.

When Elena is happy, or laughing, those subtle gold flecks in her eyes sparkle brightly even in the dimmest of light. When she's angry or upset, those flecks turn almost orange to match the fire raging in them.

Right now, Elena doesn't have any gold in her eyes at all. They're so lifeless. Emotionless. The only sign of life in her at all is the uneven rise and fall of her chest as she cries blankly in my direction. Kate and I both share a look, and silently agree that she's better suited to dress Elena, even though it feels like a fucking dagger in my chest to let someone else take care of her.

"I'm going to put some clothes on you now," Kate announces. "Shirt first."

I watch carefully as Kate puts the shirt and sweatpants on Elena, as gentle as someone would dress a newborn baby. Elena doesn't react, and I'm certain that she's so dissociated that she doesn't even realize what's happening.

Thank God Kate seems to have a soft heart for her friend, because after a lot of careful touches and tender words, she manages to convince Elena to sit up. Kate pats away some broken glass that's caught in Elena's hair. She gives her friend an encouraging smile and then takes a step back as if to say, '*all yours*'.

I shake my head. "You need to take her to the hospital. Valenti got away, and I have to deal with that fucker before I leave." I roughly point at Neil, who whimpers when he catches my fiery stare. "I can't be seen with her. Please do this for me. For her," I beg, even clasping my fingers together as if I'm praying to her. "I'll pay you—"

"You don't have to pay me. Not for this."

I swallow the lump in my throat, and nod, walking around her towards Neil, but she digs her fingers roughly into my arms. It causes me to throw my head over my shoulder, silently asking what she wants.

She lets me go and saunters over to Neil, and then harshly stomps on his dick with the pointy heel of her stiletto. She huffs and then turns around as if it didn't happen.

I wait patiently until Kate and Elena are in the elevator before my heavy boots reverberate against the floor with each step towards him. His breath quickens. If I didn't have my mask on, he'd be able to see the absolutely malevolent scowl painted across my face.

I kneel next to him, taking a deep breath before pulling out one of my pistols and reloading it. He cowers away from me, but he can't get very far. I grab him by the top of his head because he has no hair to rip out, and I tilt it back slightly before sticking the pistol in his mouth. Sweat drips down from my brow into my eyes as he begins to gag at the intrusion.

"Oh? What's that? You don't like having something forcefully shoved into your body?" He shakes his head and whines, pulling a sadistic chuckle from my chest. "There are not enough words in the English language to describe the shit I'm going to do to you."

He cowers away from me further with each passing moment as I describe in *grueling* detail each heinous method of torture I'll inflict on him. He stays quiet through my entire monologue, save for his pathetic whimpers.

"Do you believe in God?" I ask. He nods, and I laugh. "Look at me. *Look at me*. I'm your God now. Do you want to know why? Because I'm the only motherfucker on this planet that can show you mercy. Start praying. You'll need it."

I take the pistol out of his mouth and quickly replace it with a wide, serrated hunting knife. I watch as blood pools in the corners of his mouth as I slowly press it into his lips. He tries to push me away with his casted arm.

"What did I tell you the last time you saw me, Neil?" He stays quiet, and I can see it in his eyes that he has no idea what I'm talking about. I remove the knife from his mouth and press the tip of the blade over his dick. "I told you that if you ever touched her again, I would kill you."

His eyes blow wide with horror and realization. Before he has a chance to say anything, I snatch his tongue out from his mouth and cleanly slice it off with the knife, flicking the severed piece of muscle to the side and watching as blood oozes down his chin.

"This is for Elena," I declare, before slapping a strip of red duct tape over his mouth.

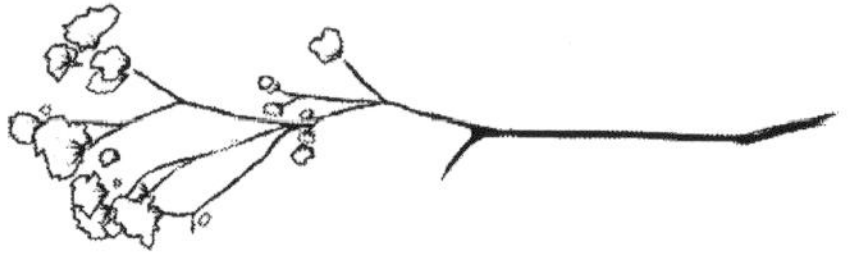

Red, white and blue flashing lights strobe against the skinny buildings lining the street below. I count seven police cars. From my position on the roof, I can see it all clearly. The scent of gasoline clings to me as I watch the detectives look up at the carnage hanging over their heads.

It's my most brutal kill yet. My body still vibrates from the euphoria of watching Neil Hayden take his last breath, my fingers wrapped around his throat. I'm still dripping in his blood. I'm not sure he has any left in his body.

I look over him in my scope.

His stiff body is hanging upside down by his ankles from the rooftop of the Hellfire Lounge. It's swaying in the cool November breeze like a fucked-up pendulum.

He's completely naked, exposing his mutilated body to the elements and the world. I removed his dick. It's shoved into his asshole. That was the first thing I did to him. Everything that followed was more sickening than the previous. There's a big gash along his belly where I sliced him open, his insides dangling out of him. I wanted to tie a noose around his neck by his own entrails, but I didn't think it would hold, so I just used a rope. He's still got that tape around his mouth. I take a sick pleasure in claiming my kills like that, especially this one.

This kill was personal, and I think my brutality shows it. I've killed people for Elena before, but killing Neil Hayden wasn't just for her, it was for me. It was revenge.

I did not make it a quick or easy death. He deserved to suffer. I took one look at Elena and knew that he and Valenti gang raped her, probably multiple times, before I even arrived at the Lounge, and then again when I got there while they looked me dead in the eye and taunted me, knowing I was powerless to stop it.

I searched every inch of that goddamn club and found Valenti nowhere. If he happens to be hiding in there, he'll be burned to a crisp momentarily, but I think he got away. I'll deal with him later, but not without first leaving a message for him.

I take a deep breath and pull a mag of tracer rounds and load them into my M4. I aim right at Neil's bald fucking head, shooting through his forehead and setting his gasoline-covered corpse alight.

Commotion breaks out on the street. The officers take cover and start looking for me.

The only downside to tracer rounds is that they're not exactly incognito. But then again, neither is an M4. My next target is the gas can I left poised neatly at the door of the Lounge, and I shoot it, igniting the cannister and the trail of gasoline I left throughout every square inch of the building. The fire spreads quickly; the liquor spilled all over the floors makes for wonderful fuel. It's not long before the entire building is engulfed in flames.

"There! He's up there!" I hear one of the cops shout, and then a barrage of bullets start hitting the brick of the rooftop ledge. I hear them start yelling commands about surrounding the building, but by the time they think they've cornered me on the rooftop, I'm long gone.

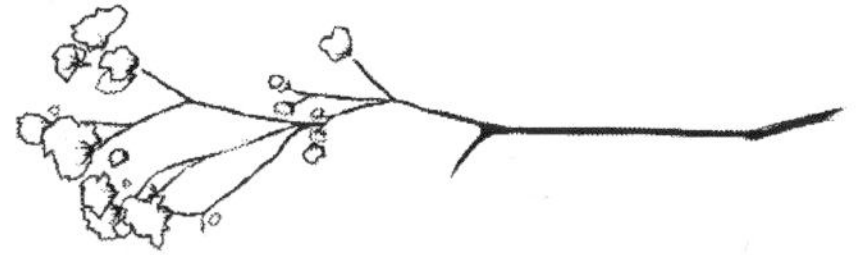

"I'm looking for Elena Young. February 11, 1990," I snap at the staff member working at the reception desk at the hospital. I didn't mean to sound so harsh, but I'm fucking exhausted, and my patience is thin. I've spent enough time away from her. Between killing Neil Hayden, my show outside of the Lounge, and then having to race home and wash off all the blood, I'm wound up tight. The woman looks up at me, and my two security guards standing behind me. I brought them along to station them outside of Elena's hospital room. She quickly types on her computer. "She's in the ER, sir."

The ER? What the fuck? She's been here for a couple hours, why is she still in the fucking ER?

I get my answer when I walk into said ER, to find doctors and nurses and security guards crowding triage room one.

And that scream.

I could recognize that fucking scream anywhere. That terrified voice that saved my life the night we met. Only this time, she's not hopelessly crying out for help, praying someone will come to her rescue.

She's crying for *me*. I hear her shouting my name over and over and over again. My heart begins to beat erratically against my ribcage as I harshly bodycheck my way through the crowd of staff members, breaking through the sea of people, only to have my heart shatter when I get a glimpse at her.

She's cowering in the very corner of the room, her IV ripped out of her arm, her hair wild and her face haunted. She's got a needle in her hand, holding it out in front of her like a knife. Kate's standing to my right, her back pressed against the wall. Our gazes collide and there's a moment where a spark of exposition graces her features. I don't get it at first, but then I catch a glimpse of myself in the small mirror directly to her left.

In my rush to get here, I've forgotten to take out the colored contacts.

Elena's eyes meet mine and the world stands still for a moment before her stance relaxes and her arms go to her side. The sound that escapes her throat is somewhere between a sob, a whimper, and a sigh of relief. She drops the needle and jumps into my arms, and I catch her easily, her legs wrapping around my waist. She's clutching onto me like her life depends on it as she shatters in my arms. Her arms tighten around me as she sobs loudly into my neck. Her violent tremors only make me hold her tighter.

My throat and eyes burn as the raw emotion crashes over us both, a hurricane of sorrow brutally pounding against the broken pieces of our souls.

I hear whispers behind me, and then a single footstep. I turn around so fast the nurse is nearly knocked over from the wind it produces. Pure rage burns in my eyes when I spot a syringe and needle in her hands. A sedative, most likely.

"Don't fucking touch her," I growl.

"Sir—"

"I said don't touch her!" I yell, like a rabid animal waiting to pounce. "She's fucking *scared*. Give her a goddamn minute."

Slowly, the staff members filter out. Kate is the last to leave, quietly shutting the door behind her.

I squeeze Elena tightly against my body, and I can feel a new wave of tears soaking through the collar of my shirt. "They're gone, baby. It's okay. I'm here now," I coo, trying to make myself sound calm and collected on the outside when I have a million other emotions coursing through my veins. Fear. Anger. Relief. *Guilt*.

"Look at me," I say quietly, and after a long moment, she pulls her head back slightly so that her red-rimmed eyes meet mine. Tears and snot and dried blood run down her face. "You were so brave, and I'm so fucking proud of you. *So. Fucking. Proud.*"

I have to know what Valenti wanted from her, the consequences so severe that she'd allow herself to be raped repeatedly rather than give it to him. I can't imagine there's anything worth that kind of torment.

I take a deep breath. "Angel, tell me what they wanted from you," I beg.

"Your name."

My brain short circuits. "What?" I ask, a dumbfounded look in my eyes because I'm almost certain I misheard her. "My name?" She hesitantly nods. My mouth falls open, breath caught in my throat, and my entire resolve disintegrates. I don't know if I should be grateful or fucking horrified that she would do that for me.

This time, I'm the one to find comfort in her neck. Her rich brown hair soaks up the stray tears that leak from my eyes. "Why wouldn't you just tell them, Elena? Why would you let them do that to you?"

"They would have done it anyways," she whispers, her voice hoarse from the emotional exhaustion. I let out a defeated sigh and look at her, *really* look at her for the first time to take in the state she's in. Her cheek is bruised. Splotched and red and swelling. She has a split lip and broken blood vessels in her left eye. There's a knot the size of Alaska on the back of her head. The large gash on her thigh is dripping blood down her leg, soaking into my pants. She's wheezing. She's sickly pale.

I carefully set Elena down on the bed, her eyes going into panic mode. She grips the front of my shirt so tightly in her small fists that she might tear a hole through the fabric. "Don't leave me!"

I use my now free hands to cup her cheeks and press my forehead to hers. "Angel, I swear on my fucking life, I am *never* letting you out of my sight again.

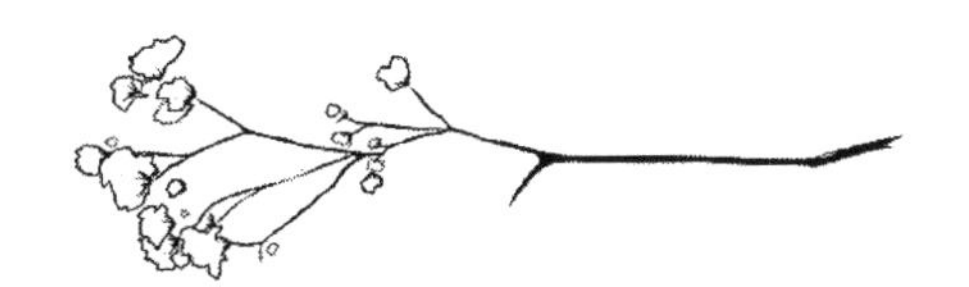

PART II

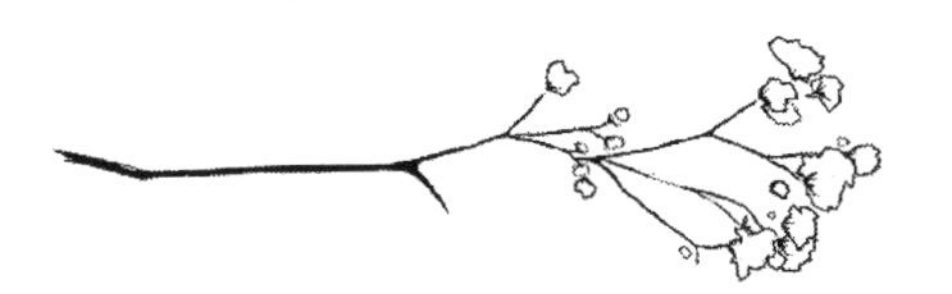

CHAPTER 23

THE EXECUTIONER

I should have burnt this city to the ground when I had the chance.

CHAPTER 24

THE ANGEL

I don't remember falling asleep, but when I wake up, the hum of a fluorescent light buzzes through my ears. It's so bright, and I wonder if that's what it looks like when you die. Everyone always talks about a light, but I'm sure their versions are much warmer and more welcoming than the harsh white above me.

My entire body feels like it's been run over. My head is in agony, the throbbing nearly unbearable and that light sends a sharp pain to my brain right under my eyeballs. I squeeze my eyes shut and rub them. An uncomfortable pressure makes itself known in the crook of my left arm. I look down. It's an IV.

I hate IV's. I know that there's not actually a needle still inside me, but whenever I see one, that's all I can think about. A tiny needle burrowing into my delicate veins with every small movement. I set my arm down and a small wave of lightheadedness washes over me, settling me back down into the bed.

I let out a shaky breath and then I jolt upright.

IV. I have an IV in my arm, which means I'm in a hospital.

I've got one of those paper-thin gowns covering my body, and a bright purple blanket draped over me. A soft pillow is poised where I was resting my head. Definitely not hospital issue.

To my right, there's a plastic chair with a leather jacket draped over the back. I lean over, my ribs aching painfully when I do, and I grab the garment. I pull it to my nose and inhale.

Christian.

A small dose of comfort settles into my heart, knowing that he's here, somewhere. I lie back down, holding the jacket close to my chest as if it were a stuffed animal, and close my eyes.

My body goes completely stiff when I hear hushed voices outside the door and pull that jacket over my head like it's a shield. I shake and tremble in my bed, hoping that if I try hard enough, I'll gain the power of invisibility. Soft footsteps approach me, and I whimper quietly under the cover, tears already welling up in my eyes.

"Ms. Young?" A soft-spoken voice asks, but I don't move for a long minute. I peek out from under the jacket. It's a woman. A tall, regal, dark-skinned woman. I meet her eyes and she gives me a sympathetic smile. "I'm Dr. Anette Portman." She takes a hesitant step forward, but only to check the bags hanging on a hook next to my bed that are attached to my IV. "Are you in any pain, Ms. Young?"

I blink at her like she's just spoken a foreign language. My heart thuds in my chest, and each breath I take is laborious and yes, painful.

"It hurts to breathe," I whisper, looking down as if it's something to be ashamed of.

Dr. Portman nods. "That's very common with broken ribs, and you have three. Luckily, they seem to be intact. No splinters. You should heal just fine. I will approve a small increase in your dosage of painkillers. Anything else?"

I take a long moment to think about it. "I have a headache."

"Also not surprising. You have a concussion. The headache will fade as long as you take care of yourself. You also came in with a large shard of glass in your leg, but we were able to remove it and stitch you up. That should heal relatively quickly and have minimal scarring."

I blink at her again. "I don't care about that."

She gives me a knowing look and takes a seat in the rolling stool next to my bed. "I'm very sorry for what you went through. It was horrific, and it is completely normal for you to feel scared, angry, worried."

She spends the next few minutes detailing STD tests, telling me that I'm clean so far, but I should do a follow-up visit in a few weeks to double check.

"Did…did you call my parents?"

"Yes, ma'am. They assured us they would be on their way as soon as possible."

My heart squeezes, and I want to ask her how much my parents know about what happened to me, so that I can prepare myself for the way they'll look at me when they get here. I already know my father will be on the warpath, and I can feel my mother crying on the other side of the country. It's going to be so hard to face them, to look into their eyes and relive that experience all over again.

Dr. Portman leaves the room, and as soon as the door shuts behind her, I let the tears fall. Clutching Christian's jacket close to my chest and letting the lining soak up my sorrow, I allow myself to be weak. I shake and my chest wheezes as I struggle to take steady breaths. It feels like my entire world has come crashing down around me, and I'm stuck in the rubble with no way to climb out. It feels like the worst kind of prison I could have been sentenced to.

Trapped in my own mind.

My punishment, being forced to relive my rape over and over again.

I hear another set of footsteps, and I'm suddenly overwhelmed with rage. Without looking, I grab the spare pillow from under my head and throw it in the direction of the door with a frustrated snarl through my gritted teeth.

"Get out!" I shout, my vision blinded by my own tears.

"I'm not going anywhere, angel."

I go stiff and wipe my eyes as I stare at Christian, lingering in the doorway. He stares back like it's the first time he's ever seen me. My chest tightens painfully. "Where have you been?" I spit out, suddenly furious that he wasn't here when I woke up. He doesn't answer me, moving to come sit in the chair next to me where his jacket was draped. He reaches for my hand, and I snatch it away so fast that the room turns ice cold with bitter tension.

Christian holds his hands up in surrender and shakes a small cup in his right hand. "I just went downstairs to the cafeteria for some coffee." A wave of sadness flickers across his gaze, gone as quick as it came before his mouth falls into a straight line and his eyes soften.

I huff. My heart is unsatisfied with the answer at first, but then I get a look at him. The delicate skin under his eyes is a dark purple. His features look sunken in, and he's so pale. One shade lighter and I'd be able to see right through him. He looks frail. Fragile. Like the smallest bit of wind will knock him over. I've never seen him without a clean-shaven face, but he's got the beginnings of a beard and his hair has seen better days.

He doesn't have to say anything for me to understand. He's been so worried about me that he hasn't been taking care of himself.

"I'm sorry," I whisper. Christian lightly rests his right arm and hand on the bed next to me. An offer to hold my hand if I choose to take it.

I don't.

"You have *nothing* to be sorry for. How are you feeling?" he asks, and I reply with the same things I told Dr. Portman. I can tell by the constant twitch of his fingers that it's a considerable effort to not reach for me and comfort me with his touch. His embrace.

The thing is, there's nothing I want more right now, but the thought feels like a million insects crawling under my skin. It makes me itchy. It makes me restless and has me gazing towards the door every few seconds to make sure the path is clear in case I need to run.

I wonder if he'll still chase me now that I'm broken and beaten. Now that I'm sliced open and had two other men forcefully shove their release inside me. I shudder at the memory of the pain and burning sensation that came along with the violation, and the utter emptiness I felt the first time Frank and Neil raped me, and then again downstairs when Christian got there, and he had to watch.

Goosebumps of anxiety break out over my body. "They got away, didn't they?" I ask, too afraid to find the answer in his eyes.

"Valenti did," he admits, and his voice breaks, turning into a whisper at the shame of it. I cringe as if I'm trapped in the room with that foul man again, letting out a shaky breath. "Elena, I swear on my fucking life I will hunt him to the ends of the earth. I will find him and I will make him suffer until even the devil himself fears me."

"He could come back."

"No, baby," Christian coos. "I promise, you're safe now. Neil is dead, and Valenti will be soon."

I blink at him, something dark and unsettling swirling in my gut. "Did…did he suffer?"

Christian's jaw tightens and I just know even thinking about it makes him feel unhinged and feral. He nods. "Yes. I made him suffer. Then I lit his corpse on fire so he wouldn't know peace, even in death."

"Good," I whisper, and something sparkles in his eyes, but before I have a chance to consider what it is, arguing can be heard outside of my hospital room door. I immediately retreat under the blankets, and Christian stands, wrapping his fingers around the pistol under his shirt. I hear something that sounds like *'get your hands off me'*. More commotion rustles outside the door, and then it's being shoved open, two men grabbing the arms of my—

"Dad!" I gasp, a sob wrecking through me when our eyes meet. "Daddy," I cry, scrambling out of the bed trying to meet him halfway, but I'm tangled in the sheets, and he makes it to me first, wrapping me in the tightest embrace he can manage. We sob into each other's necks, and I think my father might actually be more of a wreck than I am. I've never felt so much relief in my life as he holds me, and I'm clutching onto him like it's the last thing I'll ever do.

My dad pulls back a few inches, his face broken and his eyes bright red. "It's okay, sweetheart. It's okay. I'm here now."

His comfort only serves to break me down further. I don't know how long we stay hugging each other like that, but it's long enough that my back starts to ache. My head is in the crook of my father's neck, and it feels like when he used to hold me as a child when I would have a nightmare.

"Am I too old to have you chase away the monsters under my bed?" I whisper. I feel my dad shudder and shake his head.

"No, Ellie. You're never too old for that," he promises, and then pulls away again to get a good look at me, and that's when his demeanor turns dangerous. I can tell he has a lot to say, probably starting with *'tell me who did this so I can ram my shotgun up their asshole'*.

As predictable as ever, the first thing my father does when he breaks out of my embrace is grab the chart hanging on the end of my hospital bed. That's when I realize my mom's not here.

"Your mother's on her way. I was in New York for business and had a friend drive me here," he tells me as he reads over my chart, sensing my confusion.

A younger doctor walks in, holding a small plastic cup with a single pill in it. "Ms. Young, Dr. Portman asked me to give this to you. It's a Plan B."

My gaze shifts awkwardly between Christian and my father before quickly snatching the cup and swallowing the pill dry. The doctor turns to leave, but my father stops him by whistling. "Son, bring me a suture kit with the smallest thread you have available, and some local anesthetic."

"Excuse me?" The young man asks, raising an eyebrow like my father has lost his mind. "Sir, I'm sorry but—"

"My name is Elliot Thomas Young. I am recognized by the American Board of Cosmetic Surgery and have been practicing medicine for as long as you've been alive. Now, bring me the sutures."

The doctor looks stunned, and then the realization hits him like lightning. His face lights up with excitement. "Dr. Young, what an honor! Wow, this is amazing," he blabs out, rising up on his toes and then back down. "Look, I'd love to help you out, but I really don't want to lose my job here."

"If you get fired, let me know and I'll get you a job at any hospital in the country with a single phone call. Deal?"

I scoff lightly at the way the doctor darts out of the room, and my dad turns back to me with a triumphant grin.

"What do you need sutures for?" I ask as he stands up to thoroughly wash his hands at the small sink in the room. He puts on a pair of gloves just as the doctor walks back in to hand him the suture kit.

"Your chart says you have a large laceration on your left thigh. I'm making sure these quack doctors aren't condemning you to having a scar the size of the San Andreas fault for the rest of your life."

I gulp, trying to think about anything else. He's skinnier than the last time I saw him. His hair has thinned out a lot, but he's still got that silver fox thing going on that my mother goes nuts for.

As my dad focuses on preparing the sutures, I clear my throat quietly. "Um…dad? This is Christian."

My dad hardly looks up as he very slowly and very carefully unwraps the gauze around my leg, numbs the area, and removes my prior stitches. "Ah, the boyfriend." My dad offers him a curt nod without meeting Christian's eyes in lieu of a handshake.

Christian settles back into his seat like he's uncomfortable. "It's nice to meet you, sir. Elena talks about you all the time."

My dad ignores him, and I shrug subtly at Christian, offering him an apologetic raise of my eyebrows. My father isn't very friendly on a good day, and they're meeting under less-than-ideal circumstances. I can't really blame him for not being interested in my love life.

I watch my father carefully as he gives me a new set of stitches in a perfectly straight line and with such precision that I have to squint to even notice that I have a wound at all. This is why my father is the best in the country. His claim to fame is that he has a gift for completing complicated, intricate surgeries with almost no scarring. He offers pro bono surgeries to fellow veterans and active service members if they've been wounded in combat.

People flock from all over the world to his practice in Houston. He's so in-demand that his waitlist is over three years long, and there's essentially a black market for him. Celebrities and the wealthy will try and outbid each other for an open waitlist spot.

My dad acts like he doesn't know this, and does his best to appear humble, but he's good, and he knows it.

Even though my father would never even consider hurting me, every time his gloved fingers graze against my numbed thigh as he works, I want to rip off my own skin. My teeth ache from how hard I'm clenching my jaw trying to stay still. When he's done and finishes wrapping clean gauze around it, I fall back against the pillow and sigh with relief.

"Who are the men standing outside your door, Ellie?" he asks as he washes his hands again. "One of them almost got a pocketknife in their eye for trying to keep me from coming in here."

"That's my fault," Christian quickly admits. "Those are my security guards. They were told not to let anyone in but doctors. I apologize. They won't stop you or your family from coming in again."

My father narrows his eyes at Christian, as if to say, '*who are you to hire security guards for my daughter*', but he stays quiet. There's an uncomfortable tension between the two of them, and unfortunately, *I'm* in between the two of them, so it feels like an elephant has decided to take a nap on my chest.

"Christian," my father prompts. He says his name as if it tastes like dirt in his mouth. "you live here in Meridian City?"

"Yes sir, my whole life. Elena says you lived here once."

My dad nods. "I did." He narrows his eyes at Christian and furrows his brow. "Have we met before?"

Christian gives him a strange glare back. "No. I don't think so."

I try not to cringe at their attempts to make small talk with each other. Mercifully, my father's phone starts ringing. I see from the contact photo that it's my mom. As soon as he puts the device to his ear, I can hear my neurotic mother practically shouting at him for information. I hear him mutter off the room number and directions on how to get up here, and my mother comes running in. She looks wrecked like the rest of us, her deep brown hair sticking out in every direction, but her presence instantly has me weeping all over again. She pays no mind to my dad or Christian, coming straight to me and holding me in a tight, loving hug that only a mother could give.

"*Oh, Ellie*." Her warmth brings me comfort and it feels so relieving to be able to embrace her without wanting to crawl out of my skin. She shushes me and strokes my hair while I crumble into tiny pieces. I cry until I have no more tears left to give. My dad trades places with my mom so that she can sit in the chair next to me while he stands at the foot of the bed and lightly rubs my feet on top of the covers.

Even though the room feels crowded with my parents and Christian here, I've never felt safer than I do right now.

I catch a glimpse of my dad. His eyes are red. He must have started crying again. I'm sure the only thing he's thinking about is wrapping his hands around the neck of the men that raped me and killing them himself. He's thinking about all the ways they violated me and how he plans on making them suffer for it. He's extremely sensitive to seeing his family in pain. It's the entire reason he begged me not to move to Meridian City. I remember the fight we got in over it so vividly. He said, "*mark my words, Elena, by the time you realize that city is killing you, you'll wish you had listened to me*."

It sounded so cruel at the time for him to say that to me. I wasn't moving out here because I wanted to experience the world. I moved here because of my dream school and to work at Reeves Enterprises. I know he hates this city. It took his first family from him. I could never ask him to let that go for my sake, but now that I'm in a hospital bed with a broken spirit and three broken ribs, I wish I had just listened to him. While he's got tears in his eyes, I know that the second I'm discharged from the hospital, he will start dangling all of this over my head until he manages to guilt me into moving back home.

My mom holds my hands tightly and kisses my knuckles. "Ellie, what happened?"

I take a shaky breath. To be honest, I don't know what to say. Kate told the hospital staff when she brought me here that she found me in the locker room at the Hellfire Lounge naked and beaten. I haven't had a chance to try and fill in the blanks yet.

"Back at the beginning of September…I broke my phone walking home from work one night. I couldn't afford to fix it and I didn't want to ask you guys for help." I take another deep breath and look at my parents, who seem offended at the premise that I didn't want their help. "So, I got a job at this nightclub as a bartender. The owner really liked me. He offered me a promotion to be his personal bartender." I look away from them to blink away tears as my voice cracks. "He and his friends started touching me. Meridian City has this serial killer called the Silencer. I guess he had something against the owner of the club, so he killed his friends one night after I left. I think the owner assumed I had something to do with it because of the timing. I got in a car accident with my old boss, Neil, and I guess he knew the owner of the club and brought me to him. That's when they…they…" I swallow the bile in my throat. "That's all I remember. Everything is kind of fuzzy."

I hope they won't ask any more questions.

My parents look at me with wide-eyed panic at my story. I dare a glance in Christian's direction, and he tightens his jaw. I can't read the emotion on his face, but his brows are knitted together in a way that screams 'guilt'.

My dad stiffens, fury brewing in his veins. "I'm going to kill them," he spits out like he's making a promise to himself.

"Neil is already dead," Christian interjects, pulling my dad's attention to him, as well as my mother's. Christian's gaze flickers to me and then back to my dad. He takes the TV remote from the table next to me and flicks it onto a local news channel. It's an interview from a police officer. In the background, the Hellfire Lounge can be seen engulfed in flames. On the ground behind him, Neil's body is covered in a white sheet. The police officer describes the scene using words like '*brutal*' and '*inhumane*' and '*the most disturbing thing he's seen on the job*'.

The room goes silent. My mom looks horrified. My father looks pleased. Christian turns off the TV and introduces himself to my mom.

She smiles warmly at him and gives him a hug. He accepts it awkwardly. Dr. Portman comes back into my room, elated that my support system has arrived. My dad asks her five million questions, and she answers them all graciously.

She tells me that I'll be in the hospital for another 24 hours to finish out my round of intravenous antibiotics, and after that she'll send me home with several prescriptions so I can continue to heal in the comfort of my own bed.

"We're staying here, Elliot," my mother says once Dr. Portman leaves the room. She pulls out her phone and announces that she's searching for a hotel to stay in. "I'm calling the office to let them know I'll be out for a few days."

"Sorry to interject," Christian gently says to my mother. "You're more than welcome to stay with me for as long as you want. I have plenty of rooms. If you give me a list of things you need, I can have them waiting for you when you get there."

Christian's offer is so generous that my mother beams. It's not until this very moment that I realize why my father fell in love with her during the worst period of his life. Her energy is so positively radiant that it's hard not to feel better. Before my mother has a chance to accept, I speak.

"Mom? Dad? Do you think I could have a few minutes alone with Christian?"

My parents hesitate at first, but my mother nods and tugs my grumbling father out of the room to give us some privacy. When it's just the two of us, Christian stays quiet, giving me a chance to collect my thoughts.

"I was on my way to the police station," I finally admit, unable to look at him. "I was going to tell them everything about you." Christian bites his lip and nods. "Can you even begin to understand how utterly hopeless I felt to press that tracker? To know that I hated you in that moment, but you were the only person in the world that could help me?"

He looks down and then back up at me, trying to be brave and hold my searing, furious gaze.

"Why would you manipulate me like that? All I think about when I look back on our relationship is how it all feels fabricated now. None of it feels real."

It's the one question I've had bouncing around in my mind since he told me the truth.

Why would he do that to me if he truly loved me?

"It *was* real," he says, and I roll my eyes. "Just…listen. I didn't want to manipulate you. You saved my life, and from that moment, my heart belonged to you. I guess in the beginning, I thought that if you couldn't love one side of me, maybe you'd love the other. And then when you started falling for me, for Christian, the Silencer got jealous and just…lost himself." He takes a deep breath. "You have to understand, Elena, who I am when I put that mask on, isn't me. We may occupy the same body, but we're *not* the same person. He's the man looking back at me in the mirror. My alter ego. The devil that wears me as his shell. I can't escape him any more than you can."

"Why are you talking like you're two separate people, Christian?"

"Because I am!" he growls through gritted teeth, though not in anger. In *anguish*. "You're scared of him, right? Well so am I. *I hate him*. He hates me just as much. I promise, I swear on my life—on my parents' graves—that if I could go back in time and not become this monster I would. But if I wasn't the Silencer, I never would have met you. I owe you my whole fucking life and I would do *anything* to keep you in it. *Anything*, Elena."

I take a deep breath and stare at the wall in front of me for a long time, feeling numb and empty on the inside.

"What did you do to me?" I ask.

"What do you mean?"

I begin to cry. "What did you do to me, to make me so loyal, that I would let myself get raped and beaten to protect your secret?" I throw one of my pillows harshly at him. "What did you do?"

"You didn't have to keep my secret. I would have understood if you told them to save yourself. *Fuck*, I was begging you to. You *chose* not to break. You *chose* to protect me. I don't know why you did it, angel. But I know that I will never be worthy of that sacrifice, and I will spend the rest of my life making it up to you."

"You'd do anything for me, right?" I ask.

"*Anything*," he says absolutely.

"Give it up," I demand harshly, and he looks at me, confused and bewildered. "The Silencer. Let him go, right now. Today."

He gives me a defeated look and I can see the refusal deep in his eyes. "It's not that simple."

"Then let me go instead," I say, and then turn to face away from him, and pretend to fall asleep.

I hear him sigh, and then he painfully whispers, "Angel, I can't do that either."

CHAPTER 25

THE SILENCER

Elena's ultimatum sits heavy in my gut like a rock.

Her parents come back into the room as I leave. I don't stop walking until I'm outside at a safe distance away from the hospital doors to smoke. I put the stick between my teeth and light it up, trying to puff out the agony in my chest. I run my hands through my dirty hair.

I don't even know where to begin to try and fix this, but I have to. My entire life depends on it. If I don't have Elena, then I have no reason to exist.

I would do anything for her, even give up the Silencer; but it's not a matter of my willingness to do it. I just don't think it's possible. How can I rid myself of an unhinged, psychopathic, murderous alter ego that's ruled my life for the past two years? It's not a switch I can just turn off when I want. When I get the bloodlust, I can hardly think about anything else.

The one thing that makes *him* uncontrollable is Elena in danger, and Frank Valenti is still out there somewhere. I can't make her a promise I can't keep. There's no way I can let go of the Silencer while he lives. It's not possible.

It's not possible.

It's not possible.

It's not fucking possible.

"What's not possible?"

I stop my pacing and turn my head to find Elena's mother, Bethany, standing a few feet away with a soft, motherly, warm smile on her face. I hadn't realized I'd been speaking.

I blow out some smoke and then drop the cigarette to the floor and put it out with my boot.

"Nothing," I say quickly. "Is Elena okay?"

She chuckles and smiles again. “Ellie is fine,” she assures me. “I came out here for you.”

“Me?” I ask, dumbfounded. “Why?”

She sighs. “Because you look like you’ve been through hell, and I wanted to make sure you were doing okay.”

Her concern seems genuine, and an unfamiliar emotion stabs me in the chest. It almost feels like motherly compassion. The first taste of it I’ve had in thirty years. “I’m fine.”

“Christian, I can smell a lie like a shark can smell blood in the water. You’re not fine, and I’d like you to talk to me.”

To give myself something to do other than stare at her blankly, I light another cigarette. “I’m not good at talking.”

She smiles at me and places a soft hand on my arm. “Luckily for you I’m an expert at getting people to talk. I’m a therapist. And a mother.”

I scoff. “I’m not sure what you want me to say.”

Unfazed by my stubbornness, she laces her fingers with mine and squeezes my hand. “I can care about you and Ellie at the same time, you know.”

I blow out a long breath, smoke wafting in the air in front of us. “I’m not sure why you’d waste your concern on me.”

“You’re feeling guilty about not being there to stop this from happening to her.”

I give her a sardonic scoff. “Among other things. Is it really so obvious?”

She pats over our connected hands. “Only to me. Because I saw this same look that you have on your face thirty years ago, when I met Elliot and he felt guilty for not being there to stop his family from getting killed.”

I let out a shaky breath, letting the stale truth sit in the air between us like cigarette smoke. “It’s my fault,” I whisper, looking down at my feet in shame.

“Is it? Or are you finding ways to torture yourself with blame?”

“It’s my fault,” I repeat, unable to elaborate, but knowing in my bones that the blame is well deserved.

Not only did I get Elena kidnapped, raped, and beaten. Not only did I spend our entire relationship lying to her.

The worst of my sins?

I sabotaged her birth control. I was so desperate to tie her to me forever that I replaced her pills. She hasn’t been protected in a month.

If she's pregnant with Frank or Neil's baby, that's it for me. The final nail in the coffin of our relationship. There would be no saving it.

I've never prayed. Not once in my life, but I look up at the sky and blow out some smoke.

Hey, if you're listening, don't make Elena suffer any more than she already has. Please.

I'm not a man who says please often.

"Is that how Ellie feels, too?"

"Of course it is. She *hates* me."

Bethany hums. "Is that why she's asking for you?"

"That's a cruel joke."

Not saying another word, Bethany tugs on my arm until I follow her. I discard my second cigarette and let her lead me back through the hospital and up to Elena's room. When we get there, Elena is flipped on her side, facing my chair. She's holding my leather jacket to her chest like her life depends on it.

When she meets my eyes, she doesn't say anything, but I see the tiniest wave of relief ease out the tension in her body.

When I glance back up at Bethany, she gives me an encouraging smile, and a small wave of relief washes over me too.

Because maybe we'll be alright after all.

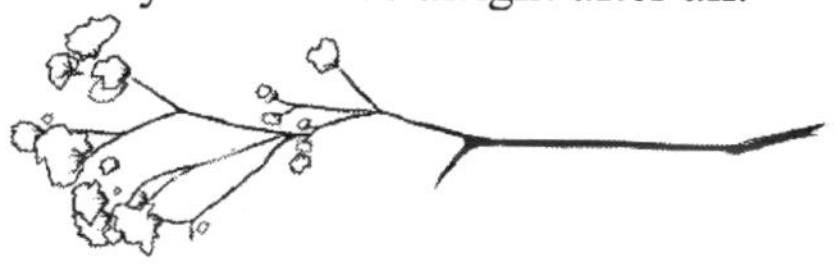

When Elena gets discharged from the hospital, her parents take me up on the offer to stay with us at the mansion.

As I drive us there, it's pretty obvious they weren't expecting a mansion.

Bethany is sitting up front with me, and Elena's in the back with her father. She hasn't said a word to me and won't even spare a look in my direction. Bethany, however, is bouncing in her seat as we cruise down the driveway. She makes small gasps of awe as she takes it all in.

Coming to a stop at the end of the driveway, I cut my losses and let Elliot help his daughter out of the car while I hold out my arm for Bethany. We walk together into my home and even though there are three other people with me, it's never felt so empty.

I take a deep breath and turn to Elena's parents. "Please make yourselves at home. Guest rooms are down that hall; pick any one you want. Kitchen is that way. If you get hungry just tell the chef, Paolo, and he will take care of you. If you need anything at all, just ask any of the staff."

One of my valets has Elliot and Bethany's luggage rolling at his sides. "Where would you like me to put these, Mr. Reeves?"

A thump and then the sound of glass shattering pulls all our attention to Elliot, who is staring down at the shards of what was once a vase of fresh flowers kept in the foyer. He's taking deep breaths and his focus is somewhere else. His grip on Elena is so tight her face is twisted in pain.

Bethany *tsks*. "Oh, Elliot, you're a bull in a China shop."

I wave my hand to indicate that it's no big deal. It's just a vase. "Don't worry about it. Are you okay, Mr. Young?"

Elliot continues to stare at the floor, breathing heavily for several seconds. Then, he takes a deep breath, stands up straight, walks right past us, and lets himself out to the backyard without a word.

"Pardon my husband's bad manners," Bethany apologizes, narrowing her eyes in Elliot's direction. Then, she takes over caring for her daughter, leading Elena towards the guest rooms. I hover in the corridor entrance, and my heart aches painfully when I hear Elena insist that she wants a very specific room.

Which happens to be the furthest away from mine.

The chasm of space between us is torture. This is my penance for everything I've done the past two years. All the lives I've taken and all the suffering I've inflicted. I had everything, and it's been ripped away. I don't think I'll ever be the same man. I thought I knew pain before. All I've done for the past thirty years is alternate between feeling numb and angry.

Elena made me taste happiness. Loving her was a drug I got addicted to after a single hit, and if I thought I've ever known what it was like to feel empty before, I was so wrong. This is what it feels like to be empty. To see my future so clearly and then watch it crumble.

She saved my life, but I've ruined hers.

I retreat to my bedroom, locking the door behind me. I pull a pocketknife out of my nightstand and then head into the bathroom.

"*Fuck*." I look like shit. It's been three days and I look like I've lost ten pounds. I guess that's not surprising considering I've put nothing in my body except black coffee and a bottle of water. My eyes are sunken into their sockets and my cheeks are hollow. Shaking my head at how pathetic I am, I roll up the left sleeve of my hoodie and hold my arm over the sink. Flipping open the knife, I take a deep breath and run the sharp edge along my wrist, slowly, forcing myself to feel every millimeter of the cut.

Then I do it two more times, until my hands are trembling and blood pools in my sink. I grit my teeth in frustration. This used to make me feel better. This used to get me through the day. Now it feels like nothing. Taking an angry breath, I slice my skin two more times. Still nothing. I throw the knife across the room so hard it impales itself into the wooden laundry hamper.

I connect my fist with my face in the reflection of the mirror. It *just* got replaced from the last time I went on a rampage in here, but I don't give a fuck. I need to make myself hurt.

Finding an abundance of partially used rolls of gauze in my drawers, I rinse the cuts on my wrists, clean the wounds, and then wrap them up. I pull my sleeves back down and rest my fists against the countertop, closing my eyes while the lightheadedness passes.

I need a cigarette. Or ten.

Seems like Elliot had the same idea, because he's six cigarettes deep when I get to the back patio, the evidence of his chain-smoking discarded in the ashtray on a small table. I take a deep breath and slump into the chair on the other side of the table and light my own cigarette. The smoke wafts into the air between us.

I glance over at Elliot. He's got gray hair, with remnants of rich brown locks scattered throughout. His eyes are blue, so Elena got her mother's eyes. He's clean shaven and his thinning hair is neatly groomed. He has the demeanor of a man that's well put-together and very meticulous about things. It must be from all the years he spent in the Army.

His hands are shaking as he lights yet another cigarette and rests his elbows on his knees while he supports his head in his hands. I can't tell if the shaking is from the high concentration of nicotine or frustration.

"Are you okay?" I carefully ask. He begins to chuckle.

"Never better," he says in a gruff voice. I can tell he's been a smoker for most of his life. I've got a bad addiction to cigarettes, but even I don't have that gravel in my voice that a lifetime smoker does. "Everything's *fuckin'* perfect." He lets out an exasperated sigh. "I should have never let her come to this goddamn city. I told her—I fuckin' told her this place would eat her alive."

Frustration it is.

I shrug. "She's committed to building her career here."

"You think I don't know that?" he snaps, finally looking at me. Our stares meet, and something flickers across his eyes. It almost looks like disappointment. He smirks with the cigarette hanging out of his mouth and chuckles. "Beautiful home you've got here."

"Thank you. My father designed it."

Elliot cocks his head to the side. "Thomas was always over the top."

That makes me pause and sit up straighter. "You knew my father?"

"Briefly," Elliot offers vaguely. Small world. I snuff out the remnants of my cigarette and Bethany slides open the backdoor. She makes a disgusted face and waves her hands in front of her nose.

"Smells like lung cancer and despair out here," she tries to lightly tease as she narrows her eyes at her husband and scowls. "Christian, Elena is asking for you."

I furrow my brow. "For me?" I ask, shocked. "Are you sure?"

She gives me a confused look. "*Yes?*"

I stand up and give Bethany a nod as I pass her to go back inside. I feel a string in my heart pulling me towards my angel, and my footsteps quicken until I'm practically sprinting to her room. Only once I'm at her door do I take a deep breath to try and relax, and then lightly knock before letting myself in.

She's curled up under the comforter. An array of medications sit on the nightstand along with her favorite snacks. A trash can full of used tissues sits next to her bed.

Her soft brown eyes meet mine, and I crumble. Literally crumble to the floor at the edge of the bed and I'm ready to beg. Beg and plead until she forgives me. As I open my mouth to do just that, she stops me.

"Shut up," she snaps. "Don't say anything."

I keep my mouth shut. She stares at me for a long time, and then her eyes go watery. "Will you sit with me?" she asks, and her voice sounds so broken and defeated it breaks my heart all over again.

"Yes," I say back. It's not even a question. I'll never leave her side again if that's what she wants. I grab a chair from the desk in the room and place it at her bedside, sitting on it backwards so I can use it to prop up my arms.

The second I settle into the chair, she burst out into loud, unhinged sobs that echo throughout the room. She's not just crying—she's *weeping*. My hands twitch uncomfortably, desperate to touch her, to bring her any comfort. But I can't.

"Fuck, angel. Tell me what to do. Tell me what I can do to help."

All she does is bury her face in her pillow and cry loudly like I'm not even there, and every second that passes feels like a white-hot serrated knife being plunged into my chest. I don't even know where to begin to try and help her.

"Even though this is all your fault, you're the only one I feel safe with." She chuckles sarcastically to herself. "How fucked up is that? How fucked up is it that all I wanted when I got to the hospital was you? How fucked up is it that when I woke up, your jacket brought me comfort because it smelled like you? How fucked up is it that all I want right now is for you to hold me? To hold me and kiss me and tell me everything is going to be okay because we're together now. I don't even know who I am anymore." She does that sarcastic laugh again. "I guess that was the point, though. Wasn't it? You wanted to strip me down raw and make me forget what it's like to exist without you."

"No, Elena," I plead, "I wanted you to *love* me."

She looks at me for a long time, and then completely lacking in emotion, she says, "I don't think you know the first thing about love."

She slumps back down to the fetal position on the bed. We sit like that for two hours, in complete silence. She's staring off into the distance, picking a hole in the edge of the comforter. It's a new nervous tick. She did it to the purple blanket I got for her at the hospital, too. The edges of it have three large holes from her fingers breaking apart the fabric.

"Christian?"

Her soft voice drives a dagger through my heart. I nod for her to continue, crossing my arms over my chest as if to shield myself from the painfully broken look she's giving me.

"When my parents go home, I'm going with them. Please don't follow me."

"Don't." My words get caught in my throat. "Don't ask me to make promises I can't keep."

"But you said you'd do anything for me," she says, her voice emotionless as she rips out my heart. "I'm asking you to let me go."

"*I can't*." I take a deep breath and make fists so tight it hurts. "You can ask me for anything else, Elena, *anything else*, and I'll give it to you without hesitation. Don't ask me to live without you. I won't survive."

"You survived before we met."

"I had a fucking gun to my head!" I shout, causing her to sink into the covers. I growl to myself. "I had my finger on the fucking trigger. If you started screaming a femtosecond later, I would have already blown my brains out." My voice cracks. "If I don't have you, then I have nothing. *I am nothing*. So if that's really what you want, angel," I pull my gun from the back of my pants and hold it to my temple, "then let me pull the trigger this time."

"Stop!" She sits up abruptly, shuddering in pain and holding her stomach from the fast movement. "Please, Christian, put it down."

"Tell me you'll stay."

"Okay! Okay. I'll stay."

My mouth does that thing where it tries to form words but can't, and I put the gun away. She sighs in relief, and I can no longer meet her eyes, because I can't stand to watch her hate me.

When she falls asleep, I place a gentle kiss to her forehead, and leave the room.

If she won't love me, maybe she'll love *him*.

And the only thing I can do to prove my love now, is find Frank Valenti, and bring Elena his head.

CHAPTER 26

THE ANGEL

I wake up panting, sobbing quietly to myself in a panic at the horrific nightmares plaguing me. I think it's the painkillers. They do something to my brain other than block my pain receptors.

It's a matter of which type of pain I would prefer.

Physical or mental?

Would I rather have my ribs ache, or have memories of rape flash across my mind every time my eyes close?

I hold my hands up in front of me and realize I'm trembling. On the bedside table next to me is a glass of water, and I down it in several big gulps.

My phone is resting on the nightstand, plugged into the charger. I grab it and immediately FaceTime my brother.

As it rings, I glance out the window. It's dark. My phone tells me it's nearly midnight. Despite it being so late, after several rings, my brother's face pops up on the screen and a small breath of relief escapes me.

"Hi," I croak.

"Hi," Travis answers quietly. "Are you okay?"

I nod. "Yeah, I'm okay." I wipe some lingering wetness from my cheek with my thumb. "I just had a nightmare."

"Do you want to talk about it?"

A fair question, but I shake my head. "No. I just wanted to hear your voice. Mom and dad are here, but I didn't want to wake them up."

"Oh, so you chose to wake me up instead?" he teases. It pulls a small smile from me, albeit a sad one. "Hey, you know I'm kidding. You can call me anytime, about anything. I'm sorry I couldn't come to see you. Justin's mom just got a heart transplant and it's been hard on him."

"Trav, it's okay. I get it."

"*But,*" he drawls out, "mom told me all about your, and I quote, *super-hot boyfriend.*"

I immediately burst into tears.

"Hey. Hey. Okay, hottie is a touchy subject. Got it."

"Sorry," I sniffle. "Shit, I'm sorry. I just…" I give him a soft, apologetic smile because what I'm about to say is probably one of the most hurtful things you can say to someone that loves you. "I've just never felt more alone than I do right now. It feels like I'm in a cage, Travis."

"That's trauma."

I tuck my knees to my chest. "You don't even know the half of it." I take a deep, shaky breath, and try to give him a convincing smile. "I'll let you go to bed. Thank you though, for answering."

"I love you, Ellie."

"I love you too."

And with that, we end our video chat. I set my phone down and cry into my knees for a few more minutes, until my head aches as much as my chest does. I'm never going to take breathing normally for granted ever again.

There's no way in hell I'm going to be able to fall back asleep anytime soon, so I take the empty glass from my bedside table to get some more water. Mercifully, my room is on the bottom floor, so I don't have to face the horrors of trying to go up and down stairs in my condition. I rub my eyes and slap around the wall of the kitchen until I find the light switch. I flip it on, and nearly jump out of my skin. I scream and drop the glass at my feet. Edwin is standing about six inches from me, balancing on a walker with a shocked expression on his face.

"Be careful. Don't cut up your feet, Elena."

I blink at him, and my body goes rigid as my arms fall to my sides. "You…you know me?"

He gives me a gummy smile. "A'course, I know you. My brain doesn't always work right, but I never forget a pretty face. Especially one my son is so fond of."

"What are you doing in here?"

"Same as you, I'd imagine. Getting some water."

"Oh," I say awkwardly, bending down to pick up the glass from the floor. Luckily it broke into three big pieces instead of shattering. I fill two glasses up to the brim with cold water, and then pass one over to Edwin. "Do you want me to find Christian?"

Edwin probably shouldn't be wandering the mansion on his own. Christian would be elated to know he's lucid. Christian once told me that it's rare these days, so he cherishes it when he can.

"No," Edwin says firmly, taking a shaky sip of water. "He's not here anyways. He went out into the city hours ago, probably looking for someone to shoot."

I start violently coughing, which hurts considering I have three broken ribs and a headache from hell. I give Edwin a strained glare, my eye twitching.

"Don't look at me like that," he huffs. "You're surprised I know about him? The Silencer, I mean. Do they still call him that on the news? I haven't watched the news in a long time."

I rub my face. "I think I took too many painkillers."

"Before you came along, he had no one else but me. He never talked to me. Not until my memory started going. He's told me everything he's ever done in excruciating detail, and I always listen." He sighs. "I pretend to forget. You see, Elena, Alzheimer's was the best thing that ever happened to me, because once my head started to go, Christian finally opened up to me. He vents to me. If confiding in me brings him a small comfort, then it's worth all the burdens I have to bear."

"He's a murderer, Edwin." I shake my head. "Why haven't you told anyone? Don't you care about all the lives he's taken?"

"Yes, I care. I pray for their souls every night," Edwin says, his eyes softening into a pleading look. "But who would believe a kooky old man with memory problems? Do I pretend I'm not lucid sometimes when I am for his sake? Yes. I'd never tell him that, and I'd never tell another soul what he's done, because all I'd be doing is betraying his trust, and he's all I have." Tears prick in his eyes. And mine. "He's my only family. He may not be my blood, but he is my son and I love him. Do you understand, Elena? Love makes people blind. It makes us blind, and selfish, and stupid."

"Why are you telling me this? Are you even hearing yourself? Is this some kind of test of my loyalty to Christian? I let myself get raped, repeatedly, to keep his secret." I laugh sarcastically. "But I'm sure you already knew that."

"Why did you keep his secret?"

"I don't know! I don't know."

"Yes, you do," he says, and his wise gaze hits me like a ton of bricks, and all I do in response is shake my head in denial. I push off the counter to leave, but Edwin stops me by saying my name. “I know you owe me nothing. I know I’m nothing to you. But I’m an old man, and I’ll die soon. I’d ask you one kindness.”

“What?”

“Don’t tell him that I know.”

“Then why’d you tell me?”

It’s quiet for a long minute. “Because I needed someone to confide in, too. You’ll never know how grateful I am that you came into his life.”

My shock must be written all over my face. Of all the things I expected him to say to me, that was not it.

“The night he met you, I woke up and I could feel something was wrong. I went into his room and found his suicide note.” A single tear falls down his face. “I thought I was too late. But then he walked through the door, panting and soaked through with rain. He fell to his knees and told me that he found his guardian angel. You are the reason I still have my son. I can never repay that debt. Not in this lifetime or any others. If you ever want someone to listen and forget, never hesitate to come to me, Elena. It’s the least I can do for you.”

Abandoning the water glass, I say, “Goodnight, Edwin.”

With that, I leave the kitchen and head back towards my room. I pause at the door. My head and eyes stay locked on Christian’s room, and before I have a chance to think twice, or even comprehend what I’m doing, my feet are carrying me to his bedroom. I don’t knock before opening the door.

It's empty and cold. The fireplace is dormant. The blackout drapes make it almost pitch black. The only light comes from the gentle golden glow of a small lamp on one of the nightstands.

I make my way over to the small bench at the end of his bed. I lie down on my side with my knees bent so I can fit my entire body onto the narrow cushion.

I fight sleep for a while, afraid of falling into another nightmare, but eventually, I let myself rest, the scent of Christian wrapping around me like a comforting embrace. The one I remember.

The one I used to crave.

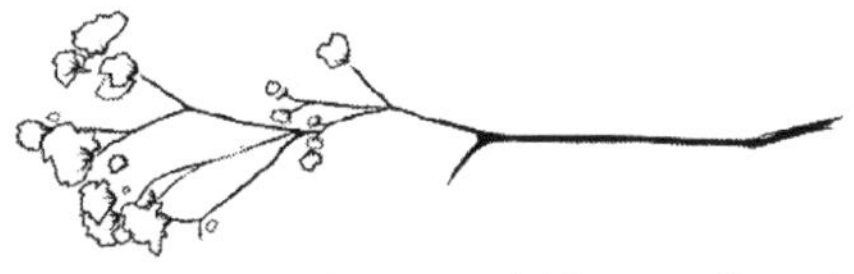

When I wake up again, as I shift, I realize I’m no longer lying down on the hard bench, but on a soft mattress, bundled up in a burgundy comforter with my face buried in fluffy pillows. I inhale deeply. *Christian*. He must have found me on the bench last night and moved me to the bed. The crinkled sheets across the other side of the mattress tell me he slept here too, though not close enough to touch me accidentally in the night.

I must have been so tired that I didn't even realize he'd picked me up to move me, and I'm grateful. I'm not sure I could have handled it. There used to be something so sacred and tender about the way he touched me. Now the mere thought has my skin crawling.

The fireplace is lit now, the soft crackling filling the silence, making the room smell of woodsmoke. The clock on the bedside table tells me it's nearly noon. I slept for almost twelve hours. I throw my legs over the side of the bed and emerge from the warmth of the blankets. I leave Christian's room to go to my own. When I get there, just as he promised before everything went to shit, all my things are neatly put away. *Right*. I had forgotten that I agreed to move in. He had to get all my stuff out of my apartment before my landlord threw it into the street.

A family photo I kept on my bedside table at my apartment now sits on a desk near the window. An array of notebooks and textbooks from my law school days are stacked on a bookshelf. My purple blanket is folded neatly on the foot of the bed. I suspect all my clothes are hanging in the closet already, and as I enter the bathroom, all my toiletries are there. My toothbrush and half-used tube of toothpaste are perched by the sink. I brush my teeth for much longer than necessary, getting lost staring at the girl looking back at me in the mirror.

I'm thin in the face. Ghoulish. Dark circles have become permanent fixtures under my eyes, blending into splotches of purple and yellow bruises across my cheek. One of my eyes is still bloodshot from where the blood vessels busted, and I poke the corner. The tender skin there is swollen. I rinse out my mouth and unbutton my sleep shirt. Dark purple bruises cover my torso where my ribs cracked in the car accident.

The scar on my thigh from the glass is, regrettably, the only part of me that looks like it's healing. That's because my dad did the stitches. It's a long, thin scar in a perfectly straight line. My body is littered in small cuts from when the glass shattered in the car accident and the club.

I take off my shorts, until I'm left in just my panties, and I stare at the space between my legs in the mirror. I can practically feel the exact moment Frank and Neil forced themselves into me. My eyes fill with tears, rolling down my face and dripping off my chin to land on my bare chest.

There's a saying that every seven years, your body will be new. The same, but all your cells will be replaced.

In seven years, I'll have a body that Frank and Neil would have never touched.

I wish that gave me comfort.

I take off my panties and turn on the shower, tears still streaming down my face as I wash myself. I scrub until my body is red and irritated. I scrub until it becomes painful, and my skin feels raw. Once I'm clean, I sit on the floor of the shower, under the hot spray of water, and stay there staring at the grout in between the stones on the walls until the water runs cold.

And in a billionaire's mansion, the water does not run cold for a very, very, very long time.

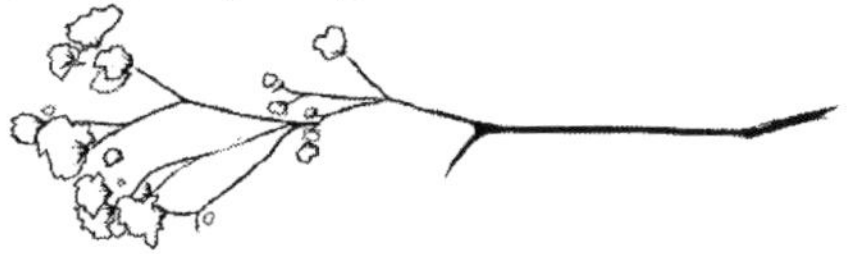

I think my father is avoiding me, and it hurts. It hurts because I know the only thing he sees when he looks at me now is a vision of two men mounting me from behind while I writhe and scream.

That's not how I want my father to look at me. It makes me feel dirty.

I find my mother in the study doing a puzzle with Edwin, who seems besotted by her. I guess that doesn't surprise me. My mother's energy is like a magnet. He's taken to calling her Helen, and when I greet him, he simply gives me an awkward smile like I'm a stranger.

If Edwin is still lucid, he doesn't make any indication of it at all. In fact, there's so little recognition in his gaze that I'm half convinced I dreamt the whole conversation we shared last night.

I ask my mother where my father is, and she shrugs before telling me that he said he was going for a walk around the property early this morning and hasn't been back in hours.

I leave them to go find something to eat. I want to be alone, and thankfully, Paolo isn't in the kitchen when I get there.

I'm not in the mood for polite conversation with the staff. Now that I've gotten a good look at myself in the mirror, I don't want them to stare at me and whisper or ask questions. Christian always has staff on the property. Maids. Chefs. Security Guards. Gardeners. Valets. I wonder how many of them have suspicions about Christian's double life. Maybe they're just paid too much and under too many NDAs to concern themselves with what Christian Reeves does in his spare time.

Even if it's murder.

I rifle through the kitchen, searching through every pantry, cabinet, fridge and freezer. After I've finished my thorough examination, I don't have the energy to make anything complicated, and choose to have some tomatoes sprinkled with salt and pepper. Simple. I grab the three ingredients along with a knife and a cutting board, and begin slicing the plump, perfectly ripe tomato into evenly sized pieces.

Halfway through cutting the tomato, I pause and stare at the knife in my hand. Tomato juice drips down the sharp blade and for a moment, an image of that blade against my wrist flashes across my mind. I take a deep breath and my eyes flicker between the knife in one hand and the veins on my wrist in the other.

"Elena."

I yelp at the voice behind me, and without thinking, I turn and swing the knife with my eyes shut. My swing is stopped, and I peek open one eye to find Christian standing there in a black hoodie, looking down at me with concern and confusion in his eyes. I look to where my knife is poised just inches from his face, and I gasp.

He's caught the knife by the blade.

I let go of the handle, and the knife clatters to the ground, covered in his blood.

"I'm so sorry. I didn't–"

"It's okay." He picks up the knife and tosses it into the sink before running his hand under cold water, and then taking a dish rag from a drawer and wrapping it tightly around the cut. "I didn't mean to scare you." My eyes are transfixed on his hand. "I've had worse. Don't worry about it."

He takes another knife from a drawer and finishes chopping the tomato for me. He looks around the counter and furrows his brow. "What were you making with a single tomato?"

I pretend I don't hear the accusation hidden in his words.

He thinks I wanted to hurt myself. Maybe I would have if he didn't walk in when he did.

I'm not going to admit that, though, so I stay quiet.

He looks at me for a moment, finally conceding and then passes over the slices of tomato. I season them with salt and pepper, and I try not to cower under the intensity of his stare as he watches me eat them.

I sigh, frustrated with the way he's looking at me. I slam my palms down on the countertop. "*What*?"

"I want to show you something. Will you let me?"

"No."

"Just give me five minutes" he begs, pulling his cellphone out of his jeans.

I roll my eyes. "Fine."

He gulps and then taps his phone screen several times, pulling up a video. He places the phone in my hands and presses play.

It's a strange point of view. There's a timestamp in the bottom corner. 9:15. It's bumpy footage of someone walking on a rooftop in circles aimlessly as it rains.

"There's a camera in my mask," he says quietly. The strange point of view makes sense. Not quite eye level, and not quite chest level. There's no sound, just several long minutes of a whole lot of nothing. I drop the phone to the counter and step back.

"Elena," he begs. "Just watch."

I rest my elbow on the counter and then rest my chin in my hand, watching the video bored out of my mind.

Something about the footage begins to look vaguely familiar.

Then it hits me. This is my neighborhood. My old one. My spine goes rigid, and I stand up straight, still staring down at the phone. "This is the night we met, isn't it?"

His silence is loud.

I watch the footage carefully, my heart falling to the floor when he pulls out a black and silver pistol. The mag is empty. He checks the chamber. There's a single bullet inside.

I feel sick to my stomach. This is the moment he was getting ready to shoot himself. My arms erupt into goosebumps and tears prick in my eyes.

His shaky hand puts the gun to his temple. He goes unnaturally still before he glances over the ledge of the building he's standing on, just in time to see me get cornered by three men in the alley.

I can't bring myself to look away from the video, not even when he puts a bullet in the skulls of those men and their lifeless bodies crumble to the ground.

He stares down at me. I'm soaking wet from the rain. Shaking. Tears stream down my cheeks as I try to cover myself with my ripped top. His hand reaches up to gently stroke my cheek and he pushes a wet strand of hair out of my face. I run away from him, and he watches from the shadows until I'm safely inside my apartment building.

I cover my mouth with my hand and finally look away from the phone, crying softly. I don't even know why I'm crying at this point. For him? For me? For us? It doesn't matter. None of it matters. Not anymore.

That girl in the video—the one he tried so hard to get to love him? She doesn't exist. She's gone. Replaced by this scarred, broken version of me.

"You never told me you stayed until I went inside."

"I told you I would make sure no one else followed you."

He did say that. I remember. At the time, I thought he was just saying it to make me feel safe enough to go home. I have no doubts in my heart that he would have killed anyone else who approached me that night without hesitation.

"Now you've experienced the exact moment you saved my life from your eyes, and from mine."

I turn around to face him, and the icy blue of his eyes is filled with a tenderness I've never seen before. A sob wrecks through me, and despite my severe aversion to touch, and my anger towards him, I throw myself into his arms and weep into the curve of his neck. His hands snake around my waist and he pulls me so tightly into his chest that it hurts my ribs. I can't bring myself to care. My skin tingles and crawls uncomfortably at the sensation of being touched, but the violent tremors wrecking through my body are no match for his iron grip on me.

"Your parents died on September 6, 1989, and we met thirty years later, on September 6, 2019. That's why you said you started believing in soulmates when you met me."

I feel a sob wreck through him too. "Do you understand now why I can't let you go?"

"Do you understand why I can't stay?"

He sighs, but he doesn't fight me this time. I feel him nod against my neck.

"I'm going home with my parents tomorrow. Promise me you won't hurt yourself."

He's quiet for a long time as we hold each other. Only after I feel him nod do I pull away and leave the room without another word.

CHAPTER 27

THE SILENCER

Elena,

I don't think I've ever been in so much pain.

I want to be there when you leave, to say goodbye and tell you I'm sorry and beg you to stay. But I'm weak, so instead, I'm writing this letter and committing your sleeping face to memory. I couldn't bear it if the last memory I had of you was the way you look at me now, after discovering the kind of monster I am.

You look disappointed. Scared. Angry.

But you're angelic when you sleep. The perfect embodiment of the endearing nickname I've given you.

I wish I wasn't the root cause of the burdens you bear.

I never believed in love at first sight. I never believed in soulmates. I made peace with the idea of being alone, and I had even made peace with death.

And then I met you.

I remember looking into your scared, tear-filled, honey-brown eyes the night we met and feeling an ache in my chest I had never felt before. I didn't immediately realize it, but that ache was my soul latching on to yours, intertwining itself so deeply that no force on heaven or Earth could ever truly separate us again.

That ache was my heart's way of telling me that you would be the first and only woman I would ever love.

You became my guardian angel. I will never let that sentiment go. If I wasn't meant to love you, then fate would have let me pull that trigger.

I may have saved you that night, but you saved me too.

My heart has been yours ever since. I don't just mean my love. I mean the actual, functional, beating heart in my chest is yours.

You're taking it with you when you leave, and I'll be nothing more than an empty shell with a gaping hole in my chest in the shape of you where my heart should be.

I know it's not healthy, and it sure as hell isn't fair to put this kind of pressure on you—to make you the essential anchor of my mortal life. To make you the tether to which I stay on this Earth. But you are.

I made you a goddess, Elena, and I worship you. You are my religion and my whole life is dedicated to loving you. That's what the most loyal disciples do, right? Dedicate their lives to their divine savior.

If you never find it in your heart to trust me again—if you never believe another word I say—believe that I love you. My love isn't perfect, and it isn't beautiful. It's broken and scarred and ugly, but all of it is yours. I will always be yours.

I will always be here ready to bow before the holy master of my soul.

I would do anything for you. If you ask me to move the sun out of your eyes, I will push it with my bare hands. If you ask me for the moon, I will wrap it in a purple ribbon and hand it to you. If you ask me for all the stars in the sky, I will create an entire galaxy, just for you.

But if you ask me to let you go?

Angel, you know I can't do that.

If you're gone, then what else do I have to live for?

Hope.

That's what I have to live for. Hope that one day I might get to hear you say, "I love you too."

So I'll wait. I'll wait as long as it takes.

Forever yours,

Christian

CHAPTER 28

THE SILENCER

I have always used violence or money to get what I want.

What I want, I can't put a price on.

As for violence? Well, that wouldn't exactly work in my situation, either.

I wonder if Elena will ever forgive me for ruining her life.

Anger has always been my go-to stage of grief. A short fuse and a heartbreak are a volatile combination.

Which is where addiction comes in.

I've smoked an entire pack of cigarettes, and it's not even nine in the morning before I'm dying for another one. The withdrawals are so bad that I'm itchy and restless, and I can't tell if it's because of the nicotine or because there's a giant fucking chasm in my chest where my heart once sat.

I came to the office at three in the morning in a black hoodie and jeans, too brokenhearted to make the effort to look like a CEO. I couldn't be there when she left the mansion with her family. I don't think I could have just sat there and accepted it. I would have done something stupid to keep her there, and I don't want her to hate me any more than she already does.

With a loud, feral roar, I flip my glass desk and watch it shatter into millions of pieces across the floor. Something small and black catches my eye on the floor in the middle of all the glass.

It looks like a spider.

Well, it *is* a spider, but not a living spider. A plastic spider. One of the rings Caroline gave Elena and I when she demanded we get married. I squat down to grab it, dusting off tiny shards of glass, and I let out a sad scoff before putting it around my ring finger like it actually means a goddamn thing.

I slump into Elena's desk chair, plucking off a large picture frame from her desk. It's that drawing Caroline gave her, the one with the three of us together on a bench. *Fuck*. Elena and I love that little girl. We were going to adopt her, but by losing Elena, I lost any hope I had of having a daughter, too.

You don't have to be married in New Jersey to adopt. But what would I say to Caroline? How would I explain that the woman she desperately wants to be her mommy isn't ever coming back?

I can't do that to her. It would be cruel and confusing.

Not to mention the fact that I'm a cold-blooded murderer.

Elena told me I'd be a good father, but that was before she knew how sadistic I am. Heartless, ruthless creatures like me don't make good parents. Or good lovers.

Several stray droplets of water fall onto the frame, and I realize I'm crying. I wipe the teardrops from the frame with the sleeve of my hoodie and then push them up to my elbows. I frown when I see the gauze wrapped around my left wrist soaked with blood.

After I wrote that letter to Elena, I spent an hour working up the strength to leave the mansion, and during that sorrowful hour, I annihilated my wrist. Tonight, I'll have to move on to my other wrist, because I've run out of space. Elena made me promise I wouldn't hurt myself, but that was only because she couldn't bring herself to say what she really wanted to. She doesn't want me to *kill* myself.

I can't understand why. What am I to her except a serial killer and a liar? Who am I except the man responsible for putting a target on her back? The man responsible for getting her kidnapped and raped.

I stand up to walk to the private bathroom of my office, to run my arm under cold water and use a hand towel to soak up the blood until it clots. The steady stream of the faucet stings when it trails down my skin, taking blood with it. The pristine white porcelain of the sink is painted in a faint rust as my blood dilutes in the water.

From around the corner, I hear the faint whoosh of the elevator door opening, and my face twists into a snarl.

"If you value your job in any way, you'll get the fuck out," I warn the intruder. I'm not in the mood to play CEO. I'm not in the mood for anything except a pack of cigarettes and an entire bottle of single malt scotch.

I rest my knuckles against the cool marble of the countertop and turn my head slightly, waiting for the distinct unease of an empty room to settle in the air. But it doesn't. Growling, I stomp out of the bathroom.

And I collide with an angel.

She stumbles backwards a few steps, and I freeze. I feel like all the air in my lungs has been knocked out of me, and I stare at her as if I've seen a ghost.

She's got big tears in her eyes, the subtle gold flecks in her irises shining brighter than I've ever seen them, twinkling like they're a light source. Clutched in her delicate fingers is the note I left on the bed for her detailing all the things I didn't have the strength to say to her face before she left me. Her perfect, pouty bottom lip quivers and she sways on her feet like she can't quite keep her footing steady.

I take a step towards her. She takes a step back, and without thinking, I reach out to take her cheeks in my hands. She cowers away.

"Don't touch me," she says, smacking my hands away. When that doesn't stop me, she holds out an arm to keep me at a distance. When that doesn't stop me either, she punches me in the chest and then smacks my cheek. I catch both of her wrists and hold them firmly at her side. She whimpers and trembles, and the closer my face gets to hers, the less she breathes, until she's nearly purple.

When my lips brush across her forehead with a soft kiss, she begins to hyperventilate and sob.

"Let me go! Christian, let me go!"

I don't say anything. She's staring up at me, tears streaming down her pink cheeks, her nose red and flaring with fear and fury. I let her hands go only to cradle her cheeks instead. Her small hands wrap around my wrists.

"Listen to me," I plead. "*I love you.* I will love you forever. Even when we're nothing but bones in the ground, I will find you in the afterlife and cherish you like I always have. I will hold you and kiss you and fall asleep with you wrapped in my arms. I will spoil you and give you a wedding ring with my last name to match. I will buy you yachts and islands and mansions all over the world so you can feel safe. I will do all of this even if you fight me because you know better than anyone that boundaries have never stopped me. One day, only when you're ready, I will fill you with my love again, and I promise I will do it so thoroughly you will forget all that pain you went through for me. You'll forget about the secrets and the lies and how betrayed you felt when you found out the truth. I will chase away all your demons because you know I'm scarier than they'll ever be. I'll do everything for you until the only thing you know how to do is love me back." I take a deep breath and wipe away her sorrow with my thumbs. "But I can't do any of that if you leave me, Elena, so I am *begging* you to stay."

"I know why I did it," she says, her voice breaking.

I just poured my heart out to her, and she's making no sense.

She stares at me with those big brown eyes with so much intensity it feels like she's burning a hole through my body straight to my soul, like she's ready to grab it by the throat and shake it until I understand.

"Ask me why, Christian."

I open my mouth to tell her I don't know what she wants, but I stop myself when the realization hits me like a truck. She wants me to ask her why she let Frank and Neil do those horrible things to her.

I let out a nervous scoff, my own voice cracking when I ask, "Why did you keep my secret?"

She sucks in a sharp breath, flattening the letter I wrote her against my chest, her words coming out as pathetic whimpers.

"Because I love you, too."

The sound that escapes me is somewhere between a prayer, a whimper, and a scoff. I think I've gone into shock. I think I've gone into cardiac arrest. I think I'm dead.

She cries out a hurt laugh, shrugging her shoulders as her hands fall to her sides and the letter falls to the floor. "You're not going to say anything?" Her face twists painfully into a look of betrayal and defeat. Tears fall off her cheeks and onto her shirt as she tries to pull away, but I don't let her move a single inch before I'm crashing our lips together.

I can taste her tears on my tongue. Or maybe they're mine. She's fighting me. Struggling to break free of my grasp but at the same time, she doesn't stop kissing me. Not until we're out of breath and panting.

Her sad eyes look up at me and all I want to do is kiss away her tears and hug her until I've fused us together.

She takes a deep breath and pulls away from my hands. "Will you give up the Silencer?"

We're in a quiet standoff. She's so brave for keeping her eyes locked on mine. Not many people can hold my stare without breaking, but she can. She knows that right now, in this moment, she's the one with all the power.

"Yes. If that's what it takes to get you to stay, yes."

"Don't say that if you don't mean it."

I take a deep breath and ask, "What about Frank Valenti?" It's an important question. If she asks me to spare that fucker, then there's no point in me pretending I can give up the Silencer. I will kill him, it's just a matter of when. As soon as he stands downwind and I catch his scent, I will hunt him to the ends of the Earth until he is nothing but a mutilated heap of flesh in my hands.

She's quiet for a heartbeat. My blood thrums in my veins, pulsing loudly in my ears.

"Kill him," she finally says. "But he's the last."

I nod. "Okay. He's the last," I say, examining her. She looks frail. Not necessarily malnourished or skinny, but her spirit, her aura, looks *frail*. I've never seen her look so uncomfortable in her own skin. "Did your parents bring you here?"

She shakes her head. "Gavin."

Thank fuck for Gavin.

Carefully, I place a kiss to the crown of her head and whisper, "Let's go home."

A few minutes later, we're in my car and headed towards the estate. Elena is rigid in her seat, staring blankly out the window. "Do you want to talk, Elena? About what happened to you?"

Without looking at me, she says with a monotone voice, "You know what they did to me. You saw it."

"That's not the same thing and you know it. You know I'm here for you, right? If you ever want to talk, or cry, or scream or hit me. I'm right here."

She shakes her head. "There's nothing to talk about, Christian."

I nod. "Okay. I understand if you don't want to talk right now, but it's not good to keep it bottled up. Just…I'm here for you. Whenever you're ready."

She sighs heavily, messing with the frayed ends of her shirt. I'm going to have to replace her entire wardrobe and all my blankets at this rate.

"My father will be mad," she says quietly. "I used to always suspect he was hoping something bad would happen to me out here. He'd never admit it, but when I told him I wanted to come home…I watched a burden lift off his shoulders. It's going to be a fight."

"You're a grown woman. You can make your own decisions."

"Like how *you* let me make my own decisions?" she snaps, turning her head to look at me. There's truth to her accusation, but it still stings. I've always let her make her own choices, but I've used fear to steer her in certain directions. I'll admit it. I'm ashamed of the methods, but not the outcome. "You remind me of my dad, you know. Your inability to take '*no*' for an answer. You'd both do anything to get what you want. And worst of all, you're both smokers."

I glance at her before setting my eyes back on the road and scoff. "I don't think your dad likes me very much. Last time I talked to him, it seemed like he'd rather be doing anything else. Every time I walk in the same room as him, he walks out."

"It's not you. My dad doesn't like anyone." Elena shrugs. "He'll come around. My mom likes you, though." She laughs quietly to herself, and it's the first real sign of life I've seen in her in days. "She thinks you're cute. I also think she has a crush on Paolo."

"It's the eggs," I deadpan. "Told you they were the best on the East Coast."

A short while later, we pull into the driveway of the estate. Elena lets herself into the front door without waiting for me. It shouldn't hurt as much as it does. She doesn't like me right now. In fact, I'm probably one of her least favorite people on the planet.

But she loves me, and those three words are the glue holding our relationship together. Holding *me* together.

I wonder what's holding *her* together.

When I walk into my home, Elena's parents are lingering in the foyer with their luggage. Bethany smiles when she sees us. Elliot frowns. At me.

"Whew!" Bethany exclaims. "Thought we were going to miss our flight. Ellie, I packed a bag for you with the essentials. We can get a moving company to get the rest of your things."

Elena clears her throat. "I…decided to stay."

The room instantly goes still, and Elliot's face turns bright red. Elena sighs and her shoulders slump. "Dad—"

"Elena, I say this with nothing but love in my heart. Grab the damn bag and say goodbye."

My body is strung tight with the need to say something, starting with '*don't talk to your daughter like that*' and ending with '*fuck off*'. But this is her father, and I can't make enemies with her family. Not if I want her in my life. I've always known her family was important to her, but I didn't quite understand how deep that love went until her father arrived at the hospital and she nearly jumped out of the bed to hug him.

I guess after spending almost my entire life without a real family, I had forgotten how important it is to the people that have them.

I keep my mouth shut. For now.

I watch Elena shrink into herself, as if getting ready to shield herself from his verbal attacks. "No."

Bethany and I clash awkward gazes, and she puts a hand on her husband's shoulder. "Honey—"

Elliot turns abruptly to face me. "I need to talk to you," he growls, and then stomps away to the glass door leading to the back patio. I share another awkward look with Bethany and Elena, and then follow him outside.

He's already halfway into a cigarette by the time I get out there. His shoulders bounce like he's warming them up for a fight. "What the fuck have you done to my daughter?" he asks. No bullshit, no sugarcoating. A very direct question that demands a response.

"I don't know what you mean, sir."

He points into the mansion. "That woman in there is not my daughter." He stares me down with a glare that could melt steel.

I sigh. "She just went through a traumatic experience. She's not going to be herself. It's normal."

"You think I'm stupid? I'm not talking about her being kidnapped and raped. I'm talking about the fact that you had something to do with it."

"Me?" I take a step back from him to keep my fist from connecting with his face. "Are you insane?"

"Are you or are you not the *great* Christian Reeves?" he prods, his mouth curling into a sneer at my name. "The great Christian Reeves that took over his dad's empire. The CEO."

I shrug. "What the fuck does that have to do with anything?"

"Neil Hayden was your employee. Elena is your employee. I know she hated that dickhead. She vented to me about him all the time. But tell me, Reeves, what's the common denominator here?" I stay quiet and take a deep breath, my hands trembling to keep myself from knocking him on his ass. "You were arrested for assaulting him. Twice. You're dating my daughter. He kidnaps and rapes my daughter."

My jaw tightens and I have nothing to say. He's right. This is my fault. Even if Frank Valenti had a part to play in it, Neil targeted Elena because of her connection to *me*.

"Gears turning in your head?" Elliot asks. "You're forcing her to stay. Why? What do you have over her?"

"I'm not *forcing* her to do anything. We talked. She chose to stay on her own."

"*You talked*," he parrots back sarcastically. "I'm going to go home with my wife. My daughter is going through a lot, and I don't want to stress her out any more than necessary. I want you to remove yourself from her life before she comes to Texas for Thanksgiving. In case my phrasing wasn't clear, that isn't a request."

"I'm not breaking up with your daughter, Elliot."

God, I want to throttle him right now. I want to wring his neck.

I muster up every ounce of self-control I have for Elena's sake and try to sympathize with him. "I understand that you're upset about what happened to her and want to take care of her. You're a loving father and it hurts to see your daughter like this, but I'm not ending things because you're jealous that I can take care of her, maybe even better than you can. Elena has a big heart. She's more than capable of loving the both of us." I take a deep breath. "I'd like us to be friends, Mr. Young."

Elliot forcefully grabs me by the front of my shirt and pulls me so he's speaking into my face. I stand quite a bit taller than him, so if he's trying to be intimidating, it's not working. He's angry, practically breathing fire when he spits his next sentence out.

"I'd rather chew glass than be friends with you. I'll be damned before I let a Reeves tear apart my family again."

He lets me go, and this time, I grab him, shoving him against the exterior brick of the house. "What the fuck is that supposed to mean?"

Elliot chuckles. "It means the apple doesn't fall far from the tree, and you remind me so much of Thomas. I wonder if you'll end up with a bullet in the chest, too."

My brain short circuits, and now *I'm* the one breathing fire. "Keep my father's name out of your mouth and get the *fuck* out of my house."

CHAPTER 29

THE ANGEL

When Christian and my dad come stomping back into the mansion, they're both furious. I can see it written all over their faces. Christian's so mad that as he passes a shelf, he swipes a glass vase and sends it shattering to the floor before disappearing behind a corner without even sparing a look in my direction.

"What did you say to him?" I demand.

My dad ignores my question and then cracks his neck. "Elena, listen to me. You are my only living daughter and your safety and happiness mean everything to me. I love you. I'm going to ask you something and I am begging you to tell me the truth."

I spare a confused glance at my mom, who looks equally confused. "Okay…"

"Do you want to stay here with him?" he asks. I open my mouth to answer, but he cuts me off. "Don't tell me what he wants you to say and don't tell me what I want you to say. Tell me the truth."

"Yes," I answer immediately. "Yes, dad. I want to stay."

He tilts his head back as if to silently pray to God before locking eyes with me again. "If you change your mind, you call me, and I will come get you. No questions asked. I don't care if I'm in the middle of surgery. Call me and I will save you from him."

Save me?

I let out a nervous laugh. "Dad, I don't need saving from Christian."

The look in my dad's eyes is a complete contradiction to what I just told him, but he doesn't say anything. He pulls me into a tight hug which my mother joins.

We say goodbye, and I wave as Gavin takes them to the airport. Something feels so wrong about the past few minutes. I don't expect Christian to shine much light on the situation either, but I go to find him anyways. He's in his home office, resting his head in his hands and rubbing his scalp like he has a headache.

"What did he say to you?"

Christian's head snaps up as if he's only just realized I'm standing here. That's very uncharacteristic of him. He's got almost magical awareness. I don't think he's ever been snuck up on in his life.

He doesn't say anything. I take a seat in the chair opposite him and fold my arms on the table and rest my head on them, staring at him. He's gone back to being zoned out.

Finally, he runs his fingers through his hair and focuses his eyes on me. "It doesn't matter."

"Okay," I say quietly as he goes back to his blank stare.

I stand up to leave him alone, since he's clearly not in the mood for conversation, but he says my name to stop me in my tracks. I face him and wait for him to continue.

"Did you know that your father knew mine?"

I shake my head. "No. He doesn't talk about his life in Meridian City."

Christian nods, and I take it as my cue to leave. I spend the rest of the day nursing the ache in my chest from my broken ribs. I use a few ice packs to help ease the swelling and take a few medications. Drowsy and low energy, I find myself in the theater room. A movie plays in the background while I scroll through my phone, not paying attention at all to whatever's on the big screen. Several long, lonely hours pass, and I get a text from my father that they've landed in Texas. I type a quick reply back, telling him I love him and that I promise I'm okay.

But the thing is, I don't feel okay. I've never felt lonelier. I've never felt more unsettled in my own skin. I've never felt so numb inside.

I pull my favorite purple blanket up to my chin. I carry this blanket around like a toddler. The poor thing has soaked up so many of my tears over the past few days. It needs a good wash.

But right now, I need it to soak up more of my tears. I cry softly into the fabric. I'm not even sure what I'm crying for. Ever since Kate brought me to the hospital, I get in these moods where it feels like a bucket of raw emotion has been dumped over my head. It's brutal. I can't think straight when it happens, and it feels like my world is collapsing in on itself.

Neil Hayden is dead. Frank Valenti is alive. To be honest, I don't know if his death would bring me any comfort. That doesn't mean I want him alive, necessarily, but if they're both dead, I'm the only one that has to live with this. I'm the one that has to bear the burden of remembering what they did to me.

If they're dead, they're free, and I'm not.

I'll never be free again.

Soft whimpers escape my throat and tears blur my vision. I wipe my face and sit up, and movement from the corner of my eye startles me.

"I hate it when you're sad," Christian says, carefully approaching and then lowering himself into the space next to me. The lounger is plenty big for the both of us. Even though we're technically sitting in the same seat, there's a comfortable expanse of space between us. Christian leans over to take a bite of the quickly melting ice cream next to me. I haven't touched it since I opened it. The top has gone soupy. He looks me over like he's committing my sorrow to memory so that he can torture himself with guilt. "Is there anything I can do to help you?"

I turn my head to look at him, my blanket still tucked under my chin like a shield. "Will you stay with me?"

"Can I hold you?"

"No. Stay on your side."

He nods in understanding, and we sit in complete silence watching the movie. I'm absorbing nothing, but something about his presence is comforting. In a careful experiment, I subtly scoot a tiny bit closer. I'm pleased when I don't burst into flames and want to crawl out of my own skin. The movie ends and I pick another one randomly. Little by little, I scoot closer to Christian. Once I'm as close as I can bear, with about a foot of space between us, that's where I stay until my painkillers put me to sleep.

When I wake, I'm still in the theater room. The screen hums with the menu of the streaming service, casting the room in a soft purple glow. I'm lying down now. My head is in Christian's lap. My body seizes up at the thought of being so close to him and I sit up abruptly, scurrying to the other side of the lounger. Christian doesn't move. He's asleep. I check my phone. It's only six, so he must have fallen asleep after I did, and stayed so he didn't disturb me.

It's only now that I realize I didn't have a nightmare.

Trying to make the least amount of sound possible, I slowly make my way off the lounger and out of the theater.

Since it's too early to try and fall back asleep, I decide I should probably humor myself and try to study for the bar exam. I haven't been as diligent with studying as I should have been the past couple of months. The exam is towards the end of February, so I still have almost four months to get my head back into focus.

It also might be a good way to keep my mind off everything—to keep me from thinking about Frank Valenti. This is something I just simply don't want to face. Not to mention that he's still somewhere out there. There's no telling what he's planning or who he might be with. I know his influence runs deep in this city, but I wonder how much loyalty he still has now that the club is gone.

Taking a deep breath, I search my guest room for a few textbooks, a notebook, and a pen, and get to work. It's hard at first. Getting back into studying after taking a long break is never easy. I read and take notes until my hand is cramping and my eyes are crossed.

At ten, when my eyes are so heavy that I can't think straight, I set down the pen and stand up to stretch my limbs. Pulling my arms over my head makes me wince in pain. I can't wait for my ribs to be healed. I haven't had a satisfying stretch in days.

There's a light knock on the door. Christian slides through, closing the door behind him. "Hey."

"Hey," I reply. He spies all the books and notes on the desk and then looks to me for an explanation. I shrug. "Thought it would be good to get my mind off things, so I've been studying for the bar exam."

He nods, and something hopeful flashes across his eyes. Probably on account of me doing something as mundane as studying. I'm willing to bet he's relieved that I'm not screaming and crying and trying to crawl out of my own skin. I rock back and forth on my heels and clasp my hands behind my back. "I know it's late but…do you want to do something? Together?" He raises an eyebrow at me. "Don't look at me like that. I'm not made of glass."

He's quiet for a beat, and then quietly asks, "What do you want to do?"

"Anything. I just…want to feel normal for a little bit."

He rubs over his jaw while he thinks of something to do, never taking his gaze off me. After a while, he gives me a weak smile. "How about a drive?"

"Okay," I nod. He tells me to get dressed, so I change out of the silk pajamas I've been living in. I put on jeans and a hoodie, fix my braid, and swish some mouthwash around to freshen up. Christian is waiting for me in the hallway, and I follow him to his massive garage.

We walk down one of the long lines of cars to the very end where a charcoal-gray motorcycle waits. Something that's made to go *fast*. Christian pulls two helmets off the rack hanging on the wall besides the bike and tries to hand it to me. I stare at him blankly.

"What?" he asks.

"When you said drive, I assumed heated seats would be involved."

He gives me a patient smile and hands me the helmet. "You'll love it. I promise."

I shake my head. "I'd have to hold onto you."

"Do you trust me?"

"Not really," I say back. "Not like I used to."

Christian rests the helmet on the handle of the bike, shoving his hands in his pockets. "I'm still the same person, Elena. The same man you fell in love with. I think you know that, and it scares you, but I told you that very first night in your apartment that I'm the one thing you never have to be afraid of."

"But I *am* afraid of you," I whisper. "I'm afraid of what you'll do to yourself if I leave and I'm afraid of what you'll do to me if I stay."

He considers that for a moment, and then throws his leg over the bike. "Give me a chance to fix this." He pats the seat behind him.

I let out an exasperated sigh. "Where are we even going?"

"Who says we need a destination?"

He throws his helmet over his head and then balances the bike so I can climb on. He's so tall and broad. He looks way too big for it. It takes me a few long minutes, and I do take a step backwards like I'm going to leave him there, but I eventually concede. With a deep breath, I put the helmet over my head and take careful steps towards the bike. He doesn't pressure me or rush me; he just patiently waits.

I've never been on the back of a motorcycle, so I throw my leg over in a very uncoordinated fashion. I have to use Christian's shoulders to pull myself up. The position hurts my ribs, but it's not unbearable. Once I'm comfortably in the seat, I give him a thumbs up.

"There's a microphone, angel. You can talk to me. Are you ready?"

"No," I say with a nervous laugh.

"I'll go slow. You can hold onto me as much or as little as you want."

"What if I want you to stop?"

"You won't."

With that, he turns on the bike and revs the engine a few times before slowly pulling out of the garage. It is a painstakingly slow pace. He drives in steady circles in the driveway until I get used to it, and then I experimentally wrap my arms around him. The solid feel of his muscles flexing under my touch sends a comforting sense of security through me. With me now less likely to fall off the bike, Christian drives a bit faster, testing my comfort level.

"I'm okay," I say quietly into the microphone, and I feel him lightly pat my hands on his stomach before speeding off down the driveway.

I take a deep breath and let the tension in my shoulders fade, and once we leave the estate, I rest my head against his back.

Because I feel safe.

That really pisses me off, because the most infuriating thing about Christian Reeves is that he's always somehow right.

I do love it. Riding with him on the back of his motorcycle, letting him race through traffic while I sit and watch the cars whiz past gives me a pleasant adrenaline rush. It's thrilling.

He knows the streets so well. Knows exactly how fast he needs to go to beat all the lights, knows exactly where to turn to avoid traffic, not that there's a lot of traffic this late, and knows which parts of the city are worth driving through and which streets are worth avoiding. We drive for what feels like an eternity, mostly staying on the South Side, where the buildings aren't covered in graffiti and the windows aren't boarded up to combat the robberies.

The rich side, to put it bluntly.

Though the memories and the fears are still in the back of my head constantly, I cherish this moment where Christian and I just get to be a man and a woman, driving through the city, pretending things are normal. Leaving everything that happened behind us for a while. I'm getting the chance to try and convince myself that I'm free from all that pain and suffering.

It's dark and chilly outside. When we're stopped at a light, I know Christian can feel me shivering because he shrugs off his leather jacket and lets me wear it.

We drive for another hour before Christian comes to a stop outside of the Reeves Enterprises building. He props the bike up and then climbs off. He removes his helmet and shakes his hair out before helping me off the bike. I remove my helmet and ask what we're doing here. He shushes me and leads me inside. We take the elevator all the way up to the top floor—to our office—and then he takes me into the emergency stairwell that has roof access. On the rooftop, we're met with a cold breeze.

"I come here sometimes to think," Christian says, putting his hands in his pockets and standing at the ledge, looking down. There are thick iron bars to keep us from falling over, but it's still nerve-racking to be so high up. Reeves Enterprises is the tallest building in Meridian City. I thought the view from our office was beautiful, but something about being on the rooftop is so liberating.

"Can I ask you something?" I prompt. He nods. "When did you know you loved me?"

"Truly?" He laughs to himself. "I think Caroline knew before I did, but it was when she gave you that drawing. I had a very vivid flashback of giving my parents a crayon drawing when I was that young and remembered how my mother looked at me when she accepted it. That's how you looked at Caroline and that was the moment it hit me that I wasn't just obsessed with you, but that I loved you. That I wanted a life and a family with you. I decided right then and there that I wanted to marry you, and I contacted a jeweler that night and told them to find me the biggest purple diamond money could buy. I took my mom's wedding ring, removed her stone, and replaced it with yours."

Then he pulls the ring out of his pocket. It's a silver band with the biggest diamond I've ever seen. Pear cut, with two other baguette diamonds jutting off on either side. It's beautiful. Sparkly even in the dark of night. My breath catches in my throat as I stare at the thing like it's going to bite me. I look up at Christian from under my lashes. "If you brought me up here to propose, my answer is no."

He shakes his head. "I didn't bring you up here to propose. I just wanted you to know I was telling the truth, since I'm no good at it."

"You're very good at telling the truth," I say as he puts the ring back in his pocket. "You're just also very good at withholding information." I stare up at him, and it begins to drizzle. "That Monday morning after we met, when you came up to my desk, were you there to see me?"

"Yes. I didn't have a plan for what I was going to do when I got there, but I just wanted to see you again. As myself. But Neil fired you and then I had to do damage control."

"If I had taken the bait and started falling for Christian Reeves from the very beginning, what would you have done about the Silencer?"

He thinks for a while. "I like to tell myself the Silencer would have left you alone. In some ways, I think it would have been easier if I had met you as Christian Reeves first. I feel like I could have saved you so much pain these past few months." It begins to rain harder, but neither of us moves. "When did you know that you loved me?"

I suppose it's only fair that he knows, though my story is less romantic than his.

"When they asked me who you were." I take a deep breath. "The moment Frank pulled down my shorts, I knew I would have never given either of them the satisfaction of breaking me. Of getting me to tell them your name." My voice breaks. "They tried very hard. And when they made you watch and I saw how desperately you were trying to get to me…I knew you really did love me, and that only made me love you more. I just didn't want to admit it to myself. I didn't want to admit that I was keeping a serial killer's identity a secret at the expense of being haunted for the rest of my life. Only love can hurt that bad and still be worth it."

He hangs his head down in shame. Rain drips from the ends of his hair. We're now completely soaked through. Cold.

"I'm sorry. For everything. For the lies and the secrets and the pain I've put you through. I will never be worth that sacrifice, Elena. Never. Not even if I lived a thousand lifetimes trying to make it up to you."

With careful fingers, I reach up to caress his cheek. His eyes find mine, his expression pained and guilty. "But you *are* worth that sacrifice. That's why I'm still here."

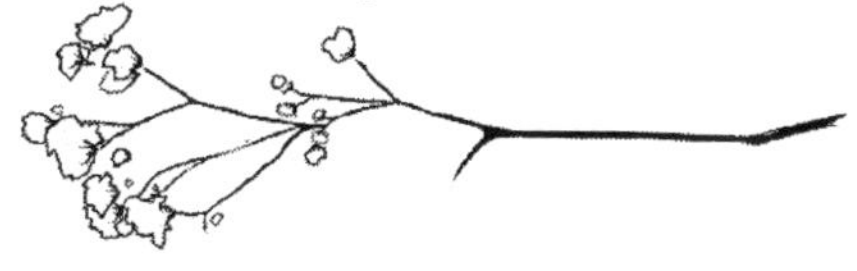

The next morning when I wake, Paolo graciously brings me breakfast and coffee in bed. I study from the time I wake up until I go to sleep.

That's my routine for two full weeks. Christian bothers me very little. I think he knows that I need some space. He checks on me, but he doesn't stay with me unless I ask, which isn't often. This back-and-forth emotional roller coaster I've been feeling since he admitted he was the Silencer has exhausted me. Physically. Mentally. Emotionally.

But at least physically, I am healing. My ribs feel mostly back to normal. I take a walk in the mornings when it's not raining, bundled up in a blanket as I walk around the perimeter of the property, usually with coffee in hand. It's the middle of November now. The weather has gone cold. Thanksgiving is in just a few days. A few weeks after that, it'll be my brother's wedding, then Christmas, then New Years. It's a busy time of the year, which is exactly what I need.

In the weeks since my parents were here, I've visited a clinic to double check for STD's and let out a huge sigh of relief when all the tests came back negative. I also started my period right on time, which was another huge relief. I think after I knew I wasn't going to be stuck with a physical reminder of my rape, a huge burden got lifted off my shoulders.

Christian asked me why I was crying the morning I got my period. When I told him, he hugged me, and I felt him try to hide his tears from me as he silently sobbed into my neck. I didn't realize it would be such a relief for him, too.

Now that I'm certain I'm not pregnant or diseased, the good days don't seem so impossible to reach anymore. It's only been a few weeks, but I'm feeling more like myself than I thought I would.

Logic says that rape victims don't like to be touched. Now that I'm living through the aftermath, I've discovered that, for me at least, it's not about being touched. All I want to do is hug Christian. All I want is for him to kiss me. All I want is to sleep in the same bed as him and wake up with his arms wrapped around me.

Christian has got me so reliant on him for everything. Food, shelter, clothing, work, love, comfort. My entire life is controlled by him, and with that, my emotions too. He's very good at saying all the right things. I don't think he's consciously making an effort to manipulate me; it just comes second nature to him now, and I will bend every time because I don't want to know what it feels like to break.

I think that's why I crave him so badly, despite everything I'm going through.

Today is the Monday before Thanksgiving. My family's group chat has been blowing up with texts of excitement. It's been a long time since we've all been together. I wasn't expecting my brother to be at Thanksgiving this year, but he told me that Justin's mom is healing surprisingly well after her transplant, so we'll all meet at my parent's house in Houston in three days' time. I've already started packing. I can't wait to get away from this city for a few days. I think it will do wonders for my mental health.

I leave my room to go to the kitchen to hunt for a snack to eat while I study. On my way to the kitchen, I hear very loud music coming from down one of the halls, towards Christian's private gym. I don't know why I'm like a moth to a flame, but I abandon the hunt for snacks and walk closer to the music. It's so loud my ear drums hurt, and by the time I get to the gym, I don't know how Christian hasn't lost his hearing entirely.

I stand in the doorway and watch him. He's in the middle of a set of pull-ups. Shirtless and dripping with sweat. His gray sweatpants cling to all the muscles in his legs deliciously.

The thought smacks me in the face. Christian is ridiculously attractive, he always has been, but I've been so disturbed by the truth about him being the Silencer that I stopped seeing it. I didn't let myself acknowledge that I was attracted to him. It was hard enough admitting that I was in love with a serial killer. I don't have any room for desire right now.

Christian finishes his set of pull-ups and drops to the floor, using a towel to pat dry his sweaty face. He turns down the music and faces me, all his scars on display. His wrists are almost completely scabbed over.

"Are you okay?"

The question stuns me. "Yeah. Why?"

"You look like you're going to be sick."

"And here I was thinking I was beautiful," I say, crossing my arms over my chest. I'm embarrassed. Is it really that obvious that I'm struggling to come to terms with normal human emotions again?

"You *are* beautiful," he says without hesitation. "So beautiful it hurts."

I shrug. "I was just going to the kitchen for a snack and heard the music." I cautiously take a step towards him.

I had almost forgotten that he carved my name into his chest. I reach out a hand to trace over the letters and then grab one of his arms to look at the healing wounds there.

"Do they hurt?" I ask.

"Not enough."

His honesty feels like a dagger in the heart. My eyes snap up to his. He looks completely nonchalant about it, meanwhile I'm sure I look horrifically disturbed.

"Before me...when was the last time you did this?"

He thinks for a second. "I was in my mid-twenties. I can't remember. It's been a solid ten years or so," he answers, and then quickly adds, "Don't you dare blame yourself."

I let his arm go and it falls to his side. "I'll let you get back to it. I'm sorry if I bothered you."

"You could never bother me."

My eyes trace down his body from head to toe. I don't understand how it's possible for a man to be so huge. He's literally Hercules. His shoulder to waist ratio is insane. He's got that kind of build that's tanky, but not necessarily super lean and shredded. He's got a healthy, strong body, built for sheer power rather than aesthetics.

"I never told you this, but you're hot."

He laughs. "Thanks for noticing."

I give him a half-hearted smile. "This is going to sound really out of place considering everything we've been through, but…do you want to come to Texas to spend Thanksgiving with my family? I know we're in a weird place in our relationship, but it would make me happy if you came with me."

"I'll come. Am I even invited though?"

"Why wouldn't you be?"

"Because last time I saw your father he was very clear that he didn't like me."

I think back to how furious they had both been when they came back inside after talking in the backyard. That feels like a lifetime ago. "You're invited because I want you to be there. My dad will get over it."

"He told me to break up with you, and practically cursed my family name. He said he doesn't want a Reeves involved with his family again."

"Again?" I ask in confusion. "Well, you did say that our dads knew each other, right? Maybe they didn't get along. My dad is dramatic. He will take a grudge to the grave."

He takes a deep breath and nods. "I'll have the jet ready to fly us to Texas on Thursday morning."

This time, when I smile, it's real. It's genuine. I'm happy Christian is coming. I internally laugh at myself.

I'm happy that a serial killer is coming to my family home.

There is something seriously wrong with me.

I cross my arms over my chest. "Have you been looking for Frank?"

He nods. "Every night." He takes a deep breath, already anticipating my next question. "I haven't found him. It's like he's vanished. I'm sorry. The longer he's out there, the more he haunts you. The sooner I find him, the sooner we can put this chapter behind us. I *will* make you feel safe again. I promise."

CHAPTER 30

THE ANGEL

I go back to my room with a snack in hand and a strange feeling in my chest. Something warm that makes my heart race. I think it might be satisfaction. I think I'm looking forward to the day when Frank's dead. He deserves whatever suffering Christian brings him.

I study for several more hours, mulling over the rule against perpetuities until my brain feels like it's going to fall out of my skull. Paolo brings me dinner, fresh tomato soup and a grilled cheese. The corner of my mouth quirks up into a small smile. Christian really is doing his best to try and close the canyon between us.

He was so focused on the chase. So focused on getting me to fall in love with him that he had no idea what to do once he actually caught me.

And here I am, stuck between loving one side of him and hating the other. Edwin was right. Love makes us stupid.

A sudden wave of emotion hits me, and I close my textbook, pinching the bridge of my nose to try and stifle my tears. Taking a deep breath, I send a text to my father, asking if it's okay to take a bath with stitches. He asks for a clear picture of my leg, which I send to him. His reply comes a few minutes later.

Dad: I would say no. You're healing, but a bath might brew bacteria in the wound. You can take a bath, just don't submerge it.

Me: But you're the great Elliot Young. Aren't your stitches magic or something?

Dad: Don't be obtuse, Ellie. It's called sorcery.

Dad: Take the bath. Promise me you'll clean it with alcohol when you're done. I'll write a prescription for an antibiotic.

I smile triumphantly. Am I putting myself at a massive risk for infection? Sure. If it earns me another trip to the hospital, so be it. Worth it.

There isn't a bathtub in my guest room, just a shower, so I pad out of my room and down the hall to Christian's room where I know his bathtub is to-die-for. I knock on the door and hear no response. When I push in, Christian's standing in the doorway of the bathroom, dripping wet from a shower with a towel wrapped around his waist, running another through his hair. We lock gazes and he freezes.

"I came to commandeer your bathtub, but I can come back later."

"No," Christian gasps, as if he thinks I'm going to disappear. "It's fine. Stay."

He steps into his closet without a word and closes the door behind him. I sigh, my heart aching slightly, and I step into the steamy bathroom. I flip the switch on the wall to make the floors heat up. Against my sock-covered feet, it instantly warms me. I filter through all the different bubbles and bath salts in a small cabinet next to the tub. I can't imagine Christian soaking in rosewater scented bubbles, so he must have bought all of this for me.

I open a container of bubbles, my mouth watering slightly when I inhale the scent of tangy oranges. I turn on the bath water, nice and hot, and pour the soap into the stream. The citrusy scent fills the room as the tub begins to overflow with bubbles.

I undress and then check the temperature before stepping into the water. I hold my breath with anticipation as I lower myself into the tub, the cut on my leg burning. I hiss at the sensation. After a few long seconds, the burning becomes tolerable, and I settle comfortably against the slope of the tub. A thick layer of bubbles covers my naked body. I sit there in silence for a few minutes, staring out at the Atlantic Ocean, gray from the dark rainclouds overhead.

A soft knock on the door has me bolting upright and covering my chest. Christian slides in and closes the door behind him with his foot. He's holding a glass of white wine and a plate of chocolate-covered strawberries.

We stare at each other while he sets the wine and plate on the edge of the tub, and then kneels on the warm tiles next to me so we're eye-level.

I gulp. "What are you doing?"

He uses a small remote to dim the bathroom lights to a warm, soft glow. Then, he takes one of the strawberries and holds it to my lips. He gives me a small smirk when I continue to stare at him in confusion.

"Trying to be romantic," he finally replies. I cautiously bite into the strawberry and chew slowly, like I'm waiting for the punch line.

"There are more subtle ways to try and see me naked."

He shakes his head. "I'm not." He holds up three fingers. "Scout's honor."

I scoff. "You were a Boy Scout?"

"No. I was way too much of a savage to be a Boy Scout." He feeds me another strawberry and I settle back into the tub, making sure the bubbles are covering all of me. He looks down at the water and raises an eyebrow. "Should you be taking a bath with stitches?"

"My dad says as long as I clean it well afterwards, I should be okay. He's writing a prescription for me just in case."

Christian nods. "I'll have someone go pick it up for you."

He folds his arms on the edge of the tub and rests his chin on them, staring past me towards the ocean. I take a deep breath and shift until I'm sitting in front of him, and then I mimic his posture, resting my chin on my forearms. Our noses are almost touching.

"Are you still in any pain?"

I subtly shake my head. "No. Well, maybe a little, but it's tolerable."

The corner of his mouth quirks into a soft smile. "I don't want your pain to be *tolerable*, I want it to be nonexistent. I wish I could take it away," he whispers, as if he's reminding himself that he's the reason I'm in pain in the first place.

I can't blame him for what Frank and Neil did to me, but I do place some of the blame on him for putting me in the middle of his war with them.

I trace the line of his arm with my eyes. His biceps bulge against the cuff of his t-shirt. A pinkish scar peeks out from under the fabric, from that first night in my apartment when he used fishing wire to stitch himself up. My eyes continue to follow the lines of his muscles until I focus on the scars and fresh cuts all over his forearms. My heart aches when I see them.

"I have a confession," I whisper. His blue eyes fixate on me, his attention completely undivided. "I miss you. I don't mean in the way that people miss someone they love when they're apart.

I miss you because I want to go back to that time when we were just two people falling in love. I miss when you were just Christian to me."

"We can go back. We can be just two people in love."

I shake my head. "No Christian, I don't think we can. You're a full package. I can't love you without loving the Silencer. You'd think that would be an easy choice. When I was going to the police station to turn you in, I felt like I would have been doing the city a favor, but at the same time, it felt like I was betraying you. Does that make sense, in the most illogical way possible?"

Christian scoffs and smirks. "That, my angel, is called Stockholm Syndrome."

I stare at him in disbelief. "I'm not a kidnapping victim." I huff. "Well, I am, but *you* didn't kidnap me."

"Sometimes people develop feelings for their captors because it's easier than fighting them."

"But you're not my captor," I say, and then my eyes widen with realization. He *is* my captor. I just never saw the chains because they were covered in diamonds. My gaze on him saddens, my chest aching. "Does that mean I don't really love you?"

He shakes his head. "You love Christian Reeves."

I love Christian Reeves. Right. Because he says they're not the same person. But how can someone be two completely different people? How can one side of him be so perfect and the other side be so vicious?

He silently feeds me another strawberry. I close my eyes and rest my head on my arms, staying with him in a comfortable silence for a few minutes before he speaks again.

"Elena? Can I…can I wash your hair?" My first reaction is to shake my head, and I sink further into the bubbles away from him. "I promise I won't touch you anywhere other than your head and neck."

I swallow the lump in my throat. "I can't."

"You trust me, right?"

"Christian, you know this is different. I'm sorry. I can't."

He shuffles on his knees until he's behind me, and I sink further into the water, my body tensing up and even under the cover of the bubbles, I use my arms to shield my breasts and in between my legs. From behind me, he leans over, his breath fanning over my neck right below my ear. "Trust me," he whispers. "Close your eyes, Elena."

"No."

He gently removes the clip holding up my long strands of hair, and they tumble over my shoulders and land in the sudsy water.

"Trust me," he repeats as tears start streaming down my face.

"Christian, *please*," I beg. He hasn't even touched me beyond unclipping my hair, and I'm trembling beneath the water. I feel like I'm drowning even though my head is safely above the bubbles.

"*Trust me*," he repeats, over and over again, in that smoky baritone way that warms me straight into my bones. "Trust me."

He dips his hands into the water next to my shoulder, using them to drip the water on top of my head, until each strand of my hair is sufficiently soaked. From the array of soaps on the side of the tub, he grabs a lavender scented shampoo, squeezing a large dollop of it into his palms. He shushes me, and I tremble when his fingers touch my scalp. My body tenses up even further, and I try to think about anything else. Something to keep me from freaking out. Something to keep me from jumping out of this tub and running through the house stark naked just to get away from him.

His fingertips rub gentle circles on my scalp, lathering the shampoo on my head. The longer he stays there, just rubbing small, soothing circles in my hair, the lines of my shoulders begin to relax. I'm still breathing heavily, and I'm all too aware of every millimeter of his fingertips on me, but I focus on taking deep, calming breaths. They come out shaky and labored. I wipe my chin where tears have gathered there, smearing citrusy-smelling water across the bottom of my face.

"I would never hurt you."

My voice cracks. "I know."

"Tell me why you're crying."

The tears flow faster. "Don't you understand? I want you to hold me so badly, but I can't stand the thought of you touching me at the same time." I touch my forehead to my knees. Ugly, hiccupping sobs escape my throat.

He stops rubbing my scalp for a moment, finding a knot at the base of my neck where it curves into my shoulder, and he rubs the tension there. When he touches a particularly sore spot, I groan.

"Do you want me to stop touching you?"

I think about it for a long time.

Too long.

So long that my water has run cold. So long that I don't realize he's finished washing my hair until he moves out from behind me to unplug the drain and let the water rush out of the tub.

He takes one of the towels out of the warmer and drapes it around me as I stand up. He uses another towel to dry my hair. He holds out his arm so I can use it to steady myself as I step out of the tub onto the warm marble tiles.

"I'm going to go get you some clothes. Stay here."

I nod, and he leaves. I sit on the edge of the tub, watching the stray water from my hair drip onto the floor. I'm not even sure I really think about anything as I stare at the puddle near my feet.

An unknown amount of time passes before Christian steps back into the bathroom, in one hand, fuzzy socks, a pair of panties, and my favorite sleep shorts. Thrown over his shoulder, one of his sweaters. I know it's his because it's way bigger than I am, and it's a deep, ruby red. I have no such color in my entire wardrobe. He places the clothes on the counter and lets me get dressed alone. When I pull the sweater over my head, the familiar scent of him warms not only the chill in my bones, but the emptiness in my soul.

I open the bathroom door to find him freshly changed and dressed for bed too. He's lounging on the bench at the edge of his bed, scrolling on his phone. I clutch the long arms of the sweater and walk towards him. Once I'm close, he looks up and gives me his positively stunning billion-dollar smile.

"Sit." He nods at the space on the floor between his legs. For once, his instructions sound like a request instead of a command. I listen, sitting with my knees tucked up to my chest, facing away from him. He gathers the ends of my hair and begins to gently comb through the tangles. He's so cautious and meaningful with each stroke of the brush through my long hair. Once it's free of tangles, I feel him begin to braid it in one long plait down my back.

"Where did you learn to braid hair?"

"In the beginning, when I would come see you in the middle of the night, you'd *always* have your hair like that. Sometimes, you'd have it in one down your back. Other times you'd have a side braid with strands loosely framing your face. And sometimes you'd have two braids. I imagine at some point in our lives, like when we're old and gray and your bones ache, you would have been too tired to do it yourself, so I taught myself so that I could do it for you."

A new wave of tears escapes my eyes. "You're so perfect it's infuriating. It almost makes up for all the murder."

I hear him laugh behind me, draping the finished braid over my shoulder. I twist it in between my fingers and turn to look at him from my place on the floor. "Goodnight, Christian."

I get up to leave, but my name on his lips stops me. "Sleep here with me tonight." I open my mouth to protest, but he beats me to it. "I promise I'll stay on my side."

I take a deep breath. "Okay."

I let myself into his plush bed, sliding under the comforter and lying rigid on my back, staring at the ceiling. After a moment, he crawls into bed, on the far side of the California king, and clicks off the bedside lamp.

"Goodnight, Elena. I love you."

"I love you, too."

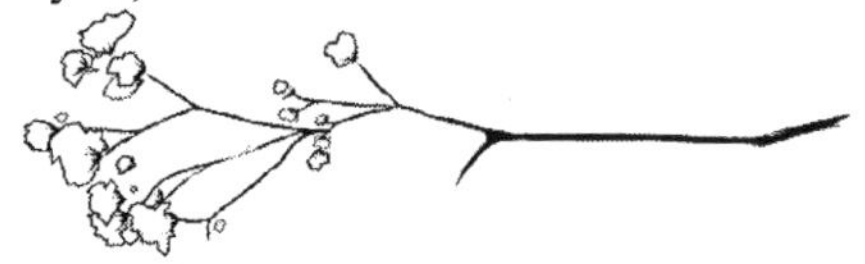

I wake up surrounded by soft sheets and a masculine scent. I wiggle against a warm body. I lift my head, meeting Christian's eyes and a soft smile, with his hands thrown behind his head, his biceps flexed. He's lit by the soft morning light from the windows in such a way that he's basking in a golden glow.

The kind of glow that makes him seem safe.

I gasp and sit up quickly, my face turning down into a scowl, ready to scold him for cuddling me in the night. But when I sit up, I realize that he's on the very edge of his side of the bed, one of his legs thrown over the side and resting on the ground. I look behind me, finding a large expanse of space.

I was the one who came to him in the night, and I slept better than I have in days.

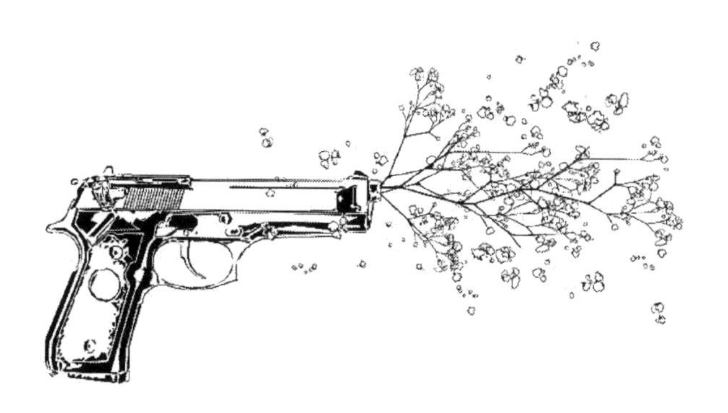

CHAPTER 31

THE SILENCER

Sometimes when I look at Edwin, all I can see is his face the night he picked me up at the police station after my parents were shot. That was thirty years ago, but I can still see the precise shade of horror in his eyes. I think that's the worst part of his memory fading.

For the most part, he knows who I am. He knows I'm Christian and he knows he's the man who raised me.

But sometimes he calls me Thomas, and those are his worst days, because I have to tell him that my parents are dead and watch him take that news like a car wreck. Edwin loved my father. They were like brothers, which is why he's my godfather. It hurts to watch him relive his grief, because Edwin may not remember it, but I certainly do. I was only six, but so many times I remember catching Edwin with a rosary and tears in his eyes, praying to God that my parents find peace. He also prayed for me, and prayed for himself to find the strength to raise me.

I was a demon after my parents died. I only got away with so much because, frankly, I was rich and could afford to. My juvenile record is sealed, but if I recall correctly, I was arrested seven times before the age of ten. By the time I was sixteen, I had a record the size of a phonebook and they started charging me as an adult. Edwin always came to my rescue though, pulling every string he could to keep me from sending my life down a drain.

I think he understood I was only acting out because of trauma, so he let most of it go. The only time he was ever hard on me was the one time I put another kid in the hospital for saying something vulgar about my mother.

I've always wanted to do something for him to say, '*thank you for not giving up on me*', because without him, I would have no one. The only thing I can think of is taking him home. To Ireland. He hasn't been there in fifty years.

As much as I hate to think about Edwin dying, he's fucking old. He's eighty-seven and has about eight hundred different health issues. Just about the only thing he can do is take a lap around the mansion once a day for exercise. He uses a walker, and it takes him about half a century to get from his bed to his bedroom door, but the last time I tried to get him a wheelchair he threw his dentures at me. Took them right out of his mouth and hit me in the forehead with them.

The point is, he can't do anything on his own. He has nurses to take care of his every need. I would have to arrange for an entire flock of them to come to Ireland with us which seems like a logistical nightmare, but I'd love to see the smile on his face when he gazes upon the beautiful green hills of his home country one last time. I think it would make him happy.

I care about Edwin. Deeply. I love him. I wouldn't consider him my father, but he's damn close. He raised me and taught me how to be a man. He did his best with me, but sadly, I still ended up really fucked in the head. I don't blame him for that.

When I was younger, I fought him tooth-and-nail about going to therapy. I didn't want to. In fact, I had such a strong aversion to it that on the one occasion he managed to get me into a room with a professional, I was so awful to the poor woman that she left the room in tears. I was only eleven.

He never tried again after that.

Now that I'm older and have real life experience under my belt, I regret not talking to him about what I was going through or how I felt. I would never entertain the idea of talking to a stranger, but I wish I had talked to him all the times he begged me to.

I talk to him now, though, not that he remembers anything I say. I tell him everything. I hold nothing back. Not even the ugly truth about the monster I've become. I talk about Elena—God, I talk about Elena so much that I think her name is permanently glued to his ears, even if he can't remember it.

Tomorrow is Thanksgiving Day.

I swallowed my pride and promised Elena I would come with her to Texas to spend the holiday with her family. I'll get to meet her brother, Travis, and his soon-to-be husband, Justin.

Unfortunately, I'll also be trapped in a house with her father, who is not my biggest fan and frankly, I'm not his either. All the times Elena talked about how he was controlling and overbearing, I always thought she was being dramatic. It only took about twelve minutes in that hospital room with him to realize that wasn't the case.

There are pros and cons to leaving Meridian City for a few days. The pros: it will be good for Elena. She needs time away from this city. Her life has been a rollercoaster since we met, and some normalcy will undoubtedly breathe some life into her. If Valenti is still lurking in the city, she'll be far, far away from him. I don't know if he's done any research on her or her family to be considered a threat to her parents or brother, but it's not on my list of worries at the moment. The cons? I'm spending two days away from Meridian City, which means I have two less days to track down the fucker.

I go out every night looking for leads. Old business associates. Regular club patrons. Even a few corrupt police officers and judges. I promised Elena that I wouldn't kill anyone else except for Frank, but my methods of interrogation aren't any less bloody.

Not that it's done me any good. It's like he vanished into thin air, and it's really starting to piss me off. The urge to commit homicide surges through my veins like it's my life's essence. It's so strong that I've even considered not claiming my kills with red tape so Elena doesn't find out and I can sate the desire for blood wrapping around my spine like lightning. I can't do that though. I feel like life would give me the middle finger and she'd find out somehow, and I'm on such thin ice with her that if I betray her trust again, I really will lose her forever. Maybe not physically, because she'll never escape me, but emotionally? I'd never get her back.

I have what I call a workshop hidden in the basement of my home. It technically doesn't exist. I paid a shit ton of money to falsify the property records to indicate the basement was sealed off a decade ago. I did seal it off, in case anyone ever comes snooping around, but I opened up another entrance just a few short feet away from the original, behind a false bookcase.

To get out of the workshop and into the city, I jackhammered into an abandoned sewer tunnel from the nineties that runs below the property.

With the exception of my guns, knives, and explosives, everything I use when I'm the Silencer has been made and forged by me, from my mask, to the hidden knife in the sole of my boot, to the clothes I wear.

Yes, I learned how to sew clothes for the Silencer. After I got an unexpected visit from the CIA a year and a half ago about my '*suspicious purchases*', I couldn't risk buying things anymore, so I had to learn to make them.

The things I do purchase off the dark web are paid for with a foreign bank account that's connected to so many false identities that there's absolutely no way to trace it back to me, and I always meet my sellers in person so there's no risk of packages getting intercepted at my front door. I'm very careful.

I've been out all night. It's six in the morning when I arrive back to the mansion sweaty, covered in blood. I take a long shower in my workshop, wiping away the black paint from my eyes and the blood splotches covering my body. I watch it all get sucked down the drain before drying off and dressing in a hoodie and jeans.

It's still early on a weekday. I gave most of my staff an extra day off since I won't be here, but a few of them are still lingering around. Mostly the maids, making sure the mansion is spotless before heading home. I sit on a stool at my computer desk in my workshop while I wait for everyone to clear out of the library so my sudden reappearance goes unnoticed. I throw a stress ball at the wall with my feet propped up on the table, scrolling through my phone while I wait.

The only form of social media I have is Instagram, and I'm rarely active. I only follow six accounts. Reeves Enterprises, POTUS, Hugo Boss, Armani, Lamborghini, and Elena. The internet weirdos who have no life instantly took note when I followed a person instead of a company, and God help me, her life story popped up so fast on Reddit that it gave me whiplash.

Prior to meeting Elena, my last post was of me cutting the ribbon to the new administrative wing on campus at the orphanage seven months ago. Now, my most recent post is from our trip to Mykonos, where the world lost their shit when they found out I was with a woman, and then subsequently lost their shit again when photos emerged of my brand-new yacht which was clearly named after her. I got tagged in so many articles and posts about it that I had to mute my notifications because they were driving me nuts.

I still can't believe posting a picture of Elena is what pushed my net worth over 500 billion. An astonishing number, even for me.

Believe me, I thanked her for it very thoroughly. With my mouth. And my fingers. And my dick. And a twenty carat Harry Winston necklace. *And* the entire Chanel catalog that was waiting on the jet for her the morning we left Mykonos.

And then she thanked *me*, wearing nothing but that diamond necklace and a fresh coat of red Chanel lipstick that ended up smeared all over my cock.

I squeeze that stress ball so tight it bursts. I can't be having these kinds of thoughts. Not now. Not when Elena was fucking gang raped less than a month ago because I couldn't keep a lid on my violence. I take a deep breath.

Thanksgiving in Texas will be good for her. Everything's going to work out; even the weird standoff between her father and me.

I've been hanging on to the last thing he said to me.

I've had a sour taste in my mouth about it ever since he left. The manner of my parents' deaths isn't any secret. Everyone knows they were shot. Everyone knows I was there.

What bothers me about what Elliot said is that it seemed like he knew something about my father's death that I didn't. But I was right there. I watched him get shot. I watched him take his last breath.

I have an unsettling feeling in my gut that Elliot is getting ready to start dangling information over my head like a carrot on a stick.

I never like to be at a disadvantage, so I've torn apart every file I can find from when my father was alive trying to find some connection to Elliot. My father was never in the Army, so it can't be that. Elliot is not in the employment records for Reeves Enterprises in the eighties. I even went so far as to pull up old property records and managed to find the apartment he lived in with his wife and kids back when he had a life in this city. The building no longer exists. It was torn down when I gutted the northern half of the island. Elliot and Diana were dirt poor. They didn't run in the same circles as my parents. I don't know how they would have crossed paths.

I must be missing something obvious. I don't take Elliot for a liar. A hardass, sure, but not a liar.

I even went so far as to pay a visit to the Chief of Police. I flashed my checkbook in his face, and in exchange for a large donation to the department, my first one in years, he let me have access to the full police report of Diana's murder.

Unfortunately, it was a bust. The records were redacted by hand and then scanned in just like the version I've already read. There's no way to uncover the names.

A few million dollars wasted on a bad lead.

I wonder what Elliot will do when I show up at his house with his precious daughter. I don't expect him to be surprised. I did tell him that I wasn't going to end things with her.

One thing I never thought about when I dove head-first into this relationship was the fact that I would have to get comfortable with the idea of having a family again. I've always hated 'family' holidays. Edwin stopped trying to celebrate them with me when I was twelve. We always just danced around each other during the holiday season and hoped neither of us would mention it. Elena, though, loves Thanksgiving and Christmas. She says November and December are her favorite months of the year because she gets to see her family.

I wish I could relate to that feeling.

I glance at the computer display that shows me the security cameras in the house. The staff has finally cleared out so I can go upstairs to get some sleep.

I'm exhausted. I haven't been sleeping well. In fact, I haven't been sleeping at all. When I'm not out chasing down Valenti, my attempts at sleep are pitiful at best. I have nightmares that begin and end with the way Elena was screaming for me in the hospital. I'll never get that sound out of my head. It haunts me. Makes my blood run cold when I think about how scared she had been—when I think about what she endured for me. What she sacrificed for me.

I don't know if I should be grateful. It doesn't seem like the right word. I don't know if it's guilt, or shame, or relief I feel. Maybe all of it.

She said she did it because she loves me, but if I put her in that position in the first place, am I really worthy of it?

My perfect little guardian angel is the strongest fucking person I know for gluing herself back together so quickly. But her cracks are still there and I'm trying to save the woman I fell in love with from becoming what I did. From becoming hollow and bitter and angry.

I take a deep breath as I use my shoulder to nudge open my bedroom door. Elena's sleeping in her own room, so I don't have to worry about disturbing her.

When I take a step towards the shower, I hear the devil on my shoulder.

Hey dumbass, we showered downstairs.

"*You* showered," I hiss as I strip and turn on the water.

I rest my forehead against the cold stone wall of the shower, and for the first time in a long time, I allow myself a moment of weakness.

My sobs come out ugly and broken, my breath getting caught in my throat as I gasp for air.

I can't decide what's worse, her shattered silence when I found her in the club, or her bloodcurdling scream in the hospital room.

I press my hands into my ears to try and bring some silence to my head, but her scream is still echoing in my mind, and I can't make it stop. My knees go weak. I fall to the ground, my forehead pressed against the shower floor, and my hands wrapped tightly in locks of my hair. I hit the side of my head to try and knock the sound out.

Here I am having a complete mental breakdown because of something Elena went though, when she's practically already built herself back up.

This is why I fucking hate you. Pathetic asshole.

"Shut up!"

None of this would have happened if you let me have her. She left that day because of you. Because you just had to be the good guy. How's that working out for you, Reeves?

Let me have control. Let me in. I'll fix this. That's what I do. I fix our problems.

"I promised—"

We're a package deal. She can't love one without the other. That's just wishful thinking on her part. She doesn't want to be strong for you all the time. She knows she can be weak with me, and I'll keep her safe better than you ever can.

"Get out of my head!" I roar at my reflection of the glass panes of the shower. Then my knuckles connect with the wall, hard enough to crack one of the milky white stones—and probably a knuckle too.

My shower's run cold, and I wash myself quickly before stumbling into my room. I don't even make it to the bed before I collapse and the world goes black.

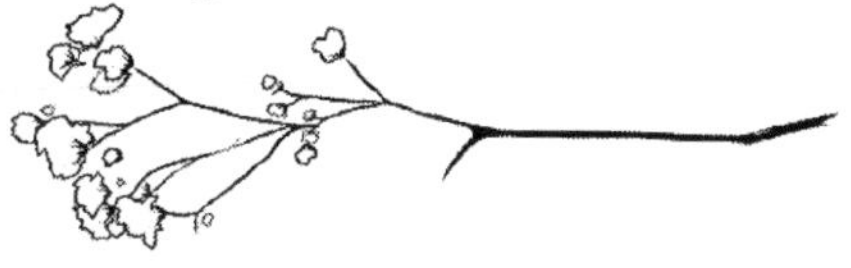

"Christian, please wake up," I hear Elena say. There's something…worrisome in her voice. "Please, Christian. Wake up."

I crash back into reality, and I sit up with a sharp inhale. I nearly crack my skull against hers.

Her mouth is open and unshed tears are in her eyes. That's when I realize we're on the floor, and I'm stark fucking naked. I blink once, twice, three times, and I focus on her face.

"Why are you crying?" I ask, and her mouth gapes open.

"Are you serious right now?" She sounds halfway furious and halfway scared. She shakes my head in her hands. "I thought you were dead. You weren't waking up and you weren't moving."

"I was just asleep, angel."

"*Asleep*?" She scoffs. "Christian Thomas Reeves, I want to strangle you right now for scaring me like that."

I sleepily blink at her and grin. "I like it when you're violent."

"Are you sure you're okay?" she asks, ignoring the teasing quip in my tone.

I nod. "I'm just tired, Elena."

I take in her attire. She's fully dressed in jeans and a nice sweater. I raise an eyebrow. "Are you going somewhere?"

She looks at me with confusion. "Are you losing your memory too? We're going to Texas."

"Our flight isn't until Thursday."

"It *is* Thursday. Our flight leaves in an hour."

I rub my eyes and look up at her again. I blink rapidly to try and orient myself. "Right. Sorry. Let me get dressed."

She sits on the bench at the foot of my bed as I go into the bathroom to brush my teeth and try to save my hair with some water and hair gel. The stubble on my cheeks and chin will have to stay.

When her family was here at the estate, I looked homeless. I would wear old hoodies, sweatpants, and mud-covered shoes. I still have massive purple circles under my eyes from worrying about Elena.

I want to make a better impression this time, so when I go to my closet, I opt to dress with some finesse.

Black trousers, black belt, navy blue dress shirt, and a nice pair of shiny black shoes. I unceremoniously throw a few days' worth of clothes into a suitcase and grab a tie from my large selection. It's black silk with small gray polka dots. As I'm fidgeting with it in the floor length mirror, I can see Elena staring at me from the reflection. She eyes me suspiciously as she walks closer.

"Got a hot date or something?"

"Or something," I purr, smoothing the crisp tie over my chest.

"Why are you dressed so fancy?"

I shrug and then wrap my father's watch around my wrist. "I wanted to make a better impression than I did the last time I saw your parents."

She giggles and steps in front of me, tugging slightly on my tie. "A little formal, don't you think?"

"You tell me. This is my first Thanksgiving since I was a kid."

She smiles, loosening the knot of the tie at my neck and tossing it to the side. Then, she unfastens the top two buttons of my shirt. She rubs over the planes of my chest to smooth out my shirt and then runs her fingers through my gelled hair to ruffle it a bit. She crosses her arms and looks me up and down, nodding with satisfaction. "Better."

We find Edwin in his room to say a quick goodbye. Elena insisted it would be fine if he came with us, but then it would be a whole thing with the nurses and it's too much to logistically work out at the last minute. Besides, we've never celebrated Thanksgiving.

I don't know if Edwin even remembers what Thanksgiving is.

"Hey old man," I say to him as we stroll into the room. Elena pokes her head in the room to wave and then gasps, announcing she forgot her phone charger in her room and runs off to get it. I give Edwin a small grin. "I'll be gone for a couple days. Do you need anything before I go?"

Edwin nods, languidly pointing in the direction of the newspaper on his bedside table. I point at it for confirmation, and he nods again. I hand it to him, and he rolls it up into a tight tube and then hits me over the head with it before laughing like an old prospector.

"Ow!" I exclaim, even though it didn't hurt. "What was that for?"

"So you know what'll be waiting for you if you don't take care of our girl."

"*Our* girl?" Weird phrasing on his part. "Do you even know who you're talking about?" I ask teasingly.

"A'course, I do. The lovely Elena."

My head snaps up to look at him, my eyes wide with shock. "Edwin—"

He bonks me over the head with the newspaper again. "Shut your yap and listen to me, boyo. That girl loves you to death. Don't you mess it up or there'll be the devil to pay."

Fuck. I can't go to Texas. Not anymore. Edwin is rarely lucid. I can't miss this opportunity to—

He pokes me square in the chest, pulling me out of my thoughts. "No."

"No?"

"No."

"But—"

Another smack to the top of my head. "Your stubbornness has always irritated me something terrible. You'd best get out of here before I put my foot up your arse and kick you out myself. Make her happy. She deserves it, and so do you."

I hesitate, and although we have a flight to catch, I need to hear his wisdom. I never valued it when I was growing up, but it's like gold to me now.

"She's so close to slipping away, and I can't lose her, Edwin. I can't. I wouldn't survive it." I take a deep breath. "I didn't know love could be so hard. I feel like no matter what I do, no matter how much I love her, it will never be enough."

"Aye, love is hard. But that's why we cherish it so much." He takes my hands in his. "Your happiness means everything to me, you know, and I want what you have with her to last for an eternity."

I squeeze his hands and suck my bottom lip in between my teeth as I think. "So how do I make it last an eternity?"

"By remembering that a gilded cage is still a cage."

I tighten my jaw. I want to defend myself, but what is there to defend? He's right. He's so right and I don't think he even realizes the extent of it. Wisdom is what Edwin does best, and he's never let me down in that regard.

I gulp. "How do I open the cage?"

"Give her the keys."

"What if she leaves? I *just* said I couldn't handle that. If I lose her, then my entire life means nothing. I might as well have…"

I trail off, because I don't know if Edwin remembers my suicide attempt the night I met Elena, and if he doesn't, then it's better for it to stay that way.

"If she leaves, then you didn't love her the way she wanted you to."

I huff. "How am I supposed to know the way she wants to be loved?"

Edwin smacks me, *again*, with the newspaper. "By *listening*. Something you've never been good at."

CHAPTER 32

THE SILENCER

When Elena and I board the jet, she has a certain…pep in her step. Like a child walking into a toy store. She seems happy.

The flight to Texas will be short. Two hours, give or take a few minutes to account for the crazy Thanksgiving air traffic.

After my conversation with Edwin, I made a silent promise to myself, and to her, that I'm going to do better. I've been selfish throughout our entire relationship. I've manipulated every part of it into my version of perfect, or at least tried. But Elena's version of perfect is different than mine. She wants trust. She wants that sickeningly sweet kind of love that gives her cavities.

I've never had a cavity, but I guess it's never too late.

"How's the studying going?" I ask. "Every time I walk past your room you're buried in a textbook."

"You know…I actually feel great. I know what to expect this time and now that I've got a few months of experience working in the field, I feel a lot more prepared than I have in the past."

That makes me smile. "I'm proud of you."

She scoffs. "I haven't passed anything yet."

"That doesn't mean I can't be proud of you. You're committed to your career, and I've always admired that about you. I offered you a chance to be my personal secretary and you wanted to stay in the legal department because you knew that was better for you and your goals. The test is in February, right?"

She nods. "Yeah, end of February. A few days after your birthday."

"Your birthday's in February too." I point out. "Tell you what, after you pass the exam, we'll take a trip to celebrate our birthdays and your accomplishment."

"You know the exam results don't come out for up to three months, right?"

I hum. "Details, details." Elena's shoulders sag suddenly, and I set my glass of whiskey to the side to give her my full attention. "What is it?"

"Nothing. It's stupid."

She looks down at her hands in shame. I sink down to the floor from my seat and kneel in front of her. I brace my hands on the armrest on either side of her. "Tell me."

She bites her pouty bottom lip to try and hide her nerves. "I want you to kiss me," she whispers, and then she scoffs humorlessly, as if she's being ridiculous. "But I'm scared."

"Of me?"

She shakes her head. "No. I'm scared I won't like it anymore."

"That's not true. You know I'm a very good kisser." I tease, and it pulls a sad laugh from her. "What if you kissed me, instead?" I suggest.

"What if I can't?"

"Then you can't, and we won't. Hey, look at me. Angel, it's been less than a month. You don't have to push yourself to do anything. Not kissing, not holding hands, not anything. I'm sorry I didn't respect your boundaries after…" I gulp. I can't even say the words. "I will respect them now. I promise."

She considers me for a long time, taking deep breaths and trying to blink away the gloss in her eyes before I notice it. Very slowly, she leans forward. I stay so still that I'm practically made of marble. She kisses my cheek, so soft and featherlight I barely feel it. She pulls away and stares at me, and I continue to stay immobile. I keep my eyes locked on hers in a warm, encouraging way.

She reaches up her hand to run the very tips of her fingers along my jaw, feeling the stubble there. She lets out a quiet, open-mouthed exhale. She wets her lips with her tongue and leans in again. This time, when her mouth touches mine, it's still slow and hesitant and cautious, but there's more life in her.

She pulls away abruptly and slumps into her seat, crossing her arms and looking away from me to hide the tears welling in her eyes.

I move to sit in the seat next to her. It is agony to not reach for her and comfort her with my embrace. "Elena, it's okay," I assure her. "Most people in your position wouldn't even go that far."

"It's not about the kiss," she croaks, sucking in a breath through her teeth. "I want you to hold me so bad. I want you to kiss me and I want you to have sex with me and I want to sleep in the same bed with you without wanting to peel off my own skin. But I can't do any of those things because they took you away from me."

Her voice breaks on the last part of her sentence.

"I'm right here. I'm not going anywhere. I promise."

She lets out an exasperated sigh and then faces me, tucking her feet under her in the seat. "No. I mean every time you touch me all I can see is them." Her pouty bottom lip begins to quiver. "*They took you away from me.*"

"They can't hurt you anymore."

"The damage was done the moment Frank pulled down my shorts." She begins to cry. "Neil had a gun to my head, and I couldn't do anything but take it. I didn't even put up a fight."

"Hey. Don't go there. *Nothing* about what happened to you is your fault. It doesn't matter that you didn't fight back. You were scared and injured. The only people responsible for this are Frank and Neil."

And me.

I take a deep breath. "Elena, I can't tell you how sorry I am. The moment I found out about that car accident I was going insane trying to find you. I would have torn apart Meridian City brick by brick if that's what it took."

"How long did it take you to find me after I pressed the button?"

"Forty-nine minutes. I was at the scene of the accident when the alarm went off. I had to go home and get weapons, gear, anything and everything I could get my hands on. I came into that club ready for war. Every second after you pressed that button was fucking agony for me. I can't imagine what it was like for you."

She sniffles and wipes her face with the back of her palm. "I'm sorry about your McLaren."

"Fuck the McLaren. I couldn't give less of a shit about that stupid car. All I cared about when I saw it was the fact that *you weren't in it.*"

"How did you even know about it?"

"All of my cars have trackers on them. When one leaves the property, its location is tracked by my security team. Gavin said the GPS went dead and police were responding to a major accident in the area. I put two and two together."

It's quiet for a long time. Elena's fingers tap nervously against the leather seat.

"Do you think I'm...*dirty* now?"

My face twists, offended at the suggestion. "No. You're not dirty. I can prove it if you'll let me."

Her eyes find mine with a curious gaze. I stand up and make my way to the bedroom in the back of the jet. Elena follows close on my heels and when we're both in the room, I lock the door behind us. I lean against the thin door and put my hands in my pocket, pulling out my cigarette case and lighting one of them. Elena looks shocked.

"Are you nuts? You can't smoke on a plane!"

"You can't smoke on a *commercial* plane," I point out. "This is *my* plane. Now I need you to look into my eyes and tell me that you trust me." She nods and I shake my head back. "I need to hear you say it."

She gulps. "I trust you."

I take a drag of my cigarette and lean my head back against the door. "I'm making you a promise that I won't touch you, but I want you to take off everything except your panties."

She doesn't move, suddenly looking like a cornered rabbit waiting for escape. "You won't touch me? No tricks?"

I shake my head. "Swear on my life."

She hesitates. "Do you want a strip tease or something? Turn around."

"No, angel. I want to watch."

All the curiosity falls from her face, and her skin turns a shade lighter with nerves. "Please turn around."

"You said you trusted me. Go as slow as you need to, but I'm not turning around." I continue to slowly smoke, one hand holding the stick and the other tucked into my pocket.

She takes a deep breath and with unsteady hands, she hooks her fingers into her jeans and tugs them down her legs. Her shirt comes next.

She's standing in her lacy bralette and panties, both a peachy pink shade. Her cheeks turn red, and I can see the exact moment she begins to reconsider this whole thing. I hold her stare and wait patiently to see what she does. If she tells me to fuck off, I will, but I don't think that's what she wants. She's just nervous. Embarrassed. Shy.

Her shaky hands unhook the bralette from the back, and she pauses for a long time before letting it fall to the floor. Her arms fall slack at her side, and she watches me intently, like she's waiting for me to become predatory at the sight of her body. But I don't. She's a beautiful woman and I love her body, but this isn't about me and my desires. This is about making her feel wanted.

"Now what?"

"Now get on the bed and wait for me to finish this." I wiggle the cigarette between my teeth. She frowns but lies down on the bed to wait for me. I finish the cigarette so slowly it's agonizing for me, and infuriating for her.

I place the nub into the ashtray in the small bathroom, and then approach the bed. Her eyes stay glued to my hands like she expects me to break my promise. I kneel on the bed and then lean over her, propping myself up on an elbow. Her breathing becomes erratic.

"Relax, angel. Relax," I coo. "I'm going to move around the bed, but I'm not going to touch you. I'll get close, but I promise, I'll keep my hands and mouth to myself."

"You're missing an important body part from that list."

I scoff. "I promise I'll keep my hands, mouth, and dick to myself." Then my face drops so she knows I'm serious. "Mykonos. That's your safe word. Say it, and I stop. Say yes if you understand."

"Yes," she shudders. "But why do I need a safe word if you're not going to touch me?"

"Because maybe you just want to use it. You don't need a reason. If you use the safe word, I stop, no questions asked."

She takes a deep breath and then nods. "Okay."

I allow myself to let my eyes leave her face, to drink in her chest. "Move your hair." It's covering her breasts, and it's in the way for what I'm about to do. She moves the strands and I make a small noise of satisfaction. "Every inch of you is beautiful, my perfect little angel." My eyes meet hers again. "I love you."

Her eyes go glassy. "Be careful?"

I nod. "I promise. Close your eyes."

She does as instructed, and I watch her entire body fill with tension. Carefully, I prop myself up with my hands and lean down far enough that my breath fans across her neck.

"I miss kissing you here, where I can feel your heart flutter under my lips." My words have the desired effect. Her entire body erupts into goosebumps. I shift again, until my breath is hot against the center of her chest, between her breasts. "And I miss kissing you here, because this is precisely how far I need to kiss down your body before you start squirming. Before you start rubbing your thighs together to try and get some relief."

Again, my words have their intended effect, and her nipples perk up, the soft pink rosebuds hardening, begging for my attention. She takes a deep breath, taking her bottom lip between her teeth. My cock begins to fatten up in my pants.

Slowly, I move further down her body. Her legs clench together in fear and her eyes shoot open. I anticipated this, and I lean back on my knees.

"Please don't," she pleads, looking green and nauseous.

"Use your safe word if you want me to stop."

"You can't touch me there."

"I won't. I told you, no tricks." I lean back down, licking my lips at the sight of that feminine softness between her belly button and the seam of her panties. Where one day she might grow my child. I glance up at her. "God, Elena, I fucking miss kissing you here."

My breath fans across the top of her panties before I move further down until I'm millimeters from her core. Tears well in her eyes, and I pause for a second, allowing her the chance to use her safe word if she wants. She doesn't, so I continue.

"I miss kissing your pretty pussy, angel. Your taste sends me straight to heaven. My mouth is watering just thinking about it."

That's a very true statement. I'm salivating at the thought like it's my first meal in months. My cock is painfully hard in my slacks, trying it's best to drill a hole through the fabric. I stare at the space between her thighs, right where her clit is, twitching and achy and needy like the rest of her.

"Do you miss it too, baby? The feeling of my face buried between your thighs until you're shaking with pleasure instead of fear? Don't you remember how good it feels?"

A single tear escapes from her eye and she shakes her head.

"No?" I hum. "Don't you remember all those times you came apart on my tongue? All the times my fingers were deep inside you while I sucked on your puffy clit? All the times you had your fingers tangled in my hair, pulling me closer and begging for my cock? You don't remember any of that?"

Something clicks inside her in that moment. I think my words have set her on fire, because she takes a long deep breath, and I can fucking *smell* the way she opens up for me under her panties. I look and smile wickedly at the wet spot forming there. "*There she is,*" I murmur to her core as if it's a separate person. "Oh, angel, you should see how wet you are." My eyes flicker back to hers. "Take off your panties and I'll show you."

"Not a chance."

I crawl back up her body, staying a respectful distance from her naked skin. The hard length of me is aching and I'm going to have to sneak away to the bathroom to rub it out before we land. I settle on top of Elena, holding myself up so not a single part of me is touching her, not even a single thread of my clothes. My lips ghost over hers.

"I was really…wet?" she asks in disbelief.

"Feel for yourself," I suggest. She pauses, but then I can feel one of her hands trace down her own body to touch the space between her legs. She lets out a gasp of awe, like she can't believe it, and looks back to me with sparkling, shy eyes. I smirk. "You were a *very* good girl—"

She cuts off my sentence by smearing her arousal-coated fingers across my bottom lip. I freeze, my eyes surely going sharklike with lust. I lick the taste off my lips and groan. I'm four seconds away from losing my shit, so I quickly push off her and sit on the edge of the bed, facing away.

From behind me, I hear her breathy voice whisper, "Touch me."

I turn around to glare at her. "No."

My cock is straining against my pants-shaped prison. I feel her shift behind me and then tug on the back of my belt. "Christian, *please* touch me."

I still make no move to touch her. Something shifts in the air, and she suddenly shatters.

She tucks her knees up to her chest and lets tears fall down her cheeks. Her breath is coming out so uneven and frantic I'm afraid she's going to pass out. "Elena, you're trembling."

"*I knew you wouldn't want me anymore*."

My heart shatters in my ribcage at how defeated and humiliated she sounds.

She thinks I don't want her because she was raped. Because she thinks she's dirty. But nothing could be further from the truth and that's what I tried to prove to her just now.

"Look at me."

She shakes her head and makes a very obvious effort to do anything but that, to the point where she turns on the bed to face away from me completely.

I sigh. "I will always want you. I've wanted you every day from the moment we met. That will never change." I get off the bed and circle around the mattress to kneel on the floor in front of her. "I think every day about burying myself inside you and filling you with my love again. I think about chasing away all the memories of what they did to you. I want to erase them from your head. I want to replace the fear they made you feel with the desire I make you feel. I *do* want you, and you know better than anyone that I will give you whatever you want." I reach up to tuck a strand of hair behind her ear. "I just don't want to hurt you in the process."

My throat burns. I wish I knew how to help her.

I gather her clothes from the floor and help her get dressed. We leave the bedroom and go back to our seats, only this time, Elena takes the seat next to mine and rests her cheek on my shoulder.

We sit in silence until we land.

CHAPTER 33

THE SILENCER

When we pull into the long driveway of Elena's parent's house, I begin to sweat.

This is going to be an entirely different setting than the last time I saw her parents, and I don't really know what to expect. I want her family to like me. Not just because of who I am and what my money can give Elena, but because they see how much I cherish her. I want them to know in their hearts that she's the most important thing in my life. I want them to know I'm devoted to making her happy.

I park the SUV in front of the house and take a deep breath as I look it over.

Two stories. Gray brick. Two car garage. Large front porch. The house is sitting on a big plot of land, with a fancy gate and expensive fences surrounding it. Their closest neighbors are half a mile away. Big oak trees dot the land around the house, and I can see a pond a short distance away.

The house is…warm. Inviting. Elena told me she grew up comfortable, and I suppose I can admit I'm a little jaded when it comes to money, because her idea of comfortable and my idea of comfortable are two very different things.

I step out of the vehicle and circle the front end of the car to open Elena's door for her. She slides out of her seat, and I can tell just from her energy that she's elated to be home.

Elena leads me up the small steps, up to the porch and then through the front door. She doesn't knock. It's unlocked. I scoff. Nobody in Meridian City would leave their front door unlocked. Not even me, and I have 24/7 security.

Elena walks inside without a second thought, but I find myself lingering in the doorway like a vampire that hasn't been invited in.

"Stop being weird," Elena says, and I cautiously take a step through the threshold. She leads us further into the house.

"Ellie!" Bethany squeals when she sees her daughter, leaving her spot at the stovetop to capture Elena in a big hug.

Her mother turns to me. "Christian!" she exclaims, squeezing me into an equally tight hug. I wrap my arms around her shoulders to hug her back. "I'm so glad you could come." She looks me over and tugs on my shirt. "And look how handsome you are. You shine up like a new penny."

"Thank you for having me, Mrs. Young."

"*Bethany*," she corrects in her thick southern accent, and I give her a nod.

I watch Elena carefully as she steps towards her brother. She twitches once, and slowly pulls him into an embrace, and I see Travis' lip quiver as he hugs her back. What a relief it must be for her family, to know that she has been healing since they last saw her.

She lets go of her brother and I shake his hand, introducing myself, and Elena skips over to her dad and throws herself in his arms. "Hi sweetheart," he says, a big smile painted across his face. "I missed you."

"I missed you too, dad."

I notice that her father looks a lot older than the last time I saw him. Probably on account of him worrying about his daughter. He peeks out from over Elena's shoulder at me, and the scowl he gives me is so hot with fury he could dry up oceans. He squeezes her one more time before releasing her. She comes to stand next to me and another man emerges from a powder bathroom.

He smiles at Elena and waves. "Hi, Ellie."

She waves back. "Christian, this is Justin, Travis' future husband."

I shake Justin's hand and then he takes a seat next to Travis at the kitchen island. I can still feel Elliot staring at me like he's trying to get my head to explode. I glare back at him as if to say, '*knock it off*'.

Bethany sighs loudly. "I'm so happy the whole family's here."

Family. That word feels equal parts icy cold and burning hot in my chest. Family is such a distant concept for me that it feels wrong. It feels like I'm betraying my parents somehow by using the word.

Elena moves to the kitchen to help her mother with the food, leaving me alone under the burning glare of her father.

"Well Christian," Bethany starts, stirring a pot on the stove, "we were all so preoccupied with taking care of Ellie that I feel like I know nothing about you. How did you two meet? I mean I know it was through work, but that can't be the whole story. Tell me everything!" She throws her head back and makes a squeal of delight. "I bet it was romantic. Was it romantic?"

Elena and I share a look. I give her a strained smile. "Sorry to disappoint you, Bethany. I saw her in the office one day, thought she was the most beautiful woman I've ever seen, and I haven't left her alone since."

Elliot lets out a sound between a sarcastic laugh and a dangerous growl. His arms are crossed over his chest, his mouth in a hard line.

"Oh my God!" Justin loudly exclaims, gathering the attention of everyone in the room. "Holy shit. You're Christian *fucking* Reeves!" Justin lightly swats at Travis' arm. "Babe, what the fuck? You told me Ellie was dating some rich guy, you didn't tell me he was a fucking billionaire."

Travis chokes on his water. "Billionaire? Like…like with a B? *Billionaire*?" They look at Bethany. "Mom! You said he lived in a *really big house*."

"Don't look at me!" Bethany defends herself playfully. "Ellie's the one dating the man. She didn't tell you he was a billionaire either!"

"Yeah, Ellie, what the fuck?" Travis tosses a crumpled-up paper towel at her.

She narrows her eyes in their direction. "Can you two stop making it weird? You're telling me you didn't connect the dots when I told you I was going on a business trip to Mykonos and staying on a yacht?"

"You didn't say you were going on a business trip with the *CEO*!"

Elena shrugs. "Oops."

I can understand Elena not telling her parents I'm a billionaire. I think that would send most parents into cardiac arrest. I'm shocked she never told her brother though. They're very close. They talk all the time. I figured he would have been the first person she told. I'm sure her parents googled me the second they stepped into my mansion. Her mother at least. Her father doesn't seem to be all that interested in who I am—only that I stay far, far away from his daughter.

Elena goes back to helping her mother, and Bethany sends me a wink before turning her attention to the stove. I smirk. At least her mother likes me.

I take in Elena's childhood home. How cozy it is. My mansion is pretty much stripped of all signs of living. No family photos on the walls. No souvenirs from vacations. No '*Live Laugh Love*' signs. The only family photos I have are on the bookshelf in my room. I don't even have that many since my parents have been dead for thirty years. The only other 'family' photo I have is one of Edwin and I when I graduated from MIT.

I remember that day so vividly. I walked across the stage, and then got drunk in a bar and had a threesome with two tall blondes. Only after I stumbled back to Edwin's hotel room at 3 PM the next day did I realize he had gotten me a cake and a gift. The cake was left uneaten, and the gift was my father's Breitling. The one he was wearing the day he was murdered. The police had kept it for almost twenty years as 'evidence'.

That was the first and only time I've ever hugged Edwin.

I'll never be able to give Elena the simple life her parents have. Their world seems so disconnected from mine. From ours. Simple won't do. Not for her. Not after what she's been through for me. Pretty soon I'll have to start carving her name into mountains to prove my love.

I watch my angel with a smile on my face as she dances around the kitchen with her mother.

"You're staring at my sister."

Travis' voice pulls me out of my besotted stare, and I look at him. I nod down at him, turning my gaze back to her.

"She talks about you all the time, you know. All good things, I promise. Be good to her, okay? She deserves happiness."

"I know. *Fuck*, I know she does. She deserves everything. I'm…trying my best."

Travis nods. "You coming to the wedding with her?"

"Didn't know I was invited."

He chuckles. "You kidding? It's every couple's dream to have a billionaire come to their wedding." Travis pokes me with his elbow. "I'll be expecting no less than a quarter of a million as a wedding present."

I'm the one to laugh this time. "I'll keep that in mind."

From across the room, Elena licks mashed potatoes off a spoon before throwing it into the sink, and I wink at her and mouth '*I love you*'.

She winks back.

When dinner is ready and the table is set, Elena pats a chair next to her for me to sit in. Elliot and Bethany sit on the ends of the table. Elena and I sit on one side, and Travis and Justin sit on the other. I get the questionable luck of sitting next to Elliot. Once Elena is in her seat, I drag her chair a bit closer to me.

Her family settles into soft chatter while they fill their plates. I go rigid in my seat, staring at the dishes blankly.

"Christian," Bethany says from her side of the table, and I look at her. "Don't stand on ceremony, honey. Please help yourself."

"It's not that," I tell her, and Elena looks at me. I don't break her stare as I explain. "My parents died when I was a kid. I haven't spent Thanksgiving with a family in a very long time."

"You're welcome to come spend time with our family whenever you want." Bethany lifts her wine glass. "*To family*."

We all repeat her toast, clinking our glasses together.

The backs of my eyes begin to burn, and I excuse myself from the table to run to the bathroom before the tears fall out of them. I wipe my face with a tissue and glance at myself in the mirror.

For the first time in a long time, the man in the mirror staring back at me isn't so bad.

When I emerge from the bathroom, Elena blows me a kiss. I take my seat next to her again, and midway through dinner, Elliot clears his throat around a bite of stuffing.

"Beth, you know I love your cooking."

"Oh, no," Bethany teases.

Elliot gives her a grin, but there's something...malicious about it.

And I don't think it's directed at Bethany.

"I just can't help but remember the best Thanksgiving stuffing I've ever had. When I lived in Meridian City, my Diana loved this diner on the North Side. They had a Thanksgiving food drive every year, and the owner made the best stuffing." Another unnerving smile crosses his face and his eyes flicker to me. "You been to the North Side recently?"

"The North Side doesn't exactly exist anymore." I shrug. "I turned that side of the island into an orphanage in memoriam to my parents."

Bethany puts her hand over her heart. "That's beautiful, Christian. Truly beautiful."

Elliot sighs. "Man, that's a shame. I *loved* Fat Lou's."

My heart falls straight out of my chest and onto the floor. I can't find it in me to tell him that Fat Lou's doesn't exist anymore.

Because I burnt it to the ground when I was eighteen.

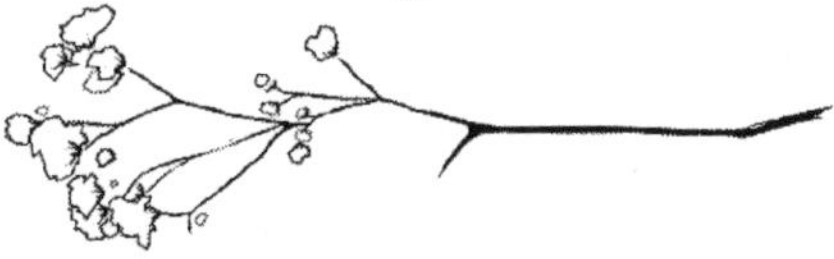

It's the middle of the night. I'm staring at the ceiling of Elena's childhood bedroom, painted a soft shade of pastel purple. She's sound asleep next to me, facing away. Her cold feet are pressed against my warm legs.

I can't sleep.

I need a cigarette.

I carefully shift out of the bed, quietly throwing on a shirt and finding my cigarette case and lighter before stepping out of the bedroom and softly closing the door behind me. I walk downstairs and out the front door, inhaling deeply when a soft breeze meets me.

I sit down in a rocker and light up a cigarette that I finish in two drags. I light another and savor this one, rocking back and forth gently.

I'm sitting outside for an hour and on my fourth cigarette when I hear the door open behind me. I turn to look. Elliot walks out with a strange combination of things in his hands. Two glasses of scotch. A pistol. A manila file folder. He sets it all down on the small table between us and slumps into the other rocker. Then he hands me one of the glasses.

"Thanks," I say cautiously.

Is he trying to poison me or something? Seems out of place for him to be so cordial with me.

I take the tiniest sip and then rest the glass on my knee to resume smoking. Elliot lights his own cigarette, takes a drag, and blows the smoke out of his nose.

"Can't sleep?"

I shake my head. "I don't sleep much."

"Nothing like smoking a cig in the middle of the night while you brood."

"I'm not brooding. I'm just…thinking."

"And that's why I brought the scotch. To loosen the tongue. Why don't you tell me what's on your mind?"

I take another drag and sink into my chair a little further, letting my head fall against the back of it. "Your daughter is one extraordinary woman. She ripped open my soul and made me a better man but…" I look down and flick some ashes over the railing of the porch. "I'll never be good enough for her. I don't know what she sees in me."

"Danger is my guess," Elliot says, and I try not to react. "She's always liked the guys that were a little bit bad for her."

I laugh out the smoke from my lungs with a cough. "That explains it."

From the corner of my eye, I watch as Elliot sits up and grabs the gun from the side of the table, and my blood runs cold when he points it at me. We both go still, and then he flips the gun upside down and tells me to take it.

"Pretty, isn't it?" He takes a sip of his drink and squeezes his eyes shut before rubbing one. "It was my very first piece."

I examine the gun, my heart still thudding wildly in my chest after being held at point-blank range. It's a deep, obsidian black. Custom engraved with his initials. It's pretty common for people who live or have lived in Meridian City to get their initials engraved or etched into their guns. Less likely to be stolen. I nonchalantly check the chamber. Loaded.

"Pretty," I agree, extraordinarily unimpressed. I have seven of the same model in my basement. And *many* guns that are *far* prettier.

He nods towards my glass of amber liquid. "Finish that."

I raise my eyebrow. Now I'm suspicious. "Why?"

He picks up the manila folder and hands it to me. "Because you'll need it, kid."

Elliot patiently waits while I down the rest of the drink he gave me, and then I take the manila folder from him. I give him a questionable look, but his gaze is off into the darkness of the night, nursing his drink while he rocks in his chair and chain-smokes. I snuff out my own cigarette and then open the folder.

I go unnaturally rigid in my chair when I realize I've seen these words before.

This is the unredacted version of the police report for Diana Young's murder.

I only have to get to the first sentence to understand why Elliot said I needed the scotch, but I can't stop myself from reading the entire thing, clearing my throat uncomfortably when I see my dad's name. Clear as day.

"*Thomas Caledon Reeves, when interviewed, admitted to the murder of Diana, Lisa, and Mary Young. He was taken into custody on three counts of first-degree murder.*"

I drop the manila folder, spilling the papers all over the porch. I look at Elliot, still gazing out into the darkness.

My chest hurts so bad that I can hardly breathe, and I clutch the arm of the rocking chair so hard I can hear it warp and groan under my grip.

"My father did *not* kill your first wife," I growl. "This is some sick fucking joke. He was a good man, and a loyal husband."

"He was a spoiled prick who couldn't take no for an answer," he snarls back. "Look at me, kid."

As if I wasn't already shooting daggers at him with my eyes, my gaze is laser-focused on him.

"I remember your face."

I feel like I'm freefalling through space. The edges of my vision go black.

And I realize I remember his too.

CHAPTER 34

THE SILENCER

Wednesday, September 6, 1989

"*Please*," I beg, clasping my hands together, pouting my lip, and giving mommy the biggest puppy dog eyes I can manage. "Please, mommy. I'll die without it."

Mommy gives me an amused smirk. "You'll die?" she asks, bending down and zipping up my jacket for me. "Well, my sweet boy, I can't allow that, can I?"

"Elizabeth, don't encourage him. He's already spoiled rotten."

The diamond on mommy's finger sparkles under the harsh fluorescent lights of the diner. Her wedding ring and pearls stick out like a sore thumb against the chipping paint and the worn-off vinyl of the bright blue booths surrounding us.

Daddy has always been the authority of the family. Which is why when he says no, I give mommy the puppy dog eyes until she says yes.

Only this time, she doesn't say yes. She listens to daddy. She's been doing that a lot lately.

They've been fighting when they think I can't hear them. But I'm an only child in a giant mansion with nothing better to do than get into trouble. I know all the best hiding places in the house. That means I hear things I shouldn't. Like how Edwin *like like's* Judith, my governess, but Judith says Edwin kisses like a chicken.

That made me laugh so hard that chocolate milk came out of my nose, and almost gave away my hiding spot inside the cabinets where daddy keeps the cigarettes he hides from mommy.

Mommy stands up, and I pout to her back. After daddy pays and we turn to find a table that isn't unnervingly sticky, I give my puppy dog eyes to Fat Lou, the owner, in a last-ditch effort to achieve my goal.

Mommy says that's a rude name, but that's the name of his restaurant! Everyone calls him that. How can it be rude?

Fat Lou smiles warmly behind the counter at me. He winks, tosses something high in the air which I catch with ease, and then he turns away to make our order. I open my tightly clasped hands to reveal an orange lollipop. My mouth waters. My parents don't keep candy in the house. I'm only allowed to have it on Halloween, my birthday, and sometimes when we're out in the city and a business has a bowl of it, mommy allows me a single piece.

Sometimes Edwin sneaks me one of those weird strawberry candies that only old people have.

I squeal with glee and shove the candy in my jacket pocket for later, trailing behind my parents into the booth.

What feels like an eternity later, Fat Lou brings us our food. Mommy of course, always prim and proper, has a salad with no cheese, no croutons, no anything other than lettuce, tomatoes, and stinky dressing. I ordered a burger just like daddy, because burgers are man food, and I am nothing if not a big strong man like him.

I smile wide-eyed at my burger and eat it as messily as expected of a feral kid with no social manners. Cheese sauce is smeared all over my face when I'm done, and mommy wipes me clean with a wet wipe she pulls out of her purse. After I'm deemed spotless again, I crawl under the table to sit next to daddy. I wrap my arms around him tight and squeeze as hard as my six-year-old body can manage.

"Thank you, daddy. You're the best."

He wraps an arm around me and pats me like fathers do their sons. "Why don't we get you a cheeseburger to-go? That way you can eat it tomorrow."

"But daddy!" I whine. "It will be soggy and yucky from the veggies."

He shrugs. "We'll get it plain and then the chef at home can give you fresh veggies tomorrow. How about that?"

I nod enthusiastically. He stands to go place the to-go order, and a small orange light outside the window catches my eye. I press my face against the greasy windowpane. There's a man outside with a red bandana slack around his neck, smoking a cigarette, staring at me with the same intensity as I am him.

Mommy makes a noise of disgust. "Bleh. Smokers. Promise me, Christian, you won't smoke when you're older."

"I promise, mommy," I say absently, not even really comprehending what she said.

Once daddy has my to-go order, he gives me the box to hold, and mommy leans over to kiss my forehead before I slide out of the booth. We step outside onto the dark street, lit by only a few dim streetlamps. Mommy grumbles as we begin to walk, complaining that her feet hurt in her heels. I hold her hand, not paying much attention to anything when we abruptly stop. I look up to see the same man that was smoking outside the restaurant standing across from us.

He's got his red bandana over his face now, covering his nose and mouth. A black jacket with the collar popped sits heavy on his frame.

"Get lost," daddy warns. "I don't have any cash."

The masked man laughs and then pulls a gun from his jacket pocket. Mommy shields me behind her, and then daddy shields us both with his body.

Though I'm confused and scared, I peek around daddy's legs to watch the man across from us.

"Do you really think I want your money?" He begins to cry. "I want my wife and kids back."

"I'm sorry to hear that, sir," daddy says calmly. "But I can't help you with that, either. Please leave us alone."

"You have no idea who I am, do you?" he asks, and then shakes his head. "You deserve this, Thomas."

And then I hear a loud '*pop*', followed by mommy screaming.

And then I hear another '*pop*', and then silence, before my parents fall to the ground.

I drop my to-go bag. "Mommy. Daddy?"

Daddy is looking up at the dark sky. I've never seen him look so…blank. Mommy is crying. Shaking. Bleeding. They're both bleeding.

The man with the bandana takes three large steps towards me, and then he points the gun at my head. It shakes in his hand, and I simply stare up at him and sniffle. He takes a shaky breath and then lowers the gun before turning and running away.

I kneel next to mommy. Warm, red, sticky blood coats my jeans. I lay my head on her chest and listen to her weak heartbeat, until there isn't one.

I glance at daddy's watch. His favorite. Gold face. Navy blue leather strap. It says it's 9:21 PM.

I don't know how long I sit there in a puddle of my parents' blood. It feels like forever. I look at mommy and place my left hand over her heart. She's not moving.

I don't know why, but I use the same hand to close her eyes. Her warm sticky blood smears across her eyelids from my hands.

Five policemen show up and stare at me, sitting on the dirty concrete in between my parents. One of them kneels down a few steps away. "Hi, kid. I'm Officer Harold Fischer. What's your name?"

"Christian," I say politely. Mommy says I should always be nice to a policeman.

"Do you know your last name, Christian?"

"Reeves."

The policemen all share a look with each other, and then the one kneeling holds out his arms and waves for me to come closer. "Come here, Christian. It's okay. You're safe now."

I blink at him, unmoving. "Are you going to help mommy and daddy?"

"Yeah," he says, his voice strained. He points up at the sky. "Hear those sirens? Ambulances are coming to help them. Come on." He waves again. "Have you ever been in a police car before?"

I shake my head.

"Do you want to sit in mine? I'll let you turn on the sirens!" he taunts excitedly. I finally stand up and reach into my pocket and pull out the orange lollipop with my bloody left hand.

"Can I eat this in the police car?"

Officer Fischer nods. "Whatever you want, kid."

Next thing I know, I'm sitting in his police car, playing with the sirens and lights. And then I'm at the police station, petting a German Shepard named Lucy with a K-9 vest on.

Then Edwin's there, and I look up at him.

"*Edwin, when are mommy and daddy coming back*?"

CHAPTER 35

THE SILENCER

The memory hits me like a truck, knocking all the wind out of me. It takes my sanity and rationale with it, if there was any left to take. I rise out of the rocking chair to my full height, breathing fire like a dragon as I snatch the gun from the table between us, and shove it under Elliot's chin.

My molars feel like they're going to crack under the pressure of my jaw as I stare Elliot down. I wait. I wait and wait and wait for him to say something. Anything. To defend himself. To beg for his life. But all he does is scowl, his dead eyes staring back at me.

"Do it," he taunts.

I shove the gun even further into his chin, causing his head to tilt back slightly. My finger is on the trigger one fucking millimeter from painting the gray brick of this house with his blood.

"She'll never forgive you."

That sentence makes me pause, because he's fucking right. If I pull this trigger, Elena will *never* forgive me. It doesn't matter if it's justified revenge.

All she'd see is that I murdered her father in cold blood.

I bare my teeth and tears prick in my eyes.

The man who killed my parents is Elena's fucking *father*.

"*Fuck*," I spit through gritted teeth.

I've imagined this moment so many times. How poetic the justice would be to hunt down the man in the red bandana and show him that I have a mask now, too. That *he* is the reason my mask is red.

I became a monster because I wanted the man who killed my parents to witness the same inhumanity he showed me thirty years ago.

It's no wonder he hates me. His punishment for killing my parents is having to watch his precious daughter fall in love with the son of his mortal nemesis.

Slowly, I lower the gun from his chin.

His revelation has made all the missing parts of the memory of that night fill in. I had lost it from the trauma. Forced myself to forget. But now I see his face so vividly. Thirty years younger, but Elliot is the man who was staring at me through the window of the restaurant, waiting for my father to emerge. He wanted payback, and he got it.

And now he must live with the punishment.

We're both murderers, and now we must face our consequences: each other.

"Why did you leave me alive? Why didn't you just fucking shoot me and leave the Reeves family in the past?"

"Because I saw the look on your face when I had that gun to your head, and I saw the face of my daughters when your father shot them. All I can see when I look at you is the man who killed my wife and little girls. The moment I walked into that hospital room I knew you looked familiar, but now that I know who you are, it's like your father still found a way to haunt me. My family."

I bite the inside of my cheek hard enough that I taste blood. "If you expected your *revelation* to convince me to let Elena go, you were wrong."

I take a deep breath, sagging my shoulders. This entire situation is so fucked. Not only did I just find out that murder runs in my veins, but the man who killed my parents is the father of the love of my fucking life.

Letting her go is not an option.

If someone had told me twenty minutes ago that I was about to extend a white flag to the man who ruined my life, I would have ripped out their spinal cord through their throat.

But, well, here we are.

"Look, we both love Elena. Don't mistake my love for her as forgiveness for what you did to me. For her sake, I am willing to *tolerate* your presence in my life. I'm going to slowly torture you by making you watch as I become a permanent part of your life. This is your first, last, and final warning. If you try to tear us apart, my love for Elena won't save you."

After my ultimatum, there's a long silence. Elliot lights another cigarette and brings it to his mouth. "If you're anything like your father, your relationship will fall apart at the seams with no effort on my part." There's another long pause. "This has to stay between us. Elena can never know. Not about any of it."

"Because you don't want her to find out her dad's a murderer?" I taunt, even though the irony of this conversation is killing me. "Or are you afraid she won't take your side?"

"What the fuck does it matter? Keep your mouth shut about it. I gave you the truth, now you owe it to me. Tell me what you did to my daughter. You didn't know about my involvement in your parents' deaths, so meeting her is just fate giving us both the middle finger, but there is a reason she's so glued to your side. She did not want to be with you when we stayed in your mansion. She couldn't wait to leave. Then, suddenly, on the day we're supposed to fly to Texas, she wants to stay. How does that happen?"

Fine. I can give him the truth. A very, very, *very* watered-down version, but the truth, nonetheless.

Sighing, I take the rest of Elliot's scotch and down it for him.

"I've been suicidal for the better part of my life. I met Elena shortly after a suicide attempt. It's…why I call her angel."

I'm hoping it's not obvious that '*shortly after*' actually means '*during*'.

"I'll tell you the same thing I told her. I had been living in the past for three decades and I didn't think I had a soul left. I didn't think I was capable of feeling anything other than pain and anger. She came into my world and tore down the walls I spent so much time building up. She made me feel worthy. She let me be vulnerable. My life was empty before she came into it, but now that I have her, I can't imagine how I lived this long without her. I messed up along the way. I was selfish. I was a bad partner, and even though I love her with every fiber of my being, I didn't love her the way she deserved. So, she left. And that's the day shit hit the fan."

I let out another heavy sigh. "She *did* want to leave, Elliot, and I was going to let her go. That morning when you were supposed to get on that flight back to Texas, I left and went to my office on the other side of the city so I wouldn't be tempted to beg her to stay for my own selfish reasons. She *chose* to stay all on her own. I didn't force her."

Elliot clicks his tongue. "I don't believe you."

"Ask her yourself."

Elliot gives me a dead, lifeless grin. He takes his gun back and waves it in the small space between us. It's languid and unthreatening, unlike his words. "I should have put a bullet between your eyes thirty years ago and been done with it."

"So do it now," I taunt sadistically. "*But she'll never forgive you.*"

He blows the last of his cigarette smoke in my face and then body checks me before walking back into the house.

My molars ache from how hard I'm clenching my teeth and I have so much pent-up aggression in my body right now that if Elliot was anyone but Elena's dad, every one of his bones would be broken.

My blood pounds in my ears as I stumble down the steps of the wrap-around porch, my bare feet loud against the loose gravel driveway. I walk aimlessly into the trees surrounding the property and lose myself in them.

I pick a poor, unsuspecting tree, and I let myself go. I use the rough bark as a punching bag until my fists are bloody and trembling and numb. Until I'm so exhausted and sweaty that I can barely hold myself up. I fall face-first into the bloody tree and onto my knees. I lightly bang my fists against the bark as I growl and weep for myself.

For the first time since I met Elena, I feel doubt. Not in my love for her. That's unfaltering. It's absolute. It's undeniable. But I do doubt my ability to be a part of her life and still keep my fucking head on straight. I've got enough screws missing already.

I'd love to get back at Elliot for what he did to my parents, but I don't know if my sanity would survive, and I have so little to start with. I don't know that I have the strength to keep this to myself, and I don't think telling Edwin just for him to forget minutes later is going to be enough.

If I told Elena, would she even believe me? She may have her differences with her father, but she told me herself that she's a daddy's girl. Her father is her hero, more than I will ever be.

I know one thing is certain: if my father hadn't killed Diana, then Elliot would have never met Bethany, and then I would have never met Elena.

And honestly? I think that would be more tragic.

I take almost two full hours to collect myself, slumped against that tree in the chilly November air. Weirdly enough, this isolation is comforting in a way that brooding on rooftops in Meridian City never is. A soft breeze filters across long grass, providing a soothing white noise to accompany my sorrow.

Taking a deep breath, I tell myself that I need to be careful. Elliot is extremely perceptive; in a way I didn't expect. He knows I'm hiding something from him. Does he suspect that

I'm a serial killer? Probably not. But he's going to be watching Elena and I. Monitoring our relationship and going through it with a magnifying glass.

If he finds out that I'm the Silencer, there will be war.

When I get back to the house, the police report papers are still haphazardly scattered on the porch. I lift them into my hand along with the folder, crumpling it all into a tight ball, and set it alight with my cigarette lighter, leaving it to burn in the ashtray.

I sneak into the house and into the upstairs bathroom to shower and wash away the blood and the poison of the truth from my skin. Dripping wet and empty on the inside, I step back into the bedroom. Elena is still sleeping like the perfect little angel she is, unmoved from where I left her. Her presence soothes me. The smallest bit of tension fades from my shoulders. I watch her sleep as I dress, and then crawl into the bed next to her. I carefully place a kiss to her hair.

Elena's forehead wrinkles and then she flips flat on her back. Her eyes flutter open, adjusting to the darkness of the bedroom. Soft moonlight casts her skin in a pale bluish glow. "Did you shower?" she asks, yawning.

"Yeah. I was drinking and smoking with your dad for a while. Didn't want to smell."

"With my dad? Really?"

"Really," I mumble, lying flat on my back next to her. "He's a very intense man."

Elena responds with a hum, already falling asleep again. "He's just protective of me. Trying to make sure the great Christian Reeves has good intentions for me or whatever."

I smirk. "Then he has reason to be concerned, because Christian Reeves has the worst intentions for you. He plans to make you his wife one day. That means you'll be stuck with him forever, and that's just cruel."

She laughs softly, the sound going straight to my heart.

She goes quiet again, and I look in her direction. Her breathing is even, her face is smooth. She's curled up on her side facing me. Sound asleep.

I fold my arms behind my head on the pillow and stare at the ceiling until morning, thinking about how fucked up my life is and how desperately I wish I could fix it.

As I watch Elena sleep, I finally understand Caroline's drawing.

Safe isn't a place.

It's the people that love you.

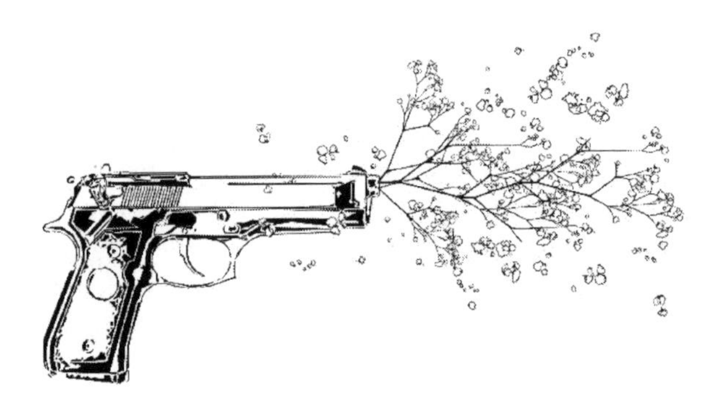

CHAPTER 36

THE ANGEL

I wake up to the subtle sound of pans clanking together downstairs in the kitchen, the smell of bacon, and warmth at my side. I lift my head, finding Christian staring down at me. I rest my chin on his chest.

"Good morning," I whisper.

"Morning." His voice sounds cold. Distant. "How'd you sleep?"

"Fine." I sit up, propping myself up on my elbows. "What's wrong?"

"Nothing." His eyes trace over my face and then he gives me a sign of humanity. A smile. "You look beautiful, angel."

Sensing his teasing tone, I run my hand through my hair to find it sticking out in every direction, knotted and messy. "Bleh. I think you mean I look like a biblically accurate angel."

I sit up completely, the comforter pooling around my waist. I rub the sleep out of my eyes and pause, crinkling my forehead when I notice my left hand feels heavy. I stare at my hand in shock when a ring is wrapped around my finger. Not just any ring, but the engagement ring Christian showed me that night on the rooftop of Reeves Enterprises. I turn to face him.

"Okay, I know I was a little tipsy last night after one too many glasses of wine, but I wasn't drunk enough to agree to a marriage proposal and not remember."

Christian grins. "I didn't propose. I just wanted you to have it."

"You wanted me to have my engagement ring before we're engaged?" I raise an eyebrow in suspicion.

"Yes."

"If I know anything about you, it's that you don't do anything without some ulterior motive, so spill."

"I just wanted you to have a symbol that you're mine. Figured an eleven-carat purple diamond delivers the message sufficiently."

I snicker. "Yeah, if you intended to break my wrist. Next time we go to Mykonos I better wear a life jacket. If I fall off the deck of the yacht I'm going to sink straight to the bottom of the ocean."

His jaw tightens as he looks at me, still lounging on the bed with his hands folded behind his head. "We could do it, you know. Get married."

I sigh, cocking my head to the side. "You are positively the most insane man I've ever met."

He raises an eyebrow. "That wasn't a rejection."

"*No*, Mr. Reeves," I tease with a small laugh.

He sits up abruptly, his face so close to mine that the tips of our noses are touching. "New rule. You're not allowed to call me Mr. Reeves until I can call you Mrs. Reeves."

"Rules are made to be broken," I say on an exhale, and then hold my breath. "How about a deal?"

He chuckles in amusement. "I'm listening. Intently."

"*Give me time*. I'm not going anywhere. Let our love be simple and let it be complicated too. Let me see all of you, the parts of you that you keep hidden under your scars. Make me fall even more deeply in love with all the dark parts of you. The parts you think are unlovable. Then one day, ask me properly, and I'll say yes." I gently tug the ring off my finger and hold it up for him to take.

With a twinge of sadness in his eyes, he takes the ring back and nods. "Okay."

I softly grin. "What's your rush to get married? I've known you since September, Christian."

"I can't live without you, Elena. My heart will never belong to anyone else. I'm not religious and I don't believe in an afterlife, but if there's even a slight chance that I get to spend an eternity with you, I want to do it properly. For whatever amount of time we have to spend together, I want to be yours. Fully. In your heart and on paper."

I let out a teasing, frustrated growl. "You always know the exact thing to say to make me putty in your hands."

"So does that mean you'll marry me?"

I laugh. "Can you at least wait to ask until *after* my brother's wedding?"

"Sure thing, angel."

We both get up to get ready for the day. We brush our teeth together, staring at each other in the mirror with the same romantic tension of two teenagers the same age at the same hotel resort on vacation.

I bite my bottom lip lightly. "I'm going to take a quick shower. You can…join me if you want."

He rinses his mouth and shakes his head. "I took a shower last night."

"I didn't mean to get clean."

He looks at me in the mirror, his eyes wide and confused. His knuckles tighten into fists and that's when I notice the fresh bruises and scrapes across his fingers. "What happened to you?"

He puts his hands behind his back and turns to face me instead of the mirror. "Nothing."

"That doesn't look like nothing."

"Do you want me to get in the shower with you, Elena?" he asks, changing the subject. I nod. "Use your words."

"Yes."

"I would see you naked. Fully."

"It's nothing you haven't seen before."

"This is different. I don't think you're ready for that."

I huff. "I think I know what I'm ready for."

"You know what you want, not what you can handle. It's different and you know it."

My shoulders slump. "Please, Christian? Do this for me."

He considers me for a second. "Kiss me," he commands. "Kiss me like you mean it, and if you can handle a kiss, I will get in the shower with you."

I know why he's doing this. He has every reason to be concerned for me and my ability to handle being seen fully naked by him for the first time. Any other time that I've been undressed, he's averted his eyes or held up a towel so he didn't see anything. I've had that layer of protection, but I'm ready to shed it.

I appreciate his caution. I really do. But I desperately miss the way he pushed me. How he so easily manipulated me into the perfect little angel he sees in his head. I miss the way he took without asking. It brought me security in a strange way. Maybe it's wrong to feel that way. Maybe it's wrong to want him so badly—but I just want him to look at me with that feral desire I had grown so accustomed to.

When I ask him to touch me, I don't want him to hesitate.

He keeps his hands clasped behind his back and stares down at me with such intensity that my bones feel like they're melting.

Carefully, I rise up on my toes to press my lips to his. He's so much taller than I am, so he shows me mercy and meets me halfway. I press my lips to his as hard as I can, hoping it will translate to eagerness instead of fear. It doesn't. He pulls away, but I grip the front of his shirt tight in my fists. With a trembling breath, I kiss him like I never have before, as passionately and as confidently as I can manage. Until we're breathless and his fingers are tangled into my hair to tug me closer.

"Are you okay?"

"Yes. I'm okay. Promise."

"Kiss me again."

I do. I kiss him until we're breathless all over again, lips swollen and hearts burning with desire.

"Get in the shower," he commands.

I undress slowly as he watches, my cheeks turning red under the blue heat of his eyes. After all, blue flames are the hottest.

He shrugs off his shirt, followed by his sweatpants and his boxer briefs until he's as naked as I am. His full erect length extends towards me, like it has a mind of its own and knows it belongs between my legs.

Pulling my eyes away from his delicious cock, I get into the shower. He follows close behind, standing as far away from me as he can, his back against the tile wall, arms crossed, face blank. The only evidence of his comfort with the situation is the tightness of his jaw and his hardness.

My eyes trace over my name carved over his heart as I wash myself, lathering up the soap so thoroughly that it's a thick white layer of suds covering my body. I turn around to rinse off the soap and wash my face, and when I face him again, he's holding his cock in his tight fist, slowly stroking it from base to tip. He inhales as pleasure twists up his body. I watch him for a second before sinking to my knees.

He stops what he's doing. "No. Get up."

I shake my head. "Trust me."

"It's not you I don't trust," he grits out.

"Keep going. Please," I beg. Reluctantly, he takes himself in his fist again and pumps as I settle down, resting my butt on my feet, just watching him.

This is how I am choosing to submit to him, in a way that doesn't require any contact. In a way that makes me feel secure and gives me an easy opportunity to stop if I decide I want to. I nod for him to continue, looking up at him with pleading eyes from under my lashes, keeping my hands resting on my thighs.

I swallow the thick lump in my throat as I watch him pleasure himself, towering over me like the god he is.

"Fuck, angel. You're so fucking pretty down there." He leans his head back against the tiles, pumping his fist faster. "I miss watching you take my cock in your mouth. You're such a good girl when you're on your knees for me."

I let out a whimper when that ache begins to form between my legs, but I make no effort to relieve it.

"Fuck, baby, move. I'm going to cum."

I shake my head, instead opening my mouth and sticking my tongue out as an invitation. His face goes slack with need.

"Please, angel, I can't wait," he groans, and when I don't move, thick white ribbons of cum shoot out of his crown in the space between us. None of it lands on my face, but a few errant strands do land on my chest. Christian goes slack against the tile walls, breathing deeply for a few seconds before meeting my eyes.

"Are you okay?"

I nod. "Yes."

He makes a motion for me to come to him with his index and middle finger on both hands. "Stand up."

I make my way to my feet and stare up at him. With his thumb, he very slowly reaches for one of the drops of release on my chest to wipe it away. I nod that it's okay.

He gathers the drop on his thumb and then lifts his hand to my mouth. I get the idea, sucking on his finger until it's clean.

"Are you wet, Elena?" he asks. I hesitantly nod. "Do you want me to touch you?"

Sighing, I shake my head. "No."

He nods. "Good girl. You're not ready for that." His hand that was in my mouth tenderly cradles my jaw. "I used to get off on the thought of breaking you, but now it fills me with fear. I have to be gentle with you now. If I break you one more time, I may never find all the pieces again."

"What if I want you to break me?" I ask, my eyes not leaving his. "What if I don't want you to be gentle?"

"Then I'll love you violently instead."

CHAPTER 37

THE ANGEL

We filter into the kitchen right as my mother finishes breakfast. Everyone else is already gathered, including my father, who already has two fingers of scotch in a glass next to him at the table. I give my mom a look, and she rolls her eyes.

I know that gesture well. It's the look she gives me when my dad gets into one of his moods. The kind of mood that not even the bright shining star that is my mother can pull him out of. I tell Christian to fix us both a plate of breakfast and I tip-toe towards my dad. He's looking straight ahead. Directly across from him is a family photo from my law school graduation.

"Dad?" I ask quietly. "Are you okay?"

My dad's eyes flicker to the rest of the family as if to see how close they are. Like he doesn't want anyone but me to hear the next thing out of his mouth.

"Does he make you happy, Ellie?"

He's drinking because of my love life. Big shocker there. He's been in a foul mood since Christian waltzed through the front door.

"Yes," I offer as a short response. One that doesn't open the door for elaboration, because I'm honestly not sure I can give him that. It's crazy that Christian makes me happy. It's crazy that I'm with him.

It's crazy that I stayed with him after everything I've learned and everything I've been through.

But here I am. I've made peace with it. My father should too.

He sighs as if my affirmative was the last thing he wanted to hear. "Figures," he mumbles, then he looks up in his hazy state and scowls at the ceiling as if he can see God.

"Does this have something to do with Christian's father?"

His eyes snap to me, wide-eyed and shocked. "What about his father?" he asks through gritted teeth, still quiet.

I furrow my brow. "Did you not get along with Thomas?"

My dad chuckles and takes a drink of his scotch. "That's one way of putting it."

I give my dad a sympathetic smile. "Dad, Christian isn't his father. Whatever your issue is with Thomas, don't take it out on him. I want you to like him. I love him."

"Because of his money?" He raises an accusatory eyebrow. "Because he lives in a big house and can take you on vacations and buy you jewelry?"

"*No*!" I whisper-shout, offended. "He has done more for me than you could ever possibly know. Can you not, just for once in my life, be supportive of a decision I made for myself? You didn't support my choice to go to law school, and you supported it even *less* when I got into Meridian Law and moved. Now you aren't supporting me when I'm telling you I'm in love with a man who would move the sun with his bare hands if it meant giving me a little shade."

"A man like Christian Reeves will get tired of you eventually. When you stop giving him what he wants."

Seething, I grab my father's scotch glass, throw the amber liquid into his face, and then slam it back down to the table so hard it cracks. Hot, angry, embarrassed tears fall out of my eyes and soak the collar of my shirt.

"Funny. That sounds like the same thing Neil Hayden said before he raped me," I croak out, and then I turn, pushing past everyone else and running out the front door.

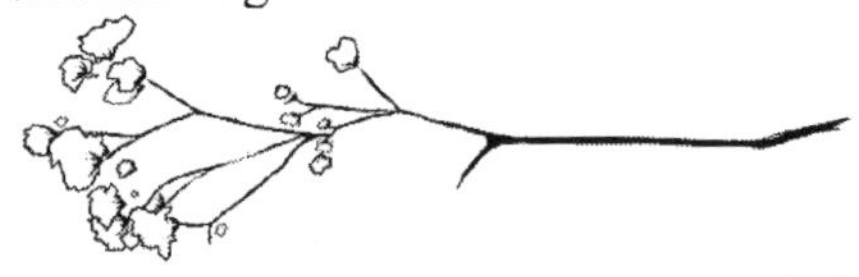

When Travis and I were younger, my dad spent three weeks building us a treehouse that any kid would envy. It's got a wrap-around porch and a tower jutting off the side. The wood is well sealed, so years of rain haven't made it moldy.

It still looks the same as the last time I saw it, only the rope ladder is frayed. I climb up the tree and crawl into the house. I'm small, but the actual space inside the treehouse is even smaller, so I have to pull my knees up to my chest to fit comfortably.

My father is a harsh man. Some people might even call him cold and cruel, but I never once thought he could be that way towards me.

As with most people, he thinks Christian only cares about me because of what's in between my legs.

I hear someone begin to crawl up the steps of the ladder and I groan. "Go away."

I hear heavy breathing and then my brother's blonde-dyed hair pokes up from the edge of the porch. "My body doesn't feel like it used to," he huffs as he crawls into the tiny treehouse with me, leaning back against the wooden wall to catch his breath. Travis turns his head to look at me with his bright blue eyes and chuckles. "We had to abandon ship. Mom is ripping dad a new asshole for what he said to you. She was threatening him with a spatula when the three of us ran out."

That makes me laugh. "How'd you know I'd be here?"

"Because I used to come here to cry too, before I came out to our parents."

I look around the tiny space of the treehouse. I remember when we could both stand up comfortably in here. Now it feels like we're sitting in ancient ruins of the past. "I don't understand what dad's problem is. Ever since he met Christian, he's been so...*impossible.* Not that he's the friendliest guy you'll ever meet, but you know what I mean."

Travis shrugs. "You're his baby."

"I'm older than you."

"Yeah, but he's already lost two daughters. He's just scared of losing a third. Maybe not to gunfire, but I think he's finally realized that we're all grown up. I'm getting married, and I've seen the way hottie looks at you. You're not going to be long after me and then who will he have left to inflict his iron will on?"

"I think it's more than that. Dad knew Christian's father and I think there's some history there that he's taking out on our relationship. I don't think that's fair."

"It's not." My brother shrugs. "But love always prevails, doesn't it? Hottie loves you to a fault. I've known him for like, a day and a half, and I can see it. You could ask him to cut off his left leg and there would be no hesitation on his part."

I laugh again. "You have no idea how right you are about that."

"I always was the genius of the family," he jests. "Dad will learn to tolerate your tall, rich, mysterious boyfriend. Give him time."

"Tall, rich and mysterious, huh?"

"Oh, and hot. Did I mention he's hot? I'd still hit that even if I was straight. Is he that big and thick *everywhere*?"

"Oh my God. Get out!" I yelp, poking Travis in the chest. He giggles and begins to climb down the ladder, and right before his head disappears, I whisper, "Yes."

He snickers. "Ha! I knew it."

Travis disappears, and then after a minute of silence, I hear someone else come up the tree. Christian's head pops up over the porch. He pauses when he looks at me.

"Well come on. Don't tell me you're scared of heights."

He scoffs. "Elena, my right foot could not fit through the door of this treehouse. I get myself in there, and I am never getting back out."

I meet him halfway, lying on my stomach so our faces are just inches from each other as he balances himself on the rope ladder and holds himself up with his arms on the porch.

"Heard my mother was defending my honor," I say dryly.

"I have never heard so many insults strung together in one sentence. Also, what the fuck does '*I'm gonna show you how the cow ate the cabbage*' mean?"

I giggle at his attempt to mimic my mother's thick accent. "It means you're about to hear the hard truth."

"Oh," he says, seemingly still confused. "You southerners are strange." I smile and then my face falls. He notices immediately. "Are you okay?"

I shrug. "Not particularly. I honestly just want to go home."

Christian nods. "Just say when, and I'll make sure the jet is ready for us." He sighs with his mouth in a thin line. "I'm sorry. This was supposed to be a nice getaway from the city with your family. Your father and I ruined it."

"*You* didn't ruin anything. He's always been like this." I lean a bit closer to press my lips softly to his. "Let's go pack."

Christian and I walk side-by-side back to the house where things have seemingly calmed down. My dad is in his home office with the door shut and my mom is cleaning up the breakfast no one ate. When she spots us, she gives me a sympathetic smile.

"I wish I could tell you I knew what his problem was."

"It's me," Christian answers. "He doesn't like me."

"That is no excuse for the way he's been acting. You're with Elena, which means you are part of this family now. He's going to have to accept that." My mom rubs Christian's arm. "I will not let him make you feel unwelcome in our home."

I am so relieved that my mom is on our side when it comes to our relationship. I don't know what I would do if both of my parents disliked Christian. She has the best chance out of any of us to knock some sense into my dad.

I sigh. "Christian? Do you think you could give my mom and I a minute alone?"

He nods. "Of course. I'll go pack our things."

Christian leaves the room, and my mom and I sit on the back porch for some privacy. It's chilly outside. I tuck my hands into my sweater and thank God for whoever invented fuzzy socks.

"I know this isn't very ethical but I'm coming to you as a patient and not your daughter." She nods and I continue. "After I was raped, the worst part of it all was the fear of being pregnant. I took the morning after pill at the hospital, but I was constantly worried about it until I got my period. Now…God, how do I say this?" I mumble to myself, playing with a split end in my hair. I suppose the best way to say it is just to say it. "I feel dirty. And not just because of what happened to me, but because I don't think I've ever wanted Christian more in my life than I do right now. Isn't that wrong? Isn't sex the last thing I should want?"

My mom blinks at me. We've always been close. I've never hidden anything from her, but she looks just as stunned to hear my words as I am to say them.

"Well, everyone reacts to trauma differently. It's true, many people who have been raped find touch intolerable. For months, years, even for their remaining lifetime, the idea of sex becomes unimaginable for them, even if it's with someone they love and trust. The very nature of sex demands that someone must give up control, at least to some degree. Many survivors of sex crimes find it hard to give up that control again."

I let out a defeated sigh. "That's my point. What if all I want is to give up that control again?"

My mom gives me a warm smile as my leg bounces nervously. "I can't say I've ever come across this situation before, but if you want my professional opinion, just because your body is ready to take that step doesn't mean your mind is. Some survivors of sex crimes distance themselves from touch while others act out sexually in order to regain the control they feel like they've lost. I know nothing about your sexual relationship with Christian, but perhaps you feel this way because your sex life involved giving up control to him, and you trusted him to make you feel safe. Maybe that's what you crave now. Not sex. *Safety.*" She pauses for a moment. "I think you're very brave for tolerating touch and affection at all."

Brave.

That's the word people use to describe you when you're a victim and they want to support you but don't know how.

But I don't feel brave.

I feel broken.

"So you think if I had sex it would do more harm?" I ask nervously.

"I think you would never recover if you had sex right now, Elena," my mom says firmly. "If you truly crave pleasure that badly and want Christian to be a part of it, just start slow and be careful, okay? He loves you. He will do anything for you, even have sex with you if you ask—but don't unintentionally make him the bad guy by rushing into things. You have a lifetime to have sex. Give yourself the chance to recover, and your future self will thank you for it."

Well, that's it then. The verdict is in. I have problems for wanting sex less than a month after being raped. Maybe my mother is right, though. Just because my body craves pleasure doesn't mean my mind does. I might just be experiencing normal, human wants and desires, but acting on them is an entirely different situation.

"Ellie, have you thought about getting a therapist out there in Meridian City? You are first and foremost my daughter. Talking to someone without an emotional connection to you will help you far more than I ever could."

I nod, though it's a complete lie. I haven't once considered a therapist. The hospital gave me some pamphlets with information on how to find one, along with a sexual assault crisis hotline and, disturbingly, the suicide hotline. But I never thought about calling them. I ripped them up and threw them in the trash. Not because I didn't want a therapist, but because there is so much I can't say to them.

I'd have to leave out so much of the story to continue to keep Christian's alter ego a secret, and I haven't put much thought into what my story would be if I left him out of it. I wasn't randomly targeted off the street and raped by strangers. I was taken because of who Christian is, as himself and as the Silencer. I was taken because his enemies knew how important I was to both sides of him. It's a miracle they didn't do the math and find out about him themselves.

"Do you think I should talk to dad?" I ask.

My mom scoffs. "Absolutely not. I'd give him the cold shoulder until he apologizes to you."

She immediately looks like she wants to take it back. It twists uncomfortably my gut as she shifts awkwardly in her seat.

"I don't like when we fight," I say, staring down at my fingers with sadness.

"It's not a fight. He said something horrible to you, and he owes you and Christian both an apology."

"Christian is a good man." I quietly reconsider my words and then add, "*To me*. He's a good man to me. I wish dad could see that."

Christian is objectively not a good man. He is a serial killer and though I've made peace with that after everything we've been through, it doesn't change the fact that he's got so much blood on his hands he could fill a lake.

Seventy-three people, by my count. Twenty-one of those have been since he met me.

Maybe that makes *me* the bad guy.

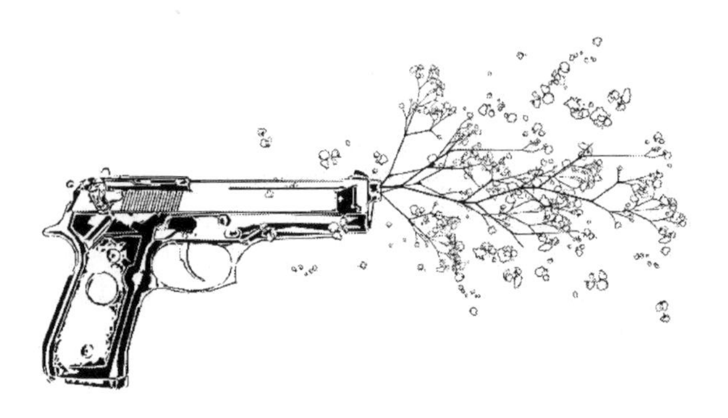

CHAPTER 38

THE SILENCER

Elena's father didn't come out of his office all morning. Not even to say goodbye.

Good riddance.

It took every ounce of my self-control to not knock his teeth out this morning when he very clearly told Elena that he thought she was only good enough for me because it was easy to get her to spread her legs.

I understand that he has issues with me, but he has no right to take that shit out on his daughter. If anything, all his attitude is doing is pushing her further into my arms, which is fine with me. It's where she belongs.

As I drive us to the airport, Elena picks at a few split ends of her hair and sighs. "Hey Christian?"

"Yeah, baby?" I reply absently as I take a sip of water from the bottle I took from her parents' house.

"What did you talk about with my dad last night?"

It takes considerable effort to keep my demeanor calm and unassuming. "My father, mostly."

"They really did know each other?"

"Briefly," I say quietly, mimicking the exact thing Elliot said to me the first time he mentioned my dad. I shrug and take another sip of water, like I'm trying to play it off as nothing. I don't want to lie to her, but I don't want to admit the truth either. It's quiet in the space between us. She's expecting me to elaborate.

I blow out a long breath. "My dad knew Diana too."

"Oh," she says, laughing nervously. "That's surprising. They weren't really…you know…in the same social class."

I scoff and shrug again. "It was really nothing."

"Then why are you acting so weird?"

My fingers grip the leather steering wheel tighter. "What your dad said to you this morning…I almost snapped his neck."

"Thank you for not doing that," she says lightly, but there's no sarcasm in her voice. She knows that if he was any other man, it would have been the last thing he ever said. "I love my dad, but I also know he's a huge jerk. I'm sorry you two aren't getting along."

"Don't apologize."

"When I was up in that treehouse with my brother, he said something that really stuck out to me. He said that my dad is just afraid of losing another daughter."

"I would never—"

"I know, but *he* doesn't."

I feel Elena's tiny hand wrap around my forearm, and I wish the fabric of my hoodie wasn't blocking her skin from mine.

On the one hand, she's got loyalty to her father, and on the other, she's in love with me. That can't be an easy place for her to be.

"Will you tell me what happened to your knuckles?"

I lift my hand slightly to look at them and chuckle. "A tree."

"*Why*?" she asks, raising an inquisitive brow.

"It was either the tree or your dad's nose." I cock my head to the side and grin at the thought of punching that man in the face. "I made an educated guess on your preference."

She seems satisfied with that answer, because she drops the subject. I subtly let out a breath of relief when she begins to ramble on about some case law she's been studying in preparation for the bar exam. I listen intently.

I consider myself a very intelligent man, but law is one of those subjects that just goes straight over my head. I could talk engineering, technology, economics, and the minutiae of politics all day, but the second someone brings up the New Jersey Court Rules my brain checks out. That's why I hire the best lawyers in the country to do the thinking for me.

I don't regret killing Neil Hayden, but I can't lie, he was fucking good at his job.

Give Elena some time, and I'm confident she'll be better. There's an associate position with her name on it waiting for her the second she passes her bar exam.

When we board the plane to head back to New Jersey, I get a glimpse at Elena's sad eyes and before I can think twice about it, I cradle her cheeks in my hands and roughly kiss her like my life depends on it. We fall into the plush seats and she sits on my lap. We kiss until we're breathless, but it's not lustful. It's frenzied and passionate, like we're both afraid we'll never get the chance to kiss each other again. My way of telling her all the things I can't say out loud.

Something sinister and cold crawls down my spine. It's fear. Fear that the Silencer will take his revenge on her father for what he did to me, and I'll lose her.

I have to make sure that doesn't happen, even if it means stripping away at her free will until she's perfectly pliable clay in my hands.

I can give an angel her wings.

But I can clip them, too, if it means I get to spend forever with her.

"I love you." I say through gritted teeth, her hair wrapped tight around my fist. "I love you so much it makes me insane. I love you so much it makes me dangerous. I love you so much that I would burn this world for you and all the people in it just to keep you all to myself. Do you understand me? If it comes down to a choice, you *will* choose me. I don't give a fuck if it costs the remainder of your soul. You are *mine* and only *mine*."

She sucks in a sharp breath when I kiss the side of her neck. "What about the Silencer?"

"What about him?"

"I belonged to him first," she whispers.

I nip at her neck and then lightly lick the red spot. "But I loved you first."

She whimpers and I kiss her until we can't breathe. I kiss her until she pulls away, and then I kiss her more, holding her to my chest in an iron grip that will never loosen.

"Christian," she breathes. "Christian, stop."

With reluctance, I let her go and release her lips. She's looking down in shame and crying. I cradle her cheeks in my hands. "Angel."

She lightly bangs her fists against my chest. Not in anger directed at me, but frustration and emotional exhaustion.

"I just want to kiss you without seeing them!"

She buries her face in my neck and sobs. I wrap my arms around her and rub soothing circles on her back as she weeps. I can tell she's putting everything she has into trying to make our relationship normal again. It's never been normal for us, but the façade that I built before I told her the truth about the Silencer was her safe place, and she wants it back.

I shush her quietly, rocking her best I can in the seat as if she were a toddler that just woke up from a nightmare.

After a long while, she settles down and pulls back to look at me. *Christ.* Even with tears in her eyes and her nose and cheeks flushed red from emotion, she's still *so fucking beautiful*. She's a pretty crier. Though I can't stand it when she cries, she looks ethereal when she does. The sheen of tears in her eyes adds a glimmer to the brown of her irises that could only look stunning on her.

She really is the embodiment of simple elegance. She doesn't turn heads because she's beautiful, she turns heads because she's regal and sophisticated. She's the exact opposite of me. The real me, at least. I can put on a suit and fake the charm all day long. But take off the suit and strip away the smile, and what's left?

A savage. A savage beast that fell in love with an elegant beauty that I will never be worthy of.

I could give her the entire world and everything in it and it still wouldn't be enough.

Her voice hoarse and quiet, she asks, "If we hadn't met the way that we did…if you didn't think I was your guardian angel, do you think you still would have fallen in love with me?"

My first instinct is to say yes. But *yes* isn't enough to describe the way our souls are intertwined.

"When I told you that you made me believe in soulmates, I didn't just mean in this lifetime, or even in this universe. My heart has always belonged to you, even if I didn't know it at first. I would love you even if I had no heart to give you, because you are the sole reason for my existence. My soul would love you if we lived on different continents and spoke different languages. My soul would be tethered to you across oceans and mountains and harrowing canyons as black as my heart. My soul would be yours if I pulled the trigger the night we met, because not even death could keep us apart. God couldn't keep me from you, because God isn't real, but *you* are, and that's all the motivation I would have needed to find you."

Elena trembles in my lap, weeping like I've just lifted a burden off her shoulders.

Do I think our relationship would be less intense if we met under different circumstances? Absolutely. But I would still love her just as much, and I am so confident in that statement that I'd bet my pathetic life on it.

Sniffling, she looks at me with a wistful smile on her face that makes my throat burn and my heart ache. "I love you."

I let out a sad laugh and push her hair out of her face, rubbing away her tears with my thumbs. "Good."

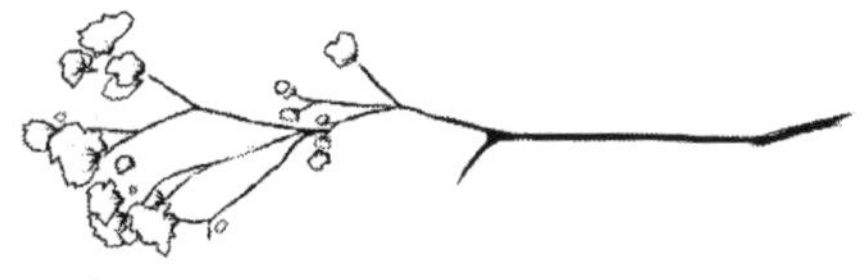

Two weeks pass.

They haven't been good weeks.

In fact, they've been fucking awful weeks. Elena has been completely inconsolable for days and days on end. She hasn't been sleeping because she's been plagued with nightmares that wake her up in the middle of the night, screaming at the top of her lungs in a thick sheen of sweat. The lack of sleep has made her irritable and even more volatile.

I can't get within ten feet of her without her body going into survival mode. Two days after we got back from Texas, I kissed the crown of her head, and she had the most intense panic attack ever witnessed in human history. She ran away from me, screaming like she was being murdered, and hid. For two days. Nobody could find her.

For two fucking days.

I nearly went into cardiac arrest, tearing apart every square inch of my house. I found her hiding in the back of my closet, inside a laundry hamper that she had hidden behind a rack of my suit jackets. She had a pocketknife clutched in her fist and blood coating her arm.

She slit her wrist.

She was dehydrated and unconscious from the lack of food and water and had to be admitted into the hospital where she underwent an extreme psychological evaluation. They recommended her for a seven-day outpatient program, which only made her panic again and she had to be put to sleep with a sedative. When she finally woke up twelve hours later, she was sent home with a prescription for anti-anxiety medication, anti-depressants, and I was given strict instructions to keep her under 24/7 supervision.

I haven't let her out of my sight since.

It's not until the middle of December as we get closer to Travis' wedding that she begins to settle down.

I still keep a careful eye on her, leaving her alone for no more than five minutes at a time. All she does all day is study, only she has to write her notes with child's markers because I don't trust her to hold a pencil yet.

Elena is the strongest person I know, and to see her so deep in her depression kills me inside, because I know I am the root cause of it.

Two days before Travis' wedding is the first time I leave her alone for more than a few minutes.

I've got a lead on Valenti.

As much as I don't want to leave her alone to chase it, I have to. Of course, the only other person I slightly trust with her safety is Gavin, so I've given him the most important assignment of his life: keeping watch while I go out for a few hours, under the guise that I'm going to the office.

In reality, I'm headed to the East Side.

I was passing by the security room in the mansion yesterday when I noticed that there was an active call on the same street as the Hellfire Lounge. Or what's left of it.

The call was regarding two arrests for Indecent Exposure. A nobody with a few extra Benjamins in his pocket was caught fucking a woman in an alleyway. The man is of no consequence to me, but I recognize the woman, even from her mugshot.

She's the bartender I choked unconscious the night I killed Valenti's friends. I found out through public records that her name is Riley Lau. If she's turning tricks in the area, she might know someone who knows someone, who knows a friend of someone else who knows where Valenti *might* be hiding.

It's a big fucking stretch, but at this point, I'm desperate.

Dressed in my Silencer gear, I find a lowlife who looks like he could use some extra money. I shove a thick stack of hundreds in his hand, hold a gun to his head, and tell him to go bond out Riley and instruct her to meet me in the same alley she got arrested in.

He took the stack of money and one look down the barrel of my gun and did what I asked. It's almost two hours later, but Riley comes around the corner, going rigid when she sees me. Then her gaze turns hungry as she saunters towards me, swaying her hips seductively.

"What an honor," she says. "I knew you'd come crawling back to me."

"I'm not here for your services," I hiss. "I need information."

She eyes me, unimpressed, and holds out her palm. I slap a stack of cash in her hand. And then another. And then another, until she finally stuffs the money in her bra before crossing her arms.

"What do you want to know?"

"Frank Valenti's whereabouts," I demand, like I already know her answer, even though I know jack shit. I won't get the information I want by asking nicely.

She sighs heavily and sticks a piece of gum in her mouth, chewing it obnoxiously. "I think he's still on the island. He was paranoid about banks, even offshore ones. He only ever dealt in cash. He kept it all hidden around the Hellfire Lounge. All his money burnt to the ground along with the club, but I'm sure he had stashes in other places too. He was paranoid, but he wasn't stupid. I don't know where he is, but I don't think he would leave the island. All the people in his pocket think he's still rich and powerful. He can't buy that influence anywhere else." She shrugs. "That's all I know."

"You're sure? You haven't heard anything about where he might be?"

She shakes her head. "Sorry. Maybe ask some of the other girls that were close to him. He kept his dick wet. There was Kate and one other…she wasn't there long. Elena! Her name was Elena. Short. Brown hair. Really innocent looking. Frank was obsessed with her."

I scoff. *Thanks for fucking nothing.*

I leave her in the alley without another word.

I'm bent out of shape about people thinking Elena's still working for him, but it's comforting to hear that no one has made the connection between her and the Silencer, except for maybe Kate, but we haven't seen her since Elena was in the emergency room.

My phone rings with a text. I expect it to be Gavin. He's meant to give me updates on Elena every fifteen minutes.

But the text is from her.

Elena: I have an emergency.

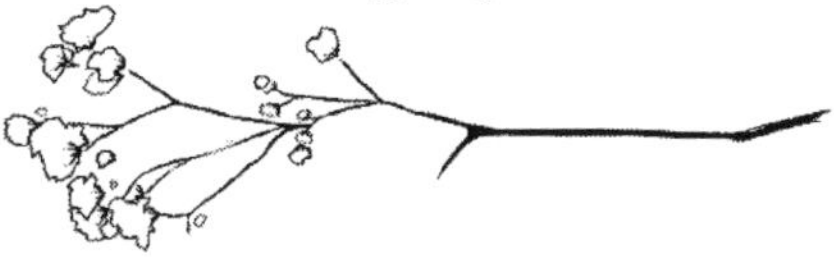

I'm in such a rush to get back to her that all rational thinking goes out the window. I risk getting myself shot by sneaking onto my own property as the Silencer and crawling through the damn window of our bedroom. I use my administrative override on the security systems to force restart them. They're down just long enough for me to get inside without raising any alarms.

I'm panting and sweaty when I land with a thud on my hardwood floors, gun raised, ready to shoot anyone that's not a five-foot-tall brunette.

My eye twitches when I spot Elena standing in the center of the room between two rolling racks of designer gowns. She gives me a sheepish, guilty smile.

"I guess I could have worded that text better."

I let out a relieved breath. "You fucking think? Jesus fuck, Elena, you gave me a heart attack."

"I'm sorry," she says, looking down at her feet in shame. I put the gun away and pop my mask off, letting it fall to the ground with a thud.

"What's the emergency?" I ask. She glances between the two racks of dresses. I scoff. "A *fashion* emergency."

If I wasn't so in love with this woman, I would strangle her.

She slumps her shoulders in feigned annoyance. "You said my dress for Travis' wedding was heinous."

I laugh. "I don't think that's the word I used, but yes, that dress was a crime against humanity."

She shrugs. "Help me pick out a new one?"

I sit on the bench at the end of the bed, peeling off my gloves and letting them fall to the floor. I nod at her to start, and she begins trying on dress after dress. She gives me a chance to comment on each one while she looks over herself in the mirror she set up near the racks.

Forty minutes later, she emerges in a sleek black satin dress with thin straps and a plunging neckline. The twelfth just like it.

She spins in a circle. "What do you think?"

"I think you look beautiful."

She playfully rolls her eyes. "Stop being such a diplomat. You've said that every time."

"That's because you're beautiful."

She huffs and then grabs another dress, disappearing to try it on. When she emerges two minutes later, my heart stops.

She's wearing a floor-length, emerald-green velvet dress that hugs her body from her chest all the way down to her thighs. The sleeves are tiny ribbons of chiffon that drape off her shoulders in an elegant way that's both sexy and tasteful. When she turns around, the chiffon of the sleeves connects at the center of her back and then falls to the floor in a train of delicate tulle.

"This one," I say, my throat barely forming words. "Choose this one. You look perfect." She gives herself another look in the mirror. "I'll get a matching bowtie and pocket square."

She narrows her eyes at me in the mirror. "Didn't realize you were a '*matching my girlfriend*' kind of guy. Where are you going to find a matching bowtie in two days?"

"Angel, never underestimate the power of a black American Express."

She leaves to change back into her normal clothes. I stay sitting on the bench, rubbing my jaw with my fingers as anxiety turns over in my stomach. When Elena comes back out, draping her chosen dress over one of the racks, she gives me a confused look.

"What?"

I sigh. "We need to talk about the last two weeks."

Instantly, she subconsciously hides her wrist from me and no longer allows herself to look me in the eye. "Are you mad at me?"

"*Mad*?" I scoff. "No, baby. I'm fucking worried about you."

Tears well in her eyes. "I'm sorry."

I stand up and take a few steps towards her. "You don't need to apologize, but I am *begging* you to talk to me. You can tell me anything, Elena."

She sniffles. "That is the problem." She looks up with pleading eyes. "You're the *only* person I can talk to. Not my parents, not my brother, not even a therapist. I can't tell anyone the truth except you and that doesn't make me feel supported. It makes me feel alone."

I swallow the burning lump in my throat. Her pain always, *always* stems from me being the Silencer. She can't talk to anyone because he's such a big part of her story, and nobody would understand it the way I can.

She sighs. "Do you know why I cut myself?" she asks, though she doesn't wait for my answer. "Because I wanted to be in control again. I wanted to be in control of my body, and I wanted to be in control of when and where I felt pain."

Control. The thing she lost when she was raped. The control of her emotions, the control of her reaction to touch.

"You want to be in control," I repeat. "Let me give it back to you."

CHAPTER 39

THE ANGEL

I go still as I stare up at the man I love, dressed as the man who once filled me with fear. The dark paint in his eyes makes the colored contacts he's wearing look even brighter.

He's different when he's the Silencer. Even with his mask off, he holds himself differently. He looks bigger and infinitely more dangerous than Christian Reeves.

I gulp. I can't describe the emotion I feel in my chest. Anticipation, maybe?

Christian is a master manipulator. I used to see that as a bad thing. Now, all I want is for him to manipulate my life, my feelings, my emotions, my heart. I want him to make me feel whole again, and sometimes I want it so bad that I don't care what it will cost me.

Christian takes a cigarette from his silver case discarded on a small table near us. He takes it between his teeth before lighting it and letting the smoke waft in the air between us.

"Take the gun in my left thigh holster. The silver and black one," he commands. I blink up at him, confused, but he raises his eyebrows in an encouraging sort of way that says, '*trust me*'.

I look over his body and then grab the gun. I hold it out to him like an offering. Like it might bite me. He doesn't take it.

Instead, he uses his strong legs to move the bench at the foot of the bed a few feet to the left, until he can sit with his back straight against a thick wooden post of his canopy bed. He tosses a zip tie at my feet and then lifts his arms over his head.

"Tie me to the post."

"What?" I ask, because he's clearly gone mad.

"Look at me. *Look at me*. Take a deep breath and trust me."

My body breaks out in a nervous tingle, but I swallow heavily and comply. I use the white plastic to fasten his wrists against the wooden post.

He tugs on the restraint a few times to check that they'll hold. "Tighter."

I tighten them, and he tugs again. When he's satisfied, he looks me straight in the eye. "Grab the gun and come straddle my lap."

Yeah, he's gone insane. I don't move. All I do is stare at him in shock.

"Elena," he says huskily, in that way that makes me melt. "Trust goes both ways, and I want to prove to you that I trust you too."

After a few more moments of uncertainty, I take the gun in my hand and walk to him, slowly settling on his lap, our faces inches apart. I'm trembling, but I trust him.

"Put the gun to my temple," he instructs, and tears well in my eyes when I do.

"Please don't ask me to pull the trigger," I beg. "I can't."

"I won't. I promise. It's there to remind you that you're in control. I can't do anything right now that you don't want me to. Take a deep breath, keep the gun to my head, and make yourself cum on my lap."

I shake my head, but his intense stare is unfaltering. He flexes his pelvis slightly, to show me that he's got a growing erection. He's showing me he's not scared. His throat bobs as he swallows slowly and drinks in my face with his eyes. I can see that he's waiting for me to panic and back off.

He's giving me control of my pleasure, *and* his.

I pull the tiny nub of the cigarette left between his teeth and put it out on his sleeveless jacket, burning a tiny hole in the fabric. I look at him, expecting him to be upset, but of course he isn't. He gives me a small nod of encouragement. I lean forward and press my lips softly to his, the gun feeling heavy in my fingers.

I pull away and I can see the lust in his dilated pupils. Can feel it against my center. I adjust myself on his lap so that I'm only straddling one of his thick, muscular thighs.

I experimentally drag my center over his thigh. We're both fully clothed, my leggings and panties another layer on top of his tactical pants, but the sensation still shoots through me like lightning.

He flexes his thigh under me and smiles with satisfaction when I hiss. "Use me. Take whatever you need from me, baby." He kisses the underside of my jaw. "You want to rub that greedy pussy on my thigh while I describe all the ways I'm going to fuck you when you're ready?"

I nod, and I feel him laugh against my throat. He kisses down my neck until he reaches the base and sucks a mark into my skin.

"I've thought about all the ways I want to make you come apart in every room in this house." I feel him smirk against my skin as I grind down on him once more. "I think I'm going to start on the kitchen counter, because you're just so delicious." My heartbeat speeds up and I moan softly as my clit rubs against his muscular leg. Even with all the layers of fabric between us, it still makes my blood molten hot. "And then I want to make love to you in front of the fireplace in the entry way. And then I want to finger you in the hot tub. And then I want to bend you over the dining room table."

I whine as I feel the coil in my stomach tighten, his words making me gush inside my panties with each breath.

"Fuck, angel, look at you," he whispers against my throat. "You're so beautiful when you're desperate to cum. Is that what you want? Want to cream in your panties while you rub yourself on my thigh?"

The filth of his words only makes me want it more.

I shift again so that I'm straddling his lap fully and grind myself onto the considerable length at the front of his pants. He groans and throws his head back against the post. I grind until he's panting and bucking up against me. He wants me, bad. I can see it in the way he bites his lip and I feel it with every pass of my center over his.

He sinks his teeth into the flesh of neck. "Angel, show me some fucking mercy and ride me harder."

"Why should I?" I whisper, and he bucks up against me, causing me to moan again. "This isn't about you."

"Yeah? You like being in charge?" he asks, his face red as he grits his jaw. He squeezes his eyes shut tight and opens them again as if he's delirious. I bury my face into his neck and moan. I'm so close, and I don't have to say it for him to know. "Go ahead. Cum for me." He bucks against me, but I force myself to freeze.

"You first."

I can hear the earth spinning with how silent it is. Christian glares up at me with frustration, roughly tugging against the restraints holding his arms in place. "You want to repeat that, Elena?"

"I said, *you first.*"

"Yeah, that's what I thought you said." He laughs at me like a fucking sadist, before attacking my lips with his own. "Naughty girl. You want me to cum in my pants, is that it?"

"Yes," I moan, throwing my head back as I grind on top of him harder.

"Not fucking happening, angel." He bucks his hips against mine. "Unless you plan on letting me sink my cock into that perfect cunt, you better cum and you better do it now, or I can't be held responsible for what I do to you."

"You can't do anything except sit there and take it."

He gives me a wicked smile. "Good girl," he growls. "Such a good fucking girl. Do you want to know the most important thing to remember when it comes to control?"

I nod, and with his unimaginable strength, he pulls against his restraints so hard that the plastic snaps, falling to the floor while I stare at him with wide eyes. I gasp when he grabs my neck with his left hand to tug me closer, my fingers now trembling over the trigger of the gun.

"*It's an illusion*," he whispers against my quivering lips. Then, he moves his finger over mine on the trigger of the gun, and he makes me pull it.

I shriek in fear and shock, but he's still staring at me, his artificial green eyes sparkling with adoration and pride.

The gun wasn't loaded. He knew that.

He let me *believe* I had the power, and it's *liberating*.

This is the man I fell in love with. The man who takes what he wants. The man who doesn't respect my boundaries because he knows them better than I do. The man who pushes me because he knows my strengths even more intimately than he knows how to exploit my weaknesses.

The man who would burn the world for me without so much as a second thought if I asked him to.

His love and his devotion have corrupted me.

I grab his cheeks and look into his eyes as intensely as he's staring into mine, and against his lips, I mewl, "*I love you.*"

I begin to grind on his lap at the same moment I crash our lips together in a frenzy of passion and lust. His hands tangle in my hair, keeping my mouth pressed to his as we swallow each other's moans. He's so hard underneath me, and my body is screaming to feel him again. The mere thought of his thick length inside me sends me careening over the edge so fast that I don't even realize what's happening until I cry out against his lips in pure euphoria.

I cum so hard I nearly go blind, burying my head in his neck and whining in pleasure. His hands rub up and down my back in soothing lines as I ride out the aftershocks of my first orgasm since I was taken. My panties and leggings are completely soaked through.

When I pull back to look at him, I catch his gaze as he licks his teeth and smiles triumphantly.

"How do you know me better than I know myself?"

"Because I see more than you think I do. And I see an angel who just got her wings."

CHAPTER 40

THE SILENCER

It's Travis and Justin's wedding day. We're in California bright and early in the morning. Elena places a quick kiss to my cheek. "I love you, see you soon."

She gathers her dress bag and I open the door to the venue for her so she can head into the suite where she and her brother will get ready for the day. She's not technically a bridesmaid, but she's been tasked with helping the four-year-old flower girl down the aisle. A cousin, if I remember correctly.

Despite having an early flight this morning, Elena is far too energetic for her own good. She's elated that her brother is getting married, happily exclaiming that she loves weddings, and vows to steal at least fifteen favors.

It warms my stone-cold heart to see her so excited about something. It makes my chest tighten, because I know it means that what she's gone through hasn't stolen all her happiness.

I stand in the cool morning breeze and smoke outside of the venue.

"You and my husband are going to kill yourselves with those things."

I turn around to see Bethany standing behind me with a warm smile on her face, masking something deep inside her that I can only describe as sorrow.

"We do share some bad habits," I reply with a smirk. She moves to stand next to me, looking out over the lush green hills of the vineyard where the wedding is taking place.

"How's Elena?" Bethany asks, her face falling slightly. "She never calls anymore."

I sigh sympathetically. "She has good days and bad days. She told me she feels lonely, which is insane considering how loved she is, but I understand. She doesn't want anyone to see her as weak."

"Elena hasn't been weak a day in her life. She's got her father's thick skull. She'll endure anything if it means that people won't see her differently."

I scoff, the backs of my eyes burning. "I think I know that better than anyone. What happened to her is entirely my fault and she somehow thinks she's done wrong by me."

I probably shouldn't have admitted that, but Bethany is a therapist, after all. She's easy to talk to. She pats me on the shoulder. "I know it's none of my business, but if I could offer you any advice about Ellie and this family, don't try and come between her and Elliot. I don't think you intend to, and I'm not making any accusations, but you and Elliot are so similar in your convictions. If either of you try to make her choose sides, both of you will lose her."

I stare down at the woman next to me, trying to find any hint of untrustworthiness in her eyes. She has the same deep brown eyes as Elena that make her easy to read. She's telling the truth.

"What makes you think she'd have to choose sides?" I ask. There's hesitation in my voice that I'm not trying to mask. Elena means everything to me. If Bethany is saying there's a chance I could lose her, she has my full attention.

"Because I know. About Thomas."

My hands fall limp at my sides. "All of it?"

"All of it."

I blow out the last remnants of smoke in my lungs. "I swear, I didn't know when I met Elena that our families had a past."

Bethany shrugs. "If you did or didn't, it makes no difference to me. What matters is what's in your heart, Christian. Elliot will take a grudge to the grave, but I have nothing against you. Elena loves you, and I can see in your eyes that you love her too. So long as you keep making her happy, you're just as much a part of this family as any of us, and Elliot will have to make peace with that someday."

Bethany rubs my arm once and then steps away to go back into the venue.

"Hey, Bethany?" I laugh nervously. "Need any last-minute help with the decorations? I could use something to do."

Bethany taps her fingers together mischievously. "Boy, do I!" She pulls me by the arm and into the reception area, where she instructs me to finish hanging string lights.

And then set up the party favor table.
And then set the place cards.
And then the centerpieces.
And then. And then. And then.

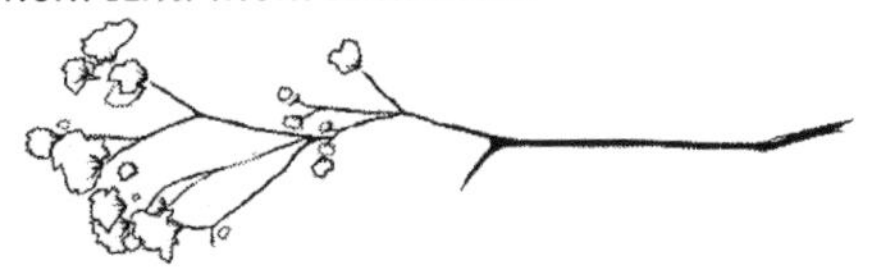

I sit uncomfortably in my reserved seat of the ceremony space in the very front row, just two seats between myself and Elliot. I even tried to shake his hand when he came to sit, and he completely ignored me. Pretended he didn't even see me. Glared right through me like I wasn't even there.

Since when am I the reasonable one?

I continuously check my watch as if it will make time go faster, and no less than a minute before the ceremony starts, Bethany comes to put me out of my misery by taking a seat between Elliot and me.

With her between us, I glance at Elliot again, and take him in. He looks cold. Distant. With me, I expect that because he clearly can't stand me, but he's not normally like this around Bethany. I don't like it.

My thoughts are cut off by the sound of processional music and the officiant begins to saunter down the aisle before taking his place at the altar. I turn my head, and just like always, when I see my angel, my heart stops.

Elena is standing at the end of the aisle, walking down with the small flower girl. Her loosely curled hair cascades down her back, the top half pinned back and out of her face. Her makeup is done so elegantly, with maybe just a little bit too much blush. That really doesn't matter though, artificial or not, she's stunning when she blushes. She's stunning always, but I've never seen her so formal. She's beautiful.

I start to imagine how heart-stopping she would be in a wedding dress, walking down the aisle towards me at *our* wedding.

The thought alone makes my heart squeeze and my dick hard.

Halfway down the aisle, the little flower girl begins running and lets out an excited squeal when Elena catches her, scooping her up into the air and blowing raspberries on her cheeks before plopping her down into her aunt's lap. Elena takes her seat next to me, a big smile across her face. I press a soft kiss to her cheek.

"You look beautiful," I whisper, just loud enough for her ears only. She winks at me and then turns her attention to Justin and Travis, who opted to walk down the aisle together. I rest my arm on the back of Elena's chair and hold her hand in mine as she watches her brother recite his vows.

I couldn't tell you a single word either of them said. All my attention was on Elena. I place a kiss to her cheek and tell her I love her, to which she turns her head and places a soft kiss to my lips.

After the ceremony, people begin to filter out of the space and Elena's family sticks around to take some photos with the newlyweds. I linger in the doorway of the ceremony space waiting for Elena, and when she's done, she skips over to me and loops her arm with mine. She leads me towards the reception space, and I begin to wonder if she'd want a big wedding or a small, intimate one. I'd prefer the latter, of course, but if she wanted a big wedding, I'd invite the entire state of New Jersey, and maybe even Texas too. I'd give her absolutely anything she desired if I got to call her my wife at the end of the day.

When we arrive at the reception hall, we stop at the bar for champagne and hors d'oeuvres. We make polite conversation with some of the guests. By the end of cocktail hour, I've got just about everyone in this room in my pocket, with of course, one exception.

Elena's father.

I've had six glasses of champagne, needing one every time I catch him glaring at me. Elena notices.

"Are you okay?" she asks with amusement in her voice. "I'm usually the one drinking up all the champagne."

I blow out air from my mouth through puffed cheeks. I lean against one of the tall cocktail tables, crossing my ankles and trying to relax. "Your father hasn't stopped glaring daggers at me all night."

She rolls her eyes and looks in his direction. "He's being unreasonable. He still hasn't apologized to me for Thanksgiving."

I take a deep breath and remember what Bethany said to me, about not making Elena choose sides. I don't want to do that, even unintentionally. "Maybe you should talk to him," I suggest plainly. "My loyalty is with you, not your dad, but I don't want him to think I'm filling your head with distaste for him. I'll be his son-in-law one day, so he's going to have to get over his issues with me."

Not that I've gotten over any of mine with him.

Elena hums. "You seem very confident that we're going to get married, Mr. Reeves."

I growl and push her lightly with my chest until her back is against the wall. I grab a handful of her thigh and squeeze, hovering my lips over hers with a smirk.

"I seem to distinctly remember getting married months ago with a four-year-old as our witness, wife."

"*Wife*?" a gruff voice repeats from behind me. I pull back to find Elliot standing there. I can practically see the steam coming out of his ears. Every time he looks at me, it's like he thinks I've just committed a horrific crime.

I've committed a lot of those. Just none he knows about.

Elena clicks her tongue. "It's just an inside joke," she seethes. Elliot's right side of his mouth twitches up in a jealous sneer, and he simply grumbles to himself before walking away. Elena reaches up to rub the base of my neck. "Don't worry about him." She rubs down the well-fitted fabric of my suit jacket. I'm wearing all black from head to toe, with an emerald-green velvet bowtie and pocket square. "You look good. I like when we get dressed up together."

"Not as good as you, angel. You look spectacular. Especially your makeup." I nip at her ear. "That blush matches the exact color of your chest when my tongue is inside you."

CHAPTER 41

THE ANGEL

After dinner, Justin and Travis do a raunchy, energetic tango as their first dance. The DJ invites all the couples in attendance to the dance floor. I stay firmly in my seat, picking at the last of the vegetables on my plate. Christian stands and holds out a hand for me to take. I look up at him with a fork halfway in my mouth and raise an eyebrow at him. "*You* want to dance?"

He nods. "What kind of wedding date would I be if I didn't ask you to dance?"

He takes my hand and pulls me to my feet, then leads me to the dance floor where a few dozen other couples are all swaying together. Christian pulls me close and places his warm hand on my back, and despite the layer of fabric between us, his touch sends a shiver up my spine. With my right hand laced with his, and my left hand on his shoulder, he begins to spin us in a simple circle.

I nuzzle into Christian's chest, breathing in his expensive cologne and sighing at the warmth of him seeping into my cheek. We sway for two songs, even the more upbeat one, ignoring everyone around us.

I'm the first to break the comfortable silence. "Can I ask you something?"

"Anything."

"Would you ever consider moving? Away from Meridian City, I mean."

He's quiet for a long time, but his hold on me tightens. "If that's what you wanted."

"Really?"

"The logistics would be difficult since my company's headquarters is in Meridian City, and the orphanage is there too, but I'd make it work." He rubs his hot fingers down my back. "Do you want to move?"

I shrug. "Sometimes I think about it."

He lifts my chin up and rubs my bottom lip with his thumb. "Where would you want to go?" He leans down to brush his lips against mine. "To Italy?" Another kiss. "To France?" Another kiss. "Australia? Brazil? Scotland? I speak ten languages, my angel. We could go anywhere you wanted."

"*Ten*? Since when?"

"Since always. English was my first language, obviously. French, Italian, and Spanish came next. Edwin taught me Gaelic, and then I learned Portuguese, Japanese, Mandarin, German, and Greek."

I giggle. "I got a 'C' in Spanish."

He chuckles. "Learning languages has always come easy to me, and I make an effort to at least make meaningful conversations with foreign investors. Makes me seem cultured." He pokes me in the side to tickle me. "What's the verdict? Where are we moving, angel?"

"Nowhere for now," I say with a smile, looking up at him from under my lashes. "Maybe when we have a family though?"

"Whatever you want."

"You're always so quick to say that."

"That's because I'm thoroughly pussy-whipped for you."

I can't help the giggle that escapes my lips.

"What's so funny, Elena Reeves?"

"Nothing. You just admitted I wear the pants in this relationship, is all." He spins me in a circle and then pulls me tight to his chest. "It sounds nice, you know. My name with your last name." His fingers trace down my body to rest on my waist. His large hands feel massive against my small frame.

"Then let me give it to you," Christian whines, practically begging. He dramatically looks around the room. "Bet the officiant is still here somewhere."

I roll my eyes playfully. "Maybe if it wasn't my *brother's* wedding, I might humor you."

He grumbles. "At least it wasn't an outright '*no*' this time. We're finally getting somewhere!"

I bring his head down a bit so it's easier for me to whisper in his ear, because even in my heels, he still towers over me. "Hey, baby?"

I feel him shiver and he kisses my neck. "The words that come out of your mouth after you call me baby are always naughty."

"Want to know a secret?" I feel him nod against my neck. "I may wear the pants in this relationship, but I'm not currently wearing any panties."

I lean back as redness blooms across his cheeks, and I slightly adjust his bowtie. I scrape my neatly manicured nails down his chest and abdomen, stopping right above his belt before taking a step away from him. "I think I need some more eyelash glue." I pull slightly at one of the falsies attached to my eyelid. "I'll be in the groom's suite if you need me."

I wink at him and turn to walk away, making it out of the reception hall and to the door of the suite before Christian catches up to me, pressing his chest into my back. I can feel his length straining behind the belt of his pants, aching to be free against the curve of my ass. He flips me around, pins me against the wall and crushes his lips against mine while he fumbles for the doorknob. When he finds it, he pushes the door open, drags us inside, and closes it behind him.

Still against the wall next to the door, he leaves messy, eager kisses all over my neck and the exposed part of my chest. He sinks to the floor and starts to push up the fabric of my dress. I help him gather it around my thighs. He licks his lips when he sees I wasn't lying. My pussy is bare. Hot. Aroused.

He stares at me for a long time, like he's committing the sight to memory. "Let me taste you," he begs. "Just one taste."

My body starts to tremble, but I gulp and nod. "*One*."

He nods back, and with a feral growl that emanates deep from his throat, he kisses my clit gently and then licks along my slit. I whimper. It feels so good. A new wave of arousal comes crashing through me. My legs feel weak when he pulls away and stands.

Then he kisses me. His lips are soft and languid against mine. I can taste myself on his mouth. I wrap my arms around his neck and pull him closer. He lifts me up, wrapping my legs around his waist so I can feel his massive erection between my thighs.

His lips move from my mouth to my neck, where he licks and sucks and nips until I'm squirming in his arms, until my hands are tugging on his hair, so hard I'm surprised I haven't ripped it out. He looks straight into my eyes. His are lust-blown. Needy. Hungry. He uses his hips to press me into the wall hard enough that when his hands leave my thighs, I don't move an inch. His hot, ravenous hands trace up my body, feeling my breasts through the thick fabric of my dress.

"What's your safe word?" he asks, looking straight at me.

"Mykonos," I breathe. "I trust you."

"*Don't,*" he whispers back, and then his hands wrap around my back to pull down the zipper of my dress just enough to expose my breasts. I can feel his hot breath as he lets out a delicious sound of satisfaction at the sight. His hands cup both of my breasts, thumbing gently over my nipples until they're both hard peaks. The sensation is pleasurable, but not overwhelming.

His lips go back to my neck before he squeezes my breasts together and opens his mouth wide to bite one hard enough that it leaves an imprint of his teeth in my skin. I let out a breathy moan as he continues to rub my nipples with his thumbs and covers my chest in hungry, desperate kisses. His erection is pressing so tightly into my core he might burst straight through his slacks.

He experimentally takes one of my perky nipples in his mouth and sucks gently. I moan louder this time. Christian is a generous lover, but he's never given my chest so much attention before.

I can feel how wet I am between my legs. My hot, sticky arousal is surely coating his slacks, and all he's doing is flicking his sinful tongue against my nipple.

"More," I beg. I don't even really know what specifically I'm begging for, but I trust him to figure it out for me. He shoves his middle finger into my mouth and commands me to suck. I do, and while I circle my tongue around the digit, he goes back to giving my nipples his complete attention.

My veins feel like molten lava and my core is dripping when he removes his finger from my mouth. He leans back just enough to see the mess I've made on his slacks. He sets my legs down and then looks at me.

"Use my hand to make yourself cum," he commands, brushing my hair away from my face tenderly. He doesn't give me a chance to ask questions, nor does he elaborate. He goes back to sucking and licking and lightly biting my aching nipples. I'm so desperate for release right now it feels like I'm on fire.

I take Christian's hand in mine, his finger still wet with my saliva, and I bring him to the apex of my thighs. He doesn't move his fingers unless I make him. He wants me to use him as a toy. He wants me to use his fingers and trust that he won't do anything that I don't allow him to.

Taking a shaky breath, I close my eyes, and lead his finger to graze over my clit.

I moan loudly at the contact. Almost obnoxiously. Like a virgin discovering pleasure for the first time. I had forgotten what his fingers felt like.

Swallowing my nerves, I guide his finger to trace gentle circles on the sensitive bud. I grind against his finger, seeking out pleasure on my own. With my free hand, I dig my nails into his back, running them down the smooth fabric of his suit jacket. I grind harder, moan louder, pull him closer and closer until I feel myself reach that peak.

And then I let myself fall. It's wild and beautiful and safe. Unable to help himself, Christian cups my pussy as I ride out my orgasm, grinding against his palm until I'm panting with sweet relief. He holds his hand in the space between us. It glistens with my slick and like the beautiful savage he is, he sticks his fingers into his mouth and licks himself clean. The skirt of my dress falls back to the floor with a soft whoosh as I let the fabric go. My chest is still exposed, my breasts spilling out over the top.

My lipstick is smeared all over his face. A sheen of sweat gathers along his hairline. He grips my hips with so much desire it's bruising. He's still painfully hard in his pants and the look on his face screams for relief. I rub my palm against his erection through his pants and that simple touch alone nearly brings him to his knees.

The door opening stops us both and has me scrambling to pull up my top to try and maintain some dignity as the newly married couple comes stumbling in, apparently having the same idea as us. The four of us stare at each other, and Justin and Travis break out into loud laughter.

"Sorry! We're sorry!" Justin bites his lip to keep himself from laughing harder and pulls Travis back out of the room by his tie. "We'll find another room!"

Christian growls and pulls the door shut after they leave, being very careful to *lock* the door this time. He rests his forehead against mine and takes a deep breath. I grab his cheeks and twirl us in a small circle until he's flat against the wall, and I sink to my knees.

He says my name through gritted teeth. "You don't have to."

"But what if I want to?" I ask as I unbuckle his belt.

"I can't promise I will be still."

"I didn't ask you to."

"Elena," he warns. "Do not fuck with me right now."

I say his name and he opens his eyes, looking down at me like he's unhinged and a millisecond away from losing his shit. Looking up from under my thick eyelashes, I give him big, simpering eyes and ask, "What's your safe word?"

He laughs maliciously, which turns into a growl, which turns into a sharp inhale. "Do you remember what happens when you get mouthy with me?"

I shake my head, pretending I have no idea what he's talking about as I continue to stall and mess with his belt like I'm struggling to get it off.

"Do you need me to show you?" he asks.

I shake my head and run my nails down his thighs, bulging against his slacks. Then, I rub my fingers along his clothed cock again, feeling it twitch under my hand. His chest heaves and he's getting ready to snap my neck if I don't do something about the situation in his pants immediately.

I flutter my lashes and smile at him. He whimpers and laughs at the same time. "That look means trouble."

"No," I say. "It means I'm in charge."

And then I lick along the length of him, still clothed.

He lets out a guttural, ferocious grunt, and trembles beneath my tongue. He looks down at me, bright red and completely embarrassed.

Because I made him cum in his pants.

CHAPTER 42

THE SILENCER

Elena and I sneak back into the reception hall after our rendezvous in the groom's suite. She's so fucking proud of herself and I'm over here feeling like a damn teenager that just saw a pair of tits for the first time. My boxers are sticky with my cum, despite my attempts to clean up in the bathroom as Elena fixed her smeared makeup.

It was embarrassing and erotic all at the same time. She was in a submissive position, yet completely turned the tables on me and stole the control right out from under me.

That's my good fucking girl.

I have the unfortunate luck of making eye contact with Elliot as soon as we walk into the reception hall, to which he frowns at me. His gaze burns into me like he somehow knows I just defiled his daughter. Or rather, she defiled me.

I take a deep breath and lean over to whisper in Elena's ear. "I'm going to go talk to your father."

I kiss her cheek. She gives me a squeeze on the bicep of encouragement and snags a couple of glasses of champagne, bringing one to her mother and dragging her to the dance floor.

Elliot notices me approaching him and goes to the bar for another drink. I stand at his side while the bartender hands him one of the '*His & His*' drinks, Justin's version. An old fashioned. Good taste.

"Elliot?"

His eyes flicker to me, but he doesn't respond. "Look, you've got to stop acting like I'm your enemy. If I can keep the past in the past, you sure as hell can too. If not for me, for Elena."

He turns to face me and then abruptly throws the drink in his glass directly into my face. The small crowd around us gasps.

"Get out of my face," he sneers.

I take a deep, angry breath and rub the alcohol off my face. If we weren't in the middle of a crowded reception hall, I'd knock him on his ass right now. I bump shoulders with him, *hard*, as I walk around him and towards the bathroom. Elena is right on my heels and follows me inside, locking the door behind us.

"Christian…"

I ball up my fists and lean over the counter, gritting my teeth and conjuring up every ounce of self-control I have so that I don't bust down this bathroom door and break Elliot's nose.

"I'm fine," I lie through gritted teeth. I feel Elena gently rub down my back, because she *knows* I'm lying to her. And myself.

I'm not used to tolerating this kind of disrespect. If he was anyone else but her father, I would have had him laid out on the floor, maybe even with a bullet in his head.

He did it because he knew I couldn't do anything about it. He knew he would get away with it with nothing more than some disappointed looks from his family.

"Do you want to leave?"

I turn around and face her and lean against the counter as she takes a napkin to wipe up some of the amber liquid from the front of my suit. At least I'm wearing black, so it's not super noticeable. "No. We don't have to leave. It's fine." I give her a half-hearted chuckle. "Come on, let's go back. I don't want to make a scene."

"If it makes you feel better, my mother never shuts up about you. This morning I went to say hi, and the first thing she did was ask where you were. She really likes you."

I nod. "I'll ask her for a dance."

We leave the bathroom and I go straight to Bethany with a charming smile and my hand outstretched towards her. "May I?" Bethany nods and gleefully takes my hand. Every time Elliot and I make eye contact, we scowl at each other.

"I'm sorry about my husband," Bethany says, noticing my stare-off with him. "He's got a temper, but he shouldn't have done that."

I shake my head. "It's okay."

"You might not have won over Elliot yet, but I'm in your corner."

I laugh. "Thank you for saying that. I really do love your daughter. More than I ever thought I was capable of."

"She's crazy about you," Bethany quips. "Talks about you nonstop. Tells me how happy you make her, and I'm not just talking about the expensive gifts and the trips and that big house she's living in, Christian. You make her happy, deep in her soul, even if your relationship was hanging on by a thread after what happened to her. Don't ever doubt the way she feels about you. She'd do anything to make you as happy as you make her."

"The feeling's mutual." I look over my shoulder towards Elena and sigh. "Bethany, tell me what I can do. Elliot isn't going anywhere, and neither am I. You know him best. What is it going to take to get him to understand that I'm not my father?"

Her face falls slightly, but it perks right back up into a sad smile. "I think all you can do is give him time to see for himself how much you love our daughter. Give him time to understand that fate brought you back into his life for a reason. I think that reason is forgiveness. For both of you. I think he will come to his senses soon. If not..." She trails off and begins a new train of thought. "He told me that you almost killed him, but you didn't for Elena's sake. I can't say the same about my husband. You showed restraint where he didn't. That makes you a good man."

I scoff. "I have bad news for you, Bethany. I am not a good man. Please don't get it in your head that I am. I love Elena and I would do absolutely anything for her. Anything. That makes me the worst kind of man. Love is the most volatile poison in the universe. I'm not a saint by any stretch of the imagination, but I make you a promise on my life, that Elena will always be safe with me, even if it costs me everything in the end."

"I believe you," Bethany says, her voice morphing into that of a concerned but hopeful mother. "I trust you. Don't make me regret it."

"Understood," I reply curtly. She seems content with my answer. "May I ask you something personal about your relationship with your husband?" She nods. "Diana and his kids were killed in 1989. Elena was born in 1990. How long were you two together before you married?"

Bethany laughs. "Elena was an 'oopsie' baby, as was her brother. Elliot craved distraction from his grief, so I gave it to him. He asked me to marry him when I found out I was pregnant with Elena, but we didn't actually have a ceremony until 1993."

I chuckle mournfully. "Elena once told me that you call Elliot your soulmate because you fell in love with him despite him being so hard to love. I guess she didn't realize the true meaning of that statement."

"Her father is her hero. He's been a good dad, even if he says hurtful things sometimes. Remember that he loved her first,

Christian. He'll have a permanent place in her heart, no matter what."

A smile tugs up the corners of my lips. "Maybe by the time Elena and I get married, he might be able to tolerate me."

Bethany perks up at the thought of her daughter getting married. "How old are you?"

Quite a change in topic.

"Thirty-six," I answer with a raised eyebrow.

She laughs. "I expect at least two grandchildren by the time you're forty. If she doesn't have a ring on her finger by next Christmas, I think I will die."

I chuckle, pulling out the engagement ring that's been burning a hole in my pocket for weeks. I present it to Bethany for inspection. She twists it and bounces on her toes in delight at the way it sparkles.

"Does it get your seal of approval?"

She sighs, and dramatically puts her hand to her head and pretends to fall over. I catch her easily. "If Elena doesn't marry you, I will."

"You know, I don't think Elliot would appreciate me stealing his wife *and* his daughter. I might start World War III."

She hands back the ring. "You'd start a war for love?"

"For Elena? I wouldn't just start a war. I'd win it."

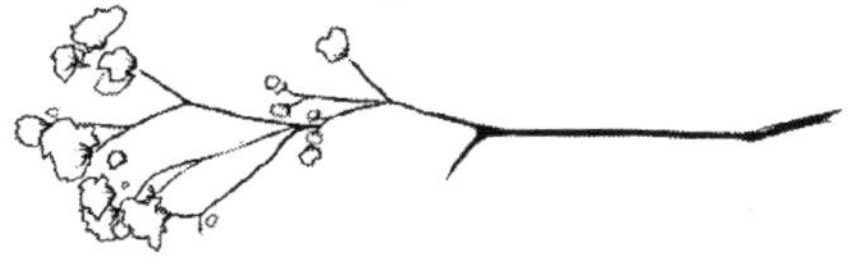

I dance with Bethany for a few more songs, grab my own old fashioned at the bar, and make small talk with a few of the insufferable businessmen who recognize me.

Elena and I take a few polaroid photos together. One for the guestbook, and a few just for us that I put into my wallet for safekeeping. She's become a little bit tipsy, dancing with her equally tipsy mother to a few pop hits. I smile at her when she catches my gaze across the room and I flash my cigarette case at her, indicating that I'm going outside for a smoke.

I leave the reception hall and step outside into the chilly December air, and light one. Cigarettes are objectively awful for me, but something about the action of smoking helps me think.

I really hate this situation with Elliot. I think Bethany was right. There's a reason I fell in love with the daughter of the man who killed my parents. Probably a lesson in restraint, if I had to guess.

For the past two years of my life, I've committed dozens of murders because I felt like I had no choice. The only way I could keep up the act of the charming CEO during the day is if I committed brutal savageries at night. I always justified my kills by telling myself I'd only kill other bad people.

But now that I know the truth about my father, I don't think my urges were uncontrollable at all.

Because I hesitated when I put that gun under Elliot's chin, when I *always* promised myself that if I found the man who killed my parents, they wouldn't live to see another second.

I didn't kill him, but only out of my love for Elena. I knew it would tear us apart.

Loving her is more important than revenge.

While I wouldn't hesitate to kill anyone that harmed her, I've shown mercy to the man who ruined my life. I think that's a testament to just how tight of a grip Elena has on my soul.

I never want to come between the two of them. He's a good, loving father. At the end of the day, I'm the outsider, and if she had to choose a side, I can't say with certainty that she'd choose mine, even though I've threatened otherwise.

I take a long drag of my cigarette and I hear the venue doors open behind me. I glance over my shoulder to find Elliot stalking towards me. I open my mouth to say his name, and I'm met with a fist in my jaw that knocks the cigarette out of my mouth. I stumble backwards a few steps, and Elliot raises his fist again, aiming for my nose this time. I let him hit me, blood dripping down my face and onto the concrete.

The third punch he winds up, I catch his fist in my hand and twist his arm behind his back. I drag him around a corner behind a wall, slamming his face into the pristine white stone of the wedding venue far away from the doors.

"What the hell is your problem?" Elliot tries to fight my grasp, and he's a strong man, but I'm stronger, younger, and a fuck ton angrier. I could flip a damn semi-truck if I wanted to. "Huh? What's your fucking problem, Elliot?"

Elliot begins fighting against me and we begin struggling and growling like two wild animals.

"Whatever's got your panties in a twist, you need to get over it. The only reason I don't knock your lights out and make you eat concrete is because of your daughter."

"Weak." Elliot smiles against the wall. "You're weak. You can't even handle her being a little mad at you for giving me what I deserve after all that disrespect."

"Is that what this is about? You were trying to provoke me so I'd give you a pavement facial? I thought we were at a ceasefire?"

"*Ceasefire*," he chuckles, and then his face falls into a hard scowl. "I can't figure out what kind of fucked up psychological hold you have on her, but I can see the devil when I look in your eyes, boy. Something is seriously wrong with you, and I'm going to figure out what it is before you get her killed."

"You killed my parents. You tried to kill me. I was a fucking kid! The only devil here is you," I seethe, practically breathing fire. "You know absolutely nothing about Elena's relationship with me. You have no idea what we've been through together or the lengths I would go to keep her safe. She's *mine*, Elliot. My relationship is none of your damn business. Swing at me again and I'll give you permanent brain damage."

Elliot spits on the ground and grabs me by the front of my jacket to pull me close. "You listen to me, Thomas, stay the *fuck* away from my family."

Both of us freeze, staring at each other as we both come to the exact same conclusion. Elliot has dissociated from reality, and he thinks I'm *Thomas* Reeves.

"Elliot…"

He lets me go and pushes me away from him, staring at me, but staring through me, too.

Then he simply walks away.

I lean my back against the stone wall of the venue and sink down to the floor, taking deep breaths to try and calm myself down. *Goddamn it.* Elliot is clearly exhibiting symptoms of extreme PTSD for what my father did to his family. My relationship with his daughter triggered it. It's so bad that he can't even tell us apart.

Elena is fortunate that she has two men that love her with all their hearts,

It's also incredibly unfortunate that we're both delusional bastards.

"*Fuck*," I whisper to myself. I stand up and sneak back into the venue and then into the private bathroom in the groom's suite to wash off my face and rinse out my mouth. I thoroughly inspect myself in the mirror to make sure I don't miss any blood.

I rejoin the party and find Elena now *thoroughly* drunk and handsy, and just a little too out of it to notice my shift in mood. I settle her into the same chair she sat in at dinner, and Bethany joins us, plopping down in the empty seat next to me after proclaiming she's danced-out for the night.

They both slump into my arms, sweaty and tired from the full day of festivities. I rub my hands against their shoulders and arms, until they're both yawning and succumbing to their exhaustion.

Elliot walks into the room, and the world goes quiet as he stares me down with his wife and daughter snuggled up in my arms.

Just to get back at him for nailing me in the face, I wink at him, and subtly give him two middle fingers.

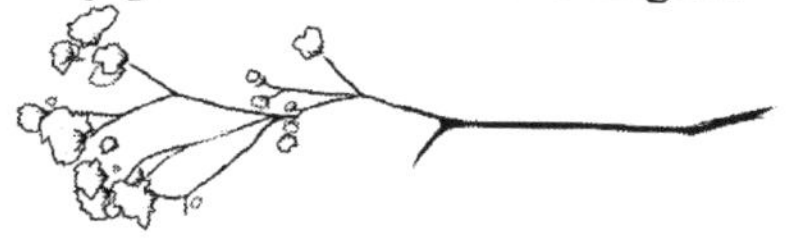

The second we get back from California, I'm stopped by one of Edwin's nurses, who tells me that he's lucid and asking for me.

Perfect, because I've got some shit to say to him.

I've got fury coursing through my veins as I stomp to his room, thankful Elena has made herself busy with unpacking. When I get to his room, I tell his nurses to get out. Seething, I approach his bed and point an accusatory finger at him.

"Edwin, look at me," I demand. The old man's lucid for the first time since Thanksgiving. I don't have time to beat around the bush and I don't have time for bullshit. "Did you know my father killed Diana Young and her two kids?"

Edwin looks at me, and his face goes ghost white, telling me everything I need to know. I walk around in a small circle, rubbing the stubble on my jaw. I prop my fists on the edge of his bed and lean over.

"Why the *fuck* didn't you tell me my father was a murderer? You lied to me my whole fucking life. You let me believe he was this perfect, lawful man that loved my mom. Loved *me*! But he was so obsessed with another woman that he killed her when he couldn't have her!"

"I did what I thought was best," Edwin whispers.

"Best for who? Because it sure as hell wasn't for my sake!"

Edwin slow blinks. "Please don't yell at me. I don't feel well."

"Don't try and change the subject," I growl, pointing at him again. "Answer the question."

He settles into his bed and tugs the covers up to his chest. He smacks his lips together and looks at me. His face screams guilt and regret. "I thought it was better if I didn't ruin the last memories you had of your parents. You were already so angry at the world." He smacks his chapped lips again. "How did you find out?"

Seething, I growl through gritted teeth. "Because Elena is the daughter of the man that fucking killed them!" I sit in the chair and pinch the bridge of my nose. "*Fuck, Edwin*."

"Are you mad at me?" he asks quietly.

"Yes," I grit out. "Yes, I'm mad at you. Are there any other skeletons in my father's closet I should know about?"

Edwin shakes his head. "No. Does Elena know about this?"

"No, she doesn't, and we're keeping it that way. It's better that she doesn't get caught in the crossfire," I mumble, though my angel couldn't be any more in the middle of this shitstorm if I dragged her there by her wings.

Edwin's head snaps towards me so quickly that for a second, I'm scared he broke it. He scowls for the first time in decades and points at me right back. "You don't get to be mad at me for keeping secrets when you're doing the same thing."

I ball my fists up and my face turns red with fury, because he's right, but I'll be damned if I admit it. *I fucking hate when he's right*. I scoff angrily.

"*Fuck that.* I think I have every right to be pissed that the man I've trusted for my entire life has turned out to be a goddamn liar. Elena is the only person in my life who has never let me down. I don't need your bullshit anymore, Edwin. I have her, and she's all that matters to me now."

As I leave the room, Edwin calls after me, sounding out of breath and tired.

"What?" I call back, without turning around.

"Will you do a puzzle with me?"

I scoff. "Do it yourself," I sneer, and then slam the door shut behind me.

CHAPTER 43

THE ANGEL

"Hey…um, it's me. Well, of course it's me. You saw my name on your phone screen…which is probably why you're ignoring it. Look, just…just call me, okay? I miss you."

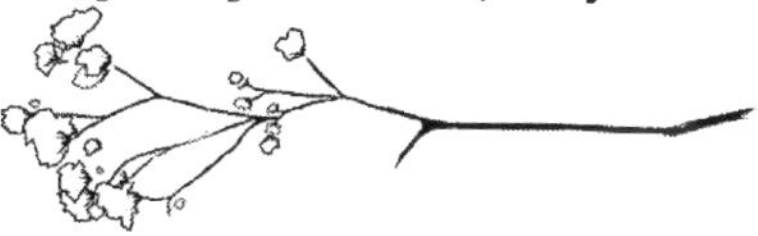

"I don't understand why you're still ignoring me! I just want to talk to you! Please!"

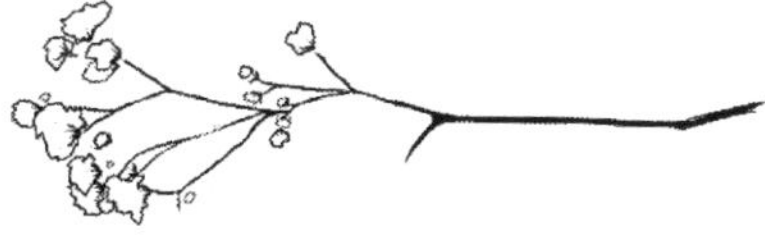

"I saw on the news this morning that you were awarded Clinician of the Year. For the tenth year in a row. Congrats. That's really exciting. I….Please, dad. Please just call me back. We've never gone this long without talking. I know it's only been a few days, but it's killing me. I just really need to hear your voice. Please."

"Is this really how you want to lose another daughter? Fine. This is the last time I'll ever call."

"Please…"

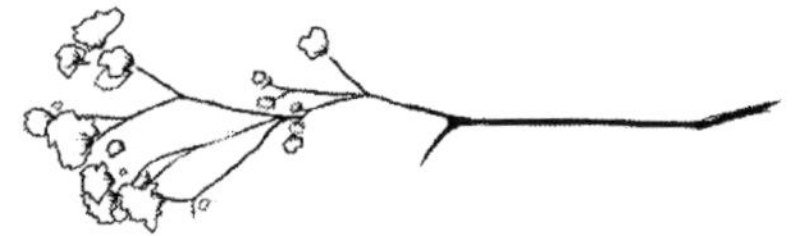

I'm sorry. Mailbox full. Goodbye!
I'm sorry. Mailbox full. Goodbye!
I'm sorry. Mailbox full. Goodbye!

CHAPTER 44

THE ANGEL

"Hi, Edwin." I say cautiously to the man sitting in front of me. He's tucked into his hospital bed, covers up to his chest, with a wet rag on his forehead. He slowly turns his head to look at me, and when our eyes meet, he gives me a warm smile.

I pull up a chair next to his bedside and take his hand in mine. It's so cold, and it's worrying. I give him a warm smile back as I use friction to heat up his hand. "The nurses said you aren't feeling well."

"Oh, don't you worry about me. It's nothing."

I suck in a sharp breath. *Hold it together, Elena.* "Edwin?" He hums back in response. "Do you know who I am?"

He lifts his head slightly to look at me, and that's how I know he can hear the break in my voice and see the welling tears in my eyes. He simply nods.

I let out the breath I was holding. "Do you think you could…pretend not to for a few minutes?"

He blinks at me twice, and then rests his head back on his pillow and gives my hand a squeeze. "I hate it when you're sad, my dear Helen."

My shoulders slump, and the dam breaks. My head falls to the bed and I let the sheets soak up my tears as I weep for myself. Weeks and weeks of emotion that I've let build up hit me all at once and Edwin is the only one who could possibly understand the sacrifice it takes to love Christian.

And after the wedding, I feel like that sacrifice is my family, and I don't know if I can live with that.

Edwin removes his hand from mine and uses his boney fingers to rub along my scalp in a comforting gesture.

"Do you remember the day we met?" Edwin asks. I lift my head and wipe my cheek. "It was the most beautiful sunny day. You were painting the lovely coastline of Spanish Point, and that gust of wind sent your brushes into the sand. Do you remember?"

My lip quivers, because I know that he's not really asking me. He's telling me the story of how he met his wife.

"I helped you clean off your brushes, but I was a clumsy lout and knocked over your paints. Your precious blue paint spilled all over the sand. You smiled and said it was okay, but I could see the heartbreak in your face. I spent the next week trekking all over County Clare looking for your special blue paint. Do you remember? The one made of lapis lazuli. It was so bright and beautiful."

I sniffle and nod. Edwin smiles wistfully.

"Cost me a month's salary, it did, but I bought it and found you a week later in the same spot, still trying to paint the water, even without blue paint. Your face lit up brighter than the sun. I had never seen something so beautiful. Your emerald eyes were the most flawless gemstones on God's green earth. You were insecure about the gap between your two front teeth, so you'd hide your smile with your hand, but all I could see was that beautiful smile and those flawless eyes behind a white veil. I begged for your name, but you told me to come back in a week. So I did. You were still in the same spot. You gave me your finished painting. Do you remember what I promised that day, sweet Helen?"

I shake my head.

"I promised I'd buy you all the paint in the world if you told me your name."

I sniffle again. "And then what happened?"

"You're telling me you don't remember!?" Edwin boasts, and then he laughs. "You said a man never made you feel like that before!"

I squeal and cover my ears as my face heats up and Edwin bursts into louder laughter, which sets off a chain reaction in me.

I can't even remember why I was crying.

CHAPTER 45

THE SILENCER

There is something very peaceful about opening the hood of a car and changing all the fluids yourself. It's always calmed me down, given me something to do. Nothing like the feeling of grease all over your arms while music bumps through the speakers. If anyone needs an escape right now, it's me. My life has suddenly become one big pile of shit, and the few days that have passed since the wedding have been absolute hell.

I've been taking it out on my cars. I smashed the Bugatti's windshield in with a crowbar just to feel something. Then I spent three hours changing the oil on several of my vehicles. Even the ones that didn't need it.

I'm elbows-deep in a Corvette's engine when tiny, freezing toes gently nudge my bare back. I glance over my shoulder with a raised eyebrow to find Elena standing behind me, eying the Bugatti suspiciously.

"Whatcha doin'?"

"Changing oil," I murmur.

"I didn't realize the oil reservoir was located in the windshield."

I grab the rag that's flung over my shoulder and wipe off some of the grime that's built up on my hands and turn to face her.

I use my thumb to point behind me. "Want to learn how?"

She narrows her eyes at me, revealing her manicured fingers from her sweater paws. "Do these hands look like they were made for manual labor?"

I chuckle. "Spoiled brat."

She sticks her tongue out at me.

My face falls when I notice how red the tip of her nose is, and the small smudges of mascara under her eyes.

"Have you been crying?"

She shakes her head. "Nope," she quips unconvincingly. "Okay, fine. You got me. Edwin was just telling me about how he met Helen. It was a really cute story."

"Until he gets to the part where he rocked her world, huh?"

Elena smiles and laughs. Something genuine sparkles behind her eyes and my shoulders instantly relax to see her happy, if only for a second.

I pull her to my side, not caring that she's wearing my sweater or that my dirty hands are mucking it up. She wraps her arms around my neck and hugs me.

I move my hands up to rest on the small of her back. She kisses the tip of my nose. "Tell me why you're upset."

My shoulders sag with regret. "When we got back from California, Edwin and I got in a fight." I look up at the ceiling and sigh. "Okay, *I* was doing the fighting. I got upset with him and stormed out. I said some shit I didn't mean in the heat of the moment."

She gives me a strained smile. "He doesn't feel good."

"I know."

Fuck, I know. I shouldn't have gotten mad at him, and I shouldn't have blown him off. At his age, not feeling good can turn into not being alive so fast it's frightening.

"Why are you mad at him?"

I close my eyes and let out a long breath, trying to buy time to find any plausible explanation without telling her the truth.

I'm not withholding information because of Elliot. I have no loyalty to that man. I'm only keeping my mouth shut about his revelation because he's her father and I'm not so confident she'd even believe me.

"Elena, angel, I can't tell you."

She blinks slowly at me, as if she's not surprised. I'm a master at keeping secrets after all.

"Okay," she says quietly, rubbing her hands across my bare chest. I purr in satisfaction when her nails scrape along my abs. "I understand."

"You do?"

She nods. "Your secrets with him are none of my business."

I wrap my hands around her waist, squeezing lightly. "I'm just not ready to talk about it."

She cups my cheeks in her hands and gives me a soft kiss. "Go take a shower and meet me in the study."

"Why?"

"Because I said so."

I chuckle again. "So bossy."

I rub my thumb over her cheekbone before standing. I throw on my dirty shirt and go to our bedroom to shower. Once clean, I get dressed and meet her in the study like she told me to.

When I get there, she's sitting at a table with Edwin, helping him with the border of one of his puzzles. He's wheezing hard, like every breath he takes seems to cause him pain. I lock eyes with him and look down at the floor in shame.

"I'm sorry," I say, my throat burning slightly from the distaste of an apology. I never liked apologizing.

Edwin blinks at me. "For what?" he asks, his Irish accent extra gravelly from the phlegm in his chest and throat. My eyes glance over to Elena, and she gives me a flat-lined smile, and shakes her head.

And now I feel like more of a dick, because I tarnished his last lucid moments together with anger.

I've always taken him for granted.

Silently, I take a seat at the table with them, and help them with the puzzle border.

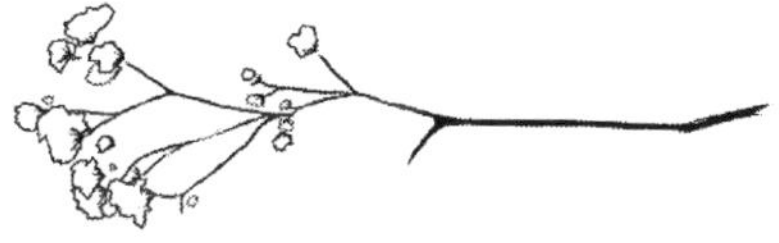

On Christmas Eve, I wake up with Elena's side of the bed ice cold. My first instinct is that something's wrong. That she's had a nightmare and is hiding somewhere in the mansion with her wrists slit.

I get out of bed immediately and shrug on a shirt before practically sprinting out of my room. When I get to the foyer of the mansion, my senses are hit with woodsmoke and peppermint, and horrid, mind-numbing Christmas carols floating through the house. My floors are covered in shopping bags and tissue paper, along with a long, rectangular box.

I can hear giggles and conversation coming from the main living area. When I round the corner, I'm hit with an odd feeling in my chest. My heart swells with something that I can only describe as domestic bliss.

There's a large Christmas tree set up in the middle of the room. Elena's on her butt decorating the bottom of it. On the other side of the tree, Bethany is decorating the top. Edwin is sitting at a small table attempting to glue two sides of a gingerbread house together with frosting.

I stay quiet and lean against a column and watch the three of them, lost in their own little bubble of holiday cheer.

I finally make myself known and pad into the room, going straight to Elena and squatting next to her to place a kiss to the top of her head. "What's all this, angel?"

Bethany peeks out from behind the tree. "Elena said you didn't own a Christmas tree, and I said that was unacceptable, so we've been working hard to keep you from being such a grinch. With the help of your credit card, of course."

I laugh. "I'm not a grinch! I just…never cared about Christmas after my parents died."

Bethany sighs and gives me a sympathetic look. "Well I'm going to make you care! So put yourself to work and use that height of yours to decorate the top of the tree!"

"Yes ma'am." I give her a big hug. "It's nice to see you, Bethany. Where's Elliot?" I ask, noting his absence.

"*Being a grinch*," Bethany mumbles to herself, and I don't bother pressing the issue, pleased with the fact that he's not here. I go back to my room to brush my teeth and then pour myself a cup of coffee in the kitchen before rejoining Elena, Bethany, and Edwin in the living room.

I'm no good at decorations, but I put the star on top of the tree because I'm the only one who can reach without a ladder. That's got to be worth something.

It's raining outside, pretty heavily, but it adds a nice ambiance to the room. I haven't felt this…content in a long time. I guess the absence of family has made me so numb to the simple joys in life. I'm a bit embarrassed to admit that decorating this damn tree made the list of my favorite memories this year.

Once the tree is decorated to Bethany's standards, she grabs two presents from under the tree and shoves one in my hand and gently places the other in front of Edwin. I stand there, awkwardly staring at the neatly wrapped box. Edwin and I don't do gifts. It isn't a thing for us.

Bethany clicks her tongue. "Well? Open them! I'm leaving soon and I want to see you two open your Christmas presents from me before I go."

My eye twitches in Edwin's direction, and he takes one for the team and opens his first. The three of us watch him carefully as he tears through the paper.

Inside, a 5,000-piece puzzle that's completely white, making it extra challenging. Edwin's face lights up like the star on top of the tree. He shoves the pitiful attempt at a gingerbread house to the floor. It lands with a '*plop'*, and he immediately dumps out all 5,000 pieces of the puzzle and gets to work, exclaiming proudly that he'll finish it by New Years and starts giggling like old people do until he gives himself a coughing fit.

Bethany turns to me. "Your turn, Christian."

With a deep breath, I tear into the small package. When I lift the lid of the black box, sitting against red tissue paper is a Christmas ornament. It's a sleek black circle with a small golden plaque at the bottom with the year etched into it. In the center, a family photo that we all took together at the wedding. I lift the ornament out of the box and hold it up by the delicate golden ribbon. It spins, revealing a message etched onto the back.

"Family's First Christmas"

I clutch the small ornament carefully in my fist and take two long strides across the room to Bethany, pulling her into a tight hug.

"Thank you," I whisper to her, quiet enough that only she can hear it, and when I finally let her go, I place the ornament right in the center of the tree, so that every time I walk by, I'll remember what it feels like to have a family.

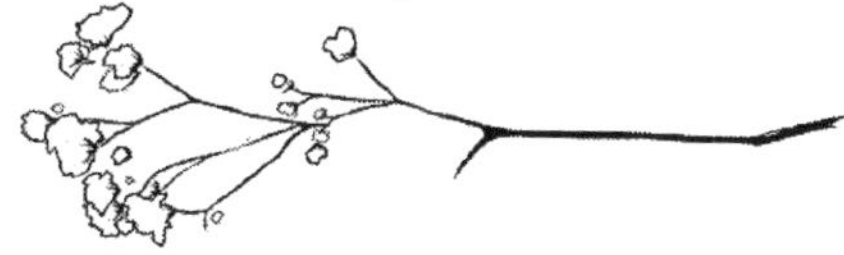

It's Christmas Day.

Bethany left soon after we finished the decorations. I gave her an extra-long hug before she left and sent her back to Texas on my private jet as a small gift to her. I didn't get her, or anyone in Elena's family, a gift for Christmas. I got Elena something, of course, and I suppose the million-dollar check I wrote for Justin and Travis as a wedding gift was enough, but I didn't even think about getting her parents anything. When Bethany landed, I texted her letting her know that her next vacation was on me.

Elena and I spend Christmas morning cuddled up on one of the couches in the living room near a fireplace, going through old family photos. I don't have nearly as many as her, so most of the time is spent listening to her tell detailed stories about every photo in the album.

I laugh at her relentlessly when we get to her middle school days, where she went through her 'emo phase' and there was no purple to be found in her life for two whole years. She shows me the first time she won a gold medal at a dance competition, reminiscing about how tight her bun was and how bad it hurt to take it out.

We go through her senior prom photos, and she is sorely disappointed to find out that I did not attend my own senior prom, because I got suspended for three days for fighting. I crinkle my nose in disgust at a photo of her and her ex-boyfriend at her college graduation.

Elena starts getting fidgety halfway through the day. Restless. Her nervous energy comes off her in waves.

I use a hand to brush some of her loose hair off her shoulder and place a soft kiss to the curve of her neck. "What's going on?"

"I'm nervous."

I chuckle. "I couldn't tell."

She smiles and then presses her lips to mine. "I need you to go to our room and stay until everything's ready. I'll text you when you can come out. Oh! And make sure you're wearing a suit."

"What are you up to? You're acting suspicious."

She playfully rolls her eyes. "Go!"

I do as she says.

About forty-five minutes of waiting pass, and I get dressed as instructed. I put on one of my best-fitting suits, my shiniest shoes, and my nicest Rolex.

As I straighten my tie in the mirror, I look around the room in the reflection and realize how accustomed I've become to sharing my home with the woman I love.

Her bar exam prep books and notebooks are scattered across the table. A stray bobby pin is discarded on the floor. A cardigan is draped over the sofa to my left. That picture of her dad she used to have in her office sits on my bookshelf next to my own family photos.

Everything about her presence in my life feels *right.* Like this is exactly where I was always meant to end up.

For the first time, I regret nearly ending my life. I almost missed out on the best thing that's ever happened to me.

I get the text to come out, and I do one final look in the mirror to make sure I look sharp. I leave the bedroom with my footsteps echoing through the quiet corridors of the mansion. When I get to the foyer, I pause, raising an eyebrow at the state of the floor.

White rose petals create a path, winding through the foyer, lined by tea lights. I follow the path slowly, and it comes to a stop in front of the fireplace.

I hear the distinct sound of heels clicking against the floor behind me, and when I turn, the entire world and everything in it fades away. Elena's hair frames her face in big, loose curls down her back. She's wearing a white satin dress. It has thin straps and a cowl neckline and ends mid-calf. Shining brightly around her neck is the Harry Winston necklace I bought her in Mykonos, accompanied by tiny, diamond studs in her ears. Her lips are painted in bright red lipstick, making her slight pout look absolutely irresistible.

I let out a shuddering breath, because I don't think I've ever seen anything so beautiful. So magnificent. So stellar.

So perfect.

She walks down the little rose petal path towards me, and when she's close enough that I can touch her, I cradle her jaw, look into her eyes, and whisper, "Stunning."

A glossy sheen coats her eyes, and those honey-brown irises sparkle up at me.

"Ask me properly."

I don't understand at first, but then the pieces start to fall together. The rose petal path. The white dress.

She's giving me a *wedding* as my Christmas present.

Pulling out the ring I had made for her out of my pocket, I slowly sink down to one knee without breaking eye contact.

"I'd offer you my heart and my soul, but you've had both of those from the moment we met. What more of myself do I have left to give that you don't already possess?" I sigh wistfully. "I have my last name, if you think it's worthy enough to follow the five letters you've carved into my heart." I take a deep breath. "Elena Louise Young, my angel, my love, my life, will you marry me?"

Elena nods, giving me her finger. "Yes, I'll marry you."

I slip the eleven-carat purple diamond onto her delicate finger, kissing it before standing to my full height and then taking her lips in mine.

"You're supposed to save the kiss until after we say, *I do*."

"I do," I whisper, taking her lips in mine again. "I do. I do. I do."

Elena giggles against my lips. "I have a ring for you." She leans over to grab a tiny red box hidden behind a pillow on the sofa.

She opens the box and then turns it so I can see inside.

It's a simple black band. I lift it from the plush red velvet. Inside the band, engraved in gold, are our initials on either side of a monogrammed letter 'R'.

Adoration fills my heart as I let her slip the ring onto my finger.

Technically this isn't a marriage, it's an engagement. We will have to apply for a marriage license and have an officiant hold a ceremony for us properly. Blah, blah, blah, none of the specifics matter.

She's pledged her life to me as I've done to her, and it's more than enough for me.

I begin to laugh as I kiss her again.

"What's so funny?"

"Nothing. Just my present to you seems so stupid by comparison."

She smirks against my lips. "Show me."

She yelps as I lean down to pick her up bridal style. She is my bride, after all. I carry her through the mansion, to the garage. Parked directly in the middle of the room is a pearlescent white McLaren 720S, and a custom license plate that simply says, '*ANGEL*'.

"Christian, you didn't!" She gasps as I set her down. "This is too much, you bought me a yacht two months ago!"

"Perks of being super rich." I kiss the curve of her neck again. "I get to spoil you rotten. Ostentatiously and often."

She tangles her small hands into the front of my jacket and pulls me in for a kiss. It's hot and needy and she drags me backwards until her legs hit her new car. Then she lowers herself onto the hood of the car and spreads her legs to reveal that she's not wearing any panties.

"Come here and spoil me," she commands.

Jesus fuck, this woman is going to be the death of me.

I fall to my knees in front of her and then I spoil my angel with my mouth and hands, right there on the hood of the car, all damn night.

Best Christmas ever.

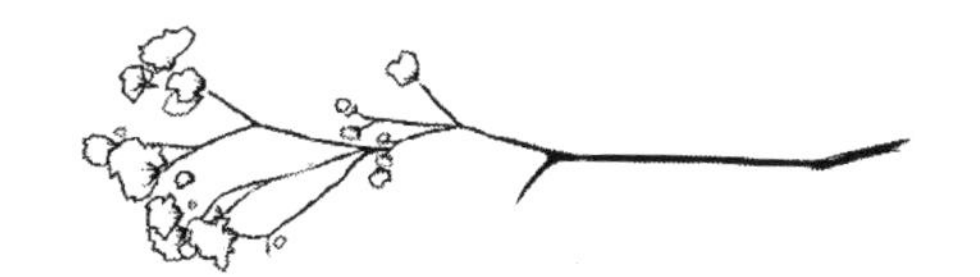

PART III

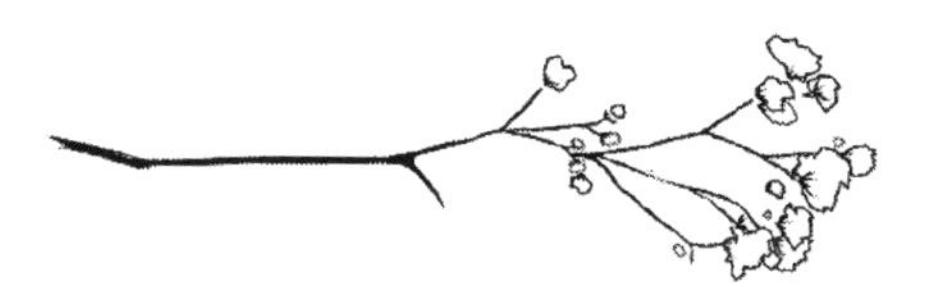

CHAPTER 46

THE SILENCER

Every night for ten days, at precisely 3 AM, like clockwork, I hear my least favorite sound.

Elena wakes up screaming at the top of her lungs until she starts gagging on the sounds coming from her throat, and then runs to the bathroom and barely makes it before emptying her stomach into the toilet.

I go with her to hold the loose hair that falls from her delicate braid away from her face. I rub her back, murmur how much I love her into her neck. It never takes her long to come back to reality, but when she does, it's always in tears.

Elena slumps into my chest and I stroke her hair. "Same as last time?"

She nods, smearing the wetness on her cheeks across my bare chest, right against the name I carved into my heart.

It's always the same nightmare. She's back in that glass cage with Frank and Neil.

I don't know why she suddenly started having these nightmares. She hasn't had them consistently since November. The worst part about not knowing what triggered them is that I have no idea how to stop them. I have no idea how to help her, and I hate feeling helpless when it comes to her.

It's almost like I'm stuck on the opposite side of that glass cage from her. Reliving the worst few minutes of our lives right there beside her.

She has dark circles under her eyes, and I can just see it in her demeanor that she wants nothing more than a good night's sleep.

I help her to the sink, but she's so tired that she can hardly lift the toothbrush. My throat burns as I watch her brush in slow, uncoordinated strokes. When she's done, I pick her up and carry her to bed to tuck her in again. She stares at the space above her, almost like she's in a trance. I crawl into bed next to her and pull her tight to my side. She wraps her arms around me and whimpers once before the tears start falling again.

I use one hand to draw mindless patterns on her back with my fingers and use my other to unlock my phone.

I open the search engine and look for the closest local pharmacy. It's not far, less than ten minutes away.

I kiss the top of her head and sit up. She grabs me frantically, her eyes darting around my face in a silent panic.

"Where are you going?"

I run my thumb gently along her cheekbone. "I'll be back in thirty minutes. I promise."

She lets me go, and I leave the bedroom to go downstairs to my workshop.

Elena made me promise to stop killing, and I haven't been, but the Silencer isn't any less useful to me. I still go out and use his presence to intimidate information out of people.

But it hasn't gotten me anywhere.

Frank Valenti vanished without a trace, and if something else killed him before I did, I'm going to raise him from the dead just to kill him again.

The thing about the Silencer is that he doesn't need to kill to put the fear of God in someone. Just because no one's found a body with red duct tape in two months doesn't mean they aren't out there, and that fear is more than enough to make up for the lack of bloodshed.

Before I put on my mask, I crack my neck and stare at myself in the reflection of a blank computer screen.

"In and out. We're there for one thing, got it?" I pause, waiting for an answer that never comes. I chuckle to myself. "Quiet tonight. That's a first."

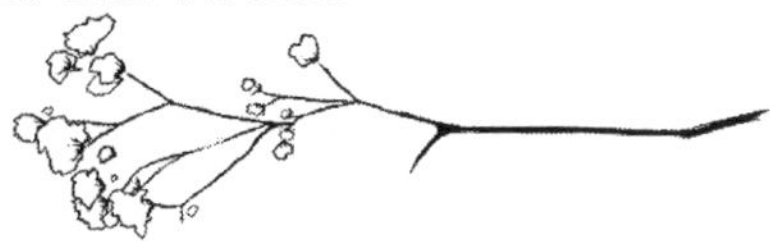

The parking lot of the pharmacy is dead quiet. There are four cameras surrounding the small white building, one on each side. The one closest to the door is easy enough to take out with a well-aimed bullet.

The sound of that gunshot will have lowered the property value of the apartments across the street, but a broken camera is a lot less shocking than a body.

When I was at MIT, I spent a lot of my studies learning how security systems work. At the time, security was Reeves Enterprises' specialty. It still is one of the main pillars of the company, and our biggest source of income globally.

Fortunately, it's one of my specialties too. I could break into the Pentagon with a glowstick and a ballpoint pen if I had to. A pharmacy? Child's play.

I shut off the security cameras inside with a jamming device I stick into the computer at the checkout desk. Then it's literally as simple as searching through the walls of medications behind the pharmacy counter until I find what I'm looking for.

Eszopiclone. Sleeping pills.

I reach for the bottle but freeze when I hear hushed voices. I squat behind one of the lower shelves. In the distance, between the breaks in the racks of medications, I can see two flashlights approaching the counter. Two men in ski masks stare at the opened security gate separating the pharmacy from the rest of the store. One of them scratches the top of his head.

"I don't like this," he whispers. "What if there's someone else in here?"

"Then unload your nine into them! Idiot. So long as they haven't taken the hydros, I don't give a fuck if there's someone else here."

"But the camera outside—"

"Shut up and start looking."

The two of them jump over the counter and start wandering up and down the aisles of medications.

Okay. No problem. Just let them take the painkillers and leave.

I shift behind a different rack when one of them turns down the aisle I need. He starts casually observing all the bottles and chuckles to himself when he grabs *my* bottle of pills.

He waves the bottle in the direction of his friend and then tosses it to him. "You ever tried these with some liquor?"

His friend tosses them back. "Nah, man. The high any good?"

He unzips his backpack to stuff them inside. "Fucking phenomenal—"

I press my gun firmly to his head. "Hand it over or lose the back of your skull."

The man drops the pills and puts his hands up in surrender as his friend stares at us in horror.

"Hey, I don't want any trouble man."

I lower my gun and pick up the bottle before shoving it into my tactical pants. It rattles with each step I take away from them.

"Hey, asshole!"

I pause mid-step and turn my head slightly to look over my shoulder. I can see the muzzle of a gun flash against the flashlights they're holding.

"Give me the pills," he demands.

He called his friend the idiot, but he's the only one making stupid decisions right now.

His friend will live longer, that's for sure.

I turn around fully. The one holding the gun definitely has a Napoleon complex. He's got to be at least a foot shorter than me. I reach into my pocket and pull out the bottle.

"These pills?" I ask, shaking them tauntingly. He gives me a curt nod back. I start walking in his direction, slowly. I'm not intentionally trying to be threatening, but it's easy to see in his eyes that he's suspicious. He's not honestly expecting me to hand over these pills, and that's probably the first rational thought he's had in the last five minutes. I approach him until his pistol is pressed directly into my sternum. I hold the pills above my head. "Well? Since you wanted them so badly, go on, take them."

He tightens his jaw at me and hilariously reaches up to try and grab them from me. I'm just being a dickhead now, knowing there's no way in hell he can reach.

"Man, fuck you!" he shouts, pressing his gun further into my chest.

"Come on, man," his friend begs, "let's just go."

"You got five seconds to hand me the pills or I'm blowing your head off! Five."

I roll my eyes and take a deep breath.

"Four."

I crack my neck.

"Three."

I catch my reflection in the security mirror hanging on the wall.

"Two."

What took you so long?

I was hoping he'd use the shelves to climb for them.

I won't tell if you won't tell.

Deal.

"One—"

The asshole never stood a chance. His arterial blood is splattered all over me and the bottles of medication before he even manages to fully get out the single syllable.

His body slumps to the floor, and his friend stares at me in shock, his gaze fixated on the knife in my left hand. His terrified brown eyes meet my noxious green ones, and I growl out another deep breath as I hear the blood dripping from my body down to the floor.

I throw my arm over his shoulders like we're best buds, and then lean in close to him.

"*Run.*"

He takes off like a bat out of hell, tripping over his friend's dead body, abandoning his backpack and flashlight.

As he's climbing over the pharmacy counter, I shoot him in the back. I yawn as I watch his body fall backwards over the counter, landing with a crack on the white tiles of the floor.

I did say he'd live longer, didn't I?

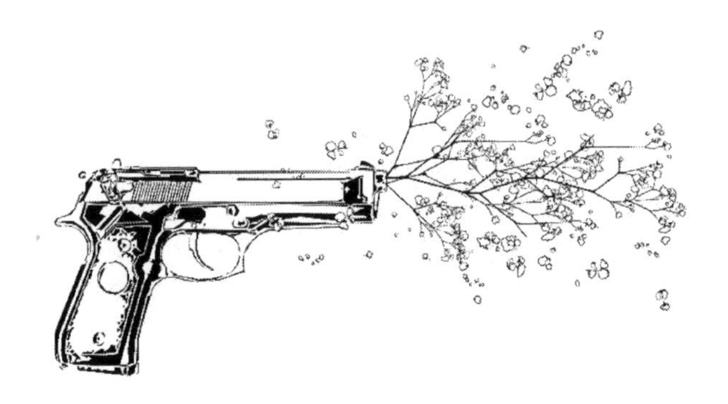

CHAPTER 47

THE ANGEL

"I'm going to puke."

Christian squeezes my hand and gives me that billion-dollar smile. "Elena, relax. Everything's going to be fine."

"But what if it's not? What if—"

He shuts me up with a kiss. It does nothing to calm my nerves. My foot bounces nervously against the marble floors of the courthouse. I watch people walk by. They all look so unhappy to be here. I guess that's understandable. Courthouses aren't exactly a place where good things happen. Especially not here in Meridian City.

I stand up abruptly and pull my phone out of my purse. Hesitantly, my finger shakes as I slowly tap the name of the one person I really need to hear from right now.

I'm sorry. Mailbox full. Goodbye!

My head sags as I drop my hand to my side, phone clutched in my fingers like a lifeline. I've heard that automatic message so many times at this point that I don't know what I'd do if my dad actually answered.

I drop my phone back into my purse and take my seat next to Christian, tucking my head in the crook of his neck. I breathe in the scent of his expensive cologne and run my fingers along the soft fabric of his suit.

"Just give him some time. It's only been a few weeks."

I let out a shaky exhale, refusing to let tears fall. Today is going to be a good day. It has to be. *I need it to be.*

The doors next to our bench open and the bailiff walks out. He glances around the hallway and his eyes land on us.

"Christian and Elena Reeves?" He motions towards the door. "Please come in."

We stand and walk into the courtroom. It's so….dull. Cherry brown wood that hasn't been updated in decades makes up the entirety of the room, from the walls to the benches to the floors.

Christian and I take a seat at the assigned table with our attorney, Jason Lockhart, and wait several long minutes by ourselves before the doors open again, and three lawyers, a social worker, and representative from the orphanage enter, along with a tiny blonde head of hair.

"Hi Elena!" Caroline shouts, loud enough for it to echo off the wooden walls. Her bunny stuffed animal is tucked into her elbow like it always is.

The representative shushes her and ushers her into the table opposite of us. Christian and I give her a small wave, and I suddenly feel those nerves kick into overdrive.

Another few minutes of waiting, and the judge takes her place at the front of the room.

"Good morning," she greets. "We are here for cause number MC-2020-06378-A, *Ex Parte in the Matter of Christian Thomas Reeves and Elena Louise Reeves For the Adoption of a Minor Child*." The judge clears her throat and looks towards Caroline and the five adults surrounding her. "The Court has reviewed the Petition for Adoption filed by Christian and Elena Reeves for the adoption of a minor child born August 23, 2015, in Meridian City, New Jersey. In addition, the Court has reviewed numerous reports and recommendations of the Child and Family Services Agency, the Thomas and Elizabeth Reeves Memorial Orphanage, and the Meridian City Advocates for Orphaned Children."

I begin to shake and Christian squeezes my hand again. I squeeze his back so hard I think I might dent my wedding ring.

"Having reviewed the aforementioned Petition and reports, the Court finds that the following statements are *true*. The child is physically and mentally suitable for adoption. The petitioners are fit to financially provide proper shelter, food, and education to the Child. Petitioner Elena Louise Reeves has had no arrests in the six months preceding the Petition."

The smile falls from my face when that's where the judge stops. I look up at Christian, and all the color has drained from his face.

The judge looks at us from over the glasses perched on the tip of her nose. "Having reviewed the aforementioned Petition and reports, the Court finds that the following statements are *false*."

Oh no.

"Petitioner Christian Thomas Reeves has had no arrests in the six months preceding the Petition. Petitioners have no conflicts of interest with the Thomas and Elizabeth Reeves Memorial Orphanage. The Child has resided with the Petitioners for at least six months preceding that date of this hearing."

The courtroom is dead silent, but I still think I can hear my heart breaking as tears well in my eyes.

"Christian," I whimper. He's stiff at my side. I dare to look at him, and I wish I hadn't. I've never seen him look so hollow.

"It is the opinion of this Court that the Petitioners have not met the requirements for Adoption in the state of New Jersey. The lengthy criminal history of Petitioner Christian Reeves raises concerns about his temperament. There are complications arising from the relationship between Mr. Reeves and the Thomas and Elizabeth Reeves Memorial Orphanage that may form an inherent bias in favor of this adoption."

Christian tenses like he's ready to jump over the table and strangle the judge right there on the bench, but I clutch my hand into his suit jacket. There's no need to fight. This is over.

I told him that we couldn't just skip the entirety of the process. Even with his influence, it was foolish for us to get our hopes up. He paid off this judge, but it wasn't enough.

We have to do what's best for Caroline, and what's best for her isn't us.

"However," the judge continues, shifting everyone's focus back to her, "just this morning, the Court received a letter from the Thomas and Elizabeth Reeves Memorial Orphanage. I'd like to take a moment to read it aloud." The judge unfolds a piece of paper and leans forward into the microphone.

Dear Mister or Missus Judge, my name is Caroline. Miss Kelly said I have lived here for fourteen months, but I told her it feels like fourteen years, and I'm only four years old, so that's a long time.

My very first free period here, my class went to the arcade, and I tried to win a toy from the claw machine, but I was too small to see inside. I used all my tokens and didn't win anything.

A really tall man saw me in the arcade and asked what I was trying to win. I said I didn't know because I couldn't see! So he lifted me up and asked me to choose a toy. I picked the purple bunny because purple is my favorite color, and guess what? The man won Mr. Bunny on his first try!

A few days later, I saw the man again and ran to him because I wanted to show him that I still had Mr. Bunny. Miss Kelly got mad at me for disturbing him. She said he was a very important person, and I shouldn't bother him while he's doing adult business.

He said his name was Mr. Reeves and that I could show him Mr. Bunny whenever I wanted. I started carrying around Mr. Bunny everywhere so I could show Mr. Reeves that I was taking good care of him.

Mr. Reeves and Mr. Bunny were my only friends. Mr. Reeves never brought his own friends, but one day, he had a whole bunch of people with him. One of them was wearing a purple dress. Her name was Elena.

Elena said that she was just friends with Mr. Reeves, but I knew that Mr. Reeves like liked *her. Now guess what? She's Mrs. Reeves, just like I said from the start. I knew it!*

Elena is my best friend. She's so pretty and nice, and she loves purple just like me. One time I gave her a picture I drew. It was me, her, and Mr. Reeves sitting on a bench. One day I want to take a picture just like the one I drew.

I don't know what Mr. Reeves' first name is, but I am tired of calling him Mr. Reeves. I want to call him daddy instead, and I want to call Elena mommy.

Miss Kelly says that in two days there will be a hearing for me, but I said that's silly, because my ears work just fine.

Can you please read this letter and make sure you check your ears? It's very important that everyone hears that I want a new family.

Love, Caroline

P.S. Can I bring Mr. Bunny? He has big ears, so he's good at hearing.

I have to cover my mouth to stifle the sob crawling out of my throat.

That girl on the other side of the courtroom could ask the President for the nuclear codes, and he'd give them to her.

The judge clears her throat again. "Well…it's clear to me from this letter that this child has a special bond with Mr. and Mrs. Reeves. Therefore, having considered all the facts and opinions of this case, the Court finds that the Final Decree of Adoption should be granted. From this moment forward, there is an established legal parent-child relationship, and the name of the child is hereby legally changed to Caroline Delilah Reeves."

The judge, now with a big smile on her face, points to Caroline. "Miss Caroline, if you could have any gift in the world, right now, what would it be?"

Caroline bites the tip of her finger for a long moment, pondering all the possibilities. Then she gasps and throws her hands up in the air, Mr. Bunny landing with a plop on the hardwood. "I want to go to Disney World!"

The judge laughs. "It is further ordered that the Petitioners shall take their new child to Disney World."

Then, she bangs the gavel on her desk.

And an hour later, we're on our private jet headed towards Orlando.

CHAPTER 48

THE SILENCER

Working from home is unnatural. I hate it. But not seeing my office at the Reeves Enterprises headquarters for a few months is a very small sacrifice to make in the grand scheme of things, considering the life I've built since Christmas.

Working from home does have its perks, though. Like getting to see my family whenever I want. My godfather, my wife, *and* my daughter.

In the two months that have passed since Christmas, Elena and I had a small marriage ceremony at the courthouse. After that, we applied to adopt. The Thomas and Elizabeth Reeves Memorial Orphanage has an adoption program sponsored by the State to match eligible children to prospective parents. It's the same process as a regular adoption. Interviews. Background checks. Home inspections.

The only major difference is that in order to adopt a child from the campus, a board composed of fifteen members from TERMO and the State have to unanimously vote 'yes' to approve the match before a final adoption hearing is held in court.

Considering I am a member of said board, that was all just logistics. Caroline was always meant to be a part of my family.

All it took was a few million dollars in bribes to finalize it within a month. Pocket change.

Those vetting processes are in place for the benefit of the child. Should I feel bad that I used my money and influence to bulldoze my way through them? Probably.

Do I? Fuck no.

The judge at our adoption hearing did order me to take a six-week anger management course within the year as a condition for the adoption. It upset me, considering I paid that judge seven figures to grant the adoption despite knowing we didn't meet the criteria, but Elena and I got what we wanted in the end, so I suppose it's a small price to pay.

She jokingly ordered us to take Caroline to Disney World, but I took that very seriously, and we were at the park for a week straight.

The first night we were there, as we were tucking Caroline into bed, she looked me dead in the eyes, kissed my cheek and said, "*I have the best daddy in the whole wide world.*"

I almost fucking *bought* Disney World for her after that.

One thing that Elena and I have realized after Caroline moved in with us is that she doesn't like to be alone. I don't think she has any sort of separation anxiety from us, at least not yet, but she's always in the same room as me or Elena, and if we're not available, she's with Edwin.

I suppose it makes sense. She was always glued to Kelly's side at the orphanage, most likely because she was the most consistent adult in her life at the time. She had a penchant for wandering off to look for candy, so now I keep stashes of Tootsie Rolls hidden around the house for her.

Elena doesn't know that though, it's our little secret.

Caroline is sitting on my lap, coloring a piece of paper bright blue. Streaks of marker are covering my desk from where her vigorous artistic hands have run off the page. This desk is solid mahogany and cost me fifteen grand. Do I care? Not in the slightest.

Caroline can do, quite literally, anything she wants.

I think I might be more whipped for my daughter than I am for my wife.

Said wife comes busting into my office looking like she's ready for war. She has a newspaper gripped so tight in her hand that she might tear a hole through the entire stack of paper.

Spying Caroline on my lap, her face softens, and she comes to squat next to us.

"Hey Caro, go to the kitchen and tell Paolo that I said you could have a cupcake before dinner."

Caroline gasps, immediately dropping her marker. "Really?" she asks in disbelief. Elena, despite her own weakness for sugar, limits Caroline's intake of it.

Though, if mommy says no, Caroline knows that daddy will *always* say yes.

Elena nods. "*Really*. But only one."

Caroline hops off my lap and darts out of the office like the roadrunner from Looney Tunes.

Once we're alone, Elena's face hardens again, and she shuts the door. She's angry. I can see it in her face. The only other time she's ever had that fury in her eyes was before she knew I was the Silencer, when she told me that she wished I would die.

"Angel—"

"Don't fucking '*angel'* me," she growls. "Is there something you want to tell me, Christian? And think about your answer *very hard*, because if you lie to me…"

She doesn't finish her sentence, because she doesn't need to. Message received. I glance between her furious face and the newspaper Edwin reads every morning. There's only one explanation for why she's so upset.

She's found out that I'm still killing.

And not even because I'm still looking for Frank Valenti.

I'm killing because I *want* to.

I'm pathetic for lying to her. I know that—and I know this isn't just *us* anymore. We have Caroline now. She will never forgive me if she finds out what I've been up to when she's under the influence of the sleeping pills I give her every night.

She couldn't have. I haven't done anything to land my kills in the paper. I don't even claim them anymore. An intentional decision I made to avoid this exact situation.

I honestly don't know what to say.

"No," I answer quietly.

"No?" She scoffs, and then throws the newspaper in my face. "Then tell me why you're on the front-page fucking news."

I flip it so I can read the large font on the front page, and now I'm concerned.

The Silencer is back! Double homicide claimed by infamous killer!

I look between her and the newspaper again, and then lay it flat on my desk. I take a deep breath.

"Elena, this wasn't me."

"Don't fucking lie to me again," she snaps, banging her tiny fists on the desk. "You promised me you wouldn't do this anymore!"

She paces around in a small circle and runs her fingers through her silky hair. She sucks in a sharp breath and lowers her voice. "We have a daughter now, Christian. If anyone finds out about you, forget *me*, think about how much danger you're putting Caroline in."

I bite the inside of my cheek at the insinuation that I would ever let anyone with ill intentions come within a lightyear of our daughter. I have to clench my fists to keep my head on straight. "It wasn't me."

"Do you think I'm stupid? Am I supposed to believe that some random person has decided to steal your M.O.?" She scoffs. "If it was just you and I, fine. I get it. But not with Caroline in the picture. If you still want to play psychopath, then maybe I should take—"

"Don't finish that fucking sentence," I hiss. I shoot up from my chair, round the desk, grab her by her neck, and pin her against the wall. "You knew *exactly* what I was when you let me put that ring around your finger. You knew exactly what I was when you sat there and let me play the the entire fucking adoption system like a fiddle so that Caroline would be ours. Don't you dare try and act like you're on some moral high ground here. And don't you ever even fucking *think* about threatening to leave me again. *Ever*, Elena, or you can kiss your freedom goodbye."

"I haven't been free since we met," she spits out.

I grab the newspaper and toss it into the fireplace to my right. I sigh and let go of her neck. I press my forehead to hers and take a deep breath. "I swear on my life, on our marriage, on our family, on everything, that those kills are *not* mine."

My declaration makes her pause. She knows with absolute certainty that our marriage and our daughter mean everything to me. I wouldn't say that if I didn't mean it.

I can see in Elena's eyes that she still doesn't believe me, or at least doesn't want to.

I resign. With a sigh, I say, "Obviously you need to cool off before we talk about this. I'll be back for dinner." I graze her bottom lip with my thumb. "*I love you.*"

"I love you, too."

She chokes out the words like they're poison on her tongue, and it sends a dagger straight through my heart.

I leave the room and find Caroline in the kitchen with frosting on her cheeks and I kiss the top of her head before I head to the garage.

Inside my car, I hit the steering wheel with my fists.

It wasn't me.

I didn't kill them.

It wasn't. Fucking. Me.

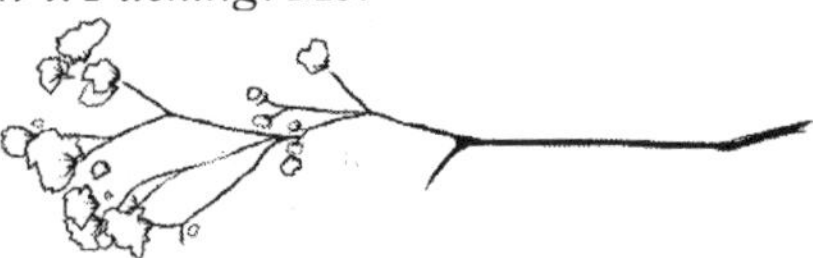

Now that I'm a family man, people find me more approachable. When I arrive at Reeves Enterprises, I'm greeted dozens of times.

I've always been able to turn on the charm when I needed to, but there used to be a wall between myself and other people. I only ever got spoken to by outsiders about business.

I think people can see that I'm human now. They can see I have a life outside of my company that's made me happy.

Happy. Still such a strange feeling. I was completely numb for thirty years. That tug on my hollow chest—that squeeze in my black heart when I look at Elena still feels foreign sometimes.

When I step into the elevator, I check my phone. No missed calls or texts. No voicemails. No anything. Complete radio silence from the only person I care to hear from.

I stare at my lock screen with a sad smile on my face. It's a photo of the best day of my life. Our courthouse marriage ceremony. The moment the judge officially declared us husband and wife, I took Elena into my arms, dipped her backwards, and gave her the kiss of the century.

In that moment, she became officially, thoroughly, indisputably *mine*.

All the boring paperwork came next. Updating my will. Adding her to all my bank accounts and credit cards. Applying for a new deed to add her as an owner of the Reeves Estate. Giving her the same authority and privileges at R.E. that I have as CEO. Complete and untethered access to anything and everything that was mine. I wanted her to have it all.

Not that she's taken advantage of any of it. The only thing she's purchased with her black card is a bar exam prep course, and a set of highlighters because all of hers ran dry. She takes the bar exam in three days, which is another reason why I've been working from home. I wanted to watch Caroline while she does her last-minute studying. It's been beautiful to watch Elena blossom under the stress, but now that it's imminently upon her, she's freaking out.

But I know she'll do great. Perfect. There's no way in hell she won't pass with flying colors.

I *might* have something to do with that, but I'll take that secret to the grave.

The elevator dings and the doors open. I walk into the office, still focused on my lock screen like staring at it will somehow make Elena less upset with me.

I'm immediately hit with the foul, unmistakable odor of decaying flesh.

When I look up, I freeze. My stomach turns and I don't think I've ever seen something so horrifying in my entire life.

I'm a serial killer, so that's saying something.

In front of me, two people are slumped over in chairs taken from the conference table. One man. One woman. The woman is wearing a short black wig and has red lipstick on her lips. The man is wearing a suit.

Both of them have a bullet hole in their heads and a sheet of printer paper stapled to their chests. Big, bold, red letters spell out Thomas and Elizabeth.

There are not many things on this earth that disgust me. I've done enough maiming of my own that blood and gore don't bother me.

But whoever did this is clearly trying to send a message to me, and it's working.

For the first time in my life, when I look at dead bodies, I lean over and puke.

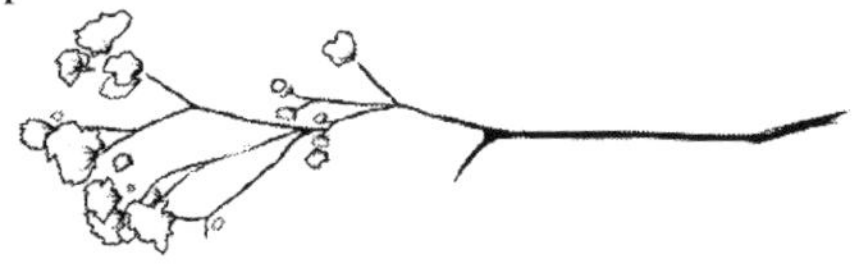

A half-hour later, I'm sitting outside the building on a bench, trying to smoke away the horror while I give interview after interview to the police. There's a huge commotion on the sidewalk outside. Bystanders and police and coroners and media vans.

"Christian!"

I stand up at the sound of my wife's concerned voice. She nearly faceplants when she exits the SUV before it's even fully stopped. Gavin brought her here, probably after hearing about the situation on the police scanner.

Elena cups my cheeks and forces me to look at her. I do, but I'm sure I look like shit.

"Are you okay?" she asks quietly.

"Do you have any mints? Or gum?" I ask, my reluctance to answer her all the confirmation she needs that I am in no way '*okay*'. She pulls a tiny tin of mints from her purse and hands them to me. I put seven of them into my mouth and use my tongue to brush them along the inside of my teeth while the spearmint flavor envelops me. I shove my hands in the pockets of my slacks.

"It was my parents," I say, laughing cruelly at this sick joke someone has decided to play on me. "I don't know who they were, but they were made to look like my parents. Dressed up like dolls." I take a deep breath and I lean my forehead against hers. "Are you still mad at me?"

She lets out a sardonic scoff. "Are you still lying to me?"

I shake my head. "It wasn't me."

Her silence tells me that she still doesn't believe me.

Something in the air goes stale. All the commotion falls quiet. I look up and around, and just a few feet from where Elena and I are standing, there's a man and a woman. Crying. Dried blood crusted along their hairline. Zip-tied wrists. Red duct tape over their mouths.

But this isn't just any man and woman.

It's my parents. My mother and father are staring back at me with terrified looks on their faces that I haven't seen in thirty years.

No. *Not* my parents.

It's worse than that. It's just a visage of them. Delicate stitches along the high points of their faces, bruised and bloody and mutilated. The woman begins to make choked sobbing sounds, like she's trying to speak.

I use one arm to push Elena behind me. She's staring at the two people in shock, along with Gavin and all the witnesses. I slowly reach my hand up to pull the duct tape off the woman's mouth.

When I do, she has bright red lipstick on, just like the woman in my office, and her lips are sewn shut. She's moaning incoherently, her brows furrowed like she's begging me to hear what she's saying even though she can't get the word out.

An irritating red flash buzzes around my vision and I rub my eyes to try and clear it away. Probably just a reflection of the police lights in the glassy haze of wetness gathered in my eyes.

The woman keeps moaning, crying harder now. And then one bullet enters her forehead. And then another enters the man's chest.

I stumble backwards in shock, feeling like I've just watched my parents die all over again. I'm unable to form words or thoughts or feelings.

After what feels like a miserable eternity, but is probably only a millisecond, I hear Gavin shout, "Mr. Reeves, get the fuck down!"

And that's when a bullet hits me, too.

CHAPTER 49

THE ANGEL

I don't think I've ever made such a high-pitched, horrified shrill in my life. I can't hear anything except the blood pounding in my ears and screams coming from my throat.

Everything happened so fast.

I heard two gunshots, then heard Gavin yell for Christian to get down. After that, all I remember is the sound of a third gunshot and my husband's skull hitting the concrete.

Gavin pulls me to the ground and covers me with his body. It's his job. I understand his concern for me, but I don't care about *my* safety. Not when Christian is just a foot away, struggling to breathe with blood soaking into his shirt.

Oh my God. Oh my God. Someone shot him.

My first instinct is to crawl to him, but Gavin won't let me. He holds me down on my stomach, flat against the concrete and shields my entire body with his own. His pistol is tight in his hand. Gavin is a large, strong man, so I can't move out from under him despite my non-stop squirming and bucking to get him off me. I reach for Christian's hand as people scream and run around us. I don't care about any of them. I don't care about possibly getting shot.

All I care about is my husband staring up at the sky, struggling for his life. I'll never forgive myself if the last thing he sees is the sky instead of my face.

"Gavin, please!" I cry frantically. "Please let me help him."

"You *can't* help him," Gavin growls, looking around at the buildings overhead, mumbling to himself. "That sounded like an M24. Army issue."

"I don't care about your fucking gun lesson!" I shout, digging my nails into his arm as hard as I can, though it does nothing. "Let me go right now or you're fired."

"Then consider me fired because you're not fucking moving until I'm positive it's safe."

I cry out in frustration and squeeze Christian's hand. "Look at me," I beg. "Please look at me."

His head turns to me, and I breathe out a sigh of relief that he's still somewhat conscious. The blood seeping from his chest is pooling onto the sidewalk. He blinks at me slowly. Tears spill out of my eyes as I watch his chest rise and fall raggedly and painfully. I can see it in the paleness of his face and the distant look in his eyes that he's fading.

"Gavin, let me go."

"No."

I growl and turn abruptly under him and kick him in the shin. "If it were your wife bleeding out on a sidewalk, you wouldn't let *anyone* stop you."

Gavin hesitantly lifts his weight off me. I scramble to Christian's side and hold his cold cheeks in my hands. Gavin shrugs off his jacket and uses it to press down on the gaping bullet hole in Christian's torso.

I sniffle and breathe in a shuddering breath. "I'm here. I'm here," I coo. His eyes close and I become frantic. I slap him across the face. "Don't you dare," I growl. "Please don't leave me. We haven't been through so much together just for you to get taken out by a bullet."

My heart aches painfully when I feel him trace a shaky hand up my arm. He growls through the pain, breathing like each intake of air might be his last. His calloused hand meets my cheek, and he rubs the back of his fingers along the delicate skin there. This feels like a goodbye and my heart can't take it.

"*Please*," I whimper quietly, sobbing and trembling as he feels over my cheek and rubs a thumb over my lip.

"Angel," Christian says, his voice a mere whisper. The resignation and the feebleness of his tone sends a jolt of white-hot fear through me.

I shake my head. "Don't give up on me."

"I would never," he chokes out. "My soul belongs to you."

I wince. "Which is why it's going to stay right here where it belongs."

He shakes his head, then moves his hand from my cheeks to rest over my heart. I understand what he means, but I shake my head right back.

"Please don't. I need you. Caroline needs you. Please don't…don't…don't!"

When his eyes close again, I throw my head up to the sky, and I scream.

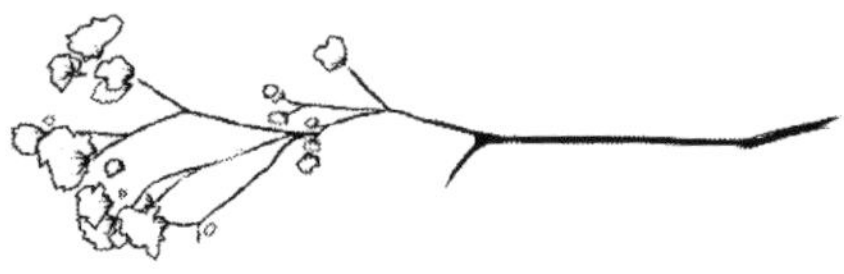

I never pray.

My family and I never put much into our religious lives. My father stopped believing in God after his first family was killed. My mother believes but doesn't attend church. Travis steers clear of religion because of his sexual orientation.

Me? Well, I suppose I'm the worst of all of us, because the first time I've ever prayed in my life is because I need God to show me mercy.

This is my fault.

This is my punishment for not believing Christian when he swore to me that he didn't kill those people in the papers.

I'm sitting in the front-row pew of the chapel. My head dipped down in shame, a box of tissues to my left and one clenched in my fist, soaked through with tears.

I haven't stopped crying in days. Six, to be exact.

I hear the door open behind me. Maybe it's an assassin, coming here to finish the job. Maybe it's an apparition. A spirit here to torment me with my grief. Maybe it's simply another person needing to pray.

I hear them take a seat behind me, and it goes quiet. I sniffle and blow my nose into the tissue, discarding it in the trashcan filled to the brim with used tissues and grabbing a clean one from my side.

"Mrs. Reeves," a woman's voice says from the pew behind me. I take a deep breath and wait for her to say whatever it is she has to say. I don't have the strength to reply. "It's time."

Those two words fill me with such dread that I think I might die from a broken heart. As a violent sob wrecks through me, I stare up at the cross hanging on the wall. I shake my head. "No."

"We need to—"

"I said no!" I shout, my sorrowful voice echoing off the walls of the small room.

I hear her sigh. "I'll give you some more time."

I hold my hand over my mouth to muffle my weeping as I hear her stand and begin to walk away. I take a deep breath. "Wait." The footsteps stop. Being strong has never been so hard. "What if he doesn't forgive me for giving up on him?"

It goes quiet for a long moment again. "Letting go can sometimes be more merciful than holding on."

I nod, looking down at my feet. "Thank you, Dr. Portman. Please leave me alone."

She leaves, and as soon as the chapel doors close behind her, I begin to sob loudly.

"Why are you so cruel to him?" I ask the cross hanging on the wall. "If you're real, you have so much more to apologize for than he ever will. When people talk about forgiveness, *you're* the one that should be asking for it."

I stand up from the pew and dust off my jeans. I've been wearing them for six days. Disgusting, I know, but I can't find the will to take care of myself when I've lost my heart. I leave the small chapel and make my way through the sterile corridors. Beige paint. White tiles. Empty. Soulless.

Like me.

I freeze at the doorway of ICU room 15. Not because I'm shocked, but because every time I step through this threshold, it feels like one less time I'll have a chance to. I take a deep breath and walk into the room, taking a seat in the chair that has my assprint embedded into it from the past six days. I slump over against the hospital bed and take Christian's hand in mine. It's so cold and limp.

I watch every breath he takes intently, afraid he'll stop at any moment. His wedding ring is heavy in the back pocket of my jeans, reminding me how fragile everything is. How precious the time I've gotten to spend with him is. It doesn't matter how it began, all that matters to me is doing everything I can to make sure that this isn't the end. It can't be.

He lost so much blood. I remember watching Gavin do chest compressions while I put pressure on the wound. When the paramedics arrived, I remember fighting against Gavin to let me go with them. I remember my hands and arms being covered in my husband's blood and feeling so powerless. I didn't know how to help him.

They told me that his heart stopped during the emergency surgery they did to try and repair the damage. While they got his heart beating again, he was clinically dead for three minutes.

Three minutes without oxygen. Three minutes without a heartbeat. Three minutes without his love.

That's all it took to shatter me.

His pupils are responsive, which the doctors keep telling me is a good sign, but he doesn't react to any other stimuli.

They can't guarantee that he'll wake up. Even if he does wake up, the lack of oxygen to the brain could have caused irreversible damage. I've had nothing to do but sit and watch my husband for six days, sitting by his side and begging him to come back to me. So I can apologize for not believing him about those murders. I don't want him to die thinking I was mad at him for something he didn't do.

I sniffle and squeeze his cold hand, running my free hand along his equally cold cheek.

"Is this what it felt like for you? To not know if I was going to be okay?" Another sob wrecks through me. "Because I don't know how you got through it. You'd do anything for me, right?" I scrape my nails gently along his scalp. "I'm asking you to come back to me, because I don't know how to live without you, either."

I pause, waiting for any sign of life from him, but there's nothing. I want him to wake up more than I've ever wanted anything, but I think I know deep in my heart that he's gone.

It's been eight days since I've heard Christian tell me he loves me. It only makes me feel worse about all those months ago, when I couldn't tell him I loved him in Mykonos. I understand now, the agony of wanting to hear those three words from the person you've given your heart to. I understand the unimaginable pain of not hearing it back.

Sitting down in my seat, I lay my head down on Christian's arm and shut my eyes, remembering all the little moments we shared together that made me fall in love with him. From our first kiss to our first visit to the orphanage, all the way up until our marriage ceremony, and everything in between. The steady beat of his heart monitor lulls me into a light sleep. Enough to be considered restful, but not enough that I'd miss a twitch of his fingers in mine.

I feel a small hand shake me. "Mommy?"

I perk up at the sound of Caroline's voice. "Yeah, honey?"

"When will daddy wake up?"

Never.

Her blue eyes are sparkling like they always are. She's so innocent. A part of me, a part I would never admit out loud, regrets adopting her. I love her so much, but if I had known that she would know this kind of loss so soon after being adopted by us, I don't know if I would have gone through with it. It seems cruel to put a child through this.

I sigh and straighten the bow in her ponytail. "I don't know yet," I answer. It's the same response I've been giving her for eight days, and the way she so easily accepts that answer feels like a serrated knife in the sternum.

How am I going to tell her that he's not going to wake up?

Caroline looks up at Christian in the bed and then back to me. "Can I hug him?"

I swallow the painful, burning rock in my throat. My first instinct is to say no, because what if she accidentally hurts him? At this point, would it even really matter?

I give her a sad smile and help her into his hospital bed. I tell her to be careful, and she is. She simply snuggles up next to him, using his arm as a pillow, and falls back asleep.

I cry silently for a few more minutes and then find Dr. Portman in the hallway. I cross my arms over my chest and look back at Christian and Caroline through the window.

"We'll do it tomorrow morning," I say, feeling defeated and hollow. Dr. Portman says nothing; simply rubs my arm in a comforting gesture and leaves me alone.

I walk back inside the room and decide that if this is the last night I get to spend with him, I'm going to spend it in his arms where I belong. I crawl into the bed on the opposite side from Caroline, and before I fall asleep, I kiss him one last time.

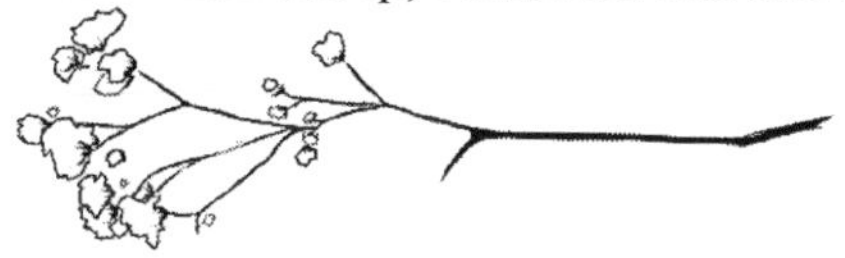

At six AM, I gently wake up Caroline and ask her what she wants for breakfast. She happily announces that she wants strawberry ice cream.

I let her have all the strawberry ice cream she can eat, because I don't know any other way to soften the blow for what's to come. After breakfast, the mood shifts in the air as the doctors start filtering into the room.

I get it. No one wants to pull the plug on Christian Reeves.

Shaking, I help Caroline back up onto the bed. Trying, and failing, to hide my tears, I tell her, "Okay, Caro." My voice cracks. "Say goodbye to daddy. Tell him you love him and give him a big hug."

Caroline stares at me, confused. "Where is he going?"

A pained whimper escapes my throat. "He's going to go see his parents."

She doesn't understand, and I'm not sure I want her to. She gives him a hug and a kiss.

"Bye-bye, daddy. I'll miss you."

I tug Caroline into my chest and hold her head in the crook of my neck, facing away from him, because she doesn't need to watch this. I hold her as tight as I can and stroke her hair while I sob quietly and nod at the doctors and medical assistants to just get it over with.

Dr. Portman clears her throat quietly. "We're going to administer a sedative to make sure he's comfortable."

I nod, unable to open my eyes. It goes eerily quiet for a few seconds, and then I think I feel my own heart stop.

"I can't believe you'd let me go without a goodbye kiss, angel."

My eyes fly open, and I go stiff in complete shock. Christian's eyes are open. He's smiling at me, with that same charming smile I fell in love with and those icy blue eyes full of *life*.

"Daddy!" Caroline giggles, pulling out of my arms and receding into his. She lands on him with a thud and he grunts in pain.

I can't move. I can't breathe. I can't think.

And then, all at once, that shock is replaced with pure, unfiltered relief. If he wasn't in that bed with a bullet hole in his chest, I would have launched myself into his arms and squeezed him until it hurt.

Instead, I choke out a garbled, ugly sob, hold his cheeks in my hands, and kiss him. "What took you so long?"

Christian circles my wrist with his cold fingers. "I met Death."

I take my bottom lip in my teeth. "And?"

Christian brushes a strand of hair back from my face, and looking deeply into my eyes, he whispers, "I told him to go fuck himself, because I'm not going anywhere without you."

CHAPTER 50

THE ANGEL

"Drink," I command, handing Christian a water glass.

He lightly chuckles. "*Yes*, Dr. Young."

We've been home for a few days now, and I haven't let Christian lift a finger since we got back. I know I'm driving him insane.

He doesn't like being taken care of. It makes him feel helpless and weak. He thinks it's dehumanizing. I've lost track of how many times he's grumbled about how he's supposed to be the one taking care of me.

I run my fingers through Christian's messy hair and smirk. He needs a haircut. So unkempt. "How are you feeling?"

"I'm fine."

"How many times must we have this conversation? You're not fine. You've been shot. You *died*. Once in my arms and then again in surgery. You were unconscious and unresponsive for *eight days*." I take a deep breath. "Eight days, Christian. So do not tell me you're fine. Tell me how you're feeling."

He licks his teeth, a glimmer in his eyes in response to my defiance. He playfully rolls his eyes. "It hurts."

"How bad?" I ask, grabbing the orange prescription bottle.

"Seven out of ten."

I huff out a breath and run my fingers through his hair again, rubbing soothing circles on his scalp as I hand him two painkillers with my other hand. "Thank you for being honest with me."

"How much longer do I have to sit in this bed?"

I giggle at his restlessness. "Until your wife says so."

"Is that right?" he asks, tangling a fist in my loose hair and pulling my lips to his. "Then my wife should know that my chest isn't the only thing in pain. I need medicine only you can give me."

"Baby, the doctor said no sex."

"I'm not talking about sex." He shrugs. "But I wouldn't say no if you're offering."

I give him a mischievous laugh and lightly nip at his ear before trailing slow kisses down his neck. I suck a mark into the section of collarbone where his gray Henley exposes the hollow of his throat.

I cover his neck in kisses, and then carefully trail down his body, staying far away from the healing wound in his stomach. He lets out a small groan of pain when I reach the waistband of his sweatpants and he flexes his abs. I pause, looking up, concern poised on the tip of my tongue.

"Angel, if you stop, I will risk internal bleeding just to hold you down and shove my cock down your throat."

"You're not the boss of me," I say, licking his hard cock over his clothes. He throws his head back and lets out a heavy breath.

He reaches to tug down his sweatpants, enough to expose his throbbing, aching length. "Put me in that pretty mouth, Elena."

I place a featherlight kiss to the tip. "What did I just say?"

Christian looks down at me with blackened fury in his eyes. He grinds down his molars, and I raise an eyebrow at him. He gets the message. I'm not moving. Not until he gives me what I want.

"You're in charge, Mrs. Reeves," he purrs, his voice sensually wrapping around my spine. "But remember what I said about control, sweet angel. It's only yours as long as I give it to you." He rubs a thumb across my bottom lip. "Enjoy it."

I keep full eye contact with him as I lick along the underside of his delicious cock, humming at the familiar manly taste of him. I swirl my tongue around the head, spreading the fat drop of precum and moaning at the saltiness of it.

"More," Christian demands through gritted teeth, his hands in white-knuckled fists.

"Say please."

He growls in frustration and grabs my hair, jerking my head back to force me to look at him.

"More. *Please*."

I laugh at his desperation, and throw back words he's said to me many, many times before.

"Beg for it, Christian."

My poor husband whimpers. He wants me so bad. "Please, angel. Please, baby. Be a good girl for me and suck my cock."

I take as much of him as I can manage in my mouth, and he shudders immediately, groaning wildly and tangling his fingers in my hair. I suck and lick him savagely.

"Oh *fuck*," he moans. "Yes. Yes, just like that. Fuck, your mouth is heaven. Touch yourself, angel. Put your fingers in that pretty pussy."

I indulge him, not letting up my pace despite my jaw beginning to ache from his size. I run my hands down my body until they reach my shorts. I tug them off and slide my fingers along my slick cunt and I moan against his cock when my fingers graze my swollen clit.

I feel a delicious pressure building in my core, coiling up and begging to snap.

"I'm close," Christian breathes. "Are you going to be a good girl and swallow all of my cum, baby?"

"*Mhm,*" I mumble against his length. His hands shove me down as far as I can take him as he spurts ribbons of his hot cum down my throat.

I dutifully swallow it all, just like he wants me to.

"Fuck. Come up here baby, sit on my face and let me taste that perfect cunt."

I crawl up his body, minding his wound and straddle his face. He immediately sucks on my clit, making me throw my head back and cry out loudly in pleasure. Christian's hands snake under my thighs to roughly squeeze my ass, dragging me even closer to his mouth. I feel his tongue taste every inch of me.

"I couldn't die without tasting this delicious pussy. I couldn't die without feeling my cock inside you again. God, I've been dreaming about it." He moans at my taste, like it's the sweetest thing he's ever feasted on. The vibrations send a new wave of pleasure through me, and I grind down on his face. "That's it, angel. Ride my face. Make yourself cum."

I moan loudly, using both of my hands to tug his hair and pull him impossibly closer. He suckles on my clit and traces a finger over the tight rosebud behind me. He shoves his finger inside without warning, up to the first knuckle, and I tremble against his face, cumming hard all over his mouth and chin.

After a long moment, I sigh in relief and climb off, lying on my side in the space next to him. I place a kiss to his cheek.

Our bodies buzz with the sweet bliss that follows the kind of high only we can give each other.

"What's your pain now?" I ask, tracing my fingers along his collarbone.

"Always zero when I'm with you."

I giggle. "Now that we've had our fun, you know what time it is."

Christian groans. "No."

"Yes," I say quietly, tapping his nose and sitting up. "I'll get the water ready."

I stand up and go to the bathroom, running the water until it's warm and then wait for the tub to fill up, just enough to cover his legs and hips because he can't get his stitches wet.

He hates baths. Not just because I have to bathe him, though he hates that too because it's just another thing that makes him feel worthless. He just hates baths in general. He finds them distasteful, which is a bit hypocritical of him considering he has the largest bathtub on the East Coast.

I help Christian out of bed, staying close by his side in case he needs help walking, though he'd rather fall on his face than admit it. We slowly make our way to the bathroom, and he sits on the edge of the tub while I undress him, and then carefully remove his gauze.

We both stare at his wound and then meet each other's eyes at the same time. He looks so ashamed, like getting shot has made him less of a man.

I give him a strained look and instruct him to get in the tub. He lowers himself slowly into the warm water and then I remove my shirt. I lower myself into the tub too, straddle his lap, and pour a dollop of unscented soap onto a sponge. I begin to slowly wash his body with deliberate caution.

"How are you doing? Mentally, I mean."

Christian huffs. "Angel, can we *please* talk about something other than the bullet hole in my torso?"

"Like what?"

He shrugs. "Like…have you spoken to your father?"

Trading out one touchy subject for another I see. I shake my head and bite the inside of my cheek.

It's true. My father and I haven't spoken in months. I called him to tell him that Christian and I were getting married by the court in January. I invited him, along with my mother and Travis and Justin, to be witnesses with Edwin.

My father was the only one who didn't show up.

It broke my heart so badly I almost couldn't go through with it. My mother was the one who got me to appear for my own ceremony.

Don't cry over something he will grow to regret. You're getting married for you, not him.

She was right of course, but it still hurt. He didn't show up for the ceremony, or the small dinner we held afterward in the penthouse suite of *The Black Palace*, the largest and grandest of the hotel chains Christian owns across the world.

He didn't even call to offer his congratulations.

It almost feels like I'm dead to him.

When Christian and I shared the news that we had adopted Caroline, he was the only one in my family who didn't come to meet her.

Christian takes a deep breath. "I'm sorry, angel."

I nod. "I know. It's not your fault. I made my choice. I chose to love you. He chose to disown me."

"He didn't," Christian says as I carefully clean around the entrance wound. "His issue is with me. He *loves* you." He taps his fingers along the edge of the tub. "Maybe you should call him."

"He won't answer." I let out a sad laugh. I tap my fingers up Christian's chest and smile sheepishly. "Maybe another grandchild will make him soft?"

Christian smiles back at me. "Don't tempt me Mrs. Reeves. I wasn't kidding about opening my wound. Whenever you're ready, I'll fuck you, and I won't stop until I put a baby in you."

My face falls as I think about children and babies, and tears glaze over my eyes. "Caroline…God, I can't even imagine what it would have done to her if you died. She didn't even understand what was happening and I didn't have the strength to tell her."

He cradles my head in his large hands. "I know," he whispers against my lips. "But I'm right here. I'm not going anywhere." He swallows the thick lump in his throat. His chest begins to puff out with anger. "I will find out who did this and make them meet the same fate as Neil Hayden for trying to take me away from you. That's a promise. No one who tries to tear apart my family will get away with it."

After I help Christian out of the bath, I pick up my phone and call my father. The phone rings, and rings, and rings, just like I knew it would.

I'm sorry. Mailbox full. Goodbye!

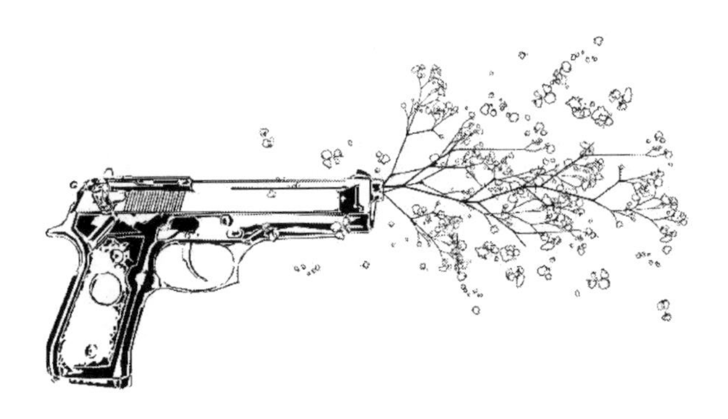

CHAPTER 51

THE SILENCER

"Goddamn it," I growl, giving up on the 45-pound dumbbells at my feet. I'm pissed off. I haven't been able to lift anything heavier than a goddamn pitcher of water in weeks.

I've lost so much of my strength—and my dignity—since I was shot. Elena did everything she could to keep me pain-free, clean, fed, and entertained in the initial weeks after I woke up in the hospital. But every meal she fed me, every time she bathed me, every time she changed my bandages, it felt like I was losing more and more of myself.

I'm supposed to be the protector.

Unfortunately, I've failed at every opportunity.

Just like I'm failing at this workout.

I can't do pull ups. I can't do deadlifts or squats. I can't use free weights. I can't jog on the treadmill. I can't even hold my fucking daughter.

Frank Valenti is still out there, somewhere. I don't think he's the culprit behind the assassination attempt, but he's still got a target on his head for far worse than that.

He touched my wife. Raped her. Beat her.

I haven't forgotten the fear on her face behind that glass.

I will never forget it, and rest will never come easy to me until I kill him for bringing her that fear. For haunting her nightmares.

He is one of two reasons why I'm pushing myself so hard to heal and become strong again. Valenti is on my shit list for touching my wife, and the fucker who shot me deserves a bullet in the brain for good-old-fashioned revenge.

Elena would kill me if she found me in my home gym trying to lift a dumbbell when I still can't even shower on my own without help. Lifting my arms above my head is next to impossible. It feels like my chest is getting ripped apart every time I try.

The bullet entered me at an angle on my left side, directly below my ribcage. Tore straight through me. Caused massive internal bleeding.

I'm alive because even with a laser sight, the fucker who shot me has shit aim. The police confirmed that an M24 was used after finding the bullet soaked in my blood a few feet away from where I collapsed. Whoever shot me probably camped out all day, waiting for me to see the carnage he left in my office, knowing I'd have to come outside where he could get a clear shot. He wanted the police to be there. He wanted *Elena* to be there. He's trying to send a message.

It's my job to figure out what that message is before he does any more damage to my family.

This entire mess already fucked up Elena's chance at taking the bar exam. She missed it because she was in the hospital with me. Her next opportunity won't be until July.

Just one more way I've failed her.

Gavin clearing his throat at the entrance of the gym pulls me out of my thoughts. I wipe the sweat off my face with my shirt. "What is it?" I ask, noting the hardened expression on his face.

"The name Katherine McGinnis mean anything to you?"

I take a second to search through my mind. I shrug. "Should it?"

Gavin hands me his phone. On the screen, a photo of a tall, strawberry-blonde woman with a sultry smirk on her face. "Oh. Kate. She's one of Elena's friends. Why?"

"Mrs. Reeves and I went into the city to pick up a refill of your prescriptions. We stopped at a café so she could grab us a coffee. This woman approached her, and they seemed familiar with each other."

"*Okay*," I say, hoping he will get to the point.

"It seemed like Kate was…distracted while Mrs. Reeves spoke to her. Constantly on her phone and looking around like she was waiting for the boogeyman to pop out. I ran her through facial recognition. She's a known associate of Frank Valenti. Thought that might interest you."

I give him a tight-lipped blank look. I appreciate his vigilance, but everything he's telling me, I already knew. "She worked at the Hellfire Lounge with Elena. Everyone who worked there is a known associate of Frank Valenti."

Gavin nods. "Just thought you wanted to know."

"Thank you," I say, in true gratitude. Gavin has gone above and beyond to keep Elena safe from the moment I met her. He's loyal and trustworthy. I chuckle lightly. "Elena told me she fired you for not letting her come to me after I got shot."

He chuckles back. "I was just doing my job. You would have done a lot worse than fire me if something happened to her."

I tap my fingers against the seat of the weight bench I'm sitting on. "When was the last time I let you have a vacation?"

Gavin tilts his head and thinks. "Couldn't tell you."

I nod and give him a friendly smirk. "I think you're overdue for one. Make some plans with your wife and your baby. Let me know the details and your entire trip is on me. Food, travel, hotel. Everything."

"You don't have to do that," Gavin says. I shrug it off and hold out my hand. He takes it in his and we shake.

"You're a good friend, Gavin. You're one of the few people on this earth I trust. I don't say that lightly."

"I know, sir. I'm glad for it."

Gavin turns away to leave, and as he's stepping through the threshold, I stop him. "Hey, Gav?"

"Yes, sir?"

"Do you trust Kate? With Elena?"

Gavin turns to face me and his face drops. "Didn't you tell me you once paid her to cover for Elena at the Lounge?" I nod. "So her loyalty can be bought."

"*And*?" I prompt, knowing there's more.

"And I think for the right price, she'd hand over Elena on a silver platter to the highest bidder."

I'm sitting on the bed, propped up against the headboard, reading through last quarter's report on my subsidiaries in Asia. I make a note of which regions are growing the slowest and start an email chain with my people to arrange a visit to that side of the world once I'm completely healed. Or at least enough to wash my own goddamn back.

Elena pops in and hops onto the bed with me, holding four paint swatches next to her head. "Which do you like best?"

I smirk. We're converting one of the lesser-utilized rooms in the mansion to her own home office, and she is very serious about getting the paint color perfect. I look at the four small papers next to her head. I tap one on the left. "*Old World Gray*."

She takes a look at the swatch and purses her lips. "You like that more than *Electric Violet*?"

"I'd need an eye transplant every time I walked out of your office if you painted it that color."

She sticks her tongue out at me. "You're no fun," she says, setting the paint samples to the side. I set down my report, too. Elena takes my hand in hers and we play a gentle game of thumb war.

"You'll never believe who I saw today."

"Kate," I reply casually. She narrows her eyes at me. "Gavin told me."

Elena sighs. "Feels like a lifetime since I've seen her."

"What's she up to these days?" I ask, wanting more information. I need to know if Gavin's suspicions are well-placed.

"Still bartending. I didn't ask where, but she seemed to be doing alright. She had a brand-new Prada bag and a limited-edition Cartier bracelet. She wants to meet for another coffee soon, to catch up."

I pause, my entire body tensing. "Angel, I don't think that's a good idea."

Elena furrows her brow. "Why not? It's just coffee. I need some girl time, and she's my only friend in this city."

"You can find other friends. Who wouldn't want to be friends with *the* Elena Reeves?"

Elena pulls her hand away from mine. "Kate was there for everything. You asked her to take me to the hospital and she stayed until you got there. She's the only other person I can talk to about what happened to me."

"If you need to vent, you can come to me. Do not go anywhere with her."

Elena chuckles. "Last time I checked, we were married, and that makes us equals. You can't just forbid me from seeing my friends."

"Well, I just did," I say back, earning a scowl from her. "Don't make me lock you in a cage, because I will if you try to go somewhere with her."

Elena stands up abruptly, clenching her fists at her sides. I move to sit on the edge of the bed. "I'm already in a cage! I've been in a cage from the moment we met."

I laugh, filling the room with darkened fury. "You don't seem to mind that cage when there's diamonds and yachts with your name on them."

A sharp sting on my cheek makes me freeze. I blink up at my angry little angel, her face full of defiance. She slapped me. I stare at her until her quivering lip finds the words she's looking for.

"*How dare you*," she growls through her teeth. "Do you really think any of that has ever mattered to me? Do you really think I'm that shallow?" Tears spill down her cheeks. "Did you forget that I let two men rape me because of my love for you?"

I press my shoulders back, growing a few inches from my posture alone and I give her a dangerous glare, standing up to my full height, fighting through the pain. I shake my head. "Don't even go there. That is *not* a card you get to play when you're mad at me. Of course I haven't fucking forgotten, Elena! I think about it every goddamn day!"

She bites down on her molars so hard I think she's on the verge of chipping her teeth. I wet my bottom lip as she stares up at me with that defiance that always gets me hard as a rock. As the blood rushes to my groin, I stop caring about all of it. Valenti, Kate, the assassin, her father. Everything that causes tension in our relationship melts away until I'm nothing but a beast lusting after her.

I wrap my fingers around her delicate neck. I'm significantly weaker after being out of the gym for weeks, but I could still snap it like a toothpick if I wanted to. With my tight grip on her throat, I drag her to the bed and shove her down on the mattress before ripping at our clothes like a wild animal until we're both naked. My cock juts out in the space between us, begging for attention just as her pussy is.

I lean over to kiss her roughly, all tongue and teeth and then roll onto my back.

"Apologize for hitting me," I demand. She opens her mouth to speak, but I shove two fingers inside and press down on her tongue like I've done countless times before. "Not with words."

I had only meant I wanted her to suck me off, but my perfect wife is full of surprises and straddles me instead, her pussy so close to my cock that when it flexes, it brushes against her wet slit. My fingers dig roughly into her thighs.

"Elena, don't play with me," I growl, and when we meet eyes again, she shakes her head, grabs my cock, and lowers herself onto my throbbing length. I groan loudly, open-mouthed and wild. She doesn't even put the full tip in and I'm already about to shoot my load into her.

"*Fuck*." I use one of my hands to lightly graze my thumb over her swollen clit. She lowers herself a tiny bit more, and now my head is fully engulfed in her tight, warm, wet hole.

It's been months since I've been inside her, and it's even better than I remember. I can feel her trembling slightly. I can see in her eyes that she's scared. I throw away the rough, possessive side of me for just long enough to reassure her that she's safe.

"Trust me, angel. It's just you and me. Let me make you feel good. Take that cock like a good girl and let me fill you with my love again."

Elena opens her sparkling brown eyes and shakes her head. "I can't. You have to make me."

I swallow the lump in my throat and try to relax my breathing so I don't end this before it begins.

"What's your safe word?"

"Mykonos," she sighs. "It's Mykonos. Please, Christian, just do it."

I make her take a deep breath with me, before I roughly grab the soft flesh of her hips and slam her down on my cock.

CHAPTER 52

THE ANGEL

I cry out loudly, from both pleasure and fear.

It's been so long. My body takes its time adjusting to his size. I'm trembling. Scared. Trying so hard to keep Frank and Neil out of my head and only allowing myself to see Christian.

He lets go of my hips and laces his fingers with mine. "It's just me and you."

I nod, not yet having the strength to look at him. I experimentally rise up a bit, gasping at the light friction. Then back down.

Up and down. Up and down. Up and down.

It's awkward at first. I can't find any sort of rhythm. I pause to wipe tears out of my eyes and then I slump my shoulders in defeat.

"I'm sorry," I whimper.

"Elena, look at me."

"I can't."

"Do it anyway."

I take a deep breath and look at him. "Grind," he commands softly. "Don't think about me. Think about you."

I tremble as I roll my hips in a circle. He squeezes my hands in encouragement, our fingers still tightly tangled together.

"That's it, angel. I'm all yours to use, to devour, to hit and to scratch. However you want to love me, that's what I'm here for."

"I shouldn't have hit you," I whisper.

He uses one of his hands to run his thumb across my clit. "It made my dick so hard I could have shattered diamonds across it."

I exhale with a tremble. "You like it when I'm rough?"

He chuckles, and I can feel it deep in my core. "I like it when you're *defiant*. I always have."

I lean over, careful of his wound, and lick the column of his neck. The new angle has me seeing stars when I grind against his dick. He's reaching parts of me I had forgotten existed. With each sharp prick of pleasure, moving becomes a little easier. I get wetter. Slicker. He can feel it too, because I can feel him flexing his abs under me even though it hurts.

I lean back again, adjust my legs, and start to bounce on him, slowly at first until I find a steady pace that has him stringing curses together as he grips my hips so tight it hurts.

"That's it, angel. Oh, *fuck*, I'm going to cum."

"Not yet," I beg. "We do it together. Please."

He hisses, gripping my hips impossibly tighter. "Okay, baby. Okay."

I throw my head back and bounce a little faster, trying to be mindful of his gunshot, but I think I could stab him right now and he wouldn't care.

I take him harder. Deeper. Faster. I let my free breasts bounce shamelessly in his face. I lean over again, grinding against him at a relentless pace, my clit rubbing against his pelvis with each sway of my hips. I kiss him, hot and frenzied as my body explodes with love and passion and safety.

Christian lets out a pained grunt, and then digs his hands into my ass, holding me tight against him while he paints my wet, velvet walls with his release. I moan into his mouth, having forgotten how erotic it is to have the man that loves me cum deep inside me. To claim me. To mark me as his and only his, like I've always been.

A rush of emotion envelops me, and I begin to cry. Not because I'm sad. I'm crying because I'm relieved. I feel like a new person.

I feel like a survivor.

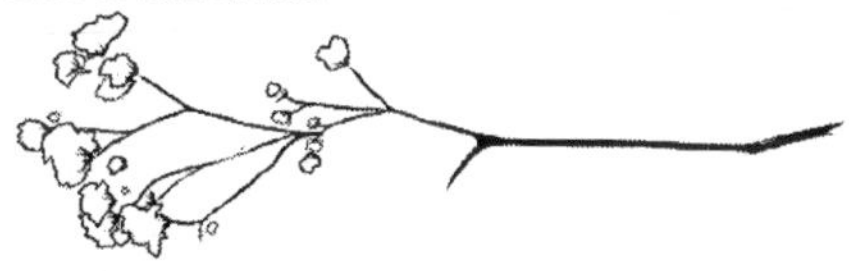

Christian and I haven't discussed our fight about Kate, and I haven't attempted to see her or contact her. She gave me her phone number the other day, but other than texting her my name so she knew it was me, she hasn't said a word to me.

I'm sitting in the downstairs study. Edwin is with me, working on a new puzzle. He finished the one my mother got him for Christmas in less than a month, so every month since, I've gotten him the same puzzle in different colors. The one he's currently working on is a pretty sunset orange. Caroline is helping him.

I'm sorting through the mail. Well, my mail, at least. Christian gets so much mail here from fanboys and people begging for money that he has two staff members sort through all the letters once a week. They pass on my private mail to me, and anything else they think is important, they put in a pile for Christian to go through.

I hardly get anything exciting. Student loan correspondence, mostly. Postcards from Travis and Justin. They cashed in Christian's wedding gift and took a year off to travel the world. They're in Aruba, planning on visiting Ibiza next.

With only one letter left, I take a long sip of the fresh-squeezed lemonade Paolo made for me.

I feel a kiss on the top of my head and smile.

Christian has been more active over the last few days. He can shower on his own now, which instantly brightened his mood. I laughed so hard I snorted when he told me to, quote, '*get the fuck out so I can wash my nutsack in peace*'. He's been in the gym trying to get his range of motion back in his arms after not being able to lift them above his head for weeks.

Christian takes a seat next to me and scrolls through his phone. He gets about a dozen emails a day asking when he'll be back in the office, and he simply tells them all that he will be back when he's back. He was shot, for Christ's sake, but they're acting like he had a cold or something.

Christian sips my lemonade, humming at the taste before going back to mindlessly scrolling. I open the last letter. Well, not a letter. It's a big envelope. Plain white. The return address is something random in Meridian City that doesn't ring any bells. I think it might be on the East Side, but I'm not sure. Postmarked two days ago. The handwriting is extremely neat, almost like someone traced a font from a computer. Red ballpoint ink. Addressed to me directly.

I open the ridiculously well-taped envelope and pull out a single thick piece of paper. It's a glossy black and white photo of Christian's mugshot from the night he broke Neil Hayden's arm. I recognize the date. My stomach turns over. Bile rises in my throat.

Because it's not just his mugshot.

In the center of his forehead, in red marker, a bullseye is sketched onto the paper.

Christian's eyes flicker to me and then he stiffens when he notices the horrified look in my eyes. "What is it?"

I hand him the photo, and he looks at it for a long time. His jaw tightens and he looks at me through the fire burning in his eyes. "This was addressed directly to you?"

I nod silently. He takes a deep breath, and he doesn't have to say anything for me to know what he's thinking.

He's tired of me ending up in the middle of things.

Frankly, so am I. I stand up and take Christian's hand in mine, tugging him out of the room and away from Edwin and Caroline so we can talk privately. He crumples the paper and throws it into the fireplace.

When we're alone, I cup his face in my hands and press our foreheads together. "Tell me what's going on in your head."

"I'm going to burn this fucking world to the ground just to get some goddamn peace."

I nod, looking up at him from under my lashes. "Let's burn it together."

As soon as the words leave my mouth, Christian pins me to the wall and kisses me savagely until our world falls into frenzied, passionate chaos.

Midway into our intense make-out session, I hear footsteps approach. Gavin clears his throat, looking away slightly as Christian adjusts himself in his sweatpants.

"This better be important," Christian warns.

Gavin meets Christian's eyes and then his gaze falls to me. "Your parents are here."

"What?" I ask, completely shocked. Not that I wouldn't be happy to see my mother, but Gavin said *parents*. Plural. As in, my father is here, too. As I try to collect my thoughts, I see my parents at the end of the corridor. My mother has her signature bright smile painting her features, and my father has his signature scowl.

If you look up the term '*resting bitch face*' in the dictionary, all it has is a picture of Elliot Young.

My mother hugs me and gives me a kiss on the cheek before greeting Christian with a hug as well. It's cautious and full of concern. They exchange an unknown look.

She holds out her arms in front of her as if expecting a gift. "Now where's my grandbaby?"

I giggle and as we all turn towards the study, a tiny head of blonde hair launches itself into my mother's arms at the speed of light.

"Hi grandma! Look!" Caroline gives my mother a big smile to show that she's missing one of her front teeth.

She lost her first tooth two days ago. That night, the tooth fairy, also known as Christian, put a one-hundred-dollar bill under her pillow, a cupcake on her nightstand, and a custom Swarovski-crystal Lamborghini Sian electric car at her bedside.

How did Christian find a Swarovski-crystal Lamborghini Sian electric car in less than 12 hours? It's as he once said, never underestimate the power of a black American Express.

That electric car is currently at the bottom of the pool because Caroline didn't know how to turn it off once she grew tired of it. She stepped out, and there it went, right into the deep end.

The tooth fairy doesn't know that part yet, and Caroline made me promise not to tell.

After my mom gushes over Caroline's missing tooth, she looks up at my father with a curious gaze. To my surprise, he squats down and gives her a gentle smile. To ease into this conversation, I squat down to her height with them and lightly tap her nose.

"This is your grandpa," I explain. She blinks at my father, studying him, and then, because she's adorable and trusting, she leaves my mother's arms and goes straight into his to hug him. My father wraps his arms around her as if it's the first time he's ever hugged a child, and something strange flickers across his eyes. Gone as quick as it came.

It almost looked like guilt.

Caroline takes my parents' hands and leads them into the study to show them the puzzle she's working on with Edwin. Christian and I linger in the hallway. He's got his hands tucked into the front pocket of his hoodie, and a sheepish grin on his face.

"You called them," I say quietly. He nods. "Why?"

He runs the back of his hand along my cheek to brush away a loose strand of hair framing my face. His soft smile falters for a millisecond before returning. "You've done nothing but take care of Caroline and I all on your own since I got shot. I wanted you to relax for a minute. I didn't think your mom would have any objections to coming to see her grandchild for a few days."

"And my dad?"

He gives me a half-hearted smile. "Maybe he's had a change of heart." He looks towards the study and chuckles to himself. "Did you see the way he looked at Caroline? That kid could end wars with how cute she is."

"She gets it from me," I lightly tease, and his smile in return is so bright it can be seen from space. I tangle my hands into the fabric of his hoodie, rise up to my toes, and press a soft kiss to his lips. "Thank you for bringing them here." I wrap my fingers around his wrist as he cradles my jaw. "I guess I should extend the olive branch."

Christian shakes his head. "He owes you an apology. If he doesn't tell you he's sorry, just say the word, and I'll take care of him."

I almost snort from how nostalgic those words feel. "My father being a dickhead isn't grounds for murder."

Christian licks his lips and then takes his bottom lip between his teeth before giving me that devilish smile he's mastered. "You're no fun, angel."

Both of us walk into the study together, and instead of using my words, I give my father an unmistakable look that says, '*we need to talk.*'

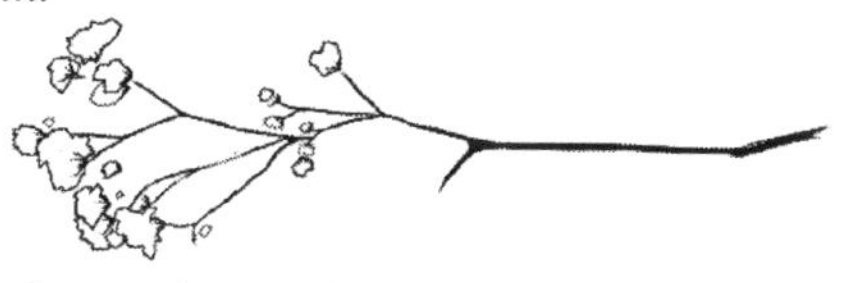

My father and I stand awkwardly on the balcony on the second floor of the mansion, overlooking the backyard. We have a clear view of the gray ocean and the impending storm clouds on the horizon.

My father digs into his pocket and pulls out a cigarette. I take it from him and break the stick in half before handing it back.

"No smoking on the property. We don't want Caroline around it. Which you would know if you bothered to come meet her two months ago."

My father looks up at the sky and sighs. "I regret what I said to you at Thanksgiving. It came out…bad."

"That wasn't an apology," I say with a curled lip, staring off into the distance.

"*I'm sorry*," he apologizes, though I can tell he said it through gritted teeth.

"Are you also sorry you weren't there to walk me down the aisle at my wedding?"

He scoffs. "That wasn't a wedding. You deserved more than five minutes in a decrepit courtroom. You deserved flowers and a first dance and a veil the length of Australia."

"I didn't *want* those things," I croak, finally looking at him. "Dad…I'm not the same girl I was five years ago, or even six months ago. You've got to accept that. I've been through a lot these last few months and you're killing yourself for not being there for me, but I'm okay. Do you know why I'm okay?" I ask, but I don't give him a chance to answer. "Because of *Christian.* His love is brutal and intense, but it's made me strong, dad. You're my hero. You always have been. But Christian is my hero too."

My father lets out a long exhale. "You're his, too. He told me. About the suicide attempt."

I blink at him, and my spine stiffens. "Christian told you…about the night we met?"

"At Thanksgiving," he confirms. "It's beautiful, you know. The story of why he calls you angel. Reminds me of your mother and me. How she pulled me out of the darkest part of my life."

It all begins to make sense to me in that moment, and it feels like a weight has been lifted off my shoulders. "That's why you don't like him," I say, almost laughing at how obvious it is now. "You thought he was a danger to me. You thought I was going to be one of his victims."

It goes quiet for a long minute as he stares at me.

Suddenly and without warning, he pulls me into a tight hug. He's shaking, like he's overwhelmed with emotion.

"I'm sorry, Ellie. I'm going to fix everything."

I hug him back. "Promise me nothing will ever come between us again?"

His hand strokes over the back of my head, and he takes a deep breath. "*I promise.*"

The next morning at breakfast, I catch my father, more than once, giving Christian a death glare that tells me he still doesn't like my husband.

Baby steps, I guess.

In my father's defense, Christian and I haven't been together long at all, and suddenly we're married with a kid. I can recognize that it's weird. It doesn't make sense, but Christian and I were always meant to end up together. I see that now. My love for him might not have been instant the way his was, but after everything we've been through, I know it in my soul that this is where I belong.

After breakfast, Caroline takes my parents and Edwin to the theater room, where she picks three Disney movies and proclaims that none of them are allowed to leave until they finish watching them with her.

With everyone else preoccupied, Christian takes my hand. "I want to show you something," he says, and then leads me upstairs to the library and stops us in front of a bookshelf.

"First edition *1984*. Nice."

"How do you know it's a first edition?"

"Because you're Christian Reeves."

He chuckles, and then pulls out his phone. He opens an app I've never seen before and presents the screen to me. It's asking for a password.

"Your birthday. Year, Month, Day," he prompts.

I give him a strange look, but I type in the numbers. A simple green checkmark appears on the screen and then I jump backwards when the bookcase starts moving, revealing a narrow spiral staircase.

I raise an eyebrow at my husband, who simply nods at me. I step into the staircase, and he follows close behind. The bookcase shuts itself behind us and it's nearly pitch-black in this stairwell.

"Lights," Christian mumbles, and small bulbs lining the steps turn on. I follow them down, down, down, until I reach a dark basement.

"Lights?" I say apprehensively, and, shocker, the lights turn on. "Woah," I announce as I take in the space.

A computer with massive hard drives and a dozen screens is directly across from us, his Silencer mask connected via USB to the tower. Tables with tools and wires and half-built projects sit in the center of the room. A rack of every kind of ammunition is on the far wall, next to an equally massive gun display. There's a refrigerator with strange vials of liquid, syringes, bottles of water, and electrolyte bags. I open a set of drawers to find a plethora of medical supplies. To my left, a makeshift shooting range.

I admit, while I was still in my initial recovery stage and unsure about how I felt about Christian, I snooped around the entire house looking for an entrance to a secret lair just like this, or at least his mask or some other evidence of his alter ego hidden away. I never found anything, but that's because I always expected the entrance to be in or around his room to be discreet. I suppose that's why he has the entrance in the library on the second floor. Who would look there for a secret lair?

"I have a request," Christian says as I peruse the space. He takes one of the pistols from the rack hanging on the far wall and loads it. He waves me over to the makeshift gun range and sets the pistol between us. "You once told me you were a good shot. Prove it."

It's a challenge. I suck in my cheeks and give him a grin before looking at the paper targets down range. "Which one do you want me to hit?"

"All three. In the head."

"What do I get if I hit them?"

"Whatever you want."

I smirk and then take the gun and aim at the first target. Then the second. Then the third. I put two bullets in each, and I think I've thoroughly surprised Christian. When he presses a button on the wall to bring the targets closer, I've hit all three in the head, *and* in the dick.

He chuckles to himself. "You're full of surprises, Mrs. Reeves."

I set down the gun and wrap my arms around his neck. He grips my waist as I rise on my toes to kiss him, hard and heavy and passionately like we kissed in the hallway before my parents arrived.

"We never talked about that photo."

Christian growls, as if that's the last thing he wants to talk about right now. "I'm not scared of a threat drawn on one of my mugshots."

"I am," I croak. "I already almost lost you once, Christian. I can't go through that again. I can't live without you."

He takes my bottom lip between his teeth and we both groan. "You won't have to."

His fingers slide down my body sensually, leaving a path of hot desire in their wake. He pops the button of my jeans with ease, and he slowly makes his way to my core. I suck in a sharp breath when his fingers slide across my slit, already wet and needy. He smiles against my mouth and withdraws his hands before pushing me by my waist to the computer desk and pressing me against it. He doesn't have to say the words for me to understand.

I lift myself onto the table and he shoves away loose papers and pens to give me more space before tugging my jeans and underwear down my legs and throwing them to the side. He kisses me again, his right hand around my throat possessively, but I stop him. He pulls away, and when we make eye contact, he sees that I'm holding his Silencer mask in my hands.

He pauses and something dark and sexy flickers across his eyes. My body responds by clenching around nothing and growing wetter. I put the mask on him, and this is the first time

I've ever understood what he means when he says Christian Reeves and the Silencer are two different people.

The second the mask is secured to his face, he's not my husband. He is rage. He is danger. He's not the King of the East Coast.

He's the Harbinger of Death.

And God help me, he's beautiful.

He switches the hand that's holding my throat, tilting my head back and staring hungrily at the heartbeat pounding against my throat.

His eyes find mine. The fire in them is nothing short of wild. Uninhibited and raw with desire. I look deep into those icy blue eyes as my eyes fill with tears from the lack of oxygen.

"I'm not afraid of you. Not anymore."

He tugs his own jeans down, just enough to free his throbbing erection, and without another word or warning, he takes me like he's always wanted to.

"Do you love me?" he growls into my throat as he thrusts ravenously.

"Yes," I whimper. "Yes, Christian, I love you."

"What's your safe word?"

"Mykonos."

The moment it leaves my lips, I feel a sharp sting on my cheek. I look up at him, wide-eyed and shocked. He slapped me. Not enough to hurt me, but enough to sting.

Enough to make me want him even more.

"I didn't ask if you love *Christian Reeves*." He says the name like it is a bitter poison on his lips as his hand returns to my throat. "I asked if you love *me*."

I let out a shuddering breath and reach for his face. I cup his masked cheeks in my hands and press our foreheads together.

"Yes," I whisper. "I love you. I love every piece of you. Even the parts I shouldn't love. Even the parts of you that have unraveled all the parts of me. *Especially* the terrifying parts that you've tangled into my soul."

There's a stray gun resting on the table next to me. I loosen his grip on my throat and make him point it at my head, not caring that it might be loaded.

I breathe through my teeth and whimper. "Now break me so you can love me back together."

His free hand cocks the gun, and he places it back at my temple. "Say it again."

"I love you."

"Again."

"I love you."

"*Again.*"

"*I love you*!"

He begins to fuck me like a savage, grunting into my neck, making sure I feel every inch of him inside me for days. He finishes inside me with a feral roar, and I follow right behind.

I take a deep breath, and before I remove his mask, I kiss him, hoping that even through the material, he can feel that I told him the truth.

I've fallen in love with the most unlovable, virulent, tragic parts of him.

And I've decided I love the taste of poison.

CHAPTER 53

THE ANGEL

Today is the first time we've stepped foot on the Reeves Enterprises property since Christian was shot. We couldn't bring ourselves to drive around the front of the building, to see the place where Christian's heart stopped beating. To see the rusty bloodstain on the concrete.

Meridian City has a thing about bloodstained concrete. No matter how much you power wash it, no matter how many times it rains, the stain remains.

Our office was thoroughly cleaned after the investigation, of course, but there's still an eerie, heavy, unsettling feeling in the air as we sit at our desks. It smells like bleach, and it takes me back to when I woke up after my car accident in Valenti's private suite. That room smelled like bleach too.

Bleach and my own despair.

Once we settle into our respective desks, the first thing on the agenda is working through the backlog of meetings Christian missed while he was out after he was shot.

He was good about working from home right after we adopted Caroline, but I told him he wasn't allowed to work while he was healing. He needed to relax if he was going to get better. He's stubborn, so he's pushed himself more than he should have to get back to functioning on his own.

Yesterday he raised his arms above his head without whimpering. It's such a small thing, but for me, it was everything. He still has a long road of recovery ahead of him, but it was solid proof that he was getting better, and this gunshot wasn't going to come back from the past to haunt us.

"…fifty-eight, fifty-nine, *sixty* requests for meetings with…" I pause for a moment to count again, "forty of them claiming *urgent* matters."

Christian groans and stares up at the ceiling of our office. He's tossing that spider ring Caroline gave us at the orphanage up above his head. It hits the white ceiling tiles with a small thump each time he throws it.

"I say we start with the oldest requests first and work our way up from there."

"Sure. Sounds great."

I huff from my desk across the room. "Are you even listening to me?"

"Yep. I'll be there."

I stifle a giggle and take the initiative to set up the meetings myself. I'm only about halfway through coordinating the calendar when Christian stands from his chair and saunters over to me.

"I want to go home," he whines.

I give him a sympathetic smile. "We need to make a dent in this work or you're never going to catch up."

"So?"

"*So*, as CEO, you need to do CEO things like rescheduling all these meetings."

"What if I don't want to?"

I scoff at his indifference. "This is your company."

"Elena, I don't care about this stuff anymore. I have a family now. You and Caroline are the only things that matter to me."

I smirk. "Well if you want to continue buying Caroline everything she looks at, you're going to have to care about this stuff."

"Angel, I have enough money stashed away in an offshore bank account that our great-great-great-great grandchildren will never have to work a day in their lives."

I lean back in my chair, cross my arms over my chest and look up at him. "If you're implying that you want to step down as CEO, I am vetoing that decision."

"But if I'm the CEO and you're going to be my top attorney, who's going to take care of Caroline?"

I take his hand in mine and squeeze it. "She's going to start preschool in the fall. We'll have to pick her up every day in a different colored Range Rover to assert our dominance."

Christian goes completely stiff, as if he's only just remembered that his daughter can't just sit at home and steal cake frosting from the kitchen. "Holy shit, you're right."

"She'll be okay," I assure him. "I'm sure Meridian Academy will be thrilled to have another Reeves attend their school. They'll take good care of her."

"*They better*," Christian grumbles. "They're going to hate me with how much I'm going to micromanage that school. God help them if anyone there so much as *breathes* in Caroline's direction wrong."

I laugh softly. "Have you ever considered not jumping straight to violence?"

"No," he deadpans. "Violence is what I do best. It's why you fell in love with me."

I scrape a nail across the thigh of his slacks. "I fell in love with you because of the diamonds, actually," I tease, flashing my left hand and wrist to show off my wedding ring and the first piece of jewelry he gave me—the diamond tennis bracelet.

I wear it every day, and instead of making me wear that ugly panic alarm he gave me as the Silencer, Christian replaced one of the diamonds with a stone that functions the same way.

It's a blood red ruby.

His way of saying the Silencer will always be with me, and a subtle way of letting his alter ego claim me.

Christian pulls me up to a standing position by my jaw and sucks a small mark onto the curve of my neck. I moan softly, but our moment is interrupted by my office phone ringing. It's the receptionist. I click the answer button and put the phone on speaker.

"Yes?" I ask, Christian still kissing my neck in the way that makes my legs feel like jelly.

"Mrs. Reeves, sorry to disturb you. I have a young woman insisting she has an appointment with you, but I can't find her on your calendar. She's being rather…abrasive. Her name is Kate McGinnis. Shall I have security remove her from the premises?"

"No!" I answer, before Christian has a chance to protest. "She's right, my mistake for not putting her on the calendar, please send her up."

"Yes, ma'am."

The phone goes dead, and Christian looks absolutely enraged that I'd allow her into our space, but I know Kate, and I don't think she'd insist on seeing me here at work unless it was for something important.

Even so, the look on Christian's face makes me defensive.

"I didn't call her."

"Then why are you letting her up here?" he asks through gritted teeth.

"Because she's my friend," I snap back. "Christian, I don't want to fight about this. Just let me see what she has to say."

He bites the inside of his cheek in a way that tells me he has a lot to say but is holding his tongue. The elevator door opens, and Kate timidly steps in, looking around the office in awe.

We make eye contact, and she gives me a soft smile. "Hey pipsqueak."

"What are you doing here?" I ask.

Kate swallows in the kind of way that guilty people do when they don't want to admit the truth. "Valenti is still in the city," she admits. "On the East Side."

"How do you know this?" Christian asks, the lines of his body now tight and on edge.

She looks down in shame. "Because I still work for him." I take a big step away from her, recoiling from shock and bitter betrayal. "I'm sorry! I came here to try and make it right," she whimpers, looking between Christian and I.

That's when I notice the large purple bruise on the side of her face that she's tried to hide with makeup.

"Look…I started working for him when I was nineteen, almost ten years ago. He had just opened the Hellfire Lounge, and no one knew about the bidding house underneath the club, or that he was the island's drug lord. My sister and I started working there together."

I do remember her telling me that she had a sister that used to work at the Lounge with her, but that she didn't last long.

"My sister wasn't pretty enough by Valenti's standards. She had really bad cystic acne and she got a lot of complaints from the men there. Valenti was going to kill her as punishment for costing him money, but I got on my hands and knees and *begged* for him to keep her alive. I told him I would do anything." Kate's face twists painfully. "I let him have sex with me whenever he wanted and promised I'd help him get his club off the ground so long as he kept my sister alive. I would flirt with the patrons to keep them coming in until he established his clientele. I would spread my legs, suck his dick, bang his friends. Anything he wanted, I did it without question." She faces Christian now. "I'll tell you where he is, but only if you make me a promise. My sister means everything to me. You have to protect her. Please. I swear, it's the *only* reason I'm still working for him."

"Done," Christian says. "If you help me take Valenti down, I promise that your sister will be safe."

Kate looks up at him from under her lashes and takes a deep breath. "There is a shipping port on the East Side of the island. It's got hundreds of shipping containers that move in and out of the place weekly. Valenti has a safehouse there. You'll know it by three blue containers in the dead center of the port." She takes another heavy breath. "It's not heavily guarded. Maybe a dozen men at the most. He hasn't left the safehouse since you burnt down the Lounge."

My heart begins to thud erratically at the thought of all of this being over. Valenti could be dead *tonight*, and months of fearing when he'd show up will die with him. I stare at Christian with hope in my eyes, but he looks distant. I reach for his hand and squeeze. He squeezes back.

"Thank you, Kate. You can leave now," Christian says, his tone leaving no room for argument. I don't fight him on this, but only because I begin to shake. Kate leaves, and I step towards one of the windows and stare out over the city. Christian wraps his arms around me in a way that says, '*I'm here'*.

"I'm going to say something, and you're not going to like it."

"You don't trust her," I inquire, though less of a question and more of a statement. "Tell me why."

He takes a deep breath and presses a soft kiss to my temple while he holds me. "If she's been working for Valenti all this time, why is she only just now coming to tell us? Everyone in this goddamn city knows where we live and work. It's not like we're hard to find. The Lounge has been a pile of ashes for *months*. If you hadn't run into her the other day, I doubt she would have come here to say anything. If she really wanted to help, she should have come to us a long time ago."

I sigh. He's right. Kate knows what I went through. She knows Christian is the Silencer, and she knows exactly the kind of person Frank is. He's not going to give up on getting revenge. She should have said something months ago.

"What do you want to do?" Christian asks, and I turn slightly in his arms to look up at him in confusion.

"What do you mean?"

"Do you want me to trust Kate and go look for him, guns raised, or do you want me to do some recon on this safehouse first?"

I think about it for a long time.

Kate is my friend. Would she lie to me for Frank?

She's always been honest with me about what a monster he is. I don't see why she would lie now, even if she is still working for him. I know firsthand that escaping his clutches isn't easy.

I turn completely in Christian's arms and run my hands down his torso, pressing roughly into the healing wound in his stomach. He winces and shifts away from my touch.

"Obviously it's going to hurt if you're shoving your fingers in it!"

"I can't risk losing you again," I whisper.

"I'll wear my suit. It will protect me. It always has. Do you know how many times I got shot when I killed Valenti's friends for touching you?"

"You hadn't been bedridden for weeks." I close my eyes and rest my forehead against his chest. "I want Valenti dead, but I want you alive more."

"Those things are not mutually exclusive, Elena."

"It's too risky."

He huffs. "You expect me to just sit here and," he shrugs his shoulders and twists his face in a disgusted expression, "let him *exist* in this city after what he did to you? Tell me that's not what you want."

I scoff humorlessly. "What I want is for you to remember that you have a family now. If revenge means you're risking Caroline growing up without you, then no, I don't want revenge."

"One bullet. That's all it will take for it to be over."

He cradles my face in his hands, gently and comforting like he always has, but for some reason, I find it hard to look him in the eye.

"Let me ask you something," I prompt, pausing to take in a heavy breath and find the courage to meet his gaze. "Do you want revenge because of what Frank did to *me*? Or do you want revenge because *you* want to kill him?"

"What's the difference?"

"One is for me, the other is for you."

Christian is quiet for a long moment as he reflects on that. His eyes never leave mine as he does.

I know when he's found his answer, because his hands drop from my cheeks, and now, he's the one that can't find the strength to look at me.

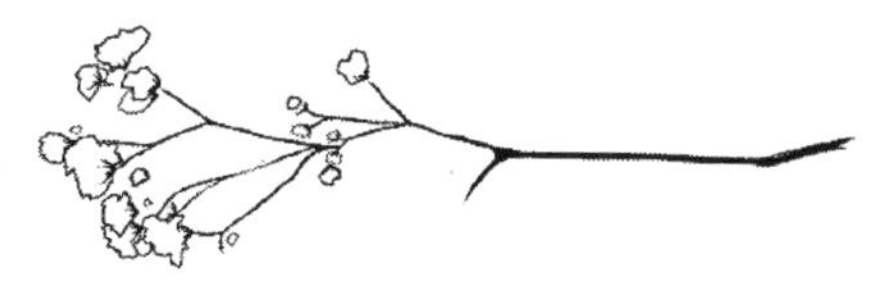

"Mommy!" Caroline squeals as she meets us in the foyer. Christian doesn't make an effort to say hi or even look at anyone, making a hasty exit up the stairs.

I know where he's going, and I don't try to stop him.

If he stays here or if he goes out to try and find Frank, I won't know. The latter wouldn't surprise me, but I don't intend on asking.

Christian is stubborn, but I'd honestly be more surprised if he *didn't* go looking for Frank. He won't rest until he's dead, especially now that it's confirmed he's still lurking in the city.

My mother notices Christian's sour mood instantly, watching as he disappears upstairs. I suppose she can relate to having a stubborn, moody spouse.

"What's for dinner?" I ask Caroline. It's Monday, and on Mondays, we let her pick the meal.

"Pizza! With lots of cheese!"

I pick her up and carry her towards the kitchen to find dinner almost ready. Paolo is sprinkling fresh-grated parmesan on top of the steaming pies. I set Caroline on the counter and glance around the room.

"Where's dad?" I ask.

My mom crinkles her nose and shrugs. "He said he had an emergency with a client. Something about the mayor's wife, I think?"

"Oh, Jeannine!" I reply, just to fill the awkward tension that suddenly seeped into the room at the mention of my father. "She's lovely."

My mom gives me a half-hearted smile and helps Caroline pick a slice of pizza.

"Tell me," I prompt, because I can see that she wants to say something but won't.

"I…" She takes a deep breath. "It's nothing."

"It doesn't seem like nothing."

She stares down at her granddaughter and sighs. "I remember when you were this little. You and Travis were always fighting over who got to ride on your father's shoulders when we would go somewhere. I've never seen someone love their children the way he loves you."

"Mom…" I choke out, my throat burning.

She sniffles. "Feels like yesterday we were sending you off to chase your dreams in this city. Now you have a beautiful family of your own. Time just…flies by."

I reach across the counter to rest my hand over hers. "Someone's feeling sentimental," I tease. She gives me a sad smile and blinks away the wetness in her eyes as a heavy set of footsteps come around the corner. Gavin walks in, pausing when he spots us at one of the double islands.

He nods to greet us. "Mrs. Reeves. Mrs. Young."

I point with my pinky towards one of the three pizzas Paolo prepared. "Want some? The three of us can't finish all of this."

He shrugs. "Why not?"

With Gavin's help, we get through two of the three pies. He tells us that in one week, he's taking his wife on the honeymoon they never got to have. A gift from Christian for protecting me when he was shot. They're going to Belize.

"Sounds like fun," I quip. "Going to make another baby while you're there?"

Gavin chuckles. "All my wife talks about is having another baby, so probably."

"Mommy?" Caroline asks. "Can I have a baby brother?"

I cock my head to the side in amusement. "Sure, I'll get right on that," I say, tapping her nose.

Christian and I agreed when we adopted Caroline that we'd wait at least a year before we started trying to have a baby, but I'm not sure if a year is enough time for me.

Not because I don't want a baby, but because I don't think I'm emotionally ready to have my genitals poked and prodded by strangers throughout the pregnancy.

Sex with Christian makes me feel safe. Loved. Free. His touch is comforting. The thought of anyone else coming near me fills me with ice-cold fear, and he knows that. The last time we talked about it, he promised me he'd wait as long as it takes for me to be ready.

As for Caroline? Well, she's only been our daughter for a couple of months, and we haven't quite gotten around to explaining how that's perhaps not an appropriate question to ask.

But when have we ever said no to her?

My train of thought is interrupted by two loud *pops* coming from the foyer. My blood runs cold. I know a gunshot when I hear it.

Instantly, I lunge for Caroline and tightly hug her to my chest as I squat to the floor and shove her inside one of the large cabinets under the island.

"Caro, look at me," I say, trying to keep my voice calm. "We're going to play a game of hide and seek, okay? You hide right here, and daddy is going to come find you." I take the diamond bracelet off my wrist and hit the panic button, clasping it around her ankle. "Don't make a sound, and don't come out for anyone but daddy. Okay?"

"Okay, mommy."

I shut the cabinet door and grab my mother's hand as Gavin, with his gun out, puts himself between us and the door closest to the foyer. It goes quiet for a few long seconds, and then I hear one more *pop*.

Gavin slumps to the floor, clutching at his shoulder. It doesn't look like it hit anything vital, but he could easily bleed out.

I'd bend down to help him, but I can't.

Because across the room, pointing a gun at us, is the Silencer.

I don't mean Christian, because whoever this is in front of me, it's *not* Christian.

His body shape is wrong. His build is wrong. His height is wrong. I can tell from across the room that he's too old. His mask is wrong. His eyes are the wrong shade of green. *Wrong. Wrong. Wrong.*

This is the man who shot my husband. I know it in my bones.

"What do you want?" I croak, my mother and I clutching onto each other like a lifeline.

"Come with me. *Now*. Or the Irishman dies."

God, even his voice is wrong.

Christian's mask has a slight voice changer too, but his is sexy and gravelly. This one sounds like a cheap knock-off of Darth Vader.

My heart crawls up my throat at the peculiar nature of that threat. *The Irishman.* He's threatening to kill Edwin, *not* my mother, who's standing right next to me.

Whoever this person is, and whatever their motivations are, he's trying to lure Christian into a trap.

And I'm the bait.

CHAPTER 54

THE SILENCER

I don't mind blood. I never have.

But when there's blood all over my home and I wasn't the one to spill it? Yeah, it's fucking infuriating.

I should have known shit would hit the fan. Last time I left Elena alone for more than two fucking minutes, she hit her panic alarm and I had to watch helplessly as two men got their revenge on me by raping her.

And once again, that fucking alarm is going off and I'm damn near ready to raze this city to the ground. If Elena has so much as a hair out of place, I can kiss my last bit of self-control goodbye.

When I get to my mansion, there are two security guards on the ground. They're bleeding from gunshots in their stomachs. These are big guys, big targets. Whoever this is that's trying to ruin my life, they have terrible fucking aim. First they can't land a fatal hit with a damn military-grade sniper, and now they can't even get a clean hit on my security guards. They're alive, just unconscious from blood loss.

I check my tracking device. It shows Elena's location in the kitchen. I slowly make my way through the house, listening carefully for any voices that shouldn't be here. Any sounds of struggle or fear.

I don't hear anything until I get to the kitchen. Bethany is crouched over Gavin, holding a dishrag against what I can only assume is a gunshot wound at the curve of his shoulder.

She turns her head and whimpers when she spots me. She looks terrified, they both do.

Then it hits me. I've made a big fucking mistake.

I forgot to change.

They're looking dead in the eyes of the Silencer.

Shit.

It's too late to try and fix it now. With my gun at my side, I kneel next to Gavin. "Where is she?"

From the corner of my eye, Bethany swings at me with a frying pan. I catch her wrist easily. She tries to tug it out of my grip, but I don't let her go until she drops it. I turn my attention back to Gavin.

"Where is she?" I repeat, my patience dangerously thin. When he says nothing, I seethe. "Fuck! Code Lilac."

Code Lilac is reserved for the high priority emergencies involving Elena or Caroline. We came up with the term when I promoted Gavin to their permanent bodyguard.

There are only two people on the planet who know Code Lilac.

Gavin Miramontes and Christian Reeves.

Gavin stares at me in utter disbelief. He tries to sit up straighter, his back slouched awkwardly against the cabinets now coated in his blood. "He took her."

"Who?"

Through gritted teeth, he hisses, "*The Silencer.*"

I tighten my jaw. "Where's Caroline?"

"What the hell is going on?!" Bethany screeches as she covers Gavin's mouth with her hand.

Gavin tilts his head to his left, towards the cabinets under the kitchen island. I scramble over to swing open the door of the largest one.

Precious Caroline lets out a whine of pure fear and curls up into a tight ball in the very corner of the cabinet. "Babygirl, it's me," I coo before letting my mask fall to the floor. "It's daddy."

Caroline blinks in confusion, but then she relaxes. "Oh, hi daddy," she says, before crawling out of the cabinet and into my arms. I hold her tight to my chest, a small wave of relief coming over me now that I know she's okay. From over Caroline's shoulders, I make eye contact with Bethany and Gavin.

"Beth—"

"Give her to me," Bethany demands, her eyes flickering to Caroline. When I don't move, her gaze and tone turns dangerous. "Christian, give her to me *right now.*"

As much as it hurts my still-healing gunshot wound, I make my way to my feet as I hold Caroline in my arms, making sure to keep her facing away from Gavin and all his blood.

I shake my head. "You'll take her."

"She's a baby, Christian," she begs as she takes a step closer.

I take a step back. "She's *my* baby. I'm the way I am because of *your* husband, Beth. You don't get to judge me."

Bethany recoils as if I've just slapped her across the face, because she knows I'm right. I take a deep breath and nuzzle my cheek against Caroline's head. "Take her," I instruct, my eyes a silent warning that if she leaves the property with my daughter, I will violently dismember her.

Bethany takes Caroline from my arms and takes her out of the room. I pick my mask up from the ground and secure it onto my face. "Hey Gav?" His eyes flicker up to mine. "Do you remember what you said to me in the gym after I was shot? About how if anything happened to Elena, I'd do far worse than fire you?"

His face turns three shades paler as I crack my neck and point my gun at his forehead.

"Consider yourself lucky that I'm making it quick."

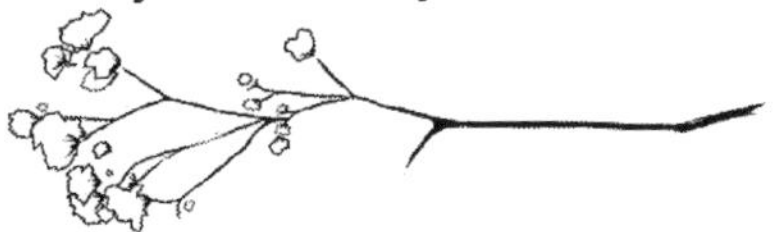

The strawberry blonde bitch steps away from the ATM on the corner, having made what looked to be a deposit of bills worth a few thousand.

Gavin was right. Kate's loyalty is with the highest bidder, but she's made a mistake. No amount of money is going to save her from me.

As she passes by the alleyway, I emerge from the shadows and grab her by her hair, ruthlessly slamming her down against the concrete sidewalk.

I love the sound of her skull cracking against the ground, and the pained scream that comes after. She tries to fight me, but she's disoriented and scared. I drag her into the alley by her hair kicking and screaming. I cover her mouth with duct tape and tie her wrists and ankles together as blood from her head seeps down into her face. I drag her through dirty alleys, making sure to put her in the path of garbage and stagnant water before we come to a stop at an abandoned warehouse.

I set up a chair in the center of the empty space and secure her limbs to the wooden supports.

I take a moment to catch my breath and clutch the burning flesh where my gunshot wound is aching. When I pull away my hand, there's blood.

Fuck.

I move to the window, sighing in content at my work. In the distance, I can see black smoke rising from the bridges leading off the island. All but one. Forcing anyone wanting to leave through a single choke point that the FBI is closely monitoring. They're handling it as a terrorist attack.

They've got bigger problems than bombs I've planted under bridges if there's so much as a scratch on Elena.

I turn back to the lying whore, and Kate is hyperventilating. I pull off the tape and stand directly in front of her, arms crossed, and I wait.

After a long bout of silence, I remove my mask and let it fall to the floor. "Well? Do you have anything to say?"

"Please, I haven't done anything!"

I chuckle, and without any shred of remorse, I punch her in the face. She should consider herself lucky that I pulled that punch. If I had let her taste the full brunt of my fist, I probably would have broken her jaw.

"Where is she?" I growl. When she says nothing, I get a little excited. It's been too long since I've had a good torture session. "Come on, Katherine. For every second of my time you waste, I'm going to spend a minute fucking up your sister. I hope she likes the taste of her own teeth."

Kate whimpers. "I don't know where he took her. Please, I swear on my life that I don't know anything."

I kneel next to her and pull out a serrated knife, tracing it down her leg, slicing open her thigh and watching the blood seep out of the deep wound. Kate starts crying. From pain or from fear, it doesn't matter. All that matters is that she's going to sit here and suffer until she tells me what I want.

Then, and only then, I will *consider* putting her out of her misery.

Who am I kidding? She's going to die the second she gives me any useful information.

I'm not torturing her because I want to. I'm doing this for Elena, because this lying bitch betrayed her by allying herself with the wrong man.

"Do you remember what I did to Neil Hayden?" I ask, the fury in my voice sharp as razors. "Do you remember his body hanging upside down outside of the Hellfire Lounge? Exsanguinated. Mutilated." I take her forearm and easily snap the fragile bone and sigh in satisfaction when she screams. "Broken." I stand up and punch her again. "Beaten. Bloody." I chuckle to myself. "Tell me what you know, and I'll spare you at least *one* of those things."

Yeah, she's fucking lucky.

I'm being really fucking patient right now. I need information, and it's the only reason this bitch is still breathing. I'm going to hunt down her sister and take it out on her, too, because I'm that fucking enraged.

I don't know who I should be more pissed off at.

Kate?

The fucker that broke into my house and kidnapped my wife?

Or maybe I'm just mad at my own stubborn ass for being on the other side of the fucking city chasing a fake lead when Elena hit her panic alarm, because I was stupid enough to let rage towards Valenti overtake my reason.

"Frank is paranoid about being found," Kate admits, slurring her words as her hazy mind tries to form coherent thoughts through the pain. "He doesn't have any electronics in his safehouse because he's afraid of getting hacked. Just a few dozen guards on rotation. One of his men brings him the newspaper every morning, so he can keep up with what's happening in the city while he's in hiding. The morning after you got married, he put the pieces together that the Silencer and Christian Reeves were the same man. After the ruthlessness you showed Neil Hayden for touching Elena, you wouldn't have let any other man have her. You made it easy to figure out. *I didn't tell him.*"

"I don't believe you. But continue."

"He wants her. Not…not like you think. Not to rape, but to control you. He knows you'd do anything to get her back, even work for him."

"You're more delusional that I am if you think I'd *ever* make a deal with Frank fucking Valenti after what he did to Elena." I grab her by her jaw, the flesh there already starting to swell. She winces at the contact.

"Pipsqueak has a way of attracting psychopaths."

"Ah, so you do know about my twin." I muse, moving her neck from side to side, contemplating if I want to break it when I'm done here.

Kate nods frantically. "He was dressed as the Silencer when he met with Valenti. He loved it. Poetic justice or some shit. Valenti wanted you, your twin wanted Elena. I think he stole your act to cover his tracks when he tried to kill you."

I cock one of my guns and shove it under her jaw. "Your story isn't making sense. If Valenti wants me, but Junior wants me dead, how would they ever make a deal?"

"I don't know, but I do know that your shadow is *obsessed* with Elena. All he talks about is saving her from you. If you ever meet, it will be a bloodbath."

I crack my neck. "Good. Been too long since I had one of those. This man dressed like me, what does he look like?"

Kate lets out a sickly cough. "Older—he had grey hair. Lean. Just about as tall as me. I only saw him once as he walked past me. I didn't get a good look."

"That's not helpful, Kate," I taunt, pressing the gun harder into her skin. "Scars, tattoos, eye color. Anything."

"Blue eyes. I remember that because Valenti told him about the contacts."

"So you swear on your sister's life, you didn't tell Valenti about me? He found it out on his own? Because I find that really fucking hard to believe. If he learned all that information himself, what does he need you for?" I pause to give her a chance to answer. She doesn't.

I put my gun away and circle around her slowly, trying to intimidate any further information from her. I can tell by her defeated gaze that she's got nothing.

"Just tell me why, Kate. Why would you help Elena one minute, and then betray her the next? She trusted you. If it was about money, you were stupid to think that anyone's allegiance pays better than mine."

"It wasn't about the money! He threatened my sister and said if I didn't find a way to get you out of that mansion, he'd kill her and make me watch!"

"Your sister is a dead girl walking either way."

"Do whatever you want to me. Just don't hurt my sister."

"Not only did you stab your friend in the back, but you put my kid in danger. Give me one good reason why I shouldn't put a bullet in the head of everyone you've ever loved."

"Please! My sister is innocent. Just like El—"

Her words are cut off with a guttural gargle when I slit her throat and blood spurts from her neck across my chest and arms. I push her backwards, and she goes plummeting to the ground in the chair, still gasping for air when I place a strip of red duct tape over her mouth and leave the warehouse.

What I've done to her is a mercy compared to what I have planned for my shadow.

God help the man who took Elena, because she belongs to only one psychopath.

Me.

CHAPTER 55

THE ANGEL

My limbs feel heavy and my head is fuzzy, most likely from whatever sedative that psycho injected me with when he dragged me from the mansion.

I'm getting really sick of going unconscious and then waking up in a different location.

This time, instead of Frank's private suite atop the Hellfire Lounge, I'm in an unassuming motel room.

I'm not handcuffed or gagged or bound in any way, which is honestly more unsettling. I wasn't tied up when I was with Frank either.

The first thing I do is pick up the phone on the bedside table to call for help, but the wires have been cut. Angry, I throw the bedside lamp across the room and watch it shatter against the wall. Then I stand up, wobbly on my legs from the sedative, and limp to the door.

It's locked from the outside. I don't even think that's legal. The door is a bust, so I go to the window. It's got bars on the outside. I'm effectively trapped.

I sit on the edge of the bed and rub my face with my left hand. My blood runs cold when I notice that my wedding ring is missing. I would blame Kate for stealing it, but I'm certain that she's already gotten paid a pretty penny for lying to Christian and I to separate us.

This is exactly what she wanted.

And we were stupid and desperate enough to fall for it.

I've never been stabbed in the back by a friend. Or at least someone I thought was a friend. I don't understand why Kate would do this to me after everything she did to help me after I was raped. She kept Christian's secret for me—or I thought she did. Now I'm not so sure.

If she told Frank or anyone else that Christian is the Silencer, then I let myself get raped for nothing, and that feels like bitter poison in my mouth.

A single tear falls out of my eye and trails down my face until it falls onto the ugly comforter tucked into the bed.

I suppose falling in love with a serial killer has desensitized me to murder, because all I can think about is how satisfying it would be to get revenge.

I look stupid now for letting her come between my marriage. I was so convinced she only had good intentions, but Christian sniffed out the lie like a shark smells blood in the water.

Last time I didn't listen to him, I got him shot. Now I've gone and gotten myself kidnapped.

I can only imagine how insane Christian is right now. I gave my tracker to Caroline to make sure he'd find her and my mother safe, but in doing so, I severed the only direct tie he has to me.

I know first-hand the kind of carnage he's capable of when I'm threatened. He's proved that time and time again.

The last time I was taken from him, I had only been gone for a few hours and he killed thirteen people and burnt down the Hellfire Lounge. I can only imagine what kind of hell he's putting Meridian City through trying to look for me.

While I'm alone, I start searching the room for anything I can use as a weapon. There might be cameras in here watching me, but it doesn't matter if there are. I'd rather slit my own throat than let Frank or any other man who isn't my husband touch me again.

I find nothing. Not even a goddamn cord I can use as a rope to hang myself with. They've all been cut too short to be of any use.

With that idea out of the question, I begin to look for notepads, a map, business cards—anything that might indicate where I am.

While I'm digging through a dresser, the door opens, and I freeze. The Silencer—the imposter enters the room and shuts the door behind him with uncharacteristic gentleness. The only sound it makes is the soft clicking of the lock.

He takes a few steps towards me, and I sink to the floor in fear, because all I can imagine is that at any second, he's going to lunge for me and rip off my clothes.

"Who are you?"

"Don't be scared," he coos. "I'm going to save you."

"I don't need saving! What do you want with me?"

He paces around the room with his hands in his pockets for a minute. The tap of his feet against the floor is unnerving.

"Nothing, sweetheart. I just want to make your husband sweat. *Relax*," he prompts. "I have a gift for you, to prove that I'm on your side."

He leaves the room for a second, and when the door opens again, my body goes rigid and tight with fear.

Frank Valenti is tied up as he's dragged into the room by his thinning hair and shoved down a few feet from me. I make eye contact with my rapist, and for once, I see fear in his eyes.

He knows that one way or another, this is the end for him, and that feels beautiful.

To my complete shock, the man approaches me and hands me a gun with a single bullet in the chamber, and an empty mag.

It's a message. I can kill the man who shot my husband, or I can kill the man who raped me.

Unfortunately for him, he's forgotten that there's a third option.

I show him his mistake by pointing the gun at my own head, staring up at him with a burning defiance that would make Christian proud.

He holds his hands up in surrender. "Don't be stupid."

"You're the stupid one for handing your captive a gun."

I'm trying to sound brave, but my voice is shaking as badly as my hand is. I don't want to die, I just don't want to be raped again.

Frank is bound by his wrists and ankles, and the imposter takes another set of zip ties and secures Frank to the bed frame.

Then he leaves the room, leaving us alone with a single bullet to decide our fate.

Blinded by fear and rage, I point the gun at his head. This is it. Payback. Revenge. *Justice.*

"I've imagined doing this so many times," I whisper, tears streaming down my face. "I've imagined what I'd say to you *hundreds* of times. Now that you're here and defenseless, the only thing I have to say to you is what I wanted to tell you the first time you raped me. That I will *never* let you have the satisfaction of thinking you broke me."

Frank whimpers, his face screaming out in confusion and fear for what's to come.

"Christian is the only person on this planet that's allowed to break me, because he's the only person on the planet who knows how to put me back together again."

Then I fire a shot.

Into the mattress above his head.

"I'm not a killer, Frank, but I'm going to enjoy watching him kill you."

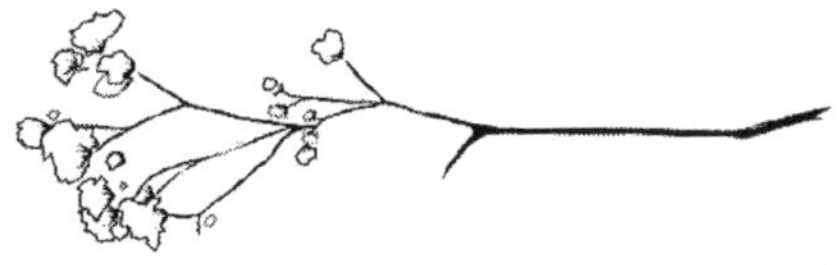

With Frank secured to the bedframe and the masked imposter still absent, I find a few short hours of sleep before the sun comes up. It was restless, and every small noise woke me up, but it was sleep, nonetheless.

In the morning, I find the TV remote hidden under the mattress and flip on the ancient, boxy screen and scroll until I find a local news station.

It brings me a small comfort that I'm still in Meridian City, because I recognize the station. What's on the screen takes my breath away.

Helicopter footage shows the unprecedented carnage Christian has inflicted on the city in the few hours I've been gone. It looks like an active war zone.

Black smoke rises from the streets and skyscrapers in thick plumes. Police cruisers are upside down and smashed in. Looters are running around with crowbars.

Traffic is backed up, circling the entire island. Three of the four bridges leading off the island are disintegrated. He blew them up.

God, I love it when he's unhinged.

As the news coverage plays in the background, I pace around the room in a small circle trying to think of a plan before the imposter comes back.

All I have to defend myself with is a gun with no bullets. I take it and tuck it into the waistband of my leggings.

When I have my back turned to Frank, I hear him yell, and then my vision goes black when I'm hit in the back of the head and tossed to the floor.

I scream and flip over onto my back, kneeing him in the nuts and pushing him off me. My eyes catch on his restraints. He's chewed through the zip-ties on his wrists to get them free, but his legs are still bound together.

I'm able to move freely, but I only have so much space to run around in this tiny room. While he's catching his breath from being hit in the groin, I bang on the door of the room and beg for someone's help.

No one comes.

I pull the gun from my waistband and go to plan Z. When Frank approaches me again, I use it as a bludgeoning tool as best I can.

He's old, but he's still a lot stronger than I am, and once he catches my wrist, it's game over. Blood is streaming down his face from where I got a few hits in, but he's still coming for me.

He grabs me by the throat and slams me into the window hard enough to shatter it with my body.

"Bitch!"

I cry out in pain as glass shards dig into my head and back, but I'm in pure survival mode and grab one of the shards with my bare hands. The shape of it is awkward, and as I hold it, it does more harm to my hands than it does to Frank when I shove it into his gut. He staggers back a little, but his hands don't let up on my throat.

I stab again, not aiming for anywhere in particular, managing to get him in the temple. He loosens his grip on me enough to send us both toppling to the floor.

As I'm catching my breath, I feel Frank grab me before he flips me onto my back and tries to pin me down by my wrists. I'm kicking and screaming and we're both covered in each other's blood, but I fight. I fight with all my strength.

And then there's a gunshot, and things go still. I freeze when Frank's blood drips onto my face from the wound in his forehead. His dead body falls limp on top of me and I push him off, flipping onto my stomach and catching my breath before looking up to find the imposter staring down at me with, dare I say, *concern* in his eyes.

He approaches me slowly, squatting down near me and tenderly grabbing my hand. He observes the cut from the glass.

"You need stitches," he mumbles. "Don't move."

When he stands up and turns his back to me, I stand up too, and with every ounce of strength I have left in my body, I jump onto his back, and like a rabid animal, I start biting and clawing.

I won't stop until I'm free.

Or dead.

CHAPTER 56

THE SILENCER

It's been a full twenty-four hours since Elena was kidnapped, and I'm on the verge of just putting a bullet in my skull because *I can't take it anymore.*

Except I can't do that, because I have Caroline and she needs me.

But Elena needs me too and *I can't fucking find her.* I thought nothing could be worse than watching her get raped and being powerless to stop it, but this? Not knowing where she is or if she's okay?

Fucking torture.

I went out into the city for seventeen hours straight looking for her and found nothing. I would have stayed out longer, but Bethany kept blowing up my phone because Caroline wanted me, and I was stuck choosing between my wife and my daughter.

Thank fuck for Bethany for taking care of Caroline while I've been out searching. She's not talking to me, but that's an issue I'll deal with later. I didn't tell Bethany that Elena's bracelet is a tracker, and Caroline's been using it as a necklace for her stuffed rabbit, and she carries that raggedy stuffed animal everywhere, so I'll know the second Bethany decides to do something stupid like skip town.

Elena and I never talked about what my priorities should be in this situation because I never thought we *would* be in this situation. It has been agony and I don't know how I'm going to make it another minute without knowing where Elena is or if she's okay.

When I find her, I'm going to fucking embed that fucking tracker under her skin so that this never happens again.

I'm outside in the backyard smoking through a pack of cigarettes, trying to think logically about how I'm going to search the entire fucking island by myself.

Elena's going to be mad at me for smoking, because I quit for Caroline, but I'm so close to losing my shit and this is the only thing I can do to try and keep my head straight.

I'm breathing through the beginnings of a panic attack when I feel Caroline tug on the side of my jeans.

"Daddy? Did you find mommy yet?"

Jesus Christ, is this what Elena felt like when I was in the hospital and Caroline would ask when I was going to wake up?

"No baby, but I will. I promise," I say, picking her up and blowing out my smoke to the side. "I'm going to find her."

Caroline wrinkles her nose at the smell of the cigarette smoke as I put it out in the ashtray. "Those are stinky."

"I know, I'm sorry."

Caroline's blue eyes stare into mine for a second, and then she crosses her arms and huffs. "Mommy is the best at hide and seek."

I laugh humorlessly. "Fuck yeah, she is." I suck in a harsh breath and cover my mouth. "Do *not* tell her I said that in front of you."

Caroline furrows her brow at me. "Can I have ice cream for dinner?"

I scoff again, amazed at how well this four-year-old child can manipulate me already.

She got that from me.

I'm so proud.

"Yes, you can have ice cream for dinner," I concede.

Caroline does a zipping motion over her mouth to indicate she will uphold her end of the bargain, and I wistfully laugh and kiss her cheek, hugging her even tighter to my chest.

"Grandpa says I can help him choose his next puzzle. Will you show me where they are?"

I take a deep breath and nod. I take her inside and lead her to the game room on the first floor where I keep a cabinet full of puzzles for Edwin. I wait for her to dig through the boxes. She chooses the one with the most purple pieces. Big shocker there.

I lead her to where Edwin is waiting in the study for her, and Edwin gives me a big grin that tells me he has no idea what the fuck is going on.

I have a meeting with the public information officer at the MCPD to, at the very least, have them put out an announcement that Elena's missing and that I'm offering a seven-figure reward for anyone who brings her to me.

When he arrives, I greet him at the door but insist we talk outside in the driveway. One, because I need a smoke, and two, I don't want Caroline to see him. I feel like if she sees a cop and hears Elena's name, she'll put two and two together, and I don't want her to worry.

I understand now what Elena said to me after I was shot, about how she didn't know how to explain the situation to Caroline. Do all parents find it this difficult to protect their child's innocence?

"Five million," I confirm through a puff of smoke to the officer. Officer Jackson? Jacobs? Johnson? Something with a J. I didn't listen.

"Alright. Is there anything specific you want people to be on the lookout for? We have what she was last seen wearing from the missing person report, but is there anything else? Scars, jewelry, deformities?"

Elena's name and *deformities* do not go in the same sentence, and I think Officer Jerkoff picks up on that from the death glare I give him.

"She would have been wearing her wedding ring; purple diamond the size of the iceberg that sunk the…Titanic…"

My voice trails off as two of my security guards run out the front door and down the driveway, towards the front gate. Confused, I follow them, jogging slowly with the cop until we reach the front gate, where a dozen of my men are walking in a circle with their guns raised in caution.

When they see me, they split apart, allowing me a look at one of my security guards holding a small lump in his arms.

She's covered in blood and dirt. Messy and nearly unrecognizable.

But when our gazes collide, I know it's her.

"*Oh my God*," I mumble.

She scrambles out of the guard's arms so fast he partially drops her, catching her only inches before she hits the ground, which is moot on his part, because I practically tackle her myself.

"Fuck, angel, are you okay?" I pat over her body as she collapses in relief into my arms. "You're freezing. Are you hurt? Is this your blood?"

My questions come out in rapid succession, but she only ever gives me one answer.

"I don't know."

Her voice is quiet, and her gaze is distant.

"Angel, talk to me," I beg, pushing her messy hair out of her face and tucking it behind her ears. I make eye contact with one of my guards and instruct him to tell Bethany what's happening and to keep Caroline occupied while I sneak Elena into the house to clean her up. The last thing I want is for Caroline to see her like this.

I pull my wallet out of my pocket and throw a fat wad of cash at the officer still carefully watching the interaction. "Not a damn word," I warn. I stare him down as his eyes flicker between Elena, my guards, and the money at his feet.

Predictable as always, he takes the cash.

Against my body's protests, I try to pick Elena up to carry her myself.

I can't, and it hurts my fucking pride to ask another man to carry my distraught wife into the safety of our bedroom.

When we're alone behind the locked door, I lead Elena into the bathroom and she slumps against the wall, sitting on the ground with her legs tucked up to her chest.

I take a hand towel, soak it in warm water, and use it to clean the blood from her face while she sits. It almost feels like a more fucked-up version of that night I forced her to take me to her apartment. I wiped blood off her then, too.

When her face is clean, I can see that she's hurt. She has a thin slice across her cheek, bruises in the shape of fingerprints around her neck, and glass stuck in her tangled hair.

"Please tell me Caroline's okay," she pleads, a single tear falling down her cheek.

"Yes," I whisper. "She's fine, I promise."

Elena lets out a long sigh and whispers, "Okay. I'm okay. I'm okay. I'm okay."

She says that, but I don't believe it. Not with the way she's on the verge of dissociating. "Forgive me for not being fucking convinced. You're shutting me out. Don't do that."

"Gavin?" she asks. I sigh as I shake my head and rub the back of my knuckles along her cheekbone. "He died because of me."

"No. No. Hey, look at me. Don't go down that hole. None of this is your fault." Frustrated that she doesn't seem to have any concern for herself in this moment, my patience begins to wear thin. "Elena, *talk to me*."

She says nothing, and I snap. Fuck Kate and fuck Valenti and fuck the Silencer imposter. Fuck everyone on this goddamn planet. I drag Elena up to her feet and pull her into the shower with me, fully clothed, and turn on the water so hot it turns our skin red on first contact. I rip at the dirty fabric covering her until she's naked and then shed my own clothes.

While I wash her body and hair, I kiss her.

Savagely. Ferociously.

"Do you have any idea what I went through?" I ask, my voice a venomous rumble. "You gave your goddamn tracker to Caroline, and I had nothing to tell me where you might be." I roughly squeeze the curve of her ass and she gasps, seeming to finally come alive at the roughness. At the safety only I can bring her using the most unhinged parts of me. I kiss her again, pressing her tightly against the walls of the shower. I wrap my hands around her throat and very gently squeeze.

She hisses and whimpers at the soreness when my hands touch the bruises there. "Who did this? Huh? Who put marks on my angel?"

"Frank."

My blood runs cold at that man's name on her lips, and I pull away to look down at her, the hot water carrying dirt and blood along her body and down the drain.

The fury in my stare could light buildings on fire.

"Is some of this his blood?" I ask.

She nods. "He tried to kill me. Your shadow killed him first."

"Shame. I wish I could have killed him myself," I whisper against her lips, hiking her leg over my hip and trailing my fingers into the space between her legs. My eyes flicker to hers, half-lidded and hazy. "Did he touch you, Elena?"

She shakes her head, and to prove it, she tangles her fingers in my wet hair and grabs my dick, causing me to groan into her mouth.

"Then what is it you're not telling me?"

Instead of saying a word, she pulls back to look at me and then slowly sinks to her knees. Without hesitation, she takes me into her mouth as deep as she can manage. I lay my hands flat against the stone walls as she sucks me off.

"Stop trying to distract me," I grunt as her lips leave my cock with a lewd '*pop*'.

"He took my wedding ring," she whispers, water from the showerhead falling into her face, gathering on her eyelashes, and irritating the delicate whites of her eyes.

"Fuck the ring. I'll get you one twice as big." I groan as she puts her mouth on me again. "God, you look so pretty on your knees," I praise, before grabbing her jaw and forcing myself down her throat faster, causing her to gag and choke. Then I do it again.

And again and again until spit leaks out of the sides of her mouth and sloppily lands on her chest.

"Get on the fucking floor," I growl. When she isn't bent over in three milliseconds, I grab her by her hair and roughly push her over until her ass is in the air and her pretty pussy is on display for me.

The smooth floor digs into our knees as I lick her from behind. *Fuck*, she tastes perfect. So sweet and feminine. She moans loudly, the sweet sounds echoing off the walls. I suck on her clit, hard. Probably so hard it's not even pleasurable, but this isn't about pleasure. It's about control. It's about safety.

I lick one long stripe from her clit to her pussy to her virgin hole between her ass. All the way up her back until I reach her throat and then I bite her hard enough to leave a mark.

I take my angry cock in my fist and stroke it twice, and then line the head up with her cunt.

Her entire body freezes and she abruptly flips over and shakes her head. "Not that way. Any position but that one. Please."

I grit my teeth and kiss her again, my tongue messily exploring her delicate mouth. "I won't be gentle," I warn, and in response, she tugs so hard on my hair it makes my eyes water. I groan, which turns into a lustful growl. "I'm going to fuck you so hard you won't be able to think about anything other than *me*. I want to feel you cum around my cock, and I want to put a baby in that soft belly of yours and then fuck you some more."

I line myself up with her again, sinking into her tight pussy and fucking her ruthlessly with no regard for her pain. She screams beautiful expletives of pleasure, dragging her nails down my back so hard that she draws blood.

I don't even care that blood is dripping from my gunshot wound onto her stomach. I don't care that it hurts. I don't care that I've earned myself another trip to the hospital.

If fucking my love back into her is the last thing I ever do, it will be a satisfying death.

That's how every man wants to go.

In between the legs of his lover.

My world explodes into pleasure as a lightning rod strikes the base of my spine, causing me to lose my rhythm at the exact moment her pussy flutters around my cock, and I coat her insides with everything I have to offer. I fuck her until my cock goes completely soft and even still, I stay inside her, breathing deep against her neck as the hot water rains over us.

I kiss down her body all the way to her glistening, swollen, fucked-out pussy and place soft kisses to her sensitive clit. I growl in satisfaction at her tiny mewls as I deliver little kitten licks to that delicate nub.

I flick my tongue against her clit and lick her in slow, deliberate circles. I alternate between fast and slow strokes, keeping my eyes glued to her angelic face. I want to watch her when she comes apart on my tongue this time.

Her cheeks are flushed, and her eyes are hazy and fucked out, like I've sent her to heaven.

It's where she belongs, after all.

CHAPTER 57

THE SILENCER

Elena still seems…off. Something is bothering her, and it's taking everything in me not to reach down her throat and just pull out whatever she's not telling me.

Did they touch her? Are there injuries I haven't seen? Did they threaten her family?

My mind goes through every possible scenario, none of them good.

Elena is still bleeding from her hand, and with her hair still dripping wet, she leaves our bedroom to say goodnight to Caroline.

Elliot is lingering in the hallway, his skin gray, looking like he's one heartbeat away from passing out. He's wearing a jacket zipped up all the way to his neck, making him look stiff and awkward.

Nice of him to show up. I haven't seen him since the morning before Elena was taken. Beth said he had a work emergency.

But what could be more important than your daughter going missing?

"Let me see," he whispers, grabbing Elena's bleeding hand. She seems shocked by the action, stumbling when he grabs her. He blinks rapidly a few times before squeezing his eyes shut and shaking his head as if trying to shrug off an intrusive thought. "Doesn't look like there's any glass fragments. Come on, I'll stitch you up."

"How do you know it was glass?"

Elena's question has Elliot's eyes flickering to me and then back down to her hand. He chuckles, cutting himself off with a wince that sounds painful. "Sweetheart, I've been a surgeon longer than you've been alive. I know what a laceration from glass looks like." He throws his arm around her shoulders and leads her to his guest bedroom. He sits Elena down at the small desk against the far wall, and I grab a chair and sit next to her, placing my hand gently on her thigh in a gesture of comfort.

From his backpack, Elliot pulls out an entire hospital supply closet's worth of medical supplies. Gauze, sutures, needles, vials of local anesthetic. Weird shit to keep in a backpack.

Maybe it's a surgeon thing. We're the type of men that like to be prepared. He has Band-Aids, I have bullets.

He begins to delicately clean Elena's wound, and I watch. Maybe I'll learn a thing or two. Most of the time, if I'm hurt, I stitch myself up. It'd be nice to have a scar in a straight fucking line for once.

Midway down the line of stitches, Elliot's hands begin to tremble, and he starts to blink rapidly again, shaking his head every few seconds.

The second half of Elena's stitches are slightly crooked.

"Elliot," I warn. He looks up at me, disdain clearly on his face. I tilt my chin down in a subtle nod. He has to tell her.

But he shakes his head. "Not now."

"Yes, *now*."

Elena's gaze flickers between us, her eyes finally settling on her father. "Dad?"

He gives me another death glare and purses his lips before beginning to wrap her hand in gauze. His shoulders slump as he takes a deep breath. "All those years of smoking finally caught up to me." Elena stiffens in her seat as he finishes his sentence. "Stage four metastatic lung cancer. It's spread to my liver and brain. I have a tumor pressing against my optic nerve and I will lose vision in my left eye completely within a month."

Elena's mouth hangs open in shock. "What?"

"I started having blurring vision and tremors when I was in the OR. Weakness. Fatigue. Hallucinations. Bloody mucus when I cough. Beth took me to the doctor, and I lit up like a Christmas tree."

I close my eyes and let out a deep breath. Not exactly how I would have told my own daughter that I'm dying. You'd think as a doctor he'd know better.

Instead of questioning him further though, she roughly pulls her hand out of his and faces me. *Fuck*. Her eyes are already red and glassy, and full of accusation. "How long have you known?"

"Angel—"

"*How long*?"

I open my mouth, trying to buy more time to try and soften the blow, but that would only upset her more. I sigh. "Beth told me three days before I was shot. We were all going to tell you after the bar exam but…"

"*Months*? You've known for *months*?" She turns to her father. "And you? You've been ignoring me since *December*. You didn't think once to answer one of the thousands of messages I've left you to tell me you were dying?"

She stands up abruptly and I reach for her. "Elena—"

"Don't touch me!" she shouts as she looks between us both before scoffing. "I've never felt so unloved and betrayed by the two men who claim to love me most."

As she stomps out of the room, Elliot tosses the dirty medical supplies in the trash can at his feet before reaching into his pocket and, ironically, pulling out a cigarette. I smack it out of his hand before he has a chance to light it.

"What the fuck was that?" I growl. "On what planet is *that* how you tell your daughter that you're dying?"

"I don't need shit from you, Reeves," he grumbles, packing up the spare supplies. "My family is none of your business."

"I *am* your family!" I shout, my teeth clenched so tight it hurts. "Whether you like it or not, Bethany, Travis, Elena, you, me, Caroline…we are family and I'm sick of your past lingering over us like a fucking storm cloud all the damn time. The only crime I've committed is being born a Reeves, and yet I'm living a life fucking sentence having to be tied to the man who stole my entire life from me. The least you could do is not make us all so goddamn miserable."

Elliot begins cackling like a goddamn maniac, clutching his stomach and using the desk to hold himself steady on his feet. He's looking frail again. Sweaty. Labored breaths. Wheezing coughs.

He looks worse than Edwin, and Edwin's got thirty years on him.

He stops laughing abruptly when he sees the unamused scowl I'm giving him. "Oh, you were serious." He clears his throat. "You really think you've done nothing wrong." He scoffs. "What I wouldn't give to go back in time to that Wednesday night." He sighs wistfully as his eyes focus on my torso. "I'm not a good shot anymore. Not like I was when I killed your parents."

"Hey Elliot?" His head cocks to the side right as my fist connects with his jaw. "Go to hell."

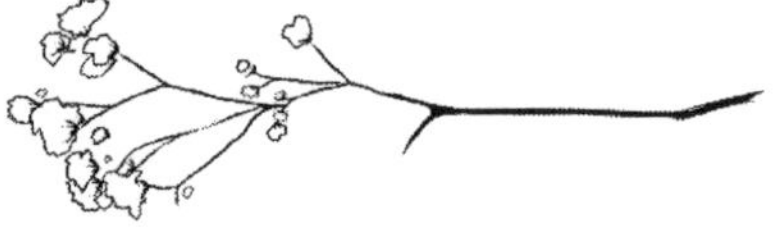

I quietly open the door to our bedroom. Elena is sitting in the center of our bed, looking particularly small with her knees tucked into her chest in the middle of the California king.

She's crying. Not sobbing, not wailing, but her face is painted in the kind of sorrow that only appears when someone's had enough. When she's been hurting and suffering so long that she's no longer living—just surviving.

"Do you know when he was diagnosed?" she asks quietly.

"Your mom said it was the middle of September."

Her face twists painfully and her head falls to her knees. She sniffles and rocks gently back and forth.

"The night of our first date…he called me. He said…he said he wasn't going to live forever, and he sounded so sad when he said it. I was so excited for our date that I blew it off. All this time…"

I tuck a strand of hair gently behind her ear.

"He doesn't want to fight it, does he?"

I sigh. "It's too late for that, angel." She closes her eyes and throws her head back, as if trying to drain the tears gathered in her eyes back into her skull.

"Mommy?"

Elena and I both look towards the edge of the bed where Caroline has managed to sneak up on us. I beckon her to climb onto the bed. "Come here, baby."

Caroline crawls up the bed with one arm, the other holding Mr. Bunny. She crawls and sits at Elena's side.

"What are you doing out of bed, sweet girl?" Elena asks.

"I missed you," Caroline answers easily, snugging into Elena's side. "I have something for you." She holds up Mr. Bunny to show Elena's bracelet is wrapped around the toy's neck like a necklace. She takes it off the rabbit and places it around Elena's wrist. "I kept it safe for you."

Elena kisses the top of Caroline's head. "Thank you. Now it's bedtime. Let's go to sleep, and we'll have pancakes in the morning. How does that sound?"

"Can I sleep here tonight? *Please*?" she drawls out, rubbing her sleepy eyes with her fist. Elena wordlessly nods and we help Caroline under the covers. Elena wraps her arms around our daughter protectively, almost like she's afraid someone will pluck her right out of this bed.

Caroline looks up at me with sleepy blue eyes, silently waiting for me to join their cuddling session. I tug off my hoodie so I'm left in my t-shirt and sweatpants, and crawl into the bed so that Caroline is in between Elena and I. I use my long arms to pull them both closer to me.

In the milky moonlight coming in from the windows, the scars on my wrist seem to glow. The pinkish skin there has a soft sheen that reflects the light, and Caroline traces her small fingers along the rough ridges. New scars and old.

"What happened to your arms, daddy?"

For some reason, the corner of my mouth tugs up into a small smile. I've never had to explain the scars on my wrist. The few people I've let see them didn't need an explanation, and I never thought I'd have kids, so I haven't quite figured out an age-appropriate answer to tell her. I always have long sleeves on around her. This is, quite literally, the first time she's seen my arms.

I can tell by the tension in Elena's body that she's curious what my answer will be.

"When I was a kid, something really bad happened to me. I was really angry and sad. Those feelings like to fight a lot." I stretch out my arm and use my fingers to trace along the scars. "All of these remind me of when I was in the middle of the battle and didn't know how to stop them."

"What stopped them from fighting?" Caroline asks through a yawn.

"Love did, Caro," I whisper, kissing the crown of her head. "Love did."

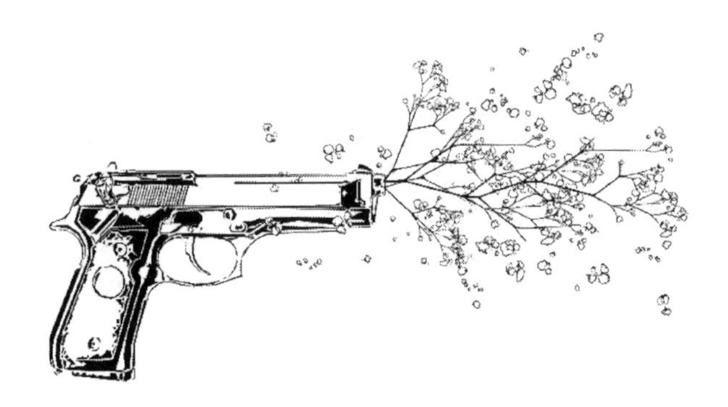

CHAPTER 58

THE ANGEL

Panic.

Ice cold panic.

That's all I feel. It grips me with its frigid fingers and won't let me go.

I can still taste his blood in my mouth. Can still feel his skin under my fingernails.

Can still see the way he looked at me when I shoved a shard of glass into his chest.

It's the middle of the night. I can't sleep. I can't even close my eyes without seeing the terrifying reality of what I've done.

"Christian?" I whisper against Caroline's hair. I know he's awake. He's always awake when he's worrying about me.

"Yeah, angel?" he whispers back, and I can't bring myself to say anything else. The air goes quiet and stale. Anxiety creeps up my spine. It feels like spiders with their long legs dancing across my skin.

"Tell me about the first person you killed."

The resonating silence that follows feels heavy. I've never asked Christian to relive his kills. I've always been curious, but a part of me always accepted the fact that the less I knew about that part of his life, the better. The less complicit I would feel.

Because that's what I am. The complicit, docile wife of a serial killer.

Christian lightly pokes Caroline in the cheek to check that she's still asleep, and then lets his head fall back against the pillows.

"His name was Peter Sims. Drug dealer. I was out looking for noses to break and came across a man holding another man and a young kid at gunpoint. I don't know—the trauma just hit me, and I snapped. I broke his neck before he even realized I was there." Christian takes a deep breath. "I buried him near the shoreline. Body washed up a week later and the police identified him."

I don't know why I expected his first kill to be ceremonious or meaningful in some way. "Did you ever feel bad?"

"No," he answers immediately. "I've never regretted any of my kills. I've never lost sleep over them. The only time I ever felt anything was when cops would stumble across a body. I was always afraid they'd somehow tie it to me, but eventually, I stopped caring about that too. Now it's not even an afterthought."

I wish I could be nonchalant about it like he is.

"I killed the Silencer."

Christian scoffs. "We're already married. You don't have to flirt with me."

The silence that follows his joke is nearly tangible.

Christian sits up slightly, his face twisting into an unknown emotion when he looks at me, to find tears on my cheeks and a terrified look in my eyes. With careful precision, he gets out of the bed and comes to my side, helping me to my feet and then quietly walking us to the bathroom and locking the door behind us.

He turns to face me, his body relaxed, but the look on his face is a mixture of concern, disbelief, and maybe even a bit of pride.

"Tell me *exactly* what happened." Even though I trust him, I find it hard to admit it out loud. He takes a step towards me and tries to reach out a comforting hand. "Elena—"

"He didn't give me a choice!" I take a big step backwards as the dam breaks and the tears fall harder. "Frank was there and tried to kill me and I was scared and had all this adrenaline in me and I just…" My hands grip the sides of my hair and begin to tug as the distress sinks into my bones. "I killed him. I killed him. *I killed him.*"

"Angel…" Christian croaks as he wraps his arms around me, right as my legs collapse and I fall to the floor in shame and panic. Christian cradles my face in one of his large hands as we settle on the ground. "Baby, I would *never* judge you for doing what you needed to do to survive." He kisses me softly, and the salt from my tears mixes with his taste. "Tell me what happened."

I jump onto the back of the imposter and do the first thing I can think of. I bite him. I bite him in the curve of his neck so hard

I feel the skin rip unnaturally when he throws me off him and I land on my back on the floor with a hard thud.

He lunges for me, anger in his eyes, and I begin clawing at him. It's not to hurt him, or even to try and stop him. It's so that when the police find my body, his skin will be under my nails.

My body hurts, my throat burns when I scream in frustration, and my limbs feel heavy with exhaustion. Not even the adrenaline is fighting it anymore.

If I don't escape now, I'm going to share this tomb with Frank Valenti, and I'll be damned if he's who I arrive in Hell with.

I'm kicking and fighting against my captor so hard that I wrestle him to the floor. He lands on his back. I land on top.

The only thing I can think to do is pull the small drawer completely off the track of the dresser and hit him with it. I get one good hit in before he grabs it from me and tosses it away. It lands on Frank's dead body.

"Stop!" he shouts, and even though he's wearing a mask, I can tell he's gritting his teeth. "I'm trying to protect you!"

"Protect me? You shot my husband and then kidnapped me! You're a fucking psychopath!"

"I need to save you from him!" he shouts, catching my wrists and flipping us over so that I'm flat against the floor.

"I don't want to be saved!"

That makes the man pause. Sweat from his salt-and-pepper hairline drips onto my face as we both try to catch our breath.

"It's not a choice I'm leaving up to you anymore," he replies. It's cryptic as hell, but the enraged sneer on my face doesn't falter. My body is tired, my adrenaline gone.

In the brief millisecond between the end of his sentence and his next breath, I rip my wrist free from his grip, grab a shard of glass, and I stab him in the gut. Five times.

He slumps over with agony. I scramble to my feet, my legs shaky with exhaustion.

I don't know why, but before I leave the room, I pause and turn back to face him. He's clutching his stomach, his breaths shallow from the pain.

"Ellie, I'm going to save you even if it's the last thing I ever get to do. I promise."

And then he goes limp.

And it hits me that I lied to Frank, because I am *a killer.*

Christian stares at me with an unknown emotion in silence as I stare at the ground, entranced by the soft blue cotton of my socks.

"Do you remember where he kept you?" he asks.

I shrug. "I don't know the address, but I could show you on a map. I remember the cross streets."

Christian nods and hands me his phone. I scroll through the bird's eye view of Meridian City and zoom in on the area. I hand the phone back, and Christian commits it to memory before putting it away. He takes a deep breath.

"I need to go take care of the bodies."

"Why?" I ask. He's never been the type to clean up his messes.

"Because I reported you missing to the police, Elena. One cop even saw you when you got here. If they find two dead bodies covered in your blood, they're going to start asking questions that you can't answer."

"It was self-defense."

"Yes, but you didn't go to the police after you escaped. You came here. That already makes you look suspicious, and I'll be damned if I let them start pointing fingers in your direction." He tugs me close to his chest and kisses my forehead. "It's over. Frank is dead. This man that's been tormenting us is dead. Let me deal with the messy part so we can move on."

I begin to cry, not because I'm sad, but because I'm overwhelmed. I don't know how I'm going to deal with the reality of murdering someone, even in self-defense. I can't talk to anyone but Christian, but unlike the last time I was recovering from trauma, I don't think he can help me.

Christian doesn't feel guilt. Not when it comes to murder. It's as mindless as brushing his teeth.

I don't want to be a killer.

But I've been one from the moment I met Christian.

When he killed those three men in the alley and I didn't report it out of fear, I became just as much of a killer as he is.

Finally, I concede. Christian leaves me alone in our room, and I stay standing in the same spot for over an hour. I glance at the digital clock on the nightstand. It's past five AM. The sun will be up soon.

The only thing I want right now is my mom.

I find her in her guest room, alone, sipping coffee and sitting up in bed. When she meets my gaze, she sets down the mug.

Her gentle thumb traces across the cut on my cheek. I flinch away from her touch slightly, and I can see the exact moment her heart breaks from the reaction.

"You didn't tell me dad was dying."

"You didn't tell me you married a serial killer."

My head snaps to her and I stare at her with wide eyes. My mom lets out a sad laugh and shrugs. "We keep secrets to protect the people we love."

I look away with a guilty stiffness in my posture. "How did you find out?"

"He came looking for you and found Caroline under the cabinets. She wouldn't come to him until she saw his face."

"You don't seem bothered," I point out quietly.

"Christian and your father are so alike that it's scary sometimes."

I scoff. "Are you trying to say dad's a serial killer?"

She shakes her head. "No. But all the things he's done in his life have led him—led *you*—to this point. You know I believe everything happens for a reason. I think we're all exactly where we belong, even if it doesn't seem like it right now."

I rest my head on her shoulder, and we're quiet for a few minutes. My mom begins running her fingers through my hair and lightly scraping my scalp.

"Are you okay, Ellie?"

"I don't know how to feel okay anymore," I whimper.

"It's okay to not be okay, Elena."

"It's easier to pretend I am, though."

"Easier for everyone but you."

Her voice is soft like a concerned mother's should be. It's both a blessing and a curse that she's so good at reading people. I've never been able to hide anything from her.

I've never had to. Not until I met Christian.

"I think that's the harsh reality of being a woman," my mother continues, "we're always so focused on everyone else, that we forget we need to take care of ourselves, too."

I take a deep breath, soaking in the truth of her words. The sun has come up, and the pretty yellow sunrise trickles past the curtains, casting the room in a warm glow.

I haven't gotten much sleep in the past two days, and as a result, I've got a massive headache.

"Do you have any aspirin in here?" I ask.

My mother nods towards the bathroom. "In my makeup bag on the counter." She throws the covers off her and stands. "I'll go get you some water."

"Oh, I promised Caroline we'd have pancakes for breakfast. If you see Paolo, will you pass on the message?"

My mother's face lights up and she wiggles her eyebrows at me. "I'll pass on more than just your message to the cute Italian in the kitchen."

That brings a soft smile to my face as I quietly giggle. “Mom!”

She giggles back. “Kidding. Kidding.”

I take a moment to close my eyes and relax in the quiet loneliness before I stand to find the aspirin. I walk to the bathroom, rubbing the exhaustion out of my eyes. I collect the aspirin and then leave my mom’s room to check on Caroline. She’s still fast asleep, clutching her bunny to her chest. The burgundy comforter is twisted around her, so I fix it and kiss her forehead. She looks so small on our massive bed.

Sometimes I feel guilty about playing the system to adopt her, but there’s no denying that even with how dedicated Christian is to the orphanage, that we can give her more. More love. More opportunity. More happiness.

I hope life never steals the way she sees good in everyone.

My mother should have made it back here with some water by now, but I assume she’s flirting with Paolo, so I’ll just drink from the bathroom faucet instead.

I blindly slap around the wall for the light switch in the bathroom. The room lights up, and my stomach turns at the sight before me.

On the mirror, written in blood are the words *I PROMISE.*

CHAPTER 59

THE EXECUTIONER

I've had time to consider that maybe I'm going about this wrong. I'm a man with many regrets, and I've always let my failures eat me alive. It's in my nature.

My biggest regret is failing to end this before it began.

All the pain and suffering I could have saved her from. All the abuse and the fear I could have spared her.

Christian Reeves has everyone fooled. Elena especially. He's got his claws so deep in her that she will never be able to escape him. He's broken her apart and haphazardly glued her back together to the point that she's unrecognizable. To the point that the pain is so normal she doesn't even realize she's hurting.

But I can still save her. I can. I will.

I promised.

Even if it costs me everything, I can't let the ghosts of my past do any more damage to her future.

Christian Reeves is not afraid of many things, but he is afraid of losing Elena. It's one of the things we have in common and his only weakness I can exploit.

I loved her first, and while he would do anything to keep her in a gilded cage, I'd do anything to release her from it.

He's delusional. He's twisted the meanings of love and obsession, justifying to himself that they're interchangeable, and they're not. I suppose that's a genetic predisposition he inherited from his father.

Thomas couldn't tell the difference either—and he paid the price for it.

As I stalk through the halls of this mansion, finality settles in my bones. This is it. The grand finale.

I turn a corner and watch the radiant woman before me dance around the kitchen, a mixing bowl on her hip and a whisk in her hand as she hums to herself.

She always did love cooking.

I stifle a pained grunt and clutch my stomach. I'm still bleeding. The jagged edges of my skin where the glass ripped it apart rubs uncomfortably against my thick shirt.

With her back turned, I silently step into the room. It's been nearly three decades since I've had a need to be so stealthy.

I know I've lost my touch when Bethany turns with a gasp and drops the mixing bowl, the beige batter spilling all over the floor and her ankles.

Her face has gone ghost white. She's scared.

She tries to run, but I grab her and cover her mouth, holding her still and shushing her until she calms down enough for me to explain.

"It's okay. It's okay," I coo. "I'm not going to hurt you." My voice sounds wrong coming out of the mask, but I have no choice but to wear it. If I want things to be normal after this is done, I have to pretend this is who I am. Just for a little longer.

It will all be over soon.

I lean down to whisper in her ear. "Where is Christian Reeves?"

"I…I…I don't know. Please."

"Do better."

"Please…whatever you want, we will give it to you. There's a child in this house. You don't have to hurt anyone else."

"Where is Christian Reeves?" I demand again, carefully annunciating each word.

He wasn't in his bedroom. Or Caroline's room. Or in the backyard or in any of the other rooms I've checked.

Sweet Bethany, she's terrified, but if I know one thing about her, it's that she isn't a liar, and while she's a fierce protector of her family, she knows as well as I do that Christian can take care of himself. She doesn't need to protect him. If she says she doesn't know where he is, then she doesn't know.

"What do you want with him?" Bethany asks, still shaking in my arms.

"It wouldn't matter if I told you, because you're under his spell. Just like Elena. Just like this entire fucking city." My molars grind roughly against the force of my jaw as anger boils in my blood. "The Reeves legacy is good for only one thing Beth, it's murder. If I don't save her now, he's going to kill Elena. He's going to kill our baby."

I didn't think it was possible for any more color to drain from her face, but it does, and I've realized my mistake when she flinches in my arms.

She begins to sob, shaking and scared and defeated. I let her go, just enough to turn her around and cup her cheeks.

"I *have to* do this," I tell her, and her face softens for a moment.

"No you don't. Please…let's just talk about this. Let's just talk. No one else has to get hurt."

"He's the Silencer, Beth."

She whimpers. "I know, but—"

My brain short circuits. My muscles tighten. My vision goes black around the edges. I don't control my limbs as I grab her neck and squeeze. She starts fighting, trying to scream, but I knock her skull against the wall until she falls limp and slumps to the ground. I set her down gently.

Then she grabs the mixing bowl and hits me with it. I pull it out of her hands and throw it across the room as she starts screaming bloody murder. The only thing I can do to get her to stop is wrap my hands around her throat again.

With her lungs already out of breath from screaming, her face quickly turns red, and then purple. She slaps me with weak arms.

"You knew!" I growl, the fury making me squeeze harder as tears prick in my eyes. "And you chose his side instead of mine. Why would you betray me like that, Beth?" When she doesn't answer, I crack her skull against the floor. "*Why?!*"

"Please…" she begs, her eyes rolling from disorientation as thick tears fall from the corners and into her hairline.

I soften my face and shush her, like a parent would soothe a child. "It's okay. It's okay. I'm only doing this to save her."

"El…El…" She croaks, choking out the first syllable of my name with the last of her oxygen.

As my fingers dig into her delicate throat, I find myself getting choked up, but I can't find it in me to stop. "I have to save her, Beth, I have to. You just…you got in the way. But I promise, baby, we'll all be together soon."

CHAPTER 60

THE SILENCER

I've got to act quickly. The motel Elena was taken to is on the other side of the island, and the sun is coming up, which means there will be a lot of foot traffic, and dumping a body when anyone could turn a corner at any second isn't exactly ideal, mask or no mask.

On top of that, I have an entire cleaning crew scrubbing out the blood from my floors. After I take care of the bodies, I'm going to my presidential suite at The Black Palace, where Elena, Caroline, Bethany, Elliot, Edwin and I will stay until my house is spotless again.

I huff to myself. Damn, that's a mouthful. This time last year, it was just me and Edwin. I never thought I would be able to say this, but I'm so fucking glad I didn't kill myself the night I met Elena. Sometimes when I think about how close I had been, I get phantom guilt, because I worry about what her life would be like if I died like I intended to.

I wonder if she thinks about that night as much as I do.

As I'm fastening my mask to my face, I see fast movement on one of my monitors. I don't normally have the internal cameras on in the mansion, mostly because I've never had a need to. Perimeter security and external cameras were more than enough.

But since Elena was kidnapped, I can't be too careful. There aren't many. Just a handful in the common areas. The foyer, the dining room, the study, the kitchen.

That's where the movement is coming from. The kitchen. The movement flashes out of frame, so I use the mouse to select the circuit with the kitchen cameras and scroll until I see what's going on.

"Fuck!"

I race upstairs, full Silencer gear, and sprint to the kitchen. I tackle the motherfucker just as he's getting to his feet, looking down at Bethany's still body.

The plummet to the ground is brutal on my torso, and I instantly feel the warm, sticky blood seeping from my gunshot. I reel my fist back and nail this imposter in the face, holding him up by his shirt.

He goes limp, and I crawl to Bethany.

Shit, shit, shit. Please, please, please be alive.

I take off my glove and put two fingers at her neck and wait for a pulse. A pulse that never comes. My first thought isn't sadness. It isn't guilt. It isn't even anger.

It's fear, because what the hell am I going to tell Elena?

I hear movement behind me and turn just in time to feel a bullet graze my right arm. I fall to my left side and groan.

And then the fucker shoots me again, this time in the leg. And then again in the other leg. And then again and again and again into my chest. Thank fuck for my body armor.

The man twitches unnervingly, like he's shocked I'm still alive. And then he does what all other people have always failed to do—he points the gun at my head.

I let out a heavy breath. My chest feels like it's on fire. My vision is going black from the pain. I can hardly breathe.

Is this really how I'm going to die? Killed by my own shadow, in my own home.

Oh, the fucking irony.

Well if this is how I'm dying, I'm not going down without a fight. My fingers twitch towards one of the guns strapped to my legs, but soft, delicate hands beat me to it.

I wish I could say I'm proud of Elena for being so strong, but I'm not, because she's put herself between me and a loaded gun, and I'm in no position to do anything about it.

"Take it off," she demands, nearly shouting at the top of her lungs as she points the gun at him. "The mask, take it off!"

"Move," the man demands, "Let me finish this, Elena."

There's sweat dripping down his temples, and blood is seeping out through his shirt and dripping onto the floor. His hands are shaking. I can see it in his posture that he's not going to shoot Elena.

But she will happily shoot him, and after glancing down at her mother's body, that's exactly what she does. She shoots him in the same spot he shot me. He falls flat on his back on the floor, and when he does, the cheap locking mechanism of his mask breaks, and it pops off his face before landing with a plastic clatter on the floor.

Elena gasps and her arm falls to her side. "*Dad?*"

She collapses to her knees and completely drops the gun, crawling over to Elliot. Her hands shake as she feels over his torso where she shot him.

"Dad…I—wait. Dad, no, I'm so sorry." Her sharp cries begin to fill the stale air and I manage to sit up, propping my back against the kitchen island.

Elliot reaches up a hand to stroke Elena's cheek, and I watch as thick tears stream down her face that cover her cheeks in a million different conflicting emotions. Guilt, fear, confusion, anger, disbelief, regret.

He begins to sob, too. "Do you remember the first thing you said to me when I came to the hospital after you were raped?"

Blinking away the tears in her eyes, she shakes her head.

He gives her a sad smile. "You asked me to chase away the monsters under your bed. But the monster was never under your bed, was it? It was in your heart."

She shakes her head again, this time from denial. "Dad, you tried to kill him. *You killed mom.*"

She keeps calling him dad, but the man lying there isn't her father. It isn't Elliot Young. They may look the same. They may sound the same.

But her father died the moment I pointed that gun at him on Thanksgiving.

"I just wanted to save you."

Elena shudders as she violently sobs. "I never asked you to save me." She turns to look at me, pleading for me to help her.

I'd do anything for her. But not this. He killed his wife and four innocent people. All for what? To send a message that he doesn't like me?

She looks down at her father again, and his eyes plead for mercy that he doesn't deserve. She knows it. I know it. He knows it, too.

Something off-putting crawls through my veins. I don't like this situation.

I see a tiny shred of humanity in his eyes when she helps him sit up next to me against the island. Both of us breathe shakily through the pain. Elena once again begs with her eyes for help.

"Christian, I don't know what to do."

"Sweetheart," Elliot says as he presses her head to his chest. "Don't you worry about me. I'll be fine."

"I shot you!"

He laughs dejectedly. "Yeah, you're still a good shot after all these years." He strokes her hair. "I'm proud of you, baby, you know that? So proud."

She whimpers and hugs him with the same fervor she hugged him with in the hospital. Filled with love and sorrow and hope. Filled with forgiveness.

Not that he deserves it.

Elliot pulls away from her, holding her cheeks in his hands and giving her a sad smile. "I'm so sorry," he whispers. "I didn't realize until this very moment that killing him won't save you." The gulps. "The only way I can save you is by letting you go."

He presses his forehead to hers as she cries, and then softly kisses her cheek before turning his head to look me straight in the eyes.

"How's this for misery?"

He reaches for the gun Elena dropped, and before I have a chance to comprehend what he's doing, he places it at her temple.

And he pulls the trigger.

My entire world goes red. My body goes numb with rage. I've gone deaf. My only working sense is sight, and I watch in horror, unable to move as Elliot lets Elena go, and her lifeless body slumps directly into my lap.

I see her dead eyes staring straight up at the ceiling, and I snap.

Without thinking, without caring, without feeling, I lunge for Elliot, grab him by the throat, and land my first punch. Then the second. Then the third.

I stop counting after I hit twenty, and I use all that uninhibited feral rage coursing through my veins to land punch after punch after brutal punch directly into his face. Elliot doesn't bother fighting back. All he does is sit there and take it.

And I kill him.

I kill him with my bare fists. Beat him until his skull is deformed into useless shattered bits of bone, and until his soft tissue and blood squelches under my hands, splattering back into my face with every reel back of my fist.

I beat him until he's simply an unrecognizable limp mound of blood and tissue under my fist.

I let out a heavy sigh followed by a loud, unhinged, blood-curdling scream. I catch my breath, and then crawl back to Elena's body, sitting in a pool of her blood. I pull her body into my lap and kiss her forehead, and then I reach for my gun.

"Daddy?"

My world freezes as I peek over my shoulder to see Caroline standing in the doorway of the kitchen. Her rabbit is in the crook of her elbow as she stares at me with her index finger in her mouth.

"Mommy said there would be pancakes."

My entire chest feels like it's being stabbed over and over again. With every beat of my heart, it only prolongs the pain.

I look back down at Elena before glancing back over my shoulder.

"Okay, baby. Just…turn around and count to one hundred, and I'll get you some pancakes, okay?"

"But daddy, I don't know how to count to one hundred."

"That's okay, babygirl, just turn around and count as high as you can."

I've been hanging on by a thread named Elena, and now she's gone.

I hold my angel to my chest and wait for Caroline to reach ten before I put the gun to my head.

And like I was always meant to, I pull the trigger.

EPILOGUE

THE FATHER

Thunder rumbles in the distance, and cold rain pours down over the quiet cemetery. The wet dirt turns the freshly covered grave into a pile of mud.

A new granite headstone sits on the soft ground, decorated with flowers.

Behind me, I can hear the click of cameras as the media surrounds the grave, trying to sneak photos of my grief for the morning paper. I use a handkerchief monogrammed *CTR* to wipe the tears from my face. I stare at the grave, my heart aching as memories flash across my mind like a movie, drawing more sorrow from my soul.

Christian Thomas Reeves

February 20, 1983-May 8, 2020

Son. Husband. Father.

It was the only appropriate message I could think of to put on the headstone. It's how I want him to be remembered.

Even with Christian's lacking sense of self-preservation, I never imagined there was a possibility that I would outlive him. I always wanted Christian to die old and warm in his bed.

I feel responsible for the carnage and pain Elena experienced, caught between a man who only knew how to love violently, and a father who couldn't let go of the past, driven to madness with his own grief.

Behind me, footsteps approach. My neck aches as I look up at the man next to me. Elena's brother, Travis, stares down at his sister's grave, next to Christian's. I hear him suck in a sharp breath as his umbrella shields him from the relentless rain.

I don't want an umbrella. I want to feel the ache in my bones from the cold tears of a million angels weeping for me.

The rosary in my hand shakes as I pray for Elena and Bethany. I pray that Christian and Elliot find peace in the afterlife. I pray to God to have mercy on all of them.

Most of all, I pray for myself. For forgiveness.

Because none of this would have happened if I had been a better father to Christian.

Travis wraps a hand around my shoulder and lightly squeezes. He doesn't know that I remember every painful detail. No one does. Not even Christian, because Elena was loyal and never told him that I knew what he was. Another debt I owe to her that I'll never get to pay.

I blink rapidly, my eyes puffy and red. I've not yet accepted this reality. I hope when I wake up tomorrow, this will all just be a terrible dream.

Next to me, a pair of sparkly, bright purple rain boots stand in the mud next to my wheelchair. Caroline's tiny hand holds mine as she looks between me and the headstones.

After a long while, she crawls into my lap, her blonde hair gone sandy brown from the rain. She looks up at me with big blue eyes.

"Grandpa, when are mommy and daddy coming back?"

With a shaky breath, I hold the handkerchief to my face, hug her to my chest, and weep with the angels.

A NOTE FROM THE AUTHOR

In the process of writing the second manuscript of this book, my father committed suicide. This book is a direct reflection of the darkest part of my life.

I was struggling to cope with the guilt, the anger, the grief. I consider myself lucky, because I had support from every person in my life. My mother and stepfather, my husband, my best friend, my boss. All of them stepped up to do what they could, and I am eternally grateful for the help they offered when I wasn't sure I wanted to live anymore. While I was blessed with that love and compassion, I still felt hopelessly numb and empty.

Therapy wasn't helping. The endless google searches of increasing desperation hoping to find some magical cure to depression weren't helping either.

I was struggling to find anything to cling to, to live for, and it wasn't until I was reading my half-finished, typo-filled second draft with tears streaming down my face, that I realized this story is what kept me here.

As Christian believes he owes his life to Elena, I believe I owe my life to you, the reader.

Thank you from the bottom of my heart.

ACKNOWLEDGMENTS

My first and biggest thank you goes to my husband, who encouraged me every step of the way and let me bounce ideas off him constantly. You kept me motivated when I was convinced I would fail, and you've been my number one supporter on this journey. I couldn't have done it without you. I love you so much and I'm so lucky I get to call you my husband.

I'd also like to thank my mom, who has always supported me and my dreams. We've been through a lot together. You've made me the woman I am today, and every accomplishment in my life is a direct result of your unconditional love.

Another huge thank you to my internet friend, Shelby. You helped me out of a four-year inspirational slump, and I never would have written this book if it wasn't for you. Shelby also helped build the playlist for this novel, and has been here from the beginning, when this story was just an idea in my head, all the way up to release day.

A million thank you's to the Battinsimps (IYKYK).

I'd also like to give a quick shoutout to my friend Seth, who graciously let Christian steal his last name and provided insight on what it takes to be a lawyer.

CONNECT WITH ME

If you enjoyed Christian and Elena's story, please consider leaving a review. It would mean the world to me!

Instagram: @ariel.n.anderson
Bookbub: @ariel_n_anderson
Goodreads: Ariel N. Anderson

Printed in Great Britain
by Amazon